A Surgeon's Heart:
The Conflict

by
R.W. Sewell, M.D.

Copyright © 2014 R.W. Sewell, M.D.

All rights reserved.

ISBN-10: 0990405109
ISBN-13: 978-0990405108 (Robert Sewell)

DEDICATION

To my children and grandchildren. It was my intent in this book to emphasize the importance of retaining one's character and integrity in all situations, especially in the face of adversity. I am so very proud to have witnessed these unwavering traits in each of you. I know that the future of our family and our nation is secure.

INTRODUCTION

Each summer since they were married, Dr. Jack Roberts and his wife Elaina traveled to the small community of Ciudad Sandino, just outside Managua, Nicaragua. There they assist their friend and local pediatrician, Dr. Domingo Ramirez, in providing basic health care to hundreds of impoverished families in his free clinic. During one of these medical mission visits, Domingo was called to evaluate a critically ill newborn in the private hospital in Managua. Jack, a highly experienced heart surgeon, accompanied his colleague into the third world hospital's neonatal intensive care unit. They determine the infant is suffering from a life threatening heart defect, and that she is the only daughter of Franco Gutierrez, a wealthy and allegedly ruthless businessman. Desperate to save his child's life, Franco was compelled to trust this American doctor to repair the child's heart. Following the successful operation, the two men became life-long friends, and that relationship further solidified Jack's ties to Nicaragua.

The Conflict is the second book in this series titled ***A Surgeon's Heart***, and continues the story of Jack Roberts as he struggles with an evolving heath care system where corporate profits and government controls threaten his practice and the entire medical profession. Jack is highly motivated by the traditional values and ethics of his profession, which he holds sacred, and he feels compelled to defend them against a system controlled by outsiders who are driven by profit and politics. Jack takes on the challenge of defending his profession, and Elaina provides him with unwavering emotional support and stability.

Jack's adopted son, David, aspires to follow in his father's footsteps, but the health care environment in America has changed dramatically since Jack finished medical school in 1972. He fears his son will be swept up into a system that treats young physicians simply as interchangeable parts in a complex health care machine. He decides that he must do whatever he can to reverse the trend toward excessive regulations and restrictions on his profession, and as the story unfolds, Jack's attempts can only be described as ***A Surgeon's Heart: The Conflict***.

The story of American health care is constantly changing, and the physician's role is being challenged by a system that is increasingly centered on the payers, both private insurance companies and government agencies. Every physician, nurse, technician and administrator is influenced by that environment, and it is the author's intent to demonstrate the impact of those rapidly changing conditions on all those who rely on the health care system, both now and in the years to come.

Please enjoy.

R.W. Sewell, M.D.

ACKNOWLEDGMENTS

A Surgeon's Heart: The Conflict, like all of the books in this series, is a work of fiction. It is the product of the author's imagination and is based, in part, on his own experiences as a practicing general surgeon for the last thirty-five years.. None of the characters described in this story are real people. Any similarities with any real persons, either living or deceased, is purely coincidental. Likewise, each of the facilities and specific situations portrayed in this story are fictitious.

Although the author's story might suggest otherwise, the care delivered in America's hospitals continues to be exemplary, and our health care system remains the envy of the world. The author wishes specifically to point out the extraordinary care his own son received at Cook Children's Hospital in Fort Worth, Texas, in the summer of 2007. The incredible dedication and expertise of every physician, nurse and staff member were directly responsible for saving his sixteen-year-old's life from the clutches of the rare, but deadly, hantavirus pulmonary syndrome. He and his entire family are extremely grateful to the incredible people who cared for Ryan, and it is in that spirit that the author has pledged a percentage of any profits that might arise from the sale of this work to that facility.

Pictured on the cover of this book are two close friends of the author, Howard Harris, M.D. and Harrell Moten. Their willingness to participate in this project is greatly appreciated.

I want to thank my family once again for their love and inspiration. My children, Julie S., Julie L., Ashley, Tyler, Ryan and Chase, are each special to me, and are a source of constant pride. My wife, Donna, has been my constant support for nearly thirty-two years, and she remains the center of my world.

CHAPTER 1

The large windows of the tenth floor suite in the Worthington hotel looked out over Sundance Square and the east side of the city beyond. Jack moved his gaze down toward the street below and saw two horse drawn carriages lined up silently in front of this Fort Worth landmark. He was immediately taken back twenty two years, to the night of his first date with Elaina, and realized just how much his life and the world had changed since that night.

Dr. Jack Roberts was wearing his best blue suit tonight, but he had yet to put on the tie and jacket as he stood quietly, staring out the window. Physically he felt very much the same as he did that night back in the spring of 1990, at least he tried to tell himself that was true. His muscular six foot three inch frame wasn't as strong as it had been just two years out of the Air Force, partly because he hadn't found time to work out much over the last year and a half. All in all, he felt like he was still in pretty good shape for a man just two weeks shy of his sixty-fourth birthday. He had a few lines and wrinkles around his clear brown eyes, which were still as sharp as ever, and his dark brown hair was now generously sprinkled with gray. The stresses of the eighteen month long political campaign had clearly taken their toll.

He looked over at Elaina as she sat quietly reading another novel in a series by one of her favorite authors. At fifty-two, her shoulder length, strawberry blond hair now required some renewal of the color periodically, but it still framed her glorious features the same as it did on their wedding day twenty-two years before. He was able to see her emerald green eyes with those glorious flecks of gold, as they darted back and forth across the pages, but he had long ago memorized their every detail. She remained the most beautiful woman he had ever known, and he loved her more today than ever. She'd been so incredibly supportive of all his efforts over the years. He knew it wasn't easy being the wife of a heart surgeon, and he was certain that living with him had been especially challenging in recent years. This campaign to win a seat in Congress had been more stressful on both of them than he had ever imagined, but tonight that was all coming to a close, one way or the other.

The lights of the city had only just begun to illuminate the streets as the first hint of twilight began to dim the early evening sky. Darkness fell much earlier this time of year, and as the sky gradually lost its brilliant blue, on this 2012 election day, his own refection in the glass of the window grew more obvious. As he saw his image staring back, he couldn't help asking himself how he'd been drawn into all this madness.

****

It was mid-June of 2008 and Jack and Elaina arrived back in Managua, Nicaragua for their annual mission trip. They would be staying with their friends, Dr. Domingo Ramirez and his wife Felicia, for the fifteen or sixteen time. Jack had lost count. This time they were accompanied by their twenty year old son, David, and his girl friend Amy. While the handsome young man had come with them once before, three summers earlier, Amy had never been to this part of the world. She was excited to see the part of Nicaragua she'd heard so much about, but when they arrived, the stifling summer heat was more than she had anticipated.

"I know you said it would be hot," she groaned, as they hauled their luggage out of the terminal, "but this is unbelievable." It was only 95 degrees but the oppressive humidity made just the act of breathing difficult. "I can't imagine living in a place like this."

Jack had decided to rent a car this time, rather than rely on Domingo for transportation, and it took forty-five minutes for them to find the outdoor rental counter and sign all the forms required to get the Ford Explorer. It was three or four years old, but it seemed to run okay, and fortunately the air conditioning worked great. Once in the cool car, Amy's mood improved considerably.

The four Americans were greeted warmly by Domingo and Felicia at the front door of their home. With the significant increase in elevation compared to the shores of Lake Managua, the air had cooled to a very pleasant eighty degrees, so that evening they enjoyed a home cooked Nicaraguan feast on the patio.

"It is so great to have you back," Domingo said to Jack and Elaina. "We have missed seeing you."

THE CONFLICT

"I thought you said you were going to come visit us some time in Fort Worth." Jack stated with a smile.

"We will, we will," he replied quickly. "I just need to find a week when I can get away."

"That's never going to happen, and we all know it," Jack laughed. "There is no way to drag you out of that clinic."

"I know I need to get away, but my patients depend on me to be here for them." The diminutive Domingo was the only pediatrician in the region, and he cared for most of the children west of the capital, all the way to the Pacific Ocean.

"You are one of a kind, my friend. One of a kind."

"I wish my doctor was that way," Amy offered. "When I called his office to get a refill of my medication, no one called me back for three days." She added, "When the nurse finally did return my call she told me I would need to come in to be seen by the doctor before they could refill my prescription. I told her I was in Austin and wouldn't be home for two months, and I argued with her for ten minutes before she finally put me on hold an asked the doctor what he wanted her to do."

"Unfortunately, that is how American medicine is practiced these days. The patient is no longer the center of attention," Jack said sadly.

"It's not just an American problem. I know many doctors here in Nicaragua who are like that as well," Domingo stated sadly.

"Why do you think that is?" David asked.

Jack and Domingo looked expectantly at each other before Jack nodded toward his long time friend. Domingo offered his opinion saying, "Some doctors enter the profession mostly for themselves. Whether for money or prestige or a sense of self importance. Their reasons vary, but for many of them it isn't about the patient. At least that's what I have seen. I'm sure there is a lot of that in the US as well." He then looked back toward Jack for his opinion.

Jack said, "I agree, but I think the problem is more wide spread than that. Most physicians entering the profession have no idea how the system works and once they finish their training they realize they're totally unprepared for all the bureaucracy and red tape, as well as the vast number of government regulations. The result is most doctors are gradually beaten down. They lose their youthful enthusiasm for the profession as their spirits are tested by the realities of the system."

Domingo nodded in agreement, but Jack wasn't finished. He added, "Proverbs 18:14 says, 'The spirit of a man will sustain him in sickness, but who can bare a broken spirit.' I believe our profession has a broken spirit. It has been systematically torn from our hearts. The patient physician relationship is the key to that spirit. It's the reason most of us chose this career. That relationship once existed between every patient and their doctor, but it has been systematically destroyed by any number of intruders. Whether it's an insurance company or a government bureaucracy, they each strive to make money or political points by controlling that relationship. Most of us have become nothing more that helpless pawns in a system that has steadily sapped our individual and collective resistance. When you add to that the rising influence of hospital executives, lawyers and huge corporations, all of whom have their own reasons for manipulating physicians, it's no surprise that many have lost their focus. The patient is no longer the center of every medical decision."

"You know, Dad, I've heard you talking about this for as long as I can remember. I understand the problems, and I agree, but what can be done to fix it?" David asked. He had just finished his second year at the University of Texas as a premed major.

"The answer is very simple. We need to change the system," Jack said, "but the current group of physicians is unlikely to do it. Many seem to have forgotten their ethical roots. They've become dependent on insurance and government payments."

"Isn't that what this next election is all about?" David asked. In the early summer of 2008, the primaries were rapidly winding down, and health care reform and the wars in Iraq and Afghanistan had been the main topics of debate.

"Everybody, including the current crop of politicians, talks about change, but until the mechanism of payment changes, a true patient physician relationship will not exist. I believe changing the system and renewing the medical profession will need to start with your generation. If you'll just refuse to sign contracts with anybody, or any entity, other than your patients, you will change the system. You and your generation are the only ones who can, and if you do, I predict you will be far more satisfied with your life's work and ultimately you'll get the rewards you deserve."

"Who is going to teach them that lesson?" Domingo asked.

There was silence as everyone looked toward Jack. After staring down at his folded hands for a few seconds, he looked up with a questioning smile and said, "I guess a few of us old farts will have to be the ones."

****

The next morning, Amy was amazed by what she witnessed at the free clinic in Ciudad Sandino. The people who came, whether as patients themselves or those who brought their children, were incredibly polite and patient. She watched one young woman with three children, the oldest was about five, all sitting patiently, waiting all morning and into the early afternoon. She held an infant and periodically nursed the infant, while quietly entertaining the other two with nothing more than a small rag doll and a ball made of yarn. She had produced a thick, handmade corn tortilla from her bright colored cloth bag, and used small bites as rewards for the well behaved children. When her name was finally called, she carefully gathered her children and her belongings and made her way into the exam room, where she spent less than fifteen minutes with Dr. Ramirez. She left with two small bottles, one was liquid ampicillin and the other liquid Sudafed to treat the two year old's ear infection. She thanked the doctor and every one of the staff members as she made her way out of the clinic.

"I've never seen anything like that," she said to David after describing the four hours she had observed the woman.

"These people are so appreciative of everything, none of the entitlement mentality we see back home," David replied. "I think that's why my mom and dad love coming here so much. My dad calls it his vacation from Americans."

"Most of my friends won't wait twenty minutes for a table at their favorite restaurant," Amy said, "much less sit for nearly four hours in a crowded clinic. I was most impressed by the way her children were so well behaved. I didn't see any of them acting out the way they do back home. There weren't any kids running around unsupervised."

David thought for a moment then suggested, "Maybe those mothers are more attentive to their children because they aren't texting or talking on their cell phones all the time." He laughed as he imagined a clinic filled with screaming youngsters while their mothers were busily texting away on their smart phones.

Amy offered a questioning smile, not sure she understood exactly what he meant. She continued, "The other thing I noticed was how closely your dad and mom worked together. They seemed to each know exactly what the other was going to do next, and their level of cooperation was amazing."

"Yeah, I noticed that too when I was here a couple of years ago. Mom, especially, seems to love working with my dad," David explained. "She was a pediatric ICU nurse, and I know she helped him with a few of his hospital patients before they were married. But afterward, apparently it was unacceptable for a husband and wife to work together in the hospital, so its only when they come down here that they have that opportunity."

"I just think its cool watching them together," Amy said. She smiled broadly at David and added, "Maybe I should consider changing my major to nursing or premed."

She thought he knew she was kidding, but David's response came quickly. "No way. I need you to get your degree in finance so you can help figure out how I can make a living without all those financial contracts my dad has warned me to stay away from."

****

"Franco and Gabriella have invited us to come stay with them in their home for a few days," Jack said as he came in from the patio after hanging up his cell phone. "I told them I'd let them know, but I'm inclined to just stay here. I don't want to offend Domingo and Felicia."

Franco Gutierrez was quite possibly the wealthiest man in Nicaragua. Three years earlier, Jack had corrected the congenital heart defect of his desperately ill newborn daughter, Christina. Since then Franco had become a dear friend, and in appreciation for what Jack had done, he gave a million dollar donation to the children's hospital in Fort Worth. He wanted to make sure that other Nicaraguan children, who were in need of Jack's expertise, would have access to that facility.

"Why are they asking us to stay with them?"

"They are having a big party of some sort, and they want us to be there."

"When do they want us to come to their house?"

"He said tomorrow afternoon, and they want us to stay until Sunday."

"Wow!" Elaina exclaimed. "I can't imagine three nights in that huge mansion." She remembered vividly, every detail of the dinner they'd had at the palatial estate two years earlier.

"I need to talk to Domingo about it."

Just then Domingo came into the kitchen and said, "I just got off the phone with Franco Gutierrez. He called to invite Felicia and me to a reception at their home on Saturday evening."

"I just spoke to him as well," Jack replied. "They want us to come and stay with them starting Thursday evening."

"Yes, he told me. What a wonderful opportunity. I have heard that the only people they ever have stay in their home are wealthy business associates and high ranking politicians. I know President Ortega has stayed there on several occasions."

"I'm not sure we'll be able to get back to the clinic on Friday morning," Jack explained.

"The clinic is closed on Friday for a national holiday, so after we close at noon on Thursday you will be finished," He explained. "I think you should go. David and Amy will likely never have such an opportunity again."

"Are you sure Felicia will not have her feelings hurt?" he asked cautiously.

"Of course not."

Jack stepped back out on to the patio and called Franco's number on his cell phone.

****

The uniformed guard walked slowly all the way around the black Ford Explorer, looking carefully in through each window. Jack understood Franco's need for security, but this seemed a bit excessive. Once the gate was opened, he began the drive up the long winding blacktop road. The first time they'd visited this estate he hadn't noticed the small surveillance cameras that were mounted on dark green, metal polls at every curve, perhaps because on that occasion he was not the one driving.

As they pulled up to the front door of the massive three story mansion, three men in white shirts and dark trousers hurriedly came toward the car. One opened Elaina's door, while another approached Jack as he exited the driver's side, saying, "I'll park your car in our garage, Dr. Roberts." The young man spoke in perfect English with just a hint of a British accent. "Please, go on into the house. Juan and Enrique will bring in your luggage." He quickly found the rear hatch release and the other two men removed the bags from behind the rear seat.

"Please come in, come in out of the heat," the housekeeper said with a distinctive local accent. "I'll let Señor Gutierrez know you are here."

Amy was mesmerized by the incredible grandeur of the entryway and the adjacent great room with the frescoed ceiling. "This place is unbelievable!" she said.

"I know," Elaina replied, "don't you just love it?"

"I can't imagine living in a place like this," Amy said, not recognizing the irony of her words. They were the exact same one's she'd uttered a few days earlier when exiting from the airport in Managua. Now, there was obvious wonder in her voice as she continued to turn around repeatedly, taking in the artwork and furnishings and the huge sunset fresco painting in the domed ceiling.

"Welcome back my friends," Franco said enthusiastically as he approached Jack and Elaina from a hallway off the foyer. He shook Jack's hand vigorously and then embraced Elaina warmly. "I am so happy to have you here."

"It is very kind of you to have us," Jack replied.

Elaina said, "It is so good to see you again. I think you may remember our son, David," she added, gesturing toward the younger man who had stood politely back until he was introduced, then quickly stepped forward.

"Of course!" Franco said. "It is so good to see you again, young man." He took David's hand and shook it firmly.

"Thank you for inviting us into your beautiful home," David offered. Then before Franco could respond, he added, "I'd like for you to meet my girlfriend, Amy Callahan."

The gorgeous young woman with green eyes and golden hair stepped forward with a timid smile, extending her hand. "It's very good to meet you, Mr. Gutierrez," was all she could think to say.

Franco accepted her hand in his with a tenderness in his touch she had not expected. "We are honored to have you with us. I hope all of you will make yourselves at home here. Gabriella has taken Christina into town for a few things, they should be back in a couple of hours. I'm sure you would all like to get settled into your rooms." He gestured toward the housekeeper and added, "Maria will show you to your rooms. Please feel free to explore the house and the grounds at your leisure, and I'll see you again at dinner."

Jack thought Franco was more formal than he had seen him previously. It was almost as if he were greeting some foreign dignitaries. They all followed Maria up the winding stairway to the suspended landing that overlooked the great room. Through the huge floor to ceiling windows they could see the pool area and a portion of the magnificent grounds that stretched out toward the lush green hills in the distance.

"I can't wait to take a walk around," Amy said excitedly, smiling up at David.

"This place is just unbelievable," He replied, trying to take in the grandeur of the massive home and estate. The rooms assigned to David and Amy were across the hall from each other. Each room was more than large enough to serve as a master bedroom in most American homes, and they were furnished with old world antiques. Each had its own marble bathroom with a huge walk-in shower. Amy thought they could be quite comfortable sharing one room, but it was obvious that would be totally inappropriate.

Jack and Elaina's room was at the end of the hall. The arched double doors opened into the guest suite. The corner living room had two large sofas that were arranged to take full advantage of the views of a lush flower garden on one side and the pool and surrounding landscape in back of the house on the other.

"This must be where the President stays when he comes to visit," Elaina said.

"Si, Mrs. Roberts," Maria replied. "*El Presidenté* has stayed in this room many times."

The opulent bedroom had a single window looking out onto the garden below with a large, but delicately hand carved oak desk in front of it. The king-sized four poster bed was covered with a beautiful silk spread with a rich burgundy background and floral designs in rich shades of orange and blue, with gold accents.

"Please let me know if you need anything," Maria said. "Your luggage is in the closet."

"Thank you so much," Elaina replied as the housekeeper left them to get settled.

"We've never stayed in a Presidential suite," Jack said, followed by a sly crooked grin. "I wonder...?"

"You won't have to wonder," Elaina said as she moved quickly into his arms. "You'll find out later tonight."

****

During dinner, Franco announced, "We are hosting a reception in your honor on Saturday evening."

Jack looked up with astonishment. "What? Why would you do that?"

"Most of our friends and many people of considerable influence in Nicaragua know you by name and by reputation, but they have never met you. We thought it only appropriate for them to meet you and your lovely family."

"I didn't bring anything to wear to a formal reception," Elaina half whispered to Jack, almost in a panic.

"We recognize that you were not prepared, so we have taken the liberty of having Gabriella's dress maker come here this evening to take measurements and allow you and Amy to pick your fabrics and style. It will only take her one day to outfit you both, but that is why we needed for you to come here today."

Elaina sat with a stunned expression. When she looked at Gabriella she saw her smiling with a reassuring nod. Amy was grinning broadly at the thought of her first custom made dress.

Franco turned to Jack and continued, "My personal tailor will be here this evening as well, to fit you and David for your tuxedos."

Jack was stunned by what he was hearing. "I brought a dark suit," he said. "It just needs to be pressed."

"This is a formal event, so your suit would not be appropriate," Franco explained. "Frederick will take care of everything."

After dinner the entire group moved into an ante room off the master suite, where the women were greeted by a an Italian woman in her mid-forties who was sharply dressed in a gray business suit. Marta was introduced to Elaina and Amy, then immediately asked the younger woman to step up onto a low platform to allow for measurements to be taken. At the same time the men were introduced to an older German gentleman who wore a dark vest and white shirt with the sleeves rolled up and a yellow tape measure draped around his shoulders.

Within a few minutes all the measurements had been performed and each of the clothiers brought out samples of materials and several books of designs for each of them to choose. Within an hour all the decisions were made and Marta and Frederick left quickly, anxious to begin the process of creating the formal garments. They explained that they would return by mid-afternoon the following day for a final fitting, and indicated the formal clothing would be ready on Saturday morning.

When they were finished with the selection, Elaina and Jack followed their hosts back into the living room for a drink. The women enjoyed Champagne, while Franco insisted Jack try a glass of a truly rare scotch whiskey he'd found during their trip to France. He explained that a Frenchman, by the name of Michel Couvreur, had purchased several barrels of twelve year old malt whiskey from one of the more famous highland distillers, He'd brought it back to his estate in the burgundy area of France where he transferred it into his own fine Sherry casks, and aged it an additional thirteen years before bottling this unique prize under his own proprietary label. The top of the square bottle had been sealed with a heavy red wax, making entry into this treasured vessel a challenge. After cutting through the heavy seal, Franco managed to get the bottle open and poured them each a generous measure of the dark, golden amber liquid.

"To my very good friend, the man who saved the life of my beloved Christina," He said as he raised his glass in salute toward Jack. The women raised their glasses as well, holding them high until Jack acknowledged the toast by nodding and reluctantly lifting his glass slightly.

The smoothness of the warm liquor was unlike anything Jack had ever tasted. He had no idea what Franco had paid for this incredible whiskey, but it was clearly the best of the best, so the price was not an issue.

David and Amy had left the fitting together to take a walk out around the pool. It was a beautiful evening, and this far up the side of the mountain, the air was cooler with little of the oppressive humidity down in the valley. The nearly full moon was just emerging over the mountain as the last orange glow of the dying sunset faded to purple on the other side of the sky.

"This is like something from a fairy tale," Amy said as she and David strolled hand in hand through the perfectly manicured garden. David's mind was reeling from the events of the day. In his wildest dreams he could never have imagined a more romantic setting or series of events than what was unfolding here in Nicaragua. In the three months since the incredible week they'd shared in South Texas at Elizabeth's home, he had been thinking about his future and how much he needed Amy to be a part of it. He wasn't sure of how or when, but he was sure he would ask her to marry him. This seemed like such a perfect place, and it would be an unforgettable way to complete her fairy tale, but unfortunately he didn't have an engagement ring, and had no way of getting one. He thought he might just ask her, and then let her pick out the ring she wanted when they got back home, but he decided that wouldn't have the kind of memorable effect he wanted.

"Are you okay?" Amy asked, sensing David was distracted.

"Yeah, I'm fine. I was just thinking about stuff."

"Stuff? Like what kind of stuff?"

"Oh, it's nothing important," he lied. "This sure is a beautiful place, isn't it?"

"I've never seen anything like it," she said. "I guess this is what its like to have more money than you know what to do with."

"They seem like such generous people," David added.

"I know. I can't imagine having formal clothes made for your guests and hosting a reception for them. Stuff like that just doesn't happen, at least not to people like us."

David stopped and turned to face her. Her youthful face and her golden hair were reflecting the silvery moonlight, giving her a truly angelic appearance. "Do you know how much I love you?" he asked, his voice only slightly above a whisper.

She stared up into his face, with the moon over his shoulder. "How much?" she asked playfully.

"More than anything in this world," he replied with a heavy sigh. He was tempted to drop to one knee right then, but it just wouldn't be right without a ring. After a moment he drew her close to him and kissed her welcoming mouth as tenderly as he ever had. Their bodies moved together, merging as one. This was not an embrace of passion. It was one of love and oneness. They both understood they already belonged to each other.

"Let's go back inside," he whispered softly as they broke the seal between their lips.

Franco had been watching them through the huge window as he sipped his drink. "They make a beautiful couple," Franco said, as he watched them slowly make their way back toward the house.

"Yes, they do," Jack added. "If I don't miss my guess, David is just about ready to ask her to marry him."

"Really?" Franco asked, trying to sound surprised. "I remember when I asked Gabriella to be my wife. It was on an evening very much like this one, but the setting was a bit different. We were walking on the beach, and I had just closed a deal to buy out my main competitor in the construction business, he said, reminiscing about that night, eighteen years earlier. "I had purchased a rather small diamond ring, and was unsure whether she would accept it," he laughed. "What a special day that proved to be."

As David and Amy entered the room, Amy joined Elaina and Gabriella on the sofa, while David walked up beside his father. "Would you care for a drink?" Franco asked.

David had tried some of his dad's scotch on a couple of occasions, and with Jack's nod of approval he said, "Sure, I'd like that."

Franco poured some of the precious liquid in another crystal glass and handed it to David. He then added another measure to Jack's glass and then his own. David sipped slowly and smiled, indicating his approval. Franco grinned, recognizing the young man had yet to understand the difference between typical scotch and what he was now sampling.

"Come with me into my study, I have something I'd like to show you," Franco said as he motioned for the two men to follow him. They left the women to sip the champagne and talk about the dresses that were being made for them.

"Your father tells me you are considering asking for Amy's hand in marriage," Franco said as they stepped into the dark, wood paneled room.

David stopped momentarily and looked questioningly at Jack. "How did you know that?"

"Well, let's just say, old guys like me have a way of knowing such things about young guys like you."

David turned toward Franco and said, "Well, the thought had crossed my mind."

"Do you have an engagement ring?" Franco asked.

"No sir, not yet," David said, sounding rather dejected. "I was thinking about letting her pick one out when we get back home."

"No, no, no," he replied quickly. "Women don't want to pick out the ring. That takes all the romance out of it. They want the man to do that."

"I'm sure you're right," David responded. "I guess she'll just have to wait."

Franco made his way behind his huge mahogany desk and opened a drawer on the far side. He produced a small black velvet box and handed it to David.

"What's this?" he asked as he opened it slowly with a questioning look on his face. Inside was an incredible seven millimeter star sapphire in a solitaire platinum setting.

"That is a ring I bought several years ago from a dealer in the Bahamas. I bought it because I liked the way it captures the light, and as an investment."

"It is very beautiful," David said as he handed it back to Franco.

"No, I want you to have it. I understand Sapphire engagement rings are very stylish these days."

"Oh, Mr Gutierrez, I couldn't possibly accept something this valuable," David replied as he sat the box on the desk.

"That is precisely why I'm giving it to you. The value is not in the thing itself. It is in the meaning of its use. I saw you both out there in the moonlight this evening. If you are planning to ask Amy to marry you, it should be in a setting such as that. If all you lack is a ring, then I'd suggest you not miss the opportunity."

"But, this is too much."

"Nonsense!" Franco exclaimed. "When it comes to love and romance, there is no such thing as too much." He picked up the box and pressed it firmly into David's hand. "I insist that you take it. If you decide not to use it while you are here, then you can return it to me on Sunday before you leave. Fair enough?"

David looked at his father who shook his head slowly and shrugged his shoulders. He knew that giving gifts such as this was more satisfying to men like Franco than accumulating wealth or possessions for themselves.

"I don't know how I can ever repay you," David replied.

"Like I said, I consider this ring to be an investment. Just promise me that when you have finished your training as a surgeon, you will continue the fine work your father has started here in Nicaragua."

David smiled broadly and said, "That is a promise I will gladly make to you, sir."

****

"Well?" Elaina asked softly. "Was that what *El Presidenté* expected?"

Jack was still trying to catch his breath. Laying on the smooth Egyptian cotton sheets next to the woman he loved so dearly, he wondered if life could offer more than this to any man. "Madam, you are most definitely the First Lady of my realm."

She rolled over, placing her head on his heaving chest, feeling the strength of his arm around her bare shoulders. "I can only hope and pray that David and Amy can be as happy together as we are."

"I know David is committed to her. I just hope she can deal with him pursuing his career with the kind of patience you've shown."

"She and I talked about that when we were in Austin. I think she understands what she's getting herself into. It's part of who he is, just like when you married me. David was part of who I was."

"What a package deal that was," Jack said with satisfaction. "I got a terrific wife and a brilliant son, and I didn't have to put up with the nine months of hormonal swings."

Elaina punched him playfully in the ribs, and said, "That's not very nice. I suppose my hormonal swings over the last couple of years have also been pretty hard to take, right?"

"You've had your moments, but over all the years they have only served to make you more desirable."

No matter what the circumstance, he always seemed to know the right thing to say. "You are just saying that so you can get me into bed."

"In case you weren't paying attention, I already have you in my bed, the Presidential bed at that."

She raised up and brought her face to his again and kissed him aggressively. After a few moments she said, "Is *El Presidenté* ready to take charge again?"

He smiled, then kissed her passionately as he rolled her over on her back.

****

The next morning Christina joined the group for breakfast. She talked almost incessantly as her mother tried to interest her in a bowl of Cheerios. As a three year old, she had become quite a handful. She refused to sit in her high chair any longer, insisting that she was a big girl. Eventually, Gabriella had to make her stay belted into her booster seat, otherwise she would have continued to run from one guest to the next, seeking the attention that was so freely given based on her outgoing personality and beauty. Her raven hair was parted down the center and pulled into two large "dog ears," one on each side of her head. They were tied with bright red ribbons that matched her tee shirt and tennis shoes.

"Your daughter grows more beautiful each time I see her," Jack said. "She looks so much like you."

"Thank you," Gabriella said with a demure smile. "Everyday, Franco reminds me how much we owe you for the blessing of Christina."

"As I have told you repeatedly, it was God's intervention that saved your daughter. I wish Franco would stop giving me the credit. All you have to do is look at her now, and it is obvious she is one of God's most precious creations."

After a moment she added, "The tailor will be here with the tuxedos for you and your son to try on around ten."

"That sounds great. Have you seen David this morning?"

"Yes, he and Amy were up early. They were dressed for exploring, so I told them about a natural spring fed pool about a quarter mile up the slope. The last I saw they were headed up the path."

Jack looked a bit concerned, "Will they be all right up there?"

"Oh yes. I take Christina up there at least twice a week when the weather is nice, like today. She loves to throw pebbles into the still water and watch the rings they make."

"Did you tell David about the fitting time?"

"Of course. He said they would be back well before then."

Elaina had slept late for the first time in recent memory. When she finally came downstairs her breakfast was waiting. Gabriella had remembered the breakfast Elaina had prepared for her and her husband, and how delicious it had been, so she had instructed her cook to prepare a Belgian waffle, with strawberries, powdered sugar and maple syrup.

"Good morning," she said, smiling as she wearily sat down to a fresh cup of locally grown coffee that was amazing. The fruit juice was a surprising blend of mango and freshly squeezed oranges. When the toasted waffle was served she could not believe her eyes. "How did you know?" she asked Gabriella, then looked suspiciously at Jack, who just shook his head, indicating he'd had nothing to do with it.

"This is what you served us in your own home, so I assumed it was your favorite. Would you like something else?"

"No, this is perfect." She sampled the juice and then the waffle before saying, "I feel as though I have died and gone to heaven. You have made us feel so incredibly special."

"You and your family are very special to us, besides, it was you who first extended an invitation to us to share your home, remember?"

"These accommodations, and the food, and everything hardly compare."

"This is the least we can do to return your kindness. By the way, the dressmaker will be here around noon for your final fitting. Amy knows to be here as well. After that, you and your family are welcome to do whatever you like. We have some four wheelers in the garage that you can use to explore the property, or you can go for a swim in the pool or play some tennis. We have a media room upstairs if you want to watch a movie. Feel free to do whatever you like. For dinner this evening Franco is going to try his hand at preparing some steaks on the grill." She turned to Jack and said, "You may need to give him a few pointers. That is not something he has much experience with, but he insists on trying."

"I'd be delighted to help in any way I can, but I don't sense that Franco is one who takes directions well," he laughed and Gabriella smiled in agreement.

****

On Saturday morning, both the tailor and dress maker showed up with the custom made garments. Elaina had told Jack that he couldn't see hers until that evening, and Amy did likewise with David. The woman also brought a selection of shoes to go with the gowns, and Gabriella insisted that Elaina wear one of her jeweled necklaces. Amy preferred her silver cross, but was persuaded to also wear a diamond tennis bracelet made with petite princess-cut stones.

The tuxedos were of the finest Italian wool, and the crisply starched, pleated white shirts were simple, yet elegant. The black satin cummerbunds and matching bow ties were of the finest quality. David's shirt studs and cuff links were rather simple design, but made of solid and highly polished gold. Jack's were also gold with center mounted black pearls. Both men were also fitted for their new shoes. David's were black patent leather, while Jack's were made of the finest crocodile, that had been brought to a brilliant shine.

"This is over the top," Jack said to his son as the garments and accessories were brought out for them to try on.

"I can't believe this is happening," David replied. "None of my friends in Austin will ever believe it."

"So," Jack interrupted, "are you planning to ask her tonight?"

"I ... think so," he replied hesitantly.

"If you're not sure, you should wait."

"Oh, I'm sure it's the right thing to do. I'm just worried about finding the right time and the right words."

"The best advice I can give you is to speak from your heart. Don't go into it with some rehearsed speech. You'll stumble all over yourself. Just tell her how you feel and what she means to you. If you do that, the rest will take care of itself."

"What if she says no, or if she says she wants to think about it?"

Jack laughed out loud then said, "There is no way that is going to happen. She obviously loves you, and has been waiting for your proposal for a long time. She may faint when she sees that Sapphire, but there is no chance she'll say anything but yes."

****

Guests were due to begin arriving around eight that evening, but Domingo and Felecia arrived a half hour early and were waiting for their hosts in the great room. Through the two story windows at the end of the room, the cloudless evening sky had taken on a soft pink glow, offering a complementary color to the sunset painting in the huge domed ceiling that loomed over their heads. All the furniture in the massive formal living room had been moved to the perimeter, and the two large Persian rugs had been rolled up and taken away temporarily, exposing the polished white marble floor. In one corner of the room the members of a six-piece string ensemble hurriedly tuned their instruments in anticipation of providing the evening's entertainment. A professional photographer was also moving rapidly setting up his lighting for the photographs of their guests that Gabriella had requested.

Despite having all day to prepare, Elaina was feeling rushed to be ready on time. She and Amy had spent a good portion of the afternoon in Gabriella's private sitting room, having their hair and nails done by a small bevy of attendants brought in just for this occasion. One of the young women accompanied Elaina to her room to assist with dressing and make-up, while another did the same for Amy.

The men had dressed earlier and were gathered in the study enjoying another fine scotch from Franco's private selection. Franco's tuxedo was similar to Jack's and David's in every way except for the huge diamonds in the studs and cuff links, and his iridescent eel skin shoes.

David was convinced that the small box he had placed in his coat pocket would be visible to everyone, and he worried that the bulge would give away his plans. "Just quit worrying about it son," Jack reasoned. "No one is going to notice. They will be too busy checking out those gold buttons on your shirt."

The butler came to the door of the study and announced to Franco that the women were about to make their entrance. The three men strode quickly into the foyer and right on queue Gabriella walked slowly down the hallway toward them, holding Christina's hand. She wore a floor length black satin gown that was perfectly fitted in every detail. The spaghetti straps over her shoulders were attached to the bodice just above her ample breasts with round platinum broaches, covered with pave diamonds. She also wore her four karat diamond solitaire necklace with its fine platinum chain. With her shiny black hair arranged elegantly up off her neck, she was simply stunning.

Christina wore an expertly tailored black velvet dress with a white satin sash and white patent leather shoes. Her head was covered with black curls with a white ribbon around them and a large white bow on top. She was also wearing white lace gloves and held her free hand out away from her body with her fingers fully extended, just as her mother had taught her. She didn't seemed to the least bit phased by the frequent flashes of light as the photographer captured at least a dozen images as she entered the foyer.

Franco crouched down and motioned for her to come to him. Her mother released her hold and the adorable three year old ran as fast as she could directly into her father's waiting arms. He lifted her high in the air and as she came down he kissed her tenderly on the cheek before holding her to his side with his left arm around her waist. He embraced Gabriella with his other arm and kissed her briefly. "You are still the most beautiful woman in the world," he said to her as he looked at her again from the hem of her gown to the full extent of her exaggerated height, due to the five inch spike heels she wore.

"Thank you darling," she said. "You look very handsome as well."

Then Amy appeared at the top of the stairs, and began the slow descent. She was wearing a strapless cream colored satin gown with a very subtle peach and burgundy swirl pattern that accentuated her athletic yet petite figure. The side of the sleek skirt was slit along the right side up to the mid-thigh. When combined with the four inch heels, the glimpses it offered of her legs made them appear longer and more seductive than ever before to the only man in the room whose interest she was seeking. She wore her hair down in a tumble of gentle curls over her shoulders, the way she knew David liked it. Around her neck was the simple silver cross he'd given her, but on her left wrist she wore the sparkling diamond tennis bracelet she'd borrowed from Gabriella. As she reached the final step, he was there to offer his hand, which she took with an unfamiliar air of formality.

David held her hand, and stepped back a half step to admire the full view, before pulling her gently toward him and kissing her softly on the cheek. He whispered, "You are absolutely gorgeous,"

"Why, thank you, sir," she replied with a somewhat exaggerated Texas drawl. She raised up on her toes and whispered, "You look pretty amazing yourself."

Finally, it was Elaina's turn. Making an entrance had never been her thing, but Gabriella had insisted. She came down the opposite side of the stairway from Amy. Her backless gown was made from a shimmering pale golden silk with an overlaid layer of fine emerald green lace. The full bodice narrowed quickly to her tiny waist and was held up by a pair of gleaming golden cords that were joined behind her neck with an elegant gold clasp. The tightly fitted material hugged her hips smoothly, accentuating what Jack always told her was her best asset. With each stride the center slit in front that extended up to just above her knee exposed her shapely legs and the sparkling emerald green sandals with four inch heels. As she turned the last few steps Jack noticed the necklace. It was a solitaire eight-karat emerald that seemed to float just above her ample cleavage, suspended from a fine gold chain. She wore her strawberry blond hair in an elaborate up-do style reminiscent of a Katherine Hepburn movie. A matching pair of four karat emeralds were suspended from the two karat diamond stud earrings by nearly two inch long gold chains. They accentuated the graceful curve of her neck perfectly. The photographer made sure he captured her entrance with nearly continuous flashes from his camera as he moved rapidly into different positions.

Jack stepped forward to meet her at the bottom of the stairs and took her hand gently, as if she were a delicate jewel that might break if handled too harshly. As she stepped onto the white marble floor, Jack held her left hand up and took a full step back and said, "Let me take a look at you."

With little prompting, she slowly turned all the way around to give him a view of the backless dress. For the firsts time in her life she felt like a Hollywood celebrity.

"Wow! You take my breath away," Jack uttered too softly for the others to hear.

He placed his hands on her waist and gently pulled her toward him, kissing her softly on the cheek before looking into her hypnotizing green eyes with their golden highlights. It was clear the dress and the jewels had been chosen specifically to compliment them.

"How do you feel?" Jack asked through his crooked smile.

She leaned forward and whispered in his ear, "I feel naked. I'm not used to being seen in public wearing only high heels and a form fitted gown." She gave him a sly, yet anxious grin.

"You look just like Cinderella," he said, this time loudly enough that the others could hear.

"I agree," said Franco. "You and Amy both look spectacular."

The guests had begun arriving, but Franco had instructed the butler to hold them at the door until the ladies had made their entrances. Domingo and Felicia joined them, and the four couples formed a receiving line in the foyer.

As the dignitaries passed through the line, Franco introduced them first to Gabriella and then to Jack and Elaina, who in turn introduced David and Amy. The brief conversations began in Spanish, but most of the guest took the opportunity to demonstrate their limited English when speaking to the Americans. While Jack and Elaina both spoke to each of the guests in Spanish, David and Amy were only able to converse in English, despite having taken classes in Spanish both in high school and college.

Among the early arrivals was the familiar Director of the government hospital. He was not accompanied by anyone, causing Jack to wonder if he even had a life other than his appointed position. "It is very good to see you again, Dr. Roberts. I do hope you will come by the hospital while you are here to see our newest addition. We have just installed our first CT scanner."

"That's terrific," Jack replied. He was certain it was at least 10 year old technology, but it was bound to be better than nothing. "Unfortunately, we are scheduled to return home tomorrow. Perhaps next time we are here."

"Of course! You know you are welcome any time," he said. He quickly shook Elaina's hand then all but ignored David and Amy, since they clearly had nothing to offer him. His remarks to Domingo in Spanish were obviously formal and seemed to be offered out of necessity, lacking any real sincerity.

The Nicaraguan Ambassador to the United States arrived in an official vehicle, having flown in from Washington just for this event. Over his dark suit, the distinguished gray haired gentleman wore a blue and white sash across his chest. When introduced to Jack he spoke easily in English. "I am delighted to finally meet you Dr. Roberts."

"It is good to meet you as well, Mr. Ambassador," Jack replied.

The older gentleman smiled broadly and added, "You have done more to promote positive relations between our two countries than you can ever know."

Jack replied, "I don't know about that, but I truly appreciate the assistance you and your Department of State here in Managua have given us the last few years. You have made it possible for several children to get the care they desperately needed."

"Franco can be quite effective at cutting through the diplomatic red tape," the Ambassador said with a smile and a nod back in Franco's direction.

"Yes, I have come to appreciate that fact. He is quite an asset to your country."

"And this gorgeous woman must be Mrs. Roberts," he said turning his attention to Elaina. He took her hand and kissed it formally as he bowed slightly at the waist.

"I'm delighted to make your acquaintance Mr. Ambassador," Elaina said as she blushed slightly when he held her hand just beyond the point where it became awkward.

"I do hope you and Dr. Roberts will continue to grace us with your presence in the years to come."

"We plan to," she replied, "and this is our son, David, a future Dr. Roberts."

"Excellent!" he exclaimed. As he shook David's hand he said, "I trust you will continue the fine work your father has been doing to improve health care here in this country."

"Yes, sir," David replied with a youthful smile. "I can think of nothing I'd like better." He then turned to Amy and said, "I'd like to introduce Amy Callahan." He thought about saying something like, my girlfriend, but thought better of it, assuming their relationship was implied by her mere presence.

"It is nice to meet you Mr. Ambassador," Amy said as confidently as she could manage.

"I hope you will continue to honor us with your visits here to Nicaragua."

"Thank you, sir. I hope so as well."

Over the next hour more than twenty individuals and almost twice that many couples came through the receiving line to meet the host and the guests of honor. They included the Ministers of several government departments including Agriculture, Education, Foreign Affairs, Industry and Commerce, Transportation and Infrastructure as well as the Minister of Health. They all offered their appreciation to Jack and Elaina for the volunteer work they had done, but in each of their remarks it was clear they were looking for some means by which their department could benefit politically by associating with this now locally famous American doctor. After offering his greeting, the Minister of Health asked if Jack would allow him a few minutes later in the evening. He had several things he would like to discuss with him.

Other guests included prominent local businessmen and two European investors who were looking at a project Franco was considering in the nearby coastal town of Masachapa. Jack was certain he would never remember any of their names, but he doubted he'd ever see any of these people again. While he didn't doubt Franco's sincerity, it was clear to him that this reception was intended to maintain Franco's strong ties to the government. That fact became obvious when the Presidential limousine, preceded and followed by large black sedans filled with security guards pulled up in front of the house.

A pair of armed guards came in first and did a quick visual sweep of the area then nodded toward their colleagues standing near the limo. President Daniel Ortega and his wife were escorted to the door, while two additional armed guards stood flanking the entrance facing the driveway.

"Welcome, *El Presidenté*," Franco said as he bowed formally toward the stockily built, yet rather diminutive man. He wore a black suit with his customary open collared white shirt. His dark hair was showing signs of gray in the temples as was his heavy mustache. He smiled broadly at Franco, his long time friend and political supporter. His wife, who was four or five inches shorter than him, followed a couple of steps behind. She wore a modest bright blue dress with a turquoise scarf around her neck.

Jack could not make out what Ortega said to Franco, but it appeared they were truly good friends. The President crouched down to say hello to Christina who had become quite tired and bored with all these people parading by her. She hid partially behind her father's leg, clinging to him without making a sound. When Ortega stood up again he greeted Gabriella, kissing her on each cheek and telling her how lovely she looked.

"I would like to introduce my good friend, Dr. Jack Roberts," Franco said, once he got the President's attention again.

"Ah, yes," Ortega said, "I have heard much about this Dr. Roberts."

Jack extended his hand toward the man whom he too had heard a lot about. As the recognized leftist dictator of this country, his history was not something Jack found especially appealing. However, he also understood that in recent years, Ortega had actually moved the country a bit to the right and toward a somewhat more democratic republic.

"I am happy to make your acquaintance Mr. President," Jack said. "This is my wife, Elaina."

She extended her hand as well and Ortega took it firmly, looking into her eyes with a piercing gaze. She wondered whether he sensed a threat by the way he was looking at her, but quickly his eyes softened along with his grip on her hand as he said, "You are a very beautiful woman." She felt intimidated, then realized that had been his intent. He was a man who ruled by intimidation, even when there was no threat to him.

"Thank you, sir," she said shyly, not knowing exactly what to say in response to such a greeting.

He turned back toward Jack and said, "You are a very lucky man to have a wife such as this."

"Yes, I am, sir," Jack responded with a broad smile.

"Very much like my friend, Franco. He too has been lucky in love, don't you think?" he nodded back toward Gabriella.

"Absolutely," Jack replied. "But, I suspect one day their daughter, Christina, will out shine them all."

"You may be right, time will tell," he said as he moved passed Elaina. "Who is this young man?"

Before Elaina could speak, David held out his hand confidently and said, "Hello, Mr. President, I'm their son David Roberts,"

Ortega looked closely into the young man's face and said, "Are you sure, you don't look anything like your father."

Again Ortega was using his typical blunt words in an attempt to intimidate everyone he met, but David was not the least bit intimidated. He responded the way he had countless times before. He had no memory of his biological father. He was well aware of the fact that Jack had adopted him shortly after marrying his mom, but that had never seemed all that relevant. "I know," he said, "I'm afraid my father hasn't aged well." His brilliant grin was completely disarming, even to this third world dictator.

Ortega smiled and nodded without further comment. David then introduced Amy who received much the same treatment as Elaina, but her handshake was stronger and more confident and was accompanied by a more assertive greeting. "It is a pleasure to meet you, Mr. President."

Sensing that his standard intimidation wasn't working well on these young people he shifted to a more subtle method, flattery. "Are all American women as beautiful as you two?"

David responded, "No sir, we only brought the two most beautiful women in Texas here to your country."

"I believe you did," Ortega replied with a smile, then repeated more softly. "I believe you did."

He moved on to speak briefly to Domingo and Felicia, who offered their continued gratitude for the support his government had provided through funding of the hospital. Over the next several minutes he mingled with his Ministers and other government officials, each of them groveling in their own way. While he was in the room, no one else seemed to be engaged in any meaningful conversation. The staff members were not allowed to approach him with either drinks or hors d'oeuvres.

Once the President had made his rounds he indicated to his staff that he was ready to leave. On his way back toward the foyer, he made a point of finding Franco who was standing with Jack, very near where they had stood the last hour and a half. As he approached them, Franco again extended his hand and said, "Thank you so much for coming by, *El Presidenté*. I know your schedule is very busy and I'm honored that you would make time for us."

Ortega smiled and said, "I always have time for you my friend," and he patted him on the shoulder. He then turned toward Jack and nodded slowly, saying, "Dr. Roberts, I'm happy to have met you and I hope you will take a moment to speak with my Minister of Health this evening."

"I will, Mr. President." Jack wasn't sure what this was about, but whatever it was, Ortega had just made it clear the Minister would be speaking on his behalf.

CHAPTER 2

"The polls are due to close in half an hour," Jason said. "Do you guys want to order some dinner?" Jason Williamson was Jack's campaign manager, and he was trying to ensure his candidate would be ready to address his supporters down in the ballroom later that evening.

"I'm not really all that hungry," Jack said.

"Well, I'm starving," Elaina countered as she took the room service menu from Jason and started looking through the choices. After a few seconds she said, "I think I'll have the Cobb salad and a glass of sweet tea."

Jason looked at Jack, as he continued to stare out the window. "You really should eat something Jack," he said.

"Okay," he replied, sounding completely uninterested, then he turned to Elaina and asked, "Angel, would you order me something?"

He turned back toward the window and was lost once more in the darkness and the memories of that night when it seemed he and his family had been at the very center of Nicaraguan society and politics.

****

After *El Presidenté* left Franco's home, the gala event went on for another two hours, with most of the dignitaries getting thoroughly plastered on champagne or vodka martinis. The musicians played a variety of classical music selections, including several familiar waltzes. Franco carried his daughter into the middle of the room and danced effortlessly around the room, holding her gently in his arms. Before the first dance was over, Christina had fallen fast asleep, her head resting on her father's shoulder. He smiled at the adoring crowd as he danced his way toward her room, where her nanny was waiting patiently to put her to bed

When Franco returned to the gathering, he found Gabriella talking with Elaina and Jack. The familiar Strauss waltz prompted him to seize the opportunity to pull his wife away to the make-shift dance floor.

"Would you care to dance, madame?" Jack asked, extending his hand toward his wife.

"Yes," she relied, "as long as you don't dip me. I'm afraid I might split the dress if we do anything too acrobatic."

They joined their hosts on the floor and quickly picked up the rhythm of the classic dance. It had been nearly two decades since they had taken those Arthur Murray lessons, but the movements seemed to come back quite naturally. The smile on Elaina's face lit up the room as Jack guided her expertly across the floor.

"This has to be one of the best evenings of my life," she said. "Its like a fairytale."

"The best is yet to come," Jack said calmly. She assumed he was talking about their private time together after the evening was over. She gave him a sly grin and a wink, but she had no way of knowing the other surprise that was in store.

The Minister of Health was one of the few who was drinking Ginger Ale. When he saw that Jack had taken a break from dancing he approached him quietly and asked if there was someplace they could talk. Jack led him into Franco's study and closed the heavy wooden doors behind them.

"What's on your mind?" Jack asked.

"My government understands that the health care provided to most Nicaraguans today is far below the standards you are accustomed to in the United States, and it's somewhat lower than many of our neighbors. You have been coming here every year for many years now, and I'm very interested in getting your opinion on how we can improve both the quality and the availability of health related services in our country." When he was finished with his opening question, the Minister took a seat on the dark leather sofa across from Franco's desk and waited for Jack's response.

"I have thought a lot about this issue, especially over the last couple of years, and I have to say I don't know the answer," Jack stated with true concern in his voice. "I have been all around the world and witnessed a variety of health care systems. What I can tell you for certain is that every one that is run by a government becomes less efficient. Generally, the quality also suffers because the people providing the care are more motivated to follow directives from their government supervisors than they are to serve the needs of their patients.

Medicine simply cannot be micromanaged by bureaucrats. It is a personal service, best provided by highly trained and compassionate, independent practitioners. Government programs don't allow for the kind of independent thinking and actions necessary to allow individual physicians to care for individual patients."

The Minister sat quietly listening to Jack's monologue, but his expression betrayed his feelings. He had asked Jack how the government could make things better, and Jack was telling him that governments were the problem.

"A good example of what I mean is the way Dr. Rodriquez runs his free clinic up in Ciudad Sandino. He does not accept any public money, so he is free to treat those patients the way he was trained. Granted, he would potentially have access to more support services and treatments if he accepted government funds, but that always comes with political strings attached. If he did, it wouldn't be long before someone would be telling him how he could better utilize those resources. We are seeing this in the US with our Medicare and Medicaid programs. It's what happens when personal medical services cross paths with politics."

"So, what you are telling me is the government should not provide for its citizens? That seems rather cruel, don't you think?" the Minister asked somewhat sarcastically.

"I'm not saying the government shouldn't play a roll. What I am saying is that most governments don't know how to play a limited roll. By definition, governments always exercise control over any situation in which they are involved. They pass laws and develop regulations, right?"

"Of course, that is our responsibility. The society could not exist without a government."

"Exactly," Jack confirmed, "and the laws and regulations must be applied uniformly to all citizens, correct?"

"Yes, so what is your point?"

"Let's say your young son needs a heart operation or he will die," Jack said emphatically, holding the Ministers attention. "His doctor tells you that there are few options, none of which are available locally. He will have to go somewhere else to get the care he needs. You would likely do whatever you could to obtain the very best specialists and the finest hospital available, even if that meant flying him to another country, you'd find a way, right?"

"Certainly."

"You would use whatever money you had in savings, or borrow from family or friends or a bank, whatever it took?"

"Yes, if it meant saving my son's life."

"Okay," Jack agreed. "Now let's say there is another child, the son of a poor farmer near Ciudad Sandino, who has exactly the same condition as your son. You would want him to have the same access to the same treatment as your child, wouldn't you?"

"Yes, it should not matter what his economic situation is. He should get the care he needs."

"So, would you use your personal resources, or borrow the money yourself on behalf of that farmer to save his son?"

The Minister sat silently with a questioning expression.

"I dare say you would not, and no one could blame you. He is not your responsibility. You might be willing to offer some assistance, because you are a kind and charitable man."

The Minister nodded slowly, not certain where this was going.

"So, what happens when the farmer can't come up with the money to pay for his son to go to the finest hospital and be treated by the very best specialist?"

"That is when the government should step in to provide for his needs."

"I agree," Jack said, "and let's say, for the sake of argument, that the government bureaucracy is willing to act with the same sense of urgency that a father would for his own child. That is another issue entirely, but I don't want to complicate this discussion further."

The Minister looked to be growing impatient, but Jack continued. "The very best care involves an operation that is available at Johns Hopkins University hospital in Baltimore, Maryland, and including transportation and temporary housing for the child's family, it will cost approximately one hundred thousand dollars. That is money your government could otherwise use to build a water treatment plant, or a new school that would benefit many more people. So, naturally, the government would try to negotiate a lower price, or find some alternate treatment for the young boy. Let's say the American hospital is willing to accept half the usual fee, but in your research you find another facility in Cuba that claims they can perform a similar treatment for the farmer's son, and it will only cost your government ten thousand dollars. What do you suspect would happen?"

"Assuming the Cuban facility was legitimate, we would pay for the boy to have the treatment there," the Minister responded.

"Would you consult with the father before making that decision?"

"No, the decision would be made by our experts in the Ministry of Health."

"So, the father would have no choice but to accept the Cuban treatment, even though you chose to have your own son treated at the more expensive American hospital?"

"I understand the point you are making Dr. Roberts, but governments must be practical when spending public resources. Besides, who is to say the Cuban treatment isn't just as good or perhaps better than the over priced American hospital?"

"You could be right, and that is an easy argument to make when gambling with the life of an unknown farmer's son. My question to you is why didn't you make that decision when it was your own son we were talking about?"

"If I have the resources, I should be free to use them however I see fit," the Minister objected.

"Precisely!" Jack exclaimed, "but, that is not what happens in government run health care. Take for example, our Medicare program in the US. When a person turns sixty-five years old they are automatically enrolled in Medicare. They are no longer free to use their own resources under that program, no matter how wealthy they are unless they choose to give up any and all claims to all the Social Security benefits they have paid into over their lifetime. The government controls virtually every aspect of their care, including what it will pay hospitals and physicians, all of whom are paid the same. By law, participating facilities and physicians must accept what the government determines to be a fair price, which is often considerably less than what other insurance policies pay. The system is so pervasive and so controlling that virtually every hospital and almost every doctor is compelled to accept what Medicare pays, along with the mountain of federal regulations, as a condition of participation."

"But they have access to care, do they not?" the Minister interrupted.

"Yes, everyone has access, but the care tends to be rather impersonal, and patients have few options and very little to say about their own treatment, because again, by law, they are not free to spend their own resources, as you so aptly put it. They essentially become wards of the state."

Jack knew the Minister was a committed socialist, so he knew much of this argument was bound to be lost on him. He, and every other elitist like him wanted nothing more than to have a system where all citizens were dependent. All, that is, except for the ruling class.

"That is a very interesting scenario you describe, but how else would you propose the government take care of those who cannot care for themselves?"

"I recognize that was what you asked to start with, and I apologize for taking a long winded approach to giving you an answer, but I felt the need to provide some context for my ideas. The first thing I would do is make any government assistance voluntary. No one should be forced to accept any help they don't ask for and perhaps don't want. Second, assistance should only be available to those who are truly in need, and then only to the extent of their need. We have people in the US who are quite wealthy, yet are compelled to accept government run medical care, then they complain about the lack of personal attention. That would be eliminated by appropriate means testing. Third, the program should define how much it will contribute, rather than artificially fixing the prices. This will create a free market where providers of the service will compete based on price and quality. Finally, for those who need total assistance, there needs to be a hospital system, like the one you currently have, where people can go without charge, but with the understanding that those are teaching hospitals. The care will be delivered by medical students and doctors who are in training, supervised by a faculty supported by the state, but academically independent from bureaucratic controls. If you can create such a system in this country, you will ultimately have the finest health care anywhere in the world. At one time that was what we had in the US, but that was before our government decided it was time to take control."

Jack had little hope that the Minister even comprehended his recommendations and no expectation that they would be considered, much less implemented.

"I will convey your thoughts to the President," he said as he rose from the sofa. "You have a very idealistic outlook on life."

"I guess I do," Jack replied, "but as a surgeon, I must always remain optimistic and think in terms of what is possible. I fear that such a system will never exist, largely because of the desire for power and control by those who have the opportunity to make such changes happen."

****

David and Amy had spoken to most of the dignitaries before silently slipping out onto the patio. They walked slowly beside the pool, where the turquoise light radiated up from twin underwater sources. The soft evening breeze caused the surface to shimmer and the light to flicker playfully off their young faces.

As they made their way down the flagstone walkway that led into the gardens, the lights from the house slowly faded until they were merely faint silhouettes, alone in the darkness. David held her hand, hoping that she wouldn't notice the growing moisture in his palms. They came to a broadened area in the path where the landscape designer had strategically placed a wood and iron bench.

"Would you like to sit for a minute?" David asked. "I know your feet a probably killing you by now."

"Absolutely," she replied, quickly taking a seat on one end of the bench. David continued to stand, looking down at her. Just then the golden full moon appeared as the cloud that had hidden it moved silently off to the east. The soft glow reflected off the fair skin of her face and shoulders, and David was convinced this was the time. He slowly knelt down on one knee, not moving his gaze as her eyes widened in surprise that initially bordered on fear.

"Amy," he began, "you are the only woman I have ever loved, and the only one I ever will love. Those few months we were apart made me even more certain of that fact. I can't imagine my life without you."

She looked straight into his anxious eyes, anticipating that his next words might be the ones she had longed to hear since they first started dating in high school.

He released her hand and searched the pocket of his jacket for the small black velvet box. As he brought it forward, he opened it slowly, and as he did she looked down and saw the brilliant star shaped reflection of the moonlight off the bright blue stone. For the next few moments she forgot to breathe. This was beyond anything she had anticipated and for the first time in her young life she was truly spellbound.

"Will you marry me?" he whispered softly.

She was so mesmerized by the sight of the ring, she didn't even hear his proposal and simply stared down at the prize he was holding. When she offered no immediate response, David was suddenly filled with panic. Had he screwed this up somehow? Was she going to tell him no? As these thoughts raced through his mind she suddenly looked up and said, "What did you say?"

He couldn't believe what he was hearing. Was this some kind of test? "I asked if you would marry me," he said, sounding somewhat impatient.

"Of course I will, silly," she said as she looked back down at the brilliant stone that seemed to shine from some magical light inside.

"You had me worried for a minute," he replied, as he took the ring out of the box and placed it carefully on the third finger of her left hand. His hands were trembling, but so were hers. He leaned forward and kissed her waiting lips, as she finally took her eyes off the stone that rested so comfortably now on her finger.

He quickly became aware of the uncomfortable hard surface on his knee, and broke the connection between their lips. As he stood up he drew her up into his arms and resumed exploring her mouth with his, this time more aggressively. Her body responded to his touch as he reached around her tiny waist, and lifted her almost off her feet. She threw her arms around his neck and held her face back from his long enough to say, "I love you more than you can possibly imagine, and I will try to make you as happy as you have made me."

They resumed their kiss, but for only a few moments. She pulled back again, as another cloud moved silently overhead, hiding the moon once more. "Let's go inside. I can't wait to tell your mom and dad."

"Before we do, I think we should talk about when," David said, always the one for details. "You know they are going to ask."

"Any time is fine with me. What did you have in mind?"

"I think it would be best to wait until we finish college. I'd also like to have a better idea about where I'll be going to med school."

She wasn't surprised by the fact that his career plans were part of the conversation, even at this unique moment in their lives. Surprisingly, she was okay with it. She had come to see him and to love him for what he was, and what he aspired to be.

When the couple returned to the gathering David nodded toward his dad, indicating he'd completed his task. Jack smiled as he acknowledged his son's accomplishment. He immediately walked across the room and politely caught the attention of the leader of the musicians, indicating he wanted to address the group. In response the musicians rested their instruments allowing Jack to assume the floor.

"Ladies and gentlemen," he began. "May I have your attention please?"

When the gathering had quieted he said, "Thank you. I apologize for the interruption, but I have an important announcement to make."

Elaina looked at him quizzically, wondering what he was talking about. He continued, "First I want to thank our wonderful host and hostess, Franco and Gabriella, for an unforgettable evening. Elaina and I have enjoyed meeting each of you, and appreciate all of you being here."

The group offered a polite round of applause, directed toward Franco and Gabriella as they stood in one corner of the room, surrounded by several members of the government.

When the applause quieted, Jack said, "And, as you know our son, David accompanied us on this trip to your fine country, and he is here with us this evening." The audience again applauded politely, which Jack acknowledged with a gesture toward his son. When the room quieted again, he added, "And it is with his permission that I am excited to announce that just this evening, Amy Callahan has accepted his proposal of marriage."

Elaina's expression was one of total shock, but quickly changed to an excited joy filled grin. She ran to the young couple as fast as she could manage given the four inch heels and the tight garment she was wearing. She hugged her son tightly, then shared a warm embrace with her future daughter-in-law. Jack watched her enthusiastic reaction as she took Amy's left hand in her's to examine the ring.

****

THE CONFLICT

The rest of the summer of 2008 passed rather quickly. Amy and her mother spent hours looking through books and magazines, planning a wedding that was still nearly two years away, and David followed his dad around the children's hospital at least two days each week, until he and Amy returned to Austin for their junior year of college.

Every evening Jack resumed his habit of watching the news and commentary regarding the upcoming elections. It was obvious that John McCain was going to get the Republican nomination, but the Democrats remained fairly evenly split between Hillary Clinton and Barack Obama. For the life of him, Jack couldn't understand how either of them had the credentials to be President, but he wasn't terribly worried. Barring something catastrophic, McCain would almost certainly win. All the polls showed him leading except the New York Times, and that liberal rag always favored the Democrats, he thought.

In late August the Democratic National Convention was held in Denver, Colorado and to the surprise of many on both sides of the political spectrum, Obama emerged as the nominee. He was the first black man to be nominated by any major political party for either President, or Vice-president, a fact that was being hailed as a monumental step forward in a post-racial America.

Like most republicans, Jack thought it was great that a black man was running for the highest office in the land. He wished it had been his party that had nominated someone like General Colin Powell or Representative J. C. Watts from Oklahoma. He supposed it didn't really matter, and to him, race was irrelevant anyway. He was far more concerned about the candidate's policies, and as far as he could tell this Obama guy was pretty liberal, but he'd had such a brief time in the world of politics it was hard to know exactly where he stood on major issues, like health care. He gave a lot of speeches, emphasizing hope and change, but he never really said what he would change or how.

By mid-September Jack got the answer he needed. During the second Presidential debate, the moderator, Tom Brokaw of NBC News, offered up the question, "Do you consider health care to be a privilege, a right or a shared responsibility?"

Mr. McCain was first to respond, saying he believed it to be a shared responsibility, and he was adamantly opposed to the government mandating that people buy health insurance or face a fine.

Obama's response was quite telling, and reflected the socialist views he knew were pervasive in Europe and elsewhere in the world. He said, "Well, I think it should be a right for every American. In a country as wealthy as ours, for us to have people who are going bankrupt because they can't pay their medical bills..." He went on to talk about his mother not getting treatment for cancer. He talked about a wide variety of vague ideas about regulating insurance companies, and compared them to the banking industry, but he offered no specifics about how he would ensure what he claimed to be the right of every American to have access to healthcare. Jack couldn't help smiling to himself, believing this political upstart had just tipped his hand. If given the chance he would certainly try once more to push through the kind of socialized medicine program Clinton had introduced back in 1993. It had been defeated soundly back then, in no small part because the American Medical Association opposed it. Unfortunately, based on his recent experience, he wasn't sure the AMA would take the same stance if confronted with a similar threat to the independent practice of medicine again.

****

"It has been months since we've been to Claude's," Jack said as he and Elaina headed across town to their favorite country French restaurant.

"I know," she replied. "The last time we were there you complained that it was too expensive."

"No, I didn't. I just said Claude had gone up on his prices."

"Yes, and then you went into a tirade about how your fees keep going down while the price of everything else is going up."

"I know. I said I was sorry at least a dozen times."

"Well, I hope we can talk about something other than medicine or politics this evening."

"I promise. We can talk about whatever you want."

For the next hour they sat at their favorite table, talking about David and Amy and how Jack's mother's memory was failing. She had been displaying early signs of Alzheimer's syndrome for several months, but still insisted on living alone in the same house where Jack had grown up.

When Claude brought out his signature strawberry soufflé Jack objected, saying, "But, we didn't order this."

"I know," Claude responded. "You have not been in for some time, and I want you to know how much I appreciate you coming back tonight."

"We have been very busy this summer," Elaina said, offering an excuse for their absence.

"I hope you will not stay away so long in the future."

"We won't. The food and the service is still special, as always," Jack said with a smile.

"I'm glad to hear that," Claude said. Then he asked, "Do you mind if I ask you a question?"

"No, not at all."

Claude pulled out one of the empty chairs at their table and sat down casually, next to Jack, but well away from the table. "I am certain you are familiar with the issues in this coming election."

"Yes, of course."

"Well, as a physician, what do you think of this new health care plan Mr. Obama is proposing?"

Jack looked tentatively toward Elaina, who reluctantly nodded her permission for him to enter into the forbidden topic. "I don't think we have any idea what he's proposing, because he hasn't given any specifics. He claims he can offer insurance to more than forty-million people who don't currently have it, and at the same time reduce the cost of healthcare for everyone. I don't think that's possible, but it sounds good, and that's all politicians are interested in. They don't expect people to analyze what they say. They simply say what they think people want to hear."

"I know you're right, but all my employees are supporting him because they currently do not have health insurance, and he claims his plan will provide it for everyone," Claude replied. "I can't afford to buy it for them, but I worry that he might make me provide it. The restaurant business does not offer high profit margins, and if I'm forced to raise my prices any further, people like you will not come. The only other option would be to cut the quality of the food, and I will simply close my door before I will do that."

"I don't think you'll have to do that," Jack said confidently. "I don't think there is any chance he's going to be our next President. He will be exposed as unqualified between now and November. The American people will see through his empty promises of hope and change." Jack was offering his opinion as if it were obvious to everyone, but he realized that politicians had frequently been successful at fooling the public with promises of government give-aways. Surely that couldn't happen on the scale necessary to elect a President.

"I hope you are correct my friend," Claude said as he slowly stood. "I'm sorry to have interrupted your dinner. Please enjoy your soufflé."

"Thank you," Elaina said, indicating to Jack that her approval of this conversation had been revoked, clearing the way for Claude to leave.

She then turned to Jack and smiled. "I appreciate the fact you kept it short. I'm very proud of you."

"I appreciate the fact that you didn't kick me under the table."

****

With only six weeks to go before the election, McCain held a six percentage point lead over Obama, in no small part because of his controversial selection of

Alaska Governor and conservative political bombshell, Sarah Palin, as his vice-presidential running mate. Attempts by the Democrats to portray her as a beauty pageant bimbo weren't working. She had held her own very nicely during her debate with Senator Joe Biden who had been tagged by Obama over Hillary Clinton as his choice for vice-president.

Jack's prediction seemed to be coming true until the major catastrophe that he feared actually happened. The national economy went into a tail spin, carrying most of the rest of the world's economies with it. No one understood exactly what happened, but it was apparent that the declining value of real estate was at the center of the collapse. For more than ten years the banks and mortgage companies, specifically the government backed Fannie Mae and Freddie Mac, had been lending money below the prime rate to low income home buyers who simply couldn't afford them. A tipping point was reached as the number of foreclosures caused the value of the properties to fall below the amount of the loans. These massive bad loans had been packaged and sold off to most of the major financial institutions. When major corporations like AIG and Bear Sterns declared they were insolvent, the panic caused a dramatic drop in the stock market, prompting the Congress to authorize nearly a trillion dollars to bailout the financial institutions, allegedly avoiding a total meltdown.

Both McCain and Obama suspended their campaigns to return to the Senate to vote on the controversial bill, authorizing the funds, known as the Troubled Asset Relief Program, or TARP bailout. Jack hated the idea of the government bailing out private companies, and he knew he wasn't alone. It was obvious the bill was going to pass, but he hoped that McCain would oppose it, if for no other reason than to separate himself from the herd of politicians who were running for cover, including Mr. Obama. He was disappointed when McCain announced his support, and within a few days of the vote on the TARP bailout, the polls showed a complete reversal. The unimaginable was now inevitable, and on election night the anger of the American people directed at the establishment, headed by the republican President, George W. Bush, was demonstrated, not only by Obama's victory, but also by the establishment of clear majorities for the democrats in both the House of Representatives and the Senate.

He sat quietly, watching the returns, and the giddy liberal commentators, all of whom were convinced that the country had finally seen the light. All he could think of was how a similar election result had occurred in 1992 when Bill Clinton defeated George Herbert Walker Bush in his bid for reelection. When Elaina came into the family room to tell Jack she was going to bed, he said, "I fear this time they have the numbers to push socialized medicine down the throats of the American people."

She was tempted to suggest that he was exaggerating, but thought better of it when she saw how frustrated and saddened he was. "Why don't you come to bed?" she suggested.

"I'll be there in a few minutes," he mumbled, but she knew it would be hours.

****

It was well after midnight and thirty-eight year old Michael Horvath, the administrator of the children's hospital, and his boss, seventy-five year old James Fitzgerald, the chairman of the board, sat comfortably in the two leather wingback chairs in the high rise office building that Fitzgerald previously owned. Now, he only half heartedly worked at running the oil company that no longer bore his name. His interests had turned from oil to healthcare, but this too was little more than a game to him; one that involved power and money.

The two men had been watching the returns together on television, and when the election was called for Obama, Fitzgerald broke out one of his prize bottles of bourbon to celebrate. Now the bottle was more than half empty as the men toasted each time a democrat was declared the victor in either the Senate or the House.

"This is going to be a great four years," Fitzgerald said with satisfaction. "We are finally going to be able to get some meaningful change accomplished."

"I certainly hope so," Horvath added. "I'm sick and tired of having to pick up the tab for every deadbeat, low life who thinks their kid should get free healthcare."

"Clinton couldn't get it done because he wasn't shrewd enough," Fitzgerald said. "He knew he could con the people into believing a government take over of their medical care would be good for them, but he didn't anticipate the AMA opposing him. This guy, Obama, and the Chicago crowd he runs with, will cover every base, of that you can be sure. He will have the AMA eating out of his hand before he makes a move. This is a done deal with the Dems now in control of both houses." Fitzgerald raised his glass and said, "To the American taxpayer! May he remain clueless!"

They clinked glasses and both threw down the smooth liquid. Horvath then added, "All we need to do to be in position to take total control of our local market is complete the takeover of the specialists' practices."

"Have you made any progress with the surgeons?" Fitzgerald asked.

"Yes, and no. I think the younger guys are about ready to sign on. They are scared to death that our primary care group will cut them off if they don't join, but the older guys are still being rather stubborn."

"Is that Roberts character still their ring leader?"

"I don't think they have an actual leader. Roberts is certainly one of the more outspoken critics of our whole system-based care initiative."

"How about the medical specialists?"

"I've got commitments from the GI docs and the pulmonary group, but the cardiologists are being a little resistant. I think their leader, Buzz Jackson, is pretty tight with Roberts, and he's influencing his decisions."

Fitzgerald turned away from the television and faced Horvath. His eyes narrowed and his lips curled slightly into a sinister smile. "Initially, I planned to break this Roberts guy using a direct economic assault, but I think it will be more fun if we attack him from the perimeter. I want you to leave him alone. Don't make any more attempts to pull him into the fold, but I want you to increase the pressure on everyone around him. Eventually, when he's the last one standing, we'll squash him like the little pest he is."

****

The impact of the historic economic downturn was felt throughout the country, with unemployment at ten percent and underemployment at nearly twice that level. Black communities were especially hard hit, with an unemployment rate in excess of twenty-five percent. The auto industry had required a huge government bail out, including the once invincible General Motors. Sales of cars and houses dipped to levels that hadn't been seen in decades. Everyday the news was filled with reports of massive layoffs, home foreclosures and bank failures. Jack had been barely able to watch the news, even FOX, since the election. The media was totally enamored with the fact that a black man had been elected President of the United States, and railed on about how he was going to fix the economy and the healthcare system and end the wars in Iraq and Afghanistan. Obama's face was on every newscast, and the underlying message he offered was that all of this was the fault of his predecessor. Few could argue that the collapse of the stock market occurred under Bush's watch, and virtually everyone seemed willing to let Obama have the freedom to do whatever he wanted.

Healthcare reform immediately took center stage in every political and economic discussion. While it had been the cornerstone of the Democratic platform, since the election, the new administration had still not revealed any specifics. Obama had campaigned on the promise that everything would be discussed openly and with complete transparency. He said that all healthcare debates would be televised on CSPAN, but throughout the late winter and early spring of 2009, nothing new was released to the public. All the White House did was restate the same talking points made during the campaign. He repeatedly said, "If you like your current insurance plan you can keep it. If you like your doctor, you can keep him or her. Insurance premiums are going to go down. All preexisting conditions will be covered, and every American will have access to affordable healthcare."

There was also the continuing problem that plagued the physician payment system under Medicare. For the last decade, the Sustainable Growth Rate formula, known as the SGR, had been used to adjust what the government would pay physicians based on the funds available. Jack, along with every other physician in America knew that something had to be done to change the way Medicare paid doctors, because the current method called for significant across-the-board cuts every year each of the last seven years. On every occasion, Congress had acted in late December to delay the cuts because they feared physicians would drop out of the Medicare program if their fees were lowered any further. These annual reprieves continued to add up, and the total was now more than two hundred billion dollars. Given the current economy, it was highly unlikely that the Congress would authorize that kind of money to accomplish what was unaffectionately called "the doc fix", despite the fact that every physician group, including the AMA had publicly insisted repeal of the SGR be part of any healthcare reform.

In June, Jack attended the annual meeting of the AMA at the Grand Hyatt hotel in Chicago as the sole delegate from the Association of Thoracic Surgeons. Elaina had always enjoyed these trips to the windy city, but this time she stayed home to help complete the final details of their church's annual charity event to raise money for an orphanage in central Mexico.

The more than five hundred delegates and nearly that many alternates, along with hundreds of visitors, including many members of the press gathered in the huge ballroom in the basement level of the Grand Hyatt. The main topic of this meeting was scheduled to be the AMA's position on healthcare reform. Now that the Congress was taking up the task of writing new legislation, the entire medical community was excited over the prospects of helping fashion the new law. As the meeting started, the Speaker of the House announced that there was going to be a change to their usual schedule. The four day meeting was to be compressed into just three days of working sessions, because, as he announced excitedly, "For the first time in twenty-seven years, the President of the United States will be coming to personally address this House of Delegates."

Immediately, there was a loss of order in the House, as physicians shared their surprise with one another. Jack turned to the delegate seated next to him from one of the other surgical associations and said, "Its pretty obvious what this is about."

The young man was at least twenty years younger than Jack, and was attending his first AMA meeting as a delegate. "What do you mean?" he asked.

"In 1993, Clinton tried to expand the role of government in medicine, but his effort failed, largely because the AMA opposed it. Obama is coming here as a preemptive strike. He knows he can't get his plan through unless this organization endorses it."

The young man looked at Jack with a questioning expression. "Do you really believe he cares what we think?"

"No, I'm certain he doesn't, but he's a politician, and he has to make it look as though he does."

As the Speaker began to conduct the business of the House, he introduced the Executive Vice-president of the AMA who spoke for about twenty minutes on the actions that had been taken by their organization since the last meeting. He was a known Obama supporter, and he droned on about how the AMA was working closely with the new administration to fashion new legislation that would help accomplish one of the organization's highest priorities, insurance coverage for every American. He concluded, almost as a foot note, how the AMA leadership was going to do everything they could to ensure that the independent practice of medicine would not be destroyed in the process.

Next to the podium was the current President of the AMA who gave the annual state of the profession speech. She talked about the historic nature of this particular meeting, and how the members of the House had a "great responsibility to change the system, which left so many in our country without health care."

Jack just shook his head slowly. He was amazed how easily these amateur politicians confused health care with health insurance. It was as if they were saying the countless children, as well as many adults, that he treated every year, weren't getting real care, because they lacked some kind of insurance.

The following day, security was extremely tight in preparation for President Obama's appearance before the AMA House. Jack had to pass through two separate metal detectors as he wound his way through a maze in the lower level of the massive hotel to gain access to the meeting hall. Eventually the delegates were all seated, and after another fifteen minutes, the President suddenly appeared from around one side of the curtain behind the huge podium that occupied one end of the massive ballroom.

Many of the delegates and all the medical student section leaped to their feet and began cheering the moment they saw him. The remainder of the crowd, including Jack stood respectfully and applauded as Obama was introduced. As he took to the lectern, he flashed his engaging grin, and held both hands up in appreciation.

The President spoke for about forty minutes, but for the most part his message was simply a reiteration of the material he had used during the campaign. His speech was interrupted on multiple occasions by standing ovations, particularly when he talked about greedy insurance companies, and access to affordable healthcare for all Americans. Jack thought he was attending a political rally, as the audience was being whipped into a frenzy, with exuberant applause and cheers, creating frequent breaks in Mr. Obama's remarks.

Near the end of the President's speech, he said that it was important that physicians not have to practice in an environment where lawyers were constantly looking over their shoulders. Immediately every delegate and alternate rose simultaneously with shouts of "yes" and "about time" amid the loud applause. They all assumed he was about to announce some new national medical malpractice reform. The President seemed startled by the crowd's exuberant reaction, and raised both hands above his head in protest.

"Wait, wait," he said, deviating from his prepared remarks that were being displayed on his teleprompter. "I want you to know that I am not in favor of any caps on damages."

Those words were no sooner out of his mouth than the vast crowd of physicians let out a collective groan. A few isolated boos could be heard, but they quickly subsided. It was clear that the President had raised a great expectation that he was going to address the nearly universal problem of liability within the medical community, but he had dashed that hope very quickly. His solution turned out to be the allocation of a meager fifty-million dollars to study the issue. Jack was not surprised that Obama wasn't willing to put a hot-button issue like tort reform into the healthcare bill. After all, the trial lawyers were among his biggest supporters. However, he was shocked by what appeared in every online news report, less than an hour after the President left the hall. "Doctors Boo The President" was what they chose to emphasize in their headlines. They said little of the generally warm reception or the number of standing ovations he received. It was clear the media was going to continue their attack on physicians as the root cause of all that ailed the American healthcare system.

The President had left it to the leaders of the House and Senate to draw up the new healthcare bills, and both chambers had begun the process shortly after his inauguration. Throughout the 111th Congress, healthcare reform was the major topic, and both houses eventually came up with their own versions behind closed doors. Each bill was written by Democrat staffers, with considerable input from major lobbyists, including the American Hospital Association, the giant pharmaceutical manufacturers, the massive insurance industry and powerful labor unions. The writers didn't seek the opinions of practicing physicians, or even physician groups like the American Medical Association. The minority party Republicans were not involved, and none of the negotiations were open to the public. CSPAN coverage was simply no where to be found.

Just a month following the conclusion of the AMA meeting, the House of Representatives rolled out its version of healthcare reform. HR 3200 was titled "America's Affordable Health Choices Act of 2009" and it contained the public option as a prominent component. It was clear that this idea of a government run insurance plan was designed to become a single payer system, similar to what existed in Canada and Great Britain. Within days of its introduction the newly elected President of the AMA was quoted in every major newspaper in the country as favoring the new bill.

Jack was livid! He wrote the AMA President a rather scathing e-mail, criticizing his willingness to publicly throw the support of the AMA brand behind this one thousand seventeen page bill before they'd even had time to read it.

The reply he received was actually more thoughtful than he'd expected. The AMA President stated that he had been contacted by the press to comment on the bill, after having been provided with a summary of its provisions. He explained that there were many parts of the bill that mirrored long standing AMA policy, and while there were other parts that needed to be changed or deleted, he believed it was a good first step.

Clearly, the AMA was not going to oppose Barack Obama the way it had Bill Clinton two decades before. Something fundamental had changed, either inside the governing board of that organization, or perhaps in the minds of the physicians they supposedly represented. When asked by his colleagues back in Fort Worth about what they saw as the AMA's traitorous position, Jack had no response except to shake his head in obvious disgust.

****

"Dr. Roberts?" the reporter asked when Jack picked up the phone.

"Yes, what can I do for you?" was Jack's rather terse response.

"I'm with channel 8 news, and I understand you are a delegate to the AMA. I'd like to ask you a few questions about your organizations endorsement of the healthcare bill recently introduced in the House." The reporter was one of those who cut straight to the point, and Jack appreciated that fact.

"I don't think it was really an endorsement, but I'd be happy to discuss what I know."

"That would be great," the reporter replied excitedly. "On Saturday afternoon we will be taping a thirty minute discussion of healthcare reform to be aired on our Sunday Opinion Makers program. Would you be willing to participate as one of our panelists?"

"Who else is going to be on the panel?"

"You are the first one I've contacted. Do you have any other recommendations?"

"Not really," Jack responded. He didn't want any of his friends getting upset with him for recommending they appear on television.

"Well, that's okay. I have several more people to contact."

Jack gave him his email address and asked that he send him all the specifics. As soon as he hung up the phone Elaina entered the family room from the kitchen and asked, "Who was that on the phone?"

"A channel 8 reporter. They want me to be on one of their Sunday morning programs to discuss the AMA's endorsement of the healthcare bill."

"What did you tell them?"

"I said I would."

"I thought you agreed not to make any more public statements without talking with me first," she said more in frustration than in anger. She recalled the way he had been treated after he testified before a Medicaid hearing in Austin two years ago.

"I'm sorry. You're right," he said sheepishly. "I can call him back and decline."

"No, after what you told me about what happen with the AMA in Chicago, I suspect the public needs to know the truth, but they'll never hear it unless it comes from somebody like you."

****

Elaina had set the digital video recorder to record the Sunday morning program because it was scheduled to air right in the middle of their church service. When they got home, Jack flipped on the television and used the DVR controls to watch it for himself.

"Are you going to come watch this?" he asked, calling loudly into the kitchen.

"Yes," she replied. "I'll be there in just a minute.

He paused the DVR as the program was starting, and waited for Elaina to finish what she was doing in the kitchen. He had been quite anxious during the taping when he saw that he was the only physician on the panel, and that one of the other participants was Herb Nichols. He hadn't really spoken to Herb much since the whole Lupe Alvarez ordeal. He knew Herb was still steaming over the fact that his hospital had written off a large bill for that girl's care, while the children's hospital had received a million dollar grant from Franco Gutierrez less than a month later. Their only other recent conversation had been about the purchase of the two million dollar surgical robot, which was currently not being used, just as Jack had predicted.

He had known the administrator for many years. Herb had even been among the small group in attendance when he and Elaina were married, but over the last few years he had changed. Since being elevated to the head administrative position in the big general hospital, Herb seemed to be absorbed by the financial aspects of everything. Jack expected their differences of opinion would come out during the panel discussion, but after the taping he realized those differences were far greater than he'd thought. The other two members of the panel were a CEO of one of the regions larger employers, and a professor of sociology from Southern Methodist University.

Once Elaina joined him, he hit the play button and they both sat down to watch the thirty minute program. The moderator moved quickly into the topic of healthcare reform and the proposed legislation. Not surprisingly the professor was in favor of any legislation that would provide healthcare for everyone. He made it clear that the insurance industry was to blame for most of the gross inequities of the current system.

"There is no excuse for the wealthiest nation in the history of the world to allow even one of its citizens to be deprived of health care, simply because they can't pay for it," he said, repeating the democratic campaign lines from the summer before.

"I agree," said Herb. "It is time we came up with a plan that will make it possible for every American to receive the very best care available. As a not for profit hospital system, we simply can't continue to subsidize the poor and uninsured with uncompensated care."

Jack had made a point to bite his tongue when he heard the words "not for profit" come out of Herb's mouth. Most of the giant hospital systems in America were cloaked under that umbrella term, while they were actually enjoying record profits. Many guys like Herb were taking home seven figure salaries.

The business executive spoke up saying, "You realize, don't you, that American industry is bearing the majority of the costs? Those rising healthcare costs are making it increasingly difficult for many companies to turn a profit. Something has to be done, because the current system is breaking the back of our economy."

"Do you agree with that, Dr. Roberts?" the commentator asked as all eyes turned toward Jack, and the camera assigned to him zoomed in for a close-up.

"I agree that the rising cost of health insurance is a serious problem," Jack said, "but, I think it's important to distinguish between health care and health insurance."

"Aren't you splitting hairs there doctor?" the moderator asked somewhat sarcastically. "Since insurance provides the means by which most Americans pay for their health care, aren't they the same thing?"

"Not really. Health care is a personal service, delivered by individual physicians to the specific benefit of the individual patients they are sworn to serve. Health insurance is a cooperative financing scheme designed to profit the insurer, at the expense of a large population. It is essentially the same thing as a lottery where the company always wins. The two have completely different objectives." Jack paused to let what he had just said sink in before he continued. "The problem with our current system lies in the fact we have allowed the two to become intertwined, and for that I blame my profession. Doctors should never be involved in contracts with any entity other than their patients."

"Wow, doc!" the moderator exclaimed in surprise. "Are you suggesting people shouldn't have health insurance?"

"No, not at all," Jack explained. "I have health insurance myself, that incidentally I pay for. I buy it to provide me with a degree of economic security in the event of a costly illness or injury. Traditionally that's how insurance is supposed to work, but that's not what health insurance has become. Most policies today cover office visits, prescription medications, and a variety of other services, all of which drive up the cost, and give the patient a sense that they are entitled to these prepaid services. Unfortunately, when they go to use their policy they find restrictions on who they can see, and even what kind of treatment they can receive."

"It would seem to me as though most physicians would want everyone to have that kind of policy," the moderator responded, sounding as though he was genuinely trying to understand. "Isn't it better to get paid something for what you do than to provide charity care to all those people who are currently without insurance?"

"If you look at health care strictly as an economic issue, you might have a point," Jack offered, "but for those of us who still believe in the Hippocratic Oath, it's more about providing our patients with the individual care we were trained to give. The idea of having an insurance company or a government bureaucracy, get between us and our patients is simply unacceptable."

The businessman who had been listening intently to the dialog between the moderator and the doctor interrupted. "So, why then did the American Medical Association come out and endorse the health care bill just introduced in the House of Representatives?"

Jack turned toward the gray-haired gentleman and said, "That is not exactly true. The media has been reporting what the AMA President said as if it were a blanket endorsement. The fact is, the AMA has been on record for decades favoring the idea that everyone should have access to quality and affordable health care. Apparently the AMA leadership found some provisions in the bill that might help achieve that goal, but, the bill is more than a thousand pages long, so its unlikely that anyone has even read it in its entirety. If it turns out to be like the bill that was introduced in ninety-three by the Clinton White House, essentially calling for a government take over of the practice of medicine, I'm certain the AMA will ultimately oppose it."

"Obviously, that's not what is being reported," the moderator injected, in an effort to ensure he didn't lose control of the debate. "Just today I saw an article that quoted an AMA executive as being excited about this legislation."

"All I can say is, I've spoken to the President of the AMA personally," Jack responded as he turned to face the host again. "He assured me that their position is one of qualified support for the general idea of expanding access to affordable care to every American. That should not be confused with a ringing endorsement of pending legislation that has barely seen the light of day."

The professor spoke up saying, "In this period of economic crisis, and completely out of control health care costs, I find it hard to understand how anyone could oppose any effort to cut the cost and expand health care services to every American, especially those who are currently uninsured." There was just the hint of disgust in his tone.

"I agree," Herb injected, not wanting to be left out of the conversation. "The uninsured are creating a tremendous economic drain on the whole system. Our hospital system provides far more charity care than even the county hospitals, and we don't receive any public funding to offset those costs."

Jack wasn't sure that statement was accurate, but obviously the truth had never stopped Herb from making political points. He decided to ignore Herb and respond specifically to the professor's challenge.

"I'm not sure it's possible to provide health insurance to forty-seven million more people, and at the same time lower the overall cost of care. If that is what they are trying to do, the ultimate effect will be to decrease access for virtually everyone."

The moderator interrupted to allow for a commercial break, and when the group discussion returned, he moved them in a different direction. During the second half of the thirty minute program they talked about the number of illegal immigrants, and their impact on the healthcare system. Not surprisingly, there was more agreement on this issue. Jack had little to say, but generally agreed that the border should be secured.

When the DVR reached the end of the program, Jack quickly deleted it.

"What are you doing?" Elaina asked.

"Deleting the program, why?"

"What if I wanted to share it with some of my friends."

"Your friends don't want to watch me on television," he said dismissively.

****

Over the next several days Jack received a number of requests to appear on local radio talk shows to discuss the healthcare reform bill. In each case he indicated that he hadn't finished reading it, but only had a vague idea what was in it. The talk show hosts didn't care about that, they just wanted someone who sounded authoritative to come on their show to discuss the most controversial subject of the year.

On each occasion Jack told the audience up front that he hadn't yet read the entire bill, but he was aware of some provisions that he found troubling. Chief among his concerns was the inclusion of a government run insurance entity, called the public option. He explained how that would eventually lead to a single payer system, something that most physicians opposed. He tried to make it clear that the statements made by the President of the AMA in support of the legislation had been taken out of context, but his seemed to be a lone voice against the giant media machine that was using the AMA to promote the effort in Washington.

One radio talk show host was known to lean somewhat to the left, and he'd had other guests on his show who had praised Congress's willingness to do whatever was required to rein in healthcare spending. Early on in that interview, the host asked, "What's so wrong with the idea of the government providing for the health care needs of all its citizens?"

Jack responded very calmly, "Whenever the government says they are going to give people something, there are always strings attached. In the case of health care it will be the loss of their personal freedom to choose the who, what, and when of your treatment. To see how a government run system works, we can just look at the one they have in Great Britain. Everyone has what amounts to free health care, but they wait months or even years to get it, and it's very impersonal. People are not free to choose for themselves. It is a one size fits all system, financed by extremely high taxes and regulated by bureaucrats. Did you know the average person in Great Britain pays more than fifty percent of their income to the government in taxes?" As he spoke his voice developed an obvious edge. He sounded more preachy than he'd intended.

The host responded by saying, "Well, doc, based on the calls I'm receiving everyday, the public believes the loss of a little freedom is a small price to pay for securing the health of all Americans." The host chose not to comment on Jack's revelation about high taxes.

****

"I heard you on the radio the other day," said one of the anesthesiologists, as Jack passed him in the doctor's lounge.

"Yeah, so did I," added one of the other surgeons. "You sounded pretty good, and I agreed with everything you said."

"Thanks," Jack replied. "It sounds like you and I may be the only ones who share that opinion."

"Nonsense," came the reply from his anesthesia colleague. "I think most of us agree with you, and I suspect most Americans do, too. They just aren't hearing our side of the argument. The liberals have control of the media, and to hear them tell it we are all filthy rich and play golf three days a week."

"DId you ever consider running for Congress, Jack?" the surgeon asked. "We need somebody like you to go up there and stop this BS. I think you'd do a great job."

"You've got to be kidding," Jack retorted. "Me? in Congress? Not on your life."

"Let's start a 'draft Jack Roberts' campaign," he said to the anesthesiologist. "I'll bet we could raise at least a hundred dollars this afternoon," he offered with a laugh.

Jack smiled at the attempted humor, and said, "Don't waste your breath or your money gentlemen. I'm not running for anything."

"Yeah, you say that now," the surgeon offered. "Just wait 'til they pass that new law. You'll change your tune."

"I don't think its going anywhere in its current form," Jack replied. Then he paused and developed a worried expression. "Then again, that's what I said about the possibility of Obama getting elected."

CHAPTER 3

Their room service dinner arrived just before seven o'clock when the polls were due to close in Texas and throughout most of the central part of the country. Elaina insisted that Jack come and sit down at the table with her, which he reluctantly did. As they watched the FOX News channel team go over the early results from the eastern part of the country, the commentators repeatedly suggested that Ohio, Florida and Virginia were key if the republican presidential challenger, Mitt Romney, were to have any chance of defeating the incumbent President, Barack Obama. Jack was absorbed in their analysis, but as he watched intently he thought it sounded more like they were providing the play-by-play accounts of a football game than a professional description of this historic event in American history.

"You need to eat something," Elaina said, urging Jack to at least try the sirloin steak she'd ordered for him.

"I will," he replied, "in a minute." Instead his mind drifted back to the series of events that led to him making the decision to run against Herman Sheffield in an effort to undo the damage that had been done to the American health care system.

****

The details of the new health care reform act passed by the House of Representatives slowly began to surface, and with it the excitement of Fitzgerald and Horvath. One of the key provisions was that everyone would be forced to buy either private or government insurance.

"Once they pass this law, we won't have to conduct all those damned fund raisers," Horvath said. "All those deadbeat accounts will finally get paid, and I won't have to go around begging for money. I think we could even do away with the entire development department."

"I wouldn't stop soliciting donations," Fitzgerald said, "If people are willing to give you money, it's pretty stupid not to take it."

Fitzgerald rubbed his chin, looking as if he were coming up with a new plan to solicit donations. After a moment he said, "We should be thinking bigger than just our children's hospital network. This change in the payment system is going to offer some major opportunities. Why don't you get in touch with Herb Nichols and arrange a meeting, just the three of us?" The tone of his voice told Horvath that his boss was not just making a suggestion. He had something very specific in mind.

The following afternoon Herb Nichols joined them in Fitzgerald's office. "Come in, come in," Fitzgerald said warmly, as he walked quickly toward Nichols and shook his hand firmly. Horvath also stood and shared a cordial greeting before the three men sat down in the grouping of chairs Fitzgerald's secretary had arranged in the corner of his office. The view overlooking downtown Fort Worth spoke to the power of the man who occupied the office.

"Thanks for coming over this afternoon," Fitzgerald offered. "Can I get you a drink?"

"No, I'm fine," Herb responded. "So, what's on your mind?" Herb was not one to engage in small talk.

"Several things. First," Fitzgerald began, "I know you are well connected with the leadership of the American Hospital Association, and I wanted to tell you how much we appreciate the role they are playing in writing, and hopefully passing this new healthcare law."

"I will certainly pass along your support, the next time our board meets, but you didn't ask me up here to thank the AHA."

"Of course not, I just wanted to make sure you knew that we were aware of everything that organization is doing on our behalf."

Herb nodded his understanding, but his look remained impatient.

The other two men had worked out their plan for approaching Nichols, so now it was Horvath's turn to speak. "We think the new healthcare law is going to provide us with an unprecedented opportunity to finally seize control over the entire system."

Herb's eyes brightened slightly as he cautiously nodded in agreement.

"The problem we have always faced has been the docs," Horvath continued.

"You don't have to tell me," Herb responded. "Those damned prima donnas are nothing but a pain in the ass."

"Exactly!" Horvath agreed. "We believe, and I'm sure you agree, that the ultimate goal of all this reform effort is going to be a single payer system, and those payments will all be made on a global basis."

Again Herb nodded in agreement, understanding that the doctors fees would eventually be combined with the hospital charges and paid to a single entity with a single check.

"When that happens, we need to be able to control that global payment, and the only way we can accomplish that will be to get the physician's under contract."

"Absolutely," Herb interrupted. "We've been trying to accomplish that for years, but the damned law here in Texas won't allow us to employ them directly."

"Right, but we have found a way around that limitation."

"How's that?" Herb inquired.

Horvath smiled slyly and explained their strategy. "What we've done is to get a couple of the leaders of the big primary care groups together. We gave then some financial incentives to join forces and form a single group. That wasn't hard, since they have been struggling to make a living under managed care and government insurance programs. We then created a separate corporation to manage their practices, and allowed the head guys to have a minority ownership position in that management company. They, in turn, brought along all the other primary care docs, promising them better payments and fewer hassles if they'd turn over their practice management to our company."

"Isn't that similar to what was tried back in the nineties? As I recall those docs didn't stay with the hospital's program once they saw how they were being manipulated."

"That's true," said Fitzgerald, "but, this time we have a secret weapon."

"What's that?" Herb asked.

"I have it on good authority that the new law is going to contain a provision that will require all government contracts to be with what they are calling accountable care organizations. Under the guise of improving quality, the government will only contract with networks that contain at least one hospital and a group of physicians. This will effectively eliminate the individual practitioner. They will be forced to participate in these ACOs, or be left completely out of the new payment system."

Herb was quickly getting the picture. He said, "So, you want to create the network first, using the hospital controlled management company, then tie it up with a nice little government contract." He paused as both men smiled and nodded in agreement. "That's brilliant," he added.

"We thought you'd agree, and that's why we wanted to get you involved," Fitzgerald said. "We think this strategy can be used to finally seize control of the entire system."

Horvath added, "The docs won't have a choice except to play along, once those contracts are completed. We'll take the global payments and initially we'll pay the docs about what they are getting now, on a fee-for-service basis. Then within a year, we can start ratcheting down their payments, using some artificial quality measures that we will develop. Since we'll have control of all the clinical data contained within our computerized health record, we'll be able to do whatever we want. If anybody complains, they'll be tossed out. The physician leaders won't dare complain because each of them will be getting regular bonuses from the management company, and those bonuses will be more than they can make in their practices."

"Sounds like you've got it all figured out so, what do you want from me?"

"Obviously, we're only able to pursue this strategy for pediatrics, but we think this strategy will work for adult healthcare as well. What we'd like to do is expand the management company to include all physician services in the region. You guys have hospitals across the entire metroplex and surrounding counties, and if we work together we could create what would amount to a monopoly using this model," Fitzgerald said. He knew Herb was a very ambitious man, and like all business men he loved the sound of the word monopoly. "All we want is exclusive control of the pediatrics piece. That would mean your hospitals would need to stop providing any pediatric care."

"Hell," Herb chortled, "we lose money on virtually all kid care. I'd gladly shut down that part of my hospital and convert it into a short term rehab hospital. Talk about something that can rake in the bucks!"

"I suspect it will take a couple of years to implement this process, but we've already done all the legal work. If this is something you want to pursue, I'm willing to bring you on as a shareholder in the management company for pennies on the dollar."

"Of course I'm interested," Herb said without hesitation. "How much are we talking about?"

"The book value of the stock is currently ten dollars a share, but because we need you involved," Fitzgerald stated. "You can buy a ten percent share in the company, that's ten thousand shares for a dollar a share."

"You don't need to say any more, I'm in."

Fitzgerald reached across the table and shook Herb's hand firmly. "I'll have the lawyers draw up the documents and get them over to your office on Monday."

"I assume you will be willing to make additional shares of stock available for the key physicians, right?"

"Absolutely," Fitzgerald replied. "They will need to pay the going rate of ten dollars a share, and none of them will get more than a one percent share."

"How about the other hospital administrators? I'll need to be able to offer them a piece of the action to get them on board."

"Of course," Fitzgerald said, expecting the question. "We are prepared to offer up to five key executives that you designate between two and five percent each, at two dollars a share."

What he didn't need to explain to Herb was the fact that he was maintaining the controlling interest in the management company. He held thirty-five percent of the stock and Horvath held twenty percent. Since Horvath was his direct subordinate, he would always control how he voted on any significant issues, including how the profits would be distributed.

"I think I will have that drink," Herb said with a satisfied smile.

****

Buzz Jackson was busily preparing for his morning in the cardiac cath lab, when Jerry Grady stepped into his office. "Hi Buzz," said the head of the huge pediatrics group that had been created when the two large competing groups merged under the guidance of Horvath, at Fitzgerald's direction. "You got a minute?"

"Well, actually, I'm trying to finish up with some paperwork before I head into the cath lab," Buzz replied, barely looking up from the computer screen.

"Oh, this will only take a minute," Grady insisted, ignoring the objection.

Horatio "Buzz" Jackson was the senior member of the pediatric cardiology group. He had served in the Air Force with Jack Roberts and the two friends had moved to Fort Worth twenty years ago to establish a comprehensive pediatric heart program. The distinguished, black physician stopped what he was doing and turned in his chair to face Grady. "What's up, Jerry?" he asked in his persistent Alabama drawl. He was trying his best to be collegial and avoid showing his impatience.

Jerry Grady, the slightly older pediatrician, had put on about thirty pounds since Buzz had last seen him, and he was now wearing a dark business suit instead of the bright shirt and cartoon tie that had always been his trademark. He was obviously showing the influences of corporate medicine.

"I haven't heard from you in a while and wanted to know if you have given any more consideration to my proposal to join our multi-specialty group?" Grady said bluntly. He had been communicating with Buzz and most of the other specialists by way of email over the past few months. With the financial backing of the hospital, the pediatricians were prepared to buy the practices of the key specialists they needed to form a true multi-specialty organization. The offer was a one time purchase of their practices, and for Buzz that amounted to a million dollars. The group would then provide them a salary of three hundred thousand dollars a year, guaranteed for three years. Several of the specialists had already taken the offer, but Buzz was still on the fence, largely because of some of the things Jack had told him about Horvath and Fitzgerald, who were clearly pulling Grady's strings.

"I haven't decided yet," Buzz stated with conviction.

"Well," Grady responded, "we have been approached by the cardiology group over in Dallas, and they have offered to have a couple of their guys join our group. They want a little more money than we planned to pay, but they are ready to move forward right away. You know we'd prefer to work with you and your partners, so I thought I'd give you first shot at this." He paused briefly, then continued, "Either way, we intend to move on with the creation of our multi-specialty group as quickly as we can to take full advantage of the accountable care organization provisions of the new law."

"It isn't the law, yet," Buzz corrected.

"We both know it's just a matter of time, and we intend to be ready, even before it passes."

Buzz sat silently looking up into the eyes of his long time colleague. It was obvious he was being strong armed into joining. The pediatricians were his main source of patient referrals, and if they brought in another group of cardiologists, those referrals would dry up immediately.

"What about the heart surgeons?" Buzz asked, hoping to find a weakness in Grady's seemingly invulnerable position.

"Oh, they're on board," he exaggerated. "We already have a commitment from George Ferguson, and I'm confident Jack Roberts will come along as well." The fact was that Grady had made a preliminary proposal to both Jack and his younger colleague, but he hadn't received even so much as a maybe from George, and Jack had flatly turned him down.

"Look," Buzz said, as he stood up hurriedly. " I've got to get over to the lab. Let me think about it, and I'll get back to you."

"I need an answer by the end of the week," Grady said rather smugly as Buzz made his way past him. "The Dallas group is ready to sign," he added as a final, not so subtle threat.

Buzz turned briefly back toward him. Grady's expression led him to believe he wasn't bluffing. His practice and his life were about to change, depending on his decision. "I'll let you know by Friday."

As he left the room he could feel the warmth building in his neck and ears as his blood pressure rose. He was being blackmailed into doing something he didn't want to do, and would lose his autonomy to a group of people he didn't trust, but what choice did he have?

****

George Ferguson, a somewhat shy thirty seven year old, had moved to Fort Worth from Birmingham, Alabama, four years earlier. He had completed his cardiothoracic surgery residency and a one year fellowship in pediatric heart surgery. He'd been recruited by the children's hospital with Jack's wholehearted blessing, because the heart program had grown to the point where Jack needed help, and the other heart surgeons in town didn't really have much experience or interest in doing pediatric hearts.

Jack had more or less taken the young surgeon under his wing and helped him establish himself in Fort Worth, but the older man's shadow was difficult for George to escape. The major cases were still being done by Jack, and George had not been aggressive enough to build his own referral network. Even so, his practice had gradually grown, in part because whenever Jack was out of town, George covered for him. In the past that was no more than two or three weeks a year, but as Jack gained confidence in his young colleague, he was comfortable taking more time off.

"You remember me telling you that Elaina and I are going to Nicaragua next week, right?" Jack asked as the two men stood at the scrub sink washing their hands in preparation for a rather routine ligation of a patent ductus arteriosus on a one year old child.

"Yeah," George replied. "I got you covered."

"Barring something emergent coming in, I don't anticipate having any patients in the hospital," Jack explained. "I expect this kid will be home by the end of the week, and I don't have anything else on the schedule."

"I know I've asked you this before, but why do you go down there every summer? I thought that was one of the poorest countries in the world."

"Actually, Nicaragua is the second poorest country in the western hemisphere," he replied. "Second only to Haiti. That's one of the reasons why we go. Those people don't have much of anything, particularly health care, and Elaina and I enjoy going there and helping out a group of local docs who run a free clinic."

"So what exactly do you do? They don't have any place where you can do this kind of heart surgery, do they?"

"Not really... we did do a PDA ligation down there a few years back. It was done under pretty primitive conditions, but we managed to get it done. Most of what we do is help the primary care guys see people for all kinds of routine problems, from hypertension and diabetes to pregnancy and immunizations."

"So you go down there to play Marcus Welby," George laughed.

"More or less," Jack responded with his own soft chuckle. "It's great. There are no computerized records, no utilization review committees, no insurance forms to fill out. You should try it some time."

"Sounds like it is just the kind of break I need," George replied. "But, it doesn't sound like it pays very much."

"I don't go down there to get paid," Jack responded. "I go to get away from this rat race that has become all about the money." He wasn't sure George was yet able to grasp what he was implying.

****

Having completed all the required pre-med courses, David was fully prepared to coast through his senior year in Austin. His plan was to take some relatively easy electives so he could keep his grade point average up, helping to ensure his acceptance into medical school. Through three years his GPA was 3.92, just shy of a perfect 4.0, and he was pretty confident he would get in somewhere. He became even more convinced when he received his score from the standardized medical college admission test he'd taken back in May. His overall score of 40 placed him in the top one percent of all students who took the MCAT.

David said he really wanted to remain in the state of Texas and the med school application process was made much easier by the single form used to apply to all five University of Texas schools, including his first choice, Southwestern in Dallas. At his mother's insistence he also submitted applications to some of the big name schools including Duke, Stanford, Johns Hopkins and of course Harvard.

As he placed the huge envelop addressed to Cambridge, Massachusetts in the mail, he laughed softly to himself. He secretly hoped Harvard would send him a letter of acceptance just so he could turn them down.

Each application required a letter of recommendation from someone other than a family member. Buzz Jackson and his dad's favorite anesthesiologist, Radha Patel, had both gladly obliged. Their letters told of a brilliant young man who had all the characteristics they would look for in their own physician.

His advisor had explained that letters of acceptance didn't usually get issued until Thanksgiving or later, so once the applications were in the mail, all he could do was wait. He and Amy returned to Austin, anxious to complete that part of their journey.

****

For the next several months it seemed the only topic in the news was the status of health care reform in the Congress. In early November, the Senate finally got around to introducing their version, which they had named "The Patient Protection and Affordable Care Act of 2009." Jack had read the House bill in anticipation of discussing it at the late November teleconference of the Association of Thoracic Surgeons board of trustees. He also reviewed the summary outline of the Senate bill, since that's all that was available. As far as he could tell, the biggest difference between the two bills was the absence of a public option in the Senate version. The issues of public funding for abortions were handled a bit differently, but Jack thought they both provided inappropriate support for the what he called pre-infanticide

As the secretary/treasure of a national organization that represented cardiothoracic surgeons, as well as the delegate to the AMA from that organization, he felt he was obligated to help formulate a response to this proposed legislation. During the discussion, it was obvious that Jack was the only one on the call who had any real understanding of what was being proposed.

When the teleconference started, many of the board members expressed cautious optimism over the bills. The academic surgeons seemed eager to see changes that would reduce the amount of charity care delivered in their institutions, Jack initially held back a bit in his criticism of the public option, however, he didn't hesitate to point out that both of the bills being considered called for at least a four hundred billion dollar reduction in Medicare payments over the next ten years.

"If you combine the cuts that are mandated by either of these new bills with the cuts that are called for by the sustainable growth rate formula, Medicare payments to physicians will end up being lower than current Medicaid levels. For our members whose practices are highly dependent on Medicare, the effect will be devastating," he said.

"I thought they were going to include a fix to the SGR with the new law," said one of the other board members.

Jack responded, "If you recall, the President said he would not sign any bill that increased the deficit by more than one trillion dollars. As it stands now, the cost of this bill has been estimated at about nine hundred and fifty-billion dollars. The cost of repealing the SGR is about three hundred billion dollars, so they have completely scrapped that idea,"

"I still think we should support this effort," said one of the other board members. Jack recognized his voice as the chairman of the department of surgery at the University of Kentucky in Lexington.

"The biggest problem with this bill isn't really the cost, it will be the thousands of new regulations the government will impose on every physician," Jack stated as if it were a matter of fact.

"Perhaps we should wait to see what the final legislation looks like," said Frank Novak, the sitting president of the ATS. "We all know there will be changes made in the Senate bill when it goes to the House. The whole thing is likely to end up in a conference committee. The final piece of legislation will be very different from what is currently being debated."

"There is one thing in the House bill that we should all be aware of," Jack said, feeling that the discussion was coming to a premature end. "The House bill contains a provision that would establish a government run health insurance corporation. This was a major item of debate on the floor of the AMA House of Delegates, and it will be a major issue going forward."

"What's the problem with the government offering health insurance to people who can't afford to buy it from private insurance companies?" This question came from another board member who's voice Jack didn't recognize.

"It will lead directly to a single payer system, because private insurers won't be able to compete. I don't think any of us want to become employees of the federal government, do we?"

Still another voice was heard, saying, "Might as well, we are already slaves to the insurance companies."

There was total silence for several seconds. Even Jack had no immediate response to the biting truth of that statement. Finally, Novak said, "Well, on that happy note I would suggest we adjourn for the evening." They all agreed, and when Jack hung up the phone he was filled with a profound sadness. He had never thought of himself as a slave to anything or anyone. Yet the longer he considered that statement, the more certain he was of its truth.

The next morning Jack received a call on his cell phone, from a number he didn't recognize.

"Hi Jack, this is Frank Novak," said the ATS President in his familiar casual manner.

"Hi Frank," Jack replied. "What's up?"

"I wanted to thank you for your report on the healthcare reform legislation last night. I know everyone appreciated the time you spent reviewing those bills."

"Your welcome, I just wish there was something substantive in it that I could get excited about."

"Yeah, I know," Novak said with a subtle sadness in his voice. He then continued, changing the subject slightly. "Listen, I got a call from my Member of Congress this morning, asking me if I would be willing to come to Washington and testify before the Ways and Means Committee on the impact of the proposed healthcare reform bill."

"That's great!" Jack exclaimed. "Maybe you can set them straight on a few things."

"There is just one problem," He replied. "My wife and I are leaving on a much needed vacation next week for our fortieth wedding anniversary."

"Are you going anywhere special?"

"Yes, she's been bugging me for years to take her to Paris, so that's where we're going."

"I'm sure you'll both love it. I've been there several times. In fact, that's where Elaina and I went on our honeymoon, but that was twenty years ago."

"I was wondering if I could get you to go to Washington next Wednesday and testify on behalf of the ATS?" Novak asked. "I know this is short notice, but like I said, I just found out this morning, and that is the only day they offered me."

"I'm not sure I'm the right guy," Jack said. "What about John Stanky? He's the vice-president."

"He is tied up giving testimony in a court case that day, and he can't get out of it, so your next in line, and besides, I think you are the logical one to go anyway. You're the only one of us who knows what's in that damned bill."

Jack thought for a moment, wondering what Elaina would say. "Okay, I'll clear my schedule and make the trip."

"It's scheduled for ten o'clock on Wednesday morning, so you'll need to go up the night before." Novak explained. "I have a room reserved at the Oriental Hotel in my name, and someone from the Congressman's office will meet you at the airport. They will also pick you up at the hotel on Wednesday morning and take you to the hearing. Obviously, ATS will reimburse you for your flight and any other expenses."

"So, what am I supposed to say?" Jack asked tentatively. "If I'm speaking for the society, I'm not sure exactly how our board feels about the bill. We didn't vote on whether we supported or opposed it."

"I think we are all in agreement that government interference in healthcare is a dangerous proposition, so I think if you use that as your guiding principle, we will all be behind you. Just talk about it to the committee the way you did to us last night."

"Okay," Jack agreed, "but if I say something that somebody on our board doesn't agree with, you'll back me up, right?'

"Don't worry about George," Novak said, referring to the academic board member who had spoken out in favor of the public option. "He's in the minority, I'm sure. Besides, you couldn't please him, no matter what you say."

"I'll do my best not to embarrass the ATS."

"I know you'll do a terrific job. I really appreciate your willingness to do this for me, and by the way, good luck. Those egomaniacs in Congress can be pretty vicious when they smell fresh meat," he laughed, but was only half kidding, and Jack knew it.

"I'll give you a report at our next teleconference." With that, the call was over and Jack headed back toward his office.

That evening he told Elaina about his conversation with Novak, and asked her if she wanted to go with him to DC. He was surprised when she said she would, so he made their flight arrangements. He told his office staff to reschedule his Wednesday surgery and Thursday office patients so he and Elaina could spend two days in Washington. She had never visited the Capitol, so he planned to spend Thursday showing her the monuments and Arlington National Cemetery.

When they arrived at Reagan National Airport, the following Tuesday evening, there was a limousine driver waiting for them, holding a handwritten sign with Jack's name on it. The couple was quickly escorted to the car and within fifteen minutes they were at the posh Mandarin Oriental hotel, overlooking the small marina on the banks of the Potomac River.

It was well after eight o'clock so they decided to just order room service. During dinner, Jack was uncharacteristically quiet. He was reviewing his prepared remarks, but the more he went over them the more convinced he was that reading a prepared statement was not the best way to make the points he wanted to make.

"What's the matter dear?" Elaina asked when she saw that he had barely touched his Maryland crab cakes.

"I'm just trying to decide what to say tomorrow. I've got this written statement, but I don't want to sit there and read a statement into the record and then be dismissed like some school boy. This is too important. I want them to actually listen to what I have to say and to seriously consider what they are doing to the future of health care in this country." Jack sounded as if he was pleading for help.

"I think you should just be yourself. Just tell them what you think and why its important. You can't make them listen, but I'm sure you will get your points across just fine." Elaina said softly but with the confidence Jack was lacking at that moment. She had a way of putting things into perspective, and that was one of the many things he loved about her.

The next morning, Elaina accompanied Jack into the large hearing room on the House side of the Capitol building. They both sat near the back of the room as the formal proceedings began. The Chairman was a man Jack recognized from his numerous appearances on television. He had recently been a guest on Bill O'Reilly's program on FOX, where he argued incessantly with the host about virtually everything, especially the bailout of Fannie Mae and Freddie Mac. He was a committed liberal democrat, who had been waiting his entire political life for this opportunity to finally pass healthcare reform.

The meeting was called to order at ten a.m. sharp, but testimony didn't begin for another hour. Each of the members of the committee felt compelled to make a few remarks on the importance of the proceedings and on the future of America. The television cameras were rolling and each five minute monolog sounded like just another campaign speech. Jack thought this had all the makings of a three ring circus.

Finally, the chairman announced the committee's plan to hear from several invited witnesses who were to provide an opening statement of not more than five minutes, and then be subject to questions from members of the committee, not to exceed fifteen minutes unless otherwise ruled by the chair.

"Our first witness is Dr. Frank Novak, President of the Association of Thoracic Surgeons."

Jack couldn't believe his ears. Had they not gotten word that he was subbing for Frank? He noticed some commotion behind the chairman, as one of the other members approached him with a slip of paper. He turned back to the microphone and said smugly, "It appears Dr. Novak was too busy to come to this committee meeting, and he has sent Dr. Jack Roberts, the secretary/treasurer of that organization in his place."

This was not exactly how he had envisioned this getting started. Jack rose from his seat and made his way toward the table that faced the panel of committee members who were seated at the huge curved desk, elevated several feet above the floor level. He assumed his seat and anticipated being sworn in, but this was not that kind of hearing.

"So, Dr. Roberts, since your president couldn't be here, I guess you'll have to do," the chairman said, not hiding his well publicized lack of respect for all members of the medical profession. "What can you tell us about health care that we don't already know?"

Jack took a quick glance at his notes, but given the challenge the chairman had just issued he decided to forego his outline and speak directly to the question he'd just been asked.

"Mr. Chairman, members of the committee," he began. "First I want to thank you for the opportunity to speak to you this morning on behalf of the Association of Thoracic Surgeons. The issue of health care reform is one that touches every American, and as a physician I consider it part of my obligation to my patients and to my profession to help get it right.

"You ask what I can tell you about health care that you don't already know, and I would like to answer that by sharing a story with you. It is the story of a baby who was born in Mexico with a congenital heart defect. The child was certain to die within days, and despite a government run healthcare system in that country, there was no possibility of her receiving the treatment she desperately needed. Her father, is a poor laborer, but he was determined not to allow his daughter to die, so, at considerable peril to himself and his family, he smuggled her across the border into Texas."

Elaina sat stunned by what her husband was revealing. Even she knew that providing care to illegal immigrants was one of the biggest arguments for the rising cost of health care. Where was he going with this, she wondered?

"The father managed to find a hospital and a young surgeon in Corpus Christi who was capable of performing the life saving operation. The child survived and returned with her family to Mexico a few days later. There was no money exchanged, no insurance filed, no government forms to fill out. It was simply a caring group of individuals, led by a physician who had sworn an oath to care for any, and all who are in need, to the best of his ability. That sir, is health care."

The room was quiet, as his story had captured their undivided attention. After another moment he continued. "With all due respect, Mr. Chairman, I would suggest that health care is not what needs reforming," he stated boldly, directly at the smirking Congressman. "What needs to be reformed is the way we pay for those services. The current system is broken, we all know that, but the reason it is broken is because we have left the most important person out of the discussion, and that is the patient." He paused again for maximum effect.

"When I took the Hippocratic Oath, it wasn't directed at Blue Cross or Aetna, and it sure wasn't to Medicare or Medicaid. It was a morally binding contract with my patient. The problems we face today all revolve around the efforts made by third parties, including our government, that interfere with that social contract between patient and physician."

Elaina had heard Jack's speech about the patient physician relationship many times, but she thought this time he was making his point far more effectively than usual.

"I understand that one of the major arguments being used to promote the legislation under consideration by this committee is the need to restrain the runaway growth of spending, and I could not agree more. We simply cannot continue along the current path. However, the answer is not a bigger government role. The current set of regulations under Medicare and Medicaid are fostering higher prices because the system is not a free market. Patients have no idea what anything costs, and they don't really want to know. To them it's free, as long as their insurance or the government says they will cover it. This has led to increasing demand for services, without regard to cost. The government's solution has been more regulations, which only compounds the problem."

Jack felt the passion of his convictions might be overshadowing the message, so he took a deep breath and lowered his voice slightly. "I would like to offer Medicare as an example," he continued. "Beginning in 1998, Medicare payments to physicians were subjected to the sustainable growth rate formula, the SGR, something that some committee like this one came up with, supposedly to curb the rise in Medicare spending. More than a decade later it is obvious it didn't accomplish that goal. Instead it has resulted in payments to physicians being essentially frozen at levels that now threaten the very viability of the Medicare program, and to repeal the SGR is estimated to cost nearly three hundred billion dollars."

"I understand that here on Capitol Hill, repealing the SGR is unaffectionately known as the doc fix. Well, Mr. Chairman, docs don't want a fix,or a bailout. They want to be left alone. The way to fix Medicare, and the entire system for that matter is for the government to decide how much they will pay for services, not how much I, or any other physician, can charge. A free market will determine the cost, and as in every other aspect of our economy, prices will come down in an environment that promotes true competition."

Jack knew he was running out of time, but he wanted to drive home his point about the evils of government interference with one final point. "Over the last four decades plus that Medicare has existed, it has undergone many revisions and modifications, and I suspect future Congresses will continue to modify it. I would simply like to point out that each and every time modifications have been made, they have increased the power and control of bureaucrats at the expense of the freedom and rights of the individual. It is interesting to note, that in the original language, when Medicare was enacted as an amendment to the Social Security Act, it included very specific language that prevented Congress from interfering with the free practice of medicine or regulating what a physician could charge for any specific service. Then in 1984, Congress passed the Deficit Reduction Act, which established a new process whereby physicians were required to declare whether or not they would participate in the Medicare program. In so doing, physicians were compelled to accept whatever the assigned Medicare payment was for any covered services.

This effectively eliminated their right to "balance bill" the patient for any amount above what the government set as a fixed fee, or charge less than that fee for that matter. From there, we saw the creation of the SGR to further regulate fees. Given that history with Medicare, why should we believe that this new bill, which expands the role of government in healthcare will not further enslave the medical profession, and our patients?"

"Mr. Chairman, and members of this extremely important committee, I would like to conclude my remarks by simply asking each of you, before you pass any law that has an impact on those you are here to represent, to imagine yourself as a patient who is in desperate need of help. When you do, you should ask yourself, would I prefer a physician who has sworn and oath to do whatever he can to help me, or one that is entangled by a sea of government red tape?"

After another brief pause, Jack concluded by saying, "Thank you, Mr. Chairman, for the opportunity to speak to this committee on behalf of the Association of Thoracic Surgeons and America's physicians."

The chairman, like most of his colleagues in the Democrat party was a staunch advocate of a single payer system. In a recent interview he had been asked about the public option and he made no secret that he believed it would lead to government run health care. He began the questioning of this witness by saying, "Well, that's an interesting fantasy you describe there, doctor. Tell me, do you really believe all that stuff about free market health care?"

"Yes, sir, I do," was Jack's immediate response.

The chairman responded, "Well, that philosophy is the reason healthcare costs are out of control. Our system is antiquated and is based on inflated fees for services that are not really that much different from some of the other trades."

"With all due respect, sir. I think it is a bit of a stretch to equate heart surgery or brain surgery with one of the trades," Jack replied with a sarcastic smile.

"Isn't what you do more or less the same thing as a plumber? And, isn't the neurosurgeon more or less an electrician?"

Jack had not been prepared for this line of attack. He responded the way he always did, countering with logic and reason.

"Clearly, Mr. Chairman, you are joking, right?" The only response came in the form of a smirking shaking of the bureaucrat's head.

Jack gathered his composure and continued. "To become a physician requires years of education and training. To equate that with being a tradesman is not only incorrect, it is insulting."

"Oh, doctor," the Chairman said, feigning regret, "I didn't mean to insult you, but you must be aware that in some parts of the world, they identify young people when they are still in elementary school and fast track them to become Medical Doctors by the time their peers are finishing college."

Jack sat in stunned silence. He couldn't believe this guy was equating a Medical Degree in the US with one from Russia or China. "I have been to some of those places you talk about, and all I can say is the level of education and the care that is delivered is not the same as here."

"According to all the statistics, care in most of the civilized world is actually better than it is here."

Jack thought for a moment before responding. "Did you ever hear of a guy by the name of Samuel Clemens?"

The chairman looked puzzled and shook his head, anticipating this doctor was going to site some obscure study that would refute what he already knew to be the truth, based on data from the World Health Organization.

"His pen name was Mark Twain, and he had a saying about stuff like what you just said. 'There are three kinds of lies: lies, damned lies and statistics.' Personally, I believe there is an agenda behind those World Health Organization statistics. Otherwise, why would people from all over the world come to the US for health care?"

"Certainly, we have excellent care for those who can afford insurance, but what about those millions who don't have the resources to access care?"

"You mean people like the little girl I saw last week in the ER who has acute bacterial endocarditis. Her family has no money and no insurance other than Medicaid. She's being cared for right now in one of the finest children's hospitals in the world."

"That's not what I'm talking about, and you know it," the chairman spouted back defensively. "I'm talking about the guy who lost his job and his insurance, and his wife had to undergo emergency surgery. Now he is filing bankruptcy because he can't pay his medical bills. He is a victim of a health care system that is out of control, and he is precisely the person whose right to affordable healthcare must be ensured. That is what this bill is designed to do."

"Perhaps, this is not the place for this type of argument," injected the ranking republican member of the committee.

"I'll decide what is and isn't appropriate arguments in these hearings," the chairman offered, glaring at his political rival. "The time has come for this Congress to act on behalf of those who aren't rich doctors or insurance executives." He turned back toward Jack and stated firmly, "I'm afraid your time is up, doctor. Thank you for coming, you are excused."

"Well, that was enlightening, wasn't it?" he said to Elaina when he returned to his seat next to her.

"I thought for a minute you might go up there and punch that SOB in the nose, and I found myself hoping you would," she said with more anger in her voice than he had heard in some time.

"Don't you see? This is just a show. It's politics, where the more ridiculous the argument the more attention you receive."

When the morning session was over, the committee broke for lunch, and Jack and Elaina made their way out toward the rotunda, accompanied by the congressional staffer who had been assigned to them for the day.

"Do we have to attend the afternoon session?" Jack asked the young man.

"No, sir. You are welcome to stay if you like, but most people leave right after their testimony."

"I think we will spend the afternoon walking around the Capitol," Jack said as he looked down at Elaina and saw her nodding in agreement.

"Excuse me, Dr. Roberts?" The baritone voice was not familiar. Jack looked up and saw a very distinguished man who appeared to be in his mid-fifties. "I apologize for interrupting, but I heard your testimony at Ways and Means, and I was wondering if I could have a word with you?"

"You're not from the media, are you?" Jack inquired defensively.

"Oh, no," the man responded. "I'm Stan Blanchard. I am the chief lobbyist for two of the larger pharmaceutical companies. I'm scheduled to testify before the committee later this afternoon."

Jack extended his hand cautiously and the Washington insider quickly went into his routine, which always included what Jack now thought was an overly friendly handshake. "I guess I have a minute to talk," Jack said, glancing briefly at Elaina. "This is my wife, Elaina."

"Its very nice to meet you," the lobbyist said, moving his gaze toward her only briefly before returning his full attention to Jack. "I don't get why you guys are so against this healthcare reform package. I'd think it would be a windfall for you."

Jack looked down at the lobbyist's two thousand dollar suit and thousand dollar shoes before looking up into his eyes. "You don't get it because to you everything is about the money. For most of us it isn't about how much we get paid, its about maintaining the freedom to practice the art and science of medicine without being dictated to by people who are only peripherally involved in pursuit of power or money,"

"I see," the man said as a quizzical expression came over his face. "I'm not sure what parallel world you are living in my friend, but the fact is that money is what makes the one I live in go around."

Jack looked at this stranger, first with contempt, but it quickly morphed into pity. "I'm sorry to disappoint you, but to me ethics and integrity are more important than money."

The lobbyist smirked and replied, "Ethics, my friend, is the science of the poor. There are only two kinds of people, those who have money and those who wish they did, and it's those who have the money that always determine what happens to everyone else."

Jack understood the implication that was being made. If the doctors didn't get on board this time, the train was going to leave the station without them.

"I feel sorry for you. Without a basic code of ethics, our lives have no purpose. The pursuit of fortune is meaningless without a bigger purpose."

"Oh, there's a bigger purpose all right. We intend to use our money and power to seize control of America's healthcare system. Then you and your Hippocratic Oath will come begging for crumbs from our table."

Jack just smiled at this pathetic man in front of him and shook his head. He didn't know what to say in response to such blatant hostility and what he thought bordered on immorality.

As the lobbyist turned to leave he looked back and casually said, "You can't say I didn't warn you."

****

"I'm so glad to have you home again," Elaina said excitedly as her son walked into the kitchen and gave his mom a big hug. She was hoping he'd stay home for the entire three week Christmas break.

"I'm really glad to be home," David said, "What's for supper?"

"You're worse than your father. It's always about food," she laughed.

"Where is Dad?"

"He called a little bit ago and told me he should be home in an hour or so. He's finishing up at the office and then he has to run by the children's hospital to make rounds."

"Did I get any mail?"

David had last been home for the week of Thanksgiving, but as of then he'd not gotten word from any of the medical schools regarding his applications. He was beginning to worry that perhaps his optimism had been misplaced.

"Actually," Elaina said with a wry smile, "a couple of things came yesterday and another showed up today. They are sitting over there on the desk." She nodded toward a small pile of unopened mail on her kitchen desk.

David excitedly collected the three envelopes and sat down at the table. They were each addressed to Mr. David Allan Roberts. One was from the

University of Texas Medical Branch in Galveston, while another was from the UT school in Houston. The third was from Duke. He decided to open that one first, anticipating it would contain the bad news of a rejection. As he carefully pulled the one page letter out he broke into a huge smile.

"What's it say, honey?" Elaina asked, anticipating the answer from the look on his face.

"Dear Mr. Roberts, As the Dean of Admissions, it is my privilege to invite you to join the freshman class at Duke University Medical School, beginning August fifteenth, 2010. I ask that you please respond to this letter no later than January tenth, 2010, informing me of your acceptance of this invitation ... "

"Congratulations!" she said as she quickly came up behind him to look over his shoulder. "Duke? Wow! That's pretty prestigious."

David reread the letter again, feeling as though perhaps there was a mistake or some additional qualifier he had missed. He didn't see anything that would suggest this wasn't the real deal. He slowly placed the letter back in the envelope and opened the next one from the school in Houston.

He read is softly aloud to himself, "The University of Texas Medical School in Houston is pleased to offer you admission to our next Freshman class, beginning August twenty second, 2010. Please respond to this letter by January fifteenth ..." He folded the letter and placed it back into its envelope and said, "I got accepted in Houston, too."

"That's great!" she said, having returned to the cook top to stir the chili she was preparing. "What about UTMB?"

He looked at her questioning how she knew where the third letter was from, but quickly realized she had been anticipating these letters almost as much as he had. He ripped open the final letter and saw quickly that they wanted him as well.

"I can't believe it," he said. "Three acceptances. I didn't anticipate being able to actually choose where I'd be going."

"There are still several schools we haven't heard from. I'll bet in a few more days you'll have your pick," she said proudly.

He stood up and walked over behind his mom and placed his hands on her shoulders. He leaned forward and kissed her on the cheek, saying, "Thanks so much for everything you have done for me. None of this would have been possible without all the support from you and Dad."

She turned around and took his face in her hands and said, "We are so incredibly proud of you. I hope you know that. Your father was so excited when he saw those letters yesterday." She released her hold on him but continued to look into his youthful eyes. "He wanted to open them and then seal them back up, but I wouldn't let him. I know he'll be even more thrilled to hear the news directly from you."

"I need to go call Amy," he said, suddenly realizing she should be the first to know. "I'll be back down for dinner." He turned and hurried up the stairs to his room.

"Hey Baby, guess what?" he asked as she answered the phone.

"Uh... You decided you want to get married tomorrow," she said teasingly.

"I'm in!" he nearly shouted into the phone.

"Where?" she replied excitedly.

"Well, so far, Houston, Galveston and, are you ready for this? Duke."

"I told you. I never doubted it, not for a minute. What about the others?"

"I've only gotten three letters so far. No idea when the others will come. I just wanted to let you know. We can decide which one to accept once we know all our options."

She loved the way he said we. "What are we going to do to celebrate?" she asked again emphasizing the pronoun.

"Well, I'm going to have dinner with my folks and then I'll come pick you up, say around eight?"

"Sounds perfect."

"My mom has made chili and she would be very disappointed if I didn't stick around here and eat with them. Maybe we'll go downtown to Sundance Square."

"Okay! Can we take a carriage ride?" she sounded almost giddy.

"Of course, if that's what you want to do. I'll see you at eight."

"I love you," she said sweetly.

"I love you too, Baby"

When Jack came through the door, David was standing in the kitchen waiting. He excitedly broke the news to his dad, even before he'd had a chance to give Elaina his customary kiss.

"That's great!" Jack exclaimed, mirroring his son's enthusiasm. "I'm kind of surprised they all came in at the same time."

"This isn't all of them," David replied. "I sent out nine applications, so hopefully I'll hear something from the others in the next few days. I'm anxious to know whether I get accepted by the other Texas schools."

"I know you also interviewed at Southwestern and San Antonio. Which other schools did you go look at?" he asked, not sure whether he had been to any of the out of state campuses.

"I didn't have a chance to interview at any other schools, but really I don't think I want to leave Texas."

"I spent plenty of time at Johns Hopkins in Baltimore, and I must say its not much to look at, but then you really shouldn't choose a school based on appearance."

"I understand the campus at Stanford is impressive, but I can't see living in California. Too many people."

"Well, once you know what all your options are, then you can decide. You have some time, and if you want to go visit a couple of those places to help you make up your mind, I'm sure we can help make that happen."

"Thanks, Dad, but I've pretty well already made up my mind, assuming my first choice accepts me."

"So, where's that?"

"I've always wanted to go to Southwestern in Dallas. Its close to home and I know its a great school, and that's where you went."

Jack smiled and nodded slightly. He had always hoped that if David decided to go to medical school that he would choose his alma mater. "That sounds great. Your mom and I will certainly enjoy having you close to home."

While Jack really was excited for David, there was part of him that wanted to suggest that he reconsider his career choice. He feared that the way things were going, his son would never have the opportunity to have the immense satisfaction that comes with a truly independent practice. If things didn't change, by the time he finished med school and residency the only option available would be to work as a government employee. That thought caused him to be overcome by a deep sadness, and as his shoulders slumped perceptibly, David took notice.

"Are you okay, Dad?"

"Yeah, sure," Jack replied quickly, as he realized he had unconsciously given away his thoughts. "I was just thinking about med school," Jack lied to cover up his feelings. "When do we eat?" he asked Elaina.

"What did I tell you?" she responded toward David.

He laughed, but Jack was left wondering what he had missed.

Elaina started filling the soup bowls with the chili she'd begun preparing two hours earlier. Her men sat down at the table and immediately started adding things to the meaty dish. She had put out a bowl of shredded cheddar cheese, a package of corn chips, a plate of diced onions and a jar of their favorite salsa. Jack always wanted it spicier than she preferred, so she'd placed a bottle of Tabasco on the table.

They passed around all the extra fixings and eventually everyone had their chili just the way they liked it. As they started to eat, David still sensed that something was troubling his father.

"So, Dad," he asked, "what do you think is going to happen with the new health care law?"

Jack had just been talking about that subject with his anesthesiologist, Radha Patel in the OR earlier that day. "I don't know," he offered. "It looks like the democrats have the votes to pass something, but what that will be is still unclear."

"I heard some people in Austin talking about a public option, but I don't know what that is." David said hoping for some clarification.

"Public option refers to insurance offered by the government to anyone who doesn't want to buy insurance in the private market, from a private company like Blue Cross or Aetna, or any other insurance company," Jack explained.

"So, why is that such a big deal?" his son asked.

"When the government becomes a competitor in the free market, the free market quickly goes away. The government doesn't have to live by the same economic rules. First, they don't have to make a profit, and second, they can use tax money to subsidize their product, making it cheaper than any private product. They will quickly run the private companies out of business," Jack explained.

"Well, I thought you always said the insurance companies were part of the problem. What would be wrong with running those guys out of business?"

"There is no question that insurance companies have been taking advantage of people for many years," Jack replied. "Don't get me wrong, I have no love for the insurance industry, but if the government takes over healthcare then every physician will become nothing more than a government employee, and that will spell disaster."

"I guess I don't understand," David stated. "The way the system is now, don't most doctors get paid by the insurance companies? Why would it be all that different if they get paid by the government?"

Jack knew David had a valid point. Doctors had indeed become employees of the insurance companies when they signed contracts with the so called managed care plans. He'd been reminded of that employed relationship during the recent ATS teleconference. It was clear that most physicians had unknowingly become reliant on the big insurance companies to pay for their services, and in recent years it had been those payers that had imposed all sorts of regulations and controls on the practice of medicine. Perhaps the idea of a public option and the single payer system that would result had simply brought into focus the ethical dilemma that results when any third party is allowed to participate in the patient-physician relationship.

"That is the argument many people are making," Jack said. "I guess the only real difference is that in a free market system, everybody has choices. If the patient doesn't like one policy they can go somewhere else, and if a doctor doesn't like what some company is paying him he doesn't have to stay with that company either. If you have a single payer, those options go away for everyone."

"But, Dad," David said in frustration. "I thought most people just got whatever insurance their employer offered. They don't really have all that much of a choice, do they?"

"That is true, and that's part of the problem. The employer based insurance system is anything but a free market. That's why I've said all along that people should be able to buy their own insurance under the same rules as their employer buys it. The reason we have this system where people get health insurance through their employer dates back to the years after World War II."

"You're not going to give me another history lesson, are you?" David laughed.

"No, but it is important for you to know that it hasn't always been this way. Employers began offering a form of health insurance called, major medical, back in the nineteen fifties in lieu of higher wages. The insurance was cheap, partly because it only covered big health care expenses, like hospitalization and surgery. It has obviously evolved into a system where today, people rely on insurance to cover virtually everything even remotely related to health care." Jack paused for a moment, realizing he was getting off the point he had been trying to make. "Anyway, employer based insurance has dominated American health care ever since, largely because of the way it is treated from a tax perspective."

David now had no idea what his dad was talking about, so he asked, "What do taxes have to do with it?"

"Everything," Jack said. "The way the federal tax laws are written, employers can write off the cost of buying insurance for their employees as a business expense, and the employees are not required to report the value of the insurance benefit they receive on their personal income tax. However, if an individual goes out and buys their own insurance policy, like your mom and I do, we are not allowed to deduct the cost on our personal income tax. In other words, companies buy insurance with pre-tax dollars and individuals must use after tax dollars. That alone makes employer based insurance much less expensive. When you combine that with the fact that big companies get volume discounts based on the number of employees they have, the entire private health insurance system continues to remain employer based."

"This is such a mess," David sighed.

Jack nodded his head in agreement as he picked up his glass of sweet tea.

"Most people don't even have a clue what's going on, do they?" David asked.

"I'm afraid not," Jack replied. "They don't know, and what's worse is they don't care. The public has been hypnotized by Obama's big toothy grin when he started talking about hope and change, and how the government was going to provide health care to all Americans."

Jack knew that Elaina was getting close to interrupting, so he decided to cut off the political discussion. He turned to her and added, "Hypnotized the way your mom hypnotized me with those beautiful green eyes."

"You knew you were close to getting kicked under the table, huh?" she said, wrinkling her brow.

Jack didn't respond other than to shrug his shoulders and dive back into the chili.

CHAPTER 4

With the first few precincts reporting, Jack had a slight lead over the incumbent democrat Herman Sheffield. Elaina was almost giddy when the numbers were flashed on the screen. Roberts (R) - 247, Sheffield (D) - 163. But the number that followed was critically important, less than two percent of the precincts reporting.

"So far so good," Jason said.

"The political newcomer, Dr. Jack Roberts, has taken an early lead over the six term incumbent democrat," the commentator said. "But, the night is young, and given the fierce battle that Sheffield waged in the final days of the campaign, it's likely to be close throughout the evening."

Everyone had told Jack what a scoundrel Sheffield was, and he knew first hand just how ugly things had gotten toward the end, but he believed all along he could win. Now as he sat silently watching the votes slowly being tabulated, he allowed himself to start wondering if that was really true. He countered his doubts by allowing his mind to drift back to the excitement that surrounded his son, as his own ambitions were being realized.

****

"I wish you could be a little more positive when you talk to David about the future of medicine," Elaina said as Jack came to bed.

"I think he knows what's happening. He's the one who brought up the subject at dinner," Jack replied defensively.

"He is so excited, and I just think when you start talking about all that political stuff, it makes it seem like you believe he's making a mistake even going to medical school."

"You know there is nothing I'd rather see him do than become a heart surgeon. It isn't his decision that bothers me. Its the way my generation of physicians is just sitting on their collective butts and allowing others to dictate to them. No one seems to be doing anything to stop it, and I can't help being saddened by that."

"If you feel so strongly about it why don't you do something?"

"I'm doing everything I know how to do. I've spoken to, I don't know how many community groups. I've testified before those morons up there in Washington. I guess I could lead some kind of physicians' strike, and I'd do that, except I don't want to go to jail."

She smiled at him, appreciating his passion, and understanding his frustration. He looked at her and shrugged his shoulders, saying, "The only other thing I could do would be run for Congress myself. Several people have suggested that I do just that, and I'm certain I could have done a lot better against Sheffield than that guy who ran against him last time."

"You're serious, aren't you?" she stated more than asked.

"I never thought I'd even consider something that far out of my comfort zone, but yeah, I've thought about it." He looked intently and added. "It's obviously too late to even consider it for 2010, but if things don't change soon, I might be interested in 2012.

"Well, I think you should do whatever you feel you have to do," she replied earnestly. "You know I will support you no matter what. The only thing I'd say is, from what I've seen, you better have some pretty thick skin, because the opposition will do whatever they can to tear you apart, especially if you appear to be a legitimate threat."

"That's not what worries me," he said. "I don't want to do anything that would make things hard on you and David."

"I'll be fine," she said reassuringly. "Maybe you should ask him what he thinks before you decide one way or another."

****

"So, when do you think you might hear from Southwestern?" Amy asked excitedly.

"I really have no idea, hopefully soon. I don't want to send out any letters to the other schools until I know for sure that I have a spot there," David offered. "So, I have until the middle of January."

"What if you get accepted at Stanford or Johns Hopkins? Would you consider either one of them?"

"We've talked about this before. I really don't want to move that far away from home, and Southwestern is every bit as good a school as either of them. The only reason I even applied to them was to satisfy my mom. I think she wants to be able to brag to her friends that her son got accepted to one of those elite schools."

"Can you blame her? I plan to tell all my friends, don't you?" Amy asked with pride.

"Not really," David said honestly. "I don't see it as that big of a deal, except for Harvard, If I get accepted there I will tell some of my friends, just so I can let them know that I turned them down."

"Why is Harvard such a big deal, anyway?"

"I think its mostly because its so old and there is a lot of history there, but there are two nobel laureates at Southwestern."

"Once you get there they will soon be talking about a third," Amy grinned broadly at her future husband.

"Don't be ridiculous," he scoffed. "They only give nobel prizes in medicine to researchers. I have no intention of doing research. I just want to be a practicing cardiac surgeon, like my dad."

"I think you are going to be the greatest heart surgeon of all time," she said as she leaned over and kissed him. "Just like you are the greatest at other things." Her seductive tone and sly smile left no doubt what was on her mind.

"Are your folks still out of town?" he asked in almost a whisper.

"Until Thursday. Why, what did you have in mind? You weren't thinking of taking advantage of me, were you?"

"You said we should celebrate, and I can't think of any better way, can you?"

"Why, Rhett Butler, how you do carry on," she offered in her best southern belle imitation.

David responded in kind. "Well, Scarlet, I promise to make an honest woman out of you some day."

They decided to forego the carriage ride and headed back to David's car and her home.

****

As Jack sat in the kitchen sipping his Diet Dr. Pepper, he saw David half stumble sleepily down the stairs. "What time did you finally get home last night?" he asked.

"I don't know, it was pretty late," he said. "I was over at Amy's discussing med school options."

"Sit down," Jack said, motioning to the empty chair next to him.

David grabbed a glass of milk out of the refrigerator and made his way over to his dad, wondering if he was going to get a lecture about getting home after midnight. "What's up?" he asked innocently.

"Your mom brought up something to me last night that I think I need to clarify," Jack stated in his typical paternal tone. "I think I may occasionally give you the impression that I don't think you should go into medicine."

"I've never gotten that impression," David said with a questioning expression.

"Well, she said that some times I paint a pretty bleak picture of this profession, and ..."

"I think you just tell it like you see it, and I understand that," David said.

"I try, but ..."

"Look Dad, I understand your frustration with the changes you see coming down the road, but its okay, really. It probably won't be exactly the same for me as it has been for you, but I'm going to become a heart surgeon, not because of how its been in the past, but because its what I feel called to do."

"You know how incredibly proud your mother and I are of you, don't you?" Jack asked, not anticipating an answer. "We will support you, no matter what you do, I just feel bad that forces you can't control are likely to rob you of much of the joy that comes with being free in your life's work. To me, that is a tragedy."

"There isn't anything you can do about it, so I wish you'd quit worrying about it."

"Its interesting that you put it that way, because that's something else I wanted to talk with you about," Jack said, placing his empty soda can on the table and turning slightly to face his son.

David took another drink from his milk as Jack continued, "I can't just sit back and watch the destruction of the greatest profession in the world." He hesitated again before continuing. "I've been considering running for Congress in 2012, and I wanted to discuss that with you before I decided one way or the other."

David smiled and tilted his head slightly to the side and he asked, "What does that have to do with me?"

"Well, it could have a significant impact on you. Political campaigns frequently put a lot of strain on family members, especially if the opposition decides to get into their personal lives."

"I've got nothing to hide," David offered. "I promise, I haven't joined any fringe organizations in Austin that might prove embarrassing." He laughed and Jack joined him with his own chuckle.

"That's not what I was referring to," Jack said. "What I meant was family members are often subjected to interviews and questions that can make them feel uncomfortable."

"I hear you Dad, but I don't have a problem with anything like that. If you want to run for Congress, go for it," David said confidently. "I'll be right behind you, supporting you all the way."

Jack took a deep breath and let out a sigh, then said, "Thanks, I appreciate that. Please don't mention this to anyone. 2012 is a long way off, and things can change significantly between now and then. If, and when, I decide to run, I'll let you know."

"Oh," David said, as he stood up from his chair, "if you do decide to run, I expect you to win." He patted his dad on the shoulder as he headed back upstairs.

****

"I got it! I got it!" David was shouting as he came in the front door. He had been out to the mail box everyday since he'd gotten home from Austin for the holidays. He slammed the door behind him and held the letter out in front of him as he ran into the kitchen.

Elaina was sitting at her kitchen desk and turned to see her excited son bounding into the room. It reminded her of when he was in the fifth grade and got his first blue ribbon for winning the fifty yard dash.

"Southwestern has accepted me!" he said, louder than he intended.

She stood and hugged him saying, "I am so happy for you, son."

"I gotta go call Amy," he said. "No, I'm going to go over there and tell her in person."

"What are those other letters?" she asked, noticing he had a handful of other envelopes in his left hand.

"I don't know, and I don't really care," he said. "This is the only one I need."

He dropped the rest of the mail on her desk and ran out to the garage. Just a few seconds after the door closed she heard the squeal of his tires leaving the driveway.

She looked quickly through the rest of the mail and saw two more official looking letters addressed to David Allan Roberts. She debated for a moment whether she should open them or not. One was from UT San Antonio and the other return address had the distinctive red shield of Harvard University. She knew she probably shouldn't open it, but he did say he didn't care, didn't he?

When Jack came in through the garage around six fifteen, Elaina was in the kitchen to greet him.

"Guess what?"

Jack had had a rather long day and was visibly tired, but he perked up at the sight of her girlish enthusiasm. "I give up, what?"

"David got his acceptance to Southwestern!"

"Was there ever any doubt?" Jack said. His smile didn't come close to matching the huge grin on her face.

"And guess what else?" she asked excitedly.

"No telling." he said, unwilling to play her childish game.

"He also got accepted to Harvard!"

"Seriously? Wow!"

"I'm not supposed to know that," she said, shrinking her head down into her shoulders, "but he ran out of here to tell Amy and I just couldn't help opening the letter."

"You're terrible," Jack said laughingly. "You wouldn't let me open those other letters, but its okay for you."

"He said he didn't care what they said, so I figured it would be okay."

"Who else have you told already?"

"Just a couple of my friends from church."

"You are something else."

****

"So, what do you think of the way Harry Reid managed to push the health care bill through the Senate?" asked the host of the local Sunday television program. The entire world had been watching for months as both the US House and Senate marched steadily forward with their respective versions of what seemed destined to be the most significant health care reform legislation in American history. Jack had hoped that neither would pass, but since the democrats controlled both houses, and they had a filibuster-proof majority in the Senate, he wasn't surprised when both were passed by the democrat majority. He had been asked to appear again on this popular opinion program, and with Elaina's approval, he agreed.

"I have to give Mr. Reid credit for some of the best back room political dealing in American history," Jack said. "What we saw was far from the open debate, televised on CSPAN, like the President promised."

"Oh, come on now," replied one of the other guests, a woman who was a representative from Congressman Sheffield's office. "You and I both know that's the way politics is always done. Deals are made. If they weren't, nothing would ever get passed."

A spokesperson for the Dallas county republican party weighed in, saying, "This is the first time in modern history a major piece of legislation like this has been passed strictly along party lines. Not one democrat voted against it and not one republican voted for it. That has never happened before. Not with Social Security, not with Medicare..."

The moderator interrupted asking another question, "We all know the Senate version is considerably different than the one passed by the House, so even though Harry Reid was successful in pushing his bill through on Christmas Eve, this isn't a done deal, is it?"

Four months earlier, Senator Edward Kennedy of Massachusetts had died of a brain tumor, leaving his Senate seat open, and silencing his longstanding, and rather passionate voice in favor of health care reform. A special election was scheduled for January to fill Kennedy's vacant seat, and the health care bill was at the center of the campaign between little known republican state senator Scott Brown, and the hand picked democrat successor, Martha Coakley. It was widely assumed that Coakley was going to win based on the fact that Massachusetts was one of the democrats traditional strongholds, and the seat had been held by Kennedy for almost half a century. However, the polls showed the election would be very close.

"This clearly makes the special election in Massachusetts to fill Kennedy's vacant seat the equivalent of a referendum on this bill and the entire health care reform process," Jack offered.

"That may be, but if you think the people of Massachusetts are going to elect a no name republican to replace Ted Kennedy, you're crazier than those looney-tune tea baggers," the union rep scoffed.

This guy was another guest who hadn't previously been heard from, but given the personal nature of this challenge, Jack felt obligated to answer it immediately. Although he was not a member of the populist movement that had come to be known as the Tea Party, he certainly agreed with many of the principles they proposed urging lower taxes and less government.

"It seems to me the Tea Party is merely restating the very principles those patriots stood for when they tossed that British tea into Boston harbor," Jack said, "so, with their support, I don't think it is out of the question that Scott Brown could defeat Martha Coakley, even in Massachusetts. Admittedly, its a long shot, but I think the people of this country are disgusted by the way this thing was passed, and would prefer both houses go back and start over with a bipartisan effort."

"This whole process is going to go to a conference committee and when it comes out it will be so watered down, it will have little impact," replied the forth guest, an area business leader.

"Well, we shall see about that in the months ahead, won't we," the moderator said, effectively cutting off the discussion. "When we come back from our break I want to ask our panel how health care reform is likely to impact the economy. So, stay tuned and we'll be right back."

As the program went to commercial, Jack was taking a sip of water from the small bottle that had been strategically placed just off camera, when the republican party representative turned to him and spoke softly enough the others could not hear, "Say, doc, we need some new blood in the party. From what I can tell, you certainly know your facts. Have you ever considered getting more actively involved."

"I'm not sure what you mean," Jack replied. "I thought that's what I was doing right now."

"I'm talking about being more involved in the party. We have a number of things we are doing in Dallas county, and I know they could use some help in Tarrant county as well. A guy like you could really make a difference."

"Party politics has never been my thing," He replied. He wanted to say because there's too much butt kissing, but decided to keep that comment to himself.

"We are back, and I'd like to ask our panel how they think health care reform is going to effect the economy? Let's start with you John," the moderator said as the camera shifted to the businessman.

"Like I said in the first segment, my expectation is that this bill will be so diluted by the conference committee, that it isn't likely to have much of an impact at all," the executive spoke confidently.

"Well, just for argument's sake, let's say the Senate version ends up getting passed, more or less as it is. I realize that's very unlikely, but if it did, what would that do to your business?"

"Like most Americans, and most of the Senators I'm afraid, I haven't read the entire two thousand page Senate bill, so I can only comment on what I have read and what I've been told is in there. However, from what I understand, it would require me to provide health insurance to every one of my two hundred and fifty-five employees, or pay a fine of up to two thousand dollars per employee per year. We already offer health insurance to our full time workers, but again, as I understand it, the new law would have to extend that coverage to most of my part time employees and even seasonal workers. If that is true, I would be forced to layoff a significant part of my workforce, because I could not afford the cost of insuring them."

Sheffield's representative stated, "But, if you aren't providing health insurance benefits to those part time employees, where are they supposed to get insurance?"

"The bill calls for the creation of government subsidized insurance to be offered in each state through what are being called insurance exchanges," the republican party rep stated. "And, if an individual decides not to purchase insurance, either because they can't afford it or they just don't want it, they will be subject to a fine."

"People should be fined if they don't have insurance," Sheffield's representative stated.

"Dr Roberts," what do you think is going to happen to the economy if this bill becomes law?" the moderator asked, again turning toward Jack.

"I'm not an economist," he said slowly, "so I can't really say, but I do know it would impact the way all Americans access health care services. As I have said on numerous occasions, this is a clear intrusion of the government into the relationship between patients and their physicians. It will greatly expand the number and scope of regulations that I, and all my colleagues, will be forced to abide by, written and enforced by bureaucrats whose sole reason for being involved is to control costs."

"That's right," Sheffield's rep quickly injected. "Something has to be done to cut the fraud and abuse out of the healthcare system and you doctors obviously won't do it."

Jack took a deep breath, just as Elaina had instructed. He was so sick of hearing about 'fraud and abuse' he wanted to light into that woman, but knew he'd come across poorly if he did. Instead he held his emotions in check and replied, "I believe most Americans trust their doctors far more than they do their representatives in Washington. The polls show that the public's opinion of Congress is at an all time low, so I don't really think they trust Washington to ferret out fraud and abuse in the health care system, or anywhere else for that matter."

"Well," the moderator interrupted, "No matter what our viewers think of the Patient Protection and Affordable Care Act of 2009, it is clear the debate over this bill is far from over. That's all the time we have for today, but perhaps we can get our panel to continue this discussion once the process has come to a conclusion."

The television camera panned back to show the whole group and all except Sheffield's representative were nodding in agreement. She was still stinging from the rebuke Jack had issued.

****

"You did very well," Elaina reassured Jack when he arrived home. "You didn't lose your temper, even though I could tell you were about to at one point."

"Yeah, Sheffield's mouthpiece pissed me off with all that crap about fraud and abuse," he said angrily.

"I know, but like I said you did a great job of not getting baited into that argument."

The phone rang and Jack answered, "Hello."

"Dr. Roberts?" The voice on the phone was familiar, but he couldn't immediately identify it. "This is Sean McLaughlin. I hope I haven't caught you at an inopportune time."

"No, no, Sean. What can I do for you?"

"I saw you on the Sunday morning show on our FOX affiliate there in Dallas, and I wanted to know if you would be willing to come on my show as a guest next week. I thought you came across as a very credible voice of reason from the medical community, and I need someone to provide just that perspective on this health care reform process."

"Well, I'm flattered that you would ask, but I have an agreement with my wife not to make any public appearances without discussing it with her first." Jack turned to see that Elaina had a quizzical look on her face.

"Who is that?" she whispered.

He covered the end of the phone with his other hand and whispered back, "Its Sean McLaughlin of FOX News Network."

"I certainly understand," McLaughlin replied, "Why don't you talk with her tonight and I'll have my producer get in touch with you tomorrow morning. If you can do this I'd like to have you come to New York on Wednesday. We'll fly you up that afternoon and put you up here in Manhattan overnight, then get you home on Thursday morning."

"Let me talk with her and I'll let your producer know tomorrow," Jack said, looking directly at Elaina. "Either way, thanks for the invitation."

"I hope you'll come join me, I think you could really make a difference as we try and stop this mess."

"I agree, it is potentially a big mess."

"Give my best to your wife, and have a good evening." McLaughlin didn't wait for a reply, as Jack heard the phone click off.

"What did he say?" Elaina asked excitedly.

"He wants me to come to New York on Wednesday and be a guest on his national television show to discuss healthcare reform from a physician's perspective."

"National show?"

"Yeah, McLaughlin comes on every evening. It's an obviously conservative opinion program with a huge audience."

"Do you want to do it?"

"Part of me wants to say no, but then another part says absolutely," he replied. "I feel that physicians are not being heard when it comes to the media coverage of this whole process, and I see it as an opportunity to be a voice for my profession. That's why I did the program today and why I went to testify before Congress. This is an even bigger stage, because millions of people will be watching."

"If you feel that strongly about it I say, go. But remember, don't say anything that might reflect badly on the hospital or the AMA, or anybody." Elaina's stern expression melted into one of pride as she stepped toward him and placed both hands on either side of his face and kissed him warmly.

****

Tonight I have with me two physicians, Dr. Peter Franklin who is the chairman of the Department of Medicine at Mount Vernon State University Hospital, and Dr. Jack Roberts, a cardiovascular surgeon in private practice in Fort Worth, Texas. Gentlemen, welcome to the McLaughlin Show."

"Thanks for having me," Jack offered.

"Its a pleasure to be here, Sean," responded the younger, long-haired doctor.

"Dr. Franklin," McLaughlin began, "I understand that you support the bill passed by the Senate last week, can you tell me why?"

"Yes, Sean. I'd be glad to. Like many of my colleagues, I want to see every American have access to health care, and I believe this bill will go a long way toward achieving that goal by requiring every American to have health insurance, whether through their employer or by purchasing it themselves."

"So, you believe that it is appropriate for the government to mandate that every individual buy insurance, even if they don't want it."

"Yes, I do, and let me tell you why. Our hospitals and especially the university based facilities like the one where I work, are flooded with patients who have no insurance and never pay for the care they receive. This puts a major strain on our system, and causes many costs to be shifted to other paying patients."

"I'm assuming then, that you expect the cost of care to come down for those of us with insurance if this bill were to become law?" McLaughlin asked, using his customary sarcasm.

"It should. As the President has said on numerous occasions, the cost of health insurance should come down for nearly everyone."

"Dr. Roberts, what do you think is likely to happen?"

Sean had told Jack in advance that he was going to ask about the cost of healthcare and the effect of the law, so Jack had prepared what he hoped was a reasonable answer.

"I don't presume to know what is going to happen to health care costs. I don't think anybody knows, but what I do know is that most things that the government has tried to regulate, like oil and gas, and air travel, have become more expensive rather than less."

"That is a good point, I hadn't thought about it that way," Sean offered. "I know from talking to you, that you oppose this bill. Tell me what it is that worries you about it."

"First, let me say that I agree with Dr. Franklin that everyone should have access to quality health care in this country," Jack said, "but I believe to a large degree we have that already. Many facilities like the one he works in, receive government support to help defray the cost of caring for the truly indigent. The facility where I work is supported through private donations that allow us to also offer superior care to indigent people without having to turn anyone away. That is true of many hospitals and many physicians across the country," Jack offered, trying his best to emphasize philanthropy as a major part of American health care.

"I know that my doctor participates in a free clinic here in New York once a week," Sean added.

"Exactly! That is what I'm talking about. What I hear from those of my colleagues who are advocating for a bigger role for government sounds more like they want a guarantee that they're going to get paid. I can't find anywhere in the Hippocratic Oath where it says doctors need to be assured of payment. Actually, it is quite the opposite."

"Wait a minute," Franklin interrupted, "I didn't say anything like that. All I said was that uncompensated care was putting a strain on the system."

Jack was unknowingly being drawn into an argument that wasn't likely to end well. He replied, "That may not be what you said, or even what you meant, but the fact is uncompensated care has been delivered by physicians since the earliest days of our profession, and it wasn't until insurance, and now the government got involved, that everyone started talking about the money."

"So how would you change the system?" Sean asked Jack.

"I don't have any quarrel with the concept of insurance," Jack said, "or even government assistance for those who are truly indigent. Where our system has broken down is when the payers, contract directly with the providers, bypassing the patient. In doing so they, we, have turned the most personal service any of us ever receives into a commodity to be bartered and controlled by the payers, and where the patient is the one who gets short changed."

"So, you would go back to the old days where patients paid their doctor and got reimbursed by their insurance company."

"Absolutely. That opens up the entire process to the forces of the free market, and would lead to lower costs and better quality. It works for every other industry, why not healthcare?"

"Very interesting," McLaughlin said, as he started to conclude the segment.

"That will never work!" Franklin interjected.

"Why not?" McLaughlin asked.

"Because people are irresponsible when it comes to their health," Franklin replied. "They all think they are invincible until they get sick or injured, at which point they want and need care, and except for the very wealthy, they lack the means to pay for it. That's when they go to the ER and demand care."

"What do you say to that, Dr. Roberts?" McLaughlin asked.

"Personal responsibility is a learned behavior," Jack said. "As long as we continue to increase the role of third parties, including the government in people's lives, the further away from those time honored traditions we move as a society. If individuals don't take responsibility, in most cases its because they don't have to. Now, if the government wants to mandate that everyone have some form of insurance, that's between the people and their elected representatives. I just don't think their doctor should get caught in the middle, because when we do our ethics get challenged."

"Thank you both for coming in tonight. Great discussion, and when we come back I'll speak to one of the Senators who voted against the healthcare reform bill, so stay tuned."

As they went to commercial Sean turned to Jack and said, "That was great! I hope I can call on you again some time."

"Thanks, Sean, but I'm not sure we actually talked about the specifics of the bill all that much."

"You're right, but what you said about free enterprise and ethics, that was much better than talking about all the new commissions and committees of bureaucrats."

"Well, I appreciate you having me on," Jack said as he shook McLaughlin's hand.

"You don't really believe all that crap about freedom from third party payers, do you?" Franklin scoffed as he and Jack made their way back toward the green room.

"As a matter of fact, I do," Jack said. "I believe it is the only way we can save our profession."

"All I can say is, you live in a different world than the one where I practice. We lost our autonomy and our ability to be the patient's advocate a long time ago," Franklin said as he shook his head and his attempt to smile turned into a smirk.

****

After Christmas, Scott Brown, a little known state senator in Massachusetts conducted a brilliant door to door type campaign, driving his red pickup truck across the state. He promised to be the forty-first vote that would defeat the final health care bill in the Senate. The entire nation watched with great anticipation on election night, the nineteenth of January, and in a shocking turn of events, the people of Massachusetts elected a republican to take the Senate seat held for all those years by the ultimate democrat, Ted Kennedy. The clear message was they wanted the Congress to start over with the health care reform process. Jack and most of his physician colleagues were ecstatic. He was convinced the will of the people had finally prevailed, and the democratic controlled Congress would have to alter their plan considerably.

Although both houses had passed health reform bills, they were different in several important ways, so they would need to go to a conference committee to come up with a compromise bill, which would then have to go back to both the House and the Senate before it could go to the President's desk. Now that the republicans held forty-one Senate seats, they would be able to block any attempt to pass any compromise bill, provided they remained united.

"It looks like we dodged a bullet," said Larry Lawson, the old general surgeon, as he came up behind Jack in the doctor's lounge.

Jack was watching the commentators on CNN rehashing the election results from the night before. "Yeah, it would appear so," Jack said. "As long as the republicans can hold their ranks together they should be able to stop this fiasco."

"I can't believe the people of Massachusetts actually elected a republican to the Senate. Pigs have finally flown over Boston," Lawson said laughingly.

"Yeah, right." Jack replied with a chuckle. "I think it shows just how uncomfortable all Americans are with the idea of losing their freedom, when it comes to their personal medical care."

While he wanted desperately to believe what he was saying, Jack's trust in his fellow citizens had been dealt numerous blows in recent months, but none greater than the one delivered by his good friend Buzz Jackson. He understood the threat Jerry Grady had made all too well, but Jack was convinced that the way to answer such threats was not to cave in, and that is exactly what Buzz had done. He had sold his practice to Jerry's group, and was now effectively an employee of Horvath and the hospital. Perhaps it wasn't going to matter all that much what the government did to the system if all the doctors ended up being employees of hospitals. He was beginning to believe he was the only one willing to stand against that growing tide.

****

After his appearance on McLaughlin, Jack had been invited to speak to a number of community groups, including the local Rotary Club at their monthly meeting in February. After delivering his standard public speech for the sixth time since his testimony at Ways and Means, he entertained questions from the audience, composed of local business leaders.

"Dr. Roberts?" one younger gentleman began. "You are obviously approaching retirement age, so why are you so passionate in your opposition to what seems to me to be a much needed reform of our healthcare system? You aren't likely to be effected all that much by it."

Jack hadn't been asked that question before, at least not formally, but he had asked it of himself on many occasions. He had indeed become consumed by what he perceived as a threat to his profession, and it was fair to ask the question, why.

"There are two reasons," he said, looking directly at the questioner who was retaking his seat. "First, because I love and respect my profession. To be a physician has been the greatest honor of my life, and I believe this kind of government intrusion will eventually destroy my profession, at least as I have known it. I have a son who is in college and has been accepted into medical school. I owe it to him to do whatever I can to ensure that he has the same opportunity to practice as an independent physician that I've enjoyed for the last thirty years. The health of his future patients, and those of countless other young doctors, will depend on their ability to make independent decisions, not ones that are dictated by some bureaucrat. I have seen first hand what happened to healthcare in England and in Canada, and despite what you may hear from some commentator on the news, it isn't pretty. The average person in Great Britain pays more than sixty percent of their income back to the government in taxes, and while the National Health Service care is free, it offers them few if any personal choices. People wait months to see a specialist, even for routine things like kidney stones or an irregular heart beat. If something is seriously wrong, like unstable angina, or a leaking heart valve, they still have to wait, often until its too late. That is not what Americans want, and I believe it is my duty to stand up and tell the truth about what is happening, because the media doesn't seem to be willing to do so."

He saw a few older men in the audience nodding in agreement. They clearly understood the need for generational stewardship.

"Second," he continued, "I'm very concerned that what is going on in Washington is not really about healthcare at all. This is simply the next step toward the creation of a socialist society in this country, destroying our personal liberties and freedoms. The control of health care has been the holy grail of the progressive socialist movement for a hundred years, and if they are successful in seizing control of it now, their next targets are likely to be your businesses." Jack made a sweeping gesture over the entire crowd. "I have contended all along that this process is more about expanding government power and control, than it is about anyone's health.

A scattered applause was short lived and was isolated to those older guys who had earlier nodded their agreement. When it subsided, one of those who had been applauding stood up and asked, "When are you going to run for Congress?"

There it was. That same question he'd been asking himself. "I'm not a politician," Jack protested. "I have no intention of running for any political office. I'm just a physician. Those guys would eat me alive," he laughed and attempted to move on, not wanting to even hint of his potential interest, but the questioner didn't sit down.

"That's the whole point," the man said, with a broad grin. "You are not a politician, and that is exactly what we need. Wasn't it Jefferson who talked about citizen legislators? The problem with Washington today is that everybody up there is a damned career politician. They don't have to live with the laws they pass. We need people like you to go up there and straighten things out."

****

For the next two months, advocates on both sides of the health care debate were clamoring for action. Proponents of the reform bills continued to spout their earlier cries of *if not now, when?*, while opponents claimed the bills hadn't even been read by those who were voting on them. The President largely stayed out of the discussions, preferring to let the Congress take the heat, and it was intense.

While the democrats were initially stunned by Scott Brown's election to the Senate, they were not going to let that stop them from achieving their long awaited goal of national health care reform. House Speaker, Nancy Pelosi, pulled her party together and pushed them to pass the Senate bill without any changes. By doing so, there would be no conference committee, and no opportunity for a Senate filibuster. When asked whether House members had even had time to read the mammoth Senate bill, she responded with what became the most frequently quoted line of the debate. She said, "We have to pass the bill to find out what is in it." Even many democrats were under intense pressure from their constituents to defeat the bill, but Pelosi's majority was large enough she could allow a few of them to vote against it and still get it through.

Jack was angered by the fact that the AMA remained surprisingly silent on the Senate bill, perhaps because Senator Reid allegedly promised to take up the repeal of the sustainable growth rate formula used to calculate physician payments under Medicare, just as soon as the law was passed. In late March of 2010, the President signed the new healthcare law, and at least from Jack's perspective the practice of medicine would never be the same.

He attended the AMA meeting in June and made an effort to get the House of Delegates to call for a repeal of the law based on the fact it still had done nothing to deal with Medicare's SGR formula in the two months since the passage of what was now being called Obamacare. There was no possibility the liberal leaning body was going to reverse its course, even though it was clear they had been lied to in exchange for their implied support.

As Jack watched the proceedings, he was clearly in the minority. The independent practice advocates had been overrun by those who favored a more centrally controlled system. As he listened to their proclamations from the floor of the AMA House, it was obvious to him what they were saying. Just like Franklin had implied but refused to say outright, during their debate on McLaughlin, these were physicians who were mostly interested in being assured of payment for their services. If that security came at the price of their professional freedom, they were willing to make that trade. To him this was the ultimate ethical conflict of interest, and he couldn't understand why so many refused to recognize the dilemma.

****

David sent his acceptance letter to the University of Texas - Southwestern Medical School and received confirmation from the office of admissions, before sending out notices to the other schools were he'd applied, declining their invitations. The two notable exceptions were Stanford and Johns Hopkins. By the first of March he still hadn't heard from either school, so technically he hadn't been rejected, but he didn't really care at this point. His letter to Harvard, declining their invitation didn't have the same degree of satisfaction he'd anticipated, because somehow, it just didn't matter.

After David and Amy had gone back to Austin to complete their last semester of college, Jack and Elaina told everyone they knew about their son's accomplishments. In mid April they took Amy's parents out to dinner to work out the details of the two big events that were coming, graduation the last week of May, and the wedding, the first week in June.

Even though their kids had been engaged for a year and a half, Jack remained a bit cautious around Ron Callahan. He was certain that Amy's dad knew that his son was having sex with his youngest daughter, and the thought made him a bit uneasy.

At dinner, the two mothers talked about the wedding arrangements while the men discussed politics and the economy. Amy's dad owned a roofing company and his business had been down about thirty percent since the economic collapse of 2008. Ron was a very reserved man who seemed to have little to say, and Jack wasn't sure how to break the ice. He decided to bring up a subject he thought everyone had an opinion about. "I'm sure you're probably aware of my strong opposition to the new healthcare law," he said.

"Yeah, I've heard you on television and the radio several times," Ron said, sounding slightly intimidated by what he perceived to be an element of fame in the man who would soon be his in-law. "I really can't say as I blame you, but, not much can be done about it now, unless the Supreme Court declares in unconstitutional."

"I don't hold out much hope of that, I think the whole damned thing needs to be repealed, but I don't see the Congress doing anything until Obama is out of the White House. Then maybe we can do something."

"We? you sound like you think anybody up there cares what you or I think."

Jack laughed and said, "Your right about that. The career politicians like Sheffield don't care. If he doesn't get defeated in November, I'm considering running against him myself."

"Your kidding, right?" Ron said with a smile.

"No, I'm serious," Jack replied.

Ron just looked at him in disbelief. "Don't you know what happens to every person who runs against that democratic machine? They get drug into the gutter. That's why no one of significance has been willing to go up against Sheffield since 2000."

"Well, maybe its time that changed," Jack said boldly.

Ron turned to Elaina and said, "You need to talk some sense into this husband of yours, or before its over they will have you, and David, and your whole family covered in mud, including our daughter."

"I think you may be exaggerating just a bit," Jack said defensively.

"Look," Ron replied, "I've lived in this town my whole life, and I've watched those people chew up and spit out better men than you for the last fifty years. Jim Wright started it, and Sheffield is just the latest in a line of thugs. I'm telling you, you don't want any part of that fight, because they don't fight fair, and they don't give a damn who gets hurt."

Ron Callahan wasn't about to share everything he knew about the political machine of which he spoke, but when he first started his roofing business he was visited by a couple of what he referred to as goons from the city. They were sent out to his business to find a reason to close him down, specifically to protect one of his main competitors, a major contributor to the democratic party. They couldn't find any legal reason to shut him down after two weeks of intense inspections. A few days later, Ron nearly lost his life in what was classified as an accident on his property. A huge pallet of composite shingles just happened to fall off a storage rack on to the hood of his pickup as he was leaving work late one evening. He managed to stick it out, and the city employees finally left him alone, but only after he hired a full time guard for his supply yard.

"I appreciate your concern," Jack said, "and I promise you I understand the risk, but if we sit back and let guys like Sheffield run the country, our kids, and our grandkids, aren't going to have much of a country to inherit."

'I agree with that," he said, "I just think there is something to be said for choosing your battles."

"Your warning is duly noted, and I can assure you that if I decide to run against that guy, I will do everything I can to keep my wife and our kids out of any fight those people might wish to start."

****

"That was such a boring ceremony," David said.

"I thought I was going to fall asleep during the chancellor's speech," Amy replied. "Then the presentation of diplomas, God, I thought it would never end."

I'm glad my dad didn't bring grandma Faye. She wouldn't have been able to sit there for three and a half hours," he said.

David and Amy had taken off their caps and gowns and were making their way to the rendezvous point to meet both sets of parents. "There they are," David said, as he spotted his dad and soon to be father-in-law.

"Well, that is perhaps the single biggest drawback to going to a really big school," Jack said after hugs had been exchanged all around.

"I counted seven Smiths and nine Joneses," Elaina offered, "but only two Callahans and three Roberts," she laughed.

"Let's go," David said, "I'm starving. Where are we going to eat?"

"Your dad made a reservation for the six of us at Truluck's Seafood restaurant, but it was for thirty minutes ago, so I'm sure they've given our table away."

"I think your mom and I are just going to head on back home. I know she's exhausted, and we have a bunch of work to do tomorrow to get ready for your graduation reception on Sunday afternoon.," Jack offered with resignation in his voice.

"I understand," David replied.

"I think we're going to go home too," Joanna said. "Its been a long day." She looked up at her husband and saw him nodding in agreement.

"We'll see you kids tomorrow," Elaina added as she hugged them both once more, and then said her good byes to the Callahans.

When the two graduates found themselves alone again, they decided to grab a pizza and make the trip out to their familiar grassy spot, just to watch the sun go down over lake Austin one last time.

CHAPTER 5

"With fifty percent of the precincts reporting, Herman Sheffield, the incumbent democrat has moved into a slight lead over the republican challenger, Jack Roberts, the doctor from Fort Worth." The local news anchor was anxious to report the status of the only local Congressional race that was in doubt as the programming switched away from the national coverage. "As expected, this is a very tight race, and with many of the more rural precincts yet to come in, it doesn't bode well for the challenger. Many of those areas have a largely latin American population, which typically votes democratic."

"That has certainly been the case in the past, John," the cohost added, trying to counter the enthusiasm of her liberal colleague, "but Roberts seemed to have a very strong appeal, even in those communities, at least until recently. We aren't likely to know the winner here for some time."

Jack was back up pacing in front of the window, stopping periodically to look at the ticker running across the bottom of the television. He was obviously anxious over his own race, but he was almost as interested in the Presidential race. His hopes for a change in leadership had been dealt a series of blows when Pennsylvania, Michigan and New Hampshire were each called for Obama, much earlier than expected. There was still hope for a Romney victory as long as Florida and Ohio remained undecided, but if they both fell into the democratic column there would be no way to unseat the man he believed was behind the destruction of his profession. He hung his head slightly, wondering if his own race would even matter if Obama was reelected. There would be no chance of repealing the Patient Protection and Affordable Care Act of 2010, as long as he remained in the White House.

Elaina came over to stand next to him by the window and asked, "What have you been over here thinking about?"

"I was just thinking about how excited David was when he got his acceptance letter to Southwestern, and how his graduation from the University of Texas seemed almost anticlimactic somehow. To him, graduating from UT just wasn't that big of a deal."

"Well, I remember you telling me that you didn't even attend your college graduation ceremony," Elaina replied.

"That was because I graduated in three years. I didn't even get my diploma until after my first year of med school," he explained.

"I think its more or less the same thing for your son," she added, hoping to draw Jack out of the funk he seemed to have fallen into over the last hour. "His goal has always been to graduate from medical school, and I think he looked at college simply as a stepping stone along the way."

Jack knew what she was saying was true, and it raised another wave of unpleasant memories, beginning with that Sunday afternoon reception.

****

Their guests began arriving right at two o'clock. Elaina had asked Jack to stand with her at the front door to greet everyone as they arrived. She wanted to leave the door open but it was already close to one hundred degrees, and very quickly it became obvious having the door open wasn't an option. She'd decorated the backyard and all around the pool area with burnt orange and white crepe paper, balloons and banners, congratulating David on his graduation from UT. She'd also had his acceptance letter from Southwestern enlarged and mounted on a poster board. It was displayed on an easel near the door leading out to the patio for everyone to see.

David also stood next to his mom in what amounted to a small receiving line for the first thirty minutes, but as the house filled up with guests, he left his post and mingled with the growing crowd as they enjoyed the hors d'oeuvres and punch. Elaina had anticipated the typical first of June heat, so she had rented several large patio umbrellas and two big fans to keep the outside air moving. Her plan had been to have most of the guest gather out by the pool, but with the mid-afternoon sun blazing down, and the forecast was calling for record high temperatures, few of their guests had been willing to leave the house to brave the heat.

By three o'clock the living room was so crowded it was nearly impossible to move around. Given the frequency of the doors being opened, and the sheer number of bodies in the room, the air conditioner was not able to keep up, despite running continuously. The caterers were doing a great job of making sure everyone had ice in their drinks, but the ice cream they were serving with the graduation cake was melting almost as fast as they could serve it. Elaina, was running back and forth between the kitchen and the entry way, trying to answer questions from the servers and greet new guests as they arrived.

Jack's cell phone vibrated in his pocket and when he pulled it out it was the operating room extension at the children's hospital. "This is Jack Roberts," he answered.

"Dr. Roberts, this is Helen Newman up here in the OR, and I'm with Dr. Ferguson. He asked me to call you and..."

"What's the problem?" Jack interrupted.

"He is operating on a boy who came in through the ER with a stab wound to the chest. He asked if you were available to come in and help him. He's run into some bleeding."

"Tell him I'll be right there." Jack hung up the phone and went looking for Elaina. "That was George on the phone. He's got some kid in the OR with a stab wound to the chest and he needs my help, so I've gotta go. Hopefully it won't take too long."

She looked up at him with obvious disappointment and said, "Okay, I sure hope you can make it back by four, because that is when the formal toast is scheduled."

"I'll do my best."

Jack leaned over and kissed her cheek. There was an unmistakable moistness to her skin that betrayed her reaction to the heat and the stress. He raced the ten minutes to the hospital and quickly changed into his scrubs.

"What have you got, George?" he asked as he came through the OR door and saw his young colleague with one hand inside the twelve year old's chest.

"This kid was in the wrong place at the wrong time and some seventeen year old stabbed him. He came in with a switchblade knife sticking out of chest right next to the left side of his sternum. I left the knife in place and brought him up here to the OR anticipating the worst. When I pulled it out he almost immediately went into tamponade, so I split his sternum, evacuated the blood and thought I could see the injury. I've got my finger on it, but for the life of me, now I can't tell whether the hole is in the aorta or the main pulmonary artery. I tried temporarily cross clamping first one, and then the other, but it doesn't seem to matter. The bleeding just continues if I take my finger away. I've called in the pump tech, but I was hoping to be able to fix it without having to go on bypass."

Jack quickly put on a gown and gloves and moved in next to the patient opposite George. "Let me take a look," he said calmly, as he took the suction from George's hand and carefully cleared the small amount of blood away that had accumulated around George's left index finger. "Go ahead and remove your finger." Jack instructed.

As George pulled his finger away the area between the top of the main pulmonary artery where it branches off to the lungs on either side and the bottom of the aortic arch immediately filled up with blood, but Jack was able to suction it away quickly enough to see the problem before placing his own finger back over the open vessel to stem the bleeding. He looked up into George's face and couldn't help but smile.

"George," he said, "you're going to need to write this one up for one of our journals. I've never seen this before. I've only heard rumors of this happening."

"What is it?" George asked impatiently.

"This kid has a patent ductus and he's been stabbed right through the middle of it."

"Really?"

"That's why it continued to bleed no matter which main artery you clamped. The connection between the aorta and pulmonary artery is still open, I think we just need to ligate this kids ductus and he'll be fine."

"Do you think we can get to it from here?"

"Sure," Jack said. "There are some guys who prefer this approach to the more conventional left chest approach. I'm not one of them, but since we're already here I don't see any reason why not." He looked back up to gage the younger surgeon's reaction then added, "You do realize its much easier if you ligate the PDA before you divide it, right?" He couldn't help but smile at the obviousness of the statement.

Jack took a long narrow vascular clamp and carefully passed it down along the tip of his left index finger, then opened the jaws very slowly before advancing it over the injured ductus. While he couldn't see the vessel directly, he knew exactly where is was in his mind's eye, having an uncanny familiarity with this part of the human anatomy. He gently closed the jaws of the vessel and slowly removed his finger, and there was no sudden rush of blood as there had been before.

Instinctively Jack began to perform the necessary dissection to expose the ductus but then suddenly he stopped. He handed the fine scissors to George and said, "I'm sorry doctor, this is your case. I didn't mean to steal it from you."

"That's okay," George replied, "you can do it."

"No, I think you need to do this and I need to help."

Within a few minutes, George had the ductus exposed on either side of the clamp Jack had applied to control the bleeding. He was able to place two additional thin clamps on either side and remove the original clamp. There was no bleeding and the three millimeter hole in the center of the ductus arteriosus was obvious. The procedure was routine from that point as he completed the division of the vessel through the area of injury then sutured the two ends closed.

"Thanks a lot, Jack," he said. "I owe you one."

"You don't owe me anything," Jack said. "I'm the one who owes you. If you weren't here taking my call, I'd be the one taking care of this kiddo and I'd miss all of my son's graduation party, instead of just part."

"I've got it from here. You need to get back to your party," George instructed. "And, please tell your wife I'm sorry I pulled you away."

"She understands," Jack said. "I'll talk to you tomorrow."

He quickly changed back into his street close and headed toward the house. It was already ten after four when he left the hospital and twenty after when he pulled up in front of the house. The catering truck was blocking the driveway so he parked on the street. As he made his way up the front walk he passed two couples coming out of the door. He shook hands with both men, and thanked them all for coming. Elaina had caught a glimpse of him heading toward the house, and as he approached, she opened the door widely. There was no mistaking the fact that she was upset.

"I'm sorry, sweetie, I got back as quickly as I could." Jack didn't know what else to say. This was her big event, and he hadn't been there for her.

"Most of the people have already left," she said showing her frustration.

"Do you still want me to do the toast?" He asked, anticipating that she had simply pushed back the schedule slightly.

"No," she said sadly, "I did it."

He wasn't sure what, if anything, he could say or do at this point to change her mood.

Another coupled headed for the front door and when they saw Jack, the man stopped and said, "Where have you been? We missed you."

Before he could respond Elaina said, "He had to run to the hospital."

"Well you missed a great party," the woman added. "Your wife gave a wonderful toast to your son. You should've heard her."

"I wish I had been here," Jack said as he looked down into Elaina's eyes. He could see she was smiling but was on the verge of tears.

As the couple left, Jack tried to catch his wife's attention, but she just walked back into the living room, not sure whether she would be able to hold back her emotions if he said he was sorry one more time.

****

"I'm really sorry," Jack said softly, as he stepped up behind her. She was standing at the sink drying her hands. All the guests and all the caterers were gone, and she was just finishing up in the kitchen.

She turned around to face him, with tears streaming down her cheeks. She took a deep breath and said, "I can't believe you had to leave like that." She wasn't angry as much as she was feeling the pain of his absence during this important event. This celebration had been one of those special family moments and she was once again having to deal with the fact he'd been summoned by his other wife, who needed him more.

"I don't know what to say, Angel."

"Please, just don't say your sorry again. I understand you had to go." Yes, she understood. She had always understood, but whenever he said he was sorry it made her feel that perhaps there was a way he could have chosen her over his other wife, but didn't. She knew she wasn't logical, but...

He reached forward and placed his hands firmly on her shoulders and looked into her softening face without saying anything more. She stepped forward and buried her head in his chest, throwing her arms around him. "I'm okay," she said, before pushing herself back and looking up into his face once more. "But, I think you need to talk to your son. He was pretty upset that you weren't here when he made his big announcement about going to medical school."

"I will," Jack said almost in a whisper. He hadn't even thought about that.

After a minute, Jack released her, and headed up the stairs to speak to David. As he entered the young man's room, he saw him sitting on the bed talking on his cell phone.

"Hey, I need to call you right back, okay?" he said before hanging up the phone. "Hey, Dad." His tone was rather distant.

"Buddy, I'm really sorry I had to leave right in the middle of your reception," Jack said as he stood in the doorway with his hand thrust deep into the pockets of his trousers. "I got called into the hospital to help George with an emergency." His words sounded hollow, almost trite. David had heard them countless times before.

"It's okay, Dad," David said, forcing a slight smile. "I understand."

"No, it isn't okay," Jack replied. "That was a very important event, and I wasn't here to share it with you and your mom. I should have been here, and I know that I can't ever bring that special moment back. I hope you can forgive me."

David got up off the bed and walked slowly over to his dad. "It really is okay," he said. "Graduating from college isn't that big a deal. Now, if you miss my wedding, or my medical school graduation, then I'll be pissed." After a brief pause he laughed and gave his dad a big hug.

THE CONFLICT

****

Saturday was the biggest day in Amy's young life. As the stylist worked her magic, arranging her long blonde hair, and the manicurists put the finishing touches on her nails, she couldn't help but grin. She was reminded of the day when David had ask her to marry him. On that occasion she'd gone through much the same routine, but never suspected what was ahead of her that evening. Today, she knew exactly what was going to happen, and she couldn't wait.

She slipped into the long white wedding dress, and her mother zipped it up from the back. "How's it look Mom?" She asked as she turned from side to side in front of the mirror.

"You look like a princess, sweetheart," Her mother said softly. "That David is an awfully lucky guy."

"Yeah, that's what I keep telling him, but actually, I think it's me who is the lucky one."

"I'm very happy for you both," Joanna said, as the first tear of the day appeared in the corner of her eye.

"Don't start that, Mom," Amy said sternly. "If you start now you're going to make me cry too, and it'll mess up my makeup."

There was a loud knock at the door, and the wedding director stuck her head in saying, "are you about ready?"

"Just about," Joanna replied. "Have you seen her father?"

"I'm right out here, waiting," Ron's familiar voice came through the door.

"Okay, just checking."

The wedding party made their way down to the foyer of the church, and as they did Joanna stopped to kiss her daughter on the cheek. She pulled her veil down over her angelic face, arranging it carefully until she was satisfied that it was perfect. "I love you sweetheart," she said one final time.

"I love you too, Mom."

As the organist began to play the processional music Amy had selected, one of the ushers escorted Joanna to her seat on the front row, to the left of the main aisle. Jack and Elaina were already seated on the other side, and they both smiled broadly as the mother of the bride looked over anxiously.

Amy's brother was one of David's groomsmen, along with two of his classmates from UT. Jarrod, his roommate from the first two years of school was his best man. Amy's older sister was her maid of honor, and three of her old high school friends made up the rest of the wedding party.

David had chosen to wear the custom tuxedo that had been made for him by Franco's tailor, and as he walked to the front of the church from the side entrance he smiled broadly at his parents and his grandmothers. As he took his position, he was visibly startled by what he saw two rows behind them. Franco and Gabriella were sitting there with their six year old daughter, Christina. He had no idea they had made the trip to Texas, specifically for this occasion. Franco gave him a knowing smile and a wink of his eye.

Like all weddings, the ceremony was beautiful, especially the lighting of the unity candle. Joanna and Elaina were both crying so much they had trouble hearing the exchange of vows. When the young couple was introduced as Mr. and Mrs. David Roberts, the auditorium erupted in applause as everyone rose to their feet. The recessional music began, and David paused briefly to kiss his mother and shake his dad's hand. Then, as they walked up the aisle, David reached out to his left, touching Franco's hand briefly, as he mouthed the words, "Thank you, sir".

Following their wedding reception at the Callahan's home, they young couple left on a week long honeymoon. The Royal Caribbean Cruise was a wedding gift, from Jack and Elaina. They were excited as they flew to San Juan, Puerto Rico where they boarded the huge cruise ship for stops in Curacao, Venezuela, Barbados, and Martinique before returning to San Juan.

When they got back to Dallas, the young couple faced the financial reality of beginning their married life together. They had no income, so they were dependent on Jack to help them out until Amy could find a job. They had signed a one year lease on a small apartment near the University of Texas Southwestern medical school. Jack had helped David move his queen sized bed and dresser, along with an old sofa and coffee table that had been in the Callahan's storage unit, into their apartment before the wedding. They had also taken all the gifts they'd received at their wedding shower out of the guest house, and stacked them in the apartment. Following the reception, Jack took the rest of their gifts to what he called the kids new home, and left them there, still wrapped. Even though David had been in Austin for four years, Elaina wasn't quite ready to admit that her son now lived somewhere other than under her roof.

When the newly weds arrived back at DFW airport, Elaina insisted that she and Jack be there to greet them and take them beck to Dallas. She shared in their excitement as they recounted everything they had done and seen on the week long Caribbean cruise, recalling memories of her own extravagant honeymoon when Jack had taken her to Paris. But, these kids were starting out much differently. Neither of them had a job, they would soon be in debt beyond anything she could imagine, and they were so young. She and Jack had discussed their situation numerous times. She wanted to help them out by paying for David's medical school, but David consistently refused anything more than a few dollars to help with living expenses.

THE CONFLICT

Jack was also more than a little concerned about the kids' financial future. By all reports, recent college graduates were having a lot of trouble finding jobs given the economy. Amy's degree in finance from the University of Texas would command an excellent salary in normal times, but these were far from normal times. David had told him stories of kids he knew that had graduated the year before him, near the top of their class, who were still looking for work. David's words still echoed in Jack's mind. He'd said, "Those guys are living on food stamps and unemployment."

As they prepared to dropped the kids off in front of the apartment, Jack knew his son was anxious for them to leave. David wouldn't want his parents there when he carried his bride across the threshold. "Well, your mom and I need to run," he said as unloaded their luggage from the trunk of the car. "We'll see you both next weekend, right?"

"Yes sir," Amy said, acknowledging their plan to accompany David's parent to Nicaragua again this summer.

"Thanks so much for picking us up," David replied, pulling Amy next to him with is left arm. He then shook his dad's hand and then leaned forward to kiss his mother on the cheek, and hug her with his free arm. She noticed that he'd been unwilling to turn loose of his bride, and once again she began to tear up under the force of still another reminder that her son no longer belonged just to her.

"Here," Jack said as he handed David a check for five thousand dollars. "Your mother and I insist that you take this. It should help you guys get by until Amy finds a job, but if you need more, let me know."

"Thanks, Dad," David said gratefully. He, too, had come to the realization that they could not yet support themselves. "I'll try and stretch this as far as possible. Hopefully, Amy will get on somewhere soon. She has a couple of interviews the week after we get back from Nicaragua."

****

"Now, who is this guy I'm having lunch with?" Fitzgerald asked his assistant as he gathered his sport's coat.

"He said he was a hospital donor. His name is Miguel Hernandez," she said. "He made this appointment more than two months ago."

"And, where am I supposed to meet him?"

"I spoke with him this morning, and he asked that you meet him at Reata at twelve-thirty."

"Did you look up how much he donated?"

"I couldn't find any record of it, but he told me it was some time ago," she explained. "He indicated he might be interested in making another donation. At least that was the impression I got."

"Okay, if he wants to buy my lunch at Reata, I guess I'll listen to whatever he has to say." He quickly took a final look at his schedule before heading for the door. "I don't want to be there all afternoon, so if I'm not back by two, call me and give me an excuse to come back to the office."

Jim Fitzgerald walked confidently into the upscale downtown restaurant, and asked for Mr. Hernandez. The hostess escorted him to a booth in the back corner where a tall Latin American man was seated, facing him, with his back to the wall.

"Mr. Hernandez, I presume?" Fitzgerald asked.

The man stood without speaking, shook his hand, then motioned for his guest to be seated. The hostess excused herself, and Fitzgerald asked, "So what can I do for you?"

Before an answer could be given, the waitress came to the table and offered to take their drink orders. Fitzgerald ordered bourbon and water, but the other man just shook his head. As she left, Fitzgerald looked across at the distinguished man who was at least twenty-five years younger and got the distinct feeling that something wasn't right. His eyes narrowed as he asked suspiciously, "Who are you? What's this all about?"

"My name is Franco Gutierrez, and I have come a very long way to speak with you," came the reply.

"I don't get it. I was told I was supposed to meet a guy here named Hernandez, some donor to my hospital. What is this, some kind of a trick?" He paused and when he didn't get an immediate response he said, "Excuse me, but I'm leaving."

As Fitzgerald started to slide out of the booth, he spotted two rather large men in dark suits seated at the table next to them. Both were staring at him intently, and as he started to move, so did they.

"Just keep your seat Mr. Fitzgerald, I won't keep you long," Franco said very calmly. "I didn't deceive your secretary. I am indeed a donor to the children's hospital. Perhaps you recall the donation I made five years ago?" Franco was referring to the million dollars he had given to the children's hospital designated for future Nicaraguan children to receive heart operations. Fitzgerald had initially moved the money into the hospital's general fund to offset the cost of a new CT scanner, but when Jack Roberts discovered his deception and threatened to expose him, he'd been forced to temporarily restored the Nicaraguan Surgical Fund. When Michael Horvath took over as the new administrator, he used some shady accounting to effectively steal the funds.

THE CONFLICT

Fitzgerald had no way of knowing how, but Franco had been made aware of the deception, so he decided to use the occasion of David's wedding to correct any misunderstanding.

Fitzgerald's eyes widened as he caught himself looking again at the men sitting at the next table. "Uh, yes. I remember. That was very generous of you Mr., uh, Gutierrez, wasn't it?"

"You understood that those funds were designated by me specifically to care for children from my country who were in need of heart surgery, did you not?"

"Of course. And that is exactly what they have been used for." Fitzgerald's tone abruptly shifted from anxious to defensive.

"Can you tell me how many children from Nicaragua have been treated in the children's hospital in the last five years?"

"No, I can't, but I do know that most of those funds have been exhausted," Fitzgerald was tempted to ask Franco if he was interested in making another donation, but he thought better of it, at least for the moment.

"That is interesting, because as I understand it, there have only been two children from my country treated in your hospital since my daughter underwent her surgery there, five years ago."

"I'm not sure that is correct, but as I said, I don't really know."

"Oh, Mr. Fitzgerald," Franco said slowly, "I think you do know. I believe you know exactly how many there have been, and precisely what the actual costs were for each of their treatments." He paused again to ensure he still had Fitzgerald's full attention. "Furthermore, you know precisely how your accountants have made some rather interesting adjustments to your books, allowing you to take that money, and use it for purposes for which it was not intended. Am I correct?"

Fitzgerald did not answer. His attempt to con this guy was not working. He wanted to bolt, but from the look of Franco's body guards that was not an option.

"I must assume from your silence that I am indeed correct." Franco had been speaking with his hand folded in his lap, and as he brought them up on top of the table, Fitzgerald reflexly sat back quickly in his seat. He relaxed only slightly as he saw Franco folding his empty hands together.

"Who have you been talking to?" he asked, trying to hide the obvious anger in his voice. "Was it Jack Roberts?"

"I can assure you that Dr. Roberts had nothing to do with any of this. He is far too fine a gentleman. He knows nothing of this meeting and is completely unaware of the fact that I know anything of your treachery. Let's just say I have my sources." Franco leaned forward slightly, causing Fitzgerald to sit back again in fear, "You don't think I would be foolish enough to give a million dollars to anyone without knowing precisely how it would be used, do you?"

"So what do you want from me?" Fitzgerald asked trying to sound more in control than he felt.

"It is not what I want, Mr. Fitzgerald, it is what I intend to get." Franco leaned back slightly as the waitress came toward the table with the bourbon, but, when she saw the look in Franco's eyes, and the way he motioned to her with a single shake of his head, she turned around without attempting to serve the drink.

He leaned forward again, assuming the dominant position once more. Then he spoke very slowly, "First, I expect the Nicaraguan Surgical Fund to be restored to eight hundred thousand dollars. That is how much there should be in that account, am I correct?"

Fitzgerald simply nodded.

"Second, I understand from my friends in Nicaragua, that there are at least three children there now with heart problems, waiting to be seen by Dr. Roberts when he arrives later this month. Assuming he determines that any, or all, of them need surgery, you will personally see to it that they receive the same level of care that my daughter received when she was in your hospital."

"I can do that." Fitzgerald answered.

"And finally," Franco said, leaning forward just another inch, "you will personally notify Dr. Roberts, that you, and the man you have working for you, what's his name, Horvath?"

"Yes."

"That you have had a change of heart, and that you have restored the fund to its appropriate amount. I do not want Dr. Roberts to hesitate, not even for a moment, if he needs to bring any child here for treatment." Franco paused briefly before continuing. "And, he must never know anything of this meeting. Is that understood?"

"I understand," the older man said, trying to regain his composure.

"Good." Franco looked intently into Fitzgerald's eyes and saw exactly what he needed to see. "I bid you good day, sir."

As he rose from his seat he turned back to Fitzgerald and leaned over, placing both hands on the table, "Do not disappoint me, Mr. Fitzgerald. I promise you, I will know if you do."

****

"So, I hear you're going back down to Nicaragua next week," Horvath said in a tone that was surprisingly friendly.

"Yes," Jack replied. "My wife and I have been going there for nearly twenty years now. It is a good place to recharge your batteries. I highly recommend it."

"Well, I'm not sure that there would be much there for me to do, but I applaud your commitment." He hesitated before sitting down at his desk. "In fact, that is why I asked you to come in today."

Jack sat comfortably across the desk from this man who had, up to now, acted indifferently toward him most of the time, and occasionally had been openly antagonistic. What was this about, he wondered. Was he going to make another effort to get him to join the pediatricians' big group practice? He knew they hadn't had any success attracting the guys from Dallas, that was obvious.

"Jim Fitzgerald and I were talking earlier this week about you, and the fact that you attract so many children to our hospital for heart surgery from all across the region." Horvath spoke in a way that sounded as though he was almost in awe of Jack's fame. "We thought it would be beneficial for both you and for the hospital if we helped you market that aspect of your practice."

Jack smiled and chuckled slightly under his breath. Given everything this guy and Fitzgerald had been trying to do, did they really expect him to believe that now they wanted to try and help him?

"What we were thinking is, the next time you bring one of those kids up here from Nicaragua, and repair whatever it is that needs repairing, we could get the local media to cover the story. It would make for great positive press, and since their care is already paid for by your rich friend down there, the story wouldn't involve any of the usual insurance or Medicaid controversy. It would be strictly confined to health care in its purest form. What do you think?"

"Hummm ..." Jack hardly knew where to begin. "As of the last time we spoke about this, you told me the funds that Mr. Gutierrez donated had been almost completely ... I think the word you used was ... depleted? Am I right?"

"At Mr. Fitzgerald's specific direction, I have gone back and recalculated all the charges on the three Nicaraguan children you've treated in our facility, and made the appropriate changes to the account. As of today, there is seven hundred ninety-eight thousand, five hundred and twelve dollars available to offset future charges." Horvath said, reading from the balance sheet he had in front of him.

"And why, exactly, did he instruct you to make that, adjustment to the fund?" Jack was beyond the point of being fascinated by the tall tale this guy was spinning.

Horvath knew ahead of time that he was going to be made to look foolish, and it was all he could do not to show the inner rage he was feeling. "Like I said, Mr. Fitzgerald thought our hospital image could benefit from the kind of positive PR that a story like this would provide. He believes the best way to accomplish that would be to replenish the fund, which will allow you the freedom to bring additional children here without worrying about how their bill might be paid."

"Well, that's awfully nice of him," Jack said nodding his head somewhat sarcastically. "I suspect he has already spoken to the media."

"I know he has some significant contacts, but I'm sure he has not spoken to anyone about doing a story that does not yet exist." Horvath was lying again, and Jack knew it.

"Well, since its been a few years since I've seen any kids down there that needed heart surgery, I have no idea when, or if, I'll see a marketable case." Jack smiled and made quotation marks in the air as he spoke the word marketable.

"We are well aware of the possibility that it might be a while, but we just wanted you to know that when the opportunity arises, we've made it possible for you to do what you do."

Now it was Jack's turn to control his anger. Who was this guy to suggest that he had anything to do with allowing him *to do what he did*? As far as Jack was concerned he and guys like Fitzgerald were major obstacles. It was people like Franco Gutierrez who deserved the credit for making what Horvath referred to as health care in its *purest form* possible. Suddenly, Jack wondered whether Franco had had anything to do with this change in Horvath, but he quickly dismissed the idea, since there was no way Franco could know about the events that happened several years ago. He certainly hadn't said anything to him about it.

****

As the four Americans piled into the rent car, the faint smell of sulfur was present in the air, and the sky seemed a bit more hazy than usual, even for Managua. Well off to the south they could see a faint plume of light gray smoke rising from one of the distant volcanic cones.

"Looks like they're experiencing an eruption off to the south," Jack said, as he pulled out on to the Pan American Highway, heading for the familiar home of Domingo and Felicia.

"Wow!" David said, staring off to the left as the roadway rose onto an elevated bridge giving then a much clearer view of the horizon. "I had know idea that there were active volcanoes in Nicaragua."

"Absolutely," Jack replied. "I think I read somewhere that there are nineteen volcanoes in this country, and nearly half of them are considered to be active."

"That is amazing," Amy said. "I've never seen a volcano erupting,"

"Neither have I," Jack responded, "until now."

Just then, a small, somewhat darker cloud of smoke belched slowly from the mountain top off in the distance. After several seconds they could hear the faint rumble of the blast.

"Did you see that?" David asked. "A big black cloud just erupted into the air."

"That's not good," Jack replied with obvious concern in his voice.

As they made their way along the highway, there were no more blasts to be witnessed, but the mountain continued to produce a steady flow of dark smoke from its peak.

When they arrived, Domingo came running out to meet them. He didn't give them his usual joyous greeting. Instead he sounded quite concerned when he said, "I am so glad you made it."

"Of course we made it," Jack said with an anxious smile.

As he motioned for his employee, Guillermo, to bring in their luggage, Domingo turned to Jack and said, "I heard just a few minutes ago on the local television station that they have closed the airport due to the amount of ash in the air."

"Are you serious?" Jack asked in disbelief.

"Yes, Concepción started erupting late yesterday afternoon and this morning the wind shifted around from the south, which is bringing the ash cloud very near Managua. It is too dangerous for airplanes to fly through it, so there will be no more flights, in or out, until the eruption stops, or the wind shifts back around to the west."

"Well," Jack replied hesitantly, "hopefully this won't last too long."

"They say these eruptions usually only continue for two or three days, but we have no way of knowing." The doubt in Domingo's voice was obvious. He had seen only two prior eruptions in his many years in Nicaragua. The first was off to the north in 1999. Cerro Negro erupted for two days, but from where he lived it was simply a gray haze on the horizon, and it didn't disrupt any aspect of his life. He also witnessed the eruption of Telica in 2007, but that peak was even further to the north than Cerro Negro. This was the first time he had seen any of the visible line of cone shaped mountains off to the south erupt, and he was clearly shaken by the event.

When Felicia entered the room she greeted all her guests with her usual warmth, but she was especially excited to see the newly weds as she showed them to Rafael's old room. It remained very much as David had remembered it from the first time he'd stayed there five years earlier.

"So, how is Rafael doing?" David asked.

"He is just completing his third year of residency at Johns Hopkins University. Have you ever heard of it?" Felicia asked proudly.

"Of course," David said, electing not to say anything about his own application to that school. He had finally heard from Hopkins and Stanford back in the early spring, and he was on a list of alternates for admission at both schools, but he had immediately written back telling them he had elected to attend med school elsewhere.

"My dad spent some time there during his training, and he told me that my uncle had a heart operation there when he was just an infant."

"Yes, it is a very famous place. Domingo and I went there when Rafael graduated from medical school in 2007."

"What kind of residency is he in?" Amy asked.

"He is training to be a neurosurgeon," Felicia replied with obvious pride.

"Is he planning to stay in the US when he finishes?" David inquired, knowing that most foreign physicians chose to stay in the United States rather than return to their homelands.

"No. when he went off to college his father made him promise that he would return here to his home and help care for the people of Nicaragua."

****

"I don't care that all their television crews are off covering some damned volcano," Fitzgerald was shouting into the phone. "You tell them to get a crew out to that clinic tomorrow and get me some video footage of Roberts and his wife and who ever else he's dragged along with him."

"But, Jim," the manager of the local television station said, "I don't have that much influence over that station in Managua. I can't force them to do anything."

"Well then, I want you to get one of our crews down there to get the story. I need that video tape." Fitzgerald now owned the station, and he intended to use it to achieve his goal, and it had nothing to do with promoting the practice of Jack Roberts.

"I already thought about that, sir, but the airport in Managua is closed because of the eruption."

"So, how did Roberts manage to get down there?"

"His was the last commercial flight that was allowed to land before they shut it down," he explained. "If we're lucky the wind will shift again, or the damned thing will stop erupting, and I can get somebody in there, but for now the only hope I have of getting what you've ask for is a local crew, and like I said, this eruption is the biggest news story in that country in several years."

"There must be some freelance videographer down there that you can convince to leave that stupid volcano long enough to get me that footage. Offer them whatever it takes, but get me what I need. You hear me?"

"Yes, sir. I hear you. I'll make every effort."

"I don't want effort, I want results!" Fitzgerald spouted as he slammed down the phone.

****

Jack drove the rented Ford Bronco past the front of the Ciudad Sandino clinic on Tuesday morning, following closely behind Domingo and into the parking area beyond the missionaries' cinder block house.

"Check it out, Dad," David said.

"What?" Jack asked, wondering what his son was talking about.

"There's a couple of guys across the street with video cameras," David reported, pointing at the videographers set up across the street.

"Probably some local news station. They've been trying to get me to appear on local television almost every time we've come down here since that press conference years ago. Don't pay them any attention and they'll likely leave in a few minutes."

Jack and his family followed Domingo through the front door of the crowded clinic, and as they did, David turned to see the cameramen raising up from behind their tripods, but they showed no signs of leaving. "They are just following your every move," David said, causing Jack to turn around, briefly facing the cameras.

"Before we get started in the clinic, I've had three kids come in early for you to evaluate," Domingo said. "I am very concerned that each of them has a significant heart problem."

"Okay," Jack replied, as he followed Domingo toward the exam rooms beyond the main waiting area. David followed close behind, hoping to be included as more than just an observer, but he recognized he didn't really have anything to offer.

The trio entered the first room where a young mother was holding a baby boy who looked to be about six months old and quite thin. "Based on the history and my exam, I'm reasonably sure this child has tetralogy."

Jack asked the mother to place the baby up on the examination table as he pulled his stethoscope out of his pocket and placed it around his neck. He then asked the mother about the child's ability to nurse. She told him that he frequently seemed to fall asleep while he was nursing, and she was afraid her milk would dry up if he didn't start taking more soon. When he asked how old the baby was, he was surprised to hear that the child was actually born just over ten months ago, and that he'd been born about a month earlier than she had expected.

The baby seemed rather listless, and his face had a slight bluish hue, although his rather dark skin made it difficult to be certain. He lifted the child's shirt and placed the palm of his right hand flat against the front of the baby's chest. After a few seconds he removed his hand and placed the stethoscope in his ears. He carefully listened to several places on the front of the baby's chest, then listened carefully to both sides of his back.

"Come over here," he said to David. "I want to show you something." David stepped quickly to his fathers side. "I want you to gently place your hand over this baby's heart."

David did as instructed, trying to mimic what he'd watched his dad do moments earlier. "Do you feel that buzzing sensation under the base of your index finger?"

"I feel something, but I'm not really sure exactly where I feel it." David obviously had no experience examining the heart, and clearly wasn't able to make the kind of subtle differentiation that Jack was suggesting existed.

"Just hold your hand there a little while, and see if you can't feel more precisely where that buzzing sensation is coming from.

"After another few seconds David started to smile slightly. He looked toward his dad and said, "I think I can feel what you mean. It is definitely most prominent right here." He pulled his hand away and pointed to a spot in the upper part of the baby's chest, slightly to the left of the breast bone.

"Exactly. Now take this stethoscope and listen over that same spot."

David had used a stethoscope on a few occasions when his dad tried to show him how to take a blood pressure, and he'd listened to his own heart several times years earlier when he was just a kid, but he had never examined a patient before. He placed the plastic buds in his ears and then gently place the round metal piece on the spot on the baby's chest where he had pointed. Immediately his eyebrows rose and his mouth opened slightly. He continued to listen for a few seconds, nodding his head slowly.

"Wow!" he exclaimed as he slowly removed the instrument from his ears. "That's amazing."

"That, son, is the unmistakable sound of a very restricted pulmonary outflow tract. Based on that sound, combined with some slight congestion in his chest and the slight bluish tinge to his skin, I think Dr. Ramirez's diagnosis is right on the money. The fact that the baby is not able to nurse due to fatigue, and is not developing as he should, I'd say we need to take him home with us and fix his tetralogy of Fallot."

"That's incredible, Dad. You make it sound like solving a murder mystery."

"Well, there's no crime to solve here, but making a diagnosis involves the use of the same concepts. You work from the clues you gather. Start with a careful history, then you do a careful systematic examination. You'd be surprised how often you can make an accurate diagnosis with just that information." Jack looked at Domingo and winked.

"You are so right my friend," Domingo responded with a slight smile.

"Now days they don't really teach those fundamental diagnostic skills in medical school, or even residency for that matter. All the emphasis is on ordering the latest high tech tests, like CT scans and MRIs, and God knows how many blood tests. Physical diagnosis is becoming a lost art." Jack turned back to Domingo and said, "Have you explained to this mother what needs to be done?"

"Yes, I have, and she is anxious to do whatever it takes to get her baby healthy."

"Great. What else do you have for us?"

They moved to the next exam room where a young boy, who appeared to be about ten years old sat on the exam table with his shirt already off. He was quite thin, and appeared to be somewhat anxious and mildly short of breath. Jack approached him and learned from his father that over the last six months he had complained of trouble breathing at times, and he was now starting to lose weight.

Jack repeated the same exam he had performed on the baby, but this time he spent a little more time listening to the heart. He had the boy lie down on his back and then on his left side. Finally he had him turn over on his right side as he continued to listen carefully at several key locations. He then asked the father in Spanish whether the child had ever had any episodes of sore throat, and was informed that indeed, six months earlier he had been very sick with a severe sore throat that lasted for more than a week. When he didn't improve, the father brought him to the clinic, and Dr. Ramirez had treated him with penicillin for two weeks.

Jack looked at Domingo and asked, "Did the cultures come back group A strep?"

"Domingo smiled and said, "I don't have the resources to culture these sick kids when they come in. I must assume they have it and treat them accordingly. This boy responded well to penicillin, so I am fairly certain that's what it was."

"Well, it has sure done a number on both his mitral and aortic valves."

"What are you talking about, Dad?" David asked.

"Come hear and listen, right here." he held the stethoscope a couple of inches below the young boy's left breast. As David put the instrument in his ears Jack said, "Tell me what you hear."

David listened intently for a few seconds and while still listening he spoke a little more loudly than was normal. "I hear what sounds like a faint clicking and some rumbling noise after that with each heart beat."

"Very good!" Jack said excitedly. "That is exactly how a mitral stenosis murmur is described in the textbook. I'm impressed."

David didn't hear what his dad said, because he still had the stethoscope in his ears. When he raised up and removed the earbuds he asked, "What did you say?"

Jack wasn't about to repeat the complement, but rather said, "That is the murmur that occurs with mitral stenosis. This boy had rheumatic fever a few months ago, and it caused his immune system to attack the valves of his heart. If you listen right hear," Jack continued, pointing to a spot to the right of the boy's breast bone, an inch or so below his collar bone, "you'll hear an entirely different sound."

David placed the ear pieces back in his ears an carefully held the end of the instrument where his dad had indicated. He listened intently for a few seconds, then his face broke into a broad smile. This time he removed the stethoscope from his ears before speaking.

"I hear a swishing sound, followed by a soft thump."

"That is the murmur of aortic stenosis, so this boy has both mitral and aortic stenosis secondary to rheumatic fever. I suspect he may also have an element of regurgitation in both valves, and the combination of these ailments is why he's showing early signs of heart failure," Jack said, indicating he thought both valves on the left side of the young boy's heart were severely damaged.

"So, what can be done about it" David asked.

"He is going to need a heart cath, so we can determine whether the valves can be repaired or need to be replaced. In an adolescent like this, I'd much prefer to repair them if possible, because as he grows, and his heart grows, replaced valves won't grow along with him. That means they'd likely have to be replaced again once he reaches adulthood."

Domingo nodded his agreement and said, "I've got one more child I need you to see."

"I assume you've explained things to this father?"

"Of course," Domingo replied. "They live in Granada, but he's come here prepared to make the trip to the US, assuming you think that's what they need to do."

"Absolutely." Jack replied with a nod of his head as he made his way out into the main room again with David close behind. As the trio entered the third exam room, they saw another young mother seated in a chair with a two year old sitting in her lap. The young man Jack assumed to be the child's father stood next to her. The more he looked at him, the less certain he was of that relationship. As Domingo introduced the mother and child, the young woman said hello, but the young man next to her said nothing.

Jack turned to him and asked in his native language, "Are you the father?"

The mother replied, likewise in Spanish, indicating that the teenager was actually her brother, and that he was there to protect her baby.

Jack's expression grew even more questioning as he turned to Domingo for an explanation.

"The father of this child is an older man who does not believe in doctors or medicine. I saw this little girl here three weeks ago, and I told the mother that she should bring her back today to see you. Apparently the father threatened to take the child away and carry her into the mountains if she ever brought her to this clinic again," Domingo explained.

The brother was certainly not a large boy, and was only sixteen or seventeen years old. However, he wore the rather stern look of a seasoned body guard, as he stood silently next to his sister.

She turned to Jack and spoke passionately in Spanish, "Please, doctor, help my baby."

Jack began his examination and quickly concluded that the child was displaying signs of advanced congestive heart failure, likely secondary to a large atrial septal defect.

"This little girl reminds me of the first time I saw you," he said as he turned to David. "I'm pretty sure she's got a big ASD, and she's going to need to have it patched pretty soon, before she develops irreversible pulmonary hypertension."

He turned back toward Domingo and asked, "Is Franco's Foundation aware of the fact that we need to transport these three kids to Fort Worth?"

"Yes, I notified them two weeks ago of that possibility, and they are ready to transport the children, and one parent each, whenever you say."

"I'd say we should get them all up there as soon as possible. That way I can get Buzz to cath them, and he may be able to patch this little girl's ASD himself."

"The only problem is the airport is still closed," Domingo said. The volcanic eruption was still occurring, and the wind continued to blow steadily from the south.

"Well, as soon as they open the airport, we need to get these kids to Texas." Jack paused for a moment then added. "Come to think of it, if the wind changes and they resume commercial flights, we may want to take advantage of that opportunity to head back home ourselves," he spoke mostly to David. "Otherwise we could potentially get stuck here for who knows how long."

****

On Thursday morning, not only did the wind shift around from the northwest, the eruption also paused, except for a small amount of white smoke coming from the top of the mountain, trailing slowly off to the east. The airport opened to commercial aircraft at nine a.m., and by noon the terminal and surrounding tarmac were clogged with planes, many of them having arrived to carry away the huge backlog of travelers who had been stuck in the airport and surrounding hotels for nearly a week. Jack and Elaina discussed the possibility of leaving early, but decided to avoid the craziness at the airport and just take their scheduled flight on Sunday.

Jack called Franco to thank him again for making it possible for these three children to receive the care they needed.

"Why don't you and your family drop by for dinner this evening?" Franco asked.

"Oh, no," Jack said laughingly. "I don't think we could handle another gala like the one you threw last time."

"No, no," Franco objected. "We have nothing planned, and there will be no other guests. I insist," he said. "We didn't get much time to visit at your son's wedding, and I have a number of things I'd like to talk with you about."

"Alright," Jack responded. "What time?"

"Around seven?"

"We'll be there, but remember, no visits from the President, and no gifts. We are already far to deeply indebted to you and Gabriella."

Both men laughed before saying their good byes.

****

The air ambulance left Managua on Friday morning, and as the children and their parents boarded the plane the freelance videographers were there to film the scene secretly from the observation deck of the terminal. Fitzgerald's station manager also had his local television crew waiting at DFW to catch the image of the Nicaraguans arrival and transport to the children's hospital.

The ten year old and his father were taken to a local hotel, since he wouldn't be evaluated by Dr. Jackson until Monday morning. The ten month old was admitted to the hospital and prepared for a cardiac catheterization on Saturday morning, while the two year old was taken almost directly to the cath lab that same afternoon.

The Nicaraguan video crew securely uploaded multiple video clips to the American televisions station's server. They included scenes of the extreme poverty in and around Managua as well as clips from outside Domingo's clinic. They had also taken several shots of the government hospital, and many featuring Dr. Jack Roberts and his family, including a clip from the clinic. For Fitzgerald the most important clip was the one of Jack talking with the guard who quickly allowed him access through the gate leading to Franco Gutierrez's palatial estate. The raw media was already being viewed and edited by Fitzgerald's studio crew, long before the subjects made it back to the states.

CHAPTER 6

The possibility of another four years under the Obama administration was just beginning to sink in. Once the networks announced that he had won in Florida and Virginia the result seemed all but certain. Jack was visibly upset, not just because of the way the Presidential election was going, but also because of the almost giddy way many of the commentators on the major networks were reporting it.

"Here locally we continue to have a very tight race for the Congressional seat in Fort Worth. With seventy-five percent of the precincts reporting, the republican, Jack Roberts, holds a razor thin lead over the incumbent democrat, Herman Sheffield." The image of the talking head switched to the graphic showing Jack with six hundred thirty-three thousand, one hundred forty-seven to Sheffield's six hundred thirty-two thousand nine hundred eighty three. "As you can see, the margin in only one hundred sixty four votes."

"It's basically a dead heat." the co-anchor added. "This election is far different for Sheffield than his last several races."

"No matter what the outcome, it seems clear the people of Fort Worth and surrounding areas are none too happy with his support of Obamacare. The question is whether there was enough of a backlash to unseat him. We'll just have to wait a little longer to find out."

They commentators went on to list the results of the other area races, as Jack made his way into the bathroom. He put the tie Jason had insisted he wear for political reasons, around his neck and carefully slipped it under the collar of his starched white shirt. He began tying the half-windsor knot, and as he pulled the bright red knot up to the front of his neck, he was reminded of yet another fateful day.

****

On Sunday evening Jack and Elaina dropped the kids off once more at their apartment, then drove the thirty-five miles from Dallas to Fort Worth. On the way, Jack called Buzz on his cell phone to ask about the Nicaraguan children.

'Hey, Buzz. how's it going?" he asked as his friend answered.

"Welcome home," he replied. "How was your flight?"

"It was fine. Tiring as usual, but no problems once that eruption finally stopped. We just dropped David and Amy off at their apartment and we're on out way home."

"Great. You need to get some rest. You're going to be busy tomorrow."

"Oh yeah? Did you cath those kids?"

"Yes," Buzz replied with a somewhat frustrated tone that Jack recognized.

"What happened?" He asked, fearing that something might have gone wrong.

"Well, the two year old girl has a big ASD as you suspected, but I was not able to patch it. Every time I got the catheter in a position to deploy the patch she went into atrial fibrillation and I had to back off. So, you're going to need to fix her on Monday."

"Okay," Jack said. "What about the ten month old boy with tetralogy?"

"He is on for you to do tomorrow as well. You can take a look at the video of his cath in the morning, but it looked pretty straight forward to me. He should do great."

"You haven't seen the ten year old yet, have you?"

"No, I got your report, but he isn't due to come in until around eight in the morning."

"Terrific," Jack replied. "I figured we'd do him on Tuesday, unless you're able to fix his valves tomorrow with those magic catheters of yours," Jack replied with a chuckle in his voice.

"Don't laugh," Buzz said. "I might just be able to keep you out of trouble by solving that kid's problems myself. You know that surgery stuff you do is pretty dangerous." Buzz was making every effort to stay serious, but the lighthearted nature of his banter came through anyway.

"Oh, by the way," Buzz said, "I ran into that video crew and let them come into the cath lab a take some video footage for that piece they are doing."

"What?" Jack asked, obviously unsure what his friend meant.

"Yeah, the crew from the local television station said they were here under your direction to document the story of these Nicaraguan children, and the care they were receiving."

"I didn't ... " Jack stopped what he was saying, remembering his conversation with Horvath two weeks before. "I guess administration must have asked them to be there, because I certainly didn't."

"Really?" Buzz replied. "They told me that they were there under your orders, otherwise I wouldn't have let them in."

What was Horvath up to? Jack wondered to himself. "Its okay. I'll ask Horvath about it tomorrow."

Early the following morning Jack made his way into the children's hospital parking lot, unaware he was being filmed by a television camera hidden in the bushes near the rear entrance to the building. Once inside, he made his way up to the OR to talk with the mother of the two year old prior to taking her back for the ASD repair.

"What is going on?" Jack asked the OR supervisor, as he walked into the holding area and saw a camera man standing on the far wall. He had started rolling as soon as he saw Jack come through the door.

"Mr. Horvath told me to allow this television crew in, he said he talked to you about it."

Jack thought for a moment and decided not to cause a scene. If Horvath wanted to promote the hospital in such a cheesy way, he figured he could play along. "Its okay," he said calmly, "just so they stay out of the way."

After the preliminary discussions with the family and all the permits had been signed, Radha rolled the small stretcher back to the heart room and began the process of putting the little girl to sleep for the repair of her atrial septal defect.

"Hi Jack," George said as his mentor joined him at the scrub sink. "How was Nicaragua?"

"It was hot as usual, but this time a little hotter than usual. They had a volcano erupt while we were there."

"Really? I didn't know there were active volcanos in Nicaragua."

"Yeah, it's one of the most geologically active areas in the world?"

"Are you talking about lava flows and all that, like in Hawaii?"

"No, we didn't see any lava, just a lot of smoke and ash. They had the airport shut down for five days because of the ash cloud."

"I remember a few years ago when that volcano erupted in Iceland. They closed down most of the air travel across Europe."

"Yeah, the guy I talked to at the airline said it's one of the more dangerous situations they face. Apparently the tiny rock particles in the ash can get blown all the way up into the stratosphere and stay there for years. If a plane flies through a cloud of that stuff, it gets sucked into the jet engines. The heat causes it to bake onto all the moving parts, causing them to seize up. He called it atmospheric concrete. Obviously not good."

"Well it's good to have you home."

"Yeah, it was great to have a week off, but I'm ready to get back to work," Jack replied.

An hour and a half later, Jack strolled out to the waiting room to speak to the young mother. He explained that the procedure had gone uneventfully, and that her daughter was just beginning to wake up in the recovery room. She was very appreciative and held Jack's right hand tightly in both of hers, and tenderly kissed it before tearfully letting him go.

"So," Jack said, catching Radha as she was on her way to see their next patient. "Have you had a chance to look at this next little guy?"

"Yes," Radha replied. "He looks relatively stable, but he sure is small for ten months."

"I know. His growth has definitely been retarded, but I suspect he'll catch up once we get him fixed."

The second procedure, likewise, went very smoothly. As Jack was leaving the OR he thanked everyone by name, as was his custom. Then he turned to George and said, "I think you're ready to fix the next one of these tets that I find down in Nicaragua, don't you?"

George smiled as he removed his mask and said, "I'm ready, but I have to tell you, I don't think I'll ever be able to do that with the same ... style you do. That was a work of art."

"Oh, don't be silly. You've got all the skills, its just a matter of experience."

"You may be right, but I'm not sure I'll live long enough to gain your level of experience."

"Now you're making me feel old," Jack said with a laugh.

****

"What did you find on that boy with the rheumatic valves?" Jack asked, as he walked into the doctor's dictation area of the cath lab.

Buzz had just finished dictating his fourth cath of the morning and was writing in the last child's chart. "He had pretty tight gradients across both valves, especially the mitral." He said, referring to the greater than normal difference in the pressure on either side of the diseased valves.

"I tried to open them but I didn't have any success. They are both really stiff, and the aortic valve has a grade one regurgitation. The Mitral regurgitation is only very minimal."

"That's basically what I suspected," Jack said. "It has been my experience that when these kids become symptomatic in such a short time, the valves are usually pretty unyielding. Sounds like, at the very least, the aortic valve is going to need to be replaced. Did you take a look at his pulmonic valve?"

Jack wanted to make sure he knew all his surgical options, and if the valve between the right ventricle and the artery to the lungs was damaged, it would eliminate his best choice for replacing the diseased aortic valve.

"The pulmonary valve looked pristine, so I think you can use it if it comes down to that."

Jack was considering this young boy for what was known as a Ross procedure, named after Dr. Donald Ross, a famous heart surgeon who first performed the operation on a child back in the sixties. It was one of the more complex procedures Jack did, and involved replacing the aortic valve with the patients own pulmonic valve, and then using a cadaver valve to replace the pulmonic valve.

"A lot is going to depend on whether or not we have to replace that mitral as well. Hopefully we can do a valvuloplasty on it. I would hate to have to replace three of the four valves in this young boy's heart."

Jack knew all to well that the risk of complications increased progressively with the number of valves replaced, so if he could just remodel the one between the left atrium and ventricle, he could significantly lower the risk of the surgery.

****

George showed up early to the OR. He'd read about the Ross procedure, but he'd never actually seen one. He knew very well that since the right side of the heart was a much lower pressure system, it would tolerate a cadaver valve graft far better than the high pressure circulation in the left side of the heart. Plus, if they used the child's own pulmonic valve to replace his damaged aortic valve, it would grow along with him, avoiding the need for subsequent re-operation when he was fully grown. While a cadaver graft used to replace the harvested pulmonic valve wouldn't grow as the heart grew, the right side would likely tolerate the gradual size mismatch, far better than the left.

"Hopefully we can just open up the mitral valve," Jack said as he and George stood at the scrub sink, washing their hands prior to what promised to be a long and arduous procedure. "If we don't have to replace the mitral, he won't have to be on long term blood thinners."

The two men entered the room at seven forty-five in the morning and they left through the same door at eleven-thirty. For more than three and a half hours they worked nonstop to remodel, rearrange and replace the valves of the young

Nicaraguan boy's heart. Jack had been able to release much of the scar tissue that was keeping the mitral valve from opening fully, so it did not require replacement. Then he performed the Ross procedure, removing both the aortic and pulmonic valves, and using the normal one to replace the one that was irreparably damaged. A cadaver valve was then used to replace the pulmonic.

"That was one of the most amazing things I've ever witnessed," George said. "And, the way that kids heart came off the pump without even the slightest irregularity. That has to make you feel good. I know it does me."

"Of course it makes me feel good," Jack replied, as he looked into the eyes of his young protege, "but, like I always tell you, this is God's work we're doing, so it should make us feel good."

Everything had gone exceptionally smooth. Jack had even accepted the television crews who still seemed to be everywhere around the hospital. This certainly would make for a good human interest story, and if the hospital managed to get some positive press out of it, he thought that was probably okay. But on Wednesday afternoon, while he was seeing patients in his office, Jack got a frantic call from the ICU. As he picked up the phone, the head nurse spoke a little louder than normal, and definitely faster than he had ever heard her. "Dr. Roberts, we need you in the ICU immediately, the ten year old Nicaraguan boy has stopped breathing. We are doing CPR, but without much luck."

"On my way," Jack said as he hung up the phone and quickly headed out the front door of his office, passing several waiting patients. He literally ran the block and a half to the children's hospital and up the stairs to the ICU. As he arrived he saw the crowd that had gathered in the young boy's cubicle and immediately made his way passed the bevy of nurses who were performing all the various tasks of a full code. The monitors were sounding various alarms, indicating low blood pressure, low heart rate, and absent respirations.

"Do you have an airway?" he asked. The intensivist was working on trying to put a tube back into the young boys trachea.

"No!" he said. "There is something blocking me."

Jack knew that Jeremy was one of the best guys in the group, and if he couldn't intubate this boy, there was a good reason. The child's color was ashen and the heart monitor showed a rhythm but the rate was only twenty-four beats per minute. They were going to lose this child if he didn't act fast, so, he didn't hesitate, "Open the trach kit!" he demanded loudly.

The nurse produced a tray of instruments, and as she unwrapped them Jack quickly put on a pair of sterile gloves and painted the boys neck with an amber colored liquid antiseptic. As he did, he saw that the heart rate was down to fifteen. He used a scalpel in a stabbing motion entering the child's trachea just above the notch in the breast bone, and very near the top of the recent incision he'd used for repairing the heart. There was a slight rush of air from the new wound, and a small splattering of blood erupted out of the half inch cut in the skin. He then took a hemostat and plunged it through the opening, then spread it widely to create a passage for a breathing tube. He removed the clamp and inserted a small plastic tube directly into the trachea.

"Hook up the Ambu bag," he commanded to Jeremy, indicating he needed for the other doctor to begin breathing for his dying patient. As Jeremy squeezed the bag, Jack could see the still unresponsive child's chest rise and fall, but his color remained very blue. The heart rate had slowed to an agonizingly slow ten beats per minute.

"Atropine!" he ordered, and quickly the nurse pushed a syringe full of the drug into the child's blood stream through the large intravenous catheter in the young boy's neck, leading directly to his heart.

"Epinephrine!" he shouted.

"We already gave some," the nurse announced.

"Well give some more!" Jack insisted.

As the second medication was given, the heart rate quickened slightly, first to twenty beats per minute, then to twenty-five, but it seemed to stay there longer than Jack had hoped. "Give another dose of Atropine!" he said. Demanding they give more of the drug that would hopefully increase the heart rate soon, before he suffered permanent brain injury due to lack of adequate flow of oxygenated blood.

"Finally!" he sighed, as he watched the heart rate gradually increase above fifty. "Do we have a pressure?" he asked the nurse.

"The art line is saying its eighty over thirty-six," she said, reading the arterial blood pressure that was being monitored by a small catheter inside the main artery in the boy's right groin.

"How long ago did you initiate the code?" Jack asked.

The nurse looked at the clock on the wall and said, "its been about ten minutes.

"What exactly happened?" Jack asked, hoping to get some idea why this child, whom he had checked on less than two hours earlier, would suddenly stop breathing.

"I was out of the room when I heard the alarm going off. When I came in he appeared to be struggling to breathe, but he wasn't moving any air. It was as if he were choking"

"Choking? On what for God's sake. He was just extubated six hours ago." Jack was referring to the removal of his breathing tube earlier that morning. "You didn't give him anything to eat did you?"

"Of course not," the nurse protested. "He said he was thirsty, and he had taken a few sips of water, but nothing else."

Jack went around to the head of the bed, asking Jeremy to move around to the side of the bed as the other doctor continued to squeeze the oxygen rich gas into the boy's lungs. Jack took the long lighted laryngoscope, the instrument that is used to place the breathing tube, and placed it in the child's mouth. He elevated the tongue and as he lifted the epiglottis, he could clearly see the vocal cords. There didn't appear to be any obstruction.

"Get me some suction," he said, and soon the respiratory technician produced a hard plastic wand connected to the suction tubing. Jack placed it into the child's mouth and all the way through the vocal cords. As he did he saw something move within the trachea.

"McGill forceps," he demanded, but none of the nurses knew what he wanted. He looked in the tray of instruments in the tracheostomy set and quickly found what he needed. He inserted the long narrow instrument that looked like a distorted pistol, and worked it cautiously between the vocal cords. He opened the jaws and saw the cause of all the trouble, and very carefully grasped it. Slowly and very gently, he pulled it back through the vocal cords and finally out through the boy's mouth.

"What the hell is that?" Jeremy asked.

"That my friend is a piece of a link sausage."

"You're kidding," Jeremy said, "Where did he ... "

All eyes went toward the nurse, who protested, "Don't look at me, I didn't give it to him."

"Who else was in here?" Jack asked.

"Just the respiratory tech and ... his father." During all the commotion the boys father had been escorted out of the ICU and asked to wait down the hall.

Jack looked back up at the monitors and saw that his pulse rate was now one hundred twelve, indicating the full effect of the Atropine and Epinephrine had finally been attained. The blood pressure was also up to one hundred over sixty, and the boy's color looked much better.

"I'm going to go talk to the father," Jack said to his colleague. "Secure that trach tube, would you? And let's get a STAT portable chest x-ray"

As he approached the small Nicaraguan man, he could see the sheer panic in the man's eyes as he jumped to his feet. Jack tried to produce his reassuring smile, but without much success.

"Your son is still alive," he said, speaking slowly in his second language. The father let out a tremendous sigh of relief as he too attempted an anxious smile.

Jack continued, "I don't know yet whether he will completely recover." He needed to make certain the child's father understood that it was possible his son might not wake up. He spent the next several minutes explaining that the long period when he was not breathing could have resulted in damage to his kidneys or heart, but especially his brain. He explained how he'd had to perform an emergency tracheostomy, and that he would now need to take him back to surgery to place a larger tube into his windpipe, and that he would likely be on the breathing machine again for a while. "We will just have to wait and see."

The father bowed prayerfully as he listened to the explanation, then raised his head as Jack continued, "Can you tell me what happened immediately before he stopped breathing?"

The distraught parent looked up, and his tear filled eyes told Jack what he had suspected. The man's voice was now halting, as he could no longer hold back his tears. "He was awake and talking to me, and he said he was hungry. So I gave him a piece of meat I had saved from my breakfast. I turned around for just a moment to get something, I don't remember what, and when I returned his eyes were very wide, and he wasn't breathing. I called for the nurse, and then three or four nurses came rushing in the room. The one who speaks Spanish told me I would have to leave the room, and that I must wait here."

Jack wasn't sure exactly how to tell this distressed father that it was that piece of meat that had nearly killed his son. He feared it would destroy him emotionally if he knew he'd been responsible for what had happened, but he had no way of explaining the situation without implying the father was at fault.

"We will continue to watch him very carefully for any signs of improvement, and I will have the nurses come and get you as soon as you can see him again."

"It was all my fault, wasn't it?" the father sobbed.

"No, no, you must not think that," Jack said reassuringly. "It was an accident. It was no one's fault."

The young man looked up gratefully and nodded, but he knew the doctor was merely trying to comfort him. "*Muchas gracias* doctor. *Vaya con Dios, señior.*"

Jack quickly returned to the ICU and went immediately to the x-ray view box where the child's film was already up on the lighted screen. The dense white appearance to his lungs was exactly what Jack had feared. As the young boy had struggled to breathe against the obstruction in his trachea, he had created extreme negative pressures in his lungs. Fluid was literally sucked out of the tiny capillaries and into the small air sacs. The condition was known as pulmonary edema, and it would make it very difficult to get enough air into those fluid clogged airways to maintain critically important oxygen levels in his blood.

For the next three days Jack and the ICU doctors worked continuously to try and get the fluid out of his lungs, but the damage to them had been quite severe. Even with positive pressure ventilation, his oxygen levels remained dangerously low. Jack had consulted one of the pulmonary specialists immediately after performing the tracheostomy, and his colleague had been managing the ventilator. At one point he suggested the boy might require the assistance of the extracorporeal membrane oxygenator, known as ECMO. This was a machine somewhat similar to the heart bypass machine used in the operating room, but it was designed exclusively to function as an artificial lung. The child's blood could be pumped out of his body and through the device where it would be enriched with oxygen before returning it to his circulation. The concept was similar to renal dialysis, which was far more commonly used to treat kidney failure, but ECMO had a much higher risk, and was only used as a true last resort.

By the fourth day, the boys lungs showed some early signs of improvement, and by the following morning it looked as though the worst was over. The chest x-ray had begun to clear.

"I think we have finally gotten his lungs stabilized," Jack explained to the boy's father. "Hopefully now we can start letting him wake up."

The boy had been in a drug induced coma since the incident, so it had been impossible to tell what level of brain function he had. A neurologist had been called in several days earlier, and he'd performed an electroencephalogram to assess the child's brain activity. What he saw was not especially encouraging.

****

"Well, Dr. Roberts?" Horvath said as he encountered Jack outside the surgical ICU. "It appears we aren't going to be able to use this particular case in our marketing campaign, are we?" His tone had an extremely inappropriate air of disappointment. "Seems this is not exactly an example of the exemplary care provided here at children's, is it?"

Jack had been devastated by the events of the past week. The other two children were recovering without incident, but he had been in the ICU at least ten hours a day, tending to his problem patient for the last six days. He was in no mood to talk to Horvath, especially today. They were going to repeat the boy's EEG that morning to see whether his brain function had improved or not.

"Mr. Horvath, I don't give a damn about your marketing plan," Jack spouted as he turned to face the young executive. "And, I would appreciate it if you would get those damned television cameras out of this hospital."

"But, Jack," Horvath said, sounding as though his feelings were hurt. "We put the marketing plan together specifically to help you, at considerable expense I might add. I'm just sorry you appear to have screwed it up."

The warmth in Jack's ears had been building since he first saw this arrogant bastard, but now he could literally feel the pounding in his own chest as he faced this pitiful excuse of a man, half his age. It was all he could do to restrain his burning desire to flatten this little weasel with one quick blow to his smirking mouth, but he didn't. Instead he took a threatening step forward, causing Horvath to recoil slightly.

"Look," he said ominously, "I'm going to try and forget what you just said, but if I ever hear you mention marketing to me again, I very likely won't be able to restrain myself."

Jack turned away, leaving Horvath to wonder whether the older, but much larger man might actually make good on his threat.

****

"How's he doing?" Elaina asked as Jack came wearily into the kitchen. It was after eight-thirty, and she had once again kept his supper warm on the stove.

"About the same," Jack replied. "The EEG showed only minimal activity, and the neurologist has been talking about possibly pulling the plug in the next couple of days, but I told him I wasn't ready to give up just yet. I've seen some kids come back from things like this, but I have to admit it doesn't look very good."

This level of disappointment in her husband's voice was something she hadn't heard very often in the twenty years they had been married, and it caused a silent tear to form in her eye. She walked over and stood behind him as he sat down to face the meatloaf and mashed potatoes she had placed on the table. He was obviously not interested in eating, and merely moved the food around with his fork. As she placed her hands on his tired shoulders, she said, "You have done everything you can, Jack. Now its in God's hands."

He dropped the fork on the plate and extended his head back, looking toward the ceiling. "It just isn't fair," he said painfully. "That kid shouldn't have to die."

She massaged his shoulders gently and leaned over kissing his cheek. She loved this man, more now than ever. She had also grown to love the roughness of the bristly, fifteen hours of growth on his now almost completely gray beard.

****

"I don't know why, because the meds had been turned off for more than eighteen hours," the nurse said as Jack entered the ICU the following morning. "But about three in the morning he just suddenly opened his eyes and started pulling at his restraints. We had to sedate him again with the Fentanyl drip, just to keep him in the bed."

Jack moved quickly to the young boys side and carefully pulled open one of his eyes, noticing immediately the pupil closed slightly in response to the light. He did the same with the other eye, and the response was the same.

"Let's turn off the Fentanyl drip again and let him wake up," he said hopefully, and the nurse immediately carried out the order.

The boy's father had been asleep on the bed built into the far wall, but he awoke when he heard Jack's voice. He came around to near the head of his son's bed. The ventilator was cycling with the same monotonous rhythm that had provided the backdrop of this dramatic scene for more than a week.

Jack spoke to him in Spanish, explaining that his son had apparently shown signs of waking up during the night. The man smiled slightly for a moment for the first time in many days, as Jack resumed his examination. He placed his left hand beneath the boys right knee and tapped sharply on the tendon below the knee cap. The boy's foot jumped reflexively in response. He repeated the test on the opposite leg with the same response.

"Get the neurologist down here," Jack said, wanting confirmation of the obvious change in his patient's status. He performed several more reflex exams, and was amazed how they all seemed to have returned to normal.

After about fifteen minutes, he noticed the first spontaneous movement he'd seen since he'd plucked that sausage from his tiny trachea. He was definitely moving the fingers of his right hand, and his face began to grimace as he struggled to open his eyes.

"Get respiratory in here," Jack ordered, knowing he was going to need to make some quick changes to the ventilator.

As the technician arrived, the boy began to show signs of fighting against the machine that had kept him alive for all those days he had laid otherwise motionless. As his movements became more purposeful, he opened his eyes with a look of panic. His arms were still restrained to keep him from reaching up and pulling out any of the tubes or monitors, but his legs were free and they began thrashing about, trying to kick his way free of the external breathing machine.

"Let's take him off the ventilator and just put him on some supplemental oxygen," Jack said to the respiratory technician. She immediately disconnected the plastic tubing that had been attached to the tracheostomy, allowing him to breathe on his own for the first time. As he tried to cough, the air rushed noisily, in and out through the plastic tube in his neck. She connected another flexible blue hose onto the tracheostomy, providing a high concentration of oxygen for him to inhale. He was now using his own muscular efforts to fill his lungs with the vital molecules.

Jack spoke softly to the young boy, explaining that he would not be able to speak because of the tube in his neck, but that he was going to be okay. The child didn't understand and continued to struggle against the soft material around his wrists, but his father clearly understood. He dropped slowly to his knees beside the bed and offered thanks to God for saving his son.

****

"Hi Debi," Jack said as the receptionist answered the phone. "Is George around?"

"Let me see if he's with a patient," she replied before putting him on hold. Jack wanted to talk with George about where things stood with Grady's group and to see whether anything had changed. They hadn't really had a chance to talk about anything other than the surgical procedures since Jack's return from Nicaragua.

"I know you're busy seeing patients right now." Jack said where George picked up the phone. "I thought maybe we could grab a beer over at Ringo's after you get finished."

"Sure," George said. "I'll be finished in the office around five thirty. Why don't we meet there at six."

"Okay, I'm sure I'll be through with my afternoon rounds by then. I'll see you there," Jack said before hitting the end button on his new iPhone.

****

A little before six Jack pulled his pickup into the half empty parking lot of the sports bar on Fort Worth's near west side. As he walked toward the front door he spotted George pulling in off the street, so he waited for him outside the entrance.

"Great timing, huh?" George said as he hurried to shake Jacks hand before they headed in to find a table. The place was not very busy for a Tuesday afternoon, and they were quickly seated in a relatively quiet booth. The usual loud country music wasn't playing for some reason, and for that Jack was grateful. He didn't tolerate noisy places like he had when he was younger. He wondered to himself why he'd suggested this place because normally it was hard to carry on a conversation.

The waitress came over immediately and took their drink orders. When she left the table, Jack said, "I don't think I've ever been in here when it was this quiet."

"I know," George replied. "Maybe their stereo is broken."

"Whatever the reason, I'm glad," Jack said with a smile. "So, did anything exciting happen while I was gone?"

"Well, I did another kid with a patent ductus, this time I put the clamps on before opening the vessel," George laughed, making reference to the trauma case Jack had helped him with a few weeks before. "I also did a couple of coronary bypasses over at the general hospital. One was a bit of a challenge without your help, but I managed to struggle through."

"Oh, I'm sure you did great," Jack responded as their two beers arrived.

"It was okay, but I have to tell you, things go much more smoothly when you're around."

George raised his glass in a half hearted attempt at a toast to his friend and mentor. "To your safe return from the third world."

Jack smiled and raised the frosty mug up casually returning the salute before taking a sip of the ice cold liquid. "Speaking of cases, I have a four year old kid coming in tomorrow from New Mexico with a big ventricular septal defect. His pediatrician told me his heart started showing signs of failure within the last month, but he's gotten much worse in the last three or four days. Buzz is going to cath him when he arrives by air ambulance around nine, and if its as advertised, I'm going to want to take him to the OR tomorrow afternoon. Are you available to give me a hand?"

"Sure, just let me know when and I'll be there."

"Great," Jack replied. He was always appreciative when George could assist. He took another sip from his beer and asked, "So, you said you had a couple of things you wanted to talk about?"

"Yeah," George began hesitatingly. "You remember I told you a few months ago that I was planning to sign up with Grady's group?"

"Of course I remember," Jack said with just a hint of frustration in his voice.

"Well, they finally came back to me with what they claim is a fair offer."

"It took them three months to finalize a contract?" Jack asked.

"Yes," George said disgustedly. "I think they were waiting until they had Buzz's group on board so they could use that as a negotiating tool."

"What did they say?"

"Grady told me that his group now controls all the pediatric cardiology in the region and that since you weren't interested in joining them, they were willing to give all the heart surgery to me." he paused for a moment as he saw Jack nodding that he understood. "However, he told me that since I was still relatively inexperienced, and since I didn't bring many of my own patients to the table, they were only going to pay me a salary of one hundred and seventy-five thousand dollars a year."

"Your kidding," Jack offered as he sat his beer back on the table.

"No," George continued. "That is less than half of what they had initially talked about, and it is about thirty percent less than I made last year, even paying my own overhead. They also only want to give me three hundred thousand to buy my practice. I may be young, but I'm not that naive. I know for a fact that they paid each of the urologists more than twice that."

"So, what did you tell them?"

"I told them I would have to think about it." George said, as he saw Jack nodding slowly.

"What did Grady say to that?"

"He told me they needed a decision within a week, because they had been approached by the heart surgeons in Dallas about sending one of their guys over here."

"You realize they used that same strategy to get Buzz Jackson to sign with them," Jack said with a smirk. "I can't believe I once considered Jerry Grady to be a good friend."

"What do you think I should do?" George ask, almost as though Jack didn't have a personal interest in his young associate's decision.

"I'm pretty sure you know how I feel. In my opinion, when they contracted with the hospital, they sold their souls to the devil. I don't see any way their scheme is going to be better for patients or docs, but it will definitely be better for the hospital."

"Grady said that they were going to be in the perfect position to take advantage of the new healthcare law and its preferential treatment of so called accountable care organizations."

Jack just shook his head and said, "You realize that ACOs are not really accountable care organizations as much as they are accountable cost organizations, and it will be the docs who will be held accountable. The government doesn't want to talk about rationing care, but when they give the global payments to the hospital and its network of doctors that is exactly what will happen. Primary care docs won't refer patients to any specialists unless they can control them. They will apply pressure to cut costs, because they will get a bigger piece of the pie. This is just another gatekeeper scheme like the old HMOs. It is designed to cut costs at the expense of the physician's ethics."

"What is a guy like me supposed to do?" he asked, sounding almost desperate. "I rely on those guys to send me patients. If I don't sign with them they will just go with the guys from Dallas."

"Look," Jack said with a sympathetic tone. "I understand the threat, but its like I told Buzz, there aren't that many people in the world who can do what we do, so finding a replacement isn't as easy as they make it sound. But, even more than that, you have to decide what you can live with, and what you can live without."

"I was kind of hoping you would have had a change of heart, and we could go to those guys together, and negotiate a better deal, but it doesn't sound like that's going to happen, is it?"

Jack just smiled slightly at his young colleague, then said, "I wish I could help you, but I've made up my mind. Like you, I worked really hard to earn the right to do what I do, and I'm not going to sell it to Jerry Grady, Michael Horvath, Jim Fitzgerald, Barack Obama or anybody else. That's just me. You and every other physician have to make your own decision."

"I just don't know how I can survive without the patients they provide."

"The question is whether you can live with the idea of being their boy?"

George truly didn't know what to do as he sat there, staring blankly at his nearly full mug of beer. Before he could say anything more, Jack added, "If you decide to stay independent, I will do everything I can to help you."

"I really appreciate that, Jack," he replied. "I'm not sure what exactly you can do, but I will certainly take your offer into consideration."

The room was suddenly filled with the sound of a twanging guitar and thundering drums as a live band began playing country music in the next room, just beyond where they were seated.

"We'll talk more later," Jack yelled to be heard over the amplified voice of the singer as he belted out the opening line of a familiar Jerry Jeff Walker song.

****

Shortly after David started med school. Amy managed to land a job in one of the university's research labs, filling out grant requests. While it did involved the use of some of her finance related skills, it was mostly just busy work. She spent hours chasing down anticipated costs of everything from laboratory animals and their food, to travel expenses for the primary investigators to present their results at national meetings. It wasn't really much of a job, certainly nothing like what she had anticipated when she'd applied to several of the larger banks in Dallas. However, it at least provided them with enough to pay the rent and put groceries on the table.

David had insisted that he was going to pay his own way through school, and since he'd gone through four years of college on scholarship, he wasn't carrying forward any debt, like many of his classmates. Even so, he had not anticipated how expensive medical school was going to be. Tuition alone was fifteen thousand dollars per semester, and his books and supplies cost another three thousand. With his dad as a cosigner, he took out a line of credit loan at Jack's bank in Fort Worth for one hundred-fifty thousand dollars, hoping that would be enough to get him through all four years.

"I can't get over how expensive it is to go to med school these days," Jack said to Elaina when he got back home after signing the loan papers with his son. "It's no wonder the number of applicants is down."

"I think we should pay for it. We can afford it, with our house and cars all paid for, and its not like we spend a lot of money," she said.

"I offered to pay for it, but he didn't want it. He insists, he's going to make it on his own, and I have to say, I admire him for that." She already knew her son's decision based on her own discussions with him. Jack then added, "I think if someone had been willing to put me through med school I would have taken them up on it, rather than go into the Air Force. But, then again, if I hadn't joined the Air Force, and had that experience, there's no telling what would have happened. I likely wouldn't have met you, and my whole life would have been different."

****

As the midterm elections of 2010 grew closer, the healthcare law remained at center stage. Every Republican running for Congress made "repeal and replace" their campaign slogan. Those who were up against incumbent democrats made their votes on the increasingly unpopular healthcare law the first point of every debate. Hermann Sheffield, the six time incumbent who represented the district that included much of Fort Worth, had voted with the majority in passing the controversial legislation. He was a prime target to be defeated, but the republican candidate was a retired school teacher who managed to survive the primary process solely because she had connections with some of the higher ups in the Tarrant County Republican Party. As the campaign wore on, her weaknesses were exploited by Sheffield's team. In the end she would have no chance against the polished politician despite the healthcare issue.

Jack campaigned for her, but he was convinced she wasn't going to win. He used the campaign opportunities to speak about the problems he saw with the healthcare law, but the crowds she attracted were relatively small, and for the most part they were people who didn't need to be convinced of the problems associated with government healthcare.

During one such gathering, Jack spoke just before the candidate was due to speak. When he was informed that she had been delayed, he made an effort to extend his remarks and then took some questions from the audience.

"Why don't you run for Congress?" shouted a man from near the back of the room.

"Because I'm a doctor, not a politician," Jack replied.

The man responded by shouting back, "I think you'd have a better chance of beating Sheffield than our current candidate does."

There were several people in the audience who booed the comment, but most were nodding in agreement, and some actually shouted their approval. It seemed that even her supporters suspected she wasn't going to win, and they were right.

Sheffield ended up being one of the fortunate incumbent democrats to survive the purge of the November 2010 election. The overwhelming majority that Nancy Pelosi had enjoyed for two years in the House of Representatives was suddenly reversed, all because of the healthcare law and the way it was passed. The Senate was still controlled by Harry Reid, but the democrat majority was nowhere near what it had been.

It was clear the reason Sheffield was able to hold his seat despite his vote for the Patient Protection and Affordable Care Act was because of the huge support he received from the Latino community. He was a staunch advocate of maintaining the rather lax immigration policies that had led to the influx of more than two million illegal immigrants into Texas. His opponent had come out strongly in favor of tightening border security and opposed any form of amnesty for those in the country illegally. The way the district had been gerrymandered it included a large Mexican-American population. The immigration reform efforts became a major issue in the campaign, and Sheffield was quick to point out that his opponent favored deporting anyone in Texas illegally.

****

"It is so great to have you home, even if it's only for one night," Elaina said as David and Amy joined her and Jack for dinner on Christmas eve. They were going to spend the night, and enjoy Christmas morning with his family, They would then spend the rest of the day with Amy's parents and her older brother who was home on leave from his third tour in Afghanistan. Jack's mother, Faye, had also joined the small gathering, as they celebrated the holiday.

"Yeah," David said, "it feels good to be home." He looked at Amy and saw the question in her eyes, so he decided to clarify by saying, "Well, actually, our home is in Dallas." Her eyes softened and a small smile appeared in the corners of her mouth.

"That may be," Jack said, "but you'll both always have a home here."

"When are we going to open presents?" Faye asked in her now rather feeble voice.

"We aren't going to open our gifts until Christmas morning, Mom," Elaina replied, as she stood and began to clear the dishes off the table. When she returned from the kitchen she said, "but I guess we could each open one tonight."

"That sounds like a great idea," David said.

Jack helped his mother into the living room where the huge, brightly lit tree stood in one corner surrounded by dozens of colorful packages. When David was younger, like most children his favorite day of the year was Christmas, but in recent years it had become less about family and more about time off from school. However, there was something different about this Christmas. Now that he and Amy were married, the idea of gathering as a family was more important than ever.

"I want David to open that one this evening," Jack said pointing to a bright red box with a white bow taped to the top.

"Okay," Elaina said, pulling it from the pile and handing it to her son.

David opened the gift from his dad very deliberately. "What could this be?" he inquired playfully. "Alright! This is what I've been wanting for several years."

He held up the box that held a Canon digital camera. As he looked at the box carefully, he realized it was not just a still camera, but it was capable of shooting high definition video as well. "This is incredible, Dad! How did you know?"

"Don't you think you dropped enough hints while we were in Nicaragua?" Jack laughed. "Every time I turned around I heard you say, 'Wow, I sure wish I had a camera. That would be a great picture.' It didn't take a genius to figure it out."

"I guess we'll just have to go back there again sometime so I can take those shots that I missed last time." David laughed again, and went over to his dad who was seated in his favorite chair, and gave him a hug.

After everyone had opened one gift Jack insisted that Elaina play some Christmas music on the piano.

"I haven't been practicing at all," she objected. "And, besides, the piano hasn't been tuned in several years."

"Protest as much as you want," Jack replied, "but, you aren't getting out of it."

Elaina reluctantly stood and made her way to the white Steinway grand that had stood in the same spot for just over twenty years. As she began playing, Amy joined her and the two of them sang several carols. Both women had strong voices, and they were soon joined by David. Jack sat silently back in his chair, enjoying the scene, as the festive music filled the house for the first time in his recent memory and his mother closed her eyes and smiled.

CHAPTER 7

"This thing is not over yet," Jason said. "There are still several precincts out to the west that haven't come in yet, and with a strong showing there, we can still win."

Jack turned away from the television once more, but he could still see the reflection of the numbers in the hotel window. With ninety-five percent of the precincts reporting, Sheffield had built a lead of nearly five hundred votes. Jack smiled to himself as he realized that was only one voter for each day since he'd decided to run. Surely he could have convinced at least one more voter each day to vote for him. Perhaps he hadn't tried hard enough. Then again, maybe those trips he made last week down to Benbrook and Crowley would pay off. The leaders of the republican party in that part of the district were certainly staunch conservatives, and had initially been firmly in his camp.

****

Jack continued to contemplate a future in politics as he followed the ongoing debates over what everyone was now calling Obamacare. Even the President himself had embraced the name, accepting it as his signature legislative accomplishment. In the mid-term election the republicans took control of the House of Representatives, and they quickly voted to repeal the law, but the democrats still held the Senate, and the majority leader, Harry Reid of Nevada, refused to even take up the measure.

The March twenty-third first anniversary of the passage of the health care law was once again being celebrated by most of the mainstream media, as they continued to give the President Obama full credit for something that had yet to provide health insurance to one single individual. As far as Jack could tell the only thing the President and his namesake law were responsible for was a growing shift in the workplace away from full time employment to part time workers. Full implementation of the law was still nearly eighteen months away, but many smaller employers were already preparing for its impact by laying off workers to get below the fifty employee threshold. Any business with fewer than fifty employees would not be forced them to provide insurance or pay a fine. Larger employers simply stopped hiring and the nations economy remained anemic.

As more details of the new law were uncovered, Jack's frustration and anger grew. It was obvious the government's answer to everything was more control through regulations. He just couldn't understand why the AMA had remained completely silent when they had openly pledged to do everything possible to save the independent practice of medicine. Either that had been an empty promise, or they weren't seeing the same changing environment he was. Clearly the AMA had no plan, and even worse, they had no will to resist anything this administration wanted to do. They seemed to welcome the idea of someone else dictating things like quality metrics and mandatory electronic filing of Medicare claims. Every physician Jack came in contact with felt betrayed by the organization that once was held in the highest possible esteem. Ultimately, it was the complete lack of professional leadership by the AMA that made Jack's decision for him.

****

"There is a Mr. Fred Schneider on the phone for you," Mary Anne said, as she stuck her head into Jack's office.

He had been introduced to Schneider at one of the republican functions prior to the 2010 election. The man was a highly regarded campaign strategists, and republican insider. He'd told Jack back then to call him if he ever decided to get involved.

"Hello, Mr. Schneider," he said. "Thanks for returning my call."

"Sure, Dr. Roberts," the forty year old man replied. "What can I do for you?"

He wasn't really sure where to begin, so he decided to just jump right in. "I'm considering running for Congress against Sheffield in the next election."

"Interesting," Fred replied. "What made you decide that?"

"I don't like what is going on in Washington, and I feel like I could make a difference."

"Well, there is no question we would like to replace Sheffield with a conservative republican, but he's pretty well entrenched. It won't be easy to unseat him."

"I realize that. I saw what happened this last time, and I believe I know the effort it takes."

"Effort?" Fred questioned. "I wasn't referring to effort. I was talking about money."

"How much are we talking about to run a successful campaign?"

"Just to be considered as a serious candidate we're talking about a million dollars minimum. If you want to be successful against Sheffield you can double that or more."

"Seriously?" Jack said. He had no idea that it would cost that much to gain a job that pays about a hundred and seventy-five thousand dollars a year.

"Yeah, doc," Fred replied. "The price of real influence in America is very high."

"I don't have that kind of money to be throwing around."

"Oh, I'm not talking about you coming up with two million bucks," Fred said. "That's how much you will need to raise from supporters."

"What all does that involve?"

"Well, typically it means going to a bunch of rubber chicken dinners, talking to people you don't know and asking them for money. All of that is coordinated by your campaign manager and a small staff of volunteers."

"I see," Jack said as he pondered the idea of rubber chicken dinners.

"If you are really serious about this, you should come to our next Tarrant County republican party campaigns and candidates committee."

"When is that?"

"As a matter of fact, our next meting is on Thursday night. We meet at Nat Louder's home in southwest Fort Worth."

"Tell me where and what time, and I'll be there."

Jack jotted down the address and thanked Fred again before hanging up.

"Wow!" he thought, "two million dollars for the privilege of being abused by the opposition and the media for two years."

****

The meeting with the Tarrant County republicans went much smoother than Jack had anticipated. The committee members were all excited to have a fresh face they could see potentially beating the democrat machine run by Sheffield and his cronies. They seemed far less focused on the fundraising aspect of a campaign than Schneider had been, but instead were focused on Jack's policies.

They questioned him extensively about his views on various issues, including immigration, the wars in Iraq and Afghanistan, energy and the environment, and of course healthcare.

In general Jack Roberts was just what the GOP had been looking for, and the members of the committee encouraged Jack to declare early, if he was serious about running in the 2012 election. "The earlier you get your name out there, the more seriously you will be taken. The primary will be in early April, which is only eleven months from now," said Nat, the chairman of the committee.

"What is involved in making that declaration?" Jack asked, revealing his obvious lack of experience.

"Well, the first thing is just telling us whether you are really serious about this. Then, we will begin spreading the word out to the various Precinct chairs, so that when you meet with them you won't be a complete unknown. They will pass your name around to their committees and groups of volunteers who will in turn spread the word throughout the district. We will need to help you put together a campaign committee and get you a manager. As soon as your donations reach five thousand dollars, which is likely to be the first day after you announce your intention to run, you have fifteen days to register with the federal election commission. At that point you're off and running."

Jack took a deep breath and said, "I have talked this over with my wife and son, and I think I'm ready."

"Sounds great!" Nat exclaimed. "Let's get this show on the road."

Over the next several weeks Jack met with all the Precinct chairs and interviewed several potential campaign managers. He was especially impressed by Jason Williamson, a young man who had participated as an assistant manager in Governor Perry's most recent successful gubernatorial campaign. He was very enthusiastic and seemed to know the answer to every question Jack could come up with regarding fund raising, personal appearances, social media, and overall strategy. He hired him to initiate his campaign, and trusted him to get all the paperwork done and begin the process of putting together a staff of volunteers.

Within just a few days Jason had created a website, docroberts4congress.com, and he began scheduling speaking engagements for Jack.

****

"Hey George, you got a minute?" Jack said.

He had just walked over from the hospital to George Ferguson's office on the third floor of the professional building, knowing it was his day to see patients in the clinic. Debi showed him back to George's private office where he had been waiting about five minutes for his associate to break free.

"Of course, Jack," he replied. "What's up?"

"I wanted to let you know that I think I've found a way to help you stay busy, even if Grady's group tries to put the squeeze on you."

"Oh yeah, how's that?"

"I have decided to make a run for Congress against Sheffield."

George's jaw dropped slightly as his eyebrows jumped in shock. "You what?"

"Yeah, that's what I'm afraid everyone is going to say."

"Well, that's great, I guess. I wish you all the luck in the world."

"Thanks, I think I'm going to need more than luck. I'm hoping for divine intervention," Jack laughed.

"So, what does that have to do with me? Do you want me to run your campaign? I guess that would keep me busy."

"No," Jack laughed, "Nothing like that. I'm anticipating being pretty busy campaigning over the next year to a year and a half, so I need to know that I can refer patients directly to you."

"Of course, I'm happy to pick-up the slack any time you aren't available."

"I was actually thinking about you and I creating a more formal relationship. It might be a way to lower both of our overhead expenses, and it would make it much easier from all perspectives if we had some kind of limited liability partnership," Jack suggested somewhat hesitatingly.

"I've always thought that would be a great way to practice, but I thought you were committed to remaining solo," George said. "Actually, this is a perfect time to make a change from my standpoint. My lease is up here in two months."

"My office has always been bigger than I needed, It would be no problem to move you in there, especially when the campaign gets rolling. I won't be there more than one or two days a week at most."

George's face broke into a huge grin as he held his hand out to the man he had the utmost respect for, and now he would have the distinction of partnering with him. "You just tell me what I need to do, and I'll do it."

As Jack took his hand he felt the need to add one more thing. "You realize, if I get elected I'll be spending most of my time in Washington?"

"That's okay. I'm used to flying solo. It seems you spend most of your time now in Nicaragua or Chicago," he laughed.

****

"Ferguson has decided not to take our offer," Grady said.

"What do you mean?" asked Horvath indignantly.

"I mean he said no. He didn't say it, but I heard through the grapevine that he is going to join Jack Roberts."

"Really? Isn't that interesting?" Fitzgerald thought out loud. "Roberts must be feeling the heat, so he's trying to solidify his position by partnering with the only other pediatric heart surgeon in town."

"From what I hear, that's not what's going on. Word is that Roberts is going to make a run for Sheffield's seat in Congress."

"You're joking, right? He can't be that stupid," Fitzgerald laughed. "We've had Sheffield's seat secured for more than a decade."

"All I know is he's been heard to drop some pretty strong hints in the doctor's lounge, and I suspect he needs Ferguson to take care of his practice when he goes out on the campaign trail."

"I hope its true," Fitzgerald said with a cunning tone to his voice. "We will be able to destroy that jerk, once and for all."

"In the meantime, I need for you to go see those heart surgeons in Dallas," Horvath said.

"I don't know any of those guys," Grady admitted. "I just made up that story about them wanting to come over here to scare Ferguson into signing on with us."

Horvath turned and stared at Grady angrily. "You what?"

"I've never met any of the heart guys in Dallas. They wouldn't know me from Adam," he said timidly.

The younger Horvath couldn't believe his ears. He just stood there shaking his head. "Now what are we going to do?"

"Its all right," Fitzgerald said calmly. He turned to Grady and said, "Just call them up and arrange a meeting. Michael will go with you," He then turned to Horvath and said, "Make them an offer they can't refuse."

****

"Dr. Roberts?" Jason asked as Jack answered his cell.

"Hi Jason, what's up?" he replied.

"I have a group of potential donors who would like to meet you. They are having a cook out tomorrow afternoon. Its not far from where you live."

"That sounds great," Jack said. "Will I need to stay long?"

"No, I would recommend you only stay twenty or thirty minutes. These people are some major donors so you really need to be there, but if you hang around too long they'll sense that you're trying to milk them."

"Got it."

"They called me, and said they would like to meet you and help get your campaign off the ground."

"What exactly does that mean."

"We're talking about a political action committee that could potentially give us up to six figures."

"I thought donations over twenty-five hundred were prohibited."

"That's true for individuals, but these guys formed a PAC that allows them to pool their money and gain far more influence."

Jack thought for a moment about the need to raise two million dollars. "I guess it's time to get this show on the road," Jack added, repeating the phrase he'd heard Nat use when he first declared his intentions.

Jack hung up the phone and walked into the kitchen where Elaina was just beginning to prepare dinner.

"Who was that on the phone?" she asked, barely taking her eyes off the pot of boiling rice.

"It was Jason," Jack said. "He called to tell me about a group of local donors who want to meet me."

"That's great! When?"

"Tomorrow afternoon," Jack explained in a voice that was far more timid that usual.

"I thought you were going out to see your mom tomorrow after church?"

"The event is not far from here, so I figure I'll run out to Mom's afterward."

"Okay," Elaina said in a warning tone. "Just make sure you make it out to see Faye."

"Jason said it would only be for fifteen or twenty minutes, and apparently these guys are major donors that are offering to jump start my campaign."

"In that case, I think we need to celebrate," she said as she winked seductively before putting the package of chicken breasts back into the freezer. "I have a desire for some strawberry soufflé ... as well as what comes after."

****

It had been a couple of months since Jack and Elaina had been to Claude's, and they were welcomed warmly by their host.

"Please come in, come in," he said excitedly. I have your favorite table all prepared."

Claude made a point of personally seating them, then brought out a bottle of champagne. "Claude, please, we didn't order that," Jack protested as Claude popped the cork and poured the bubbling wine.

"It is on the house, my friend. I insist. This is for my next United States Congressman and his beautiful wife."

"What? ... How did you? ... " Jack hadn't formally announced his candidacy, but obviously if Claude knew, then half the people in Fort Worth must also know.

"I heard the news from my banker. He was in two nights ago. He was very excited to learn of your plan to run against that scoundrel Sheffield. He said he learned about it from his republican precinct chairman," Claude explained. "It is true isn't it? Please say yes."

"We aren't scheduled to make a formal announcement until next week," Jack said cautiously, "but yes, it is true."

"I am so excited," Claude said, mostly toward Elaina. "If there is anything I can do to help, please let me know."

"The thing we're going to need more than anything at this point, are donors," Jack said.

"I will definitely contribute to your campaign fund," the little Frenchman assured him. "And just as soon as you get your signs printed, please bring me some. I will post them here in my restaurant, out on the street, and in my yard, everywhere."

"I will see to it that you get some of the first ones printed." Jack was smiling, mostly because he was amused to see how excited his long time friend was.

"Ladies and gentlemen!" Claude turned away from their corner table and shouted over the noise of the crowded restaurant. "May I have your attention please!" As the crowd hushed slightly he continued. "I am so very pleased to have as my guest here tonight, Dr. Jack Roberts and his lovely wife Elaina."

Jack was in a state of shock. Claude wasn't actually going to do this, was he?

"I want you all to raise your glasses with me in salute to Dr. Roberts, as I have just learned that he plans to run for the United States Congress." Claude lifted a glass of champagne high over his head and Jack saw most of the patrons do the same with their drinks, followed by a smattering of applause.

"Dr. Roberts?" Claude asked as he turned his attention back to Jack, "would you care to say a few words?"

He was certainly not prepared to speak to the fifty or so people who were now awaiting a response, and initially he looked at Elaina for direction. When she nodded her approval he stood, facing the group of strangers who were all staring at him expectantly.

"Ladies and gentlemen, I apologize for interrupting your dinner. It was certainly not my intent this evening. Elaina and I came here to enjoy a quiet evening and some great food, not talk politics. This was completely Claude's idea."

The group laughed respectfully, and some of the diners elected to return to their meals. Most, however, remained attentive to what Jack was saying. "Next week I will formally announce that I will be seeking the republican nomination for Congress from this district. Before you ask, let me assure you that I am a physician and not a politician, and that is precisely why I'm running. The current administration is systematically destroying the finest healthcare system the world has ever known, and if they are allowed to continue, they will destroy this nation, the greatest force for good in history."

"That's right!" shouted a gentleman a few tables away.

"I appreciate your support," he said pointing to the man. When the room quieted again, he continued, "Herman Sheffield has represented this district in Washington for more than a decade, and it is time for a change. He has voted for every program this President and his party has put forward, including Obamacare, and I don't believe that his votes are representative of the majority of Texans."

Jack paused for a moment amid a spontaneous round of applause. He then said, "With your help I am confident we can take our country back, and after we repeal the current healthcare law, I want to be there to help fashion a patient centered system. There is a lot of work to do before we can make that happen, and I would like to invite each of you to join us in the effort. Thank you for your kind attention, and please enjoy the rest of your evening."

As Jack sat down there was another more vigorous round of applause, and a few more shouts of support. Elaina turned to him and said, "Very nice. Short and sweet. You earned my vote tonight." She smiled and winked at him again. "I had no idea politics was so sexy."

****

"Hello, doctor," said the host of the event in a booming base voice. "It is so good of you to drop by."

"I really can't stay long judge. I have another commitment this afternoon." Jack was speaking more rapidly than normal. He was uncharacteristically nervous.

"I understand," the judge replied, trying to sound as though he was concerned. "Let me introduce you to a few of my close friends. They are all anxious to meet you."

As Jack stepped into the huge family room of one of the oldest and largest homes in Westover Hills, he saw twenty-five or thirty well dressed people, milling around, sipping cocktails and engaging in conversation. The judge cleared his throat loudly and then spoke in his commanding courtroom voice. "Friends, I would like you to meet Dr. Jack Roberts." Everyone looked up first toward their host, and then toward Jack. He realized he was under dressed in his slacks and open collared white shirt, but he'd been told this was going to be an outdoor barbecue.

The judge continued, "With your help, Dr. Roberts here is going to unseat that scoundrel Sheffield in the next election."

There was a smattering of applause, but most of the guests still had drinks in there hands, so Jack heard only a few soft exclamations of approval.

"Dr. Roberts, would you care to say a few words?" the judge suggested

Jason had told Jack that he would be asked to address the group briefly, and that he should keep his remarks somewhat vague.

"Thank you Judge Minor," he began. "First, let me say, I can't stay long. However, I felt it was important to come here and tell you why I'm running for a seat in the United States Congress. As all of you are aware, this administration has managed to ram through a new healthcare law called the Patient Protection and Affordable Care Act. Unlike many of the representatives and Senators who voted to enact that law, I have actually read it." Several in the small audience laughed, temporarily disrupting him.

He then continued, "As a physician, I have grave concerns about how this law is going to impact, not only my practice, but the ability of physicians across this country to provide appropriate, compassionate care for their patients. I have personally testified before Congress and tried to reason with those who were behind this legislation, but obviously, without any success. So, at the urging of many of my colleagues and patients as well as other concerned citizens like yourselves, I have decided to see if I can unseat Herman Sheffield, one of the men who voted for the healthcare bill each and every time it came up in the House of Representatives during the last session, and who has voted against all efforts to repeal or modify it during the current session." Most of the men and women had set their glasses down and were now able to applaud more vigorously.

"I am not a politician, but I believe I have enough real world experience to represent the people of Fort Worth and the surrounding region in Washington. I know I have much to learn about conducting a successful campaign, but I'm anxious to get started. I am very fortunate to have an experienced campaign manager, Jason Williamson," Jack said as he gestured toward the young man who was standing several steps behind him. "I'm certain he will keep me busy, and with the help of people like you, I feel confident we will be able to prevail, not only in this next election, but in repealing the law that promises to destroy the greatest healthcare system the world has ever known. Thank you."

The applause was stronger than he'd expected and continued well beyond the time where he was comfortable nodding and saying thank you repeatedly. A number of the guest came forward to shake Jack's hand, and offer him their best wishes.

As he turned back toward Jason, anticipating they would be making a quick exit, a tall elderly gentleman tapped him on the shoulder and said, "excuse me doctor, my name is Joe Turner. I run a pretty good size oil and gas company, and I'd like to ask you a couple of questions if you don't mind?"

Jack turned around to shake the man's hand, and he said, "sure, it's nice to meet you Mr. Turner."

"You can just call me Joe," he said.

"Okay, Joe, please call me Jack."

"Well, Jack, I'm obviously concerned about this new healthcare law. I've got five hundred and fifty employees, so when this thing goes into effect it's going to cost me a bundle. I've already decided to just pay the fine, because that'll be a lot cheaper than buying the kind of insurance that meets the government's specifications for all of 'em."

"I don't blame you," Jack said. "I've heard a number of people say the same thing."

"I think it's a great idea to repeal the whole damn thing, but as long as we've got that jerk in the Oval Office, I don't think it matters what the Congress does, do you?"

"There's no doubt, Mr. Obama would never allow this law to be repealed. It is his signature legislation, and he's committed to doing whatever he has to do to keep it in place. But, I think the American people are waking up to his agenda, and I think there's a very good chance he can be defeated in 2012, provided we come up with the right candidate."

"Yeah, that's what I think too, but the real question is who that candidate is going to be?"

Jack nodded in agreement, and said, "at this point the field looks pretty crowded, but I think it'll come down to Romney or perhaps Mitch Daniels, the governor of Indiana. I really like what he did with healthcare reform in his state, but he hasn't declared his intention to run just yet."

"On a somewhat different subject, what is your position on the Keystone pipeline?"

"I really don't know that much about it, other than what I've heard reported on television, but it sure sounds to me as though it's something we should pursue in order to gain energy independence."

"Yeah, that's what everybody's saying, but I just wonder if then we will be dependent on the Canadians." The old oilman furrowed his brow just a bit as he seemed to be pondering his own position. "I wish we could just secede from the damned union, and go back to being the Republic of Texas. We've got plenty of resources here to be our own country again." He paused for a moment to judge Jack's reaction, then he said, "but we all know that'll never happen."

"It would sure make things a lot simpler," Jack replied patting the older gentleman on the shoulder and turning again toward the door.

"Excuse me Dr. Roberts," an older woman's voice came from off to his left.

Jack turned toward the rather short, petite gray-haired woman, who was making her way briskly toward him. He looked down and saw she was wearing a name tag that read, "Elsie Perkins - President - Tarrant County Republican Women's Club."

"Hello ... Ms. Perkins, right?" Jack said with a smile.

"Yes," she replied, glancing down and touching her name tag. "I'm with the Republican women's club, and I would like to invite you to come to our meeting next week. We have a significant influence in this county, and I think our members would be very interested in what you have to say."

"I would be delighted to come and speak to your group. What I'd suggest is that we coordinate things through Jason, my campaign manager." He called for Jason to join him and introduced her.

"Oh, yes, I know Elsie very well," Jason said, as he shook the woman's hand. "I've been meaning to call you to schedule a time when I could bring Jack to one of your meetings."

She looked up into Jack's face and smiled broadly, saying, "I think we've got ourselves a winner here."

"Thank you very much," Jack replied. "I just wish I shared your confidence."

"Well, one of the first things we're going to need to do is inject you with some of that confidence," She said in an almost lecturing tone. "If you don't have confidence in your own ability to win, no one else will either."

"I'm just trying to get my feet on the ground," Jack said. "This political stuff is new to me, so if you've got something you can inject me with that will help me get through this process, I'm all for it," he laughed.

"I think we better go," Jason said taking Jack by the arm.

"It's very nice to meet you, Elsie. I look forward to seeing you again soon," Jack offered.

As the two men turned to leave, Judge Miner stood near the door. He extended his hand first to Jason and then to Jack. "Thanks for coming by, doc."

"Thanks for inviting me to come and meet your friends," Jack replied. "I just wish I could stay longer."

"I'm sure we'll have plenty of opportunity to discuss things in detail over the next few months. Perhaps we can get together for lunch one day soon?"

"That would be great!" Jack said. He reached into his shirt pocket and produced one of his business cards. He handed it to the judge and said, "Just give me a call."

"I'll do that." The judge paused as he looked briefly at Jack's card, before putting it in his shirt pocket. He would make a point of contacting Jack the following week when he would tell him that his political action committee was getting his campaign started with a one hundred thousand dollar donation.

****

"I understand you are going to be out of town all next week," Jason said, as he and Jack were driving to the meeting of the Tarrant County Republican Women's Club.

"Yeah, I thought I told you about our annual trip to Nicaragua a month or so ago," Jack said.

"You probably did, I just forgot to write it down. Your wife told me about it when I spoke with her earlier today."

"You spoke to Elaina today? How come?"

Jason was trapped. He wasn't supposed to say anything, but Elaina had asked him to run Jack's weekly campaign schedule by her, just to make sure he didn't commit to something that conflicted with a family event. Jack was terrible about keeping a written schedule. For years he'd relied on Mary Anne, his office manager, to coordinate his schedule at the office, but she wasn't involved in any way with his new campaign. So, it was extremely likely that Jack would find himself double or triple booked if someone else wasn't watching out for him, and Elaina knew it.

"She just asked that I keep her updated on your campaign events. I think she just wants to make sure she knows which evenings you are going to be home for dinner."

"Nice try, Jason," Jack laughed. "She's making you run everything through her, isn't she?"

"Well, she just asked to stay in the loop."

"Actually, I think that's a great idea. That way I won't get caught over committing." He smiled to himself and said, "That's something I'm prone to do."

"She said you guys are going to Managua"

"Yeah, we've been going down there every year for the last eighteen years."

"What is there to do down there?"

"We work with a friend of mine in his free clinic, and enjoy the peace and quiet of the mountains, but mostly we just get away from the rat race."

"You know," Jason said, "I've been thinking about how we should conduct your campaign, and I think we've got a number of ways we can go."

"Oh yeah, like what?"

"Well, I think we should definitely emphasize your military service. That is always good for the veteran vote, and Sheffield has no military record. In fact I think he was a draft dodger."

"Really, I didn't know that."

"It's not something a candidate is likely to say about himself, and most opponents don't bring up stuff like that when they are up against an incumbent."

"It would seem to me to be relevant, don't you think?" Jack said with a smirk.

"Yeah, but he would just come back with how he has served his country as a Congressman."

"So, what else were you thinking about?" Jack asked.

"Obviously we focus on you being a pediatric heart surgeon."

"You do know that nearly half of my practice is adult cardiac surgery, don't you?"

"Yeah, sure, but I think we should stick with the idea that you fix little kids. Nobody really cares about whether you work on some old geezers. They don't tug at the voters' heart strings the way sick children do."

"Is that what this boils down to, appealing to people's emotions?" Jack said incredulously.

"Of course! You can't win a race for any office unless you can reach people on a visceral level. Look at Obama. He didn't get elected because he was super smart or had some great ideas. He won because he had a great smile and he talked about hope and change to a nation that was hurting from the collapse of the economy, and people wanted to be comforted. They wanted to feel better, and voting for him made them feel better."

Jack shook his head. "If people are that shallow, then we are truly in more trouble, as a nation, than I thought."

"Oh, come on Jack. Don't tell me you still think this is a nation of the people, by the people and for the people. If that were true, we really would be in trouble, given the relative level of education of most Americans."

"I don't necessarily agree with that," Jack said. "I think most folks are educated enough to know right from wrong, and that's more than I can say for some of the people I've seen in the halls of Congress."

Jason laughed softly then replied. "You have a point there, but then again, have you seen any of those man on the street interviews that Jay Leno does?"

"You mean his Jaywalking segments?"

"Yeah, now you have to admit those are some certified morons."

"Well," Jack laughed, "you have to cut them some slack. That is Southern California."

They both laughed for a few moments then Jack asked, "So what else do you think we need to build the campaign around? You mentioned military service and pediatric heart surgery. Anything else?"

"I don't think it needs to be the major focus, but I believe we can do something with the volunteer work you do in Nicaragua."

"If its just the same to you, I don't think I want to go there," Jack said with a degree of hesitation in his voice.

"Why not, I think a lot of people will find that aspect of your work and your character compelling? We have to make you a man of the people, and the average guy truly admires that kind of charity work."

"I don't know. It just seems wrong somehow to promote yourself by emphasizing stuff like that."

"I know what you're saying, Jack, but you won't have to do any of the promoting yourself. My staff, your surrogates, will do all that for you."

"It just seems like things of that nature should be kept private, you know?"

"Let me break this to you as gently as I can. From this point forward, there is nothing in your life that is going to remain private." Jason spoke as he pulled his car into the parking lot of the restaurant where the meeting was to take place. When he turned off the engine he turned to Jack and said. "If you don't want anyone to know about what you do on your vacation you have two choices. Either you don't run for office, or you don't take a vacation. Its as simple as that."

****

While in Managua, Jack stopped by the government hospital, just to see if there was anything the nurses needed. A few months earlier he had sent some old cardiac monitors down to their recovery room and intensive care unit. The general hospital in Fort Worth had finally replaced them with the latest high tech equipment, so Jack had bought the old ones for almost nothing. He wanted to make sure they had received the shipment and that they were all still working. As he walked into the main lobby he ran into Pasqual, the reporter who had interviewed him previously.

"Hello, Dr. Roberts," Pasqual offered, as he enthusiastically extended his hand.

"Hello, señor Pasqual, isn't it?" Jack asked, hoping he had recalled the man's name accurately.

"Si, I mean yes," he replied. "I had heard you were in town, and I came here hoping to run into you."

"I just came by to see how things were going here at the hospital," Jack replied.

"The nurses told me of the generous donation you made. Having that equipment is something they greatly appreciate."

"It was going to be scrapped back home, so I'm glad someone could get good use of it."

"I would like to write an article about it for our newspaper, do you mind?"

"If it's all the same to you, Pasqual, I think my name has been in your newspapers quite enough already," Jack said with a growing smile. "You can just say it was from an anonymous donor."

"I understand," the reporter replied. "I can do that." He shifted his weight as he reached into his pocket and retrieved a small notebook and pencil. "However, as a follow-up to my other articles on Nicaraguan healthcare, I would like to get your opinion on the new law that President Obama signed a few months ago."

Jack didn't really want to talk about what had happened, but perhaps this was his opportunity to speak his mind without the media filters back in the states. "Okay, what do you want to know?" he asked.

"It seems to me that many people were opposed to this law. Can you explain why you think that is?"

"Well," Jack began, "I think most Americans want the government to stay out of their personal lives, and you don't get more personal than their healthcare." Jack continued as Pasqual rapidly scrawled his notes into the small spiral notebook. "They don't want some government bureaucrat telling them what doctor they can see and what treatment he or she can provide. That is simply not the way we traditionally do things in America."

"As a physician, do you approve of the new law?" Pasqual asked, trying to get Jack to offer his own perspective,

"I understand the intent of trying to provide insurance coverage for everyone, and that is a laudable goal," Jack offered, "but, the way it is being done is anything but laudable."

"What specifically do you find objectionable?"

Jack thought for a moment and realized he was being asked to provide a critique of the more than two thousand page law, much of which was in legislative language that was yet to be interpreted by the regulators. He decided to stick with talking about only those parts that he was totally familiar with the details. "First, the way it was passed was not the way major legislation should be done. The entire law was rammed through on a strictly partisan basis and lacked any of the transparency the President promised back when he was campaigning. Second, the new law is funded in part by a half trillion dollar cut in Medicare over the next ten years. That program is already underfunded, so this new law will threatens seniors with even less access to healthcare. The way the government intends to do that is also part of the law, and its called the independent payment advisory board, or IPAB." Jack knew that even the AMA was on record as opposing the IPAB. "It is a fifteen member board, appointed by the President, with the specific task of recommending cuts to the Medicare program. Any recommendations they make must be voted up or down as a whole by the Congress. They cannot make any changes to their recommendations, and if the Congress votes them down, then by law, they are required to come up with their own set of cuts equivalent to those of the IPAB. If they can't do that, then the IPAB recommendations move forward as if they had passed. Furthermore, there is no legislative review of this process."

"Why is cutting unnecessary, or excessively expensive treatments, a bad thing?" Pasqual asked, continuing to write notes as rapidly as Jack spoke.

"The problem is, the members of the IPAB will not be actively practicing physicians. The cuts will be made to some treatments that currently save lives. I'm not going to go so far as to call it a death panel as some have done, but the impact may be just that." Jack knew he was extrapolating beyond what Pasqual and his readers were likely to understand, so he decided to offer an example.

"The IPAB is very similar to what they have in Great Britain, only over there they call it the National Institute for Health and Care Excellence, or NICE. Its a great name, but it functions as the main cost cutting arm of their National Health Service. When I was there many years ago, I witnessed first hand how it worked." Jack paused a moment to ensure that Pasqual had caught up with his notes before going on. When the reporter looked up, Jack continued.

"The surgical treatment of congenital heart disease is costly, we all know that, but it also represents the only hope for many innocent young lives. The NICE bureaucracy effectively eliminated access to highly effective surgical treatments to hundreds of children by prohibiting those procedures from being performed in all except a very few centers in the country. Children who couldn't make it to one of those referral centers in time simply died."

Pasqual looked up over his notebook with a questioning expression. "If you don't believe me, look it up," Jack said. "There are hundreds of hospitals across Great Britain, but only a few are approved to provide pediatric heart surgery, and that is exactly the kind of effect the IPAB will have in the US."

As Pasqual resumed writing, Jack said, "I could go on and talk about the cuts in medical research and taxes placed on medical devices, but I'm afraid your readers would be bored with that sort of stuff. Suffice it to say, the law will regulate every aspect of the practice of medicine, and it was written by lawyers and people in the business of insurance, not physicians. I wonder what those elitists would say if the doctors were given the opportunity to write a two thousand page law that effectively told them how to do their jobs?"

"I think I have enough, Dr. Roberts," Pasqual said as he finished writing down Jack's last quote. "You have been most helpful, and again I appreciate your valuable time."

"Even though I doubt anyone in the US will ever read it, I'd appreciate it if you'd run it by me before you publish it, especially so I can check any quotes for accuracy."

"Of course, I will do that," Pasqual said as he again extended his hand.

****

"Hello, Elizabeth?" Jack asked, speaking into his cell phone. "This is Jack Roberts."

"Dr. Roberts!" Elizabeth exclaimed. "It is so good to hear your voice. Where are you?"

"Elaina and I are still in the airport in Managua. Our flight to San José has been delayed a couple of hours due to weather."

Up to now, Jack had been communicating with Elizabeth Burke through email. He and Elaina had planned to visit her in Costa Rica the year before, but things hadn't worked out. This summer Jack had arranged to take a few extra days off for their long awaited reunion at the conclusion of their annual trip to Nicaragua. She had told him she would pick them up at the airport in San José, and Jack didn't want her waiting.

Elizabeth had sold her half of the gift shop on South Padre Island back in the summer of 2008. She and Jennifer Morgan, her business partner, agreed that the inventory was valued at two hundred and fifteen thousand dollars, but their building on the boardwalk of was worth three times that. Elizabeth's father had advised her to buy it from the developer, fifteen years earlier when the shopping area was first built. The two hundred thousand dollars purchase price was the main reason she'd asked Jennifer to join her. Elizabeth simply didn't have the money to do the deal on her own, and her friend was looking for an investment following her divorce. They had been equal partners from the beginning, but Elizabeth finally decided she wanted out and once she made up her mind, she didn't waste anytime.

THE CONFLICT

****

"I'm going to miss having you around," Jennifer said, sounding more sad than she felt.

"I'm going to miss being here," replied Elizabeth. "I'm not sure what I'm going to do with all my free time."

"Oh, I'm sure you'll find something to do. You're still planning to move to Costa Rica, aren't you?"

"Yes, as soon as I can sell my house."

"Well, I hope you'll keep in touch."

"I will, and I hope you'll come visit me some time."

Both women said all the right things, but neither meant a word of it. Their partnership had always been one of convenience, and they never really shared any interests, except the business, but even that had become quite contentious. Elizabeth had agreed to walk away with just over four hundred thousand dollars, money Jennifer had had to borrow from the bank to buy her out. Once the deal was done, they had no reason to ever contact each other again.

Elizabeth's father had passed away rather suddenly from a massive heart attack at age seventy-five, leaving the fifty-three year old woman essentially alone. She had a thirty-two year old son, but he rarely came by to see her, except when he wanted money. Several of her long time friends had retired and moved to a Costa Rica because the tropical climate was inviting, and the cost of living was low. She had fallen in love with the place during the three visits she'd made down there over the last few years, and had dreamed of moving there herself one day.

She knew her life had become boring, but it wasn't until her chance encounter with David Roberts and his vivacious girl friend, Amy, that she realized just how dull and unexciting it was. She'd met David's father, a prominent pediatric heart surgeon in Fort Worth, Texas, eight years before, when she was helping a Mexican family get treatment for their daughter. Running into his son provided a stark reminder of the excitement she had felt, and how that whole experience had made her feel so incredibly alive. When David and Amy left to go back to college, she knew she needed to do something different with the rest of her life.

Within two weeks of when she put her house on the market, she had an offer for two hundred and thirty-five thousand dollars. She was actually in Costa Rica, looking at a couple of houses in the mountainside community of La Garita, where her friends lived, when she got the call from her realtor. She couldn't believe how quickly things were working out. The sale of her home was going to be a cash deal, and the agent told her if she accepted the offer, closing could occur before the end of the month. "Sounds good to me," she said. "I'm sure I can be out by then if that's what they want."

When she hung up the phone it suddenly hit her, she needed to find a place to live right away. The two bedroom that she'd had her eye on previously had sold, but she found a three bedroom oriental style bungalow in the same neighbor hood for one hundred twenty-eight thousand. It sat on the side of a heavily forested hill and had a huge covered deck that extended across the back and along both sides. The views of the mountains to the East and the ocean to the West were spectacular. Most of the homes in the development were on one to two acres, but this one had only a small yard in the back, which separated the house from a five hundred foot drop into the canyon below. For her, it was perfect, because it provided security and didn't require maintenance.

Within two days she closed the deal on her new home, and began making plans for the move. She discovered it was going to be very expensive to move all her stuff to La Garita because the import tariff on furniture was thirty-five percent. She thought it would be cheaper to just buy all new furniture and restrict her move to only her personal items. She could pack some in her suburban, and the rest would have to fit into a six by eight foot container that she could ship directly to her new address.

When she got home she called Doris, a friend who was in the business of conducting estate sales, and by the following weekend she was rid of all her furniture along with a bunch of other junk. She pocketed another fifty-five hundred dollars, which would more than offset her moving expenses.

Elizabeth had told her son, Tommy, that she was thinking about moving to Costa Rica several months before, but he just thought she was blowing smoke.

"Hi Tommy," Elizabeth said excitedly. "Guess what?"

"I don't know Mom, what?" he replied, sounding somewhat annoyed at being interrupted during a baseball game that he was watching on television.

"I've sold my business, and my house, and I'm moving to Costa Rica."

"What? When?" he asked, sounding concerned.

"Just as soon as I can pack-up the rest of my stuff."

"You're kidding, right?"

"No, Jennifer bought me out and I'm scheduled to close on the house next Wednesday. I've already sold all my furniture in an estate sale, and I bought the most beautiful little house you've ever seen. It's on the side of a mountain just outside La Garita."

Her son couldn't believe what he was hearing. "What's the deal Mom? Are you having a midlife crisis?"

"No, I'm retiring to my dream home in Costa Rica. I've decided now is the time."

"What are you going to do with your cars?"

"Well, that's part of why I'm calling you," she said. "I need to drive my suburban down there, and I was hoping you'd come with me. I'll pay to fly you back home, and for your trouble you can have the jeep."

Tommy had wanted the old, black Jeep Wrangler in her garage for several years, but she wouldn't part with it. She always contended it was her emergency car. "So, how long is the drive down to Costa Rica?" Tommy's attention had turned to what exactly he was going to need to do to get his hands on the Jeep.

"It is right at two thousand miles, so it will probably take us five full days. I thought we would leave next Tuesday. That way you could be back home by Sunday."

"Wow! Mom," he was astounded by the huge changes she had already made and the way she seemed to have planned out the entire move. "Are you sure about all this? Selling everything you own and moving off to another country. Sounds pretty scary to me."

"I have never been so certain of anything in my life," she said confidently. There was a momentary pause in their conversation until she added, "So, will you drive down there with me?"

"I'll have to see if I can get off work, but I'm pretty sure it won't be a problem."

"Great! I want to plan to leave early Tuesday morning, to get across the border before all the commercial traffic. Can you come stay with me at the Marriott Courtyard on Monday night? That's where I'm living right now."

"Sure. I'll stop by my apartment after work and pick up my suitcase, then I'll head that way. Should be there by seven."

"Thanks," she said. "You're a good son."

"I just can't believe your moving so far away."

"Its only a three hour flight from Houston, and I expect you to come visit at least as often as you do now." She felt she had to give him some grief for the fact that he only drove across town to see her every three or four months.

"I will, Mom. I'll see you in a few days."

"Okay, see you on Monday evening."

Before she left the country she sent out email invitations to a number of people in her address book. She wanted them all to know where she was going, and that they had an open invitation to visit anytime. Among the invitees was David Roberts, and she told him to be sure to forward her invitation and contact information to his mother and father.

****

"It has been storming here all morning," Elizabeth replied to Jack's revelation that they were still in Managua. "but it appears the weather is finally improving. I called the airport and they told me about the delay." After a brief pause she asked, "You are still coming aren't you?"

"Of course, assuming you'll still have us."

"Oh, I'm so looking forward to seeing you again. The guest room has been ready for a week." The excitement in Elizabeth's voice was infectious.

"We are also anxious to see you again, but I hope you haven't gone to any trouble."

"It is no trouble at all. I will be waiting for you right outside the TACA airlines baggage claim."

"Great," Jack replied, confirming their prior email plan. "If there are any further delays I'll call you, but otherwise we should be there around five."

"See you then," Elizabeth said before hanging up. She had been so excited when she received Jack's first email two months earlier, and now that he was actually coming for a visit she was beside herself. She had only had two American visitors since she moved to Costa Rica. One was her son, and the other was an old girl friend from high school who only stayed for a couple of days. She said it was just too hot without air conditioning.

Her son's visit had come about six months after he'd helped her drive the suburban through Central America. He had lost his job and came to ask her for some money. She knew something was up when he ask if she'd pay for his airfare. Eventually she gave him five thousand dollars, and told him that if he found another job, he wouldn't have to pay her back. However, she told him that if he decided to go on welfare, that he would have to pay her back every dime, with interest. She didn't want her son depending on the government for anything, He clearly got the message, and the result was he found another job within two months.

When Jack and Elaina came out of the airport they immediately spotted Elizabeth. She looked very different from the last time he saw her in Fort Worth. Her blond hair was now streaked with gray. She no longer kept it colored the way she had back in Texas. It was pulled back into a long ponytail exposing her somewhat more weathered appearance. She wore faded jeans and a dull red tee shirt with a local restaurant logo across the front, but her smile was still as genuine as Jack had remembered.

The two friends exchanged warm greetings and Jack introduced her to Elaina. He quickly loaded their bags into the back of her suburban and they headed out to the West toward La Garita. During the thirty minute drive along highway three, Elizabeth wanted to hear all about the work Jack and Elaina were doing in Nicaragua, and how things were going back in the states since the passage of the new healthcare law.

As she heard the sadness in Jack's voice she said, "You know," she added knowingly, "I could see the changes coming, not just in healthcare but in all aspects of American culture. There is a growing sense of entitlement, especially among younger people, and I'm not just talking about the poor or minorities. I think our generation has failed somehow. We didn't teach our kids the value of hard work and the joy that comes from a life made through personal effort and responsibility."

"You are absolutely right about that," Jack said. "I really feel sorry for anyone who has never experienced the excitement of accomplishing or building something of significance through their own effort. That is what gives our lives true meaning, yet so many people miss that point altogether. They have been fooled into thinking that its all about what you have, or what you can accumulate."

"Why do you supposed that is?" she asked.

"I don't know," Jack replied soberly. "Perhaps its as you say, our generation failed to teach our kids that the world doesn't revolve around money and fame."

"I think the decline started with television," she offered. "That box has ruined more young lives than you can count. Kids don't have to read a book, they just watch the movie. They don't go outside to play games, they just watch them on television. I think its those mind-numbing experiences, that have robbed them of ambition and a work ethic."

"That may have played a part," Jack said, "but I think parents are really to blame. Maybe I'm over simplifying things a bit, but I believe that following world war two, the euphoria of having beaten Hitler and his Japanese allies, and the boom in the American economy was profound. Everyone began to believe it was possible to get rich, and many did. Naturally, they wanted their children to have a better life than they had, so they gave them the spoils of their hard work without expecting much in return. Eventually, those parental gifts translated into a sense of entitlement that has grown with each subsequent generation. The liberal politicians simply took advantage of that change in American philosophy by offering anything and everything the public wants, assuming no one would mind passing the cost on to the next generation."

Elaina had heard this tirade more often than she cared to, so she reached forward between the two front seats and hit Jack in the left shoulder as firmly as she could manage. "We are on vacation, remember," she said with a bite to her voice. "She doesn't care to hear your philosophy on the decline and fall of modern America."

"I'm sorry," Jack apologized.

"No, really, I am enjoying having some real conversation for a change," Elizabeth said, more to Elaina than to Jack.

"He just gets going, and doesn't always know when to quit," Elaina explained.

"I can't blame him, especially given what is happening to doctors."

"Elaina's right," Jack acknowledged. "We came here to see you and all we've talked about is the problems you moved here to escape."

As she pulled the suburban into the circular driveway in front of her house, Jack thought the house appeared rather small, even by local standards. She opened the front door as Jack retrieved their bags. Elaina stepped into the small atrium, and saw the stairway that led down to the main floor. The hand rail and treads were made of high gloss mahogany. The living room was more than ample, and the far wall was comprised almost entirely of windows that looked out on to a wooden deck and a magnificent view of the valley below.

"Wow!" Elaina exclaimed. "What a great house!"

"Thank you. Please come in and make yourself at home."

Jack was astonished by the size of the house that had not been apparent from the street. "This is really incredible. Seeing this from the outside, there is no way anyone would anticipate what you have here."

"That's the main reason I bought it. Nobody knows what I have, and I like it that way. Let me show you to your room."

The small kitchen and dining area were located behind the stairway, and built back into the side of the hill. To the left were two bedrooms. One was small and had only one window up high on the far wall. The other was similar to the living room, with huge windows looking out toward the mountains in the distance. A set of French doors opened out on to the huge suspended deck, which wrapped around the side of the house. The screen covered windows were open and there was a pleasant breeze wafting through the room, supported by a large white ceiling fan.

"This is beautiful," Elaina said, "but surely this is the master bedroom."

"No," Elizabeth replied. "My room is on the other side of the house. It is similar to this one, but I have a view of the ocean. Its quite a way off in the distance, but the sunsets are often spectacular."

"This has to be like living a dream for you," Elaina said.

"It's great, but I have to admit I get a little lonely now and then," she admitted. "I have several friends that live nearby, but living alone is not something I've ever grown accustomed to since my divorce."

"So, why didn't you remarry? I'm sure an attractive woman like you is bound to have had plenty of suitors," Jack offered.

Elizabeth blushed slightly before responding. "I guess when you get burned as badly as I was, its hard to ever trust anyone again."

"Elaina and I both know what you mean. I swore off women for years following my divorce, but thank God I came to my senses." He looked at Elaina and flashed that same crooked smile she had loved the first time she saw it.

"Yeah," his wife said, returning his smile with a mischievous wink. "Meeting me was the best thing that ever happened to you."

Elizabeth sensed they were still very much in love, and a jolt of jealousy surged through her heart. She longed to feel that way again, but she knew that was not going to happen, and she had resolved to live out her life without romance.

"Tomorrow I want to take you all to see where I work," she said casually, carefully changing the subject.

"You are working?" Elaina asked.

"Absolutely!" she replied. "I'd go crazy if I didn't have a job."

"What are you doing?" Jack asked.

"I volunteer at a local orphanage," she offered. "You should see those kids. They will steal your heart. For some of them I'm like the mother they never had."

"What time do we leave?" Elaina said excitedly.

"Oh, not until nine or so tomorrow morning. I'm not scheduled to work tomorrow, but I usually go in for a couple of hours nearly everyday."

Jack smiled broadly and said, "Why am I not surprised?"

"I'll let you two get settled in," she said, again blushing at Jack's remarks. "I'm going to go finish fixing dinner. It will be ready in about an hour."

As she left the bedroom she closed the door behind her. Elaina looked up into Jack's face and slowly shook her head. "That is quite a woman," she said.

"Yes she is. I feel privileged to know her," he responded, "But, she is no where near as special as you." He reached forward and pulled Elaina into his arms and kissed her passionately.

She initially melted into his arms, as he held her close to him. He pulled back and began to unbutton her blouse. As he did, she objected, saying, "She is right outside!"

"So, lets go take a shower before dinner. She said it would be an hour or so, and we need to change clothes anyway." He looked down into her gorgeous green eyes and smiled slyly. "She won't hear anything but the water running," he said, as he continued to undress her slowly, this time without any resistance.

****

The next morning the trio boarded Elizabeth's suburban again and headed west, down the winding road toward Atenas. On the outskirts of the small town, she pulled into a small dirt parking lot and up to the front of a one story wooden frame building. The three wooden steps, leading up to the porch were in need of repair, but she bounded up them, stepping over the broken middle plank. "Mind your step," she said, looking back over her shoulder toward her guests.

She opened the heavy wooden door and invited Jack and Elaina to follow her inside. The room was dark, but seemed especially so given the stark contrast with the brilliant mid-morning sunshine. Once his eyes adjusted, Jack could see a few old wooden benches along the walls, and an open door on either side of the narrow hallway. As they walked passed the doorway to the left he could see a classroom occupied by a dozen or more young children, ages four or five to mid teens. They were being led by a teacher who appeared to be only a few years older than the oldest of her students.

"These are our school age kids," Elizabeth explained. Jack could see that the older children were assisting the younger ones with a reading exercise.

"Who is the teacher"? Elaina asked.

"Oh, that's Francesca. She grew up here in the orphanage and now lives in one of the casitas out behind the main building."

"How many of these children get adopted?" Jack asked.

Elizabeth smiled and shook her head. "It is very rare for one of our children to be adopted. Most of them stay here until they reach the age of sixteen. At that point they usually leave to find a job back in San José or at one of the resorts along the coast. Sometimes we see them again if they are passing by, but that's pretty unusual."

"Where do these children come from?" Elaina asked.

"A few are brought here from the government hospital after their mothers have either died during child birth, or are simply abandoned. Others are dropped off as young children when their parents are unable to provide for them."

"See that little girl sitting over by the window?" she asked, pointing across the room to a five or six year old child, who obviously bore significant raised pink scars on the left side of her face. "That is Hermina. She was the only member of her family to survive a fire that consumed their small cinder block home about a year ago. She was burned pretty severely."

"Where was she cared for?" Jack asked.

"She spent about two months in the government hospital in San José. They transferred her here once the risk of infection had passed, and we have cared for her the best we could since then."

Jack's heart was broken. This beautiful young child had survived, but her life would never be the same. He could see by the appearance of the scars on her face and neck that they were most likely due to deep second degree burns that had become superficially infected. With proper treatment, the scars likely could have been minimized, but now the significant disfigurement was beyond repair.

Elizabeth turned and walked the few steps across the hallway to the doorway into another similar sized room. This one was filled with makeshift play pens, old wooden baby beds, and several small mats lined up against one wall.

"These are our infants and preschoolers," she said proudly.

The room contained at least twenty young children and three adult attendants who were making their way through the maze, caring for the babies. Some of the infants were crying for attention, but most were sleeping.

"How many children do you have all together?" Elaina asked, holding back her tears for the moment.

"Right now we have thirty two, which is pretty much our capacity. We have had as many as forty, but when we get to that level we can't provide adequate meals or sleeping accommodations, so we have to find other orphanages that will take them," she explained. "The director has talked about adding on to this building, but it is so old and run down, that seems pointless. I think he'd like to just bulldoze this building and build a new one on this same site, but like everything else, the problem is money."

"How is this place financed?" Jack asked.

"We get a little from the government, but as I understand it, that support has been declining in recent years. The Catholic Church also provides some support, but mostly in the form of supplies and clothing for the children. Other than that, we rely on donations and volunteers."

"Our church back home just held a fund raising event to help support an orphanage in Mexico," Elaina said, wondering whether that facility was in as dire need as this one.

"We have a few churches back in the US that hold annual fund raisers like that for us as well, and a couple of times they have even sent teams of volunteers down to help with repairs, but most of our support comes from some expatriates who live here in the area."

"Really?" Jack asked, somewhat amazed. "Are they wealthy people?"

"Oh, yes!" Elizabeth said, surprised that Jack wasn't aware of how many people of considerable means had chosen to retire to Costa Rica from Europe and the United States. "There are several in my own neighborhood who moved here for the climate and the low cost of living, but for many, they came just to escape the high taxes. One of my good friends came here from Holland. Her family was extremely wealthy and she decided she was tired of paying seventy percent taxes, so she moved here about twenty years ago."

"Doesn't she still pay taxes on her holdings back in Holland?" Jack asked.

"Nope! She moved all her holdings into an off shore account and she became a Costa Rican citizen. Her income has remained the same, but her cost of living has dropped dramatically, and her tax rate is less than a quarter of what it was."

"I'll bet she misses all the trappings of European society," Elaina offered.

"Not really, at least according to her. I've asked her that very question on several occasions, including before I started looking into moving here myself. She always says those snobs she used to run around with, can have all their high society life, and the depression and anxiety disorders that go with it." Elizabeth laughed to herself. "Of course I wouldn't know about any of that since I never had that kind of life to leave. I know she misses Holland sometimes, because she flies home to visit for a couple of weeks at least twice a year."

"What kind of place does she have here?" Jack inquired.

"Oh, my God!" Elizabeth said, raising her eyes briefly toward the ceiling. "She has a magnificent villa on the hills above here. It sits on about three hundred hectares. She has three guest houses and a riding stable. It is absolutely fabulous. And she also has another house down on the coast. I went there with her for a weekend a couple of months ago. It's on the most beautiful, pristine, private beach you've ever seen."

"I can't imagine why she'd ever want to leave here, unless it's to be with her family." Elaina said with a sigh.

"She has one son who still lives in Holland, but she brings him over to stay with her a couple of times a year, and he usually stays for a month or more each time." Elizabeth paused a few seconds before continuing. "There is also a retired American judge who lives with her. He is a widower, and he too is independently wealthy. Between the two of them they have donated more than a hundred thousand dollars to this orphanage, just since I've been working here."

Elaina looked up at Jack who was just shaking his head. "Sounds like someone else we know," Elaina said.

"Sounds like the only difference is that Franco Gutierrez built his fortune in Nicaragua and still lives there," Jack added.

"You know Franco Gutierrez?" Elizabeth asked in disbelief.

"Yes," Jack said hesitatingly. "Have you heard of him?"

"Are you kidding? Everybody in Central America has heard of him. He's about as famous in this part of the world as Donald Trump is in the US. How do you know him?"

"I operated on his daughter a few years ago, and we became friends."

"I thought I had important friends, but to be on a first name basis with Gutierrez tops anything I can claim," Elizabeth said shaking her head in amazement. She had no idea just how familiar Jack and Elaina were with Franco and Gabriella, and neither of her guests were going to explain any further.

CHAPTER 8

"Let's go," Jason said. "It's time."

Jack straightened his tie and slipped on his suit coat as Elaina moved in front of him. She did a quick visual inspection the said, "You look great."

They walked quickly to the elevators, and in less than three minutes they were on the ground floor, making their way through a hallway behind the ballroom where Jack's supporters were waiting anxiously.

As he stood silently in the holding area the events of the past year flooded his memory as he tried to remember all the people he needed to thank.

****

The first weekend in September of 2011, the Tarrant County GOP held a rally at Billy Bob's Texas, the world famous "honky tonk" located in the Fort Worth Stockyards. This was where many local political careers had been launched, and the event marked the beginning of the campaign season. All five potential candidates for the republican nomination planned to use this opportunity to formally announce their intent to run for Congress, including Jack.

He didn't know any of the other candidates, but Jason had told him there was only one other person who planned to announce that was likely to offer any real competition. He said, "John Crenshaw is a young lawyer, who was hand picked by his firm to make this run, and those guys are very good at raising money. They will have a strong support staff, but Crenshaw is vulnerable because he's so young. He's not much older than your son, and we should be able to capitalize on that if we end up head to head."

As the evening got underway, Jack was uncharacteristically nervous. He had memorized his five minute speech, but he wondered if he had included everything he needed to say. He didn't want to come across as just a doctor. He wanted people to see him as a serious candidate who wasn't just about healthcare. As his time to speak approached he stood back stage, rereading his speech one last time. When he was introduced there was more applause than he had anticipated from the nearly three thousand who were on hand. Initially he struggled to gain his composure, but eventually he moved carefully into his remarks, reciting his lines just as he had rehearsed them. When he was finished, the audience seemed unimpressed. Their response was a rather tepid applause, and none of the outbursts of support he had expected.

"What happened?' he asked Jason, his campaign manager, as he came off the stage and headed for a prearranged gathering with some of his supporters.

"You kinda blew it," Jason offered honestly.

"I thought you agreed on the content, didn't you?" Jack protested.

"The content was fine," Jason replied. "The problem was your delivery. You sounded like a high school student auditioning for a part in a senior play."

"I told you from the very beginning that I'm not a polished public speaker," he protested.

"Jack, I've watched you speak to the precincts and other small groups for the last two months, and you are a terrific extemporaneous speaker," Jason said. "What you did this evening was exactly the opposite. When you are yourself, the people love you. When you read a prepared speech, even if you've memorized it, you come across as an insincere ... well ... politician."

Jack sighed heavily. He knew Jason was right. He was trying so hard not to be the one thing he was becoming. His nerves got the best of him, and he knew it.

"Look, Jack, I know this is all very new to you," Jason said trying to soften the blow he had just delivered. "But, I don't know anyone who has a better grasp of the healthcare issues, or who has more knowledge of the facts than you. You need to play to that strength, and make it the focus of this campaign. People are all afraid of what is happening, just like they fear getting sick and going to the doctor. You need to use the same confident, comforting approach when you talk to the public about the impact of Obamacare, just like you do when you're talking to one of your patients about heart surgery. They want to trust you to fix the problem, so all you need to do is project confidence, the same way you do in the operating room."

Jack knew Jason was right, but he certainly didn't feel as confident in this arena as he did in the one where he was in control.

Elaina caught up with them as they made their way through the crowd of speakers back stage. She had her usual bright smile, but her words lacked any real enthusiasm. "Great job, honey," she said as she hugged him briefly and kissed his cheek.

"No it wasn't," he said with his head hung perceptibly.

"I thought you did just fine," she protested slightly, trying to raise his spirits.

"Jason is right. I blew it."

His campaign manager chimed in again. "Listen, this was just one speech. We can't afford to compound it by acting like we just lost the Super Bowl." He put his arm around Jack's shoulder and said, "We need to go wow your supporters with the real Jack Roberts, and soon they'll forget all about the egg you just laid."

****

Over the next few weeks, Jason arranged several meetings where Jack had opportunities to speak with small groups of influential Republicans. In these settings, he was highly effective and extremely well-liked. Initially everyone was not only interested in his opinions about healthcare, and the potential repeal of Obamacare, but they were also highly supportive. In one week he raised nearly eighty thousand dollars, which allowed Jason to print one thousand yard signs with Jack's campaign slogan, "Roberts, the right prescription for Congress."

"You know Jack," one of the local bank presidents said as he put his arm around him, "you're going to make a great Congressman, but you know, not everything is about healthcare. Those of us in the banking business have been taking it in the shorts, and we need some guys with backbone to repeal that damned Dodd-Frank Law."

Jack wasn't exactly sure what was in the law that bore the name of man who had been the chairman of the House Ways and Means committee when he testified before him three years earlier. "Yeah," Jack said laughingly, "I had a run in with Mr. Frank a couple years back. I can't imagine anything that he's had something to do with that I could support."

"He's a piece of work all right," the banker agreed, "but that law... well... if it doesn't get repealed they are going to end up regulating us out of business."

"I'm sure I'll have an opportunity to get up to speed on all the particulars once I get to Washington," Jack said.

The man replied in a patronizing way, as he patted Jack on the back. "I don't really care whether you have all the specifics nailed down, I just need to know that you're going to vote to repeal it,"

No sooner had the banker left Jack's side, than he was approached by still another older gentleman who said, "I think you've got a real chance."

"Thank you, I really appreciate your support," Jack said as he shook the gentleman's hand, but the man held on to Jack's right hand a bit awkwardly, as he reached up and placed his left hand on Jack's shoulder.

"I know you're mostly about healthcare, and I get that, but I'm in the oil business, and I need for that Keystone pipeline to get approved."

"As I understand it, the Congress has already approved it," Jack said in response. "It's the president and the EPA that are holding things up."

"That's true," the oilman said as he finally released his grip on Jack, "but Congress can certainly put some pressure on this administration, and I'm counting on you to do just that."

Jack replied quickly, "I've been on record for some time supporting the Keystone XL pipeline project. It would be good for Texas and for Texas businesses. What I'm hoping is that we'll have a different administration that will see things our way,"

"Yeah, I'm just afraid we don't have anybody running right now that's capable of taking Obama down. I don't know, maybe Rick Perry will get into the race, and we'll have somebody we can finally get behind." The oilman offered his support, and Jack nodded in appreciation as they parted.

The schedule that Jason had Jack on called for him to meet with potential donors nearly every evening. Sometimes these were small gatherings in private homes, while others involved small groups that met in area restaurants or bars. In every situation Jack understood from Jason, that the main reason he was there was to raise money. Contrary to what he had promised himself before the campaign even began, he found himself practicing the art of telling people what they wanted to hear. He repeatedly argued with himself about what he had found was some how, necessary.

As Christmas approached, Jason arranged for numerous fundraisers across the city, and at each event Jack struggled with the temptation to pander to his audience. This was especially true when he gave speeches in the Hispanic community. Jason had strongly recommended that he deliver those messages in Spanish, something Jack had no problem doing, but he felt that he was being a hypocrite. He had advocated on numerous occasions for immigration reform that included making English the official language of the US. It seemed he was saying one thing and practicing something else, but Jason told him that was politics.

The one thing that Jack refused to do was to use his history of providing his surgical services to the low income community, as a tool to win their votes. He could have easily gained considerable support by bringing up the fact that he had personally operated on dozens of children of illegal immigrants in the local community over the past twenty-plus years without receiving payment. He made the decision early on to avoid that strategy because, as he put it, doing so would make him appear self-righteous. Jason, on the other hand, didn't hesitate to use his surrogates to very carefully put out that message on Jack's behalf.

****

As January turned to February, the political season shifted into high gear. Jack was asked to be on at least three or four radio talk shows every week. The primary race had come down to him and Crenshaw, just as Jason had predicted. Jack had raised over three quarters of a million dollars, and had used about half that amount so far on media advertising.

"I had no idea it cost so much just to put on a one minute television commercial," he said, when Jason showed him the bills for ten spots on one of the local network affiliates.

"Yep," Jason responded, "It cost us forty-five hundred dollars to make the ad, and then we pay twelve hundred dollars every time it runs. And that isn't even prime time. As we get closer to the primary, we'll need to increase our exposure during peak evening hours." Jason looked up from the papers he had been pointing toward and spoke directly to Jack, face to face. "This is what I was talking about back in June when we first started. Its all about raising money. Without the resources to get your face on television, there is no way to win."

"I understand that," Jack admitted, "but I still think it's wrong. You shouldn't be able to buy an election just because you have more money to spend on television ads than the other guy."

Jason smiled and chuckled out loud briefly as he told Jack, "Wait until you see what really goes on in Washington."

The republican primary had been pushed back from April third to late May, because of litigation over redistricting. A group of activists and several democrat law makers alleged that the redistricting maps that were drawn up by the republican controlled Texas legislature, violated the federal Voting Rights Act. A panel of three federal judges decided to hold up the Texas primary for nearly two months. Most republicans believed the delay was orchestrated by the Obama administration to ensure that the result from the Texas presidential primary would come long after that race had already been decided.

Jason was concerned that their campaign might run out of money if he started too early with the prime time ads, so he waited until mid April to begin running them. By that time most of the other candidates had already been seen on the four major networks multiple times. He told Jack he was "keeping his powder dry", waiting for the right time. His strategy proved very effective, because in the last two weeks before the May primary, Jack's was virtually the only name and face seen on television. The other candidates, including Crenshaw were basically out of money.

The biggest story of the Texas primary certainly wasn't Jack's race, or even the Presidential primary. Romney had long since secured enough delegates to gain the republican nomination on the first ballot at the convention later that summer. The big race was for the republican nomination for the US Senate. Texas Lieutenant Governor, David Dewhurst was running against a field of other candidates to replace Senator Kay Bailey Hutchison, who had decided not to seek re-election. His main opposition was a constitutional lawyer and former Solicitor General for the State of Texas, Ted Cruz. There was no doubt that Dewhurst would win more votes than any other candidate. The only thing in question was whether he would reach the fifty percent level required to win the primary outright. If not, he would face a run-off against the candidate who finished second.

Throughout the campaign Jack continued to work, but he had reduced his schedule to only three days a week. He performed most of his elective surgery on Tuesday and Wednesday mornings, and he saw patients in the office all day on Thursdays. Having George in the office was a huge help, since he was able to shift much of his patient load, and George obviously didn't mind the extra business. Jack saw his income drop about thirty percent, but with another surgeon now sharing in the overhead, it wasn't a big concern. He and Elaina had saved more than enough to see them through, but so far they hadn't been forced to dip into their savings.

Jack decided to take the entire week of the primary off, making a final whirlwind tour of the entire district. He spoke at three different breakfasts, two luncheons, and three different dinners, all on the eve of the primary election. When he finally got home that evening it was after eleven-thirty.

"I just thought I was tired after twenty-four hours of trauma call," he said to Elaina as he staggered through the door.

"Well, at least you had a lot to eat," she smiled, as she brought him a cold beer from the refrigerator.

"Are you kidding," he laughed. "The only food I've had was a breakfast taquito from What-a-burger around ten, and a bowl of Wendy's chili at three-thirty. Both were in the car between stops. I think Jason is trying to kill me."

She laughed as well then asked, "Would you like for me to fix you something?"

"No Angel, I just want to go to bed. Jason will be by to pick us up at seven a.m."

"Us?" she asked.

"Yeah, he said, "we need to go to the polls together and we need to be there by seven thirty. He has notified the television stations so their cameras should be there to catch us casting our ballots. They will run that clip multiple times during the day. He says it helps get out the vote."

"Okay," she said with a deep sigh, feigning her own exhaustion. "I guess I can get up early for you, but just this once." Jack gave her a weary smile as he slowly got undressed.

After casting his vote the next morning, Jason had wanted him to make a couple more stops in an effort to get out the vote.

"Look," Jack said with finality, "If I haven't convinced enough people to vote for me over the nearly twelve months since I decided to run, another speech or another appearance isn't going to matter. Elaina and I are going home to get some rest."

"Okay," Jason conceded, "but, your campaign workers are expecting you at the Worthington around six. You will be there tonight, right?"

"We'll be there prepared for whatever happens, win, lose or draw."

That evening was one of the most remarkable of Jack's sixty-three years. He won the primary in what Jason described as "an epic landslide."

The local news commentator agreed, reporting "Nearly fifty-five percent of the votes had been cast for the political newcomer, Dr. Jack Roberts. I guess that speaks to the relative anger and frustration over the new healthcare law. At least among Texas republicans."

The co-host of the election night coverage added, "His closest pursuer, John Crenshaw was twenty points back with only thirty-five percent. We haven't seen a primary win like this by a relative unknown in a very long time. It would appear that Harold Sheffield is in for a real fight between now and November."

Shortly after seven-thirty Jack received several phone calls. Each of the other candidates called to congratulate him on his victory and to wish him well in the general election. The call from Crenshaw was particularly gratifying, as the young lawyer was very gracious in defeat.

"I am proud to have had the opportunity to run against you, Dr. Roberts," Crenshaw said. "You ran the kind of clean, issues oriented campaign we don't see that often in American politics, and I want you to know you can count on my support going forward."

"Thank you very much, John. You conducted yourself with extraordinary integrity, and I'm proud to have gotten to know you these last few months. I can't tell you how much it means to me to know that you and your supporters will be there to help us get this nation back on a proper course."

Jack's acceptance speech was delivered to his staff and about two hundred supporters in the ballroom of the Worthington Hotel. He thanked them and mentioned his conversations with the other candidates before throwing out a challenge. "This has been a great evening of excitement and jubilation, but it is important for us to recognize that we haven't won anything, yet. We can celebrate tonight, but tomorrow marks the beginning of the real campaign."

The audience erupted again his shouts of "Let's go, Jack! Let's go, Jack!"

He raised his hands to quiet them before concluding, "I'm going to need each and everyone of you to help me get this thing done!"

Again the audience broke into applause followed by the chant that continued as Jack pulled Elaina to his side before raising his arms over his head in a gesture of victory.

****

"Can you believe it?" Horvath said disgustedly. "He actually won the damned primary."

Fitzgerald smirked as he sipped his bourbon and water. "I suspect he's going to find that running against Sheffield is a bit different than that light-weight, Crenshaw."

Horvath laughed along with his boss then added, "Yeah, I suspect this is going to get nasty before its over."

"You have no idea," Fitzgerald said as he smiled broadly then took another healthy draw on his bourbon.

****

Dewhurst had not been as fortunate as Jack. He had fallen just shy of the fifty percent needed to avoid a run off with the younger, and highly energetic Cruz. Dewhurst was clearly part of the establishment, while Cruz was a populist with the backing of the Tea Party and several young, conservative Senators like Mike Lee of Utah, and Rand Paul of Kentucky. He was running a grassroots campaign, similar to the one Jack had waged in his primary, but Cruz was doing it on a state-wide basis.

"What would you say to asking Ted Cruz to come to one of our campaign rallies?" Jack asked Jason.

"Generally it's the guy that's running for state-wide office that invites the guy running in a more limited area. I haven't heard anything from them yet, but we likely will the next time they come through the metroplex." Jason knew some of the people in the Cruz campaign and he could certainly call them if the need arose. "I want to warn you though," he added, if you are seen as endorsing either candidate in their run off, it could cost you dearly if the other man wins. This isn't forgive and forget politics, no matter what they may say publicly."

So, you think I should stay out of their race, right?"

"Absolutely. That is exactly what I'm saying."

"So, the idea of inviting Cruz to my event is kind of stupid, huh?"

"You are a very quick study, Jack. You have some real potential in this business," Jason laughed.

****

With the presidential primary season over, both national parties were focusing all their energy on their August conventions. But, now that the nominees had been determined, local party activists simply shifted gears, focusing now on beating their rivals from the other party. Jack found himself surrounded by countless new supporters. It seemed that most of them understood what Jack had only recently learned - don't commit too soon.

"Hello, Domingo? This is Jack Roberts." He spoke somewhat louder than he'd intended to compensate for what seemed like a bad connection.

"Hi Jack, its good to hear your voice," Domingo replied. "When are you coming down?

"That's what I was calling about. Elaina and I are not going to be able to make it this year."

"But... why not?"

"I'm in the middle of this campaign, and there is so much going on, I'm afraid I just can't get away."

"Felecia will be so disappointed," he said. "And, I had planned to have some of the children you have helped come to the clinic, just to see you again."

"I'm really sorry," Jack said sadly. "I would love nothing more than to see all of them again, but my campaign manager tells me that this is a crucial time. We are trying to raise enough money to get me elected."

"I will tell them." The tone of Domingo's voice betrayed the fact that he was beyond disappointed. "You will let me know if you change your mind, okay?"

"I will, my friend, I will." Jack's voice sounded very sad. He and Elaina had made the trip every summer, and this would have been their twentieth year.

When Jack got home that evening Elaina could tell there was something wrong. She asked, "What's the matter honey? You look like you just lost your best friend."

"I didn't lose him, at least I don't think I did," Jack replied with a smile. "I talked to Domingo today, and explained about our not being able to get away this summer, because of the campaign. He sounded so dejected. I just feel so... empty, you know? That trip has been a part of our lives for nearly as long as we've been married."

"Well, its not too late. You could just tell Jason that you need some time off," Elaina reasoned. "What is it you always say? Nicaragua is a great place to recharge your batteries?"

"You're right," he said confidently.

Jack rose from his chair and walked out on to the patio. Elaina smiled to herself as she watched him through the sliding glass door. He was pacing back and forth, talking on his cell phone, presumably to Jason. After a couple of minutes he stopped pacing and looked down at the phone as he selected another number from his contacts list. Again he started pacing, but this time he was visibly more relaxed and she could see him smiling spontaneously for the first time in weeks.

****

As they got out of their rent car in front of Domingo and Felicia's home, the Nicaraguan couple came running out to greet them.

"Welcome my friends! Come in, come in!" Domingo said excitedly. "We have been expecting you." He motioned for his guests to go on in the house ahead of him and his wife.

Jack and Elaina stepped through the front door and saw a long banner hanging from the ceiling that read "¡*Bien Venido!*" with the English phrase "Welcome Home - 20 Years!" written in script beneath the Spanish words. Suddenly the room erupted with a host of voices shouting, "Surprise!"

The room was filled with many familiar faces as people flooded in from their hiding places in adjacent rooms. Jack was shocked. He first looked to Elaina for an explanation, but she was just as surprised as he was. He then turned toward Domingo who was grinning broadly. He had obviously been planning this reception for some time. Jack could only imagine how disappointed he must have been when he'd initially told him they weren't coming. Now, all that was behind them, and Domingo's party had been a complete surprise, just as he had intended.

"Please come and sit here," Felicia said to the guests of honor. "I will have all of the children come over to see you."

For the next few minutes several children were brought to see the man who had been most responsible for their survival. Domingo had even tracked down the father of the Ochoa boy, and convinced him to bring the child back to Nicaragua from Belize. Jack just shook his head in amazement as Domingo introduced the healthy nine year old. The boy held out his hand to the doctor and said, "*muchas gracias, señor*," despite the fact he had no memory of the remarkable events that took place in the government hospital, seven years earlier. Jack smiled broadly and took the child's hand in his and replied, "*de nada, mijo.*" Hearing the term of endearment from this stranger caused the boy's face to change from an anxious smile to a huge grin, as he stepped forward and threw his arms around Jack's neck.

Seeing this obvious spontaneous outpouring of emotion, Elaina began to cry, along with many of the clinic volunteers who had also come to pay tribute to Jack. "Don't you start," Jack spoke to her softly, fighting to hold back his own emotions.

The scene was repeated several more times, including the eleven year old boy, who bore the scar on the front of his neck from the unexpected tracheotomy. Each child was accompanied by their parents, and most brought hand made gifts of some sort. The last child in the procession was the little three year old that had required the ASD repair the previous summer. The young mother followed the child, encouraging her as she slowly walked toward Jack and Elaina. The woman's younger brother was not with her this time. Instead, she was accompanied by an older man that Jack did not recognize.

Jack leaned over and lifted the child on to his knee, speaking softly to her in Spanish. The child was clearly afraid and began to cry in protest. When Jack placed her back on the floor, she immediately ran to her mother and buried her face in her mother's bright yellow skirt.

"*Muchas gracias*, doctor," the mother said as her radiant smile caused Elaina to once more start to cry softly. "This is my husband," she said, introducing the man who had once threatened to take her child into the mountains rather than allow her to be cared for by any doctor.

Jack stood and extended his hand toward the man who was at least twenty years older than his wife. He accepted Jacks hand rather shyly and spoke very softly. "*Gracias, señor por savar la vida de mija.*" The fact that this man's mind had been changed to the point where he was now willing to stand before him, and thank him for saving his daughter's life, gave Jack a greater sense of accomplishment than any other event that day. He was convinced the ancient culture of ignorance and fear was gradually being replaced by hope and trust.

Later that evening when all the guests had gone, Jack and Elaina sat quietly on the metal glider on the patio, next to the small guest house. As the last faint glow of the sunset faded, the outline of the mountains also blended into the darkness of the moonless night. Domingo and Felicia were helping Rosa clean up the kitchen, leaving them alone as they reminisced about all the years they had been coming to this peaceful place, that their friends back home referred to as the middle of nowhere. But to them it seemed like the center of the world.

"I trust we aren't too late." Franco's voice broke the silence, as he and Gabriella came out through the back door accompanied by the now seven year old Christina.

"Oh my goodness," Jack said, rising to his feet. "What a surprise!"

Franco moved quickly to greet his friends, and as he shook Jack's hand he said, "We understood there was a party for you, and all your Nicaraguan patients, so, we simply could not miss it."

Christina ran quickly passed Jack to Elaina and gave her a big hug. Jack smiled as he pretended his feelings had been hurt by the child's obvious snub, until Gabriella embraced him warmly and kissed his cheek. "She has been asking about the yellow-haired Ms. Elaina everyday for the last week."

Once all the greetings had been exchanged Jack suggested their friends sit with them for a while and share the bottle of Chilean Syrah, Jack had just opened. They were joined by Domingo and Felicia as they all enjoyed the coolness of the late June evening and the crisp red wine.

Domingo excused himself for a moment, but soon returned with his camera and Rosa, the housekeeper. "I took photos of all the other children today, so I must have one of Christina and Jack, please."

For the next several minutes he took multiple photos of Jack and Christina, then more that included Elaina and the young girl's parents, and finally he wanted to get a group photo. He looked through the camera as he arranged the group for the shot. Once he was satisfied with the placement of everyone, he handed the camera to Rosa who accepted it nervously, trying to determine exactly where she was supposed to be looking and which button she was to push. Domingo gave her specific instructions, but she still looked confused as he ran around to stand next to his wife and behind Jack who was seated with Christina on his knee. Elaina was on one side and Gabriella and Franco on the other. Eventually Rosa was able to push the right button, capturing an image that was destined to make headlines.

****

"Thank God for Roberts," Horvath said excitedly.

"Yeah," Fitzgerald laughed, "Chief Justice Roberts."

The two men had toasted the decision by the Supreme Court, never having dreamed that it would be the Bush appointee John Roberts who would cast the deciding vote, keeping their dreams of a healthcare monopoly alive.

THE CONFLICT

"Now we just need to get rid of his namesake," Fitzgerald said, "then we can get back to the business of bringing the rest of his colleagues to heel."

****

Jack thought the week had gone by incredibly fast. They had spent each day at the clinic, and each leisurely evening was spent on the patio. There had been no challenging cases to deal with, and the trip had been exactly what Jack had hoped for, a relaxing interlude that allowed him to get reenergized for the last four months of the campaign. He had even turned his cell phone off for the first time in years.

"You looked like you were having a great time," Jason said as he walked into Jack's office on Monday morning.

"What do you mean?" Jack asked and he shook his manager's hand.

"That picture of you on Facebook. It looked like you guys were enjoying yourselves. I certainly hope it was worth it because you missed the biggest opportunity yet to close the deal on this election,"

"Whoa, whoa, slow down a minute. First, what picture on Facebook?" Jack asked.

"The one your friend Domingo posted. You have some kid on your lap."

"I didn't realize he was planning to put that photo up on the Internet, but I can't see anything wrong with it. That was one of the kids I operated on several years ago."

"I recognized Elaina obviously, but who were the other people in the picture?"

"I haven't seen it, but I assume its the one with the child's parents, and our friends that we stay with when we're down there."

"Well, like I said, it looked like you were very relaxed, but now we have some catching up to do."

"Okay, what was the big thing that I missed?" Elaina had made him promise not to watch any television or surf the Internet news for the week they had been gone, and he had been too tired to even turn on the news once they'd gotten home late last night.

"You really were on another planet, weren't you? The Supreme Court decision came down on Thursday. They held that the healthcare law is constitutional because the penalty for not buying insurance is actually a tax."

"You're kidding. I thought Obama's people insisted from the beginning that the mandate was not a tax."

"It seems that the Chief Justice didn't see it that way."

"Unbelievable." Jack said just shaking his head.

"Every local television station as well as FOX and CNN have been looking to have you on their opinion programs to talk about the decision. A couple of them even asked me if you were related to Chief Justice John Roberts."

"I don't guess I'm all that surprised at the decision," Jack said as his shoulders slumped noticeably.

Well, like I said, you missed a golden opportunity to let the world know where you stand on this issue, because you weren't here."

Jack turned sharply toward Jason and his words had an edge to them that his manager hadn't heard before. "Look, Jason, I understand that it is your job to help get me elected, and I truly appreciate your efforts and your experience, but I won't be criticized for taking a week off from the campaign to be with my wife, and to relax. I can't help it that this golden opportunity, as you put it, just happened to coincide with my being out of the country, and I won't allow you to make it seem somehow that its my fault."

"I didn't mean to imply that it was your fault. I just wanted ..." his voice trailed off. Jason was frustrated because he had been forced to find all manner of excuses why his guy, the doctor who was running on the idea of repealing Obamacare, wasn't available to even comment on the biggest healthcare news story since the law had passed more than two years earlier.

Jack was upset as well. He knew that the media attention on the Supreme Court's decision had been an opportunity missed, but he was more angry with the decision itself. The idea that somehow it had become okay to compel someone to buy something that must also meet a certain government standard wasn't right. He been beyond disappointed with his professional organizations for years, including even the Association of Thoracic Surgeons. None of them had come out publicly opposing this increasing intrusion into the practice of medicine.

He hadn't been very active in the organization for the past year, even though he had moved up the leadership ladder and was currently the vice-president. Fortunately that position had no real duties, and he knew if he was elected he would have to step aside and let someone else assume the presidency for the next two calendar years.

"Do you remember a couple of years back when you were part of a group on television talking about the proposed healthcare law?" Jason asked, breaking Jack's train of thought

"Yeah, sure I remember," Jack said.

"Well, that station called me on Saturday and asked if you would participate in a follow-up panel discussion?"

"A follow-up two and a half years later?" Jack interrupted.

"It seems the feedback they received the first time around was rather, what did he say, tepid? So they decided not to do a follow-up. Now that you are in this race and the law has been upheld, they think there will be more interest."

"That's what it's all about, isn't it? Ratings."

"For those guys, yes," Jason agreed. "For us, its all about exposure."

"Is Herb Nichols going to be there?"

"Apparently so."

Jack thought for a minute, and as he did Jason said, "We don't have to do this if you don't want to."

"No, I think its a good idea."

The following afternoon, Jack showed up at the station thirty minutes prior to the time taping was scheduled to begin. He was now very accustomed to the routine of appearing on television. He even carried his own make-up kit with him. He didn't want to hear Elaina tell him about the shine on his nose and forehead the way she had following one of his early televised events. Jason told him that his appearance accounted for more than half of how the public perceived him, so he made sure to always try and look his best on camera, even if it meant using a little foundation and powder.

Herb arrived only moments before the taping was scheduled to begin and greeted Jack casually off camera. The other members of the panel remained seated in the small green room until they were called to the set, so Jack hadn't really had a chance to interact with any of them until the show began.

"Good evening ladies and gentlemen," the moderator began. "Tonight we have with us a group of healthcare experts that we had on this program back when Obamacare was being debated in the Congress. Now that it has been determined to be Constitutional, we decided to bring them back to gain their perspective once more."

He then introduced each of the four panel members, leaving Jack for last. As he gave Jack's credentials he said, "and Dr. Roberts is now the republican nominee for Congress from the district that includes a significant portion of the DFW metroplex

Jack nodded his appreciation and said, "Thank you for inviting me."

"Let's start with you Dr. Roberts. Now that Obamacare is the law of the land, have your opinions about it changed at all? I know you were pretty adamant in your opposition a couple of years ago."

"No, Jim," he responded. "I remain very concerned about the impact this law will have on the patient-physician relationship, and that's why I decided to run for Congress. I believe that repealing the law is the only way to save the best healthcare system in the world."

The sociology professor managed to get the moderators attention and when asked his opinion he said, "Jim, despite what Dr. Roberts said about the physician-patient relationship, this law will guarantee every American access to healthcare, and that is something that has been far to long in coming."

"Mr. Nichols," the moderator said as he turned toward Herb. "I understand you sit on the board of directors of the American Hospital Association, and that organization has been a staunch supporter of the President and this law from the beginning, is that right?"

"Yes," Herb said in a relaxed style. "We believe that the only responsible policy is to compel every American to have health insurance. Otherwise the cost of caring for the uninsured will continue to fall on the rest of us. This is essentially what the law does, and I'm sorry if some doctors don't like it, its the right thing for America." Herb placed a special emphasis on the word doctors, making what amounted to a verbal gesture Jack's way.

The businessman was silently shaking his head, and when the moderator ask him his opinion he said, "I find it interesting that the doctors and the hospitals can't agree on how to split up the nearly two trillion dollars that guys like me are shelling out every year for healthcare. I, for one, have heard enough about access and cost control. The bottom line here is American business can't continue to bear the burden of paying for everyone to go to the doctor or the emergency room every time they feel like it."

"Under the new law you don't have to," the sociologist offered. "People will be able to buy insurance from the exchanges, freeing you and other employers from that burden."

The businessman replied without prompting from the moderator, "Yeah, provided we pay the government a fine of two thousand dollars per employee, every year. That is a tax on business that is simply unfair, and will drive many of this countries best employers out of business."

"What do you have to say to that, Mr. Nichols?" the moderator asked.

"Well, America's hospitals employ more people than any other segment of our economy, so we understand precisely the problem my colleague faces. We face the same thing. And I agree with his comment earlier about doctors and hospitals arguing over who is going to get paid, how much, and for what. That is why we have initiated a program to work in concert with our network of physicians to lower costs and improve quality across the board."

Jack had been afraid that this conversation was going to come to this. Herb laid the first real blow of the night, using the standard talking points designed to convince the public that having their physicians be employees of the hospital would be the best solution. It was critical that he respond, but he knew if he tried to use his standard argument of the importance of independent physicians and the old Hippocratic Oath he would come across as self serving. Instead he elected to take a different approach.

"I can't speak for every physician," Jack said, "no more than Mr. Nichols can speak for every hospital, but I do think I am representative of a large segment of the physician population. We are ready to participate in a meaningful way with hospitals, businessmen, sociologists and any other stakeholders when it comes to fashioning a healthcare policy that is good for patients. This new law does nothing to empower our patients. Instead it serves to enslave them to a government controlled process that will ultimately make quality healthcare more difficult to obtain for every American. And helping fashion a patient centered system to replace Obamacare is precisely what I intend to do when I get to Washington."

The other panel members all tried to respond at the same time, causing the moderator to interrupt and go to commercial. The taping process paused for a few minutes, and Jack took the opportunity to grab his bottle of water.

"Pretty slick the way you got in that part about what you would do if you got to Washington. I'm sure your campaign manager will be proud," Herb said. "Assuming they don't edit that part out."

Jack hadn't spoken to Herb since he announced his intent to run nearly a year before. He was well aware of Herbs support for Sheffield, and he suspected he was responsible for the fact that Jack had found it challenging to gain support from many of his colleagues. Some had even admitted to him that they feared for their jobs if Nichols found out they had supported him in any way.

"It has to be difficult for you," Jack said.

"How's that?" Herb said, taking the bait,

"Always having to take orders from the American Hospital Association, or the CEO of your hospital group, or even ... " he started to say Fitzgerald, but decided not to tip his hand. He had heard about their alliance from his friend Traci Bryan who was still a major part of the administrative staff at the children's hospital. She had also told him to expect both Herb and Horvath to actively fight him, and anyone else who opposed the new healthcare law, because they fully intended to use the accountable care organization contracting process to further pad their salaries, which were already well into seven figures.

Herb just stared at Jack without allowing his expression to change. He was not the least bit amused by this confrontation, but Jack had not intended it to be amusing.

"I think you should be careful, Jack. You could find yourself taking orders sooner than you might think."

****

"We have a new television ad that I need for you to approve," Jason said.

"Okay," Jack replied, "what's it about?"

"It features some of the video we shot of you talking with several individuals at our last fund raiser. Then we have you in the hospital, caring for a couple of kids, then we've incorporated some still shots of you and Elaina in Nicaragua. Those are some very heart warming photos of you and some kids and some of the clinic staff. The final segment is a shot of you testifying in front of Congress It finishes with a picture of you in front of the Capitol building in Washington, with our campaign slogan 'Dr. Roberts - the Right Prescription for Congress' written across the bottom."

After watching the video clip he nodded toward the computer screen and said. "I like it. I appreciate that you didn't over emphasize the mission stuff. Where did you get those pictures from Nicaragua'"

"I got them from your friend Domingo. Elaina gave me his contact info. We figured that by using still images it would convey the distant location impact we were looking for," Jason said. "I think it creates just the right combination of compassion, world experience and social awareness, all from what is obviously a family man."

"I like the part of the narrative about taking your concerns to Washington."

Yeah, that was Angie's idea to correspond with the video of you in front of Ways and Means."

"When do you plan to start running this?"

"We just need to add your audio dub that provides the obligatory approval of this message, then we'll get it out to all the local stations. It should be running by tomorrow evening."

****

With three months to go before the election, the polls showed Jack with a surprising eight percentage point lead over the incumbent democrat. Jason was confident that barring something totally unforeseen they were going to pull off the upset, but he wasn't taking anything for granted. He had witnessed first hand how elections could turn around very quickly.

On the last day of July, Ted Cruz had defeated the heavily favored David Dewhurst for the republican nomination for Senate. "Now can we invite Cruz to one of our events?" Jack asked.

"I will talk to his campaign tomorrow to feel them out," Jason said. "I suspect they may have some interest because it will cost them a lot less to piggy back on to one of our events, and I'm sure they have to be running low on funds given what it cost them to chase down Dewhurst."

Jason had some good friends in Cruz's campaign, and they were very interested in working out a joint appearance in Fort Worth, but the next time their candidate was scheduled to be in the area wasn't for another three weeks. Jason was able to get a commitment for an evening rally on Saturday, August twenty-fifth. He had already reserved the Convention Center Auditorium for that night, two days before the start of the GOP national convention in Tampa, Florida. His original plan had been to invite Mitt Romney, to make a swing through Texas on his way to Florida, but he'd been informed by the presidential campaign that they had no plans to campaign in Texas. They considered Texas to be safely in their column and were instead planning to spend their time and resources in Ohio, Florida and Michigan. Jason had also ask Rick Perry to attend, and was surprised when he received a tentative, yes, from the Governor's office. Three other republican members of Congress from North Texas had already agreed to attend, in support of Jack. Their races were not expected to be close, and they would like nothing better than to see the lone area democratic representative unseated.

"I'm working on a joint appearance with Cruz, and it's looking pretty good. But, I have some news that I think will satisfy you for the time being," Jason said, during his daily briefing with Jack.

"Oh yeah?" Jack said.

"I just got word from the Romney campaign that they plan to endorse you immediately after the convention."

"Wow! That's terrific."

"I suspect we can also get a formal endorsement from Cruz at our event. Then we'll put together a little video ad with both of them saying how much they want you to be there to help them in Washington. That ad, combined with this one will be our strategy for September and October. If we need anything else for the last week or so of the campaign we should have the resources, but it will be tight."

"Sounds good to me," Jack said. "Now, I have to see a few patients this morning before our luncheon in Arlington."

****

"We need to shift gears in your campaign," Fitzgerald said. He had arranged this meeting with Sheffield in a dark restaurant on the south side of town.

"I know," Sheffield responded, "my staff has been looking for something we can nail this guy with, but he appears to be squeaky clean. And that ad he's running, that shows him with all those kids? Its racking up support that I don't see us overcoming."

"Your staff just hasn't been looking hard enough." Fitzgerald countered, then waited for what he knew would be an objection.

"We've looked everywhere. We looked into his military record, his medical practice, his wife, his son ... nothing. The only thing that is even close to a scandal is the fact that his brother is some kind of a genius who works for some bioengineering company in Japan. We weren't able to get anywhere with that, because that's one of the most tightly secured organizations in the world." He paused for another moment then added, "We even hacked into his social media accounts, looking for a girl friend or some shady financial deal, but I'm telling you there's nothing,"

"What if I told you I had something that would derail his campaign overnight? What would that be worth to you?" Fitzgerald asked

"I'd have to see it, but obviously if you're able to take that SOB down, then I would certainly be very indebted to you."

Fitzgerald gave him a sly grin, then said, "Oh, I have exactly what you need, and I'll give it to you. All I ask in return is direct access to you and your votes in this next session. And, of course, any subsequent sessions," He laughed.

****

With ten weeks left in the campaign, the polls showed Jack with nearly a double digit lead. It was less than a week until the GOP Convention and Jason had assured him he would have the endorsements of Governors Perry and Romney within a few days after it was concluded. His joint appearance with Ted Cruz was only three days away, and Cruz appeared on his way to an easy victory in the general election. The campaign couldn't have been going any better.

"Did you see Sheffield's new ad?" Elaina asked.

"No, what's he got to say now?" Jack said.

Before she could answer Jack's cell phone rang.

"Hey Jason," he said casually.

"Where are you?" Jason half shouted.

"I'm at home, why?"

"Stay there. Do not go outside. Do not answer the door. Do not answer the phone. I'm on my way over there right now." Jason hung up, and Jack just stared at his phone.

Elaina tried to explain the one minute television ad she'd seen a half-hour before, but she was so upset it was difficult for Jack to understand what she was saying. Within five minutes Jason pulled up in front of their house, surprised there weren't any reporters there yet. Jack let him in, and he quickly escorted Jack to his study. "I don't want anyone to know you are here, so stay away from the windows."

"What are you talking about?" Jack demanded.

"I'm talking about Sheffield's ad that started running this morning."

"What? Has he taken out a contract on me?"

"You obviously haven't seen it, have you?"

"No, Elaina was trying to tell me something about Nicaragua, but she was so upset I couldn't understand what she was saying."

Jason opened his briefcase and pulled out his computer. "Sit down and watch this." He quickly pulled up the YouTube video that already had seven thousand views. He hit play and enlarged the image to fill the screen.

"Jack Roberts claims to be someone who cares about children." The video images were from Jack's own television ad, showing him at the clinic in Ciudad Sandino. "He even goes to this clinic in Nicaragua, allegedly to care for innocent children. But is that really why he goes to that Central American country?" The background music had started very cheerful and light, but it changes abruptly to a sinister military sound, with heavy drums as the scene changes showing a white Ford bronco in front of a huge iron gate. The driver is speaking to a guard who is holding a machine gun. The car is then allowed through the gate. The video is replaced by a still image of the bronco that had been enlarged and was somewhat grainy. There is no mistaking the driver as Jack accompanied by Elaina. "It appears the doctor has some very close ties to this man, Franco Gutierrez," the video shows a candid still photo of Franco getting out of a black limousine, then there is a closeup of him with his name written beneath it. Then the photo of the group that Domingo had posted on Facebook appeared, zooming in on Jack and Franco in a casual private setting. "Gutierrez is one of the richest men in Central America, and has long been suspected of having ties to organized crime. Gutierrez is also one of the men behind the return to power of this Dictator, Daniel Ortega, in Nicaragua in 2007." The video cuts to a picture of Daniel Ortega. It is an old photo and shows him wearing military fatigues and holding an assault rifle. Additional photos are shown of Ortega with Venezuelan Dictator Hugo Chavez, and then one with Fidel Castro. "Could it be that Dr. Roberts isn't telling us who he really plans to represent in Washington?" Jack is shown in a very unflattering pose, then his image moves to the left third of the screen, with the image of Franco appearing in the center and then Ortega on the right. After a few seconds, the Image changes to one of Sheffield with and American flag in the background, and the music shifts to a instrumental rendition of God Bless America. "Wouldn't it be safer to keep a proven All-American leader in Congress. Vote Sheffield on November sixth."

As the video ended, Jack stared blankly at the blackness. His mind was racing, unable to focus. Who was behind this? How could he explain his relationships? Would anyone believe him?

He didn't even hear Jason when he said, "You have got to remain completely out of sight until we come up with a way to respond. The reporters will be all over this story."

As he was speaking the phone was ringing, and Jason instructed Elaina not to answer it. Even as she was sitting back down beside her husband, the doorbell rang. Clearly they were going to have to come up with a response, and they needed to do it quickly.

****

By late that afternoon, every local news program led their telecast with the rising scandal involving the republican candidate for Congress. They all had remote video crews, and images of Jason's empty car sitting out front of the Roberts' home were being beamed into every home within a hundred miles. The story had even been picked up by CNN and was being discussed by some of their political pundits and talking heads.

"I have to go out there and say something," Jack said in frustration. "The longer I stay hiding in here the more guilty I appear to be."

Jason nodded and said, "Just make the statement we prepared, and don't take any questions."

"I'm going with you," Elaina announced and followed him to the door without hesitation.

As the front door opened, thirty to forty reporters made a mad dash across the lawn. They were followed closely by their cameramen and sound technicians. The were all shouting their questions, as flashes from the still cameras were reflecting off Jack and Elaina's faces in what seemed like one continuous bright light. Jack held up his hands and the crowd slowly became quiet.

"I know you are all here to get my response to what is clearly a vicious and extraordinarily misleading ad being run by my opponent. I want to make it clear that I have absolutely no ties whatsoever to any foreign government, including the current regime in Nicaragua. My wife and I have been involved with a free clinic in that country for twenty years, and that is the full extent of our involvement there. I do know Mr. Franco Gutierrez, but only because I operated on his daughter to repair a heart defect several years ago. I have know knowledge of his political leanings and as far as I know, my campaign has not received any support from him or any of his affiliated companies. I consider this effort on the part of my opponent to be completely baseless and malicious, and I would request that he stop running it immediately."

As soon as Jack was finished with his statements the reporters all began shouting their questions again, demanding more information. "Look," Jack said, "I have told you everything there is to say about this, and I am not going to take any questions at this time." He turned to Elaina and followed her back into the house amid the torrent of questions and continued flashes of light from the photographers.

"I don't think they were satisfied with that," Jack said to Jason as Elaina broke down crying.

"Why is our relationship with Franco and Gabriella even an issue?" she demanded through her tears.

Jack held her in his arms, but he was unable to offer any answers.

****

"Ted Cruz's campaign just called and cancelled," Jason announced the following morning.

"Why?" Jack asked, but already knowing the answer.

"They described you as, radioactive!"

"What can we do? I've offered what I thought was a very reasonable response. What more do they want?"

"It isn't about what the media wants," Jason said. "This is a story, and they will continue to follow it as long as they believe there is something more to it." He looked at Jack and asked, "There isn't any more to it, is there?"

"Of course not! I can't believe you would even ask such a thing."

"If there is you can bet they will find it, so the best thing to do is get anything and everything out in the open."

"I have told you, and them, everything there is."

"Okay, then I suggest you go back on television and tell the public once more, everything about your relationship with Franco Gutierrez. I will arrange a one on one interview with one of the guys over a channel eight. They have been very fair to us over there, and I think you'll get a chance to tell your side of the story."

****

The thirty minute interview on channel eight, on Sunday morning, had gone about as well as Jason could have hoped. He felt that Jack had done as good a job of damage control as was possible. But when the weekly polls came out on Monday, The dip he had anticipated was more like a crash. Jack had gone from being up nine points to being down by three.

"There isn't anything else to do but get back out on the campaign trail," he told Jack.

"I guess I'll have to stop seeing patients and turn everything over to George until after the election."

"That is what I would recommend if you want to get back in this race."

For the next five weeks Jack made hundreds of campaign stops. He visited every lunch counter and coffee shop in the district. He and some of Jason's staff walked door to door in parts of the district that were heavily hispanic. Jason's research had shown that it was the Latino community that had been the most influenced by what they were now calling "The Franco Ad" so, Jason thought he needed to try and restore their trust. He was amazed by the number of doors that were slammed in his face. People seemed to have had their minds made up as a result of a one minute television ad that implied that Jack was somehow connected with a Central American Dictator.

The Romney endorsement was now totally out of the question. His campaign wasn't interested in even talking to Jason. Rick Perry's office had likewise declined to even comment on Jack's candidacy. Jason had even lost some of his volunteers, presumably because of the ongoing scandal. Even so, when the polls came out three weeks before election day, Jack had recovered some of the ground he had lost. At the height of the scandal he was down five points, but with numerous television appearances and radio interviews, the gap had been closed and he was back almost even with Sheffield.

****

"Are you ready for the knock out punch?" Fitzgerald asked over the phone.

"I'm pretty sure we've got him on the ropes already," Sheffield chuckled. "My people tell me they think we're up by at least five."

"In my experience, you never rely on things like 'pretty sure' or what other people think. The only way to make sure a snake is actually dead is to cut off its head."

"What are you suggesting? There's only sixteen days to go."

"Precisely! There is no way he will be able to recover from what I have planned. And what makes it even sweeter is the fact that it comes at a price of only four thousand dollars." Fitzgerald wasn't leaving anything to chance, and in reality he would have paid a hundred times that much to get even with that bastard who threatened him. "What I want you to do is, tomorrow have your staff ..."

****

With only two weeks left in the campaign, Jack was working sixteen hour days, and he had regained some of his personal optimism.

"I agree Jack, yes, we can still win," Jason said. "Many people don't make up their minds until the last minute, so there is every reason to believe it can still happen, but we've run out of money, so its pretty much on your shoulders at this point."

"I'm up for it!" he replied. "The worst that can happen is we go down trying."

Jason's phone rang, and it was one of his assistants. He turned on the television as the young woman suggested. He switched to three different stations and on each one there it was. Sheffield's latest ad. It showed the video of Jack outside his front door telling reporters that "my campaign has not received any support from him or any of his affiliated companies." Then they showed an official campaign finance document, with two highlighted lines showing donations of two thousand dollars each, from Nicaraguan companies. The names were both allegedly subsidiaries of Gutierrez Enterprises.

On Tuesday, November sixth, 2012 Jack lost his bid for Congress fifty-three percent to forty-seven percent. The pain of that defeat was made even worse as Obama was also re-elected to the White House. Jack knew there was no longer any real hope of reversing the destruction of his profession, and the one to which his son was committed.

****

"I know you're devastated," Elaina said as she wrapped her arms around his slumped shoulders just before they walked out onto the stage of the Worthington Hotel Ballroom, "but things have a way of working out,"

"I can't see any way this is going to work out now," he said, his voice was almost inaudible.

"I think this is a sign," she said

"Maybe so," Jack replied, as he looked up into her glistening green eyes. "but its one I'm having a very difficult time understanding."

CHAPTER 9

The stresses of the campaign had clearly taken their toll on Jack. He hadn't played racket ball with Buzz, his longtime friend, for more than a year, and the lack of exercise combined with the countless late night dinner meetings, had caused him to gain nearly twenty pounds. His comfortable smile and enthusiasm for work had been replaced by a visible fatigue, and the gray hair that had been mostly confined to his temples just a year before, now gave his entire head a classic salt and pepper look. After the election, Elaina had asked him frequently if there was something the matter, and he always replied with, "I'm fine, and I'm going to be fine." Despite his insistence, she sensed he was hiding his deeper disappointment.

"Don't you think it would be a good idea for us to get away from here for a while?" she asked, as they sat at the breakfast table. It had been two days since the election and Jack was preparing to return to his practice the following Monday.

"No, I need to get back to work," he explained without looking up from the sports page of the newspaper. He brought the edges of the paper together briefly, and then continued reading an article on college football that was allowing his mind to escape the disappointing defeat he had suffered. "It's time to turn the page, and I don't want to delay the process any longer."

While Jack readily admitted he was tired, he hadn't yet admitted, even to himself, what was really weighing on him. The idea that his patriotism had been questioned, and that he had been cast as a liar in those damned political ads, filled him with an unfamiliar anger and distrust.

"I just thought we might take a long weekend and run down to San Antonio or somewhere, just to get away," she suggested.

Jack jerked down the paper and glared angrily toward her. "I'm not running anywhere! And, I don't need to get away!" His words had a bite to them that she had not expected.

"I just thought ..."

"Well, don't!" he barked. "I just need to get back to work." He immediately regretted taking out his frustration on his wife as he saw her recoil. He quickly resumed reading the paper, knowing he would apologize to her later, but he wasn't prepared to deal with what was really bothering him.

****

On Monday morning Jack decided to run by the children's hospital before going into the office. He hadn't performed any surgery there for more than two months, so he obviously didn't have any patients in the hospital, but he thought it would be best to get back into his usual routine of making rounds first. Instead of seeing patients, he planned to go by the OR, the surgical ICU and each nursing station to thank all the nurses who had supported his candidacy, and to let them know he would soon be getting back to his pre-election routine.

He was generally greeted with smiles and offers of support. Clearly, most of the people who knew him were genuinely disappointed by the outcome of the election, but there were a few who seemed to make a point of avoiding him. Perhaps they chose to believe that he was the corrupt political wannabe that Sheffield portrayed him to be.

"Hi Dr. Roberts," Traci Bryan said, as she passed him in the hall on the way to her office.

"Hi Traci," he replied. "How are you this morning?"

"Better than you I suspect."

"Oh, I'm just fine. I think its probably for the best," he replied, trying to convince himself he likely wouldn't have been able to make much of a difference in Washington anyway, since there was no hope of repealing the healthcare law with Obama still in the White House.

"You got a minute?" she asked.

"Sure," he said as he followed her into her office.

"Have a seat," she said as she hung her coat on the back of the door before closing it. Traci was the only person in administration that he felt he could trust. Perhaps it was because she had worked for many years as a nurse before becoming involved with actually running the hospital. "I know you're disappointed you didn't win, and just so you know, I voted for you," she said with a smile.

"I appreciate that, but it appears that politics is more of a blood sport than I had anticipated."

"That's what I wanted to talk to you about," she offered, as she sat down casually behind her desk. "I was appalled at the way Horvath talked about you to our staff."

"What did he say?" Jack asked, not sure what Traci was talking about.

"On more than one occasion over the last few months, he told the administrative team and the middle management staff that it was people like you who were going to destroy this hospital. He said that without the expanded Medicaid coverage provided for under the new law, we would likely not be able to continue in operation. He viewed you as a threat, especially if you were able to win the election and take your opposition to Obamacare to Washington."

"That doesn't really surprise me," Jack said. "He and I have never seen eye to eye on anything that I can recall."

"I know. I can't say as I agree with him on much either, but I got the feeling that there was more to it than just a difference of opinion."

"What do you mean?"

"The morning after the election he called a meeting of the entire management staff, right down to the individual department managers, and thanked everyone for the part they played in defeating you and in re-electing President Obama."

"Wow! That's pretty strange," Jack replied.

"That's not all," she said. "He told us that now that all the children of Texas would be covered by insurance, he was planning a major marketing initiative to attract as many patients as possible from throughout the state. He said that the hospital was planning to work in concert with the big physician group to become the sole provider of pediatric services for every child covered under the new law."

"That doesn't surprise me either," Jack said, "that's been his and Fitzgerald's plan from the beginning."

"I know," she agreed, "but, what I found most disturbing, and the main reason I wanted to talk with you, is what he said about independent docs, like you." She paused and Jack leaned forward in his chair, in anticipation. "He said that the medical staff was considering closing its membership, and gradually moving toward a completely integrated system, where only those physicians who were contracted with the group would be allowed to practice here."

"Well, he may try to do that, but I don't think he can, at least not in the short term," Jack replied. "There are still quite a few of us old guys around who will resist anything like that. Who would do the heart surgery? This place would have a tough time making it without the income it rakes in from those patients."

"He hasn't completely given up on the idea of getting the Dallas group to come here," she said, "and I know he's pushing Kent Hinson, the VP of provider relations, to change George Ferguson's mind."

Jack wondered whether George might be susceptible to their offers, now that he was busier than he'd ever been. He probably could have locked up his colleague with a long term contract with a non-compete clause, but he didn't think those kind of arrangements were appropriate between physicians. If George didn't want to stay with him, the last thing he wanted to do was to force him to either stay and be unhappy, or move more than fifty miles away, as was called for in most non-compete contracts.

"I appreciate the heads-up, Traci," he said. "I know you're sticking your neck out, just telling me this."

"Like I've told you many times, Dr. Roberts," she said, "as a nurse, I really agree with what you are doing, trying to maintain an independent practice. I think its best for the kids we treat here, but I need this job, so I can't afford to openly oppose Horvath."

"I know that," Jack replied sympathetically. He understood that since Traci's divorce she was burdened with having to help put her daughter through college. "You don't need to worry. I won't say anything to anyone about this."

"One of these days, when I don't need the money, I'm going to tell that SOB just exactly what he can do with this job."

They shared a brief laugh as Jack stood and headed out the door. As he was walking down the hallway, he passed Horvath, who was walking toward his own office.

"Morning Jack," Horvath said with an uncomfortable tone, "what are you doing here?"

"Planning to get back to work," Jack said sensing Horvath's suspicion. "I was just checking with Ms. Bryan to make sure I hadn't missed any policy changes while I've been away."

"I see," Horvath looked suspiciously back toward Traci's open door. "So, did she answer your questions?"

"Yeah, she said nothing much has changed."

"That's true," he said with satisfaction. "Everything is moving along quite nicely." Then he added, "Sorry to hear about the election results, but it's good to have you back."

Jack knew he was lying, but once more decided to play along. "It's good to be back."

****

THE CONFLICT

The airport was especially busy this time of year, and Ben's flight from Tokyo's Narita Airport had been delayed. It had been diverted to San Francisco because of weather earlier in the day that caused DFW to be shut down temporarily. Weather delays in North Texas were not unusual, but they were typically due to thunderstorms in the spring and fall. On rare occasions, like this one, the area would receive a paralyzing blanket of white, and the airport was simply not prepared to handle it. Following a four inch snowfall overnight, all runways were shut down, but as the clear morning sky allowed the sun to raise the temperature into the middle forties, the snow was almost completely gone by noon, and the airport reopened just after noon. Ben's plane finally arrived at four o'clock, nearly eight hours later than scheduled.

"Welcome home," Jack said, as he hugged his brother.

"Thanks, that was a long flight." Ben said. "What's for dinner?"

"What do you want?" Jack asked with a laugh.

"Tex-Mex! I've been craving some chicken enchiladas for at least six months."

"We can do that," Jack said as he picked up his brother's suitcase and headed for the terminal D parking garage. Elaina was waiting in the car, and when she saw the two men walking toward her she got out to greet her brother-in-law. He looked the same as he always had, a bit thinner than seemed healthy, and despite his attempted smile, he always appeared too serious. It was as if he was continuously thinking about some major problem that needed solving.

"Hi, Ben," she said warmly as she hugged him. He responded with a polite one arm embrace, holding his briefcase to his side with the other.

"Hello, Elaina," he replied. "You are looking well."

"Thank you," she said with a smile. "You haven't aged a bit."

"Unlike my brother, huh?"

"Now, that's not nice," Jack said as he climbed behind the wheel and headed for the south end of the airport.

****

On Christmas Day, Jack drove out to Hurst to pick-up his mom and bring her to their home. She hadn't felt comfortable driving the freeway for several years, and at ninety-two, he didn't think she had any business driving period, but completely taking away the freedom that her car provided wasn't something he was prepared to fight over.

The reunion between Faye and Ben was especially hard for Jack to watch. Her progressive memory loss had become a major challenge. When Ben greeted her at the front door, she didn't recognize him initially. Once Jack explained that he was her youngest son, she acted as if she hadn't needed the explanation.

"Why don't you come to see me," she pleaded.

"Well, Mother," Ben said, "I'm living in Japan."

"That's no excuse for not visiting your mother," she reasoned. "I may not be around that much longer you know."

"Oh, Mom," he objected, "you're not going anywhere."

"I am too going somewhere. I'm going to join your father," she replied.

Ben looked at Jack, questioning whether there was something going on that he didn't know about.

"She's been talking about going to be with Dad for the last several years," Jack explained.

"And don't you try and stop me either," she protested. "If anybody tries to put me on one of those machines to keep me alive, I'll come back to haunt each and everyone of you."

Jack laughed, trying to lighten the mood, but Ben sat silently, never having heard his mother talk so openly about such things.

After they finished opening their gifts, Jack and Ben went outside on the patio. It was a beautiful sunny day, and the temperature had risen to almost seventy degrees. They sat down outside the guest house where Ben was staying, and talked about their mom. She was still living alone in the same house where they had been raised. Jack had tried to get her to consider moving to a retirement community nearer their home in Fort Worth, but she would hear nothing of it. He'd even offered to have her come live with them, now that David was out of the house, but she didn't want to climb the stairs to a second floor room, and she wasn't comfortable in the guest house. She had agreed to allow her next door neighbor to come by and check on her everyday, for which Jack secretly paid the middle aged woman two hundred dollars a month.

"So, how are things going with your super secret project? What's it been now, four years since you moved to Tokyo?" Jack asked.

"Five," Ben responded. "I can't believe how long it has taken, but we are very close to having our system ready for market."

"Why is this thing such a big secret?"

"Mr. Naryama doesn't trust any other medical device manufacturers, especially his competitors in Japan," Ben explained. "He has insisted on making certain every element of our system is covered by every possible international patent before allowing anyone to even talk about the concept."

"Naryama? I knew a guy by that name when I was stationed in Tokyo, what was it, 1982?" Jack tried to recall. "He was a surgical instrument manufacturer."

"Really? You knew Shinti Naryama thirty years ago?" Ben asked with obvious disbelief.

"I don't know if its the same guy or not. The man I knew built my favorite custom needle holder, and he provided me with a set of instruments to do an emergent operation on a newborn in the military hospital," Jack explained. "He should be in his late fifties by now."

"That was definitely Shinti. I can't believe it," Ben said shaking his head. "All this time I've been collaborating with him half way around the world, and I had no idea you two knew each other. They did an exhaustive background check before offering me the position, so he must have known you were my brother."

"Oh, he probably didn't remember me," Jack said.

"Are you kidding? Naryama remembers everything, and I do mean everything. He is a brilliant man, and he has a true photographic memory."

"So, if you guys have been working so closely for the last five years, I wonder why he never mentioned that he knew me?" Jack questioned.

"I don't know, but when I get back home next week I'm sure going to find out," Ben said with resolution.

"Home?" Jack asked. "Are you now a permanent resident of Japan?"

"I don't know about permanent," Ben replied, "but it sure feels like home."

"So," Jack began, "Are you going to tell me anything about what you've been doing?"

Ben thought for a moment before responding. "I guess since you know Naryama, and since we are so close to having a working prototype, I can tell you a little about it, but you have to swear not to tell anybody about it."

"I'm not going to say anything to anyone," Jack promised.

"We have developed an entirely new surgical concept," Ben spoke now with an excitement in his voice that Jack had never heard coming from his brother. "We call it the MATRICS platform."

Jack nodded his head slowly, waiting for his genius brother to offer him some details that he could understand.

"MATRICS stands for minimal access totally robotic intra cardiac system."

"What? Intra-Cardiac Robot?" Jack asked, not sure he understood.

"You are going to love it, when you see it," Ben said.

Just then David came out on to the patio to greet his dad and the uncle he hadn't seen for two years. Ben hadn't been able to get away from work last Christmas, and he hadn't made it to David and Amy's wedding.

"Hey there, David," Ben said with surprise.

"Hi Uncle B." David replied with a broad smile. "I haven't seen you in a long time. Welcome back to the good old USA."

Ben hugged his nephew, who was three inches taller than him, and sported a considerably more athletic physique. "It's good to see you. I'm really sorry I wasn't able to make it to your wedding, but I did bring you guys a belated wedding gift."

Ben went into the guest house and in a couple of minutes he returned with an envelope. "This is not to be opened now," he instructed. "You must wait. I'll let you know when, but it may not be for a few years."

"I don't understand," David replied. "Why can't I open it now?"

"Because it isn't ready," Ben explained.

David looked at the plain white enveloped that had "Mr. and Mrs. David Roberts" written in calligraphy, and under it were a series of expertly drawn Japanese letters. "What does this say in Japanese?"

"It says 'Good fortune comes to those who wait."

"Well, good fortune would certainly be welcome. The sooner the better," David said as he laughed and placed the envelope in his jacket pocket. "Thanks," he said as he shook his uncle's hand.

"You are very welcome," Ben said, very sincerely, before adding, "Where is that wife of yours?"

"She's inside with Mom and Grandma."

"Well let's go in, I want to see her," Ben suggested. Once David turned to head for the door, Ben spoke again to Jack. "We'll talk more later."

All afternoon, and into the evening, Jack kept wondering what in the world his brother meant by intra-cardiac robotic system. Finally around ten o'clock David and Amy left for their home in Dallas. Amy thanked Ben for the wedding gift, and then added, "Whatever it is I'm sure we'll be able to make good use of it."

Since it wasn't that far out of their way, David offered to take his grandmother home, saving Jack the trip. Ben told her he would stop by to see her again on his way to the airport in a couple of days. As they drove away, Elaina looked at Jack and said, "I'm exhausted. I'm going to bed."

"I'll be up after a while. Ben and I have some catching up to do," Jack said kissing her softly on the cheek.

When she was gone, Jack turned to Ben and asked, "Can I fix you something to drink?"

"You know I don't drink," he said. "Alcohol kills brain cells, you know?"

Jack laughed softly toward his brother then said, "I don't know about that." He went into the kitchen to get some ice.

"Perhaps that scotch you love so much has already destroyed the part of your brain where that information was stored," Ben offered. "I'll just have a glass of tea if you have some."

Jack returned with a small cocktail glass with two ice cubes, and a glass of iced tea. As he handed Ben the tea he said, "You know the caffeine in that tea can cause early onset dementia."

"Ben smiled and asked, "How early?"

Jack poured himself a generous measure of his favorite eighteen year old Macallan, then settled into his familiar chair across from the couch where Ben was already seated. "So, you were about to tell me about this intra-cardiac robotic system?"

"Yeah, like I said, we just about have our first prototype finished. We plan to try it out in the animal lab starting in a few months."

"What exactly is it?" Jack asked impatiently.

"This is an entirely new robotic technology that will allow major procedures to be performed on the heart while it is still beating. It will lower the cost and the risk of many of the procedures you do. We believe we can have it ready to at least start the FDA approval process by this time next year, but it will take years to get it through the human trial phase." Ben sounded very excited up to the point when he began talking about getting approval from the federal drug administration. At that point his voice began to trail off just a bit.

"You haven't told me anything yet," Jack said, knowing his brother sometimes allowed his mind to get ahead of his mouth.

"Oh, yeah, sorry," Ben replied. "We have created a miniaturized robotic system using some of the latest carbon fiber nanotechnologies. It can be deployed on the end of a vascular catheter into any chamber of the heart."

"What's so different about it? Jack asked. "Sounds like some of the catheter based systems we already use."

"Well, first of all it is equipped with a micro-camera and a powerful xenon light source that provides direct visualization of the interior of the heart."

"That's not possible," Jack said. "You can't see through blood."

"That is just one of the issues we had to overcome."

"How?"

"We use an infrared wave length, and the camera isn't your typical light gathering device," Ben explained. "Its a bit complicated for someone without a PhD in quantum mechanics to understand, but let's just say we can see through the blood just fine."

"You're right, I don't understand, but if you say you can provide an image of the inside of the heart I believe you, but providing an image is not the same thing as actually doing something once your in there."

"That is true," Ben conceded, "but we have developed an array of devices that can be deployed through a separate channel. We've got a Neodymium YAG laser that can be used to cut through tissues and we have a mechanism to deliver a new type of highly efficient tissue adhesive. We also have an entire array of umbrellas and patches and plugs that can be used to cover or fill a wide variety of vascular defects."

"That all sounds exciting, but so much of what I do can't be done on a beating heart. There is just too much motion," Jack said.

"That was the second major obstacle we had to overcome," Ben agreed.

"Okay, I'm listening," Jack said with a smile.

"We use a combination of image synchronization and a stabilization software to give the surgeon an image that appears to be completely stationary. I think you'll be impressed when you see it."

"I'm impressed just hearing about it," Jack admitted. "I'm just not sure how its possible to make the gadgets you describe strong enough to be usable, yet small enough to put them in through a tiny catheter?"

"Like I said," Ben offered, "we use the most sophisticated carbon fiber technology. The nanotechnology makes it possible to produce cables the size of a human hair that are stronger than ones made of titanium ten times larger."

Jack was trying to get his mind around the concept of intra-cardiac surgery without the need to stop the heart or putting the patient on bypass. "Wait a minute," Jack said as if he'd found a fatal flaw in the idea. "You said this was a robotic process."

"I was wondering how long it was going to take for you to get around to asking about that."

"Well?"

"It is impossible for anyone to simultaneously use all the components of the system with the kind of precision required. That is why we created a computerized control panel where the surgeon has total control over the robotic manipulation and deployment of every element," Ben said, sounding like a teenager describing his newest stereo system to one of his envious buddies.

"I guess I can understand now why you've been over there for five years."

"We aren't finished by any means," Ben said. "We still have several major issues to work out in the animal lab. It will likely be another six to eight months before we are ready to begin clinical trials."

"Who do you have lined up to do the trials?"

"That is the newest problem," Ben now sounded dejected. "We had planned to use one of the university groups in Germany, but a competitor company brought a similar idea into the European market last year. They weren't even close to being ready, but they convinced an Italian group to use their system on five patients. Unfortunately, the first two died of intra-operative complications, so they were forced to suspend their effort."

"I'm surprised I didn't hear anything about it," Jack said.

THE CONFLICT

"The whole thing was being done in secrecy," Ben explained. "Nobody knew about it but the principles, and the Italians tried to keep it quiet after those two disasters. Eventually, word of those deaths spread throughout the European academic community, so now there's an unofficial moratorium on any new robotic technology across all of Europe."

"Why don't you get somebody here in the states to do the trials?"

"Getting any new product through the FDA has become nearly impossible. The guidelines that must be met before clinical trials can even begin are ridiculous. It would take at least five years, and probably more like eight from where we are today, just to get approval to start phase two clinical trials, and that would be at least another two year process. The phase three trials would take two or three more years, so, in a best case scenario we would be at least ten years getting this product to market. There is no possibility of making that work financially. Naryama already has more than one hundred million invested in the development of MATRICS, and he has calculated the cost of getting this through the FDA would be another quarter of a billion. Plus," Ben added, "under the new healthcare law, our device will be subject to the medical device tax, further increasing the cost to any hospital that might be interested. The combination of all these factors make it impossible to bring this product to the American market."

Jack just shook his head. "I wonder how they got the current generation of surgical robots through?" Jack asked in a rhetorical manner.

"They were brought in before this latest round of federal restrictions and taxes were introduced," Ben said, having reviewed that process several years before. "Even so, it took that company nearly ten years to get their current device to market."

"Our hospital administrator bought one of those robots a couple years back. I think it cost about two million bucks, and that didn't include the disposable components or the annual maintenance fees. They tried to get me to use that technology to do some of my thoracoscopic procedures, but I refused. I saw it as nothing more than a marketing gimmick, at least for the procedures I do." Jack explained "Plus, the hospital charges somewhere around twenty-five thousand dollars per case, in addition to all the other routine OR costs. That's how they're trying to recoup their investment, but I'm not sure how they will be able to make it work with all the cost cutting that is coming under the new law."

"I agree," Ben said, "That is why that company has been pushing to get as many robots installed as they possibly can, before the new law goes into full effect. They are selling them based on financial projections that just won't be there a couple of years from now."

"Even if the robot makes it possible to do a few procedures, like prostatectomy, I just don't see the value of it for most of the operations its currently being used for," Jack said.

"You're right, and now we're seeing new complications with the robot that are occurring because the surgeon has no tactile feedback. There is no sense of touch ... none. The surgeon can't feel any resistance through those motorized operating arms, and there have been numerous reports of instruments being inadvertently pushed through organs and blood vessels without the surgeon even being aware, with disastrous results."

"Yes, I know," Jack replied. "That is one of the things that worries me the most about any robotic system."

Ben smiled broadly as his brother took another sip from his drink.

"What?" Jack asked suddenly as he saw his brother's demeanor change.

"That is the final part of the MATRICS platform that I'm working on," Ben said proudly.

"What do you mean, final part?" Jack asked, confused by Ben's reference.

"Are you familiar with the warning systems that are now being used in some of the newer cars, that tell you when another car is behind you, or when you've wandered over into another lane?"

"Yeah, sure. Elaina and I looked at a new Lexus a couple of months ago. It feels pretty weird when the seat vibrates for a second, but it definitely gets your attention."

"They are using similar technology in some of the newest prosthetic limbs, to allow for haptic feedback when an artificial finger comes into contact with any object, allowing the person wearing it to not only feel that they are touching something, but even the relative texture of the object. It is really cool stuff."

"Don't tell me you've incorporated that into MATRICS."

"That is precisely what we're doing, and I just about have the process perfected. That's why we're not quite ready to go to clinical trials. Like I said, it will be another six to eight months."

Jack sat stunned by the details of what his brother had developed. "This sounds like science fiction," he said, unable to get his mind around all the possibilities. "How did you ... ?"

"What do you think I've been doing for the last five years, sitting on my butt?" Ben said with a laugh. "I figured I needed to come up with something that you could use to fix the hearts of little kids, without having to cut into their chests the way those barbarians cut into mine."

****

Three days after Christmas, Jack took his brother back to the airport to catch his flight to Tokyo. On their way, they stopped by to see their mother, as Ben had promised. The old house looked a bit more run down than he'd remembered on the outside, but virtually nothing had changed inside. Perhaps a bit more clutter, but the furniture was the same, and even the pictures on the wall were unchanged.

The two brothers spent about an hour and a half at the kitchen table, talking more to each other than to her, but she was satisfied serving them some rather stale cookies and some overly sweet iced tea. It was obvious she enjoyed having them back in her house, even if it was only for a brief time.

"I guess we need to go, Mom," Ben said. "My flight leaves in two hours, and I need to get through security."

"When will I get to see you again?" she asked sadly.

"I don't know, Mom," he replied reluctantly. "Probably not until next Christmas, but it is possible I might be able to make it back this summer. It just depends on work."

"I miss you," she said as a tear ran slowly down her weathered cheek. This was the first time Ben had seen his mother cry since shortly after his father died, nearly fifty years earlier.

"I miss you too, Mom," he spoke softly as he hugged her gently, feeling the frailty that now possessed her shrunken frame.

"I love you so much." Her weak voice sounded even more feeble as her words came haltingly through her tears.

"I love you too, Mom," Ben replied, sounding more strong than he felt in an effort to compensate for her frailty.

As he released her and turned toward the door, she spoke again with a bit more strength. "Wait a minute. There is something I want to give you." She stepped over to the coffee table that was cluttered with mail, some of which had never been opened. From the shelf under the glass top she pulled out an old scrapbook. "I was going through these old photos the other day and I found one that I want you to have."

She turned a few of the old plastic covered pages before finding the one she was looking for. As she pulled the old photo out from under the slightly yellowed plastic, she said "I don't think you've ever seen this picture. Your father was so upset when he saw this picture in the Fort Worth Star Telegram on that Sunday, he threw it away. I called the paper, and ask them if I could get a copy of the original picture, and they sent this to me about a week later in the mail. I never showed your father, and I guess I never showed it to you either."

She offered him the old black and white print, and he took it from her trembling hand. The image was of President Kennedy bending over slightly and shaking the hand of eleven year old Ben, flanked by his father and sixteen year old Jack.

Ben was stunned. "I had no ..." he said.

"I know, I probably should have given it to you a long time ago, but I put it in this scrapbook before your father died, and I forgot all about it until the other day. I want you to keep it."

"Thank you, Mom. I will have it framed and keep it on my desk as a reminder of a different time. Thank you so much."

As Jack pulled the car out on to the street, Ben asked, "Had you ever seen that photo?"

"No," he replied, "I had no idea that such a picture even existed."

"It is so sad," Ben said.

"What do you mean?" Jack asked.

"Watching Mom getting old. The way she seems to live her life in the past. It's like she doesn't have anything to motivate her going forward, so she just keeps reliving her memories."

"I see that all the time in my older patients," Jack said. "I think some of them are just too tired to make an effort to be productive, but more often I think they feel inadequate. I've had several older people tell me they are ready to die. They say that their lives have no meaning any more."

"That's really a shame," Ben said, "because, just sharing their experiences could make a big difference in the lives of younger people."

"I'm not sure the younger generation cares to listen to us old farts," Jack said, recalling some of the speeches he had given to college age gatherings back during the campaign. "I wish I had more time to sit down and talk with Mom about the things she's seen in her life, but it seems there's never any time."

They both sat silently for several minutes as Jack guided the car onto the freeway toward the big airport.

"I get the feeling I'm not going to see her again," Ben said, almost in a whisper.

****

Jack had been elected President of the Association of Thoracic Surgeons back in November, but his two year term didn't start until January, 2013. He was now responsible for conducting the monthly teleconferences of the ATS board of trustees, as well as the organizations annual meeting in Denver. Traditionally, that meeting was dedicated to sharing the latest clinical information, with all the speakers being thought leaders of the profession, but in recent years attendance had declined significantly. The feedback they had received indicated that surgeons were having to manage their budgets more closely, and traveling to meetings was not only expensive, but it took them away from their practices for several days. In addition, most practicing surgeons were more concerned about the impact of all the new regulations that were being implemented under the new law, than they were about the latest clinical studies.

"I think we need to include a presentation on the political situation in Washington during our next meeting," Jack offered during the January board teleconference.

One of the members quickly agreed, but then added, "I think most of our members are aware of what is happening in DC, but what they don't know is what is being done on their behalf."

Another member said, "I'm not sure I know what, if anything, is actually being done for us."

Jack responded, "I agree. We haven't really had much of a presence on capitol hill, and as a result the only thing we have to report is what is being done to us."

The newly elected vice-president, George McCarty, an academic surgeon at Georgetown University Hospital in DC, spoke up. "I think we have a great opportunity to participate in an on-going dialog as the healthcare law is gradually implemented. As you know, I live here in the Washington area, and I'm happy to meet with members of Congress and their staff anytime the opportunity arises."

Jack recalled vividly how George had been an ardent advocate for the public option, back during their debate over the AMA's stance on healthcare reform. "Perhaps before any of us goes to Congress on behalf of the ATS, we need to come up with an organizational policy. That was what I had asked for prior to testifying before Ways and Means, three and a half years ago. Without a formal position on issues like the expansion of Medicaid, and the Independent Payment Advisory Board, and a variety of other potentially damaging parts of the new law, I don't see how any of us can claim to represent our organization's position."

"I believe we will look foolish opposing things that have already passed," McCarty said. "We need to move on, to help ensure that thoracic surgeons are included in the discussion as implementation proceeds over the next few years."

"I'm sure there are others who agree with you, George," Jack replied, "but in my conversations with members across the country, most of them asked what are we going to do to fight that implementation process."

"I agree," replied another member. "We should be letting those guys in the House, and especially those in the Senate, know how concerned we are about the impact of this law on our profession and our current and future members."

"Our profession will be just fine," McCarty replied. "Provided we work with this administration. I fear that if we are perceived as obstructionists, we will find our road will be filled with even more obstacles. The Department of Health and Human Services has reached out to me on more than one occasion, asking for help implementing their policies, and I think we should be there, as an organization, to assist in any way we can."

"You know the country is very divided on this issue," Jack said. "Although the Supreme Court decision declared the healthcare act to be constitutional as a tax, it also allowed each state to decide whether to accept the expansion of Medicaid. This has created a huge controversy here in Texas, as I'm sure it has in other states. The democrats in our state house want to see Texas create an insurance exchange, and expand the Medicaid roles, but the republicans remain strongly opposed. Our republican governor has vowed to not accept the additional funds from Washington, but there is growing pressure from the other side. They claim the only responsible thing to do to deal with the economics of caring for millions of illegal aliens, as well as the urban poor, is to take the offer of more federal funds."

"They should simply recognize the reality of this situation," George said. "This is a new system whose time has come, and there is no point in resisting. The outcome is inevitable. Sooner or later we will have a single payer for healthcare."

Jack wanted to hear from other board members, but the phone line remained silent. Finally he said, "Well, I'm not sure we are going to reach a consensus this evening, so perhaps we should take up the subject of developing an organizational position during our next meeting."

****

The mid-February Saturday was the coldest morning of the year. Elaina was slow to get out of bed, but around nine she made her way into the kitchen. Jack was already dressed and was sitting at the table reading the paper and sipping his customary Diet Dr Pepper. Just as she started to fix herself a cup of coffee the phone rang.

"Hello," she said.

"This is Sally Maples," the woman spoke swiftly, "is Dr. Roberts there?"

"Yes," Elaina said with concern in her voice, "let me get him."

She covered the phone with her hand and said, "Jack, it's for you, it's Sally Maples."

Jack recognized the name immediately as the woman he was paying two hundred dollars a month to check in on his mother everyday. He jumped up from the table and quickly made his way to the phone.

"Yes, Ms. Maples," he said louder than he'd intended, "is everything okay?"

"No, sir," she said sadly. "That's why I'm calling. I went by to check on your mother this morning and I found her on the floor of her kitchen, unresponsive." The woman sounded a bit out of breath as she told the story rapidly. "I called nine, one, one, and the paramedics were here within about three minutes. They have taken her to the hospital. I have no idea what's wrong. I'm so sorry Dr. Roberts." As her voice trailed off, Jack could tell that she was crying and was blaming herself for something she couldn't have prevented.

"Thank you so much, Ms. Maples. It sounds like you did everything you could. I will call the hospital as soon as we hang up."

"They said she was still alive when they left here," she offered in a hopeful tone.

"Okay," Jack said hurriedly. "I'll take care of everything from here." He then thought to add, "Would you please lock-up the house when you leave?"

"Of course,"

As he hung up the phone he turned to Elaina and said, "It's Mom."

She knew what he meant and nodded. "Do you want me to go with you?"

"No, I'll call you when I know more."

Those were almost the same words she'd used when she'd called David, three years earlier after her own mother had been admitted to the hospital for what proved to be a fatal heart attack. She replayed that day of turmoil in her head hundreds of times, and she only hoped that if Jack's mother was in a similar condition that she wouldn't have to endure being resuscitated multiple times, before they finally let her go.

On his way to the hospital Jack called the emergency department. After being transferred twice and spending several minutes on hold, he was eventually connected to the ER doctor who was taking care of his mom.

"I understand you are Mrs. Robert's son?" the young man asked in a very detached voice.

"Yes," Jack replied, "I'm on my way out there from Fort Worth. What can you tell me about her condition."

"Well, I'm not allowed to tell you anything at this point. I'm not authorized to release any information without her direction, and that has not yet been obtained."

"Are you kidding me?" Jack spouted. "I'm her son. I have power of attorney, and I am a physician. What is going on with my mother?"

"As a physician, you know the rules," he said coldly. "I cannot discuss anything with you over the phone without her specific direction. All I can tell you is that she is here."

Jack understood the privacy laws, but this was ridiculous. His mother might be dead for all he knew, and this moron wasn't going to provide him with any information. "You are aware of her advanced directive, aren't you?"

"No," he said, sounding somewhat surprised. "We don't have anything on file under her name."

Jack had discussed with his mother on several occasions the need for her to file her advanced medical directive with the hospital and the ambulance service, and he had been fairly certain that she had done so. "I hope you guys aren't doing CPR on her."

"Again, sir, I'm not at liberty to discuss any aspect of her care with you at this time."

"I'll be there in fifteen minutes!" Jack hung up the phone and accelerated to eighty miles per hour as he headed out Airport Freeway toward the hospital.

He parked his pickup in the ER parking lot, which was surprisingly crowded for a Saturday morning. He made his way passed the security guard and the registration clerk who pressed a hidden button, releasing the electronic lock on the large metal door leading into the busy Emergency Department. The clerk had said that Mrs. Robert was in bed seven. Jack quickly located it, and as he stepped into the crowded room he heard the nurse say, "We have a pulse."

"What's going on?" Jack demanded. "I'm her son."

The nurse looked up from her clipboard and said, "Well we were able to get her back."

"You what?" Jack was now beyond angry. "You've been performing CPR?"

"Yes, and we finally got her heart restarted. I think you should wait out in the hallway sir," she said as if dismissing an annoying child.

"Didn't you know that she has a signed DNR in her advanced directive?"

All the nurses and the ER doctor turned toward him simultaneously. "We don't have any record of that under the name Faye Robert."

"Of course you don't," he said. "Her name is Faye Roberts."

The only sound that could be heard in the room was the steady beeping of the heart monitor. The nurses looked at one another and at the ER physician, but none of them were willing to look at Jack. One by one they slowly filed out of the room until only the head nurse and the physician who had been running the code remained.

Jack made his way to the head of her bed and saw that she was awake and feebly struggling against the breathing tube that had been inserted. He took the syringe that had been used to inflate the balloon holding the tube securely in her trachea, and removed the air. She responded with a weak cough, and Jack carefully removed the tube, allowing her to cough again.

"You can't do that," the ER doctor said.

Jack just glared at him and said, "I already did."

He leaned over as his mother whispered, almost too softly to be heard, "I was almost there. Why didn't they let me be with Harry?"

"Its okay Mom, he'll still be there when you arrive."

"Mom has had a stroke," Jack said, speaking into his cell phone from the hallway of the Emergency Department.

"I'm sorry," was all Elaina could say.

"Yeah, me too. The worst of it is she's now also suffering from a fractured sternum from the chest compressions they did while they were resuscitating her."

"You're kidding." she said. "I thought she had a DNR advanced directive."

"She does. They had her registered under the wrong name."

"Oh, Jack," she said, "I'm so sorry for her."

"I don't anticipate she's going to last very long," he sighed. "Her chest x-ray looks like she's in pulmonary edema from all the fluid they gave her, and other than a brief period when she was conscious right after I got here, she has been more or less unresponsive."

"Have you been able to reach Ben?"

"Not yet. But, its the middle of the night over there."

"How about your sister?"

"I'm going to call Janet next, and then I'll call David."

"Do you need for me to do anything?" Elaina knew there wasn't anything she could do to alter the stress he was feeling, but she was hoping he would give her something to do.

"No, not really," he said. "I'll be here for a while, and I'll let you know if things change."

Within an hour Faye was transferred to a private room on the fourth floor, but soon after she was moved from the ER stretcher to the hospital bed she just stopped breathing. Jack was at her side as she slowly slipped away.

"Say hi to Dad for me," Jack whispered in her ear as he gently closed her eyes.

CHAPTER 10

"So, how's school?" Jack asked.

"Its great," David replied. "This second year has definitely been more fun. I enjoy seeing how all that basic science stuff applies to various diseases, and in our introduction to clinical medicine rotations, we get to actually participate in a bunch of different stuff in the hospital."

David and Amy had driven out to his folks' house on a Sunday afternoon. It was a warm afternoon for the second week in March, signaling an early spring, and Jack had suggested they grill some steaks outside. The young couple both looked as though they had each lost a few pounds, and Elaina was truly concerned that they weren't eating enough because they didn't have any money.

"How's your job working out?" Jack asked Amy.

"Its okay," she replied. "It's not very exciting, but it pays the bills."

"Amy's gone back and reapplied for a management position at several of the bigger banks in Dallas, but they all say they aren't hiring." David felt he needed to defend her in advance of any suggestion that she wasn't pulling her weight.

"I don't know about the banks," Jack said, "but, I can tell you that here in Fort Worth, nobody's hiring. It's been that way for more than four years now. Every employer I know is scared to death about the impact of Obamacare."

"I don't understand what that has to do with it," Amy said. "I thought all that law did was make insurance companies provide insurance for pre-existing conditions and make more people eligible for government assistance, so they can buy insurance."

Jack smiled at his beautiful, but naive young daughter-in-law and nodded slowly. "That's exactly what the guys in Washington want everyone to believe, but there's a whole lot more than that in the over two thousand pages of legislative language."

"It's all too complicated for me," Amy said.

"Actually, its pretty simple," Jack replied. "The law says that any employer with fifty or more full time employees must provide health insurance for all of them, and most larger employers already do that. However, their insurance policies must now be what are called approved plans. That means they must cover certain things like pre-existing conditions and other preventative health benefits, which will raise the cost to the company substantially. The penalty for not providing insurance is two thousand dollars per employee per year, so many employers that are currently below the fifty employee threshold are not hiring. Those with more than fifty employees are laying people off to get below the threshold. Others are hiring people on a part time basis. As long as you work less than thirty hours a week you don't count toward the magic number of fifty."

"That's crazy," Amy said, her understanding of finance was beginning to kick in. "If I was an employer, I'd just tell my employees that they're on their own, and pay the two thousand dollar a year penalty. It would be a lot cheaper than buying health insurance for everyone."

Elaina got up from the table and went in the house. She had heard all this more times than she cared to admit.

"Like I said," Jack continued, "there are quite a few that are doing just that, but under Obamacare everyone has to have insurance. If they don't get it through their employer, they have to buy it themselves. That's what they mean when they talk about the individual mandate," Jack paused. "Otherwise, you have to pay a fine that is levied by the IRS."

"But, isn't health insurance really expensive?" Amy asked.

"Yes," Jack said. "Decent coverage costs about a thousand dollars a month for the average family of four. That's why a lot of young people go without insurance. They simply can't afford it, so, under the law, each state is supposed to set up an insurance exchange, where individuals can apply for government subsidies and shop for policies they can afford. The insurance companies will offer products that meet the government's minimum requirements, but they will still be more expensive than most people are willing to pay."

Amy was nodding her head, trying to act as if she understood what he was saying. "So, if people can't afford it what do they do?"

"They have to either pay a fine every year they don't have insurance, or they can apply for the Medicaid program in their state," Jack said.

"I thought Medicaid was only for really poor people," David questioned.

"That used to be the case, but under this new law, the states are being required to expand Medicaid to anyone that makes up to three hundred and fifty percent of the poverty level. Only a few states have actually done so, and many, like here in Texas, have decided they can't afford it."

"But if the money is coming from the federal government why would the states not be able to afford it?" Amy asked.

"Medicaid is basically a state run program and most of them are already overburdened by the existing Medicaid roles, despite receiving federal matching funds. If they expand the program, many states simply won't be able to pay their obligations without increasing taxes. Unlike the federal government, states can't just print more money, so their only choice will be to cut the amount they pay doctors and hospitals, and since Medicaid already pays less than any other payer, including Medicare, any additional cuts would threaten the very existence of the program, because no one will be willing to accept Medicaid."

"This is unbelievable," she said. "Why didn't anyone talk about this before the law was passed?"

"Many of us did, but the media wouldn't cover it, because they are all in this President's hip pocket. Most of the lawmakers didn't know, because they didn't even read the bill before they voted on it. It was rammed through by the liberal democrats as soon as they had a majority in both houses of Congress as well as the Presidency." As he saw the confusion in Amy's face turn to anger and frustration, Jack began to feel sorry for her, believing he was somehow responsible for allowing this blow to be delivered to her idealistic world.

"Anyway," he said. "That's why employers aren't hiring, and why the economy continues to remain stagnant."

"You certainly have a way of throwing cold water on a party," Elaina said as she returned from the kitchen with a pitcher of lemonade.

****

Horvath was addressing his entire management staff at one of his weekly meetings. "We intend to take full advantage of the new healthcare law, and the number of children who will soon be covered under government subsidized insurance and Medicaid, by expanding our marketing efforts in the second quarter to include Oklahoma, all of West Texas from the panhandle down to the Rio Grande, and into eastern New Mexico.

"I have hired a new vice-president of marketing, and our objective is to attract as many referrals of children in need of hospitalization as possible. We will be emphasizing elective surgical care and various diagnostic services," he said, assuming everyone present knew that elective surgery and diagnostic imaging were the economic life blood of the hospital.

"Obviously, the new law includes a number of new documentation requirements, so we have hired four new managers to help ensure the hospital's compliance with all the new federal regulations." Horvath seemed very confident that his marketing efforts would bring in more than enough revenue to offset this significant increase in overhead. He introduced the four new managers, then added, "I also have the pleasure of introducing Mr. Peter Grant as our new Vice-President of compliance. He comes to us from the law firm of Kleinman, Walters and Sheffield. He has been a healthcare attorney specialist for the last ten years, and we are extremely fortunate to have attracted him away from that prestigious law firm to oversee our compliance with the growing set of legal requirements."

The forty year old man stood, and quickly made his way to the podium. He was sharply dressed in a dark gray business suit, and sported a smile that was so continuous, it almost appeared to be painted on his face. Coming from Sheffield's law firm, he was obviously a staunch supporter of the newly re-elected congressman. Horvath's plan was to use him to ensure that all physicians on the medical staff would be intimidated into giving up control of their practices to the management company. Frightening doctors and hospitals with the risks of non-compliance with every legal regulation under existing healthcare laws had been the basis of this lawyer's entire career.

"I am extremely excited about this new opportunity," Grant said. "We all recognize that these are very challenging times to be in the business of healthcare, but I'm convinced that with your help, we can turn this hospital into the kind of modern enterprise that can take full advantage of our new national healthcare system. I hope to get to know each of you over the coming months."

"Thank you, Peter," Horvath said, after leading the group applause. "These are indeed challenging times, but I'm certain our team is up to the task." He looked around briefly until he spotted Traci Bryan sitting near the front of the room. He asked her to stand, and said, "One of the most important changes we will be implementing this year is a new electronic health record. I realize we already have a computer system in place, but it is not capable of meeting our needs under the new law. I have asked Traci Bryan to head-up the project of converting our current system to the new program. Traci would you please come up and talk a little bit about the new system?"

Horvath motioned for her to join him at the small podium. She had never been particularly comfortable speaking in public, and she wasn't exactly enamored with this new task she'd been assigned, but Horvath had promised her a hefty bonus if she could help him complete the transition by the end of the year. Her thirty thousand dollar bonus would come out of the massive bonus the hospital would receive from the government, as part of the new multibillion dollar federal health information technology initiative

"Thank you Mr. Horvath," she began. "Our new system is called Total Health Elements Secure Information System or THESIS. Ours will be one of the first hospitals to implement this new cloud based software program, and we have been assured that the company will provide us with all the support we need to make it operational over the next nine months. The system integrates all documentation of services in every department of the hospital and provides for immediate creation of accurate charges, for anything from a Tylenol tablet, or an MRI study, to the number of minutes spent in an operating room. Everything you do, and everything the employees who work under each of you, will be done through THESIS." The name suggested a theoretical advantage, but no one was allowed to talk about the uncertainty of this three million dollar purchase.

She looked around the room full of clinical managers and saw most of them nodding robotically in agreement. "The system is also designed to track the results of all treatments and monitor those results, allowing us to report comprehensive patient outcome information directly to the payers, using a sophisticated data analysis process. This system will offer us the kind of data we will need to monitor quality, and ensure that best practices are being followed across the entire system." Horvath had insisted she recite the script he had prepared precisely the way she had just done, and it had taken her most of the last two days to memorize it.

"Our physician partners will also be implementing THESIS in their outpatient care settings. This will offer a truly integrated healthcare record, eliminating redundancies and allow our doctors to communicate directly with you, and everyone else who has access to THESIS. Likewise, you will be able to communicate with them, provided they are logged on to the system." Again the audience seemed to accept this concept, and a few even voiced their approval.

"As I said," she continued, "all the information is in the cloud, and for those of you who may not be familiar with that term, it means the data will be stored on a remote server system, with multiple back-ups, so it will never go down. We will no longer need to maintain our own servers, which will result in a considerable savings to the hospital." She looked around once more before asking, "Are there any questions?"

The director of the operating room raised her hand, and when Traci pointed to her, she stood and asked, "You mentioned that the physicians who are partnering with the hospital will be implementing this new electronic record, correct?"

"Yes," Traci replied. "They will be switching over from whatever systems they are currently using, to THESIS. This will occur at the same time we are making the switch here in the hospital."

"What about those physicians who are not part of that group? We have a number of surgeons who operate here that are not in the big group," she said, as she sat back down.

Traci knew the answer, but she paused a moment to decide how best to respond. Horvath immediately stepped forward, assuming a position along side her and said, "It is our intent, and the intent of our physician partners, to integrate every physician who practices in our hospital under this system. We believe that when our doctors see all the advantages it offers, they will be more than willing to get on board."

It was what he didn't say that was most important. The initial cost of the new software program was fifty thousand dollars per physician, and there would be a nine hundred dollar per month maintenance fee. These expenses would all be paid for by the management company for all physicians who were working under that corporate umbrella. For those outside the group the cost would be crippling. He also didn't tell anyone, including his physician partners like Jerry Grady, that the management company had a separate contract with the software vendor. It included a seventy-five percent discount for groups of one hundred or more physicians. He knew it would be easy to show the retail cost of the system on the management company's books, and skim off the huge savings from the discount for himself and Fitzgerald.

****

"I don't care that some of the doctors are complaining," Horvath said. "We will implement THESIS, and if you aren't up to the task I'll find someone who is."

Traci bit her tongue rather than say what she was thinking. "I'm perfectly capable of getting the system in place before the end of the year," she offered calmly. "I just thought you should be aware that some of the physicians, even some of the leaders of the physician group, are unhappy with the complexities they are encountering."

"Is Dr. Grady among those complaining?"

"Yes, sir," she said. "He was in my office yesterday angry about having to change his twelve character password every sixty days. He said he can't remember twelve characters if some must be capitalized, some have to be numerals, and some have to be special characters."

"Are you kidding me?" Horvath spouted. "He's smart enough to go to medical school, but he can't remember a simple password?" After a few moments he gathered himself and said, "I'll speak to him."

Traci was about to leave when he asked her, "Have you heard anything from the cardiac surgeons?"

"No, sir," she replied. "The last time I talked to Dr. Roberts he said he would do his best to work with our new system, but he had no intention of converting his office records over to THESIS. I don't think you want to hear everything he said."

"Oh, but I do. I'd like to know what the esteemed Dr. Roberts has to say," Horvath insisted.

"He's not the only critic of this system, but he is clearly the most outspoken," she offered reluctantly. When her boss gestured for her to continue she said, "He pointed out that the only reason the hospital is making this change, and compelling all the doctors to participate is the multimillion dollar kick back the government is offering."

"Go on," he said slowly.

"He said, the new system does absolutely nothing to improve the care our patients receive, but instead will only serve to increase the burden on the staff and the physicians, taking time away from actual patient care. He says the protocols and processes are inflexible and require tedious documentation that defies all logic. He's convinced that the government wants us to collect all the data, including the outcomes information, so they can exercise total control over all of healthcare, and beyond."

"Beyond?" Horvath smiled. "What could they possibly do with our data beyond determining whether they're getting value for their money?"

"I really couldn't say, sir," Traci replied, even though Jack had told her his thoughts. He suspected that healthcare is simply the first step in changing this country into a socialist system, and having access to more and more personal information on every American is a big step in that direction. She recalled him saying, "If you don't have any secrets from the government, like whether or not you own a gun, or how you discipline your children, then the government owns you," but she wasn't about to share that opinion with Horvath.

"So, that's all he said?" Horvath asked.

"That's pretty much it," she said.

"That old man is a pain in the butt!" he proclaimed. "Perhaps he won't be around too much longer, and maybe then we can get on with the rest of the twenty-first century." He turned to her and said, "That is all for now," effectively dismissing her.

As she left his office she realized just how much she had come to loath her boss, and how much she wished she could get away.

****

Jack had settled back into his usual routine, and although his patient volume had taken a couple of months to ramp up after the election, his reputation continued to draw patients from throughout the southwest. He was just happy to be back working again. The frustration of losing his bid for Congress faded rapidly, and he was enjoying spending time in his personal sanctuary, the operating room. That was the one place he still felt a sense of control.

"Hello, Dr. Roberts," Nancy Abbott said, as she spotted Jack sitting at the nursing station. She was the head nurse on the evening shift on the surgical floor of the children's hospital. "How are you doing with the new electronic health record?"

"Do you want the truth?" he asked, as he looked up from the computer screen.

"Yes, I think I already know, but tell me anyway." she replied.

"It sucks!" he said with disgust.

She laughed briefly, then said, "I agree with you. Most of the doctors say the same thing. And I can tell you from the nurses' perspective, we hate it."

"They want me to use this same system in my office, and I absolutely refuse. It is extraordinarily user unfriendly. I've been sitting here for ..." he glanced at the clock on the wall, "twenty minutes, charting on two patients. I can't believe that I have to type in my ridiculously long password every time I write an order on a patient, just to prove it's still me, even though I'm the only person logged on to this computer. Then, virtually every medication order I write generates an automatic warning, telling me of some obscure potential risk, or interaction. It then recommends another drug from the so called 'best practices' list, which makes no sense whatsoever. Sometimes it will not even accept certain orders, unless I go back to the patient's problems list and add a new diagnosis. If that isn't bad enough, it makes me choose from a list of potential codes, before it will even accept the new diagnosis. Even though I've just written an extensive progress note explaining the change in the patient status, but that isn't adequate."

"I know, there are at least three extra steps that every nurse has to go through. My nurses hate it. They are spending all their time in front of the computer screen. We are told that all this is necessary to document every diagnosis and every treatment, otherwise we won't get paid."

"Of course," he said shaking his head slowly. "That's precisely what this is all about, getting maximum payment."

"Administration tells us that's how we stay in business," she said.

"That may be," he replied, "but, it sure as hell isn't good medicine, or good nursing."

She simply smiled at Jack, knowing that she probably shouldn't say any more. The administrator had made it clear to the entire staff that they could potentially lose their jobs if they openly criticized this new computer health record. She looked around to make sure no one else was listening, then spoke softly, saying, "I really believe this damned system was responsible for an injury one of our patients suffered last week."

"What happened?" Jack asked.

"We had a twelve year old girl who had been admitted over night, following an appendectomy. Her mother had gone home to check on her older daughter, leaving the child asleep. When she woke up, she called out here to the nurses' station saying she needed help going to the bathroom. It was right at shift change, and her nurse, Jackie Jefferson, was tied up at the computer charting on another patient. She had a number of things that she'd entered that hadn't been saved, and our instructions are to never leave a computer unattended, even for a moment. If she logged out without resolving several conflicts in the system she would lose at least half an hour's work. So she felt she had no choice but to go through all the system safeguards to ensure that her work had been saved, which took her about five minutes. By the time she finished, she hurried in to check on the little girl, and found her laying on the floor. She had tried to climb over the bed rails, gotten tangled in her IV tubing and tumbled out of bed. She landed on her arm and broke her wrist."

"You're kidding." Jack said

"No, I wish I was," Nancy replied. "Jackie is a great nurse. She's worked here for five years, but when she left that night she was in tears. She felt responsible for what happened. She came in the next morning and turned in her resignation. She told the director of nursing she couldn't work in a place that put the need for data collection ahead of the safety of the patients."

"I've known Jackie for years," Jack said. "Losing her is a big loss, but I can't say as I blame her for leaving."

"I can't either," she said sadly, "I've been here for fifteen years, and we've never had anything like that happen before. I'm convinced this damned computer system, that's supposed to make it easier for us to care for patients, is pulling my nurses away from the bedside, simply to satisfy this administration's demand that we capture every possible charge item."

Just then, a new, part-time patient attendant appeared from around the corner. She had been standing just out of sight, but near enough to hear the entire conversation. Nancy stood up straight and acted as if she had been talking to Jack about his patient, as the attendant walked by them casually. When she was well down the hall, Nancy said, "I sure hope that girl isn't a stooge for Mr. Horvath."

"Do you think he has spies?" Jack laughed.

"No, I don't think he has spies," she said seriously. "I know he does."

****

The next morning when Jack got to the office, there was a letter on his desk from the Centers for Medicare and Medicaid Services. It was a form letter that had been mailed to every surgeon in the country who participated in the Medicaid payment program. After the initial paragraph he was shocked by what he read. When he finished he slammed his palm down on his desk, on top of the brief letter. "They can't do that," he said out loud to himself."

"Who can't do what?" George said as he poked his head through the open door.

"You obviously haven't read your mail yet. I'm sure you got the same letter from CMS," Jack replied.

"No, I haven't looked at my mail in a couple of days. What did they do to us this time?"

"I'll read it to you," Jack said as he picked up the now slightly wrinkled paper. "In an effort to ensure quality care, as well as the financial viability of the nation's Medicaid program, CMS is recommending to all state Medicaid administrators that they suspend payment for certain costly surgical procedures, pending review of their comparative effectiveness with non-surgical treatments."

"What do they mean by certain costly procedures?" George asked in disbelief.

"Two of the procedures they cite are closure of atrial septal defects and ligation of patent ductus arteriosus in children. They say," Jack resumed reading from the letter. "Most of these minor heart problems will resolve with time without the need for surgery, yet nationwide hundreds of these costly, and unnecessary, operations are still being performed."

"What? Minor heart problems? Do they think we don't consider the possibility of spontaneous closure of an ASD or PDA before we decide to operate on any kid?" George was beginning to understand why Jack was so livid.

Jack hadn't even heard George's words. He was totally absorbed in his thoughts about what he could do to respond. As the president of the Association of Thoracic Surgeons he felt he had to formulate a response on behalf of all the surgeons who would be impacted by this policy decision. He used the intercom on his desk phone to summon Mary Anne into his office. When she arrived, he instructed her to call all the members of the ATS board of trustees, and arrange an emergency teleconference meeting for that evening.

He finished in the office around five-thirty, giving him just enough time to run over to the hospital and check on his three patients, before the six-thirty teleconference. As he walked on to the nurses station he saw an unfamiliar face sitting behind the desk. The new nurse who couldn't have been over thirty said, "May I help you?"

"Who are you?" Jack asked, not hiding his surprise.

"I'm Patricia Klein, the new head nurse on this shift." She pointed to her name tag with the letters RN, MSN behind her name, indicating she had a masters degree in the science of nursing. "And, who are you?" she asked.

Jack did not generally wear a white coat. He thought it scared the children, and he was wearing his name tag dangling from his belt, below the level of the countertop where she couldn't see it. He stood studying this new nurse for a moment, before he said, "I'm Dr. Roberts. Where is Nancy Abbott?"

"I don't know a Nancy Abbott ... Dr. Roberts, was it?" she asked.

"She has been the head nurse on the evening shift on this floor for more than three years!"

"It is my understanding that my predecessor is no longer employed here. May I help you?"

"I doubt it," was all he said. He looked suspiciously around the nurses' station, and sitting in the lounge area beyond, he recognized the face of the patient care attendant he had seen for the first time the evening before.

****

"I assume each of you received the letter from CMS?" Jack asked as he called the board meeting to order. Not everyone was available on such short notice, but he did have a quorum, but it consisted exclusively of the academic members.

"Are you talking about the one recommending Medicaid payments being suspended for certain procedures?" asked the vice-president George McCarty, a surgeon at Georgetown University Medical Center, in DC.

"Of course," Jack said. "That is why I called this meeting. I believe the ATS must respond to this ridiculous pronouncement. CMS has no basis for making such a recommendation, and children will potentially be denied life saving operations if this is implemented by the state Medicaid directors."

"I think your over reacting Jack," McCarty said. "We all know there are any number of ASD closures and PDA ligations being done unnecessarily."

"What!?" Jack said. "Are you siding with CMS?"

"All I'm saying," McCarty said in a very cool voice, "is that I think it's appropriate for CMS to insist that all reasonable efforts have been made to treat patients with less invasive methods before considering surgery."

"Don't you mean less expensive treatments?" Jack asked harshly.

"If you want to put it that way, then yes. This new policy recommendation is in keeping with the new healthcare law. We have to be better stewards of the government's money." The arrogance in McCarty's tone was unmistakable.

"That may be true," Jack replied, "but, just because it is in keeping with the new law, doesn't make it right. They are essentially saying that a surgeon's judgement cannot be trusted."

Another of the board members decided to way in, "I think George is right. We should just monitor this situation rather than act in haste. We don't even know whether any of the state Medicaid boards will accept this recommendation, and even if they do, I'm sure individual wavers can be obtained on a case by case basis."

"Jack, I agree with you in principle," added a fourth member on the call, "but, I'm sure if we fight this, they will trot out several examples of cases that make their point. Some kid who wasn't all that symptomatic from a PDA that was operated on and developed some major complication. They won't hesitate to share anything like that with the media, and we'll have no defense."

"What kind of defense will we have when kids are allowed to die of progressive heart failure or irreversible pulmonary hypertension, because they were denied an operation?" Jack was fuming. Had all of these guys lost their minds, he wondered.

"I would move that we table this issue," McCarty said. "We can take it up at our next meeting in two months."

"Second," came a response.

Jack had no choice but to asked for a vote. It was unanimous. The faceless voices on the conference call had all ensured that their organization would remain silent on this issue for now.

"Is that the only item of business, Jack?" McCarty asked. "I've got a dinner meeting to attend."

"No," Jack said very slowly, "that is not the only item." He thought for a moment, then spoke in a very deliberate manner. "I accepted this position with the understanding that I would make every effort to represent the surgeons who are members of the ATS. Our colleagues look to us as the board of trustees of this organization, and to me as its president to provide leadership and to act positively, any time our profession or our patients are under fire, no matter where that fire comes from. It is clear to me by virtue of your unwillingness to address this issue, that you, my fellow board members, do not share that same sense of duty." There were several voices that could be heard challenging him.

"I hereby resign as president of the ATS, effective immediately, and wish you all good luck."

"You can't do that Jack, you have a two year term." one member shouted.

"I can," Jack said softly, "and I just did. And furthermore, you can find yourselves another delegate to the AMA. I'm through with them too."

For a few moments he listened silently to the voices that were all talking at once, then he simply hung up the phone, leaving them to their own devices.

****

The next morning Jack stood on the front steps of the children's hospital, surrounded by reporters and camera crews from three of the four local television network affiliates. Promptly, at nine o'clock the news conference he had requested began. It was obvious that if he hadn't been involved in a campaign for Congress, there was no way he could have called a news conference and expected anyone to show up, but he rightly reasoned he still had enough name recognition to command an audience with the local media.

"First of all," he began, "I want to thank you all for coming today, and hearing what I have to say. I also want you to know that I am speaking strictly for myself, and not for any organization or group." The reporters looked questioningly at each other, now unsure what this was all about.

"Yesterday, I received a letter from the Centers for Medicare and Medicaid Services in Washington. It indicated that the Secretary of Health and Human Services was recommending to the Medicaid administrators in every state that certain surgical procedures should no longer be paid for under the Medicaid program. These procedures included two of the most common congenital heart defects we encounter in children." Jack held a paper with some hand written notes, but he did not refer to it.

"These are procedures that have traditionally been covered under the Texas Medicaid program, as well as by other state programs across the country. To unilaterally withdraw coverage for such critical operations is both irresponsible and dangerous. This is an obvious attempt to ration healthcare resources under a government budget, rather than considering the needs of the children. Unfortunately, the first to feel the bite of such inappropriate actions will be the most vulnerable among us. I would strongly urge those who administer the Medicaid program here in Texas, to not implement these recommendations of the Secretary of Health and Human Services. The children of Texas must continue to have access to these life saving treatments."

Jack fielded a couple of questions from the reporters, mostly about how many procedures would be affected by the recommendations, and the number of them performed at this hospital. Finally, one reporter asked, "How much do you get paid by the government to perform one of these procedures?"

"My payment for these, or any other procedures, is not at issue here, and I will not discuss that at this time."

The video of his press conference appeared on all three local news programs at noon, and was immediately posted on the Internet. By one-thirty, Jack's office phone was ringing off the wall. A few of the callers indicated they wanted an answer to the question of what he was paid for an ASD closure or PDA ligation, but most were from fellow surgeons from around the country, supporting his stance. Later in the afternoon he received invitations from the FOX national network to appear on their morning program to discuss the issue. Despite his earlier promise to Elaina that he would run all media appearances through her, he figured that since she had agreed to the press conference, she would approve. He agreed to go to the studio in Dallas to appear remotely, rather than fly to New York again.

When he arrived at the studio at six the next morning, the local producer had him sit in front of a photo backdrop of the Dallas skyline for the interview. The host spoke briefly with him off camera during one of their breaks, previewing what he planned to ask.

As the interview went live, Jack was calm and confident in his answers. He was very convincing as he talked about the decision processes that surgeons go through before subjecting any child to an operation. He made it clear that his objection to the recommendations was based on his own experience, and particularly the impact he had witnessed following similar restrictions placed by the British healthcare system nearly thirty years earlier.

The segment was brief, but powerful. After the interview was over, the on camera personalities were visibly upset by the implications. One of them said, "Are we now seeing the government death panels that we were warned about, back when Obamacare was being debated?"

****

"Dr. Roberts, I appreciate you taking time out from your busy schedule to drop by," Horvath said as he greeted Jack at his office door. Jack had reluctantly come by, but he figured this time Horvath would be on his side, since the hospital would benefit from maintaining the Medicaid coverage for these procedures. What he hadn't counted on was a phone call Horvath had received from the Director of the Centers for Medicare and Medicaid services, instructing him to, "silence Dr. Roberts or suffer the consequences."

"You've had a busy couple of days," Horvath said.

"Yes, I have," Jack replied. "What can I do for you?"

"I understand you feel passionately about this whole issue with CMS, and I don't really blame you," he lied, "but I think you should know, that all this controversy and publicity you are bringing to the hospital reflects badly on us."

"I would have thought you'd enjoy the attention. What do they say in Hollywood? "The only bad publicity is no publicity at all."

"Look, Jack," Horvath said, trying not to lose his composure, "I think all this stress is causing you to display some... let's just say, questionable judgement."

"I'm not sure what questionable judgement you are referring to, Mr. Horvath," Jack responded, trying to control his desire to respond more forcefully. "Perhaps you can enlighten me."

"I just think your attempt to take on the Secretary of Health and Human Services on your own, shows a lack of appreciation for the potential consequences. Again, I suspect it may be related to all the stress you went through back when you were campaigning, and now trying to get your practice going again, and ..."

"I'm not feeling any stress, Michael," Jack spoke in almost a parental tone.

"Perhaps not, but I think it would behoove you to take a week or so off, to reassess your perspective on all this."

Jack stood up and looked intently at the man who was more than twenty years his junior, and said, "I have no intention of taking any time off, or reassessing my perspective on anything."

As Jack turned to leave, Horvath said, "You do realize you could be jeopardizing your career, at least what's left of it?"

"And how is that?" Jack asked reflexively.

"You are bordering on being disciplined as a disruptive physician. Our bylaws are very clear." He picked up a piece of paper on his desk and said, "They define disruptive behavior, and I quote, 'as any behavior, action or effort, which draws negative attention to the facility or any of its staff members is prohibited and may result in disciplinary action.' Certainly, none of us want to see a stellar career, such as yours, tarnished in such a way, would we?"

"Are you threatening me?" Jack asked, taking a step toward Horvath's desk.

"I'm merely pointing out to you that you might consider how your actions reflect on your fellow physicians the next time you decide to appear on television. Those are the medical staff bylaws, not mine."

Jack glared at him but did not say anything further. He turned and walked briskly out of the office. As soon as he was gone and the door was closed behind him, Horvath picked up the phone and called Herb Nichols.

"Hey Herb, this is Michael. I just wanted you to be aware of what was going on with Roberts."

"Did that stuff I gave you on those Medicare patients help?" Herb asked, referring to two cases he had found of Jack's, where the admitting diagnosis didn't match the discharge diagnosis. "The feds are always looking for any irregularities to generate an investigation."

"I made an anonymous call to the FBI this morning. They seemed to take the information seriously, so we'll see."

Horvath then called Fitzgerald to share the latest. "I'm glad my contacts in the department of justice were helpful," Fitzgerald replied.

****

As Jack walked into his office on Monday morning there were three men systematically going through his computerized patient records. "What is going on here? What are you doing?" he demanded of the man in the dark blue suit.

"I am FBI special agent Murray, and these two men are investigators from the office of the Inspector General. We are here to conduct an audit of your records. Until we are finished, you and your staff are not to touch anything."

"Am I being charged with something?" Jack demanded.

"I am not at liberty to discuss any of the details of this audit at this time." He then handed Jack a copy of the court order, which gave them legal authority to search anything and everything in his office.

"I tried to call you, Dr. Roberts, but they wouldn't allow me to use the phone." Mary Anne said.

Jack turned back to the agent and asked, "How long is this going to take?"

"I have no idea, sir. Probably a couple of days."

"So how am I supposed to see patients and conduct my business?"

"You aren't. We will let you know when, and if, you are allowed access to your computers and communication devices."

Jack turned toward Mary Anne again and said, "You and the other girls need to just go home. I'll stick around."

For the next three days, Jack's office phone remained on the answering service and the front door remained locked. Mary Anne wasn't even allowed to call the patients to tell them not to come for their scheduled appointments. She placed a hand written note on the front door indicating the office was closed for an unforeseen emergency.

"What the hell is going on?" George Ferguson asked when he arrived at the office that afternoon. Jack explained what he knew of the so called "audit", including his suspicion that it had been triggered by his public stance against CMS. The two men decided they would continue with their surgical schedules as planned, and try and catch up in the office as soon as the feds were gone.

On Wednesday afternoon, Jack finished his surgical schedule and made his way back to the office. The men were gone. They had left without notifying him of anything. He called Mary Anne, and asked her to come back into work.

That afternoon she called every patient that had not been seen due to the disruption, and rescheduled them all. Several of them asked if everything was alright, whether Dr. Roberts was okay, or if there had been a death in his family. She explained that it was a problem with their computer system, but that everything was back up and running now.

The following Monday, Jack received a phone call from the office of CMS. "Dr. Jack Roberts?" was the greeting offered by the official sounding voice on the other end of the line.

"Yes, this is Dr. Roberts."

"My name is Samuel Jordan, and I'm with the Fraud and Abuse Division of CMS."

Jack did not respond verbally. Instead, he simply sat back in his desk chair and prepared himself for what he assumed was not good news.

"As you know, based on an anonymous tip, officials from the FBI and the OIG conducted an audit of your computer records, and they found several irregularities in your billing records with respect to your participation in the Medicare program."

"What irregularities? There must be some mistake," Jack insisted. "We are very meticulous with our record keeping, I would like to know which patients you are referring to, and the nature of the so called irregularities."

"Under the law, I am not obligated to divulge any of the specifics of the findings, but I can tell you they involved changed diagnoses, and procedures your office billed for that did not match the admitting diagnoses."

"That sort of thing is bound to happen all the time. Sometimes the admitting diagnosis has to be changed during a hospitalization, if the patient is found to have something other than what was initially suspected."

"I wouldn't know anything about that, sir, but what I do know is that you are being fined for multiple violations of the Medicare billing regulations. Ordinarily, the fine is ten thousand dollars per occurrence, however, since this is your first offense the director has agreed to handle all of these violations as a single event. You will have thirty days to submit a cashier's check in the amount of ten thousand dollars to the Centers for Medicare and Medicaid Services, or face potential arrest and prosecution."

Jack sat silent for a moment. He had heard of stories like this, but never in his wildest dreams did he imagine something like this happening to him. "I intend to appeal this. This is a mistake."

"Dr. Roberts, by virtue of your participation in the Medicare program, you have waved any right to appeal according to federal statute," the other man said flatly. "The decision of CMS is final and any further violations will result in your immediate removal from the Medicare and Medicaid programs and potential criminal prosecution. I must also warn you, that the findings of this audit are to be considered confidential. Under federal law you are not to discuss either the findings or the amount of the fine you are to pay." There was a momentary pause before the man asked, "Do you understand what I'm saying, sir?"

"Yes," was all that Jack could manage.

"Good day to you Dr. Roberts," the government man said with finality. Jack heard him hang up, not waiting for a response.

****

News of the conversation between Jack and CMS was the only topic of discussion among the three employees in the office. When George arrived shortly after one o'clock, they quickly brought him up to speed.

"So, what did they say?" George asked as soon as he saw Jack.

"They claimed they found several cases where the diagnosis didn't match up with the procedure. You know they just used the admitting diagnosis, so it wasn't any big problem for them to find patients whose diagnosis changed, based on what was found at surgery." Jack sounded disgusted as he described the ten thousand dollar fine.

"Are you going to appeal it?" George asked.

"I can't," Jack explained. "If you read the fine print of the Medicare participation agreement, you'll see that it makes you a government contractor, and as such you lose any right to appeal any adverse ruling by CMS."

"I don't get it," George said. "If this is what I can look forward to, I'm not sure I want to stay in practice."

"I'm certain this has something to do with what I had to say about the CMS recommendations. If you keep your head down, you aren't likely to be audited."

"I really like the idea of being independent, but it seems as though the system is stacked against us," George said.

"Yeah," Jack agreed, "things aren't anything like the way they used to be. I really fear for what it will be like by the time my son finishes his training."

George shifted in his seat, and decided he needed to tell Jack what was really on his mind. "I have been approached again by Grady and by the multi-specialty group. They have made a new proposal that is quite a bit better than their previous offer." George realized as soon as he started, that this was probably not the best day to bring this up, but he felt he needed to be honest with Jack.

"I figured as much," Jack said. "Are you going to take it?"

"I don't really have a choice. This past year I've been doing about as much as I can, and I figure I'm taking home about three hundred thousand. They have offered a guaranteed salary of four hundred thousand, plus health insurance, and they'll pay for me to go to two meetings a year. They will also pay for all my office overhead."

"Sounds like a pretty sweet deal," Jack said, realizing he was about to be by himself in practice once more.

"My wife is really pushing me to make this move," he said.

"It doesn't sound like you have much choice."

"You have been so good to me, I just don't feel right leaving, especially now."

"Listen, George," Jack said, as a crooked smile came to his face, "you need to do whatever you have to do. I just hope I can count on you to cover for me if I'm out of town, I'm sure you know that you can count on me anytime you're out of town or just need some time off."

George Ferguson was not normally an emotional guy, but this occasion was proving to be difficult. He viewed Jack like a father figure with respect to his practice. He had found himself repeating many of the same phrases he'd heard Jack use, and even some of his mannerisms mimicked his mentor.

"Of course I'll cover for you," George said holding back against the temptation to embrace his friend. "I'm really sorry. I wish you'd consider coming with me."

"Those guys don't want me," Jack offered, "and besides, I couldn't make it in that environment. I think I'd retire rather than become an employed physician."

CHAPTER 11

"Now that was just the kind of workout I needed," Jack said, as he and Buzz approached one of the small tables in the central gathering area of the health club. "Do you want a Gatorade?"

"Yeah," Buzz replied, "that sounds great."

When Jack returned from the counter with two cold drinks he sat down to begin the process of cooling off. "I know I say this nearly every time we get together," Jack said, "but, we need to make sure we find time for this every week. I can't believe how much better I feel when I get some real exercise. That year on the campaign trail nearly killed me."

"I know what you mean," Buzz agreed. "Without you to beat up on, I gained ten pounds myself."

They both laughed, but Jack still didn't like the fact that Buzz had won at least two out of every three matches since they resumed playing about six months ago.

"So, how are things working out with George Ferguson doing your cases?" Jack asked. He knew that since George joined the big group, he had been receiving virtually all of Buzz's referrals. The only cases Jack and Buzz had in common now were those patients that were referred directly to him from out of the area.

"He's doing okay," Buzz said, less than enthusiastically. "He's not nearly as comfortable with the kids as you are, and he lacks the ability to instill confidence in parents, but we haven't had any major problems, at least not yet."

"He's a good surgeon, but he's not yet convinced of that fact," Jack said. "I'm sure with time he'll gain more confidence, and that will translate into better relationships with both the kids and their parents."

"What have you been up to lately?" Buzz asked. He still saw Jack occasionally in the hospital, but not on an everyday basis like he had previously.

"I'm still doing a few redo hearts, and some of the stuff the other guys don't want to mess with over at the general hospital," he replied. "I'm also seeing three or four kids a month, coming in from west Texas and Oklahoma. That hasn't really changed much."

"So, when are you going to retire?"

"Retire?" Jack exclaimed. "I'm not planning to retire anytime soon. I'm only 64, and I can still whip you on the racket ball court, at least once in a while," he laughed. "The closest thing to retirement I have planned is my annual trip to Nicaragua. In fact, next month Elaina and I are going to extend our trip to two weeks."

"I didn't mean to imply that you needed to retire, far from it," Buzz responded. "Its just that this whole healthcare system change seems to have taken a toll on you."

"Now that, I will agree with," Jack said shaking his head silently. "Sometimes I feel like I'm the only one who is angry about what is happening to the practice of medicine."

"You are by no means the only one who feels the way you do. I think most of us are just as angry and frustrated as you are, we just aren't willing to do anything about it," Buzz said. "I truly admire the stance you've taken, I just wish I had the ability to stand up to the Gradys and the Horvaths of the world, but I can't take the risk."

Jack looked knowingly into Buzz's face. He felt a sense of sadness as he saw nothing but frustration in the eyes of his old friend. He smiled, trying to reassure him, then said, "Your time will come. You just need to be ready to make a move when the opportunity finally presents itself."

"I don't see it happening anytime soon," Buzz said as he drained the last of his Gatorade.

****

It was hard to keep track of exactly how many trips they had taken to Managua, but each time they encountered something, or someone, new. In addition to the clinic visits in Ciudad Sandino, Jack decided that this time he and Elaina needed to see more of the country side. So, starting on Friday morning of their first week, they ventured out on day trips, either up into the mountains or down to the coast.

It was on the third such day trip, this time toward the southwest, that they happened upon the Montelimar Beach resort near the costal town of Pochomil.

They parked their rental car and strolled along the beautiful, dark gray, volcanic sand beach.

"I can't believe so few people are here," Elaina said as they walked down the nearly deserted seaside, hand in hand. "This is such a gorgeous place. I could certainly see myself walking along a beach like this every morning, once you decide to retire."

Jack looked over at her and asked, "Have you been talking to Buzz Jackson?"

"No, what makes you say that?"

"He was asking me about retirement a couple of weeks ago. Do I look like I'm getting old?"

"No, I just know how frustrated you are with everything," she said sympathetically.

"Does it show that much?" he asked.

"Are you kidding? It's all you talk about," she said. "I worry that you are so caught up in it that one day you're going to keel over from a heart attack or something."

He stopped and turned her toward him, looking into those same green eyes that had captured his heart, and said, "You're not going to get rid of me that easily. I'm not going anywhere."

Her smile was the same one he fell in love with, only now there were a few more lines in the corners of her eyes, but he never noticed, and even if he had, he wouldn't have said anything.

"I know what you are doing is important to you," she offered with obvious understanding. "I just think you need to take your own advice."

"How's that," Jack said, breaking into his own crooked smile.

"Remember telling David about balance? Well, I think you could use a little more balance in your life." Her words weren't harsh, but they touched his heart directly. He knew he sometimes allowed his passion to possess him, and he knew she was right. He needed to let go of things that he couldn't change.

"So, do you think you'd like to retire here?" Jack asked.

"By here, do you mean Nicaragua?"

"Yeah, I guess," he replied tentatively, "or at least somewhere on a beach?"

"You know I love being near the water, and this is about as near the water as you can get." She realized she hadn't really answered her own question about Nicaragua. "I guess I could learn to live in this country, although, I really liked that place Elizabeth Burke has down in Costa Rica."

"Yeah, she has a sweet set-up, but we don't know anybody down there other than her. At least here we have a few friends," he stated, before he realized he was almost making it sound like a plan. "I don't know why we're talking about retirement," he added. "I have no intention of retiring, at least not any time soon."

"Maybe we could consider a vacation home down here. We could rent it out most of the year. That way we'd have a place of our own, and we wouldn't have to continue to rely on Domingo and Felicia to put us up in their guest house." Elaina offered as they resumed their walk down the beach.

"That's something I've thought about for several years, even back before David came with us his first time," Jack said thoughtfully, "but, I didn't want to say anything."

"Why not?" she asked. "Did you think I'd say no?"

"No. I was afraid you'd say yes," he laughed, "and then I be stuck house hunting."

"Are you serious?" she asked, hoping he wasn't just teasing her.

"I think it would be good to have our own place, but I wouldn't want to be this far down the coast. This is just a little too far from Managua. I'd like to be close enough to Domingo's clinic to be able to help him out."

"In other words, you'd need to be close to work," she said with a laugh.

"You know me," he admitted. "I have to work. I don't think I could ever completely retire. I can't imagine living, day after day, trying to find something to do."

"Oh, I'm sure I could find things for you to do."

He laughed along with her, then said, "Well, if we're going to find a vacation home while we're here, we probably need to get started looking."

"Are you teasing me?" Elaina said, letting her excitement show.

"Come on," he said, "let's go see what we can find."

As they hurriedly headed back toward their car, he added, "I'm not real crazy about the idea of renting out a second home. That sounds like a lot of trouble. People tend to trash rental property, ya know?"

"I agree," she replied. "I just mentioned it because I know you are always considering the investment potential whenever you buy anything."

"We've never really bought any investment property," he said, not sure to what she was referring. "The only investments we have are the Apple stock, my office building and my mom's old house. I only bought out Ben's share of Mom's house, because I knew he had no interest in messing with rental property. I'd really like to sell it, but the real estate market is so depressed right now,"

"I was referring to the opportunities you've turned down over the years. We've looked at a couple of time share investments, and you've always said they wouldn't pay for themselves," she explained.

"That is true," he agreed, "Plus, if we bought into one of those deals we'd be stuck going back to the same place every year." Jack was referring to time share deals they had looked at in Hawaii and another in Virginia. They were nice, but he didn't want to go there every year on vacation.

"Yeah," she said with a laugh. "We wouldn't want to go the same place, every year."

Somehow, Jack didn't look at these trips to Nicaragua as vacation, but they had indeed become just that for both of them.

"If we didn't rent out our place, we wouldn't have to worry about planning our trips in advance. We'd have the ability to come and go whenever we wanted," she reasoned. "I might even come down here for a month or so at a time. without you."

"You would come without me?" Jack said sadly.

"Obviously, I would rather you came along, but, now that David's not home any more, I rattle around in that big house everyday. I would love to come down here for a few weeks at a time, especially in the winter." Elaina could tell she had introduced an idea that Jack hadn't considered. "You could come visit if you want," she added playfully.

On Saturday, Domingo introduced them to a local real estate agent, and when they explained what they were looking for, she told them to give her a couple of days to get a list of properties together. She was certain she could find something that would meet their needs. Before they left her office in Managua, she recommended they open a local bank account. It would make it much easier for them to purchase any property.

****

Franco had known that Jack and Elaina were back in Nicaragua, but for their first week he had been out of town, visiting one of his construction sites near the Caribbean coastal city of Puerto Lempira. He insisted Elaina and Jack meet him and Gabriella for dinner at one of their favorite restaurants in the Intercontinental Hotel on Sunday evening.

During dinner Jack told Franco that he and Elaina were planning to start looking for a vacation home on Tuesday morning.

Franco was very excited to learn of their plans. "Please allow me to introduce you to my friend, Monique Jordette," he said. "She is the most knowledgeable real estate specialist in the region."

Jack smiled as he looked over at Elaina who was also smiling. "What?" Franco asked impatiently.

"We have already met with Monique," Jack said. "She is the agent Domingo recommended as well."

"I was hoping to be of help to you, but it appears you found the best this time without my assistance." Franco sounded quite disappointed.

"It's okay, my friend," Jack said, playfully. "I'm certain you will have another chance to help us out." He was enjoying having the opportunity to be one step ahead of Franco for once.

"I'm certain that she recommended you open a bank account here in Managua," Franco said confidently.

"Yes, we were planning to visit the Central Bank of Nicaragua tomorrow morning," Jack announced. "Domingo recommended that bank."

"I agree," he offered casually. "That is the most reputable bank in the country."

The following morning Jack and Elaina walked in the Banco Central de Nicaragua. A bright young receptionist stood as they entered the lobby, and approached them as if she had been expecting them.

"Please, follow me," she said in flawless English. "Mr. Herrera, our president, has been expecting you."

Jack looked at Elaina quizzically as they made their way toward the large corner office in the rear of the bank.

"Dr. and Mrs. Roberts, please come in, come in. Make yourselves at home. I am Edwardo Herrera," he said as he shook Jacks hand, before gently taking Elaina's and escorting her to a large leather wingback chair.

Jack sat in the other identical chair then said, "How did you know ..." He was still in shock over the familiarity of this reception.

"Mr. Gutierrez informed me you would be coming in this morning, and he asked that I take care of your needs personally," Herrera explained. "Mr Gutierrez is our most valued customer.

Jack laughed to himself. He should have known that he could never stay one up on Franco for very long.

"So," Herrera asked, "what can I do for you?"

"We are considering purchasing a vacation home here in Nicaragua, so we need to open an account at a local bank. We have been told this is the most reputable one in Managua," Jack said, sounding more formal than he'd intended.

"I see," replied Herrera. "Do you plan to finance your purchase, or will it be a cash transaction?"

"That will depend somewhat on the price of the property. We have not even started looking yet, but, it would be my preference to make it a cash transaction," Jack said, anticipating he could find something reasonably priced.

Herrera had hoped he could provide this low risk American doctor with a sizable loan. "Of course," he said, hiding his disappointment. "So, you will need a local checking account, in anticipation of paying for your purchase?"

"Yes, that's correct." Jack agreed. "That's why we're here."

"Of course." the banker said as he sat down behind his desk and pulled a folder from the top drawer. He handed it to his secretary who had joined them in his large office. "Ms. Sanchez will be happy to fill out all the forms for you, and we can have you on your way very quickly. Might I ask how much you intend to deposit?"

"Will you accept a check from an American bank?" Jack asked.

"Normally we require a bank wire when our foreign customers open a new account, however, since you are a friend of Mr. Gutierrez, I am certain your check is good."

"In that case, we'll open the account today with ten thousand dollars, then if we find a house that we decide to buy, I'll have my bank send additional funds as an over night wire transfer."

"That will be fine," Herrera said. "Is there anything else I can do for you?"

"No, you have been quite helpful. Thank you."

Herrera reached across the desk and shook Jack's hand again. As he did he said, "I trust you will tell Mr. Gutierrez that we treated you well?"

Jack smiled and said, "Certainly." He understood full well that this man was not serving him. He was serving Franco, because he needed his money, but what he didn't know was there was more to their relationship, much more.

****

"This house isn't exactly on the beach. It's abut one hundred meters from the ocean," Monique said, "but, I believe it is exactly what you're looking for. It is less than an hour from Managua, on the outskirts of the small fishing village of El Transito,"

Elaina was excited beyond words. They had started their search on Tuesday, looking at several houses near Domingo and Felicia. She thought they were okay, but they weren't at all what she had in mind. She wanted something near the water, and Jack said he would be willing to look anywhere within a one hour drive of Managua.

From Managua, Monique drove them west, on the road to Leon, up the slope of the Cordillera Los Maribios mountain range. A few days earlier, when Jack had driven across this ridge of mountains that separated the central part of the country from the coastal region, the summit had been shrouded in clouds. Today the late morning sun illuminated the lush green tropical forests and rich volcanic farmland that stretched out before them, all the way to the brilliant azure blue Pacific.

"Can we get out and take a picture," Elaina asked eagerly.

Monique found a place to pull off the road, and the trio got out of the Ford Explorer. Elaina hadn't brought a camera, but Jack always carried his iPhone, which took exceptional photos. She asked him to take several pictures of the landscape. Then Monique, ever the salesperson, suggested that she take a picture of them with the ocean as a backdrop. She could tell from Elaina's grin, that she would have no problem making a sale that day.

They headed down the western slope through the irregular terrane of this ancient volcanic formation. After about twenty minutes, they turned left toward the ocean on the road to El Transito. The surface was paved, but it could hardly be described as a highway. While the main road from Managua to Leon was not heavily traveled, this road, known as NIC 40, was nearly deserted.

It had been almost an hour since they'd left Domingo's home as they entered the fishing village of El Transito. The houses they passed were all quite small, but well kept. There was a small market near the center of town, where farmers from the nearby hillside brought fresh fruits and vegetables. Next to that was a butcher shop that offered local chickens and various cuts of beef, mutton and goat. Nearer the beach there were several open air seafood shops that sold fresh snapper, grouper, mackerel and shrimp.

Jack was surprised to see a couple of American style surf shops near the beach. He said to Monique, "I didn't know there was surfing here in Nicaragua."

"Oh, yes," she replied. "This area is famous for some of the best waves anywhere in Central America." Then she added, "There are numerous places up and down the coast where surfers come from all over the world. Most prefer to come in the winter because that is our dry season."

They then headed north from the center of town, and Elaina noticed a few of the homes were a bit larger, but she still hadn't seen anything like what she was looking for. Monique drove to the end of one street and then turned into a driveway that was sparsely covered in gravel. There was a small wooden frame structure on the right, but just ahead was a one story, white stucco house, with a clay colored tile roof. The irregular gravel driveway made a gentle circle in front of the home. The surrounding landscape included several bougainvillea vines that had been allowed to grow uncontrolled. They hung lazily over the windows and off the top of the roof over the front door.

As they got out of the car, Monique said, "This house has been vacant for a couple of months, but it wouldn't take much to get it back in shape." Along the coast the temperatures were more moderate than what they'd become accustomed to, in and around Managua, and the constant breeze off the ocean made it very comfortable to be outside.

Jack looked back up toward the front of the property then asked, "What is that other little building?"

"That is the caretaker's house," she replied. "The previous owners had an older couple living there. The man took care of the property, and his wife worked inside the home. When the owners left, the couple was forced to leave as well, but as I understand it, they would be very interested in coming back to work for any new owners."

"What does domestic help like that cost?" Jack asked.

Monique smiled and said, "Oh, the cost is very little. These people are very happy to work for little more than a roof over their heads. This couple charged the previous owners ten dollars a day, which is adequate to provide for their essentials.

"So, you're saying that it only costs about three hundred dollars a month for a full time maintenance man and an inside maid?" Elaina asked in disbelief.

"That is correct." Monique replied. "I'm told she is also an excellent cook, but they do insist on having Sunday mornings off, to attend Catholic Mass in the town."

Elaina had always envied Felicia. Her housekeeper, Rosa, had worked for her for more than twenty years, and her husband Guillermo maintained their yard and landscaping perfectly. He also performed any odd jobs around the house for Domingo.

As the trio entered the house the large living room was empty. The terra cotta tile floor was dull from lack of recent care, but otherwise appeared in excellent condition. The slightly vaulted ceiling was accented by open wooden beams, that were stained dark brown, and stood in sharp contrast to the white hand trawled surface of both the walls and ceiling. She was immediately reminded of the interior of the la Mansion de Rio hotel in San Antonio where she and Jack had stayed that memorable weekend back in 1990. Floor to ceiling windows made up the far side of the room that looked out onto a generous wooden deck.

Before Monique could show them the rest of the house, Elaina walked swiftly passed her and out through the French doors onto the partially covered deck. She gazed out over the small lawn and overgrown garden to a shallow tidal lagoon about ten feet below the level of the house, down a gentle slope. A gravel path way led from the end of the deck, through the garden down toward the water, and continued across the lagoon as a plain wooden bridge to the sandy beach on the other side. The ocean waves could be heard in the distance as they broke onto the beach in front of the huge black rocks that dotted the coastline, remnants of a massive volcanic eruption many millennia before.

"Let's go down to the beach," she said excitedly to Jack.

"Don't you want to see the rest of the house?" he asked.

"There'll be time for that later. I want to see the view from the beach."

The wooded planks of the bridge traversing the twenty-five or thirty yards of lagoon seemed quite sturdy. There was no railing so they proceeded single file, with Elaina in the lead. When she reached the other side, she slipped off her shoes and left them on the end of the bridge, preferring the feel of the warm gray sand on her bare feet. She found herself almost running through the soft sand, between several of the large irregular rocks that stood between her and the ocean. The louder the sound of the crashing waves the more quickly she moved, as if drawn like a magnet to the sound. As she rounded the largest of the obstacles, she suddenly stopped. The view of the beach was beyond what she had imagined. She stood on the edge of a small cove, in the shape of a half moon. To her right, the broad sandy beach was protected from the large waves. The sand sloped gently toward the water, which lapped lazily onto the shore. To her left the waves were propelled by the full force of the open ocean, crashing noisily on to the steeper sandy shore. The row of dark lava formations extended down toward the small town that sat on the far side of the cove. These irregular rocks had been tossed onto the beach thousands of years before during a violent eruption of one of the now silent volcanos. They created a rocky barrier between the beach and the lagoon and the other homes beyond.

She turned to face the ocean and closed her eyes. The warm sea breeze smelled amazingly familiar to her. She stood almost breathlessly for several moments, taking in the rhythmic sounds of this idyllic spot.

Jack came up behind her and placed his hands on her shoulders as she was now staring into the blue pacific beyond the waves. She felt his touch, but seemed hypnotized by the beauty of this place. After a few moments she turned suddenly to face him and said, "This is it!"

"It is beautiful," he agreed, "but you haven't seen the rest of the house."

"I don't care what the house looks like, this is where we are going to spend our final years. Even heaven will have a hard time topping this."

Eventually Monique convinced them to come back up to the house. She showed them the three bedroom layout, with the master bedroom having its own French doors out onto the large deck. The kitchen and bathrooms were equipped with modern fixtures and appliances, suggesting the house was no more than five or six years old.

"So, what are they asking for this place?" Jack asked.

"This is one of the most desirable properties along this section of the coast, but the people who own it are anxious to sell. As I understand it, they are having some financial problems, so it is priced right."

"What exactly does that mean?" Jack said, bracing himself for what he feared would be far more than the half million he had available.

"The listing price is two hundred and twenty thousand," she said, rather sheepishly, "but, I think they'll take two hundred thousand."

Jack looked over at Elaina as a huge smile broke over her face. He tried to remain stoic as he said. "Offer them two hundred thousand... but, if they hold the line, I'll pay their asking price. Just don't let this one get away."

Monique opened her purse and pulled out her cell phone. She quickly made the call to the listing agency as Jack and Elaina walked back outside. "I'm so excited," Elaina whispered. "I may spend more than a month at a time down here."

"Without me?" Jack pouted.

"Like I said, you can come visit any time you like."

He took her into his arms and kissed her passionately, realizing that this was to be their private escape from both the pressures of his profession and the boredom he knew she felt. He had secretly wanted to have this kind of retreat for many years, but hadn't known when, or if, it would ever materialize.

****

After they closed the deal on the house, Elaina decided to stay over for another week to find some furniture and work out the details of hiring the caretaker and his wife. The sixty year old man's name was Federico, and he was almost as excited by the new ownership as Elaina was. The rather small man smiled and nodded approvingly throughout the brief interview. His wife, Lucinda, was also rather short, standing less than five feet tall. She seemed cautious at first, and was even more distant when Elaina explained that she and Jack would only be staying in the house a few weeks each year. The rest of the time the house would be vacant. Lucinda looked at Federico with alarm. She assumed they would be paid only during those periods when the owners were there.

Elaina sensed her concern, and said, "You will be paid every month, whether anyone is staying in the house or not. We will need for you to keep the house and the grounds maintained. I would like for you both to start today." Lucinda smiled and quickly agreed. Elaina gave them each several tasks that needed to be done immediately, so she could move in.

Two days later a delivery truck pulled up in front of the house. It took the three men half the day to unload the furniture Elaina had purchased from the only quality furniture store she could find in Managua. She bought a large area rug for the living room and a smaller one for the master bedroom, and had them brought in first, partially covering the recently scrubbed floors.

The seller had accepted their offer of two hundred thousand dollars, but Jack wired an extra fifty thousand to their Nicaraguan bank from their savings account back in Fort Worth. They agreed on a budget of twenty thousand dollars to buy the necessities for the house. Everything was so much less expensive here than back in the states. She was able to get far more than she'd anticipated, and was able to buy everything she needed for the living room as well as a round table and six chairs for the adjacent eating area for under four thousand dollars. The master bedroom furniture was only two thousand, including a small wicker table and two chairs for the private deck area. She decided to only furnish one of the other bedrooms now, in case David and Amy decided to come down with them. She thought that was unlikely, since David rarely had any time off from school, but that didn't keep her from hoping.

She also bought a washer and dryer, a microwave oven and a coffee maker. While Jack still didn't care for it, she had to have her coffee in the mornings. She also found the perfect outdoor table and chairs for the main wooden deck area, and when she was finished she had only spent nine of the twenty thousand dollars. When she got back to the house she realized the furniture was only the beginning. She needed everything else, like pillows and linens for the beds, all the supplies for the bathrooms, dishes, silverware, pots and pans, and countless other things for the kitchen. Plus, Federico and Lucinda needed equipment and supplies to care for the house.

The next morning she arrived back in El Transito at seven-thirty to pick up Federico. She had borrowed domingo's Land Cruiser, because the rent car wasn't big enough to carry everything she anticipated getting that day. She'd never bought a lawn mower or garden tools, or anything like that, so she figured the local man would know better than anyone precisely what he would need to care for the property.

As they drove back into Managua, Federico told her the previous owner of the house was a wealthy business owner from Southern California. He had purchased the property in 2006 and built the house a year later. He and his wife lived there about three months the first year, but less and less each year since. His son lived there at least six months every year. He was a surfer, and often had other surfers come to stay with him from all over the world, but mostly they were from California. Federico wasn't sure exactly what happened, but he understood that the man's business had started to decline in the fall of 2008, so he started coming for only a week at a time. When he was there he never seemed to relax the way he had that first year. In the last twelve month he had only come twice, with the last time being three months ago.

One day a company from Managua came out with a big truck and took everything out of the house, as well as all the lawn equipment, everything. They took it all back to the city to sell at auction. The owner didn't even pay him and his wife for the last month, and it wasn't until the real estate agent came out to inspect the house, that they were told they must move out of the home they had been in for nearly six years.

Elaina could only imagine what had happened. The US economy crashed in September of 2008, and small businesses were hit particularly hard. California had been effected as much, or more than any other part of the country. She felt especially bad for Federico. He'd had nothing to do with the circumstances that led to his loss of employment and his home. She assured him, this time things would be different.

Domingo had recommended a store on the outskirts of Managua that sold lawn and garden equipment, but given the number of things they needed, there was no way for her to get everything home, even in Domingo's vehicle. Federico convinced the store manager to deliver the lawn mower, ladders, shovels, rakes, a gas trimmer, and everything else he'd picked out. He recommended that Elaina only pay him half at the time of purchase, with the rest to be paid the next day upon delivery. He explained that in Nicaragua, if you pay in advance, things had a way of never showing up as promised.

They also went to a hardware store and bought several gallons of paint. She didn't care for the stark white walls of the master bedroom, and one of the other bedrooms had been vandalized, apparently by a visiting surfer. They also bought brushes and rollers and drop cloths, so that Federico could do the job of repainting the inside of the house.

That evening they returned to El Transito with the Land Cruiser loaded down. She now had everything she needed for the kitchen and bathrooms, as well as linens, towels, toiletries, even a new hair dryer. She was determined to make this new house a home away from home for her and Jack.

Lucinda did not require any instruction. She immediately began unpacking the linens and washed them. As soon as they came out of the dryer she carefully ironed them and made up the beds. She also washed the new towels and wash cloths before hanging them in the two bathrooms and stacking the extras neatly in the linen closet.

While her new employer and her husband were gone into the city, she had walked into the market and bought things she needed in the kitchen. Elaina had given her the Nicaraguan equivalent of one hundred dollars to buy cleaning supplies, laundry soap and basic food items. She had also gone to the fish market, so while the washing machine was running, Lucinda prepared dinner for señora Elaina.

She asked her to please come and sit down at her new table. Elaina had been busy with Federico, explaining which paint was to go on which walls, and as she came back into the kitchen she stopped dead in her tracks. Out of nowhere she suddenly felt the tears welling up in her eyes.

"Where did you get that?" she asked Lucinda in disbelief.

"At the market, señora Elaina. I'm very sorry, it was the only one they had that would fit the table. I will return it tomorrow," Lucinda responded to what she was certain had been a reprimand.

"No, no," Elaina replied, looking at Lucinda with a tearful smile. "It is perfect. I only wish my husband was here."

Elaina walked over to the table, now covered in a red and white checked cloth, and sat down slowly. Jack had only been gone for four days, but at this moment she felt incredibly alone. Lucinda presented her with a plate of fresh grouper, pan fried to perfection, along with some local vegetables, plantain and her own version of gallo pinto, the rice and beans staple of every Nicaraguan's diet.

Monique had said Lucinda was a good cook, but this meal rivaled any she'd had in Nicaragua, including those at Franco and Gabriella's home. However, she ate less than half of what Lucinda had served, then suddenly placed her knife and fork on the table and stood up.

"You did not like?" Lucinda asked, alarmed that the first meal she had prepared her new employer was not acceptable.

'No," Elaina explained. "The food was delicious. I just need to go outside for a few minutes."

"Shall I keep it warm for you?" Lucinda asked, hoping she would come back and finish her dinner.

"No, I'm finished. Thank you."

Elaina walked out onto the wooden deck, and saw the sun slowly melting into the ocean just beyond the large black rocks. She was tempted to walk down to the beach, but she stopped herself. She couldn't imagine watching her first sunset in her knew home without Jack being by her side. She cried softly to herself, wishing more than anything that he would suddenly appear, pick her up in his strong arms and carry her playfully out to the beach. She decided to drive back to Domingo and Felecia's, unable to spend her first night alone in her new home

****

"Hi, George," Buzz said. "Are you busy?"

"No, Dr. Jackson," George replied, still not comfortable calling the senior cardiologist by his first name.

"I wanted to tell you about a female infant I just saw, that has a big problem." Buzz wasn't one to exaggerate, and George knew that when he said it was a big problem that wasn't good.

"What's she got?" George asked, sounding more timid than usual.

"She's got a hypoplastic left heart," Buzz said. The echocardiogram was unmistakable. The two day old had been born with only one pumping chamber. The right ventricle was pumping all the blood out through the pulmonary artery and the only blood going out into the main circulation was going through the patent ductus, the vascular channel that normally closes shortly after birth. George knew that this was one of the most challenging problems to fix surgically, typically requiring three separate operations over a two or three year period.

"Wow, Dr. Jackson," he said. "That's a tough one. How is she doing?

"She is currently holding her own, but her systemic pressure is very low, even with supplemental nitrogen." Buzz was using a complicated process to have the infant breathe gas with lower than normal oxygen levels in an attempt to shunt more of the blood flow out through the ductus, but this was only a temporizing measure. Without surgical intervention the child was certain to die within two or three days.

"I have to tell you, I've never even seen one of these. I've read about it, but I've never done a Norwood procedure, which is what she needs as a first step."

The phone was silent for a few seconds before Buzz spoke again. "I don't think she would tolerate a transfer anywhere else."

"Why don't you call Jack? If anybody around here can fix it ..."

"I already ran that idea passed the group's utilization review committee. They said they would not approve getting Jack Roberts involved in this case. They told me that's what we hired you for."

"But, there's no way I would feel comfortable doing this case. Who do I need to talk to?" George asked, again sounding almost like a resident, the first time the faculty wasn't present for a big case.

"You can call Grady," Buzz replied, "but I don't think he will budge on this. He told me that if they have to pay any more outside consultants this month, the money will be coming directly out of all the group members salaries."

Did you tell him this kid will likely die?"

"Yes, and all I got was, 'get George to fix it. If he can't, then at least we will have tried.' So, that's why I'm calling."

"I'll get back to you in a few minutes," George said.

He hung up, and immediately called Jack. "Do you have any experience with hypoplastic left heart?" was all he said.

"Well, yeah," Jack responded. "Its been a few years, but I've treated two kids here in Fort Worth, and I had another one back when I was at Hopkins. Why do you ask?"

"Dr. Jackson just called me. He says he has a newborn with that problem. He has her on supplemental nitrogen to increase pulmonary vascular resistance, but the baby isn't going to make it without urgent surgery."

"So, what are you waiting for?"

"I've never done a Norwood procedure," he said, his voice sounding almost like a teenager.

"You don't need to do that," he explained. "All the baby needs is a hybrid procedure. You can do that without even going on bypass."

"I have no idea what your talking about."

"All you need to do is stent the ductus to make sure it doesn't close, and you need to band both the pulmonary arteries. That will protect the pulmonary circulation from excess pressure and shunt most of the blood through the ductus out into the systemic circulation. That should buy you three or four months. Then you can do the second stage procedure. If all goes well, you can do the final stage when she's two or three years old."

"You make it sound easy, but I'm just not comfortable."

Jack recognized that phrase as the one this younger generation used routinely to avoid accepting responsibility. "I'll come help you," he said, trying to sound encouraging.

"I'd really rather you do it, and let me help, but our utilization review committee has already refused to allow an outside consultant."

Jack chuckled to himself. "I wonder what they would do if you were out of town, and I was covering for you?"

"I don't know," George sounded disgusted. "The way this thing is designed, it's the docs who take the financial risk for everything. They're already paying me a salary, but your fee would be paid out of the bonus pool, and that wouldn't set well with Grady."

"That's exactly why I didn't join the group. When the cost of caring for patients comes directly out of the doctor's pocket, it creates a huge ethical dilemma."

"That's seems pretty obvious now, but back when they were offering me that contract, that issue never came up."

"Of course not," Jack explained, "but this accountable care organization stuff is nothing new. All it is, is another way to shift the risk from the payers to the physicians. We saw it with HMOs back in the nineties, and the result was the same."

"Yeah, and I guess I shouldn't be surprised that my take home pay hasn't been what I was promised. They say that because of cost overruns every partner has had to assume a proportionate cut in pay."

"I thought you had a contract?" Jack asked.

"I do, but Horvath pointed out during last month's group meeting, that Medicaid payments had been reduced again. He said that all physician contracts are contingent on a minimum income to the group, and if the gross revenue falls below that threshold, all physicians must share in the shortfall."

"My guess is he doesn't participate in the sharing of those so called losses."

"One of the other guys asked that exact question during the meeting, and he was told that the management agreement is different from the physicians' agreement."

"You know Horvath is making in excess of a million dollars a year from that management contract, right?" There was silence on the phone. Then Jack added, "That's in addition to at least that much in annual salary as the hospital administrator."

"I had no idea he made that much," George replied.

"How do you think he can afford that new Aston Martin Vantage he's driving around in these days?"

"I really screwed up when I agreed to join those guys," George said, almost to himself.

"Don't beat yourself up," Jack offered sympathetically. "As you told me before you signed, you had to do what you had to do."

"Yeah, I know, but what's even worse is I can't really get out of it now. They put in a non-compete clause, so if I decided to leave, I couldn't practice anywhere within fifty miles of Fort Worth."

"Well," Jack sighed, "we aren't going to change any of that today. What we can do is fix that baby's heart. When do you plan to do the surgery?"

"Whenever you're available," George said hopefully. "I'm on my way over there to see her as soon as we hang up."

"I was supposed to pick up Elaina this afternoon at the airport, but I'm sure she won't mind taking a cab. So, I'm available anytime after one o'clock. Just have them set up as if you were doing a ductus ligation," Jack recommended. "I would also make sure you get Radha Patel to do the anesthesia. These kids can be a little tricky."

"I will let you know what time as soon as I get it scheduled."

"I'll be here," Jack said. "Oh, by the way, ask Buzz whether he got measurements of the length and diameter of the ductus. You need to make sure you've got an appropriate sized stent."

****

By the time Jack got home that evening it was after seven. He was glad to see that Elaina had made it home okay..

"How are you, my Angel," Jack said as he held her firmly and kissed her passionately. "I'm sorry I couldn't meet you at the airport. George needed my help with a baby."

"That's okay," she said, "I'm just glad to be home."

"I'm glad too. It's been pretty lonely around here the past five days."

"It was pretty lonely in El Transito, too," she said. She didn't think she could tell him about the one evening she spent alone in the new house without crying.

"I wish I could have stayed to help you get the house in order, but I had to get back."

"I know," she said softly. "I really enjoyed getting everything together. It was almost like starting over again. I wish you could see the furniture, it looks great, and Federico and Lucinda are going to be terrific."

"I can hardly wait to go back... and check out our new bed," he said, as he smiled and looked lovingly into her eyes.

"Me either," she agreed, "but, tonight I'm not thinking about our new bed. I'm ready for our old bed." she asked, as she broke away from his grasp and ran playfully up the stairs. "Care to join me?"

****

The baby with the hypoplastic left heart did very well following surgery, and within forty-eight hours she was breathing on her own, on room air. George had asked Jack if he would continue to look in on her, since he wasn't sure exactly what to expect. Jack gladly agreed, and went by to check on the baby twice a day. It was on his third afternoon stop by the intensive care unit that he ran into Dr. Grady.

"Hi Jerry," Jack said, "What are you doing here?"

"I could ask you the same thing?" Grady replied somewhat sharply. He knew exactly who Jack was there to see.

"I was just checking on that baby with the single ventricle that George operated on the other day. He asked me to look over his shoulder."

"Yeah, I heard," Grady said, making it obvious he was not happy that George had brought any surgeon in on the case who was outside the group. Jack's fee would count against their budget for out of network physicians, which, in his mind, meant he was paying for it.

Jack was acutely aware of the way things worked, so he decided to confront Grady head on. "You don't need to worry, Jerry. I'm not charging for making rounds on this kid."

"I would certainly hope not," Grady replied. "I saw your assistant fee come over my desk for approval, and I have to tell you, I don't make that much for a full day seeing patients in the office."

Jack had charged the standard assistant's fee, which is twenty percent of the surgeon's fee, even though under the circumstances he certainly could have justified charging a much higher co-surgeon fee. If George were working on a fee-for-service basis, his charge would have been about thirty-six hundred dollars for the hybrid procedure and all the postoperative care for ninety days. That is how Jack came up with his charge of seven hundred twenty dollars, which his office manager submitted directly to Grady's accountable care organization.

"From what I understand, Jerry," Jack said. "You aren't seeing many patients in the office anymore. Don't you spend most of your time working with Horvath, running your big group practice?" Jack let his contempt for the whole scheme get the best of him. He knew better than to antagonize Grady, but he just couldn't help counter punching.

"The work I do running our ACO is really none of your business, Roberts," Grady retorted.

"You're right. I didn't mean to imply that your work wasn't important in its own way," Jack returned. "I just don't see you helping patients the way you used to."

Now it was Grady who was on the verge of losing his temper. "The work I do is enabling other providers to serve patients more effectively than ever," he bragged. "Without our network, many of those who were previously without care would not be getting the care we are now able to provide."

Despite his best effort, Jack couldn't help but laugh. "That is the biggest pile of crap I've ever heard. We both know this whole accountable care organization scheme is just another way to shift control of healthcare away from the patients, and into the hands of bureaucrats." He paused, expecting Grady to return his challenge, but he didn't. "You've been around long enough to see that this is just another version of risk shifting. ACO, HMO, PPO, they're all the same thing. The only difference is this time it is designed specifically to divide physicians into those who have government contracts and those who don't."

"You know, Jack," Grady responded, the venom in his words was no longer hidden. "It's guys like you that brought on all of this. You and your fellow, ego driven surgeons, and your demand to be paid on a fee-for-service basis. Us primary care guys have been paying for your inflated fees for too long, and now we intend to even the score."

"Jerry," Jack said calmly, "you have fallen victim to the oldest tactic in history. Guys like Horvath, all the way up to the President of the United States, know there's no way they can exert any control over the practice of medicine if the physicians stand together. So they seek to divide us based on the one thing they can control, and that's money. What are they paying you? A lot more than you could make as a practicing pediatrician, I'll bet. In exchange for that big paycheck, all they ask is that you gather up your trusting colleagues into a nice controllable group, with your docs' sole reward being that they get to keep something they already have, their own patients. Anybody who won't play by those rules must be considered the enemy. Really, Jerry? Is that what you swore an oath to do? To become a patient broker?"

"Clearly, you choose not to see the changes that are upon us. Our profession is no longer what you thought it was, or what you want it to be. Quite frankly, I don't think it ever was. The world has moved on Jack, and people like you, who are unwilling to change with the times, are simply going to get run over. You can think whatever you like about me, but I intend to lead the way toward a more fair and equitable healthcare delivery system," Grady spoke without hesitation, but there was something in his voice that convinced Jack he'd struck a nerve when he brought up the Hippocratic Oath.

"I may not live to see it," Jack replied, "but, the system you are building will ultimately crumble under its own bureaucratic weight. When people who put their trust in us realize that profits trump ethics, they will turn with a vengeance, not on the businessmen, but on the physicians who betrayed them. Just remember that, the next time you're in one of those board meetings and one of those other guys in a dark blue suit refers to you, not by your name, but simply as doctor."

****

Jack walked into the ICU for the fourth consecutive day to check on the progress of George's patient, but as he approached the glass enclosure with the large number eight painted on the door, he saw the room was vacant.

"Where did Dr. Ferguson's patient go?" he asked the nurse.

"I'm not sure, sir. I just came on duty," the young woman answered.

Jack feared the worst. He pulled his cell phone out and dialed George's number. "What happened to our patient?"

"I was told I had to transfer her to the hospital's new pediatric non-acute care facility," George replied.

"What non-acute care facility?" Jack asked.

"The hospital bought that abandoned nursing home around the corner, and they did some minor renovations to make it into a step down unit."

"So, you're telling me she isn't even in the hospital?"

"Technically that is part of the hospital, but physically its a couple of blocks away."

"Why did you agree to moving her? That baby wasn't ready to leave the hospital." Jack was trying to understand what could have possibly compelled George to transfer a six day old baby with a potentially fatal cardiac anomaly, who was only four days post-op, to a renovated nursing home.

"The ACO's case manager told me the new facility has all the capabilities of our inpatient units here in the hospital."

"I wouldn't know about that," Jack said, "but that baby needs to be monitored very closely. She could still easily develop a respiratory problem, and if she does you could lose her in the time it takes to transfer her back here to the ICU."

"I argued with the case manager, but she said she was authorized to move my patient even if I didn't agree, based on the new protocol for cardiac surgery patients," George explained, sounding more like a school boy than a cardiac surgeon.

"Who developed this protocol?" Jack asked. He and George were the only pediatric heart surgeons on the staff.

"I was told they are implementing the protocol that was recently released by the Association of Thoracic Surgeons. I was going to ask you what you knew about it."

George obviously couldn't see Jack shaking his head slowly as the phone was quiet for a moment.

"That sounds like something McCarty would do," he said, almost to himself.

"Who is McCarty," George asked.

"George McCarty is the guy who assumed the presidency of the ATS when I resigned, earlier this year. He's one of the main reasons I left," Jack admitted. "He's one of those academic guys that knows everything, or at least he thinks so."

"Well, I don't know whether he's the one who wrote the protocol or not, but I read it, and it calls for any child undergoing a cardiac procedure that doesn't require bypass, to be moved out of the ICU within forty-eight hours, unless they're still on a ventilator," George explained. "It also states that the entire length of hospitalization should not exceed four days unless there are ongoing complications. That's why they insisted I move my patient to the step-down unit."

"That might be fine for an uncomplicated two year old following the ligation of a patent ductus, but for a newborn with a major defect like a hypoplastic left heart, that's absurd," Jack replied angrily.

"I tried talking to Grady, but he said he had been by to see the baby himself, and she appeared to be doing well. He's actually the one who initiated the transfer process through the case manager."

"He can't do that! That's your patient, not his!" Jack shouted.

"That's what I thought too," George replied, "but, I was told that part of my contract with the group gives the medical director the authority to act on behalf of the group to ensure quality care and appropriate utilization of resources, including determining appropriate hospital admissions, discharges, transfers and consultations."

"George, you've got to find a way out of that mess," Jack urged his friend. "They are putting you and your patients at incredible risk. I can guarantee you that there is also something in that contract that makes you the fall guy if anything bad happens."

****

Jack stormed into Horvath's office, demanding to see him immediately. "Mr. Horvath is in a staff meeting," his administrative assistant stated.

"I don't care, I need to speak to him immediately," he insisted. He was obviously upset, and his six foot three inch frame was an imposing presence as he place both hands on the front of the young woman's desk.

She picked up the phone and called into Horvath's office. "Dr. Roberts is here. He says he needs to speak to you." She listened for a moment then replied, "Yes, sir. I'll tell him."

When she hung up the phone she looked up confidently, and said, "He will see you in just a few minutes. Please take a seat." She motioned toward the chair on the wall across from her desk.

Jack continued to stand, and paced slowly back and forth a few feet in front of her desk. After about two minutes he heard obvious laughter coming through the door of Horvath's office. He looked questioningly at the woman who was trying to appear busy at her desk. She looked up and said casually, "Can I get you a cup of coffee?"

Just then came another round of laughter from the inner office. This time even louder and more boisterous than before. It sounded as though two men were engaged in a party, rather than a meeting. Jack turned to her and said, "No, thank you." He then stepped around her desk and boldly opened the door, interrupting what must have been an entertaining story.

"Excuse me, but I need to speak to you," Jack said bluntly.

Horvath was startled by the intrusion, and as he stood up from behind his desk, Jerry Grady also turned in his chair to see who had entered the room. "We are in a meeting right now, Dr. Roberts. Perhaps you could ..."

"No, this can't wait," Jack spoke, using the same authoritative tone he usually reserved for times of emergency in the operating room. "And, I'm glad you're here, too," he said toward Grady.

Neither Horvath nor Grady spoke. They were both intimidated by the dominant figure that had just entered the room, as the door closed rather noisily behind him. Jack took a few steps forward, bringing him alongside Grady's chair, and as he did, Horvath said, "Please have a seat," attempting to regain his composure and control over the situation.

"No, thank you," Jack responded. "This will only take a minute."

"What's on you mind this time," Horvath said as he took his seat again.

"The baby George Ferguson operated on four days ago, the one with the major congenital heart defect, should not have been transferred out of the ICU, much less out of the hospital. I saw her a few minutes ago over in that so-called step-down unit of yours. I couldn't find a single nurse who knew anything about caring for post-op hearts, and the child was clearly not getting the kind of monitoring necessary." He turned sharply toward Grady and continued, "You had no business moving her. You don't know the first thing about what level of care she needs. I just hope for your sake that nothing bad happens, because if it does, you can bet it will be on your head, not George's."

"Now, just a minute," Grady said, as he stood up to the challenge Jack was offering. "I was simply following the protocol that was set by the Association of Thoracic Surgeons. You really should know what your own organizations are recommending."

"I know all about that bunch. McCarty, their new president, is nothing but a lap dog for this administration. He wrote all those new protocols strictly so CMS could deny payments, not because they provide appropriate care."

Immediately after his conversation with George, Jack had called his old friend, Carol Reeves, the Executive Director of the ATS and gotten an update on what McCarty was doing. She had told him of McCarty's frequent trips to the Centers for Medicare and Medicaid Services, and the numerous dinners he had been invited to with the director of that huge government agency. He had even met with the Secretary of Health and Human Services to discuss additional ways to cut costs for treating cardiovascular disease.

"Perhaps, you would like to help us bring our new step-down unit up to your standards," Horvath suggested, choosing to change his tactics slightly.

"I have no intention of sending any of my patients to that pitiful excuse for a healthcare facility," He replied, then turned to Grady. "Have you even been over there?"

"Why, no, but I understand it's been completely renovated."

"You know they closed it down years ago because it wasn't safe for nursing home patients. I hardly think a fresh coat of paint and some new tile on the floors changes much of anything."

"We are simply responding to the directions we are given from the government," Horvath stated, carefully avoiding the safety issue. "Medicaid and SCHIP, as well as the major insurance carriers are all considering making transfers to non-acute care facilities mandatory, except in certain unusual circumstances. We soon won't have a choice in the matter."

"You may not have a choice, as you put it, but I do," Jack announced, "I consider what you are suggesting to be dangerous, and I will not subject my patients to such treatment."

"Well, the patient we are referring to isn't exactly your patient, now is she?" Horvath asked with a smirk.

"No, she is not," Jack replied. "She is Dr. Ferguson's patient, and since I assisted him in the care of that baby, I feel a certain responsibility to help him ensure her safety."

"I see," Horvath said as he contemplated his next move, "That may be true in this instance, but I will see to it that you will not be placed in this position ever again."

Jack knew exactly what he was implying, and he angrily turned and left the room, deciding he had made his point, but realizing he wasn't going to change the mind of either man.

As soon as the door slammed, Horvath turned to Grady and said, "I think its time we rid ourselves of that pain in the ass."

CHAPTER 12

"I started my clinical rotations last month," David said with excitement. Everyone had told him that the third year of medical school was the most fun and exciting. "I'm doing Internal Medicine right now, and from there I go to Obstetrics and Gynecology."

"That's great, sweetie," Elaina said, excited to have him and Amy over for a Saturday evening cook out. "Speaking of Obstetrics?"

"No, Mom, we're not pregnant," he said, knowing precisely what she was implying. "We're not ready to take on the responsibility of raising a child just yet."

"I understand," she said sadly, "you're both still very young. I just ..." Her voice trailed off before she could say how much she wanted a grandbaby to spoil.

"Once I get into a residency program we'll start considering it, but that's still at least a year away," David added. "Speaking of which," he said, as he turned toward his dad, "the dean called me into his office last week and told me it was a possibility that I could graduate in just three years."

"That's great," Jack said. "You know that's what I did," he paused briefly then added, "but, I thought they did away with that program back in the nineteen eighties."

"He said they were reviving early graduation to help fill some of the residency programs, but only on a very limited basis. Its only available to the top ten percent of the class and only if the student matches with a university based internship in either family medicine or general surgery."

"So, is that something you're interested in doing?"

"Of course!" David said without hesitation. "I already know what I'm going to do after med school, so I figure the sooner I can get into my internship and residency the better."

"I think it sounds like a great idea," Elaina said, obviously still thinking about how long she might have to wait for that first grandbaby.

"If you're sure, then by all means, go for it," Jack said, but David detected a hint of caution in his dad's voice.

"Can you think of any reason why I shouldn't skip an entire year? After all, I still have seven years of internship and residency."

Jack thought for a moment and said, "Two potential reasons come to mind. One, if you're the least bit uncertain about your choice of specialty, then another year of clinical rotations at this point might help you decide. I know you've said repeatedly that you plan to do cardiac surgery. I just think you need to be certain before you commit to starting that training." Jack was being very cautious with his choice of words. He didn't want another lecture from Elaina about being too negative. "The other reason would be if you had any thoughts of an academic career. The big time programs are not real high on guys they perceive as taking a fast track."

"I thought about both of those possibilities," David replied. "I am absolutely convinced that cardiac surgery, and more specifically pediatric heart surgery, is the career path I want to pursue." He paused very briefly to allow his dad to absorb that part of his answer. "As for being a teacher, I have no interest whatsoever in working in the kind of controlled environment that academic institutions impose on physicians."

Jack sighed, recognizing that his son sounded more like him everyday, independent to the core. "You won't get an argument from me," he said, "but, if things keep going the way they are, private practice is likely to be just as controlled as the academic world, if not more so."

"You still get to make your own decisions when it comes to your patients, don't you?" David asked.

"More or less," Jack replied. "However, that is changing."

"Is the government trying to tell you what to do?" David asked, anticipating his dad would go into one of his tirades about socialized medicine.

"Actually, it isn't the government telling docs what to do directly. They just dangle dollars out in front of people, with major strings attached."

"What do you mean?"

"Well, for example, part of the new law calls for the creation of these, so called, accountable care organizations."

"Yeah, you've talked about that before," David interrupted, "but, I haven't heard anybody else talking about them."

"That's because most of the doctors don't want anyone to know how they can potentially be a big money maker. An ACO is nothing more than a hospital and a group of doctors who contract together to provide care for a large group of patients, for an annual fee. The more they can keep their costs down, the more they stand to profit. If they spend more on caring for their group of patients than they're paid, the ACO has to cover the difference."

"But, how does that impact the doctor's decision making"

Jack knew this was complicated, and might not make any sense to his idealist son, but he decided to try and explain what was happening using the example of the Medicaid baby that George and he had operated on the week before. Once he had finished explaining what had happened, including his subsequent conversation with the principle directors of the ACO, David nodded his head slowly, indicating that he understood.

"You need to tell that story to the media. People have no idea what is happening. If they knew how the system was being manipulated against them, maybe they would do something," David spoke with a sadness in his voice that Jack hadn't heard before.

"I don't know, son. I've tried, but most people just seem to be apathetic. If it doesn't impact them directly, they just smile and move on." Jack's voice also had a sad tone. David had never heard his father sound so defeated.

"Maybe that's because they haven't had a specific case that they could relate to," David wisely pointed out. "The baby you just described could have been born to anyone, and I think people can relate to that story."

"You could be right," Jack agreed. "You could be exactly right."

****

On Monday morning, Jack called a local radio talk show that had been friendly toward him during his campaign. He was informed that the program he was inquiring about had a new host, but Jack didn't know him. The show ran from noon to two, five days a week, and since the host was still new to the area, he was anxious to have local guests on to talk about major and minor issues of the day. When the producer heard what Jack wanted to talk about, she invited him to come on the program the next day from one to one-thirty. She explained that in the first thirteen minute segment Jack could tell his story, and in the second segment they would take calls from listeners. Jack wouldn't need to come to the studio, they would just talk over the phone.

At five before one, Jack's cell phone rang and the producer told him to hold until the host introduced him about three minutes after the hour. Jack sat at his desk, listening to three minutes of news as the radio broadcast played live through the phone. The news was followed by the midday traffic and weather, then three more minutes of advertising. When the bumper music started playing he anticipated he would be up next.

"Welcome back to the second hour of the Bill Harris show. As we went to break, Kevin from Mansfield was asking about the new law here in Texas that requires motorists to slow down, and move over when passing any department of transportation vehicles, the same way you're supposed to do when passing a law enforcement vehicle stopped on the side of the road."

He continued talking to the caller that he'd held over from the previous segment. Jack remained on hold, as the host droned on about the amount of highway construction in the area. Finally, he wound up the discussion at nine minutes after the hour.

"Now, as promised, I'm delighted to have with me someone, who for many of you, needs no introduction. He ran a very spirited, but unfortunately unsuccessful campaign for Congress last fall. He is one of the areas foremost physicians and an outspoken critic of Obamacare, Dr. Jack Roberts. Welcome to the show, Dr. Roberts."

"Thank you, Bill. I appreciate you having me on."

"So, tell me," Harris said, "Now that Obamacare is about to be fully implemented, with people being able to sign up starting October first, have you changed your mind about the law, even a little bit?"

This wasn't the way the discussion was supposed to begin, but he figured he'd go with it for now. "No, I haven't," Jack responded. "Actually, like most people, the more we learn about this law the more convinced I am that it is bad for most American's."

"But, isn't it a good thing for every American to have access to affordable healthcare?" Harris asked.

"Of course," Jack replied, "and if that's what this law did, I think most of us would applaud it, but Obamacare is not about healthcare at all. This is just another episode in the centuries old struggle over power and money."

"So, you see the government providing insurance to people who can't afford to go to the doctor as just a way of controlling them?"

Jack realized this guy wasn't the least bit interested in hearing the story he was prepared to tell. He just wanted to debate philosophy, and from the condescending tone of his questions, he was anything but the conservative talk show host he was touted to be. "I don't know exactly what the motives were of those in our government who rammed this law through," Jack said, "but I can tell you that the end result is that people are losing their individual freedoms."

"From the polls I've read, it appears that many, if not most people are willing to sacrifice some choices in exchange for the security of knowing they won't be wiped out by a huge medical expense." Harris was turning this into an argument, more than an interview.

"That may be," Jack admitted, "but, when it comes to their health, people often don't realize the value of being able to make their own choices until they're faced with an actual crisis."

"So, you see this more as an individual freedom issue," Harris stated, trying to steer Jack into a discussion about collective versus individual responsibilities.

"Yes, I do think this is about individual freedom, but there are things in the law that most people are totally unfamiliar with, like accountable care organizations ..."

"But, isn't it a good thing that everyone should have some kind of healthcare available to them?" Harris interrupted. It was clear he wasn't going to allow Jack to tell the story he and the producer had agreed to the day before.

"Of course, everyone needs access to healthcare, but this law has created incentives for those who provide those services, and that threatens the quality of that care. It isn't enough ..."

"But, wouldn't you agree, doctor, that access to care trumps quality? That some care is better than no care at all, and before Obamacare, many of the poorest Americans have not had access to even basic care because they lacked insurance."

"That is simply not true," Jack replied. "We have had countless programs in place for many years, like Medicaid and SCHIP that were designed specifically for the poorest among us, but many people don't sign up for them. And, I would disagree with the premise that you must sacrifice quality for access. Those two things are not mutually exclusive."

"We're here with Dr. Jack Roberts, former republican candidate for Congress, and an Obamacare opponent. We need to take a quick break, and we'll be right back to take your questions."

Jack was hoping to use the break time to find out why he'd been consistently cutoff, and not allowed to tell the story about the infant who had ultimately died from pulmonary complications in the step-down unit. When the four minutes of advertising had concluded, the music returned and Harris began speaking again.

"We're back with our special guest, Dr. Jack Roberts, who, as most of you know, was unsuccessful in his attempt to unseat democratic Congressman Harold Sheffield last November. We've been talking about the pros and cons of universal healthcare. So, Dr. Roberts, can you tell our audience why you are so adamantly against the idea of government subsidized healthcare?"

"As I said earlier, I'm not opposed to everyone having access to healthcare, what I am opposed to is either insurance companies, or the government, making medical decisions, and that is precisely what is happening under this new law."

"Let's take a few calls from our listeners, shall we? John in Frisco, you're on the air with Dr. Roberts," Harris said, quickly diverting Jack once again, this time to a caller who had been pre-selected by the producer of the show.

"Yeah, hi." the caller said hesitatingly. "I wanted to ask the doctor, if they are somehow able to repeal Obamacare, how he would recommend I get insurance. I'm in my mid-forties, I have diabetes and two years ago I lost my job because I had a heart attack and missed a lot of work. I was only able to maintain my COBRA insurance for nine months, and now I can't find anyone who will insure me for a premium that my wife and I can afford. She has a decent job, but she works in a small office that doesn't offer health insurance. Obamacare is the only option we have."

"Dr. Roberts?" Harris said coolly, tossing the ball to Jack, anticipating that he'd have no answer.

"Well, John," he replied, with a very sympathetic tone, "your's is an all too common situation, and I'm not sure there is a good answer, but, I know one thing for sure. If you become a patient of a government program you are certain to get the minimum care defined by the law, instead of the compassionate, personal care you deserve."

"But, I can't afford to pay to go to the doctor." The caller interrupted. "We are barely scraping by on my wife's salary and my unemployment."

"As I said," Jack continued, "your situation is unfortunate, and one that is shared by many Americans who can't find a job in this difficult economy. Have you looked into applying for Medicaid?"

"I'm not interested in that," John replied. "Medicaid is for poor people. I want to have regular insurance like everyone else. I just need the government's help to buy it through the exchange."

"I hope you realize that the policies offered through the government exchanges will be equivalent to Medicaid," Jack stated. "And, even with assistance from the government, you will still have to pay a significant portion of the premium yourself."

"I thought it was going to be free," John said, sounding somewhat surprised.

"Of course," Jack said, "that's what they want everyone to believe. This whole thing has been one big sales job, telling the American people that Uncle Sam was coming to their rescue. It is simply not true."

"Let's take another call," Harris interrupted.

"Hold on a minute," Jack stopped the host, "Let me finish answering John's question."

"Okay," Harris replied sheepishly.

"Many physicians are just as frustrated with the system as you are. A growing number are breaking away from the government and insurance created straight jacket that binds their decision making. You might want to look for a physician in your area that you can see for a fee that may surprise you. Some are offering deep discounts for patients like you, who are unable to pay their usual fees. You might find it interesting to know, that under current programs like Medicare and Medicaid, the government establishes all payments, and it is illegal for a physician to charge any patient more than the established rate. If they charge anyone less, that then becomes the charge they must use for everyone. The result has been that charity has become a word that is almost never used to describe healthcare today."

"But, Dr. Roberts ..." Harris attempted to stop Jack's monologue.

Jack quickly continued, "Virtually all our hospitals, and now even most large physician organizations, have been caught up in the quest for profits, and that focus has been fueled by the fact that insurance companies and government, not the actual consumer of the services, control the money. We used to have hospitals that were dedicated to caring for those who could not pay, but with very few exceptions they are gone, swallowed up by huge conglomerates run by corporate bureaucrats. Under Obamacare, physicians are now being herded into mega-groups, called accountable care organizations, where the doctors assume the financial risk of caring for their patients. This leads to dangerous cost cutting, and even rationing measures, all under the false claim of quality and efficiency."

"I'm sure John isn't really interested in any of that," Harris interrupted once more, "He just wants to know how he can get the insurance he needs."

"That's exactly why this is such an important call," Jack added. "The idea that everyone must have insurance is a business strategy that plays directly into the hands of those who's sole motive is to profit from each transaction."

Harris felt he had succeeded in his assignment to not allow Jack to talk about ACOs, but he also knew his boss wouldn't be pleased that he'd allowed this free-market capitalist to ramble on. He knew he had to do something to regain control of his own program. He said, "Profiting from healthcare? That sounds like the pot calling the kettle black, don't you think, doctor? You've made a pretty good living practicing all these years, right?" Before Jack could respond he continued. "I dare say most of the operations you've done weren't paid for by guys like John, were they?"

"All that is true," Jack said without the slightest delay, "and, I'm not saying that people shouldn't have insurance."

"That's certainly what it sounded like to me," Harris injected.

"What I'm saying is that insurance would be a lot cheaper if our healthcare system was a free market, and if the policies were designed to cover only major illnesses or injuries. Everyone has car insurance, but it doesn't pay for normal wear and tear items like tires and fan belts. Those are things that the car owner is responsible for. If car insurance paid for new wiper blades or every oil change, none of us would be able to afford it. The reason guys like John can't afford health insurance is because most policies try to cover everything from brain surgery to a five dollar antibiotic prescription. And by the way, pharmacies now charge more like fifty to seventy-five dollars for that five dollars worth of pills. Since the customer isn't paying for it, they can inflate their charges so that when the insurance company pays them a discounted, contract rate of say thirty or forty dollars, there is still a huge profit. But when guys like John show up with no insurance, they are told the cost is seventy-five bucks. That's not right, but the only solution he's told is available is to get insurance. In a free market economy he would be able to buy the medication for five bucks. That is precisely what many people are doing. They go across the border into Mexico and buy their medication for a fraction of what they'd pay here. Eventually, the same thing is likely to happen for all healthcare services."

Jack realized he gotten a little off topic, but he was afraid Bill would cut him off again, and he wanted to make the point that possible alternatives existed to the current insurance and government controlled healthcare system.

"Well, I thought we'd have time for more calls for the doctor, but I see we are just about out of time for this segment. I want to thank my guest, Dr. Jack Roberts, and hopefully we can have him come back on with us again, sometime very soon," Harris said, filling the final few seconds, not allowing Jack to even thank him before they went to commercial break.

The producer came on the line and quickly thanked Jack, before she also hung up without waiting for a response.

****

Immediately, when Jack walked through the door that evening, Elaina asked, "I thought you were going to tell about how that baby died because of regulations and cost cutting measures?"

"I thought I was too," he replied with frustration, "but that jerk kept asking me broad philosophical questions about Obamacare, and every time I even got close to talking about ACOs, he cut me off."

He sat his briefcase down on her desk and took the few steps over to the cooktop where she was preparing dinner. He walked up behind her, wrapping his arms around her waist, he kissed her gently on the neck. She turned around in his loose embrace to face him. "Well, I thought you did a good job of explaining why people need to maintain control of their own healthcare decisions."

He smiled and said simply, "Thank you." He then kissed her softly again before breaking away, in search of something cold to drink. As he poured himself a glass of lemonade, he then added, "Traci Bryan called me at the office, just before I left to come home."

"What did she have to say?"

"She said that she overheard Jim Fitzgerald, the chairman of the board, and Michael Horvath, the hospital administrator, talking about my interview. It seems that Fitzgerald now owns that radio station. She said he was very angry that I had been invited to be on the Bill Harris show. He hadn't found out I was going to be on until this morning, and they had already done a number of promos on the air, so he allowed the interview to go through, but apparently he instructed Harris to make sure I didn't share anything about ACOs or the story I was planning to tell."

"Really!" Elaina replied.

"She said she overheard him telling Horvath that his station had been inundated with calls supporting my position, but none of them were able to get on the air. He even admitted that the caller that was asking me questions about his inability to get insurance was actually one of Fitzgerald's own employees."

"Are you serious!?"

"I don't know for certain. but I don't have any reason to doubt Traci. She warned me that something is coming but she didn't know exactly what.

****

The deadline for creating statewide insurance exchanges, as called for by the new federal law, was October 1, 2013, but less than half of the states had actually done so. Those that had, were struggling to process the massive number of applications. Others, like Texas, had simply expanded their Medicaid roles, which now included millions who were previously uninsured. The huge and sudden increase in the number of Medicaid patients forced Texas to reduce physician payments for all covered services to avoid running out of money. As a result, most of Jack's colleagues, including the pediatric surgical group in Dallas, had decided to opt out of Medicaid altogether. So, Jack's office had been inundated with referrals of children with various heart problems from all over the state, many of whom were in the country illegally.

"I'm sorry, I don't have an appointment available until mid-November," Phyllis explained, in Spanish, to a mother on the phone.

"But, I was told that with my new government insurance, I could get my baby seen right away." The woman argued.

"I understand, but Dr. Roberts simply can't see your child for another eight weeks. We have already expanded our office hours to include Saturday mornings, but since he is one of the few pediatric heart surgeons in the state that still accepts Medicaid, we have been swamped."

"Will you please call me if you have a cancellation?" she asked."

"Of course," Phyllis replied, but she already had five parents on her list to call in the event of an unlikely cancellation.

"I will be happy to drive to Fort Worth from San Angelo, but you will need to give me at least four hours notice."

"Yes, ma'am, I will," Phyllis reassured the anxious mother. "If your daughter's condition deteriorates, you should take her the closest emergency room."

As Phyllis hung up, she saw Mary Anne standing in the doorway. She had been listening to her exchange. "How many is that this week?" Mary Anne asked.

"That's the fourth one just today!" Phyllis exclaimed. "I just hate having to make these people wait. Every story is the same. They've all been told their child has something wrong with their heart, and they need to see a specialist. They've just been waiting to get the Medicaid coverage they'd been promised was coming, so, now that they have it, they all want to be seen immediately."

"I guess this is what happens when two million people go from having no insurance coverage to being covered by a government program," Mary Anne replied. "All we can do is see as many as we can."

Jack had come in the back door and was standing a few feet behind his office manager, listening to her tired sounding voice. "That is correct," he said. "We can only do so much."

Mary Anne turned around, somewhat startled by his presence. "I thought you weren't going to be here until two."

"My committee meeting finished early," he explained. "Anything else going on?"

"As a matter of fact there is," she said. "We got another letter from CMS today."

"What? Are they going to try that stupid ban on ASD and PDA repairs again?" Jack asked. CMS had been forced to reverse their earlier position on procedures to close atrial septal defects and patent ductus arteriosus, largely due to the public pressure created by Jack's press conference nine months earlier.

"No," she said slowly, "but, this new policy is just as bad, if not worse," Marry Anne said.

"What is it this time?"

"As of last Monday, they are now requiring pre-authorization for all Medicaid related services that require hospital care, even if it's an outpatient procedure."

Jack just stood in front of her desk, looking at the letter, dumbfounded by what he was reading. The letter was only one page, but to comply would require countless extra man hours, mostly from his staff. "Have you been to this web site?" he asked, referring to the government website referred to in the letter. All physicians were instructed to review the list of procedures that now require pre-approval, and what the criteria were that would need to be met to obtain payment.

"I did take a quick look at it, and I don't think you are going to like it," Mary Anne said.

Jack went back to his office to access the Internet on his desktop computer. He quickly found the CMS site and began reviewing the laundry list of procedures, the specific findings that must be present, the required diagnostic tests and the nonsurgical treatments that must be documented for each congenital heart defect. "You have got to be kidding me," Jack spoke slowly to himself.

As he scanned further down the page, it was obvious that this was nothing more than a step by step review of each condition, as if it was a test for resident surgeons. Clearly this was written by an academic surgeon who believed that every decision should be made by following an elementary protocol. At the bottom of the page he saw the notation "All recommendations for procedures in this category were developed by the Association of Thoracic Surgeons."

Jack picked up the phone and dialed the number of the STS office. "May I speak to Carol Reeves?" he asked the receptionist, expecting to be transferred to the executive director.

"I'm sorry, Ms. Reeves is no longer with the ATS. Can someone else help you?"

Jack thought for a moment before saying, "No, I don't think so. Thank you."

He quickly pulled up Carol's cell phone number from his electronic address book. He touched the number and after two rings he heard Carol's familiar voice, say, "Hello, Dr. Roberts."

"Carol, what's happened?" Jack asked.

"I couldn't take it any more," she said. "The organization has become a joke. McCarty is offering the ATS name to the highest bidder."

"What do you mean?"

"The most recent thing he did was appoint a small group of his academic cronies on the board to what he called the Clinical Review Committee. He of course was the chairman. He then offered his committee to the Centers for

Medicare and Medicaid Services as a resource to develop criteria for every thoracic and cardiac procedure," she said. "That might not have been so bad, but when I suggested CMS should pay ATS for that information, he told me he'd already worked out an arrangement with the CMS Director, and ATS would receive ten thousand dollars when the work was complete."

"I saw the criteria they came up with posted on the CMS web site. That's what prompted my call," Jack said.

"Well, I did some inquiring behind the scenes and found out that CMS actually paid up to two hundred thousand dollars to each of twenty-two separate organizations for similar work in the various specialties," she said. "When, I asked McCarty about that, he denied knowing anything about it. I suspected something was up, so I called one of the guys on his committee, and told him I was just confirming that he received his payment for the committee work. He had know idea I was just fishing. When he confirmed that he received the check for five thousand dollars directly from McCarty, I knew."

"So, McCarty took money from CMS to develop these criteria and guidelines, then paid his committee members a few thousand each, and pocketed the rest?" Jack concluded.

"That is exactly what happened," Carol replied. "I went to DC and confronted him face to face, and he denied having any deal with CMS. He tried to sound incensed by my allegations, but he's not a very good actor."

"That sounds just like that SOB," Jack said, letting his voice trail off.

"I handed him my resignation right then, and I have to say, he seemed almost pleased to accept it."

"Of course, I'm sure he was more than willing to get you out," Jack said.

"I probably should have stayed and blown the whistle on him, but I just couldn't stand to work one more minute for an organization headed by someone who is that morally corrupt. Besides, all the other key members of the board are on his committee. My guess is they would have fired me, which would have looked really bad on my resumé."

"No, you did the right thing," Jack said. "If anyone is to blame for this, its me. I should never have resigned and left that organization to him."

****

When Jack got home that evening, Elaina could tell that something was very wrong. He seemed distant and totally absorbed as he kissed her briefly in passing, heading directly into his study.

THE CONFLICT

After a few minutes, she followed him into the small room off the hallway leading to the master suite. She saw him sitting at his desk, staring angrily at the computer screen. "What's up?" she asked, with concern in her voice..

"What did you say?" Jack asked, as he looked up rather startled, her voice having broken his concentration.

"Something's got you totally preoccupied," she said, "Do you want to talk about it?"

"You don't want to hear about it," he said softly. He knew how she felt about him bringing work home, and this time he really didn't want to burden her with the whole ATS, CMS mess.

"Yes I do." she said earnestly. "Something is wrong, and I would like to know what it is. Maybe I can help."

He smiled at her, knowing there was nothing she could do, but he appreciated her concern. "It's the same old stuff, government intrusion into medicine, physicians who have forgotten the meaning of the word professional. You know. Its the same thing I've been fighting against for years."

"No, I've seen you upset by that political nonsense before," she replied as she walked over behind him and placed her hands on his shoulders. His computer screen was filled with the CMS web site, and the list of procedures he commonly performed. "There is something more to it this time, isn't there."

He explained the new mandate from CMS and the role that McCarty had played in creating the criteria that would now have to be met before any child could receive the treatments that he and other surgeons provided based on their own extensive training and clinical judgement. "Now, we are going to have to satisfy some government clerk, armed with this ridiculous check list, before we can treat any child. This is just like the system I watched unfold in Britain, three decades ago. It's designed to do one thing, reduce the number of procedures performed. That means kids are going to die unnecessarily."

He turned toward her, and looked up into her eyes that were glistening slightly from the sadness she felt, not only for those children, but also for him. He was such an idealist, but that was what she loved about him, and it was what made him a great surgeon. "I don't know what to do," he sighed. "If I hadn't resigned as president of the ATS, maybe I'd still have a platform to argue against this."

"You still have a platform. People still listen to what you have to say," she said, moving her hand to tenderly touch his cheek. "You are one of the few people who have had the courage to speak out in the past. Maybe its time for you to do so again."

"I don't know," he replied, "It never seems to do any good. People just don't listen." She had never heard her husband sound so despondent, even after he lost the election.

"I think you're wrong," she replied. "I think most people are just as angry and frustrated with what's going on as you are. Everybody's looking for answers, and I think you should keep telling them what you see. Just keep telling them the truth."

Jack thought carefully about what she had said through dinner, trying to formulate a plan in his mind. He helped her clear the dishes off the table, and as she began loading the dishwasher, he said, "I actually considered going back on the radio to try and tell this story, but I don't trust any of those guys. They just want to hear themselves talk."

"What about doing a one on one television interview with Thomas Heller?" she suggested. "He's the guy who does that Sunday morning news program on channel eight called the Bare Truth. He was very nice to you during the campaign." He looked up at her with a questioning expression. "It might be worth a shot," she concluded.

He didn't say anything more, as he sat down in his favorite chair and turned on the television. He was soon absorbed in a Dallas Maverick's pre-season basketball game, and decided to sleep on her idea, and not think about it again until the following morning.

The next day he saw a young boy in the office with aortic stenosis. He had been diagnosed as an infant, but he didn't require treatment at that time. As the child grew, he gradually began to develop symptoms. Now, as a six year old he was complaining of intermittent chest pain and dizziness. A month earlier he had passed out at school, when he was running to catch up with on of his friends. The local cardiologist in Tyler, Texas had attempted a balloon valvuloplasty to open the aortic valve, but with no real improvement. Now, with his symptoms worsening to the point of nearly constant dizziness, and an inability to walk more than just a few feet without having to sit or lay down, he had been referred to Jack for aortic valve replacement.

"We need to get this boy on the schedule for this week," he explained to Mary Anne. "His systemic pressure is so low, he's in real danger of having a major stroke. and his heart isn't going to last much longer pumping against that tight aortic valve."

"We have a spot on Thursday afternoon, but I doubt we can get approval that soon," she explained.

"Approval?" Jack said angrily, having temporarily forgotten the new Medicaid requirement. After a challenging glance from Mary Anne, he rolled his eyes and said, "Just see what you can do."

The referring doctor in Tyler had sent most of the child's records, but missing were several documents Mary Anne needed to submit to the Medicaid cardiac surgery approval hotline. She called the other doctor's office and spoke to the office manager. She told her she needed the young boy's chest x-ray and electrocardiogram reports, the dictated cardiac cath report that included a detailed description of his failed attempt to open the valve, along with all their office records, documenting the attempts to treat his failing heart with medications.

"I'll get that stuff together for you as quickly as I can," the other woman said, "but I haven't received a copy of Dr. Perkins' dictation yet. I was told they had a problem at the hospital with their dictation system last week, but I'll call over there as soon as we hang-up."

"I can't submit the pre-authorization request to CMS without it. Would you please let me know as soon as you find out about that report?" Mary Anne asked.

When she hadn't heard from them by three o'clock that afternoon, she called Dr. Perkins' office again. "What did you find out about that cath report?" She realized she sounded rather impatient, but Jack had asked her about it twice since he returned from lunch.

"I'm sorry I haven't gotten back to you," she said, "but we've been pretty busy. The hospital tells me their automated transcription program went down for a few hours last week, and the dictated report was lost. They said our doctor would have to dictate his report again."

"How long will that take?" Mary Anne asked impatiently.

"That's the problem," she explained, "Dr. Perkins is on vacation this week. He won't be back until Monday."

"Is there any possibility the hospital can recover the dictation?"

"No ma'am. I asked about that, and they said their server went down and they lost all the dictation for that day."

"That's going to be a problem," Mary Anne said, resigned to the fact that the dictated report would not be available, trying to think of another option. "Do you think we could at least get Dr. Perkins' hand written notes, and the nurses notes from the cath lab? That might be enough to satisfy these new criteria."

"I will try and get you what I can, but the cath lab usually closes at three. Let me give them a call and I'll call you right back."

Ten minutes later Dr. Perkins' office manager called back. "I'm sorry, I couldn't get anybody in the cath lab to answer the phone. It will be tomorrow morning before I can get the records you need."

Mary Anne just shook her head. She then said, "I understand. If you would, please give me a call first thing in the morning. This boy and his parents are here in town, and I'm not certain what I'm going to do with them. I can't get him admitted until I have the pre-authorization for his surgery."

"When did CMS start requiring pre-approval for surgery?" the other office manager asked.

"Last week," replied Mary Anne. "Don't ask me why, but it is going to be the biggest mess ever. I called them earlier about this case, and I was on hold for thirty minutes before I could talk to a live person. The girl I spoke to had no idea what I was talking about when I explained I had a six year old who needed an urgent aortic valve replacement. She put me back on hold for another fifteen minutes. When I finally got someone on the phone who even knew what I meant when I said I needed pre-authorization for the surgery, all she did was read me the criteria, straight off the web site."

"I'm glad we don't have to do that for every kid we cath." she said.

Mary Anne laughed silently before she said, "Obviously, you haven't read what's on the CMS web site. You do need pre-approval, even for a cardiac cath, except in certain, very specific emergency situations."

The phone was silent for a moment before Mary Anne's counterpart said, "But... we don't have the time or the personnel to do that for every Medicaid patient we see."

"Tell me about it," Marry Anne responded. "Nearly every other pediatric heart surgeon has quit taking Medicaid, so we are swamped with this kind of busy work, only to get paid about twenty cents on the dollar."

"Dr. Perkins has been considering dropping Medicaid, and I wish he would. Maybe this will be just what it takes to get him to make that decision."

"Dr. Roberts will never drop out of the Medicaid program. I think he would take care of those kids for free, but CMS won't allow that. You have to be a Medicaid provider, otherwise those patients can't even be evaluated."

"What are they going to do when everyone refuses to take Medicaid?"

"That's a good question," Mary Anne said. "There's talk that the government will tie Medicare and Medicaid participation to the physician's license. Forcing everyone to participate, but I don't know how that would help. I know several physicians in our area who have instructed their scheduling people to only schedule one Medicaid patient per week. So, while they are technically participating, they aren't really."

"Can you blame them? We looked at our experience last year, and we didn't come close to breaking even on Medicaid."

"I just feel bad for kids like this boy and his family." Mary Anne added. "The politicians promise them all this free care, but then there isn't anyone to provide it." Again there was silence for a few seconds, before Mary Anne added,

"I get to the office around eight-thirty every morning, so if you would call me as soon as you know something, I'd appreciate it."

The two women concluded their conversation and Mary Anne walked back to Jack's office. She explained the problem with the dictated report, and waited patiently for his frustrated and angry response. Instead, he gave her another assignment.

"Would you see if you can get Thomas Heller on the phone?" He saw her questioning expression, then added, "He's that guy from channel eight news."

"She nodded and left the room. A few minutes later Jack heard her voice on the intercom, "Mr. Heller is on line one."

Jack picked up the phone and said, "Tom, thanks for taking my call,"

"Sure," the reporter replied, "what's up?"

"You remember right after the election you told me if I had anything news worthy on the healthcare front to let you know?" Jack asked.

"Yeah, sure." Heller replied.

"Well, there are some things happening as we get closer to the full implementation of this healthcare reform law that people need to know about."

****

"This morning I have, as my guest here in the studio, Dr. Jack Roberts, an accomplished heart surgeon and former candidate for Congress. Welcome Dr. Roberts to the Bare Truth," Heller said.

"Thanks for having me on, Tom," Jack replied. He was dressed in a navy suit, with a plain white shirt and light blue tie. Elaina had told him that people tend to associate the color blue with the truth.

"Well, now that Obamacare is about to be fully implemented, I understand there are a few concerns in the medical community."

"That's true," Jack began. "There are so many problems that have been created it's hard to even know where to start."

"Why don't we start with the expansion of Medicaid," Heller suggested, just as he and Jack had agreed.

"As you know, the law expanded the eligibility requirements for Medicaid to include approximately two million more people here in Texas, and that includes a lot of kids."

"Much of your practice is pediatric heart surgery, isn't it?" Heller asked, creating an opportunity for Jack to connect to the issue on a more personal basis.

"Yes, in the last few years my practice has become even more focused on childhood heart disease, so currently about eighty percent of my patients are children, and more than half of them are covered either by the State Children's Health Insurance Program, called SCHIP, or by Medicaid."

"I would think that increasing the number of Medicaid patients would be good for business, right?"

Jack smiled and chuckled almost sarcastically. "You would think so, but the problem with Medicaid is that the payments for physician services are so low, in most instances it doesn't cover our costs. That's why many of my colleagues have decided not to participate in the Medicaid program. So, while many more patients now have coverage, there are fewer and fewer physicians available to provide the care they need."

"So, you still accept Medicaid patients?"

"Yes, but I'm not sure how long I can continue to do so. Three months ago the average wait to get an appointment to see me was less than two weeks, but now, since I'm one of only a handful of surgeons who still take Medicaid, my schedule is booked out more than two months. I have had to hold some spots open in my schedule for non-Medicaid patients. Otherwise that's all I would see, and like I said, Medicaid payments are so low, I couldn't stay in business if all my patients were under government insurance."

"When you say payments are low, can you give me an example?"

"Sure," Jack replied. "For a new patient office visit, my charge is one hundred fifty dollars. Most insurance companies pay between eighty-five and a hundred, and Medicare pays about sixty-five, but Medicaid is now under thirty."

"Thirty dollars to see a heart surgeon?" Heller exclaimed. "You have got to be kidding me!"

"No," Jack said calmly, "and that number has been continuing to go down steadily for the last several years, as the state budget has continue to get tighter."

"Obviously, you make up those losses with your surgical fees, right?"

"Not really," Jack explained. "Let's take for example a typical pediatric heart operation, like say, the ligation of a patent ductus arteriosus. That's a blood vessel between the pulmonary and systemic circulation that normally closes shortly after birth, but when it doesn't it can lead to heart failure in infants and small children. The typical surgeons fee for that procedure is around twenty-five hundred dollars."

"That doesn't sound like much," Heller said, "considering my plumber charged me two thousand bucks for a new hot water heater."

"The average insurance payment for that procedure is around twelve hundred dollars, but Medicaid only pays four hundred and fifty dollars."

"But, what does that take you, an hour, maybe two to do that operation?"

"That is true, but the fee includes all the pre-operative time spent with the patient and the family, the four or five days in the hospital and ninety days of follow-up after the procedure. I worked out the per hour charge, and it comes out to around fifty-three dollars an hour."

"But, I was under the impression that major operations like that cost tens of thousands of dollars."

"They do, but most of that money goes to pay the hospital. The surgeon's fee is typically less than ten percent of the total cost."

"That's amazing," Heller said, shaking his head.

"But," Jack continued, "the economics are not the only concern. In fact, for me and many of my colleagues, the main issue isn't the money, it's the regulations."

"We need to take a short commercial break before we hear more from Dr. Jack Roberts about government regulations, and what they are doing to impact your health, and the health of your children. Stay tuned, we'll be right back."

As soon as the red lights on all the cameras went off, Tom turned to Jack and said, "This is great stuff. Are we getting to what you wanted to say?"

"More or less," Jack replied, "but, I really want to use some specific examples when we start talking about the regulations. My wife and son have both told me I tend to talk too much in the abstract, and that most people can't relate. They need individual stories to be able to really understand the potential impact on them."

"They're right about that," Tom agreed, "that's the way we present the news everyday."

"We are back with my guest, Dr. Jack Roberts, and just before the break he was tell me that most physicians are actually more upset by the way the government is regulating the practice of medicine than they are with the way they are being paid." He turned back toward Jack who was seated on a navy blue sofa, and separated from his leather chair by a glass top coffee table. "Why don't you tell us a little bit about some of the new regulations and their impact on your ability to practice medicine?"

"Well, like I said at the beginning of this program, its hard to even know where to begin, but I have a couple of specific examples that I think will offer your audience some insight into what is happening."

"I agree," Tom said, "Why don't you tell the audience the story you shared with me about the little boy you saw last week?"

"He's a six year old from Tyler, Texas. I saw him in my office last Tuesday, and he has a severe case of aortic stenosis. That means the opening from the main pumping chamber of his heart that supplies blood to his entire body is very narrow. The result is the flow of blood is restricted and his blood pressure is very low."

"Is this something that came on suddenly?" Heller asked.

"No, he was born with this condition, but when he was a baby he was pretty well compensated. As he has grown, the narrowed valve hasn't grown with him, so he gradually began having trouble with dizziness and chest pain, and recently he started passing out with almost any activity. That's when his cardiologist referred him for surgery."

"Sounds like something needs to be done right away."

"That's true," Jack agreed. "His condition is not a true emergency, at least not yet. But his blood pressure is low enough that he is at risk of having a stroke due to insufficient blood flow to his brain, and his heart is also in danger of failing because of the amount of resistance it is pumping against."

"So, have you operated on him?"

"Not yet," Jack said, with a frustrated tone.

"Why not?"

"Because, the Centers for Medicare and Medicaid Services recently started requiring pre-approval of all surgical procedures, and so far we haven't been able to get them to authorize the operation."

"Why?" Heller was the one who now sounded angry.

"The process requires submission of a laundry list of documents, some of which we have yet to obtain from his doctor's office in Tyler. It's not their fault, they are doing everything they can. The problem is that no one at CMS has any authority to do anything until every i is dotted and every t is crossed. Meanwhile, this boy and his family remain in a nearby hotel room, waiting."

"Can't you just go ahead and do the surgery anyway and get the authorization later?"

"No, that would be considered fraud in the eyes of the government. Even if I decided to proceed without charging anything for the procedure, the hospital wouldn't allow me to admit him without the pre-authorization because they wouldn't get paid either."

"This is ridiculous!" Heller said disgustedly. "Who makes up these rules?"

"In this case, CMS. They are the federal bureaucracy that oversees everything that has to do with Medicare and Medicaid."

"Did they consult with the doctors before implementing these regulations?"

"The criteria used to decide whether a procedure can be authorized were developed by one of our professional organizations, but those academic surgeons were actually paid by CMS. The obvious goal of this process is to reduce the total number of procedures performed. Some might even go so far as to call it a form of rationing."

"We hear a lot about fraud and abuse of these programs," Heller said. "Do you think any of these regulations prevent fraud?"

"Absolutely not," Jack replied emphatically. "But, the vast majority of what the government is referring to as fraud is nothing more than minor errors in documentation. I was audited earlier this year, and fined for alleged Medicare fraud, but CMS wouldn't even tell me what they found in their three day review of my records. There was no appeal process. They were judge, jury, prosecutor and executioner."

"We need to take one more quick break," Heller said, "Then we'll be back with my special guest, Dr. Jack Roberts, to hear more about how the government is seizing control of your healthcare. Stay tuned."

"That is amazing," he said, as he turned toward Jack. "No appeal?"

"I don't even know what they found. Three guys showed up in my office, unannounced. They spent three days rifling through my records without asking any questions of me or my staff. When they were finished they just walked out, and a few days later I got a call notifying me that I was being fined ten thousand dollars." As Jack concluded his explanation he remembered the instructions the CMS official gave him about not discussing anything about the audit or the fine with anyone, but before he could say anything more the red light on the main camera came back on.

"We're back with our guest, Dr. Jack Roberts, a pediatric heart surgeon and former Congressional candidate," Heller said facing the camera. He then turned to Jack and asked, "So, Dr. Roberts, why did you decide to run for Congress?"

Jack smiled and shook his head. "Looking back, I guess the only reason was to try and help reverse the trend I'm seeing as our government assumes more and more control over people's lives. I was, and still am, frustrated by the lack of people in positions of authority, actually willing to stand up for what is right."

"It has to be frustrating to watch your profession being systematically turned into an arm of that government."

Jack dropped his eyes and shook his head, "It is the saddest thing I have ever witnessed. It's like watching someone die from a cancer that no one seems to even want to acknowledge exists."

"Other than the delay in treating the child from Tyler last week, are you aware of any specific examples of how patients are being impacted by government regulations?"

"Absolutely," Jack replied, "but, what I see is more subtle. For example, there is a major move to reduce the length of each patient's hospital stay. The objective is to lower hospital costs to match the lower payments they are receiving. The problem is that's not the way it's being presented. Hospitals are implementing, so called, quality improvement processes that are designed to meet some arbitrary guidelines imposed by the government. In many cases the effect is the exact opposite."

"We've been hearing a lot about quality assurance," Heller said, "and now you're suggesting it's more about cost containment?"

"That is correct," Jack said, nodding his head rather emphatically. "I'm aware of a case where an infant with a very serious congenital heart defect was moved to a nursing facility outside the hospital, just four days after heart surgery. The reason that was used for the transfer was that national guidelines call for a hospital stay not to exceed four days, unless there were ongoing complications. The baby appeared to be doing okay when they transferred her, but three days later she developed acute respiratory failure and suddenly died."

"Oh my God!" Heller exclaimed.

Jack replied, "Now, I don't know, that might have been the outcome even had she remained in the hospital, but I can't help but believe that the decision to transfer her should have been left up to her doctors, not some panel of so called experts whose sole purpose is to micromanage medical decision making."

The show's director switched to the closeup camera, focused on Heller as he sat with a stunned look on his face. After a few seconds of silence he started shaking his head slowly and said, "That is simply unbelievable."

The camera returned to Jack, who was nodding his head. His expression was one of frustration as he remained silent.

Heller gradually composed himself, then looked at Jack and spoke in a sad voice, "Unfortunately, we are about out of time, but I'd like to know, what are you planning to do now?" Heller asked.

"I'm not going to run for office again, that's for sure," Jack laughed, lightening the mood between them somewhat.

"Why not? It sounds like something has to be done."

"Politics is a blood sport," Jack replied. "At my age, I'm not cut out for that. I think my role needs to be one of sharing the facts, as I see them, with people like you and your audience. Maybe when enough people learn the truth about what is really happening, they will insist that the government get out of our private lives."

"I wish I shared your optimism," Heller replied. He then turned back to the camera, clearly still shaken by the story Jack had just shared. "Thank you for watching, and I hope you'll join me next Sunday as we continue to uncover the Bare Truth."

CHAPTER 13

"The Bare Truth," aired at nine-thirty on Sunday morning on the ABC affiliate, in the Dallas-Fort Worth area. By ten-thirty the station had received more than one hundred calls, and twice that many emails. Based on the unprecedented interest in the story, the station manager sent the video to the network in New York, and by two in the afternoon it was posted on the ABC News web site. Within two hours it had received nearly thirty thousand views and more than four hundred comments. That evening Mike Huckabee made the story part of his Sunday evening program on Fox News.

"You told me people still wanted to hear what I have to say, and by all accounts I guess you were right," Jack said to Elaina, following the tenth call in an hour. Their home phone had been ringing almost continuously since mid-afternoon on Sunday. Reporters were calling from as far away as London, all asking the same questions. "How did that baby die?" and "Is that six year old going to get his operation?" He finally unplugged the home phones from the wall outlets, assuming that anyone who really needed to get in touch with him, including the hospital, could do so on his cell phone.

"Its like David said, people want a story they can relate to," Elaina replied, "and you certainly gave it to them."

"I feel bad," Jack said, "As soon as the words were out of my mouth about that baby who died, I wanted to take them back."

"Why?" she asked.

"Because I'm afraid that case will come back to bite George."

"George isn't the one at fault. You know that," she said.

"I know, but when something like this happens, invariably they will find a way to blame the doc. George will be inundated with calls, and I'm not sure he'll know what to say to protect himself."

Almost on cue, his cell phone rang. It was George.

"Hey George," Jack said. "I can only guess why you're calling."

"I doubt it," George said anxiously. "I'm calling to warn you. Grady called me a few minutes ago. He is livid. He wanted to know if I had anything to do with that interview."

"You told him that you didn't know anything about it, right?"

"Yes, of course, but, he demanded to know why I needed you to look over my shoulder, and when I told him I wasn't comfortable taking care of that baby on my own he went ballistic. He threatened to terminate my contract with the group and sue me for non-performance under some bullshit clause in the agreement."

"What did you say to that?" Jack asked, knowing George was actually looking for a way out of that group.

"I told him, that he and Horvath were the one's who should be worried about a malpractice suit."

"You said you called to warn me... about what exactly?" Jack asked.

"He is going to come after you. I don't know how, but he sounded serious. I just think you need to watch your back."

"Well, I appreciate the heads up, George," Jack said sincerely. "He can come after me if he likes, but I haven't said anything that wasn't the gospel truth."

"I just think you need to be careful."

"Are you still going to be able to help me with that aortic valve in the morning?" Jack asked. Shortly after they taped the interview on Friday afternoon, he received word from Mary Anne that she had managed to get CMS to approve the boy's surgery for Monday morning.

"You bet," George replied. "I'll be there around seven-thirty.

****

On Monday the impact of government inspired healthcare regulations was the topic of discussion on every early morning talk radio program in America. Some right wing pundits were claiming that the government had purposefully caused a significant delay in the care of a six year old boy. One even falsely reported that the child had died over the weekend, waiting for a life saving operation that had been denied under Obamacare guidelines. Another attributed the death of the infant to government negligence, calling it "bureaucratic malpractice."

In the doctors lounge, Jack was greeted very warmly by several of his older colleagues, but the younger guys, with the exception of George, avoided him completely. They all feared Grady would find them guilty by association.

The six year old's aortic valve surgery had gone very smoothly. Jack had used a cadaver valve so the boy wouldn't have to be on blood thinners for the rest of his life, and he explained to the parents that it was likely their son would need to have it replaced with another, larger valve once he reached adulthood.

He left the hospital soon after the child was safely into the recovery room. Radha was managing the child's ventilator and IV fluids, and the young boy appeared to be doing great. When he arrived at his office there were more than fifty phone messages on his desk. It seemed that every reporter in the country had found his office number the same way they had found his home number. "I'm not taking any calls from reporters. It's business as usual today, okay?" he said to his three employees. They each nodded in agreement, but just then the phone rang again.

"Dr. Roberts' office, this is Phyllis, How can I help you?"

"This is Michael Horvath from the hospital, I need to speak to Dr. Roberts."

"Its Mr. Horvath," Phyllis said, after placing the administrator on hold.

"Tell him I'm with a patient. He can either hold for a few minutes or I can call him back."

After a few seconds she said, "He said he will hold. He sounds pretty angry."

Jack let him simmer for a few minutes before finally picking up the phone in his office. "This is Jack Roberts."

"Dr. Roberts, this is Michael Horvath."

"What can I do for you Michael?" Jack said casually. He had only called him by his first name once before, and he was in no mood to sound overly respectful now.

"That interview you did yesterday on television has created quite a stir."

"That was my intent," Jack replied. "Hopefully, it will result in some changes that will be good for our patients."

"Don't get smart with me, Roberts!" He spouted angrily. "This is serious. I have had reporters from every television station in the state calling, wanting me to comment on that infant's death."

"So, what did you tell them?" Jack asked.

"You aren't going to get away with this. Not this time." Horvath's words were sharp and his tone was clearly threatening.

"I was always taught that when you tell the truth, you don't have to worry about getting away with anything," Jack replied calmly.

"We'll see about that!" Horvath said as he slammed the phone down.

****

"Hi, Jack," Traci said, "Are you in the hospital?"

"No, I haven't made it back yet," Jack replied. "I was just finishing up in my office before coming up there to check on that kid I operated on this morning."

"Don't!" she warned.

"What do you mean, don't?"

"I mean, don't come up here right now. Horvath and Grady are waiting for you."

"What difference does that make? I'm not afraid of them."

"I'm not sure what they're up to, but I don't like the look of it.'

"Do they have guns?" Jack laughed.

"No, of course not," she replied. "But I have a bad feeling about this."

"So, what do you want me to do?" he asked reluctantly, trying to pacify the one friend he had in administration.

"I'm going to go talk to them and try to find out what their planning," she said. "Please, just sit tight for a little bit, and I'll call you back when I know something more."

"Okay, I can wait a little while, but I have to come up there sometime this evening to check on my patient."

After about fifteen minutes Jack's cell phone rang again.

"I couldn't get any information out of them," Traci said, "but a just saw both of them leave for the day."

"So, its safe?" Jack laughed again in response to her anxious tone.

"I don't know what you think is so funny, Jack. These guys are angry and they are out to get you."

"I appreciate you looking out for me," Jack replied sincerely, "but, I think I can handle those two."

"I'm just worried about you," she said, earnestly. "I've never seen either of them so upset, and angry."

"I'll be careful, I'll even look under my car for any signs of a bomb," he couldn't help but laugh softly at the cloak and dagger conversation in which they were engaged. "You are very sweet to worry about me, but I promise, I'll be just fine."

"Okay," she said with resignation in her voice.

"I'll come by tomorrow, and we'll talk," he said, again trying to reassure her.

****

On Tuesday morning, Jack went by the ICU to check on the only patient he had in the hospital. The six year old boy was doing very well. His blood pressure was normal and he was waking up, fighting against the tube in his trachea. The ventilator had been turned off and he was breathing on his own.

"Has Dr. Patel been by this morning?" he asked the nurse taking care of the young boy.

"Not yet," she replied. I spoke to her around seven, and she said to get everything ready to extubate him."

"He certainly looks strong enough," Jack said. "Let's go ahead and take out the endotracheal tube."

The nurse quickly removed the tape that secured the plastic tube to the boy's face, and spoke to him reassuringly. "I'm going to remove the breathing tube now, okay?"

The boy's eyes were wide open as he shook his head vigorously in agreement. As she slid the tube out of his throat, he coughed twice, then winced at the pain in his chest.

"That's good," she said. "Just take some deep breaths of this oxygen." She quickly placed a clear green plastic mask over his mouth and nose, discarding the now needless tube into the biohazards container.

Within a couple of minutes the child calmed down and Jack could see that he was breathing effortlessly. His oxygen saturation was ninety-eight percent, and his respiratory rate was only twenty two. "Not much out of the chest tube," he remarked.

"No, sir," she replied, "The night shift only recorded five cc's."

"Let's get him up in the chair this morning," he said, then asked, "where are his parents?"

"They went down to the cafeteria to get some breakfast," she answered.

"I'll run down there to let them know how he's doing."

Jack signed into the computer terminal just outside the sliding glass door. He went through the seven separate steps required by the new electronic health record. The program would not allow him to type a note in the chart until he documented that he had reviewed his patient's vital signs, intake and output volumes, lab tests, the nurses' notes, the physical findings, all current medications and finally his nutritional status. Only then could he type in that he was doing well, and that he had extubated him.

"Did you write the order for oxygen by face mask," the nurse asked.

"No, but I will," Jack said disgustedly, shaking his head at the wasted time spent doing things that had no impact on the actual care of his patient.

"Don't forget about the order for getting him up." she reminded him, just as he was about to finish charting.

Jack took a deep breath and let it out slowly, as Elaina had instructed him, as a means of dealing with the frustration. After another two minutes of entering passwords and reassuring his digital friend that it was still him who had typed the orders and the note in the chart, he turned toward the entrance to the ICU. As he looked up, he saw Horvath and Grady standing near the nurses station desk, obviously waiting for him.

"Gentlemen," he said, in a questioning tone as he approached them.

"Dr. Roberts," Horvath said, "We need to talk with you."

"I was just on my way down to the cafeteria to speak with my patient's family. Would you care to join me?"

"No, we need to speak in private. Please, follow me," the administrator insisted as he turned and gestured down the hall. When they reached a small consultation room, Horvath opened the door, and he and Grady followed Jack inside.

"I won't ask you to sit down," Horvath said, "This won't take long. As you know, Dr. Grady is our recently elected chief of staff, and after consulting with him we have concluded that your conduct has become detrimental to the general welfare of this hospital."

"What conduct are you referring to specifically?" Jack asked, trying to sound surprised, but not very successfully.

"I'm referring to your open, public discussion of hospital policies and specific patient care issues. Your appearance on local television, and the subsequent rebroadcast of that interview nationally and internationally, has caused irreparable harm to this hospital's stellar reputation. Based on our conversation yesterday, when you told me, in no uncertain terms, that it was your intent to create a major controversy, we have concluded that you willfully and maliciously set out to damage the good name of this hospital and its medical staff."

Jack stood quietly, letting Horvath have his say. Grady also stood quietly with his chin high and shoulders back, almost as if at attention.

"We are left with no alternative but to summarily suspend your privileges to practice in this facility, effective immediately." Horvath assumed a similar posture, next to Grady.

"Is that your response to the truth?" Jack asked, more as a statement than a question. "You get exposed for adopting a stupid and dangerous policy for the sole purpose of saving you money, and all you can think of to do is shoot the messenger? That's pitiful." His tone turned to disgust. "You want to know about irreparable harm? I'll tell you about irreparable harm. Go talk to that little baby's mother. She can tell you about irreparable harm, first hand."

"According to the medical staff by laws, you will be afforded the opportunity to appeal this suspension at a medical board hearing, to be conducted at a mutually agreed upon date and time, within the next thirty days. You may bring an attorney to that hearing, and you are encouraged to do so," Horvath added.

Jack turned to Grady with a smirk, "I suppose you are going to assume the care of my one day post op aortic valve patient?"

"We will assign the child's care to the intensivists and to George Ferguson," Grady said confidently. "It is my understanding that he is the only patient you currently have in the hospital, is that correct?"

"Yes, but I have three cases on the schedule for tomorrow."

"How you choose to deal with those patients is your problem," Horvath said, "but you will not be doing surgery on them here. You may go to the doctor's lounge and retrieve any personal items you have there, but then you must leave the building immediately."

Jack turned back toward him. It was all he could do to stop himself from punching the arrogant bastard in the face. He knew his anger was obvious, but he didn't care. "I will first go down to the cafeteria and speak with the parents of my patient," he said. "They need to hear from me exactly why I won't be seeing their son."

"I'm afraid that is quite impossible," Horvath replied. "You have been relieved of all duties in this facility with respect to that patient."

Jack took a menacingly bold step toward Horvath and glared into his eyes. "If you think you are going to stop me from speaking to my patients family, you are very sadly mistaken."

Horvath stared back with as much resolve as he could manage, but the surgeon's six foot three inch frame loomed over him. Despite his best effort, he was forced to take a step back, as Jack exited the room.

"I think it's going to be very difficult to keep him off the staff permanently," Grady said. "He has a lot of friends around here, many of whom are on the board."

"He is guilty of conduct detrimental to all of their practices," Horvath replied.

"That may be, but when it boils right down to it, he hasn't done anything wrong from a clinical stand point, and that's how most docs will judge him."

Regaining his resolve, Horvath turned to face Grady as a sly smile came quickly to his face. After a moment he said, "I don't think the medical staff will ever have to deal with the problem."

****

Jack recognized the young parents of the child from Tyler sitting near the window, and when they saw him a look of concern came over both their faces. They were sure that the only reason the doctor would come looking for them in the cafeteria was to tell them something was wrong with their son. Jack gave them a reassuring smile as he approached.

"Is everything okay?" the dad asked, rising to his feet.

"Yes, everything is fine," Jack said, motioning for him to sit back down. "I removed his breathing tube a few minutes ago, and he's doing very well. I'm sure he'll be talking to you when you get back up stairs."

"That's wonderful," the mother said with a broad smile.

"I do have some other news, that I need to share with you," Jack said calmly, trying not to alarm them. "I was recently on a television program discussing some things that I strongly disagree with, regarding the changes in our healthcare system, and some of the things that hospitals are doing in response."

"Yes, we watched that program on Sunday in our hotel room. I thought what you had to say made a lot of sense," the father said.

"Well, not everyone here in this hospital agrees with your assessment. The administration has determined that my remarks were damaging to the hospital's reputation, and they have suspended me from practicing in this facility, effective immediately." Jack's words sounded more like an apology than an explanation.

"What?" the mother exclaimed. "How can they do that?"

The father followed, abruptly asking, "Who is going to take care of our son?"

"They have the right to suspend any physician's privileges to practice, under the medical staff bylaws, and that is exactly what they have done. As to who will assume the care of your son, Dr. George Ferguson is the surgeon who assisted me during his surgery, and he will be assuming his care. George is a great surgeon. He and I have worked together for several years now, and he is very capable of taking care of any circumstance that might arise."

"Was any of this because of what you said about the delay in getting our son's surgery approved?" the father asked.

"No," Jack said, reassuringly. "This didn't have anything to do with that." he paused briefly then continued, "I'm really sorry. I feel terrible about having to relinquish your child's care to anyone else, but I have every confidence that Dr. Ferguson will take excellent care of him."

"We understand," the mother said sympathetically. "I hope you can get this situation resolved quickly. You know you were the only surgeon we could find that would accept Medicaid. I hate to think what will happen to other children who need your services if you aren't allowed to practice."

Jack wondered that as well. He shook his head and without realizing it, his shoulders slumped noticeably. The sadness in his voice was obvious as he replied softly, "I don't know either."

He turned and headed back upstairs to the doctors change room. He quickly collected his personal items from his locker and started back toward the elevator. Just as he made his way into the hallway he heard a familiar voice behind him.

"Jack!" Radha called out.

He turned and saw his long time friend walking briskly toward him. He smiled and said, "I suppose you heard."

"Yes, its all over the hospital," she replied. "I feel terrible about this."

"You don't need to feel bad," he said, "you didn't have anything to do with it."

"I feel bad for you," she explained.

"I'm sure this will all blow over in a couple of weeks. They can't make this charge stick, and they know it. I can use a little time off anyway."

"There's more to it than just the suspension," she said, almost in a whisper.

"What do you mean?"

"We can't talk here," she said looking around to see if anyone else was in the hallway. "I'll walk with you out to your car."

They both remained silent until they had made their way to the parking lot. As Jack unlocked his truck and put the items from his locker in the back seat he asked, "So, what else is there?"

Again she looked around, fearing she was being watched, then spoke softly but more rapidly than normal. "Just a few minutes ago I was in the private dining room when Mr. Horvath and Jerry Grady came in talking about you. I guess they didn't see me because I was standing in that little alcove where they keep the coffee machine. I overheard Horvath telling Jerry that he didn't think there would be a hearing."

"What?" Jack said angrily. "They can't deny me a hearing. It's in the bylaws."

"He said he had contacted CMS and the FBI himself. He told Jerry that they had agreed to another fraud investigation, based in part on the fact that you violated their instructions when you shared information about their previous audit."

Jack shook his head slowly, remembering exactly what he had revealed during the television interview. "I wouldn't be surprised," he said in frustration.

Radha continued to tell him more of what she had overheard. "Horvath said he was meeting with FBI agents and the local Medicaid fraud investigator tomorrow morning, prior to a raid on your office."

"A raid on my office?"

"He said he expected that you will be arrested and hauled away in hand cuffs. He said Fitzgerald planned to have his station post a television crew outside your office to catch it all live."

"Are you sure?"

"Yes, I'm certain. Those guys are out to destroy you, Jack. They want you completely out of their way."

Jack stood next to his truck, trying to get his mind around everything he had just heard. As difficult as it was to believe, he knew Radha had no reason to lie to him.

"Listen," he said intently, "I don't want you to share any of this with anyone else, okay? I don't want them to even suspect that there is any connection between you and me."

"What are you going to do?"

"I'm not sure," he said shaking his head, "but, I can tell you this much, I'm not going to jail."

He got into his truck and started the engine, but he sat silently with both hands on the steering wheel, thinking. After a minute he reached for his cell phone and dialed the direct line to Traci Bryan's office.

"Jack!" she said in little more than a whisper. "Have you met with Horvath?"

"Yes, about twenty minutes ago," he said.

"I'm really sorry."

"No need to be sorry, I brought it on myself."

"Well, just for the record, I agree with everything you said in that interview."

"Thanks," he replied, "Too bad you aren't still the administrator."

"I don't know how much longer I can stand being here. This place has become almost like a war room. Just yesterday I overheard Horvath talking to one of the other assistant administrators. He was saying something about having to blow the whistle on one of our long standing staff members for possible Medicaid fraud. She said he had a meeting scheduled the next morning with representatives of CMS."

"That's why I was calling. I'm sure that staff member is me. Horvath is trying to get rid of me by whatever means he can, all because I refuse to participate in his scheme to employ all the doctors."

"There has to be something more than that behind this," Traci said. "I'll keep my ear to the ground and I'll let you know if I hear anything else."

"Okay, thanks. I'll be in touch," Jack said as he hung up.

Her comments only confirmed what Radha had told him. What he didn't know was how it was really Fitzgerald who was pulling the strings behind the scenes. It was not enough to have beaten Jack in the recent election, he was still committed to extracting every possible measure of revenge on the man he assumed was responsible for that mobster, Franco Gutierrez, and his goons, terrorizing him.

His next call was to Elaina. "How quickly can you get packed?"

"Get packed, for what?" she asked excitedly. She had always dreamed of how one day, without warning, he would take her back to Paris. Was this that day?

"We have to leave town today."

By the sound of his voice it was clear this wasn't any romantic getaway. "Where are we going?"

"To our vacation home in Nicaragua. Its a long story. I'll tell you about it when I get home, but we need to leave as soon as possible."

"Okay," she said. "It will take me at least a couple of hours."

"Don't tell anyone that we're leaving town. I'll explain later."

"But..." she started to object, then suddenly realized this had something to do with the television interview. He didn't want them to be followed. "Do you want me to pack your stuff too?"

"If you can that would be great, otherwise I can do it when I get home."

"When will you be home?"

"I need to run by the office for a few minutes, so, probably in less than an hour."

"Are you okay?" she asked, concerned for his health.

"I'm fine. We'll talk about this when I get there, okay?"

"Okay," she said once more, this time unsure what exactly she was agreeing to.

"I love you, and I'll see you soon," Jack said trying to offer some reassurance.

As soon as he hung up, he drove the short distance to his office. As he stepped through the back door, he saw Mary Anne walking from the kitchen area back to her office. "I need to see you," he said using his military tone.

She understood that was not a request, but an order. She turned around immediately and stepped through his office door just as he was sitting down at his desk. "What's up?" she asked.

"You need to cancel my office for the rest of the week. I'm leaving town, but you can't tell anyone else."

"Where are you going," she asked, concerned that there must have been a death in the family or some similar emergency.

"I'm going to Nicaragua, but it will be better for you if you don't know why."

She didn't question him verbally, but her expression was seeking clarification. It wasn't like him to sound so secretive. "What do you want me to tell the girls?"

"They don't need to know anything right now, but you can tell them they will also have the rest of the week off, and they can leave as soon as they help you clear my schedule."

"Do you want us to reschedule your patients?"

"No," he replied.

"What am I supposed to tell them? Many of these people have been waiting weeks to see you."

"I know," he said, looking up from his computer screen. "The best thing to tell them is that someone will be in touch with them in a few days. You'll need to print out a list of my schedule for the next couple of months, including the patients' phone numbers so we can call them back."

"A couple of months? I thought you told me to cancel just the rest of this week? What's going on?"

He stopped what he was doing on the computer, realizing he couldn't avoid telling her. "As a result of that television interview, my privileges at the hospital have been suspended, and tomorrow the FBI and CMS are going to raid this office."

"What?" she sounded as though she'd just heard about the sudden death of a relative.

"They are out to get me, Mary Anne," he said, acknowledging out loud what Traci had suggested. "If I'm here tomorrow when they show up, there is a good chance they'll take me out in handcuffs, and I'm not going to sit still and allow that to happen."

"I'm so sorry, Dr. Roberts," she said, allowing her emotions to show. "What do you want me to do?"

Jack thought for a moment then replied. "Just cancel the rest of this week for now, and print out the rest of my schedule for the next two months. I'll let you know what to do with them, once I've had a chance to talk to George."

"Consider it done," she said and quickly returned to her office.

Jack used his cell phone again to call George Ferguson. He explained in detail what had happened earlier that morning.

"Oh, my God!" George exclaimed. "Horvath really is out for blood."

"I don't know exactly what's going on, but I'm not going to wait around here to get arrested for something I didn't do, then spend six months or more trying to prove my innocence from behind bars."

"What can I do for you?" George asked.

"Prayer would be good," Jack suggested, trying to lighten the mood, but without much success. "What I really need is for you to take care of my patients."

"I can do that." George said confidently. "Other than the kid in the ICU, what else do you have?"

"He is the only patient I have in either hospital, but there are three kids on the schedule for tomorrow. I've had Mary Anne cancel them, but they'll need to be seen by you right away. My other problem is my office. I have patients booked out for a couple of months. Since I'm about the only guy still accepting Medicaid, a bunch of these are kids that are coming in from across the state."

"I'm still a Medicaid provider," George said. "I told Grady that I refused to be bullied into resigning from Medicaid, even though the rest of the group has already done so."

"That's great! I didn't know that," Jack replied.

"They have been controlling my schedule, so I've only been seeing one or two Medicaid patients a month, but I'll see what I can do."

"Do you mind if I give Mary Anne your cell phone number? She'll have a list of all our scheduled patients and I'll have her work with you directly on getting them in to see you."

"Yeah, that sounds like a good idea," George said. "It sure would have been a lot easier if I was still in that office, wouldn't it?"

"Maybe," Jack replied, "but, if you were here, you might be a target also."

"You're right. I suspect that sooner or later I will be just that."

"I really appreciate you doing this. I owe you big time," Jack said earnestly.

"You don't owe me anything, sir. It is me that owes you. You have been the best mentor any man could ask for. I'm not sure where you're going, or what you are going to do, but if there is room for me, please let me know, and I'll join you."

"That is very kind of you, George, but at this point I have no idea what I'm going to do. Rest assured, I will keep in touch."

The two men said their goodbyes and Jack returned to his computer screen. He pulled up the Quickbooks application and reviewed his financial status before calling Mary Anne back into his office. She had run his office for more than twenty-five years, She did all the bookkeeping and wrote all the checks.

"Are these accounts current?" he asked as she stepped behind him, looking over his shoulder.

"Yes, sir," she said, "I just paid our middle of the month bills."

Between the two business accounts, Jack had just over eighty-five thousand dollars in the bank.

"I want you to pay Phyllis and Shelly each six months severance pay and let them go at the end of the day. Write them each a letter of recommendation from me, but ask them not to say anything to anyone about my absence."

"Okay, what else?" Mary Anne asked as she jotted down his instructions on the little note pad she carried around with her constantly.

"Before you leave here today, I need for you to box up all my diplomas and certificates along with that collection of old surgical instruments and ship them by FedEx to Dr. Ramirez's home in Managua. You should have the address."

"I do," she confirmed.

"When you leave the office I want you to leave your computer and everything else just as it is. I don't want any changes made to anything. I don't want the feds to have any reason to accuse us of altering records." She nodded in agreement. Then he continued, "However, I need for you to make two back-ups of our server, so you'll need to buy another two terabyte drive."

"That's easy enough. What else."

"I need for you to make two copies of all our legal paper documents as well. You can probably get Phyllis to do that before she leaves. I want one copy as well as one of the hard drives added to that box you're shipping to Nicaragua."

"What do you want me to do with the other copies and the other hard drive?"

"Take them home with you tonight, and don't tell anyone you have them. That's my insurance policy, in case they try and frame me for something I didn't do."

"That's a very good idea, sir."

"There should be enough money in the cash drawer to pay for the new hard drive and for shipping the box to Managua. Anything that's left is yours." He turned to face her and said, "I'm really sorry my career seems to be ending this way, but I don't really have any other choice. Its fight or flight, and I'm afraid I'm outgunned, so if I stay and fight, I'm going to lose."

"I understand, sir," she said sadly. "I don't blame you."

"After the severance pay to Phyllis and Shelly, that should leave about fifty thousand," Jack said. "I want you to write a check to yourself for the balance."

"I can't do that," she said with a laugh. "That is your money, and you are likely to need it wherever you're going."

THE CONFLICT

"You can, and you will take it, in part because I intend to have you remain my employee for a few more months. I'm going to need for you to monitor any additional payments that come in over the next few months, and to make sure no one vandalizes this building while I'm not around. I also need for you to contact Dr. Ferguson later this week and arrange to get all my patients appointments with him. He said he is still on Medicaid, but the clinic is trying to limit the number of those patients he is allowed to see. I'm sure he will do whatever he can to help accommodate those who already had appointments here, and any new patients that call here should be referred to his office."

She nodded in agreement. "Anything else?" she asked. When he shook his head she turned back toward her office to print out the checks for his signature.

As she was leaving he said, "Bring me a few blank checks to sign. That way you'll be able to pay any bills that might come up using the money we receive through the mail. I don't want to be a deadbeat when it comes to paying my bills."

No, sir," she said seriously, "we wouldn't want that." The both tried to laugh without much success.

When she returned with the checks he signed them all without even looking at them. He said, "I will call you in a few days on your cell phone. When you leave the office this afternoon, lock the door and do not return until next Monday at the earliest. They should be finished with their audit by then."

"This is a very sad day, sir."

"Yes, it is," he replied. "I never dreamed I'd retire like this, but things happen for a reason. I just don't have a clue what the reason is for this one."

"I'm going to miss you," she said with just the hint of a tear in her eyes.

"I'm going to miss you too, Mary Anne. You have been an incredible asset to this practice and a great and loyal friend." He stood up and walked around the desk, embracing her as she started to cry openly. "Hey, I'm not dying," he said. "I'm certain we will see each other again, probably sooner than you think."

****

On his way home, Jack called American Airlines and booked two one way tickets to Managua for that afternoon. The connection was through Miami, but the layover was shorter than the flight they usually took through Houston on United. As he drove up to the front door he could feel the adrenaline surging in his veins. He knew escape was his only option, and he knew he needed to get moving as quickly as possible.

When he opened the front door, he called out to Elaina.

"I'm up stairs," she shouted.

Jack quickly bounded up the stairs and found his wife hurriedly packing two large suitcases. Before saying anything he moved swiftly toward her, taking her in his arms, holding her closer than he had in years. "I'm sorry," was all he could think to say.

She looked into his sad eyes, returning his gaze with one of trust and understanding. "I don't need to know all the details, I just want to know how long you think we'll be away?"

"I don't know," he said. "It could be a week, a month, a year, I don't know."

"What time does our flight leave?" she asked.

"At twelve-thirty."

"That gives us barely two hours. We best get moving," she said.

She quickly finished packing their clothes, and personal items, as Jack headed down to his study to gather his personal documents from the safe, including their passports and a little over five thousand dollars in cash. As he started back up the stairs he saw his wife struggling to drag one of the heavy suitcases down the from steps.

"I'll get that," he said, as he quickly made his way back up to the top of the stairway, taking the large black canvas bag in one hand. He carried it to the front door, and when he returned to the top of the stairs she had already brought the second bag out of the bedroom.

He saw her turn away from him, and he knew she was crying. He left the bag and ran quickly after her. "Elaina, wait," he pleaded softly.

She stopped, but didn't turn around. He moved in front of her and raised her chin in his hands. Her green eyes were filled with tears. A sense of overwhelming guilt came over him. It wasn't fair that she might not see this house again. Their entire life together had taken place within these walls, and he was asking her to just walk away from everything. This was her home, her sanctuary. All the pictures on the walls, the little things they had collected over the twenty-three years they'd lived there. How could this be happening.

"We don't have to go," he said. "I can't ask you to leave all this."

Her face offered that knowing, anxious smile that a mother gives a child on the first day of school. It told him that she understood what he was doing, but it didn't matter now. "Even though I don't yet know why, I'm certain you have a very good reason why we need to leave, and that's all I need. Stuff, we can replace. You, I can't live without, so yes, we are going."

He kissed her tenderly, tasting the saltiness of her tears. As he looked again into her eyes he could not help remembering the first time he gazed into them. They were filled with tears that time as well, only then they were tears of joy following David's successful surgery. "We can call David from the car," he said.

She nodded and went back into the bedroom to retrieve a couple of books she had been reading and a family photo album.

Jack finished loading the truck and as she came out of the house he set the alarm and locked the door behind them. As they pulled out of the driveway, he looked over at Elaina. Her jaw was set and she was no longer crying. She made no effort to look back as they pulled out on to the street.

"He's not answering his phone," Jack said.

"He is probably in class, or maybe he's delivering babies," she said.

Jack tried calling David three more times, each time leaving a brief voice message, asking him to return his call. Then he called Tony Hawkins at First National Bank. "Jack, what can I do for you?" Tony said in his usual overly friendly banker voice.

"I need for you to wire some money out of my savings account to my account in Nicaragua."

"I thought you already bought that place down there?" the banker inquired, indirectly asking why Jack wanted the money transferred out of his bank.

"I did," he said, "I just need some cash for other expenses. Can you tell me what the balance is in my two accounts there, checking and savings?"

The banker's tone was considerably less jovial as he said, "Sure, wait just a minute. Jack could hear the clicking of the computer keyboard, and soon Tony's voice returned. "You have seventy-five thousand give or take a few dollars in your savings, and another thirty thousand in your checking."

"That's about what I had figured," Jack said. "I need you to wire one hundred thousand dollars to my account at the Nicaraguan Central Bank, immediately."

"But, Jack," the banker said. "That will leave you only five thousand dollars in this bank. Are you sure you want to ..."

"Yes, I'm quite sure," he said. "I'd like to leave one thousand in the savings account to keep it open and the rest in checking."

"Your serious." Tony's statement sounded more like a question.

"Yes, I'm serious," Jack said. "I'd appreciate it if you take care of it personally." After a brief moment of silence Jack added. "And give my best to your dad the next time you see him." Jack had operated on Tony's dad five years earlier. He'd performed an emergency surgery for a ruptured aortic root that was very nearly fatal.

"I'll take care of it doc," he said, as he hung up the phone.

Jack immediately tried David again, but the call went to voice mail once more. He then called his other banker at Chase and repeated the same conversation he'd had with Tony. This time the amount was somewhat less, but this banker was also reluctant to turn loose of Jack's money. He finally agreed to wire the sixty-five thousand that Jack asked for directly into his Nicaraguan account, but not before he asked Jack to verify his social security number, birth date and mother's maiden name.

As he clicked off his cell phone again, Elaina asked, "May I ask why you are moving all our money to Nicaragua?"

"I'm afraid the FBI could potentially freeze all our assets," he said. "I'm not going to let them have anything, because I haven't done anything wrong."

"Then what makes you think they would freeze our assets?"

"Fitzgerald and Horvath have been feeding the authorities a bunch of lies about my practice. They were behind that first audit, and when they saw that I wasn't going to stop opposing them, I'm certain they are behind the raid on my office that is set to happen tomorrow morning."

"Are you sure?" she asked cautiously.

"Absolutely," he replied. "I'm not sure exactly why, but they are out to destroy me. They had me suspended from the medical staff just to support their argument that I'm some kind of a loose cannon. Horvath called CMS and the FBI again, suggesting to them that I may have done something illegal with regard to Medicaid, and that I inappropriately talked about their audit last winter."

"Is any of that true?" she asked.

"I did mention the audit during my interview, but everything I said was the truth. As far as Medicaid is concerned, Mary Anne has been so incredibly careful, I don't know how they could accuse us of anything. The only thing I worry about is the fact that since virtually everybody else dropped out, our volume of Medicaid patients has gone up dramatically. I've heard that one of the first things they look for is a sudden change in volume of claims."

"If nobody else is taking Medicaid, wouldn't it make sense that your volume of patients would go up?" she asked.

"Of course, but I'm convinced that's part of CMS's overall strategy. They want to make it as hard as possible for people to access care. They want fewer docs, and then do whatever they can to hassle those who remain in the program," Jack said in frustration. "They make us out to be the bad guys. They want the public to blame us when they can't get care. This whole fraud thing is just another part of that strategy. If I was to show up at my office tomorrow, I'd be accused of Medicaid fraud even before they looked at one single chart. Since this would be the second CMS audit in less than a year, I'm sure I'd be put into the back of one of those black town cars, wearing handcuffs. Remember watching that doc over in Dallas get hauled off to jail?"

"I remember," she said anxiously.

"That's why we have to leave the country. I don't think I'd look good in an orange jump suit, do you?"

Elaina didn't answer. She continued to look straight ahead, frightened by the scenario Jack had just laid out.

"Hello, Buzz?" Jack said, as his long-time friend answered his cell phone.

"Jack!" Buzz answered, "Where are you?"

"Elaina and I are on our way to the airport," he replied.

"Where are you going?"

"I'd rather not say right now, I don't want you to have to lie if someone asks."

"Things are crazy around here this morning," Buzz said. "Your suspension is all anyone is talking about. I assume you're going to fight it, right?"

"I think the suspension was just Horvath's way of painting me as a bad guy. Their plan all along has been to get rid of me."

"Who is they?" Buzz asked, not fully grasping what Jack was saying.

"Horvath, Grady and Fitzgerald. They needed me out of the way, not only because I wouldn't cooperate with their plan to employ every physician, but also that interview I did threatens to blow up their whole scheme."

"What do you need for me to do?" Buzz asked, now beginning to fear for his friend's safety.

"I don't really need anything, I just wanted you to know I was leaving the country for a while."

Buzz thought for a moment then asked, "What about your car? Are you planning to leave it at the airport?"

Jack hadn't even thought about his truck. "I guess I'll get David to come get it and take it to the house."

"Let me do that for you," he said. "Just text me the location and leave the keys on top of the right rear tire. I'll come pick it up this evening and put it in your garage."

"That would be terrific," Jack replied, "My house key is on the same key ring. My office manager will be going by to check on the mail and she'll be watching the house for us."

"I'll just hang on to your keys until you come back."

"That might be a while," Jack said rather cautiously.

The phone was silent for a few moments before Jack added, "I'm really sorry if any of this spills over on to you."

"Don't be ridiculous," Buzz replied. "I'm your friend, remember? If you need anything, you call me. Any time, from any place. I'm here for you."

"I appreciate that, more than you know."

"All I ask is that you save me a place," Buzz offered.

"What do you mean, save you a place?" now it was Jack who sounded confused.

"I know you. You're going to start something, somewhere, and when you do I want to be a part of it."

"Trust me, I don't have any plans to start anything. I'm just trying to stay out of trouble."

"I'm just saying, keep me in mind when you decide what you're going to do."

"Thanks buddy, I'll be in touch," Jack replied, then ended the call.

Jack tried David's number again, as he pulled his pickup into the huge garage at terminal D. There was still no answer. He found a space on the second level, and quickly unloaded the two suitcases, along with his briefcase and Elaina's carry on bag. He locked the truck and placed the keys on top of the right rear wheel. He then sent Buzz a text that read simply "D-B4."

Their flight was scheduled to depart in just over an hour, and even though the first leg was only to Miami, they were still required to use the international check in process, which took nearly thirty minutes. The agent scolded them briefly for not arriving at least two hours in advance, then said she wasn't sure if their bags would make it. If they wanted to make sure, she could move them to the five twenty flight that would arrive in Managua at midnight.

"No," Jack said, "We need to go on this flight." He didn't want to risk Horvath or Fitzgerald getting wind of his escape and notifying the FBI that he was fleeing the country.

They made it through security without any trouble and arrived at the gate five minutes before boarding was scheduled to begin. Jack slumped into a chair next to Elaina and tried unsuccessfully to relax. He looked up at one of the television monitors that was tuned to the airport version of CNN. He couldn't hear the sound, but he saw the image of a young man in a business suit being led out of a huge building in New York. His hands were restrained behind his back, and the scrolling text under the video read, "Carl Thompson accused of insider trading ... All personal assets seized ..."

Jack sat up straight in his chair and pulled his cell phone out again. This time he called his stock broker, James Levit. "Hello Jim, this is Jack Roberts."

"Hi Jack, are you calling to buy some more Apple stock? If so I'm not sure I'd recommend it. It is at an all time high right now."

Levit had always been one to talk more than listen. "What is the price of the stock today?" Jack asked.

"It is trading right around six hundred dollars a share, so with the additional shares you bought last year using the dividends that were paid over the previous six years, you now have 25,056 shares. With a total value of fifteen million, thirty-three thousand, six hundred dollars."

"Sell it." Jack said.

"What?!" Levit exclaimed.

"I want you to sell it all, and wire the money to a numbered account I have in Switzerland." Jack had opened a Swiss bank account more than thirty-five years ago, when he was stationed in Germany. He had made a few small deposits over the years, but the balance in the account was less than twenty thousand dollars. He'd meant to close out the account and move the money into a trust for David, but he'd never gotten around to it. He figured he'd take care of it one day when he and Elaina went back to Europe, but that day had never come.

"Are you sure that's what you want to do?" Levit asked again. He stood to make a huge profit on the transaction, but he also needed to be certain.

"Yes, I'm sure."

"For a transaction of that size I'll need something in writing," Levit said.

"Will an email do?" Jack asked.

"Yes, I can accept an email as proof of your directive."

"Good, I'll send it to you in the next few minutes," Jack confirmed. "I need this done today, okay?"

"Yeah, sure," Levit said. "You realize there will be a three percent brokerage fee for the transaction, right?"

"Just take it out of the proceeds of the sale, and wire the rest to my account."

Levit quickly did the math in his head. His firm would make just over four hundred and fifty thousand dollars on the sale and his commission was twenty-five percent of that. He was going to make over one hundred thousand dollars that day. "I will make certain this gets done today, Dr. Roberts. You can count on it."

Jack hung up and used his phone to compose an email to Levit. He pulled out an old slip of yellow paper that was tucked into a side pocket of his wallet. He unfolded it and carefully typed in the ten characters of his Swiss account, then folded it back up and put the paper back where it had been stored, untouched for more than five years. As he hit send on his phone he heard the gate agent announce their flight was ready for boarding.

He and Elaina walked quickly to the line that was forming behind the priority access sign, and while they waited he tried calling David once more. Just as the agent took their boarding passes from his hand he heard his son's voice say hello.

"David, I'm so glad you picked up."

"What's up Dad? I saw where you called several times. Is everything okay?" David asked, sounding very anxious.

"Yes, your mom and I are fine. We are at DFW, and we are boarding a plane to Managua."

"What? I thought you guys were just down there three months ago?"

"It's a long story," Jack said. "We will be there this evening, and I'll call you then. I just wanted you to know we were leaving the country, in the event you heard anything on the news."

"On the news? What do you mean?"

"I'll tell you about it this evening," Jack said. "Don't worry, everything is going to be fine."

CHAPTER 14

By the time Jack and Elaina arrived in Managua, made it through customs, obtained their rental car and then drove to El Transito it was nearly midnight. He decided to wait and call David the next day.

The house was just as Elaina had left it. The walls were still bare, and freshly painted with the softer beige color she'd picked out, but the furniture made it feel a little more like a home. "So, what do you think?" she asked as Jack put the suitcases down, just inside the front door.

"I like it," he said. "You did a great job."

Just then Federico and Lucinda came running in through the front door. They had both been asleep, but were awakened by the sound of a car on the gravel driveway. Federico was wearing only his work trousers, without shoes or shirt and Lucinda had thrown an old pink bathrobe on over her nightgown. Federico was carrying the large machete he used to cut the vines around the perimeter of the property. He was ready to expel any intruders.

"Federico!" Elaina exclaimed, as she saw him advancing toward Jack.

"Oh, señora Roberts!" he replied in Spanish. "I am so sorry. I thought you were thieves."

"That's quite alright," she said. "This is my husband, Dr. Roberts."

Federico placed his weapon carefully on the floor before taking a single step forward. "It is very good to meet you señor doctor," he said, in the mumbled Spanish of a native Nicaraguan. He bowed politely at the waist, but did not presume to extend his hand to this man who obviously controlled his livelihood. He clearly had cause to dismiss him and his wife, putting them back out on the street.

Jack closed the short distance between them and spoke to Federico in fluent Spanish. "I have heard a lot about you from my wife. She tells me you are both very hard working people."

"Si, señor doctor," Federico replied. "We are very pleased to work hard. I hope you will forgive me for coming into your home this way. We should leave now." The older man said to his wife, obviously embarrassed, not only for barging in, but also because he realized he was naked from the waist up.

Jack smiled, understanding the difficult situation that Federico was in. "Why don't you both go back to bed," he suggested. "We can get better acquainted in the morning."

"Si señor doctor," he said as he bowed again, before beginning to walk slowly backward toward the door, his head still slightly bowed. He picked up the machete and hid it sheepishly behind his back.

"My name is Jack, Federico."

"Si, señor doctor Jack," he said timidly, as he and Lucinda both quickly exited, closing the door quietly behind them.

"I think you frightened him," Elaina said in a reprimanding tone.

"I frightened him?" he laughed. "He was the one with the machete."

Jack walked passed the new living room sofa, to the French doors. He opened them, allowing the warm, nighttime breeze to enter the house, then turned back toward Elaina. "Care to join me?" he asked.

Elaina started to object. She was beyond tired, and was anxious to get to bed, but then she realized this was the first time they had been together in their new home. She smiled and made her way across the room and out onto the wooden deck. She walked to the smooth, recently painted railing. She could hear the distinct sound of the breaking surf in the distance, as the half moon illuminated the lagoon, just a few yards down the gentle hill.

Jack followed her out on to the deck, but allowed her to stand alone at the railing for a few moments. He slowly approached her, waiting for her to turn around. Once she was facing him, he pulled her into his arms, looking intently into her beautiful green eyes. There was no longer any sign of the fear, or the sadness, he'd seen earlier that day. In the silvery moon light he detected a real peace in her face. Here in their new home, they were away from all the madness. Away from all the pressures. Together at last in their own little paradise. He leaned forward and kissed her waiting lips, softly at first, then with a new passion, one that was free of any tension or stress. It was as if in that moment they were the only people in the entire world.

"I'm sorry it had to be this way." His words were slower and more gentle than she was used to hearing.

"What is it you always say about life's most important decisions?" she said. "The why is more important than the how?"

"I think you must have known," he said.

"What do you mean?" she asked, looking up at him with just the hint of a smile.

"Buying this house was your idea, wasn't it? I think you must have known we'd need a place where we could escape."

"I definitely wanted us to have a place to getaway, but I had no idea we'd be running from the FBI."

They both laughed softly, before sharing another kiss. "I believe you mentioned something about trying out your new bed." he said, flashing his crooked smile.

"Yes, I believe I did."

****

On Wednesday morning, two agents from the North Texas office of the Federal Bureau of Investigation, along with a special investigator from the Office of the Inspector General, and the manager of the southwest regional office of the Centers for Medicare and Medicaid Services walked into the office of Michael Horvath at nine a.m. sharp.

"Please come in, come in," Horvath said as he stepped around his desk to shake hands with the three young men and the middle aged woman. One of the men and the older woman were dressed in dark gray business suits. The other two men wore white shirts, black trousers and navy blue jackets. He'd had his secretary bring in two additional chairs, not knowing exactly how many people were going to show up.

The government employees each handed him a business card with their name and agency clearly displayed. The woman was from CMS, and she began the conversation after everyone had been seated. Each of the visitors sat near the front of their chairs, with both feet squarely on the floor and hands in their laps. From their posture, it was clear they did not intend to be there very long.

"I understand you have evidence that Dr. Jack Roberts may have defrauded the Medicaid program. Is that correct?" she asked.

"Yes," Horvath said, "As I told you over the phone, I'm very reluctant to bring any allegations against Dr. Roberts, he is one of our finest surgeons, but I feel it is my patriotic duty."

"Can you explain exactly what he did and what evidence you possess that confirms your allegations."

"Certainly," Horvath said, ready to begin his well rehearsed speech. He reached into the top drawer of his desk and handed her a folder. "Two months ago, Dr. Roberts treated a child from Guatemala in our emergency department. The young boy and his family were in this country illegally. The child had suffered a spontaneous pneumothorax... that's a collapsed lung. Dr. Roberts placed a tube in his chest, then admitted him to the hospital for a total of three days. Our social workers explained to the family that they were not eligible for any government program. However, I have it on good authority, that Dr. Roberts filed a claim to Medicaid for the services he provided."

"What do you mean by 'on good authority'?" the CMS manager asked.

"I'm not at liberty to give out names, but I can assure you the information is solid," he said confidently. "Obviously, I don't have access to his billing records, but I assume that you'll have no trouble obtaining them."

The CMS manager looked through the file briefly, then handed it to one of the FBI agents. "We will look into it."

"Were you aware of the interview he did on local television last Sunday?"

She nodded once, acknowledging that she had seen the interview at some point. "I wasn't sure whether you saw it or not, but he spoke freely about the audit your agency conducted less than a year ago, and as I understand it, that was a clear violation of a CMS directive." He was sure that they would come down hard on Jack for that, if nothing else, but she seemed to ignore his rather inappropriate accusation.

"Do you have anything else?" she asked impatiently.

"No, not at this time," Horvath said. Then as the group stood to leave he added. "There is one other thing." They all turned to face him again, with almost blank expressions. "The chief of our medical staff suspended Dr. Roberts just yesterday, for behavior detrimental to our hospital."

Led by the CMS manager they all left the office without further questions or comment. Horvath was certain that Fitzgerald's plan was working perfectly, assuming the man they'd paid to break into Jack's office two nights earlier hadn't been discovered, and that he'd succeeded in planting the data on Jack's computerized office records.

****

"Mom?" David asked anxiously, "Is everything alright?"

"Yes, sweetie. Everything is fine," she responded. She was using Jack's phone. He thought it might be best for him to hear her voice first. "Sorry we didn't call you last night, but it was really late by the time we got here."

"Where exactly are you?"

"We're at our new house here in El Transito. We just woke up, and we wanted to make sure you knew we got here okay."

"I was beginning to worry. What's going on? Why did you leave so suddenly?" he pleaded.

"Let me let you talk to your father."

She offered Jack the phone, and he said, "Hey, buddy, I'm sorry for not calling you back last night, but like Mom said, it was almost midnight before we got to the house."

"What happened? Why did you guys leave so suddenly?"

"It's kind of a long story, but if we hadn't left the country, it's very likely that I would have been arrested by the FBI."

"The FBI?" he shouted.

"Yeah... the guys who run the hospital have targeted me, and I couldn't risk going to jail."

"Jail? ... What did you do?"

"Nothing," Jack said.

"Okay, then. What did they accuse you of doing."

"I'm not sure, but I do know they contacted the FBI and CMS and initiated another audit of my practice, and I know that once those people start looking, they are going to find something, no matter how trivial, and sInce this would be a second offense, they don't just fine you, they put you in jail."

"But, I don't understand. Why would those guys target you? I thought you were one of the more influential members of the medical staff."

"I know they didn't like what I had to say in that TV interview about some of their policies and procedures, but I think the real reason is that I refused to join their big group and be a part of their accountable care organization."

"There's got to be more to it than that," David reasoned.

"If there is I don't know what it ..." Jack said, then hesitated. "I wonder?" he thought out loud.

"You wonder what?" David asked.

"I was just thinking. Maybe they are still upset over the million dollar grant that Franco Gutierrez made to the hospital. They diverted the funds so they could buy a new CT scanner, but for some reason they decided to restore the fund. I'm not sure what that had to do with me, but I'm certain they weren't happy about it." Jack continued to rack his brain for a reason why Fitzgerald had changed his mind, but he couldn't think of any reason. The one thing he was sure of, it didn't have anything to do with any marketing campaign.

"A million bucks certainly might be enough of a reason for someone to come after you," David said.

Jack didn't respond. He was absorbed in his own analysis. With him out of the way, he wondered how long it would take for Horvath and Fitzgerald to pull another accounting maneuver, and line their own pockets with Franco's money. Perhaps that was it. That was certainly the reason they had gotten rid of Bob Anderson, the previous administrator.

"So, how long are you and Mom planning to stay down there?"

Jack returned from his momentary mental wandering, and said, "I don't know. I guess that'll depend on what the feds find, and whether they issue a warrant."

"Is there anything you need for me to do?" David asked, hoping he could somehow assist in clearing his dad's good name.

"I know you are very busy with school, but if you have a chance to go by the house sometime next week, just to make sure everything is okay, I'd appreciate it. The alarm system is set, and Mary Anne, my office manager, will be forwarding our mail, so at this point there isn't much else that needs to be done."

"Okay," David replied, his voice sounding somewhat helpless. "I'm sorry, but I need to go, or I'll be late for morning rounds."

"Your mom and I love you very much. We'll talk to you soon."

"I love you guys, too."

****

As soon as the international connection with David was broken, Jack called Domingo. He explained that he and Elaina were at their new home in El Transito, and he gave him a quick account of what had led to their unscheduled return.

"So, you are a fugitive from American justice?" Domingo asked, not certain of exactly how much trouble his friend was in.

Jack laughed, but in his mind, he knew Domingo's assessment was more accurate than he wanted to admit. "I guess that's true, but I don't expect the FBI will spend a lot of energy looking for me down here."

"So, are you planning to apply for Nicaraguan citizenship?"

Jack laughed again, but this time because the thought had never crossed his mind that he was now technically a refugee. "I don't think so. I feel sure we will be returning home at some point, so I think I'll hang on to my US passport for now."

"If you change your mind, I know some officials in the government," Domingo quipped.

"So do I," Jack said. "Probably some of the same people."

Domingo laughed, then asked, "Are you planning to work while you are here, or are you going to just lay around on the beach?"

"You know me, I need to keep working. Do you have an opening at your clinic?"

"I will always have a place for you, my friend."

"In all seriousness," Jack said, "I'm not sure how long we'll be here, and I'm considering applying for a temporary work visa. Do you know how I might go about that?"

"Of course," Domingo assured him. "You must have a sponsoring physician, which I will be happy to be, and you must apply to the Ministry of Health. You have met the Minister, so I don't expect you'll have any trouble securing the work visa for as long as you wish to stay in this country."

"I'm going into Managua later today. Perhaps I'll go by the office of the Ministry of Health if I have time, but I need to find a computer for here at the house. Do you have any recommendations where I can find one?"

Domingo offered him two different stores that sold computers and the other equipment he would need. The only real option for accessing the Internet from his home would be a satellite dish. He could also use it to get international television.

"FedEx should be delivering a box to your home this afternoon," Jack said. "I would like to come by and pick it up, if you or Felicia will be home."

"I won't be home until at least six o'clock, but I will tell Felicia to expect you."

"Great, I look forward to seeing her."

"Do you mind if I ask why you didn't send the box to your home in El Transito?"

"Do you want to know the truth?"

"Yes, always."

"I knew how to get here, but I didn't know the address," he laughed.

****

David was walking toward the nurses' station on the fourth floor of Parkland Memorial Hospital when he was suddenly stopped by one of the faculty members. He looked down at David's name badge, prominently displayed on the pocket of his short white cotton jacket, and asked, "Is that your dad they are talking about on the news?"

The young student looked up in astonishment, then told his professor that he didn't know anything about it. He hadn't seen any television that morning. Despite this initial denial, David was convinced, based on the earlier conversation with his dad, he knew where the reporters and cameras were. He excused himself, and found an empty patient room. He turned on the television and flipped quickly through the local channels until he saw the news coverage. In the right upper corner of the screen he saw the words "Recorded Earlier Today."

"We are here outside the office of Dr. Jack Roberts, former republican candidate for Congress," the young reporter said, as she held the microphone to her face. The familiar image of the white wooden frame house in the background was unmistakable. "We were told that he was being investigated by the FBI and the Centers for Medicare and Medicaid Services for possible Medicaid fraud. Apparently there is no one in the office. The agents have been trying both the front and rear entrances, without success, but now, a locksmith has been called in, and as you can see, he is working to open the front door."

David watched as an older man in civilian work clothes knelt down in front of his dad's office door. Soon the door swung open and two men wearing dark blue jackets with the bold letters, FBI, printed in bright yellow across the back, entered the building. A woman and another man, both wearing dark gray business suits followed them through the door.

The reporter continued, "We have been told that Dr. Roberts was audited several months ago, and was fined for an apparent Medicare violation. We do not know the specifics of what brought about that audit, or the reason behind this current raid on his office. We do know that he is one of the busiest pediatric heart surgeons in the country, and a large number of heart operations he has performed on area children were covered under the Medicaid program."

"That was recorded around nine-thirty this morning," the news anchor said, as the television image switched back to the studio. David thought it was unusual for the news to be on at ten-thirty in the morning, almost as if this were some developing crisis story. What he didn't know was that Jim Fitzgerald had instructed his station manager to cover this story exactly that way. He wanted every one to see the yellow tape being stretched out around his father's office, signifying an active crime scene investigation. There was only one conclusion the public could make, based on what they were seeing. This man, his dad, who had tried to come across as a servant of his patients, and who came close to being a representative of the people in Washington, was a criminal.

The video feed switched back to the reporter on the scene, and the words in the upper right corner now read, "Live". The bright yellow tape stretch between the old oak trees near the street, around the building, and the agents were seen carrying boxes and computers out of the front door, placing them in a black van parked in the narrow driveway.

"We have not seen any sign of Dr. Roberts or any of his employees this morning. Obviously, they must have known this raid was coming, and have stayed away," she said, drawing her own conclusion. "This certainly doesn't look very good for the doctor, Tom. Back to you in the studio."

****

"Hello, Franco?" Jack said, hoping his voice would be recognized.

"Dr. Roberts," Franco replied, having seen Jack's name appear on his caller ID. "To what do I owe the pleasure of this call?"

"Its kind of a long story, but Elaina and I are here in Nicaragua, and I was hoping you and Gabriella would join us for dinner this weekend, here at our new home in El Transito."

"I am very pleased that you have come back so soon. I will need to check with Gabriella, but I'm not aware of any plans this weekend."

"Great!" Jack said. How about Saturday evening? We'll plan dinner around seven-thirty."

"I will call you once I have confirmed it with my wife," Franco agreed.

"And by the way," Jack added, "please dress casually. We will likely be eating outside on the deck."

"That sound's very nice," Franco said. "I look forward to seeing you both again, and I want to hear all about what has brought you back to my country so unexpectedly."

Just as he concluded his conversation with Franco, Jack's cell phone rang. It was Mary Anne. She spoke rapidly, telling him the government agents had just left her house. Her voice reflected the fear and anger that lingered, even though they were now gone. He listened intently to what she said, then replied, "You did great. I don't think they will bother you any more, but if they do, or if you learn any more specifics, please call me immediately."

"I will," she said timidly. "I'm glad you and Mrs. Roberts are safe."

Jack walked back into the house and found Elaina arranging the few clothes they'd brought with them in the bedroom closet. "Let's take a walk down to the beach," he suggested.

She looked up and smiled, saying, "Give me two minutes to change."

Soon they were making their way across the narrow wooden bridge over the still water of the shallow lagoon and on to the sandy strip of land with its large black volcanic rock formations that separated them from the rolling surf just beyond. They each left their sandals on the end of the bridge, feeling the warm, soft sand on their bare feet. They walked through the narrow opening between the rocks and out onto the broad gently sloping beach. The tide was out, and the waves were small and lapped softly against the shore, more quietly than Elaina had remembered.

"I just talked to Mary Ann," Jack spoke, breaking the unusual serenity of the late morning scene.

"What did she have to say?" Elaina asked, as she gazed beyond Jack to the open ocean in the distance, beyond the mouth of the bay.

"She told me the FBI and CMS had just left her home. As we suspected they had raided the office this morning, and it didn't take them long to find out where she lived."

"Was she upset?"

"She didn't sound angry," Jack replied. "She sounded more frightened than anything. She said they questioned her for nearly half an hour, about why the office was closed on a Wednesday, and where I was."

"She must have been terrified."

"I'm sure she was, but knowing Mary Anne, I doubt they sensed it. She's a pretty cool customer."

"Did they tell her why they decided to raid your office?"

"No, but she said they had a court order, and that they had confiscated all our computers and were taking them to a CMS office for analysis."

"Do you think she is in danger of being accused of anything?"

"No," Jack replied reassuringly, "they weren't coming after her. They're looking for me."

"What did she tell them?"

"When they asked her where I could be found, she told them that I was visiting friends out of the country, but then she told them that she suspected I had finally decided to retire. That's why she wasn't surprised when she was instructed to lock up the office and pay the employees, which she had done the day before."

"Did she say anything else?"

"She said the CMS area manager had a list of all the Medicaid and uninsured patients that I've treated since their last review eight months ago. They didn't say where they had gotten the list, but it had to have been from Horvath. They told her they intended to review every case for any irregularities. The CMS manager told her that in their initial evaluation they had found at least one illegal Medicaid claim for treatment for a patient who lived in Guatemala. She told them that she knew exactly which case they were referring to, and that no claim had been filed for that boy's care by our office. She said the FBI agent cut her off. Apparently he was not at all happy that the CMS manager had shared any information about their investigation, and he told her that she was not to discuss any details of their conversation with anyone, including the press. He told her that if they found anything further, they'd be back to question her again."

"Oh, Jack!" Elaina exclaimed, as her eyes began to moisten. "She must be frightened beyond words. I can't imagine the stress of having a bunch of government agents staring down at her as they peppered her with questions."

"I know, I feel terrible about leaving her there alone, but she and I talked about it before I left the office yesterday, and she said she would be just fine. Mary Anne is a very strong individual, and hopefully the worst is over for her."

"What do you think they meant by an illegal Medicaid claim?"

"I have no idea," He replied, "I've only seen one patient from Guatemala in the last year or more, and I'm certain we didn't file a claim in that case. The family was in the country illegally, and as soon as he was well enough to leave the hospital, somebody, I presume it was Horvath, called the Immigration and Customs Enforcement guys, and ICE deported the whole family."

She just shook her head, trying to imagine being the parent of a child who was just released from the hospital and then forced to leave the country. Jack decided to move their conversation in a different direction.

"I'm going into the city this afternoon, do you want to come?"

"I don't think so," Elaina said, "I've got a number of things I need to do around the house. Why are you ..."

"I need to go buy a computer and a satellite dish so I can access the Internet, and so I can review all my office records."

"How are you going to access your records if they took all your computers from the office?"

"Mary Anne made a backup on a separate hard drive. She's shipped it to Domingo's house, along with a bunch of my diplomas and copies of all my legal documents from the office. I'm going to run by there and get it while I'm in town."

"Why did you need your diplomas?" she asked.

"I thought I might need them to obtain a work visa. You don't expect me to spend all my time walking the beach, do you?" His voice sounded playful, but she knew exactly what he meant.

"What if I want to get a work visa too?" she offered, sounding more serious than he'd expected.

"Well, I guess we'll need to have David, or Mary Anne, or somebody dust off your nursing diploma and your Texas license, and send them down here," he said as he smiled and stopped walking, then turned to face her. "Assuming that's the kind of work you're talking about."

"If you're going to work while we're here, I think I'd like to help." She flashed him a girlish smile, hoping he would allow her to be his working partner in whatever he had in mind.

As they turned around and headed slowly back toward the house, he said, "I asked Franco if he and Gabriella would like to come join us here for dinner on Saturday evening."

"What!" she exclaimed. "I'm not ready to have company for dinner yet. There are so many things I need to get done. The house is so, so, unfinished," she said hesitatingly. "The walls are all bare. There are no drapes on any of the windows. I don't even have any towels for the guest bath."

"Well it sounds like you need to come into town with me and pick out a few things," He said with a broad smile.

****

Jack found the store in Managua that Domingo suggested might carry the Apple products he needed. His medical records program was Mac based, so he bought a new fifteen inch MacBook pro, and a twenty two inch high definition monitor that he could plug it into, assuming he could find a desk. He planned to set up a little office in the larger of the two guest bedrooms. He asked the salesman what he knew about getting a satellite dish to access the Internet and television, and was referred to another store a few blocks away.

As soon as he and Elaina walked into the second store, a young Englishman came up to him and said. "Let me guess. You and your wife have just retired here and you need a way to call back home to check on those grandchildren that won't cost a fortune. Am I right?"

"Not exactly," Jack said with a smile, "but, you're close."

"How can I help you then?"

"We have a home in El Transito, and I need satellite Internet and television service."

"I have exactly what you need. Assuming you have a clear view of the southern sky, we can install a dish that will provide you with high speed Internet as well as one hundred and forty-seven television channels, sixty-three of which are available in high definition as well as unlimited telephone service to anywhere in the United States. It is even possible for you to forward your US home number to your new home here for an additional twenty five dollars per month."

"Really?" Jack said. "That does sound like exactly what we need. How much is it?"

"The dish and installation is free, assuming you sign a two year contract agreement. If you wish to just go month to month, the dish with installation will cost you seven hundred and fifty dollars."

Jack thought that sounded reasonable. "So, what's the monthly service cost?"

The service that I just described, not including the call forwarding is two hundred and seventy-five dollars a month. With the call forwarding it would be three hundred a month."

"Wow!" Jack said. "That seems a bit pricey." Nearly everything in Nicaragua was considerably less expensive than back in Texas, but satellite technology was obviously not one of those things. It reminded him of the early days of cellular phones back in the eighties. His first Motorola cell phone had cost three thousand dollars and the service was charged on a per minute basis, starting at two dollars a minute. He wondered how long it would be before competition would bring down these satellite prices the way it did cell phone prices back home.

"If you are interested in only Internet and phone service, the cost comes down to two hundred dollars, but the call forwarding would again be an additional twenty-five." The salesman anticipated Jack's next question. "We do not offer Internet service alone."

Jack looked over at Elaina for some hint as to how she felt about what the man was saying, but she had wandered over to one of the televisions that was on display. It was tuned to one of her favorite soap operas. As he watched her staring intently at the fifty-two inch screen, he had all the answer he needed.

"How much for the Samsung television?" he asked.

"That one is fifteen hundred, but we have a special this week. If you buy a fifty inch or larger plasma or LCD television, we will give you an additional twenty-four inch TV for free."

Jack knew they would need a TV for the living room and one for the bedroom as well. "Does your installation include running the cable from the satellite to two rooms in the house?"

"Normally we charge extra for the second room, but since you are also buying a television, I can have our installer include the second room at no additional charge."

"How quickly can you have the equipment installed and the service up and running?"

"Our installer will be in El Transito next Wednesday and Thursday," the man said, "but for an additional two hundred dollars, I can have it installed tomorrow."

Jack laughed to himself as he concluded that some things were constant everywhere in the world. Money gets things done. He agreed to get everything the man was offering, including the two year contract. The total came to two thousand dollars, eighteen hundred for the TVs and the first month's service, plus two hundred more to have it installed the next day. When the salesman presented him with the bill the total due was twenty three hundred. "What's this? Are you charging me an additional month's service?

"No sir," he replied, recognizing that Jack was unfamiliar with the Value Added Tax on all goods and services. "The VAT tax is fifteen percent, but if you are buying this through a business you can send in the receipt and get the tax refunded to you."

"I'm not in business here, at least not yet," he said, as he started writing the check.

****

Elaina finished her shopping more quickly than Jack had anticipated. She decided to forego any artwork for the walls, but she did find some nice sheers for the windows that faced the northwest in both the master bedroom and living room. At first Jack was dreading having to hang them, but then he remembered, he had Federico to do those tasks he didn't care to take on himself. He smiled silently, thinking he could get used to retirement, if he didn't have to do things he didn't really want to do.

Driving up to Domingo and Felecia's home added nearly an hour to their trip back to El Transito, but Jack needed what was in that FedEx box. As soon as they arrived back home, he unloaded the car and began setting up his computer in the empty bedroom that he had designated as his office. For the time being he had to work on the floor, since he'd forgotten all about finding a desk.

He booted up the computer and started going through the registration process until he realized he couldn't complete it without Internet service. As much as he wanted to start reviewing the data that Mary Anne had copied to the two terabyte, Western Digital hard drive, he decided to just wait until he could do it right. So, he left the laptop computer on the floor along with the extra monitor and joined Federico in the living room to hang the curtain rods.

****

This can't be right," Jack said to himself as he stared intently at the computer monitor. The system was working flawlessly. It was as if he were sitting at his desk in his office reviewing his patient's records.

Two men had arrived that morning and within four hours they had the dish installed. The previous owner had wired the house for cable, so it was no problem hooking up the televisions. On the way home from the electronics store, Jack realized he needed a telephone, so he had called the salesman and ordered two cordless phones, with charging bases, for another two hundred dollars, plus the VAT. One of the men had shown him how to transfer his old phone number to the satellite system, but he couldn't actually make that connection without having someone physically present at their home in Fort Worth. Jack told them he could do that himself, once either David or Mary Anne was available.

"What can't be right?" Elaina asked from the doorway.

"According to this record, Mary Anne billed Medicaid twenty-three hundred dollars for services provided for that ten year old boy from Guatemala."

"I thought you said she denied having done that?" Elaina questioned.

"She did, but here's the claim, plain as day. It shows that it was generated the day after the boy was discharged from the hospital, but so far there hasn't been any payment posted on the account."

"Is it possible she did it by mistake and just forgot about it?"

Jack looked up at Elaina and shook his head slowly. "Mary Anne wouldn't do something like this by mistake, and even if she did, she certainly never forgets anything that went on in that office." He looked back down at the screen and said, "I'm going to call her."

After just two rings, Mary Anne picked up and said, "Hello?" Her voice sounded very fragile.

"Mary Anne? What's the matter?"

"Oh, hi, Dr. Roberts," she said more confidently. "I thought you were another reporter. They've been calling here non-stop for two days, demanding I come clean on this whole Medicaid fraud business."

"I'm so sorry," Jack said compassionately. "This is all my fault."

"No, it's not. I'm convinced it's that damned Michael Horvath."

"Why do you say that?" Jack asked.

"He has been interviewed by every television channel, and several talk radio stations, over the last two days. He has been saying all kinds of bad things about you. How you were milking the Medicaid program, and how you were only running for Congress with the hope of lining your pockets. Then today he told one reporter that he had heard you were in the Cayman Islands hiding from the FBI."

"Well, he got one thing right," Jack laughed, "I am hiding from the FBI, but not in the Caymans."

"This story just seems to be growing," she said. "Today, one of the stations interviewed Congressman Sheffield, and you can just imagine what all he had to say. He made a political speech about how fortunate the citizens of his district were that a crook like you didn't win the election."

Jack couldn't think of anything more to say other than "I'm sorry, Mary Anne. I guess I should have stayed and fought this thing head on. I took the easy way out, and left you to take the heat."

"No, sir," she replied quickly, "you did exactly the right thing. If you were here, I have no doubt you would be in jail, and for me, that would be far worse than having to field these calls from reporters."

"I appreciate you saying that, more than you know," he said.

"Oh, I almost forgot," she said. "I heard from Phyllis and Shelly today. They both said that a few reporters have called them as well, and they both told them they didn't know anything, and that they don't work for you any longer."

"If you talk to either of them again, please tell them how sorry I am for all the hassles I've created for them."

"Are you kidding? Those girls would run through a wall for you. They know you didn't do any of the things people keep accusing you of doing, and they are so appreciative of the generous severance pay you gave them." Mary Anne then added, "And by the way, so am I."

Jack sat silent for a moment, unsure what to say in response to such incredible loyalty from the small group of women who had become almost like a second family to him. His silence lasted long enough that Mary Anne asked, "Are you still there?"

"Yes," he said slowly, "I'm still here,"

"I was worried that maybe we got cut off," she said, then asked, "You called me. Did you need me to do something?"

"Yeah," he said, again wondering what he had done to gain such devotion. "Actually, there are three things I need. First, the next time you go by the house to get the mail, I need for you to go into my office, and get a folder out of my desk, and send it to me. Its the one marked Elaina's Nursing. It contains her nursing school diploma and a copy of her Texas nursing license." Jack thought for a minute then asked, "You do still have a key, don't you?"

"Of course. Is the security code still the same?" She had been in their home many times while they were out of town, and was very familiar with how to arm and disarm their system.

"Yes," Jack replied.

"That's easy. What's number two?"

"While you're in the house, I need for you to call me here on my cell. We are going to forward the house number to our new phone here."

"Are you sure you want to do that? Those reporters aren't likely to leave you alone either."

"I'll deal with them. I just need to make sure people who may not have my cell number can still get in touch with us."

"So what's the third thing?" she asked, anticipating he was going to ask her to pick up the dry cleaning or make sure their trash was put out for pick-up.

"I need for you to explain how a bill could be sent to the Texas Medicaid Program from our office, for services rendered to that ten year old boy from Guatemala?"

There was a moment of silence before she responded, "I don't know what you mean. Like I told you, I never submitted a claim for the care you gave to that boy. I didn't even bother to create a charge, because you told me to just write it off." She sounded a little offended that he was questioning her word.

"That's what I thought, and I obviously believe you, but I'm sitting here looking at the copy of our records that you sent me, and it shows very clearly that a charge was created for twenty-three hundred dollars, and it was billed to Medicaid the day after he was discharged from the hospital."

"I have no idea how that could have happened," she said, trying to think if maybe one of the other girls could have entered the charge and submitted the claim. "I'm the only one who creates charges, and I'm the only one who submits those claims. What's the date of the claim?" she asked.

"July twentieth," Jack replied.

Mary Anne took a moment to check her calendar, then replied, "July twentieth was a Saturday. Not only was the office closed on that day, I couldn't have made that entry anyway. I was in Houston that weekend visiting my mother. That's her birthday."

"Someone has hacked into our system and planted this bogus Medicaid claim, knowing it would stand out like a sore thumb in an audit," Jack said, speaking mostly to himself. "It is pretty obvious who's behind this." He paused another moment then asked, "Is there anyway we can run a report of the times you logged into the system?"

"Sure," she said, then proceeded to walk Jack through the steps for creating the report. Within a couple of minutes he found it.

"I think I have exactly what I need, but just to confirm it, is there a way to see when the Medicaid office actually received the claim?"

"That's easy," she said. "Since we file all our claims electronically, the Medicaid computer system sends us an electronic receipt immediately once they receive it. It doesn't mean they actually start processing it. It just says they got it." She told him where to find what he was looking for, and as he pulled it up, a broad grin appeared on his face.

"Your the best Mary Anne," he said. "Remind me to give you a raise."

****

"Now that he is out of our hair, I want you and Grady to move forward with closing the medical staff," Fitzgerald said. "We don't want any more rebels inside our camp."

"There are a couple of older guys that might try and resist, but without their ring leader, they won't be able to hold out for long," Horvath said.

"I'm not sure why we have to go to the trouble of closing the staff," Grady stated. "Virtually everyone is now part of our group."

"Two reasons." Fitzgerald said bluntly. He was not at all happy about having to explain himself to this doctor who was trying to be a businessman. "First, a closed staff eliminates any possibility of someone like Jack Roberts even applying for privileges in our hospital. Those kind of independent thinkers must be kept out, or we risk having our whole concept fall apart because of internal competition." He paused for a moment to make sure Grady understood this was how a monopoly was maintained. "And, second, if we have a closed staff, we can better control our existing physicians. If somebody starts complaining about how much they get paid, or how hard they have to work, we can go out and recruit a replacement, but even more importantly, if we find that certain service lines are not profitable, we can cut our losses by moving out the docs who provide those services. With a closed staff, we won't have to worry about anyone else offering losing services in our facility."

Grady looked at Horvath and asked, "What kind of services are we talking about?"

Horvath tried unsuccessfully to suppress his sly smile, then said, "Well, the first one that comes to mind is facial plastic surgery. Those guys take six to eight hours in the operating room, fixing something simple like a cleft lip or removing some kind of facial birth mark, and most of the time we don't get paid anything. That is OR time that could be used to actually make money with other procedures. With a closed staff, we can easily get rid of the plastic surgeons who perform those procedures."

"Why not just tell those guys they can't do them in this hospital?" Grady asked, naively.

"The last thing we want to be accused of is denying any kind of care," Fitzgerald said defensively.

"But isn't that what we'd be doing?"

"Absolutely not!" Horvath said with a smirk. "The physicians are the ones who make those decisions, and they are free to do whatever procedures they choose. We are merely making a business decision not to include those physicians on our staff that negatively impact our bottom line."

THE CONFLICT

Grady started to object, but seeing the satisfied looks on both of the other men's faces, he decided to go along. He didn't want to say anything that might threaten his half million dollar a year salary as the CEO of the physician group, or the huge bonus he was receiving from the hospital every quarter.

****

At seven o'clock the black Lincoln town car pulled off the concrete road, onto the last driveway before the street ended. The driver pulled the car up to the front of the white stucco house, which looked far more inviting than it had when Jack and Elaina first saw it. The bougainvillea vines had been trimmed, the shrubs were neatly pruned, and the lawn appeared well manicured.

As Franco and Gabriella approached, Jack and Elaina were both standing in the front doorway to greet them.

"Welcome, my friends," Jack said excitedly. "Thank you so much for coming."

"This is a very secluded place you have here," Franco remarked. "Are you hiding from someone?"

Jack laughed and said, "Yeah, the FBI."

The two men shook hands and exchanged a cordial one arm embrace. Elaina and Gabriella hugged each other warmly before similarly greeting the men. Without them noticing, the driver retrieved a rather large package from the back of the limo.

"Please, come in," Elaina said. "I hope you'll excuse the fact that I haven't had time to do much decorating yet, but please, make yourselves at home."

"I thought that might be the case," Gabriella said, "so we brought this for you." She pointed to the three foot by four foot package the driver had leaned against the wall just inside the front door.

"What is this?" She replied with surprise, anticipating that it was a framed piece of art based on the appearance of the neatly wrapped package.

"It is for both of you," Gabriella said, "but I think it may be most appropriate for Dr. Roberts to open it."

Jack stepped forward and easily lifted the large, flat package, placing it on the nearby sofa. He quickly tore the silver paper and immediately recognized the image. He held up the heavy wooden frame that surrounded the painting of Elaina. The oil portrait had been produced from a photo of his wife on the stairs of Franco and Gabriella's home. She was wearing that custom pale gold gown with emerald green lace overlay and those spectacular emerald earrings and necklace.

"Wow!" was all he could say as he held it out at arms length.

"What is it?" Elaina asked.

As Jack turned it toward her he said, "Only the most beautiful woman in the world."

"Oh, my God!" Elaina exclaimed. "How did you?..."

"We thought your home could use a personal touch, and I was certain your husband would approve."

Elaina was speechless, so Jack responded. "I think its perfect." Jack said. "I have always wanted a portrait of Elaina to hang in the living room." He didn't comment of the fact that this one was considerably smaller than the life-sized painting of Gabriella that dominated one wall of the Gutierrez great room.

"I don't know what to say," Elaina offered as she examined her likeness.

"You don't need to say anything," Gabriella said as she handed her another much smaller flat box wrapped in red foil, and encircled with a white ribbon with a small white bow on top. "I am so glad you have come to Nicaragua, and I hope you will stay."

Elaina's eyes grew wide as she accepted the gift, "Please, open it," Gabriella urged her friend.

"You didn't need to buy me anything" Elaina said. "You and Franco just being here is gift enough, and the painting..."

"The painting is for both of you, but this is just for you," she said pointing to the unopened box. "I did not buy it. It was given to me and I want you to have it."

Elaina carefully removed the ribbon and found the seem where the foil was taped. She removed the paper, exposing the white velvet box, which seemed vaguely familiar. She opened the top slowly, holding her breath with anticipation.

"Oh my God," she exclaimed. Elaina reached into the box and removed the same huge solitaire emerald necklace she had worn once, the night of the reception. She held it up to the light, and said, "Oh Gabriella, I can't accept this." She quickly placed it back onto the white satin surface, along side the diamond and emerald drop earrings. "This is too much."

"I want you to have them," Gabriella said, refusing to accept the box as Elaina tried to hand it back to her. "As you can see in the painting, they look so much better on you than they ever did when I wore them."

She looked over at Jack hoping he would give her some direction. "But, this is too much," she protested. "I can't ..."

Gabriella, moved forward and placed her hands over Elaina's as she held the edges of the open box. She smiled with delight in her eyes as she saw Elaina struggling with the situation. Then she repeated softly, "I want you to have them."

She looked again toward Jack, who nodded reassuringly. "Thank you so much. This is beyond anything I could ever imagine."

"Why don't you put them on," Jack suggested.

"They don't exactly go with this outfit." She was wearing a white cotton blouse and a navy skirt.

"I think emeralds go with just about anything," Jack said with a boyish smile. He started to say something about them going very well with nothing, but knew better than to embarrass her with such a bawdy line. Instead he simply walked over and took the necklace out of the box and placed it carefully around her slender neck. She had started wearing her hair up, in a french twist, mainly because of the heat and humidity, making it easy for Jack to fasten the clasp of the delicate gold chain. She turned to face him tentatively, but when she saw the sly way he was looking at her, immediately she broke into a broad grin. She knew he was remembering that night in what he called the presidential suite, when she wore only these same jewels to bed.

"You'll have to put on the earrings yourself," he said, holding the box up in front of her. She quickly removed her simple pearls studs from both ears and replaced them with the large diamonds with the even larger emeralds suspended by gold chains.

"She looked up innocently into Jack's eyes, and tossed her head playfully from side to side. "So, what do you think, el Presidenté?" she asked.

Gabriella and Franco looked on with satisfaction, but were both puzzled by the reference to el Presidenté.

"I too, have something for you my friend," Franco said, approaching Jack. "Actually, it is for both of us," he said as he presented him with a narrow black gift bag.

Jack opened it quickly and produced a square bottle with a hand written label. "Wow!" he said. "This is that special scotch we shared after dinner at your home."

"Yes," Franco replied. "And, I want you to know, this is one of the last bottles of Michel Couvreur scotch in existence. He no longer is in the business of aging scotch whiskey in France, so I hope you enjoy it."

"We will enjoy it," Jack said excitedly, "just as soon as I can get the bottle open,"

Lucinda had been instructed to offer the women a glass of a chardonnay Jack had found at a liquor store in Managua, and he was planning to serve Franco an eighteen year old single malt scotch from the Glenmorangie distillery. Elaina had insisted they at least buy some decent crystal if they were going to serve drinks to their friends. As Lucinda came into the living room, Jack stopped her and sent her back into the kitchen with a new set of instructions. She returned a few minutes later with two crystal flutes of Dom Perignon champagne for the ladies and two highball glasses containing generous measures of the amber colored scotch.

Jack raised his glass and said, "To our new life here in Nicaragua, and to the best friends anyone could ever have."

After the toast, Jack led the way out on to the wooden deck, anxious to show their friends the view out to the west. The sun was just setting behind one of the large black volcanic formations between the lagoon and the beach. The jagged edge of the rock divided the sun light into distinct rays of bright golden yellow, against the brilliant blue, cloudless sky. The still water of the lagoon offered an inverted reflection of the unique image.

"What an incredible sunset," Gabriella exclaimed as she preceded Franco onto the recently stained pine decking. She seemed mesmerized by the sight, as Franco came up behind her. Her casual summer dress was worn off the shoulders, revealing her bare olive skin. He touched her cool shoulder gently with his left hand as they were both captured by the celestial vision.

After a few moments, Jack and Elaina joined them at the railing, and Jack said, "We're so glad you agreed to join us this evening, Elaina even ordered up this visual spectacle."

"This is certainly a great place to retire," Franco said.

"Who said anything about retiring? I'm not anywhere close to being finished."

Over the next several minutes, the four of them watched the light slowly fade as the golden rays gradually turned to pale yellow against a background of deepening blues, with touches of violet and purple. They savored their drinks, and chatted about Christina, David and Amy until Lucinda announced to Elaina that their dinner was ready.

As they took their seats around the outdoor table illuminated by two large candles, it was difficult for any of them to take their eyes off the last remnants of the dying daylight to the West. Lucinda served them each a combination salad of fresh local fruits and an appetizer of pan seared, yellow fin tuna sliced into planks, all served over a bed of crisp lettuce. At Jack's direction she poured them each a glass of the chardonnay that he'd originally planned for before dinner.

The main course was a filet of sierra mackerel, poached in a white wine sauce, capers and chopped cilantro. It was served with steamed julienne carrots mixed with purple onions and mild yellow peppers.

For dessert, Lucinda prepared her specialty, sugar bananas. Gabriella insisted that the woman tell her the secret of this incredible dessert. As they were enjoying the delicious treat, Lucinda explained that she sliced each banana lengthwise then rolled them in a thick slurry of white sugar and cinnamon water.

She then placed them in the freezer for twenty minutes. Just before serving, she rolled them again in brown sugar and then placed them in a very hot iron skillet to caramelize the outer layer. She then poured a thin layer of heavy cream on the plate and arranged the two pieces carefully over the cream, then drizzled a small amount of honey over the top.

"That was a wonderful meal," Franco said. "You may want to be careful about having people over for dinner. I have some friends who would think nothing of hiring Lucinda away from you."

After dinner Jack and Franco enjoyed another glass of scotch as they all walked down to the beach. Elaina and Gabriella walked ahead, chatting about everything and nothing, like a couple of school girls, as they watched the moonlight dance off the surface of the gentle waves.

"So, are you going to tell me what happened?" Franco asked.

"I'm not sure you want to hear all the sordid details, but it was pretty simple really," Jack began. "With all the changes that are occurring in healthcare back in the states, some people are choosing to try and manipulate the system by controlling the doctors. I refused to play by the rules they are trying to establish, so they decided to come after me. I'm now pretty sure they are the same people who were behind the torpedoing of my campaign last year when I was running for Congress. When I still refused to toe their line, they got the FBI after me for alleged Medicaid fraud. So, it came down to either leaving while I still could, or going to jail."

"Who are these people that are after you?" Franco said, with obvious concern for his friend.

"Oh, you wouldn't know them," Jack replied. "One is the guy who replaced the administrator you met, his name is Michael Horvath. The previous administrator, Bob Anderson, was a great guy. He wasn't the least bit motivated by money. He just wanted the kids to get the best care possible. This guy Horvath is the exact opposite."

"He sounds like some of the people we have working here in our government."

"Highly ambitious, with very low ethical standards?"

"Yes, that describes most of the Ministers," Franco agreed.

"The other guy is his boss, James Fitzgerald. He's the chairman of the board of the hospital. He's got plenty of money, so for him, I don't think this is as much about profit as it is power and control. He uses guys like Horvath to do his work for him, and I can tell you first hand that he's not one that takes no for an answer."

"Did he threaten you?" Franco asked, trying to remain as casual as possible.

"Not in so many words, but I have no doubt that he and Horvath were behind this most recent government raid on my office. In fact, I was reviewing a backup copy of my office records and discovered a bogus claim that someone had entered to make it look like I was attempting to defraud the Medicaid program."

"How do you know it was them?"

"I don't know for certain, but the only people who would have the information needed to post the claim are either my own employees or someone with access to the hospital records. I'm certain it was none of my employees, because the amount billed was more than twice what we would have charged for the services, and the entry was posted at two thirty in the morning, two days before the raid. That was almost two months after I treated the boy in the hospital."

"Why do you say it was a bogus claim?" Franco was determined to learn as much about Jack's situation as he could.

"The child was a ten year old from Guatemala, who was in the US with his family illegally. He wasn't eligible for Medicaid, or any government program, so filing a claim under those circumstances is expressly prohibited, but the Medicaid program is so screwed up they are likely to pay those kinds of claims and never catch their error."

"So, are you going to go back and fight to clear your name?"

"I don't know," Jack said in frustration. "I know I should, but I have no way to prove they were behind this attempt to frame me, and based on all the negative publicity this thing has gotten, I don't know whether I could ever really, as you say, clear my name. Maybe it is time to just hang it up." Jack's voice sounded more defeated than he felt, but he really wasn't sure what he was going to do.

"You know," Franco offered, "you could work here in Nicaragua. I'm certain the people of this country would benefit from your experience and expertise."

"I've thought about it, but the kind of work I'm best at requires a modern hospital, specialized equipment and a lot of support staff. Those are all things that don't exist here."

Franco nodded his head silently, acknowledging the truth of Jack's assessment.

"For now, I think I'm just going to apply for a temporary work visa, and Elaina says she wants to work with me. She's a registered nurse, you know."

"I remember her talking about being a nurse when we stayed in your guest house in Fort Worth," Franco said. "It does not surprise me at all that she would wish to work by your side. You two are truly made for each other."

"It would be exciting to try and build a modern hospital here in Nicaragua," Jack said, almost as if he were speaking only to himself.

"Why don't you do it? I'm sure I could help, I have many connections in this country."

"I've seen some of your connections," Jack laughed. "I have no doubt you could be a huge help, but I don't know," he grumbled. "It sounds like a pipe dream to me."

"If you decide to pursue the idea, please let me know." Franco spoke with a sincerity in his voice that let Jack know he was not just making idle conversation.

The four friends lingered a while longer on the beach before finally making their way back to the house. Lucinda had finished cleaning the kitchen, and had joined Federico in their cozy quarters, while Franco's driver waited patiently next to the car in front of the house. After a few minutes of thank you's and goodbye's, he and Gabriella stepped out the front door and into the big Lincoln. Just before he sat down beside his wife, Franco turned back to Jack and said, "Please, let me know how I can help."

Jack and Elaina waved as the limo noisily rolled over the gravel driveway and out onto the street, then quickly disappeared around the corner.

"What did he mean, let him know how he could help?" Elaina asked as Jack closed the door.

"Oh, he thinks we should build a hospital here in Nicaragua." Jack said, as he walked toward the back door to make sure it was locked.

"Well, maybe you should," she said. "But, before you start planning anything like that, I've got something else for you to do, *El Presidenté*."

He turned toward her, and she had already removed her blouse and skirt, and was working at unfastening her bra. She was still wearing the emeralds and they still matched her eyes.

CHAPTER 15

"May I speak to the regional manager?" Jack asked, as someone finally answered the phone. He had gone through the entire automated phone queue at CMS, and had been on hold for more than twenty minutes, waiting for a live person.

"She is in a meeting, may I take your name and number and have her call you back?" the young woman asked in a robotic tone.

"Just tell her Dr. Jack Roberts is on the phone."

The name was familiar, causing her to pause for a moment then she said, "Please hold."

In less than fifteen seconds, the manager came on the line and said, "Dr. Roberts, where are you?"

"Where I am is not important. I'm calling to let you know that I was set-up by someone outside my office. We did not bill Medicaid for that boy from Guatemala."

"I know that," she said. "We found the irregularity."

"Really?" Jack sounded surprised that they would have made the discovery.

"This kind of thing is not that uncommon," she said. "We understand that when doctors make enemies, one of the easiest ways to attack them is to accuse them of fraud."

"So, I'm not going to be charged with anything?"

"Of course not," she assured him. "Wherever you are you can come back home any time you like."

Jack remained skeptical. "Just like that? It's over?"

"Just like that," she said casually.

"Why is it that I don't believe you?" Jack said suspiciously.

"Why would I lie to you?" she said. "I want to close this case."

"Sure you do. You want to lure me back home so you can have me arrested. I know how you guys work. You need the politicians to think your doing your job, and the best way to show them is by arresting doctors on live national television." Jack was convinced that she was lying about finding the irregularity in his records. "Well, you aren't going to make me into one of your political prizes."

"Dr. Roberts, I can assure you that you have nothing to fear from me, or from the FBI."

"Okay," he said, "then I want you and those agents who were with you, to call a news conference in front of my office. Get all those same reporters and television cameras out there and then you can tell the world that I'm innocent as a newborn baby. Will you do that?"

"Uh, well, you know I can't do that." she replied hesitantly.

"Then I guess your case will have to remain open." When he didn't hear an immediate response he hung up the phone.

He found Elaina out on the deck and sat down in the chair next to her. "It looks like we are going to be here for a while."

"Do you think we can get David to ship some more of our clothes and personal items down here. I'm getting tired of wearing the same five outfits."

"They aren't after you. They're after me," Jack said. "Why don't you fly back home and get some of the things you need, and you can check on the house."

"I guess I can do that. I can bring a couple of trunks back on the plane, but it will probably cost us a couple hundred bucks extra."

"The other option would be to ship a container of stuff down here, but I'd prefer to wait on that until we decide how long we're going to stay," Jack reasoned.

"I hate to go back to the house alone, what with all that's been going on," she said. "Do you think Mary Anne could pick me up at the airport and go with me?"

Jack reached over and touched her gently on the shoulder, while giving her a reassuring look. He said. "I'll call her this evening. I'm sure she will be happy to help."

"Okay, I guess that probably is the best option."

"You really are my Angel," he said. "I wish I could go with you, but I'd like to be able to come back with you, ya know?"

"I don't want you to go if there is even the remotest chance they'd arrest you."

THE CONFLICT

****

Two days later, Jack took Elaina to the airport in Managua. She was armed with a list of necessities she planned to bring back with her. The return ticket was open ended, but she told him she planned to be back in no more than three or four days. They shared a parting kiss and he told her he'd try and get a few things done while she was away. Then she boarded the flight back to Texas without him.

Jack got back into the rental car and headed out on his next big chore, buying a car. Now that it seemed clear they were going to be there for more than just a couple of weeks, continuing to rent didn't make any sense. Plus, even if they went back to Texas, they were certainly going to be spending more time back here in Nicaragua. They'd need a car each and every time they were here. He had never been one to buy used cars. He always thought they were almost certainly someone else's problem. He figured that's why they were for sale. Domingo had suggested the dealership where he'd bought his Toyota, and recommended Jack get a four wheel drive vehicle, because so much of the terrain in his country included dirt roads that were often impassible in a conventional car.

The Toyota dealership had a relatively limited selection of vehicles compared to the massive number of cars that covered the huge lots back in Texas. However, as soon as he pulled in, Jack saw exactly what he wanted in the back corner of the lot. The silvery blue Land Cruiser, with four wheel drive, would be perfect for their needs. When he explained to the salesman that he was Dr. Ramirez's friend, the man decided he needed to introduce him to the general manager. Domingo had taken care of the owner's daughter a few months before, and he had told all his employees to take special care of him. The salesman wasn't sure whether that special care extended to the doctor's close friends, but he didn't want to risk being criticized if he didn't at least check with his boss.

As Jack shook hands with the general manager, the man looked at him with a questioning expression. "I've seen you somewhere before," he said.

Jack shrugged and replied, "I doubt it. My wife and I just moved here from Texas."

"Ah, yes!" he said as he made the connection. "You're the surgeon from Texas who performed the heart operation on that young boy here in Managua a few years ago. I saw you on television."

"You have quite a memory," Jack remarked. "That was eight years ago."

"In the car business it is very important to remember people's names and faces," the manager replied. "What can I do for you, doctor?"

Jack told him he was interested in the Land Cruiser, and that he would be paying cash.

"That is an excellent choice. I sell many of those vehicles to American expatriates."

Jack hadn't thought of himself as an expatriate, but technically that's exactly what he was and it certainly sounded better than refugee. The two men discussed the warranty and service arrangements, which Jack found surprisingly similar to what was available back in the US. They agreed on a price of sixty-five thousand, which was thirteen thousand less than the sticker, but once the VAT was added the actual cost was back up over seventy-two thousand. Jack handed his check to the manager, who then had the salesman follow him back to the airport in his personal car, where he returned the rented car. By the time they got back to the dealership, his new truck was ready and waiting.

Jack drove to the government complex at the Concepcion Palacio in the southeast sector of Managua. He was going there to get the necessary forms to apply for a temporary work visa. As he approached the rather small building, he once more realized how different things were here, compared to what he was used to back home. This was a national government department, yet the building reminded him of a run down sub-court house back home. The lobby area only seated five or six, and surprisingly there was no one waiting. He walked right up to the young receptionist behind a desk that looked to be a reclamation project from a used furniture store.

"May I help you, she asked?"

"Yes, my name is Jack Roberts, and I'm seeking a temporary work visa as a physician from the United States. I would also like to inquire about a work visa for my wife. She's a registered nurse."

The receptionist picked up her phone and called one of the assistant ministers to the front. The portly, middle aged man made his way slowly to the front of the office until he stood directly behind the receptionist. He asked the same question, and Jack provided the same answer.

"What did you say your name was again," the midlevel functionary asked, trying to remember where he might have heard the name Roberts before. He knew it was familiar, but he didn't know why. "Let me get the forms," he said. "Then you will need to fill them out and mail them back to this office. It usually takes three or four weeks to process the application."

Jack nodded, expecting nothing less. Third world countries had their own time schedule that simply couldn't be rushed.

The man turned back toward his cubical, and as he did the Minister of Health was coming around a partition, and nearly ran into his subordinate. "What are you doing?" the superior asked angrily in response to his underling's mere presence in his path. Jack smiled as he watched the exchange occurring, less than twenty feet from where he stood.

"There is an American doctor up front who is asking for a temporary work visa for himself and one for his wife."

The Minister allowed the other man to continue his task of finding the necessary forms, but as he made his way across the back of the room, between the rows of desks, he glanced up toward the receptionist and recognized the familiar face. Immediately he turned and walked to the front.

"Dr. Roberts, it is so good to see you again." He reached across the receptionist as if she were just a part of the furniture, and shook Jack's hand vigorously. "Please come back to my office," he said as he motioned for the American to come around the desk and follow him back to his private corner of the building.

"What brings you to the Ministry of Health?" the government bureaucrat asked, subtly emphasizing the importance of his agency and his own position.

"My wife and I have purchased a home in El Transito, and since we will be living here for a while, we thought it would be a good idea to make ourselves useful."

"You wish to work as a physician here in Nicaragua?" the Minister asked in surprise.

"Yes," Jack replied, "and my wife Elaina would like to work as a nurse. I'm not sure you remember, but you met her the night of the reception at the home of Franco Gutierrez."

"Of course I remember," he said with a subtle smile. "How could any man not remember meeting such a beautiful woman."

"Thank you, I'll give her your regards."

"So, what brings you back to this country?"

Jack wasn't about to go into all the details of his clandestine escapade. Instead he offered, "We have always enjoyed our visits here, so, the time just seemed right to buy a place here where we could spend more time. Elaina loves the beach, and we found a beautiful home in El Transito where we can both relax and just get away." Those final words were more true than his host would likely ever know.

The Minister didn't inquire further, but instead asked, "How long do you anticipate being here?"

"I really don't know," Jack replied. "It could be only a few months each year, or it could be nearly full time. We aren't sure yet, but I would like to have the flexibility when I'm in this country of working with my friend Dr. Domingo Ramirez, whom you also met at the reception."

He reached into one of the drawers of his desk and found the folder containing the necessary materials. He pulled out two official appearing documents and across the top lines he wrote in the names Dr. Jack Roberts and Elaina Roberts. He then signed each one quickly along the bottom. "I can only grant you and your wife medical work permits for one year. After that you will be required to apply for an extension, assuming you wish to remain here in Nicaragua." He said as he handed Jack both documents.

"Thank you, sir," Jack said, surprised at how quickly the process had been. "But, what about the application forms? Don't I need to fill out something?"

"That is merely a formality," the Minister scoffed. "My deputy minister will fill out all the paperwork for both of you. I will have him contact you at your convenience to get the specifics. Just give the receptionist your local contact information."

"Thank you again," Jack said as he stood and shook the man's hand once more.

"It is me that should be thanking you," he replied. "President Ortega was very pleased when I shared our conversation with him. He has asked me to work on a plan that will bring our healthcare system up to the standards in the United States."

Jack chuckled to himself, but the Minister saw what he thought was a smirk on Jack's face. "Do you not think that is possible," he challenged.

"Of course," Jack replied, realizing the Minister misunderstood his response. "I was just thinking about how the American healthcare system seems to be in decline. It may be easier to meet their new standards than you might think."

****

"Do you have any new information on those two guys," Franco asked.

"Yes, sir," the man replied in a very business like tone. "We have been following both of them, and I have their cell phones, home and office phones tapped."

"Have you identified the man who planted the data?"

"We have narrowed it down to three possible individuals in this town who are capable of pulling off that kind of operation. It's just a matter of time before we know. We are cross referencing phone logs and bank records. We should have an answer by the end of the week."

"Very good," he said. "When you find him I want a recording of him naming those two guys as the men who hired him, preferably on video, but audio will do if that's all you can get."

"Yes, sir. We'll get it."

Franco pressed the end button on his cell phone and walked out of the rear door of his study onto the patio where he could see his daughter splashing and laughing with her mother in the swimming pool.

****

"Yes, I know," Elaina said, "I miss you, too."
"When are you guys coming home?" David asked.
"I am home," she said, "I came back for a few days to get some of our personal stuff. It appears your father and I are going to be living in exile in El Transito, at least for a while." She laughed briefly at the idea of being in exile.
"I wish I could get away to come see you, but there's no way this week."
"That's okay, I understand," she said.
"Why didn't Dad come with you?"
"He believes he's still on the FBI watch list, and if he is, they likely would have been waiting for him as soon as he got off the airplane."
"This just seems so wrong," David said. "If he doesn't come home, how will he ever be able to clear his name. The longer he remains away, the more guilty he appears to be."
"He's aware of that, but he says he has no way of proving he's innocent."
"I just wish there was something I could do," David said with obvious frustration.
"You really don't need to worry about your dad, or about me for that matter," she instructed. "We are doing great. Our new house is coming along. The weather down there has been terrific. The beach is beautiful. Life is good. When I get our stuff shipped down there we'll have everything we need. Everything, that is, except for you and Amy."
"Well, it's going to be a challenge for me to come down there while I'm still in school."
"I know that, silly, but your dad and I were talking about having you guys down for Christmas. Your father emailed your uncle in Japan, and it sounds like he's coming."
"We'd really like to see your new house," David said, speaking more deliberately. There's just one minor detail,"
"I know what you're going to say," she interrupted. "You don't have the money, right?"
"Right. We're just getting by on Amy's salary, and two tickets to Managua are not in our budget."
"We'll take care of that. You can consider it your Christmas present."

"That sounds great," he said excitedly. "I'm off the last two weeks of December, and hopefully Amy can get off too. I can't imagine there will be many people around the research department during the holidays."

"We'll have your room all ready. You guys are going to just love it down there."

"I'm sure we will," he said. Then he asked, "Do you think there is any possibility that Dad will be able to make it here for my graduation from med school in early June?" His voice was almost childlike as he couldn't imagine his dad not being present for that particular event.

"There is absolutely no way he would miss your graduation. You can be certain your dad and I will both be there, even if we have to sneak across the Mexican border and hitchhike to Dallas," she said with a laugh.

****

"Jack? Can you come here a minute?" Domingo called out as he stuck his head out of one of the exam rooms. Jack was sitting talking with Domingo's nurse in the small alcove that served as the nurses station in his private clinic.

"Sure," he answered as he quickly rose from his chair and joined his colleague. "What is it?"

"I want you to take a look at this baby. He was born at home about three months ago, and his mom brought him in because he wasn't nursing very well."

Jack walked over to the exam table where the young mother was holding her baby boy very close. She released her grip slightly, allowing Jack to inspect the infant who looked to be only smaller than a typical three month old. He listened to his chest for several minutes, and then looked closely at the child's eyes.

"I'm pretty sure he's got it." Jack said.

"That's what I thought," Domingo said. "So, what do we do now. We still don't have a heart lung machine in this country and you can't take him back to Fort Worth yourself." Domingo said in frustration.

"I'll take care of it," Jack said with finality. "You just explain to this mother that her son is going to need to go to Texas for a heart operation."

He walked back out to the nurses station and retrieved his cell phone. He used the directory to find the name he needed and the number was dialed automatically.

"Hello, this is Dr. Jackson," Buzz said with his familiar southern drawl.

"Hey Buzz, how are you?"

"Jack!? Is it really you? I thought you'd fallen off the face of the earth."

"No, I'm still around, just not around anywhere the FBI might be able to find me." he laughed

"You said you were going to call me, and when I didn't hear from you I thought something terrible must have happened."

"I'm sorry, I completely forgot about calling. We've been trying to get settled into our new house, and I've started working in the clinic here in Managua. It just totally slipped my mind."

"I understand," Buzz said sympathetically. "So, I take it your not coming back?"

"Not until I'm sure that its safe."

"I can't say that I blame you. Things are getting worse around here by the minute."

"How's that?" Jack asked.

"Grady has proposed that the medical staff here at the children's hospital be closed. He and Horvath are trying to turn us into an exclusive ACO based practice. Now that they've got all the docs under contract, they want to make sure nobody can practice here without being an employee, and for those that are employed, the only way out would be to leave the area."

"Do they have the votes to get that done?" Jack asked.

"Are you kidding? Grady has all the pediatricians on board, and the specialists are all too scared to stand up to him. It's a slam dunk."

"It wouldn't do me any good to come back anyway, since my privileges were suspended, and I didn't file an appeal."

"You're right. I hadn't thought about that," Buzz said. "I understand that Herb Nichols is pushing the guys over at the general hospital to close their staff as well. You know they put together the same kind of group practice model that Grady started over here. I swear, it won't be long before there aren't any independent physicians left."

"I hate to say it, but I told you so," Jack said, with a sad reluctance in his voice.

"I know," Buzz admitted, "We wouldn't listen, and now we're paying the price." He paused before adding, "My income is down forty percent since I joined this group, and I'm working longer hours than ever."

"Just wait until the first of the year when all those government contracts switch over to global payments to the hospital and the Accountable Care Organization."

"I don't even want to think about it. I may just have to pack up my bags and come join you."

"That might happen one day. You never know." Jack paused a moment before continuing, "The reason I called is I have a three month old here in Managua that I'm sure has tetralogy of Fallot, and I'd like to get him up there to see you and George."

"Horvath has let it be known that no uninsured patients will be admitted without prepayment of at least fifty percent of the anticipated hospital charges."

"That should not be a problem," Jack said, "There is still more than six hundred thousand dollars in the Nicaraguan Surgical Fund."

"I can ask, but it wouldn't surprise me if that money isn't there any more."

"I'll call George and have him go with you. Horvath knows that both of you have knowledge of the fund, and I'm confident that George is ready to take on this case."

"Like I said, I'll try, but I'm not optimistic."

"When you know something call me, and I'll get the baby and his mother up there."

"Will do," Buzz said.

****

Jack called Franco's private number, but he wasn't in his office. His secretary answered and said she wasn't sure when he would be back. Jack decided to leave a message, "Please tell him that I called, and that I have a baby in the clinic that requires heart surgery, and will need transportation to Texas."

About an hour later Jack got a call back from Buzz. "Horvath told me that it was his understanding that the money in the fund was specifically designated to pay for children that were under your care, and since you are no longer on the medical staff the fund was being dissolved."

"That guy has to be the most heartless SOB in the world," Jack said.

"I'm sorry. There's not much I can do."

"I know. I'll figure out something," he said as he hung up the phone.

Jack sat motionless at Domingo's desk for several minutes, leaning forward, his head in his hands.

"What's the matter?" Domingo asked, as he entered the small office.

Jack looked up and just shook his head slowly.

"Were you able to speak with your friend in Texas?"

"Yes." Jack's usual air of confidence was gone. "This is all my fault," he said sounding utterly despondent.

"What's your fault? What did he say?"

"He said they can't take this baby."

"Why not? I thought you said there was still more than enough money in the fund that Franco established several years ago."

"Oh, the money's there," Jack said, "but the damned administrator is playing games with it. He claims that according to the agreement with Franco, it can only be used for patients that I admit to the hospital. He's saying that since I'm no longer on the staff, they are under no obligation to accept any uninsured children from Nicaragua."

Domingo took a moment to sort out everything his friend just said, but then he asked, "Why don't we just get Franco to call them and tell them to allow other doctors to care for this child."

"I can't do that," Jack said, "He has already done enough. This wouldn't have happened if I had stayed there and fought for what was right. Instead I ran away like a little school boy, and now that baby is ..." He couldn't finish saying what he was thinking.

"Before you came here, children with these kinds of problems were never treated," Domingo said. "This is not your fault. You have done what you could, but you are not responsible for the life of every child."

Jack looked up into his friend's concerned face. "Perhaps that's true," he agreed, "but, I am responsible for this one. I know what needs to be done and by God I'm going to see to it that it gets done." He spoke with a renewed conviction, as he developed a new plan in his mind.

"You're not going back to Texas are you?"

"No, I have another idea," Jack replied. "I know a surgeon in Buenos Aires who trained at Hopkins. I'm going to see if he will accept this child."

"Why send him all the way down there? Don't you know somebody in Houston or Miami? That would be much closer."

"Yes, and much more expensive," he said. "I think I can get this done for a lot less in Argentina."

It only took Jack a few minutes of searching the Internet to find what he was looking for, but it was more difficult getting Dr. Manuel Fernandez-Chapa on the phone. He remained on hold for more than twenty minutes while the office staff tracked down the heart surgeon.

"Hello, this is Dr. Fernandez-Chapa,"

"Manuel, this is Jack Roberts."

"Jack... how are you my friend? What are you doing these days?" The man spoke excellent English with a very distinct Argentinian accent.

"I am living in Nicaragua, working here with a local pediatrician, and I need your help."

"Anything for you my friend. What do you need?"

"I have a three month old here with tetralogy of Fallot, and I was hoping I could bring him down to your hospital and have you do the surgery."

"I do not understand. You are one of the foremost experts in that procedure. Why are you sending the child to me?"

"It's a long story, but we don't have the facilities here in Managua to do this kind of surgery, and for reasons I won't bore you with, I can't take him back to the States."

"Of course, I would be happy to take care of him," he said, then added, "the only question is whether our hospital will agree to accept him. I assume this is a charity case."

"No," Jack said, "you can tell them they will get paid, I just need some idea what the charge is likely to be."

"I can find that out and call you back within the hour."

"That would be great," Jack replied. "How soon could I bring him down there?"

"That is entirely up to you. I am here, and I have no travel plans until the holidays, so, we will be ready whenever you say."

"I really appreciate it. I'll start making the arrangements and I should know something by the time you call back."

Jack hung up after giving Manuel his phone number, then immediately called Franco's private number again. This time the familiar voice of his powerful friend answered.

"Did you get my message?" he asked.

"Yes, I was planning to call you back to see if you needed an air ambulance to Dallas/Fort Worth, or whether the child and his mother could go by commercial jet."

"I think they can travel safely on a commercial airline, but we're not going to Fort Worth. I need transportation to Buenos Aires, and I'm going with them."

"Buenos Aires?" Franco asked, "Why?"

"It is difficult to explain," Jack said. "I just need for you to trust me. I'll tell you all about it some time over a glass of scotch."

"I will have my secretary make the arrangements," he said, his voice still had a questioning tone. "When do you need to leave?"

"Tomorrow morning would be great. Will that give you time to get the necessary travel papers for the baby and his mother? They obviously don't have passports."

"Consider it done," Franco said. After a brief pause he asked, "What about the hospital bill?"

"That's taken care of," Jack said without hesitation.

He called Elaina back in Texas, to let her know he needed to go to Argentina for a few days. She was still packing two suitcases and a large trunk with her summer clothes and some things for Jack. She was also trying to decide whether to take family photo albums, jewelry and personal documents.

"I have to go to Buenos Aires. I'll be gone for a week, maybe ten days."

She was used to Jack telling her that he had to leave for the hospital with little notice, but this sounded strange somehow. "Why are you going to Argentina?" She asked, totally unaware of what had been happening at the clinic.

His response was very simple. "I need to fix a broken heart."

****

It was around ten the next morning, when Domingo's old silver Land Cruiser pulled off the street and on to the gravel driveway. He was there to pick up his friend and take him to the airport in Managua. The traffic was unusually heavy as they made their way back into the city, and it was almost noon when they finally made it to the clinic where the anxious mother waited patiently holding her baby with the slightly bluish skin. They arrived at the airport at twelve-thirty for their two-thirty flight on Copa Airlines. Jack was somewhat nervous about the nearly thirteen hour flight, not certain how well the child would tolerate the lower oxygen levels of the pressurized cabin, but there wasn't really anything he could do about it now. They had a four hour lay over in Panama City, that would at least give him a chance to evaluate how well the baby tolerated the first leg of the trip.

Throughout the hour and a half flight the child sat sleeping in his mother's lap, and his breathing remained steady. During the lay over, Jack bought sandwiches and sodas for the young mother and himself, then managed to catch a nap for an hour, sitting in a hard, molded plastic chair.

The second leg of their flight was delayed more than an hour due to weather in Argentina. Once they finally got underway, the baby seemed to become a bit listless. The mother laid the baby on the empty seat between them, and Jack kept a close eye on him. When he saw the baby struggling to breathe, he pushed the call button over his head. The flight attendant came to his side and he asked if they had an oxygen tank on board. She explained that it was for medical emergencies only. He told her he was a physician and then pointed to the struggling child. She asked if he thought they should return the plane to Panama, but he explained that the child needed an operation in Buenos Aires, and that he would be okay if she would just bring the oxygen.

Two flight attendants rolled the small green, metal canister down the narrow aisle, and Jack stood as they approached. He had them place the tank in front of the seat where the baby was laying. The tubing leading from the top of the tank ended in an adult size plastic mask.

"Is this the only tank of oxygen you have?" he asked.

"Yes," was the answer he had feared. He would have to make this one small tank last more than seven hours. Fortunately, the gauge showed it to be full, but it would never last if he used the inefficient mask.

He opened the overhead compartment and pulled his carry on bag out an placed it on his seat and opened one of the inside pockets and found his five dollar, emergency plastic poncho. It wasn't designed for this use, but it would have to do.

Jack returned the carry on to the overhead compartment and turned his attention to the clear plastic garment. He opened it fully and put the oxygen mask and the end of the tubing through one of the arm holes, then he folded the other arm in and rolled the top down tightly to seal it. He then folded the bottom under twice and turned the valve on the tank. Immediately the poncho began to rise as the oxygen inflated it like a balloon. Once it was fully inflated he slowed the flow from the tank until it was at a minimum. He waited a few minutes until he was sure his makeshift oxygen tent was going to work.

He asked the mother to hold the child again while he arranged the plastic cocoon on the seat. He unfolded the bottom and instructed the mother to place the almost motionless baby inside. He folded the end closed again, and temporarily increased the flow from the tank until the enclosure was fully inflated. Then he turned the valve back down to the minimum. Within a couple of minutes the baby seemed to be moving his arms and legs spontaneously, and even through the plastic with the limited illumination from the overhead reading light, his color seemed somewhat improved as well. The plastic gradually fogged slightly from the gathering moisture of the baby's breath.

Jack took a deep breath and sat down next to his patient. It was now just a question whether the single oxygen tank would last.

****

"How's it going with closing the medical staff?" Fitzgerald asked, as he pour two glasses of bourbon over ice.

"The bylaw change has been written and has been distributed to the entire staff. They have ten days to vote, so it should be done before the first of December." Horvath had no doubt about the outcome.

"You know the thing I'm enjoying the most?" Fitzgerald asked, as he handed Horvath his drink.

"I can only imagine it has something to do with gaining total control of the hospital. That has to feel good," Horvath replied.

"Of course," Fitzgerald said, "but that isn't what I am savoring the way I'm savoring this fine bourbon."

"What it is then?"

"It's watching that arrogant Roberts fall. Not only is he gone, out of our hair, but his reputation is gone too." He took a long draw on his whiskey then added, "Guys like that need to be taken down a notch or two, and I take great pride in being able to do that."

"I wonder what he's doing now?" Horvath asked.

"Pushing pills in some third world country I hope."

There was a knock at the door of his office, startling both men. "I thought you said your secretary had gone home."

"She did," Fitzgerald said, as he stood and moved toward the door. "It's probably the cleaning crew. They know better than ..."

The door burst open as the wood around the latch splintered from the force of the intruder's kick. Two men dressed all in black, entered the room, both carrying large hand guns that were pointed directly at the two frightened executives.

"What the ..." Fitzgerald sputtered.

"Shut up and sit down," one of the men said, motioning with his gun toward the chair Fitzgerald had previously occupied.

"There is no money in this office," Fitzgerald lied.

The intruder took three steps toward Fitzgerald who was still standing. With the quickness of a viper he struck the older man across the face with the back of his gloved hand that was holding the gun. The blow caught him totally by surprise, dropping him to his knees. "I said, shut up and sit down," he instructed.

Fitzgerald struggled to pull himself into the chair. Horvath started to help his boss, but the other man moved two steps toward him, freezing him in his seat. Fitzgerald used the sleeve of his white dress shirt to wipe the fresh blood from the side of his mouth, then looked angrily at his assailant, but remained silent. A trail of blood ran slowly down the front of his white beard until several drops fell softly onto his gray trousers.

"We are not here to take anything," the intruder said, still openly brandishing his weapon. "We are hear to deliver a message."

Horvath was visibly trembling, fearing for his life. Fitzgerald had invited him for a quiet drink before dinner at a nearby steakhouse. At first he'd told him he'd just meet him at the restaurant, but the boss wouldn't take no for an answer. Now they were alone in this secluded office on the top floor, with no way to escape.

"Mr. Fitzgerald, I'm sure you remember that you were warned once, but it appears you didn't fully understand. Clearly, you require a second, more specific warning."

"I have no idea what you're talking about," he objected.

"Oh, I think you do," he said sarcastically. "Didn't you, and Mr. Horvath here, deny care to a Nicaraguan child just yesterday?"

"I didn't ..." Fitzgerald said, as he looked angrily at a stunned Horvath.

"Mr. Gutierrez does not tolerate anyone stealing from him, especially when children are harmed in the process," he said, as he turned toward Horvath and nodded to his partner, prompting him to move menacingly toward the younger man. "You don't have any children, do you Mr. Horvath?"

"No, I don't," Horvath replied timidly.

"Then you have no idea the pain a parent feels as they watch their child suffer, or even die, when some money manager, like you, denies them treatment, choosing profits over patients."

Horvath knew better, but he couldn't help but object. "I didn't ..."

He wasn't allowed to finish his statement as the second man rapped him sharply on the front of his right knee with a billy club. There was an audible crack as his knee cap split instantly, and he cried out as the incredible pain shot through his entire body. He grabbed his knee instinctively, but he wisely made no effort to fight back.

"In the future, you would do well to remember what that pain feels like."

The man reached into his pocket and retrieved a tape recorder. "In case either of you might be thinking about calling the police, I think you should hear this first."

He pushed the play button and the voice of the computer hacker could be heard very clearly. "I was hired by Mr. James Fitzgerald and given my instructions by Mr. Michael Horvath."

The disguised voice of an interrogator then asked, "What were you hired to do?"

The hacker answered, "I was to break into the office of Dr. Jack Roberts and access his computer system. I entered a false Medicaid claim according to the specific direction of Mr. Horvath."

"Did you receive payment for the job?"

"Yes, I was paid five thousand dollars in advance, and another five thousand the day after the FBI raided the doctor's office and confiscated the computers."

"And who paid you?"

"I was paid in cash by Mr. Fitzgerald."

The man turned the tape recorder off and placed it back in his pocket. He turned back toward his captives and said, "If either of you speaks a word about our little visitation this evening, this tape will find its way into the hands of the FBI. I believe the penalty for tampering with medical records is five to ten, and malicious misleading of federal officials in the course of an investigation is ten to twenty."

He then spoke directly to the older man. "Mr. Fitzgerald you're too old to go to prison. I fear you would not fare all that well." Then he turned toward Horvath and said, "And a pretty young, single guy like you? Well let's just say your knee isn't the only part of your anatomy that will be hurting in prison."

"What does he want?" Fitzgerald asked. "Does Roberts want to be reinstated?"

"Dr. Roberts has nothing to do with any of this. This is between you and Mr. Gutierrez, and what he wants is his million dollars back."

"The account only has six hundred thousand dollars left in it," Horvath said through his pain.

"Perhaps you didn't understand me. Mr. Gutierrez wants his one million dollars back." He reached into his jacket pocket and pulled out an envelope addressed to a local post office box. He placed the envelope carefully on Fitzgerald's desk and said, "It doesn't matter to Mr. Gutierrez where the money comes from, but he is anticipating my call on Friday, confirming receipt of a cashier's check. That gives you three days. More than sufficient time, don't you think?"

He walked back over in front of Fitzgerald, whose mouth had swollen over what would prove to be two broken teeth. "If the money is not there by Friday, I have been instructed to visit you both again. Do you understand this time?"

Fitzgerald nodded and Horvath simply held his knee as he rocked back and forth through the throbbing pain.

Before leaving, the two intruders made sure neither man could call for help. They took both of their cell phones and crushed them under the heels of their boots. Then they ripped the desk phone from the wall and did the same to the secretary's phone as they made their way back to the freight elevator.

****

The huge jet began it's decent into Buenos Aires, just as the gauge on the oxygen tank reached empty. The plastic enclosure began to slowly collapse, so Jack knew he needed to remove the child from what would quickly become a death chamber. As he opened the end of the poncho the baby's mother awoke, and accepted the child who began to cry rather weakly. She held him close to her and offered him a bottle of formula she'd gotten from Domingo at the clinic, and carried on the plane in a small canvas bag.

Jack watched the frail child carefully as he seemed to be struggling to take the formula and breathe at the same time. He was certain the child was dehydrated since he'd only had one wet diaper since they left Managua.

The weather around Buenos Aires was still a bit stormy, and their descent was very bumpy. Several times he heard brief muffled screams from a few rows behind them as the plane suddenly dropped a hundred feet or more before recovering and lurching up again. The young mother held her child tighter than ever, fearing he would be ripped from her arms. Jack was afraid that the baby couldn't breathe at all, but there wasn't anything he could do to make her loosen her grasp on the child.

Finally, as they broke through the heavy clouds, the air became calm and the roller coaster ride ended. Jack reached over and encouraged the mother to relax her hold on the child. The baby was still breathing, but once again he was otherwise motionless. His eyes were half closed and his mouth half open, and the bluish tinge to his skin was more pronounced than before.

As soon as the plane was on the ground, Jack immediately turned on his cell phone and when he saw that he had service he typed in Manuel's number.

"Manuel, this is Jack Roberts." The urgency in his voice told the other surgeon that things were not going well.

"Where are you?" Manuel asked.

"We have just landed," he replied, "and I need for you to have an ambulance meet us at the gate. This baby needs supplemental oxygen right away."

"I will call the medical staff at the airport and have someone meet you with an oxygen tank and a wheel chair."

"Thanks," he said with some relief. "I don't think we are getting here any to soon. This kid is dehydrated and he needs to go to surgery as soon as we can get some fluids into him."

"We are all prepared to accept him," Manuel assured his American colleague. "It is only a fifteen minute ambulance ride from the airport to the hospital."

As they walked quickly up the ramp into the terminal there was an agent waiting at the gate with a wheelchair and an oxygen tank, similar to the one he'd milked dry during the flight. The mother sat down in the chair holding her precious child, and Jack quickly placed the cumbersome plastic mask over the child's entire face. He turned the valve on to near maximum flow and picked up his carry on, as well as her small canvas bag, and they hurriedly made their way to baggage claim.

Despite being moved to the front of the line, it still took nearly thirty minutes to collect their bags and clear customs. The child's breathing and his color had both improved on oxygen, but the tank was being depleted rather rapidly given the inefficiency of the huge mask.

When they finally passed the last check point and turned the corner into the crowded terminal, Jack could see the ambulance just beyond the glass doors. He thanked the agent for her assistance as the emergency technicians took over the process of loading the mother and child into the ambulance. There was just enough room for Jack to place their bags along side the stretcher as they closed the rear doors. Jack climbed into the passenger side of the ambulance and closed his door as the driver pulled away from the curb. As soon as they were underway the driver switched on the siren and they moved rapidly through the morning traffic.

Jack's body was tired, but his mind was racing. He recalled vividly the images, and the sounds of the ride from Hurst to Fort Worth in his father's pickup as they'd followed the ambulance containing his baby brother nearly sixty years earlier. Despite all the advances in technology, it seemed situations like this never changed. The challenges would always be there, and that was what he loved about his profession. There would always be another child who needed help.

He allowed his mind to retrace all the events of the last two months and wondered if he would ever be in a position to use the considerable talents he still possessed. The idea of being forced into retirement from surgery was unacceptable. He simply couldn't allow the desires of others to dictate the rest of his life. At that point he made up his mind to create his own future, relying on all he'd witnessed and experienced, since that fateful day when his life's course had been set for him by an eerily similar situation to the one he found himself in now.

CHAPTER 16

As soon as the three month old Nicaraguan child was admitted to the pediatric intensive care unit at the children's hospital in Buenos Aires, the staff started caring for him. Dr. Manuel Fernandez-Chapa was in surgery that morning, but the nurses went to work immediately, based on the orders he had already given. An IV was placed in the infant's tiny arm, and fluids were started after blood samples were gathered and sent to the lab. The child's breathing appeared to have stabilized with the supplemental oxygen in the ambulance, but the monitor that was taped to his tiny finger still showed his oxygen saturation level was only seventy-six percent. A portable chest x-ray confirmed the boot-shaped heart, offering additional evidence that Jack's diagnosis of tetralogy of Fallot was indeed correct.

Jack found an extra chair, and moved it to the back of the small cubicle, out of the way of the busy nursing staff. It was clear that they had things well in hand, so within just a few minutes he was sound asleep. When Manuel arrived to check on his new patient he didn't want to wake his friend. After he examined the baby he turned to leave the bedside and accidentally bumped into the IV pole, which banged into the side of the metal crib. The sound was not particularly loud, but it was enough to arouse Jack from his uncomfortable slumber.

Seeing his old friend, Jack opened his eyes and said, "Hi Manuel, how are you?" Jack stumbled slightly as he rose slowly to his feet, and reached out to shake the other surgeon's hand.

"I am very well, thank you," his friend replied. "You look like you could use some more sleep."

"I'm alright," Jack said, reassuring himself. "Just glad to be on the ground. That flight was a little dicey."

"I can just imagine," Manuel said.

"They only had one small oxygen tank on board, so we had to improvise."

"Well, I certainly agree with your diagnosis. We have his cardiac cath scheduled for this afternoon and the surgery is set for tomorrow morning."

"That sounds great," Jack said with a smile. "Your people here did a great job of getting him stabilized."

"Yes, we have a very good crew," Manuel agreed.

Jack realized the baby's mother was still asleep in the chair next to his. He pointed to the young woman and said softly, "His mother didn't get much sleep either, but I'm sure I'll have a chance to formally introduce you to her later this evening."

Manuel turned to the nurse and spoke to her in Spanish, saying, "Would you show Dr. Roberts to the on call room where he can lie down and get some sleep."

"I'm okay," Jack said in their native tongue, much to the surprise of the nurse.

"I insist," Manuel said, reverting easily back to English. "I need for you to be well rested for tomorrow."

****

It was certainly smaller than the one he was used to back in Fort Worth, but to Jack, an operating room was an operating room. He had learned long ago that it wasn't the facility that performed the acts of healing, it was the people, and from what he could tell, the people here were extremely capable. When he'd decided to accompany the baby and his mother to Buenos Aires, Jack hadn't planned to participate in this baby's care in any way, but Dr. Fernandez-Chapa had insisted that he take an active role, so he planned to scrub in and assist the local surgeon.

The baby was asleep on the operating table as the two surgeons entered the room from the scrub sink in preparation for the operation. One nurse had prepared the child's chest with the standard brown antiseptic solution and two other nurses were just finishing covering him with the standard sterile drapes.

"Ladies," Manuel said, gathering everyone's attention, "and gentleman." referring to the anesthesiologist, "this is my very good friend, Dr. Jack Roberts."

The group of six people in the room all said hello to Jack at the same time before Manuel continued. "This baby is Dr. Roberts' patient and he is going to perform the surgery and I will be assisting him."

Jack was startled by the announcement and said, "No Manuel, this is your case. I brought him here for you to ..."

"Dr. Roberts is one of the world's foremost authorities on the surgical treatment of tetralogy of Fallot," he continued his announcement to the group, "and, I am hoping to learn some useful tips from him today."

"Manuel, I don't think ..."

"Please," Manuel interrupted, "This is a great opportunity for me, and I would consider it an honor to assist you."

Jack wasn't sure if Manuel was merely patronizing him, or if he really meant what he was saying, but as a guest in his operating room he was in no position to argue further. He assumed the position of the primary surgeon on the child's right side and began by asking each person in the room to tell him their name. Once he was certain who he was working with, he asked about available sutures and vascular graft material. He made a quick survey of the instruments and equipment, and when he was satisfied he said, "Well, let's get started."

The operation took just under ninety minutes to complete, and the child had come off the pump without any difficulty. After the dressings had been applied and the chest tube was connected to the drainage system, he and Manuel made their way out to the surgical waiting area and found the baby's mother. She had been extremely anxious before the surgery, but after hearing that everything had gone smoothly, her face broke into a huge smile as tears of joy streamed down her face.

"That was truly a work of art," Manuel said.

"You are too kind," Jack replied. "I'm sure it was no different than what you would have done."

"I learned so much from you today. Watching the precision of your every movement made me realize there are many things about my technique that I can improve. You did not appear to be in a hurry, yet the procedure was completed far faster than I have ever done it."

"Speed is never the objective," Jack said. "Didn't Fleming tell you that when you were at Hopkins?"

"Yes, of course," Manuel answered, "He also emphasized the point of no wasted movements, but I have never seen that philosophy in actual practice until today."

"You are very kind to say that," Jack said. "Dr. Fleming was a great mentor, but I was very fortunate to be exposed to the best example of no wasted movements from the very beginning, even before I went to medical school. When I was just fourteen years old I had the opportunity to watch Dr. Walt Lillihei perform an open heart operation. It was the first time I had ever watched any surgical procedure, and it was obvious to me, even as a teenager, that he was truly a master. I have spent my entire career trying to replicate what I saw that day."

"Well, now I, too, have watched a master at work, and it gives me something to strive for."

"You flatter me too much," Jack scoffed before changing the subject. "I need for you to take me to the head of the hospital."

As the two men walked into the hospital director's office, the secretary asked them to be seated. Neither surgeon sat down. They both paced aimlessly around the small anteroom while she walked back to tell her boss that he had visitors.

"Hello, Dr. Fernandez-Chapa," the middle aged hospital executive said, as he came out from his office to greet them.

"Hello Jorge," Manuel replied. "This is my good friend, Dr. Jack Roberts."

"It is an honor to meet you, Dr. Roberts. Manuel has told me much about you. We are pleased to have you here in our hospital."

"Thank you, sir," Jack replied. "I truly appreciate your willingness to allow me to bring that child here for treatment. Your staff has been exemplary."

"Would you care to come back to my office?"

"No, thank you, sir, we need to get back to the recovery room and check on our patient," Jack replied politely. "I just wanted to come by and pay for the child's care." Manuel had told Jack what the hospital charges were going to be, so he'd gone by his bank before he left Managua. He reached into his wallet and pulled out a cashier's check for eight thousand dollars. "Hopefully that will take care of it. If not, please let me know."

The director accepted the check, and his secretary said, "Could I get you some coffee or tea?"

"No, thank you, we really can't stay," Jack offered, as he turned to Manuel.

"You are more than welcome to bring any of your patients here anytime you like," the director said shaking Jack's hand again.

As they made their way back toward the surgical recovery area, Jack couldn't help doing the math in his head. He'd originally had just under two hundred thousand in his Nicaraguan account, but after buying the Land Cruiser and paying for Elaina's flight, and now this eight thousand, that balance was down to just over one hundred thousand dollars. Even though this hospital was less than a tenth of what it would cost in Fort Worth, at this rate he would only be able to afford to care for a few children like this, unless he was willing to dip into his Swiss account. Clearly, he was not Franco Gutierrez, and never would be.

****

His cell phone rang, and the caller ID showed a number with an eight one seven area code.

"Yes?" he asked patiently.

"It wasn't in the post office box today."

"Do you know whether he has left the area?"

"No, he's still around. He hasn't been into his office, but I've seen him around his house. He visited that other guy yesterday at his home for about an hour. He hasn't been back to work either. He's still on crutches."

"Perhaps you should pay the old man a visit at his home. "

"I can do that," the retired Navy seal said. "His security system is pretty elementary."

"Tell him there has been a fifty percent interest penalty imposed, and he has twenty-four hours."

"Yes, sir. I understand."

"Just don't kill him."

When the call ended the caller turned to his partner and said, "The boss says we need to make our house call."

The two men already had a plan in place, they had simply been awaiting the go ahead. At two in the morning they easily disarmed the residential security system, cut the phone lines into the house, then deftly made their way into the huge home on the west side of Fort Worth.

They climbed the stairway to the master suite on the second floor and found the door locked. The second man used a rather simple tool to pick the lock and slowly started to open the door.

"I have a gun!" Fitzgerald shouted. "And I'm not afraid to use it." He hadn't been able to sleep for three nights, anticipating these men would try and kill him because he had refused to meet their demands. When he thought he heard a faint noise at the door, he pulled his nine millimeter Glock from the bedside table, just as he had done on more than one occasion each of the two previous nights, but on those occasions there was no one there.

The two men crouched low on either side of the doorway and as one pushed the door open the other tossed a small device into the room. A split second after the bright flash and loud bang, they heard a shot fired, and the bullet struck the top of the door jam, well over their heads. Both men rushed into the room, taking advantage of their disoriented target. They quickly seized his weapon, and easily restrained the older man who put up very little resistance.

When the intruders turned on the light it was clear Fitzgerald was alone. They knew he had sent his wife to stay with her sister in Dallas for a week, based on telephone conversations recorded the day after their first encounter in his office.

"My boss is very disappointed and more than a little angry that he hasn't received his money yet," the man said. "And, now that you've taken a shot at me, I'm a little angry as well."

The other man drug the captive out of his bed by his arms, which he then jerked around his back. It was obvious that his aging shoulders weren't accustomed to being manipulated, as he cried out in pain when the much larger man threw him roughly into a small chair, and expertly bound his wrists together behind his back with a large zip tie.

"You look like a smart man," he said almost casually.

Fitzgerald's only response was a grimace.

"But, based on your willingness to ignore my earlier instructions, I don't think you are nearly as smart as you look." He moved around directly in front of Fitzgerald and lifted his bearded chin with his left hand until they were face to face. "I'm sure you understand the concept of interest, right?" he said prompting a silent nod of the older man's head.

"Good, then it won't come as any surprise to you that since you missed your payment deadline, Mr. Gutierrez is charging you interest. Your payment is now one and a half million dollars."

He raised his chin a little higher and said, "That's only fair, don't you think?"

Fitzgerald nodded again, this time twice.

"I'm afraid that if your cashier's check for one million, five hundred thousand dollars is not in that envelope, and that envelope is not in that post office box by tomorrow afternoon, the interest will include at least one more digit." As he spoke the last word, his partner reached down and grabbed the little finger of their captive's left hand and jerked on it sharply.

"You can tell him he'll have his money tomorrow," he said, all signs of resistance were gone from his voice and his appearance.

"For your sake, I certainly hope so."

The second intruder pulled a large knife from his belt and flashed it near Fitzgerald's face, making sure he could see the light reflecting off the blade before he used it to cut the zip tie in a single motion.

"Just a reminder, in case you are considering going to the police, I still have that recording."

The next afternoon, the call from his man in Fort Worth was more satisfying.

"I have the check sir."

"Very good. Did you send the tape to the FBI?"

"Yes sir, just as you instructed."

THE CONFLICT

"Good," Franco said as he hung up the phone in his home office.

****

"We're on our way home," Jack said, feeling more exhausted than he was willing to admit.

"What time do you want me to pick you up?" Elaina asked in a sleepy voice.

"Our flight is scheduled to arrive around one o'clock in the afternoon," he sounded exhausted. "Would you mind calling Domingo and telling him? I think he is planning to take the baby and his mother home."

"Sure," she said. "I'll call him in the morning. Is everything okay?"

"Yeah, everything's fine."

"You just sound kinda down," she said.

"I'm just tired. Sleeping alone, in a strange bed, in a hospital call room, in a strange country, isn't my thing."

"Does that mean you want to go back to Texas?" she asked playfully.

"No," he laughed. "It means I miss you. I'll see you this afternoon."

"Have a safe flight, I love you."

"I love you too, Angel."

As he pushed the end button on his phone, he saw the time was four-thirty in the morning, which meant it was one-thirty in El Transito. Their plane was just beginning the boarding process for the first leg of what promised to be a nearly eleven hour flight through Panama, and then home to Managua. Jack was having trouble grasping that idea. The concept of home being anywhere other than Texas still seemed completely foreign to him.

****

The next morning Jack woke up much earlier than usual, not just because of the three hour time difference, but also because he had collapsed into the bed just before seven o'clock the previous evening. It was well before sunrise as he wandered into the kitchen and found a diet Dr. Pepper in the refrigerator. He silently smiled, knowing Elaina had made a special effort to find the rare liquid in Managua. He suspected she'd called Gabriella to find out where she bought them for her husband.

Jack turned on the television, but turned the volume all the way down, making sure he didn't wake Elaina. He flipped through the channels until he settled on CNN, and watched as the early morning news program silently rehashed the previous days top stories, but they were certainly news to him. The ticker across the bottom of the screen talked about the continued civil war in

Syria, followed by the account of yet another earthquake in Indonesia, but this time there had not been a tsunami. Mr. Obama was seen in another photo session in the White House with the President of Japan, who was in Washington to promote the latest Sino-American trade agreement. After a few minutes, he flipped over to the satellite feed from the Dallas / Fort Worth FOX affiliate. He had paid extra to the local provider to have access to two of the four local stations in North Texas. They were just coming on with the early morning show. With the sound down he couldn't hear what they were saying but he recognized the morning news anchor and the guy who was doing the weather forecast. He decided he'd go out onto the deck and listen to the surf, but he left the television on, just for the light it offered.

This really is a terrific place to live, he thought. In fact, he wasn't sure he cared to return to the rat race, even if the FBI were willing to announce his innocence. The way things were going with the American healthcare system, he wondered if perhaps now was as good a time as any to get out. Elaina always said, everything happens for a reason, and maybe his legal problems had a bigger purpose. He sat quietly, listening to the waves breaking in the distance and watched as the full moon slowly dropped toward the western horizon, signaling that dawn would be coming soon.

Daylight had just begun to take hold of the morning sky when he heard Lucinda come into the house through the front door. She saw him sitting on the deck and waved silently as she made her way into the kitchen to start breakfast.

Had it really just been three weeks since they'd arrived here? He thought about everything that had happen in that time, and it seemed impossible. Surely things would begin to slow down now. Part of him wanted to do as Domingo had suggested and just go lay out on the beach, but the other part of him was saying he needed to do something meaningful with the rest of his life. What that was, he still didn't know.

Lucinda called out softly through the back door, "Your breakfast is ready señor doctor Jack." The name had stuck since Federico first used it that night Jack affectionately called the night of the machete. As he came into the house he watched Elaina as she fixed her coffee at the kitchen counter, then headed sleepily toward the table. He completely ignored the television, as it was silently offering a story that would once more put his name out in front of the public.

He kissed Elaina on the cheek as he walked by, on his way to the refrigerator to get another diet DP. She said, "How long have you been up?"

"I don't know," he replied, "A few hours. Must be jet lag. I couldn't sleep so I came in here and turned on the television, and ..."

As he spoke, he turned toward the silent image and was stunned by what he was seeing. "What is Mary Anne doing on the..." He rushed to find the remote and turned up the volume.

He heard her say, "I had no idea who was behind it. All I knew is that someone hacked into our computer system and planted a fraudulent Medicaid claim."

The camera focused on the reporter who followed up on what Mary Anne had said. "We now know that the man accused of generating those false claims against Dr. Jack Roberts is local billionaire and retired oil tycoon, James Fitzgerald."

The image cut to a scene showing two FBI agents leading Fitzgerald out of his home in handcuffs. The reporter continued, "We know that the FBI received an anonymous tip that implicated Fitzgerald in a conspiracy to commit Medicaid fraud and unlawful tampering with medical records, along with this man, Michael Horvath." The screen was filled with a head shot of Horvath that looked to be from five or six years earlier, before his hair had begun to turn gray. "He is the administrator of the local children's hospital, and Fitzgerald is currently the chairman of the board of that hospital. I was told he was responsible for hiring Horvath, a few years ago."

"Has there been any comment from the doctor?" the anchorman asked.

"No. I haven't been able to find anyone who even knows where Dr. Roberts is. It would certainly seem that if he were indeed innocent of the original FBI allegations, he would want to come forward and clear his name, but so far there has been no sign of him," the reporter spoke directly into the camera.

Jack stood stunned in front of the television as the anchorman in the studio changed the subject. "In other area news ..."

Jack turned to face Elaina who had joined him in the living room. "What are you going to do?" she asked.

"I guess I need to go back, don't you think?" His look was almost childlike, as if he'd been handed a trophy for winning a game after the other team had forfeited.

"Do you plan to resume your practice right away?" Now it was Elaina's turn to offer an anxious look. He knew she was just getting accustomed to her new surroundings and their new life.

"I... don't know." he said in a hesitating whisper. "I think we need to talk about that before we make any decisions." His face regained a more confident appearance, as he said, "there's only one thing I am sure of, we need to go back to Fort Worth immediately."

She smiled cautiously and nodded her head slowly in agreement, then said, "I'll get started packing our bags."

As she turned toward the bedroom she wondered why he'd said "go back to Fort Worth" instead of go back home?

****

They'd rushed around that morning to get ready and barely made it to the airport in time for the noon American Airlines flight from Managua to Miami. Jack called Domingo as they were on their way to the airport, just to let him know where they were going.

"Do you need for me to come to the airport and retrieve your car?" Domingo asked.

"No, Federico, our caretaker is with us, and he will be driving the car back to our house."

"Please call me when you return, and I will come pick you up."

"That is very kind of you."

"Do you have any idea how long you will be gone?"

"I don't know," Jack said cautiously. "It could be a week or two, or it could be a month or more."

"Just let me know if there is anything you need for me to do." Domingo wanted to help his friends, but clearly he had no idea how.

"I'll talk to you soon, mi amigo." Jack said, responding to the sincerity in Domingo's voice.

They had to claim their luggage and clear US customs in Miami, then change planes for the flight to DFW, so despite the nearly two hour lay over, there hadn't been any time for them to talk about anything. Jack called Buzz from Miami and told him they were on their way back to Texas. When his friend offered to come pick them up, Jack told him they would just take a taxi to the house, and he would talk with him the next day. But as they came through the controlled access revolving door between the gate area and baggage claim of DFW's terminal C, Buzz was standing there, waiting for them.

Jack put down his briefcase and Elaina's carry on bag, and without a word being exchanged, the two best friends embraced each other warmly.

"I told you not to come," Jack said in a scolding tone.

"Yeah," Buzz said, "since when have I ever taken orders from you?"

Buzz embraced Elaina and said, "It's so good to have y'all home. I know this whole ordeal must have been almost more than you could handle."

"Actually, the most difficult part has been getting back here today," she said, the fatigue in her voice was obvious.

Once they collected their luggage they followed Buzz out to his car for the twenty-five minute drive back to their familiar four bedroom home on the west side of Fort Worth. On the way, Buzz told Jack what had gone on at the hospital that day.

"The whole place is a mad house," he said. "The FBI arrested Horvath at his home about two hours after they hauled Fitzgerald off to jail this morning. The hospital board held an emergency meeting to name an interim chairman and administrator."

"Did they give the job back to Traci?" Jack asked.

"No, she turned it down."

"Why!?"

"She said she didn't want it, so they appointed Norman Gardner."

"What!?" Jack exclaimed. "Isn't he ..."

"Yep," Buzz replied. "The vice president of development."

"The only experience he has is raising money. He doesn't know anything about running a hospital," Jack said, shaking his head in disgust.

"I know, but other than Traci, every other person in administration has close connections to Fitzgerald, and the board wanted to sever all ties with him. They are so worried about the publicity and their reputation. They fired every one of the guys he and Horvath hired.

"What about Judy Schneider, the director of nursing? Is she still there?"

"Yeah, she told me that she thought about resigning to avoid getting caught up in all this mess, but Traci talked her out of it. Even though she didn't accept the title of interim administrator, Traci is clearly the one running the show."

"How's George?" Jack asked with concern.

"He's okay, I guess. I haven't seen him in a couple of days," Buzz replied. "Since you left he's been very busy, but he seems more quiet and withdrawn than usual. I think he's just frustrated, kinda like the rest of us. Maybe this big shake-up at the hospital will give everybody a chance to reorganize." He hesitated as he glanced over at Jack. "I know he'll be glad to have you back."

Jack turned around and looked anxiously toward Elaina in the back seat. In the darkness he couldn't see that she had fallen asleep. "I'm not sure how long we're going to stay," he said, his voice reflecting his uncertainty.

"What do you mean?" Buzz asked, taking his eyes off the road, looking at his friend and colleague with an unbelieving expression.

"We haven't decided whether we are going to move back here or stay in Nicaragua."

There was a stunned silence in the car for a few seconds before Buzz said, "Well, I can't say as I'd blame you if you didn't come back. I don't think it's ever going to be the way it was when we first started back in eighty-eight."

"A lot has happened in those twenty-five years," Jack agreed, "and most of what I've seen in the last five years hasn't been good."

****

"Hi sweetie," Elaina said as David answered his cell phone.

"Mom!" he half shouted, "Where are you?"

"Your dad and I are here in Fort Worth," she answered calmly.

"I saw all that stuff on television yesterday, and I tried to call both of you, but I didn't get an answer."

"We flew back yesterday, and didn't get to the house until late."

"Is Dad okay?"

"Yeah, he's fine. He's still asleep. He had a rather fitful night. I don't think he finally came to bed until well after two o'clock. He was in Argentina for more than a week, and was only home one night before getting back on a plane to come up here. I know his biological clock is all screwed up."

"Argentina? What was he doing way down there?"

"Oh, it's a long story. I'll let him tell you about it."

"So, is Dad going back to work?"

"I don't know," she said cautiously. "I don't think he's decided what he wants to do, and right now, everything is in such turmoil, I suspect it's going to take some time for us to make a decision about our future."

"Wow!" David exclaimed in a half whisper. "I thought only young people. like me and Amy, had to seriously contemplate our futures."

She laughed then replied, "Hey, we're still young people too, ya know?"

****

When Jack finally woke up it was nearly ten o'clock. "Why did you let me sleep so late?" he said, sounding more angry than he felt.

"Because you needed the rest," Elaina replied in a maternal tone. "I talked to David, and told him we were here."

"Good. Have you spoken to anyone else?"

"No, I've just been sitting here drinking my coffee, and looking out the window at the overgrown lawn." The late fall temperatures hadn't allowed the grass to grow significantly, but it was clear from the distinctly greenish color of the pool water and the leaves that were scattered over the entire landscape that no one had lived in this house for at least a month.

Jack looked outside and groaned, "Oh, man. I forgot all about the lawn guys. I guess when they saw that we weren't home they figured they wouldn't get paid. I need to call them this morning, along with the pool guy. Hopefully I can get them back out here today or tomorrow to clean up this mess."

Jack turned back toward her and saw that she was intently watching him as he talked about getting the house back in order. He could see the uncertainty in her face and walked slowly but purposefully toward her, then gently wrapped his arms around her.

"What do you want to do?" he asked, subtly emphasizing his interest in her desire.

She pulled back just enough to be able to look up into his dark brown eyes. She could feel his need for direction, but she refused to be lured into making a choice. This needed to be his decision. "I want whatever you want," she said, allowing him to see the honesty of her words in her loving eyes.

Jack drew a deep breath and sighed, knowing she wasn't going to tell him what to do. She never had in the twenty-three years they'd been married. She'd always supported him, no matter what, and this time was no different.

"I guess we need to get this place fixed up," he hesitated for just a moment before completing his thought. He looked into her eyes and flashed his crooked smile, "So we can sell it."

Elaina's face beamed with the same youthful glow he had seen on the beach in El Transito. He knew that was now her home, and there was really nothing for either of them here anymore.

****

"Hi, Mary Anne," Jack said, when she answered the door.

"Dr. Roberts! What are you doing here?" she asked excitedly.

"I tried to call you, but you obviously aren't answering your phone, so I came over to thank you in person."

"Come in, please."

He stepped inside, and she quickly closed the door. "Those reporters are everywhere. When the doorbell rang I thought you were another one of them."

"I saw you on television yesterday, and I just had to come tell you how much I appreciate everything you did to help clear up this whole mess. I'm sure it must have been difficult dealing with the FBI and all those reporters, and just the whole controversy."

"How could you have seen me? I thought you were in Nicaragua?"

"We get two of your local channels, eight and four, on our satellite down there. I saw the whole thing, including Fitzgerald's arrest. He looked like he had a huge bruise on the side of his mouth."

"I didn't see that, but I saw Mr. Horvath when they arrested him. That was so pitiful. He was on crutches."

"Really? That's strange. Did they say why?" Jack inquired.

"Something about a knee injury. I don't know."

"So what did the FBI tell you?"

"The last time I spoke to them was two days ago. They said they had obtained evidence that supported my... I mean, our claim, that someone had hacked into our computer system. Prior to that they had actually issued a warrant for your arrest."

"I guess they must have uncovered something that implicated Fitzgerald and Horvath, but I have no idea what it might have been," Jack said as he tried to think through the data on his computer.

"So, are you coming back to work?" she asked hopefully.

"No, I don't think so," he said with an obvious sadness in his voice.

"Why not? From what I understand, you've been cleared of all charges."

"I know," Jack said, smiling at her naive assessment. "That's true this time, but, I'm not even on the medical staff at children's any more."

"You know they will reinstate you," she insisted.

"I don't think so. They've closed the staff except for members of Grady's group, and I'm not going to join that bunch, no matter what."

"But, you are too young to retire. What about all those patients, especially the children who need your help?'

"I know," he replied, again letting his feelings show. "I guess George, or someone else, will have to take care of them... I just can't practice medicine under the constant threat of some government agency showing up in my office and finding something that doesn't match up with their protocols or regulations."

"So, what are you going to do?" Mary Anne's question sounded like more of an accusation.

"I'm not sure, but Elaina and I are going to move to our place in Nicaragua. We've decided to sell our house and I'm going to ask you to help me liquidate the practice assets."

She nodded reluctantly, realizing his mind was made up, and she learned long ago not to argue with him once he'd made a decision.

"I figure that will take a month or so, then I'll put the office building on the market."

"I'll get started Monday," she said. "I doubt it will take very long."

"As compensation, you can keep fifty percent of whatever you get for the furniture and computers, assuming the FBI returns them."

"But, you've already paid me more than enough," she protested. "We've got more than a hundred thousand dollars worth of hard assets."

"You have done countless things for me over the last twenty-five years that you haven't been compensated for, and this is my way of trying to even the score." His smile told her how much he appreciated her, as she began to cry softly. "Besides, I'm going to need for you to keep the business open for at least six months, since I'm sure there will be a few payments trickling in from claims you've posted in the past."

"I was looking at that the other day," she said. "The current accounts receivable is just over two hundred thousand, but I know we won't collect even a third of that."

They continued discussing the process of winding down Jack's practice, and the need to maintain the medical records for at least seven years. Mary Anne's tears had stopped as she reverted back into her work mode, trying to treat this like any other assignment.

"I will keep in touch," Jack said as he stood to leave, "but what I'd like for you to do is send me an email updating what's happening every Friday, okay?"

She smiled for the first time since he'd arrived. Somethings would never change. Jack Roberts demanded organization and accountability, even now, with this systematic dissolving of his practice.

"Oh, and one more thing," he said as he turned around once more. "I need for you to contact Blue Cross and see what I need to do to convert my health insurance to that BlueCard Worldwide Program. I looked into it once before, but it was too expensive considering we were only out of the country for a week each year, but now I think its something I need to do."

He saw her nod that she understood and he knew she would take care of it.

"I want the traditional indemnity plan. I don't want any PPO program, or anything like that. Just get me something with a relatively high deductible, in the five to ten thousand dollar range, okay?"

"Yes, sir. I'll take care of it," she replied.

As he walked back out to his truck, Jack realized he had just ordered the final elements of his total retirement from the practice he had spent a quarter century building. His shoulders visibly slumped, as it suddenly hit him that his plan to one day hand his practice over to his son, wasn't going to happen.

Before he could get into his car two reporters ran up to him from across the street with cameras rolling. "Dr. Roberts!" one shouted. "Would you like to make a statement?"

The other asked, "Where have you been hiding?"

****

It took less than six hours for Fitzgerald's lawyer to obtain a hearing, and he was released on one hundred thousand dollars bond later that evening. Horvath was also released on bail the next day, after only one night in jail.

"My client is innocent of these allegations," the sharply dressed older attorney announced confidently to a group of reporters outside the entrance to the Eldon B. Mahon Federal Courthouse. Fitzgerald stood slightly behind him and off to his left. The swelling on the side of his face had mostly resolved, and the large bruise around his lower jaw was almost completely hidden by his thick white beard. "He has been a pillar of this community for many years, and we plan to do whatever is necessary to prove his innocence of these outlandish charges, and restore his exemplary reputation. We have no further comments at this time,"

"Can you tell us where the FBI got their information?" on reporters shouted.

"Mr. Fitzgerald, do you plan to remain with the hospital? another asked.

"Mr. Fitzgerald has no comment," his attorney said brusquely.

The older man and his chief lawyer quickly walked to the black sedan that was waiting for them on the street. Once inside, Fitzgerald turned to the attorney and asked, "So, how are you going to get me out of this?" He had know doubt this man, whom he was paying five thousand dollars a day, would find a way to get the federal grand jury charges dropped.

"I spoke to the prosecutor an hour ago and he wouldn't tell me anything other than they have an audio tape that names you and Horvath as paying someone to file a false Medicaid claim on the doctor's computer system. If that's all they have, then you have nothing to worry about. I can argue that the tape is inadmissible evidence. It could have been produced by anyone who was out to get you. The doctor could have done it himself, to frame you and Horvath. Unless they can produce the actual witness, they have no case. My guess is they are searching for him even as we speak."

While Fitzgerald had told his lawyer about the payoff, he hadn't told him that after his latest encounter with Franco's men, one of his own guys had seen to it that the computer hacker would never testify. He'd been assured that the young man's body would never be found.

****

On Saturday afternoon, David and Amy drove the forty-five minutes from Dallas to Fort Worth to see his parents before they left for Nicaragua again. He had talked to his mom several times over the phone in the week since they'd been home, and he knew there was no way to change his father's mind. He understood how his dad felt, and for the first time he worried that all the things he'd been saying for the last few years about the future of American medicine were coming true.

"Hey, buddy," Jack said as he embraced his son.

"Hey, Dad," David replied, happy to see his father again, but clearly saddened by the circumstances.

Jack then gave Amy a warm hug as well and kissed her on the cheek. "How's my favorite daughter?" he laughed.

She smiled broadly at his standard greeting. "I'm fine," she said. "It's so good to see you guys here at your home."

Jack was surprised when Elaina took the lead, "It won't be long this won't be our home any more. The realtor called yesterday with an offer on the house."

David turned toward her and said, "You know Mom, this is the only house I can ever remember living in."

"I know sweetie," she said, "but you haven't really lived here for six and a half years."

"It still feels like home to me. Lots of memories here."

"You know, you'll always have those memories," Jack said, "but, its time for your mom and I to move on. We're planning to make some new memories of our own."

"Speaking of memories, where's the Madonna?" Amy asked as she looked around the familiar foyer."

"It's in that container out in the garage. We're shipping a few things to El Transito. You'll just have to come down there if you want to see it."

"We are really looking forward to spending a week or so down there with y'all for Christmas, assuming we're still invited."

"Of course!" Elaina insisted. "I was planning to make the airline reservations today, while I had you both here."

"What are you going to do with all this furniture," David asked.

We have a guy coming over tomorrow to arrange an auction. My hope is it will all be gone next week." Elaina gestured with her hands, indicating she wanted everything gone.

"What about the piano," David inquired, not believing she would part with it.

"You know I love it," she replied. "That was my wedding gift from your father, but It costs too much to have it shipped down there, so..."

"I wish I knew how to play," Amy said. "I'd buy it, but then, I have no idea where we'd put it in our apartment."

"Well, if you kids see anything around here you can use, just say so."

For the next few minutes David and Amy wandered around through the house, looking at pieces of furniture, house plants, and area rugs. They didn't have all that much room in their two bedroom apartment, but Amy found a few things she really wanted.

"I don't know how we'll get them home," David protested when she said she wanted the two large brass urns that stood on either side of the doorway leading out to the patio.

"That won't be a problem," Jack offered casually.

David looked up to see his father holding two sets of keys to his two year old Chevy Pickup. "You've always wanted a nice truck, and while this one isn't new, it's a whole lot more functional than that pile of parts in the garage that I hauled off a few years back."

David's eyes lit up as he said, "you're kidding me ..."

"No, I want you to have it. I have no way of getting it to Nicaragua and besides, I have a brand new Land Cruiser down there, so here are the keys and the title."

"Wow! I can't believe it!" He hugged his dad enthusiastically, then smiled excitedly toward Amy. "Now we can sell that old Honda."

"We're planning to drive back home in your mom's BMW." Jack even surprised himself at the ease with which he talked about Nicaragua as their home. "That way we'll have two cars. Initially I wasn't too sure about the idea, but she really wants to keep her Beemer, and it's only five years old."

David laughed along with his dad before his face took on a more sober appearance. "I can't believe you guys are actually moving to another country, like, permanently!"

Jack looked at him and chuckled slightly as he said, "Who knows. We might only stay there a year or two, and then maybe we'll move someplace like New Zealand or Australia." He saw Elaina's scowl out of the corner of his eye, causing him to turn toward her but he continued talking to his son. His voice became softer and more relaxed, as he said, "over the years, I've learned that there's really only one thing that's absolutely permanent... and that is love."

CHAPTER 17

The familiar drive down Interstate thirty-five was uneventful through Austin, San Antonio, and on to Laredo, where they spent their last night in the United States. They stopped at a local Walmart and bought a styrofoam ice chest and filled it with ice and cold drinks, along with some snacks for the long drive. The next morning, they were both up and ready to get underway before daylight. As they crossed the international bridge, Jack couldn't help feeling a sense of loss as he guided the car under the sign that said, *Leaving the United States of America.*

They had closed on the house the day before they left, and Jack was surprised by the absence of any display of emotion by his wife. He knew she was only looking forward, and was ready to get back to their new home. He was also anxious to get there, knowing they would have to be in Nicaragua when their shipment arrived. The contents of the containers would be thoroughly inspected by the authorities, but they would have to be in the country to claim the retirement exemption, that allowed them to import up to twenty thousand dollars worth of used personal goods and home furnishings without paying any import duty. He was certain their stuff would exceed that number, but Franco had assured him they would not be assessed anything. He'd already seen to that. The Nicaraguan government also allowed retirees to bring one car into the country, free of any import tariff.

Their car was loaded with many of their more personal items. Elaina had put all her jewelry and other valuables in a small safe that Jack had placed into the trunk of the car, behind their suitcases and a few small kitchen items. Several of her most prized pieces of artwork and a box of her best crystal was resting in the back seat.

Despite the name Pan American Highway, in many parts of Mexico, the route seemed more like a country road. Jack had been warned not to leave the main road, and to avoid stopping anywhere that was not well populated and only drive during daylight hours. Since he wasn't sure about the availability of adequate accommodations, they stopped everyday by late afternoon, as soon as they found what looked to be a decent hotel along the route. It took a little more than two days to reach the Guatemalan border, and it was there they found out what driving through Central America was all about.

Gasoline at every Pemex station in Mexico was nearly twice as expensive as it had been back in Texas, but as they sat in the long line at the Guatemalan border, Jack was glad he'd filled up earlier in the nearby town of Comitan. After two hours they finally reached the point of initial contact with a border control officer. The uniformed agent walked slowly around their car, clearly admiring the German made luxury vehicle, acting as if he'd never seen anything like it. When he returned to Jack's window he told him to pull into one of the open bays for inspection. The man followed the car as Jack pulled into a covered parking spot. Soon, another agent came out of the building toward their car and asked for their passports. After Jack handed him the documents, he was told to step out of the car. Initially, Elaina thought she was going to remain in her seat, but the other agent opened her door and motioned for her to get out and follow her husband into the building. Jack reluctantly left their vehicle in the bay, unlocked as he'd been instructed, however, he did think to take the keys with him.

The interrogation room was void of any furnishings; no chairs or tables, only a large mirror at the far end, with another door next to it. Jack turned back toward their car and watched through the cracked window, as two agents opened each of the rear doors, the trunk, and the hood, obviously looking for contraband. He fully anticipated they would start unloading everything, but other than opening the ice chest, he couldn't see that they were even bothering to move anything else.

After about five minutes, an older gentleman wearing a perspiration stained brown uniform shirt and black trousers, that both seemed at least one size too large, appeared through the doorway on the far end of the room. Jack correctly surmised he had been observing them through the one way mirror from the moment they'd entered the room. He was holding their passports and an old wooden clipboard.

"Roberts?" He asked more as a statement, as he approached the two Americans.

"Si," Jack responded, letting the man know he spoke his language.

"What is the purpose of your trip?" His English was more than passable. His ability to communicate with American tourists was the reason he had risen to the position of shift supervisor at this important border crossing.

"We are on our way back home to Nicaragua," Jack explained.

The man nodded, indicating his understanding, then asked, "Do you have any firearms in your vehicle?"

"No," Jack said. The thirty-eight special he usually kept in the bedside table was in one of the two shipping containers that were also on their way to El Transito, by an entirely different route.

"Do you have any tobacco products with you?"

"No," Jack knew it was best to simply answer the man's questions, rather than entering into a dialogue about the dangers of smoking.

"Are you bringing any plants or food with you?"

"No, sir, only a few snacks in our cooler."

"Do you intend to spend any time in Guatemala?"

"Only the time it takes to drive from here to El Salvador."

"Do you not like my country?" The agent had used this question many times to move the interrogation in the direction he wanted. Jack noticed his voice seemed to be changing from his initial suspicious, very business like tone, to one that was more familiar, almost friendly. He had been told what to expect, so the old man's meaning was clear.

"We have never been to Guatemala before, but I'm sure it is lovely. However, this time we are simply passing through, on our way to our home in El Transito." Jack wanted the man to know that they had a very specific destination.

The agent took another step forward before he asked, "I assume you are aware of the transit fee?"

"Yes," Jack replied, wanting the man to know that he knew all about this routine method of bribing border patrol agents. "How much is it?"

The agent looked out at the BMW with all four doors and the trunk standing open and said, "For an expensive vehicle such as yours, the fee is usually one thousand dollars, US, but since you have been so cooperative, I am authorized to accept five hundred, assuming you pay in cash." Elaina gasped audibly, catching the man's attention briefly. She muttered to herself something about highway robbery. Fortunately, she was far enough away, the man didn't hear her.

Jack responded, "I assume that transit fee is good throughout the CA-four countries, and that you will provide me with the necessary papers to show as we cross the other three borders?" He was referring to the Central America - Four, Border Control Agreement, that allowed for free passage between Guatemala, El Salvador, Honduras and Nicaragua.

"Of course," the man said as he took a pen from his shirt pocket and tapped lightly on his clipboard.

Jack reached into his pocket and removed his wallet. He slowly removed five one hundred dollar bills, being careful not to allow the man to see that he had considerably more cash available, fearing he might decide to raise his fee. He handed the man the money, and once he counted the bills, satisfied with his payment, he signed a sheet of paper on his clipboard and tore it from the pad. He handed Jack the two passports and the paper and said, "I trust you will drive carefully through my country."

He motioned to the other two agents, indicating these rich Americans were now free to leave. The men left the car wide open as they headed back into the building, passing Jack and Elaina without even acknowledging them. They simply wanted to collect their share of the bribe.

It took the rest of the day for them to reach Guatemala City where they stopped for the night at the Hotel Vista Real on the southeast side of the city. Jack had hoped to be able to make it to El Transito by the following evening, but the rugged mountains of Southern Guatemala and El Salvador made that impossible. Although there weren't many cars on the highway, the ones they encountered presented significant obstacles. Most were only making twenty-five to thirty miles per hour, and passing on the narrow road was always difficult. They spent one last night in a hotel in San Miguel, El Salvador, before finishing the last leg of the trip, crossing the pacific coast portion of Honduras and then into Nicaragua. At every border crossing Jack presented the paper he had received from the Guatemalan agent to the local official, along with another one hundred dollar bill to ensure their passage.

It was just after six the next afternoon when they pulled off the paved street on to their gravel driveway. Lucinda and Federico came running out of their small house to greet them excitedly. Before they began unloading anything from the car, Elaina insisted they walk down to the beach. In the fading light of the late November evening, she inhaled the warm breeze off the ocean. The combination of the wide expanse of purple and orange sky and the smell of the salt water, was a welcome contrast to the air conditioned confines of the vehicle which had surrounded them for the last six days. This was now truly their home, and she didn't think she had ever felt more content.

****

"We're back," Jack said excitedly, once his friend answered his phone.

Domingo's surprise was obvious as he said, "That's wonderful. I wish I had known. It will take me at least an hour, but I will be there to pick you up as soon as I can get there."

"No, no! We didn't fly back," Jack spoke quickly, realizing the assumption his friend had made. "We drove down in Elaina's car. We are at our home here in El Transito.

"Wow," he said, imagining the challenges they must have encountered. "When did you arrive?"

"Last night. We finished unpacking this morning."

"Does this mean you are actually here permanently now?"

"Well, like I told our son, I'm not sure what permanent means, but yeah, we sold our house in Texas, and my office manager is in the process of liquidating my practice. So... I guess that makes this about as permanent as it gets."

"I'm so very happy to have you and Elaina here in Nicaragua," Domingo said, his voice betraying the flood of emotions he was feeling. "You are both so very dear to Felicia and me, to have you living in my country is truly an honor."

Jack hesitated, not knowing exactly how to respond to his friend's praise, so he decided to change the subject. "Have you seen our baby with tetralogy back in the clinic?" It had now been nearly three weeks since they had returned from Buenos Aires.

"He is doing very well," Domingo replied. "I saw him last week, and his mother said he is feeding normally. I'm sure it will be a while before he catches up to where he should be on the growth chart, but overall, he looked great."

"When is he due to come back in?"

"In two weeks, but I could have his mother bring him sooner if you want to check on him."

"No, that's okay. I'll just plan to see him with you during his next scheduled visit."

"Are you coming to the clinic before then?" Domingo wasn't sure what Jack's plans were for returning to work, and Jack wasn't either.

"I don't know," he said honestly. "I think I need to spend a few days here at the house before I decide what I'm going to do. Things have all happened so fast, I need some time to sort through everything."

"I understand. I think you and Elaina deserve some time together in your new home."

"Yeah, we need to get settled. I suspect that won't happen until after our two containers arrive from Texas."

"Two containers? Wow! You must have shipped most of what you owned."

"Oh, no," he laughed, "Not even close." Jack realized that Domingo had no way of knowing how much stuff he and Elaina had accumulated over the years.

The two freight containers held only a small percentage of their possessions, and only those that were irreplaceable.

Three days later Jack received a call from the Customs office in Managua, notifying him that both his containers had arrived, and had been thoroughly inspected. He arranged to have them both delivered by a friend of Domingo's who owned a moving company.

"Our stuff is being delivered tomorrow," he announced to Elaina as soon as he hung up the phone and walked back into the house.

"I can hardly wait to finally get settled in," she said excitedly. All the family photos, her mother's quilts, the rest of her clothes, almost everything of significance would be in that crate.

"I know you are anxious to truly make this house into our home," Jack smiled, hoping she would be pleased by his surprise.

The next morning a large flatbed truck rolled down the gravel driveway and stopped in front of the house. Elaina came running out the front door to greet the driver and his three helpers. When she saw the second big crate she just assumed they had another delivery to make.

As the men used a huge dolly to roll the six by eight by twelve foot container down the long ramp behind the truck, she said, "please be careful. There are some breakable things inside."

The men expertly maneuvered the large wooden box to a spot near the front door, where they began the process of opening it using two crow bars. While two men worked on the first crate, the other two returned to the truck and began removing the straps that were holding the second.

"No!" she shouted, "We only have this one crate. That's not ours."

Jack was watching from inside the house, smiling as she tried to refuse the second large container. The more the men insisted, the more she objected. She came running into the house to get Jack to stop them, and as she did, she caught him smiling his crooked little smile.

"What's so funny?" she demanded. "Those guys are trying to unload that other container. You need to tell them it's not ours."

Jack had made it very clear that she could only ship what she could fit into one container, but what he conveniently neglected to say was that he was going to ship one as well. "Let them go ahead," he reasoned. "They're the ones doing all the work. If they need to load it back on to the truck, they'll be the ones doing that as well."

"You're no help," she said as she turned around and headed back out to inspect the contents of the first crate, just as the second one was being rolled down the ramp and positioned to be opened as well.

One of the men was using a shoe truck to roll a large wardrobe box out of the first container and asked her where he should put it. She whirled around and led him into the house and into the master bedroom. She explained that all the clothing boxes were to be brought in and placed near the closet, where Lucinda would unload them.

As she returned to the front door, another man came in carrying a large box that she recognized as being filled with framed pictures and paintings from their old living room. "Put those over by the sofa, please," she instructed. It was clear that the house was going to be more than just a little cluttered for a while. She figured it would take at least a week to unpack everything, since that's how long it had taken her to prepare the shipment. Before she could get back to the front door two men came in with Jack's office desk. She showed them where to place it in the larger of the two spare bedrooms. That room was big enough to also serve as an office. Even with the desk, there was still enough room for the new bedroom furniture she'd bought in Managua. Once she was satisfied with the placement she started toward the door again, only to find them unloading the headboard and foot board of the beige bamboo and wicker furniture from their old guest house. While she had new furniture in their master bedroom, she really liked this bed and dresser much better, so when she suggested to Jack that she wanted to use it in their room, he just shrugged and told her it didn't make any difference to him.

Federico and Jack had already moved the furniture out of the master, and set it up in the third bedroom to make room for what the movers were now bringing in the house. Each time she moved toward the front door to check on the progress of the unloading, one or more of the men was bringing something in, asking for her direction. Finally, they brought in the last large box. It looked like another wardrobe box, but this one didn't contain any clothing. The man placed it in the center of the living room where she began removing the packing tape. She removed her mother's quilts that had been used to wrap the prize, protecting it from being damaged during the three thousand mile trip. "Would you please come lift this out for me?" she called across the room to her husband.

Jack stepped over to the large box, and carefully lifted the nearly four foot tall carving of the Madonna, placing it gently on the floor. "Looks like she made it just fine," he said, as he inspected it thoroughly. "Where do you want it?"

"I don't know. Somewhere near the front door, I guess," she offered. She walked toward the door, following one of the movers as he headed back outside. She almost bumped into another man who was carrying in a familiar piece of white enameled furniture.

"What is ...." she asked, not believing what her eyes were suggesting.

Jack came up beside her and said, "That's what was in my container."

The massive Steinway grand piano was resting on its side, on two large furniture dollies. Three of the men carefully guided it through the doorway, and when Elaina saw it "Oh, Jack," she said, nearly in a whisper. "I thought you sold it in the estate sale?"

"I did, I sold it to Buzz for a dollar, then I paid him to have it shipped down here. So, actually it's his piano. We're just borrowing it," he laughed.

She ran the few steps that separated them, throwing her arms around him like a young girl at Christmas.

"Thank you so much," she cried. "Losing my piano was the only thing I regretted about this move."

"I knew that," he said staring down into her tear filled eyes, "that's why I couldn't let it go."

She pulled her face up to him and kissed him through her joyful tears, then ran over to help the men move the sofa and coffee table more into the center of the room, making a place near the far wall for the new addition. She had them move the piano so that as she sat on the bench, she would face into the room and be able to see the ocean through the window wall to her right. "That's perfect!" she said excitedly as she assumed her familiar posture and placed her hands tentatively on the keyboard. She cautiously played a few notes of one of Jack's favorite pieces, but stopped abruptly. "Oh, my God," she said, as she recoiled from the keys, "that's hideous!"

"Don't worry," Jack offered sympathetically. "I have a man coming out tomorrow from Managua to tune it."

She rose from the bench and walked purposefully to her husband, throwing her arms around his neck again, the tears having gone, replaced by a sultry grin. "You've thought of everything, haven't you?"

He gazed warmly into her sparkling green eyes, and drew her closer to him, saying, "I promised, a long time ago, to spoil you for the rest of your life, and that is what I intend to do."

Their kiss had the controlled passion of two people who shared a single spirit. The movers stood at the doorway smiling at the two Americans embracing in the center of their home, but Lucinda quickly shooed them out the door as if they were stray animals. She turned back to see that her employers were still holding each other like young lovers, oblivious to their surroundings. She could not help but stare at them, smiling at their unashamed expression of love.

****

"Hi, Mom," David said, as he hugged his mother tightly.

"It is so good to have you guys here," she replied, as she released him and turned to embrace Amy. "What's wrong, dear?" Her voice now filled with concern. Amy's face had a pale greenish tinge, and her eyes were narrow and her brow furrowed.

"It was really a rough flight," David explained.

"I'll be all right in a little bit," Amy replied. "I was okay until we started down."

The last of the summer rainy season had long since passed, but the thermal wind patterns over the mountains of Central America often resulted in what the pilots referred to as "bumpy air" below twenty thousand feet.

Jack helped David with their luggage, as Elaina provided some much needed support to her daughter-in-law. They loaded the big Land Cruiser and headed for El Transito. The late December sky was a brilliant blue, without a cloud to be seen.

"The last time we were on this road, that mountain off in the distance was erupting," David remarked, looking out to the left, as they entered the highway.

"Yeah," his father responded, "nothing like that going on today, thank God."

Amy's color improved rapidly, and the seventy-five minute drive passed quickly as they each took informal turns telling what had transpired since they had been together just a month earlier. As Jack drove the big Toyota across the mountain pass near Santa Ana, the view of the vast Pacific Ocean in the distance was spectacular.

"Can we stop and take a picture?" David asked.

Jack pulled off the road, not realizing that this was the exact same spot their realtor stopped on the way to showing them the house in El Transito. David jumped out, grabbing the small camera bag that contained the digital camera his father had given him two Christmases before. He took several shots, then insisted that his mom and dad pose for a photo with the ocean in the distance. Elaina laughed as she physically pulled Jack over to the railing, and made him assume the same position he had when Monique took the same photo five months earlier.

"If this turns out, I want an enlargement of this picture. Your father and I stood in this same spot for a photo that I have on my phone, back when we first went to look at our house."

"It's a great view," Jack agreed, with an unspoken protest, "but I think there are much better photos to be taken much nearer the water."

"That may be true," Elaina agreed, "but this first glimpse of the Pacific is pretty hard to top." The excitement in her voice was obvious, but Jack was sure it had much more to do with having her son near, than it did the view of the ocean.

When they pulled onto the gravel driveway, David saw the small cinder block building and exclaimed, "Is that the house!?"

Jack laughed, but didn't answer as he made the gentle curve around the huge avocado tree that blocked the view of the main house from the street. "That's more like what I was expecting," David said as he saw the white stucco structure.

"It's not nearly as big as our old place in Texas," Elaina said, "but it's more than adequate for your dad and me."

Elaina had planned to put Christmas lights around the house, but she hadn't been able to find what she wanted at the PriceSmart store in Managua. She'd bought a membership to the huge superstore, that was similar to the Costco she'd shopped at frequently back in Fort Worth, but she was told that all the outdoor lights were gone by early November. She was able to find a great artificial tree and some new decorations to go along with the small box of personal ornaments that were part of the special items she'd included in her shipping container.

"Wow!" David said, as he stepped into the main living room. The eight foot tree was completely decorated, and dominated the room, and there were a few presents scattered on the floor beneath it.

Amy immediately spotted the ivory colored, shiny enameled piano in the corner of the room. The lid was closed, and Elaina's favorite nativity scene was carefully arranged on the small, round, embroidered tablecloth, just as it had been every Christmas for more than twenty years. "I thought you sold your piano?" she asked excitedly.

"So did I," Elaina replied, "but, mister sentimental over there decided he couldn't live without it." Jack laughed as she pointed accusingly toward him.

"I'm so glad," Amy said. "I just can't imagine your house without that piano."

"I agree," David added, "I hope you will play some Christmas music for us later."

"Of course she will," Jack added quickly. "She's been practicing everyday since we got the thing tuned."

"This is really nice," David said as he looked around the room. "It's actually a lot bigger than I expected."

"Let me show you to your room," his mother said, as she walked down the front hall toward the guest room. "Then we can take a walk down to the beach."

It was early evening before they all returned from the beach to an evening meal served by Lucinda on the deck. She had immediately taken to David and Amy, they were so different, so much more respectful than the surfer son of her former employer. She continued to serve them fresh fruit, and pan fried filets of mackerel until David insisted that he couldn't eat another bite. Although she didn't understand their English, the looks on their faces and their body language made it clear they had enjoyed it thoroughly.

"So, tell me how things are going at school," Jack said.

"I start my general surgery rotation right after the holidays. I'm really excited to finally scrub-in to a real operation."

"I thought you said you were in on several C-sections when you were on the OB service," his mom interrupted.

"A C-section is hardly the same thing," he responded. "I'm talking about real surgery."

"I suspect if you ask those women who had their bellies cut open to remove a child, they would tell you just how real that surgery is," Elaina offered in return.

"You know what I mean," he responded. "I'm talking about treating diseases and injuries." He paused briefly, then returned to his dad's question. "Everything is progressing very well, and unless something drastic happens, I will be graduating in June."

"That's great," Elaina interrupted again. "Does that mean you guys are going to start a family?"

He turned back toward her, shaking his head in mock disgust. "Mom, you have a one track mind. Amy and I are enjoying being a young married couple right now. I'm sure we'll get around to having a house full of kids one day. We'll let you know."

What he hadn't told her was that they had decided to start trying a couple of months earlier. Amy had stopped taking her birth control pills back in October. She was now more anxious to have a child than Elaina was to have a grandbaby.

"Anyway, I have started looking at potential internships and will be entering into the matching program this spring."

"That's always an exciting time," his dad said, "at least it was for me. Any ideas where you'd like to go?"

"I've thought a lot about it, and I think I would like to do my internship, residency and cardiothoracic surgery fellowship all in the same place. What do you think?"

"Well, that kind of depends on the place. When I was an intern at Parkland, I thought the same thing, but they couldn't guarantee me a spot in their cardiothoracic surgery fellowship once I finished my surgical residency. That's why I chose to go into the Air Force to do the rest of my training. They made a spot for me four years in advance. I don't imagine any program would do that now days."

"You might be surprised," David replied. "Some of the programs are really anxious to fill their residency spots. It isn't anywhere near as competitive as it used to be."

"I guess medical students are starting to wise up and take what I've heard said is the road to success."

"What do you mean the road to success?" Amy asked, unsure if she'd missed something.

David jumped in with an answer, "Radiology, Ophthalmology, Anesthesiology and Dermatology... R, O, A, D."

"Those are said to be the highest paid specialties for the amount of work required," Jack explained. "Although, I'm not so sure about anesthesia anymore, and the fact is, every medical and surgical specialty is under attack these days."

Amy turned to him and asked, "so, if you had it to do over, would you choose heart surgery again?"

"I can't imagine doing anything else," he responded. "I'm sure I could have made more money doing something else, and I'm certain I would have had more time to spend with these guys over the years," he gestured toward David and Elaina, "but, I know I've enjoyed my life's work as much or more than any man, and at the end of the day, that's all I could have ever hoped for."

"That has been obvious," David said. "I think it's interesting some of the faculty and many of the residents that I talk to seem angry and frustrated. I don't think they really like what they're doing."

"I doubt that it's that they don't like what they are doing as physicians as much as it is they hate the way the system has turned against them. Everything they do is so scrutinized now days. It isn't enough to know what to do for any given patient, now you have to satisfy whoever is writing the check for that service." Jack shook his head slowly and added, "The truth is, that was the deciding factor as to why we're here and not back in Texas. That, and your mom's desire to be on the beach."

"Don't go blaming your early retirement on me," she objected.

Jack laughed, knowing he'd touched a sensitive area. He knew she would never want anyone, especially David, to think that she had coerced him into moving to El Transito. "You know I'm only kidding, but the fact we had this place to retire to, made the decision that much easier."

"So, are you officially retired?" David asked.

Jack looked up into his son's questioning expression and replied, "No way. I'm just getting my second wind. I don't know yet what I'm going to do, but you can rest assured I'm going to do something, and it won't be oil painting."

****

"The medical staff voted eighty-nine percent to eleven percent to close the medical staff," Grady announced to Fitzgerald and Horvath. While both had been relieved of their duties with the hospital, they still held controlling interest in the medical practice management company. It was a separate business entity, and as long as they held the physician contracts, they could still dictate to the docs and the hospital every element of the accountable care organization, including how the global payments from the new government run insurance plans would be handled. Admittedly, it would have been easier if they were also running the hospital, but getting the new board to play ball would prove to be merely an inconvenience. Some of the board members were already suggesting they may have made a mistake in firing Fitzgerald so hastily. The new guy wasn't nearly as aggressive, and many of their marketing programs were being allowed to die for lack of support.

"That's perfect," Fitzgerald said. "Now, if that moron running the board decides he doesn't want to play ball with our physician group, he has no where else to turn. The docs are back in control, and we control the docs."

"Don't let any of them hear you say that," Grady warned. "They don't like to think of themselves as being controlled."

"Keeping them from figuring out they are being used is your job, Grady. That's what we're paying you more than half a million dollars a year to do."

Horvath then added, "Just remember, there's always someone ready to take over if you either decide you want to cross us, or prove incapable of doing the job."

"Don't forget," Grady responded angrily, "I'm the one that herded these cats together. You owe me."

Fitzgerald laughed briefly under his breath and said, "Now, now, gentlemen. Let's not argue over who's more important than who. This pie is already plenty big enough for all of us, and once this government run healthcare system really kicks in, we will be in complete control of all the funds. Doing whatever it takes to maintain that control should be more than enough incentive to keep your little egos in check, don't you think?"

"Yes, sir," Grady said obediently.

"I guess," Horvath replied, still hobbled by his broken patella. Since the incident the last time he was in Fitzgerald's office, he remained in a perpetual bad mood.

"It could be worse, Michael," Fitzgerald added. "You know, you could have a busted knee and be in jail."

Horvath hung his head knowing how much he owed the old man. His attorneys had gotten all the charges dropped using what Fitzgerald called "some fancy lawyering." Since they did not stand to benefit either directly or indirectly from the fraudulent claim they couldn't logically be accused of defrauding the federal government. Likewise, since the person they were alleged to have conspired to frame for Medicaid fraud was unwilling or unable to file charges against them, there was no crime committed. Finally, the recorded voice on the audio could have been anyone, most likely someone hired by one of Mr. Fitzgerald's or Mr. Horvath's many business competitors, and since the FBI had been unable to produce one credible witness, or a single shred of evidence, suggesting that either of their clients had engaged in any of the charges being leveled against them, the government simply had no case.

****

Three days before Christmas Jack was back at the airport in Managua to pickup his brother. He had flown in from Tokyo through Los Angeles and was exhausted, despite flying business class across the Pacific. Jack greeted Ben warmly as he emerged from customs and baggage claim.

"Welcome to the third world!" he exclaimed.

"That was one long flight," Ben replied, "I certainly hope it was worth it. Do they have any Mexican food here?"

Jack laughed and said, "No, but I suspect you'll be surprised by what you find, and I don't think you'll be disappointed."

As they climbed into the Land Cruiser, Ben asked, "Where's your pickup truck? I didn't think you'd ever part with it."

"I gave it to David, more or less as an early Christmas present. This four wheel drive vehicle is far more practical. The roads around here become virtually impassable when it rains, and it rains a lot from March to October."

"So, what in the world made you decide to move down to this God forsaken country anyway?"

"Several things," Jack replied. "First, this place is anything but God forsaken. I have never felt so close to him as I do when I'm here." Jack paused to let his brother understand the conviction of his statement. "Second, its about as relaxed as any place you've ever been. No one seems to be in a hurry. Third, it's cheap to live here, with a few notable exceptions, like satellite Internet service." Ben's reaction made it clear that he was surprised his brother could even get satellite communications. "And most importantly, Elaina loves this place, and when we get to the house I think you'll see why."

"I'm just shocked that you decided to retire so suddenly."

Ben was not aware of what had gone on with CMS and the FBI, so Jack proceeded to fill him in on the details of the preceding three months, and when he finally finished, Ben said, "I can't believe it. What has happened to the American healthcare system?"

"I've asked myself that same question countless times, and I've come to the conclusion that It's rotting from within," Jack's voice was filled with sadness and frustration. "It began deteriorating as soon as it became more about insurance company payments than the patients wellbeing."

"What about the drug manufacturers. Didn't they play a part."

"Sure, but when you look at what's happened through a wider lens, it is actually the physicians who failed to uphold their promise to put the patient first. As soon as physicians started contracting with anybody and everybody except our patients, we began the gradual erosion of our professional ethics. That opened the door for a wide variety of parasitic entities, like insurance companies, for profit hospitals and yes, drug companies to step in and do whatever they wanted. Without an independent physician, the patient no longer has an advocate, and the system has been spiraling out of control ever since."

"I supposed those parasites you talk about would include device manufacturers like the one I work for?" Ben asked, in a sullen tone.

"In some cases, yes," Jack replied. "I don't mean to imply that all manufacturers, or all drug companies, or even all insurance companies and hospitals are guilty of taking advantage of the public. The problem is clearly much more complicated than that, but overall the system has gotten out of control, largely because the one component that patients were told they could trust to help keep them from being taken advantage of, specifically their doctor, has been compromised."

"Whatever happened to the Hippocratic Oath?"

"Most medical schools don't even use it any more as part of their graduation ceremonies. They claim it is too old fashioned. The AMA recently started rewriting the code of medical ethics to reflect the idea that physicians are actually more obligated to manage the collective resources of the society than they are to provide for the needs of any one patient."

"Sounds to me like they're in somebody's pocket."

"Exactly!" Jack agreed. "The government takeover is only the latest in a long process that has turned healthcare from a personal service into a massive industry and the AMA and most of the other physician organizations, have been complicit in the process. So, I just decided it wasn't worth it to keep fighting the medical establishment and the rest of that perverse system. Bottom line, I could have gone back to Fort Worth, and muscled my way back onto the staff of the hospital, but it just wasn't worth it. I just turned sixty-five, and figured this was as good a time as any to get out."

"So, what are you going to do now?"

"I have no idea," Jack said with a slight chuckle. "I'm going to do something. It may sound strange to you, but I'm just waiting for God to point the way."

"What, do you think I don't believe in God?" Ben questioned his older brother.

"No, I didn't mean it that way. I just figured you'd say I should make my own decisions rather than waiting for divine guidance."

"Well, I assume you've given it more than a little thought, right?"

"Of course. I haven't thought of much of anything else since Elaina and I decided to move down here permanently, almost two months ago. Actually, the truth is, it goes back well before then."

"I'd say if you haven't been able to come up with some kind of a plan by now, it sounds like you need some divine direction," Ben offered. "The fact is, I've been trying to decide what I'm going to do, too."

"Really?" Jack asked. "Based on what you told me last Christmas, I figured you'd just about be ready to launch your MATRICS operating platform."

"The system is ready to go," Ben said in obvious frustration, "We just can't get anyone to do the clinical trials."

"Why not?"

"All the European surgeons are still very skeptical after what happen with our competitors system, and we haven't been able to find anybody in the US who will touch it."

"What happened to that other company."

"They went under. Last I heard, their investors took about a two hundred million dollar loss."

"Wow!" Jack exclaimed.

"Yeah," Ben replied, "our Wall Street investment bankers took notice too, and it really impacted our ability to get any secondary funding to conduct the clinical trials. When you combine that with the fact that all the docs are now saying the risk is too high, we haven't been able to find a single reputable institution that will even talk to us."

"So what are you going to do?"

"I'm not sure. Naryama is reaching his limit financially and he's pretty discouraged by what he's hearing from his contacts in the states. They're telling him that even if it works, their hospitals won't buy the system because of declining reimbursement. They don't see any way to recoup their investment."

"How much do you anticipate a system will cost?"

"Our initial plan was to sell the basic platform for under a million dollars, but based on the number of units we think we can sell and support, we are going to need to get close to two million each, just to reach a break-even point within the first three years. That's assuming we could sell a hundred units."

"I assume there will be some individual disposable items that will be sold separately, right?"

"Yes, of course. The average case will involve about ten thousand dollars worth of disposable catheters. As you can imagine, the tiny catheters are expensive to manufacture in small numbers, but once we reach a point where we're manufacturing them in larger batches, we anticipate that cost will decrease significantly."

Jack paused for a few seconds before saying, "I remember a time when innovation and new product development was booming. I fear those days are over."

"That is certainly the case in the states," Ben agreed. "Everyone is scared of what the government take over of the healthcare system is going to do, and from all the forecasts I have seen, there are no longer any profits to be made in the healthcare industry, unless your an insurance companies."

"That's true, but that's only going to last for a few years," Jack explained. "Those guys are making record profits now, but in a few years the government will push them out of business with a single payer system like they have in England and Canada."

"We tried to get a couple of guys in Canada interested in our MATRICS platform, but they just laughed when we told them what it cost. They said they're having trouble just getting the government to pay for the disposable supplies for the cardiopulmonary bypass machine."

"I know," Jack said, "I have a colleague up there who is actually re-sterilizing instruments and equipment that are designed to be disposable."

"What about the risk of blood borne diseases being transmitted?"

"I asked him that, and he said he has each patient sign a document acknowledging the risk, and virtually every one of them agree, because it's either that or not get the operation. Can you imagine, waiting for a year or more to get an operation, and then when your turn finally comes, the surgeon says you must agree to the use of equipment that puts you at risk for getting AIDS, or hepatitis C, or who knows what other deadly disease the guy before you might have had?"

Ben shook his head silently, "I'm afraid your right. The age of innovation may be over," he said with a discernible sadness in his voice.

"From a practical stand point that's true, but I don't think there will ever be an end of new ideas," Jack replied. "We just need a new way to get them into practice."

"Yeah, that's our problem with MATRICS. At this point I don't see anyway that technology is going to survive. I'm afraid all the work I've done for the last six years is going to end up being a complete waste of time."

As Jack navigated through some slow moving traffic and turned off the Pan American Highway, toward the west, he thought about what his brilliant brother had just said. It appeared that healthcare innovation was being destroyed by regulations as well as the risk of liability. "You know, I've been thinking about what it would take to build a modern hospital here in Nicaragua. One of my friends in Managua is a very wealthy guy, and the last time I talked to him he sounded like he wanted to help make that happen."

"I can only imagine all the red tape you'd have to go through to get something like that done here." Ben scoffed.

"Maybe," Jack replied, "but, in the short time I've been down here, I've discovered that if the right people are involved, specifically people with money and power, obstacles just seem to magically melt away."

"Well, at this point Naryama and I are willing to look at any reasonable options to get the clinical trials done. Without them, MATRICS is dead in the water.

****

"Hi Elizabeth," Elaina said as the other expatriate answered her cell phone. "This is Elaina Roberts."

"Elaina! How are you?" Elizabeth exclaimed. "It is so good to hear your voice."

"It's been far too long," Elaina said, "I must apologize for not staying in touch these last few months, but things have been extremely hectic." After their visit to Costa Rica, Elaina had spoken to Elizabeth several times on the phone and they had corresponded by email frequently, but they hadn't touched based for nearly six months.

"What are you and Dr. Roberts up to?"

"That's why I was calling. Jack has retired from practice and we have moved down here to Nicaragua."

"What!" she exclaimed,. "You guys are living in Nicaragua? You're kidding, right?"

"No, I'm serious. We've been here a couple of months now."

"That's terrific! Where are you living?"

"We bought a house in El Transito. It's just off the beach and I love it."

"I'm so excited for you."

"Thank you, I can't wait for you to see it. In fact, that's why I was calling. Jack and I were talking about you last night and wondered what you were doing for Christmas?"

"I don't have anything planned. My son was supposed to come down, but he can't get off work, so, I'm just going to have my own little private Christmas." The disappointment was obvious in her voice.

"Why don't you come up here to El Transito for a few days. David and Amy are here, and I know they would love to see you again."

"Oh, I couldn't possibly impose on you guys. Besides, y'all should be spending your Christmas together as a family."

"We discussed it over dinner last night, and everyone agreed that you are very much a part of our family. Even Ben, Jack's brother whom you haven't met, agreed. He even offered to sleep on the sofa to free up the second guest room for you. We all want you to come spend the holiday with us."

"That is so thoughtful of you."

"So, you'll come?"

"Yes," Elizabeth said hesitantly. "I would love to come spend a few days with you, but only on one condition. I assume there is a hotel of some sort in your town, right?"

"Yes, there are several hotels in town that cater mostly to the surfers who come here from all over. But, like I said we can make room for you."

"No, I'm not going to push anyone out of their bed. I will only come if I can find a room at one of the hotels."

"Let me do this," Elaina countered. "One of the places is just down the beach from us. It's no more than a quarter of a mile. Let me go down there and make a reservation and I'll call you back."

"That sounds like a good idea."

"I know this is short notice, but today is Monday, and Christmas is on Wednesday, so I was hoping you could drive up tomorrow and stay the rest of the week? Ben is going to be here until the weekend. The kids are staying until New Years."

"Like I said, I don't have any other plans, so if you can make me a reservation, I'll be there."

Immediately after she hung up, Jack interrupted her thoughts. "You're not trying to play matchmaker are you?" he asked.

"Of course not," she lied, sporting an innocent grin. "I just think Ben needs someone to talk to other than just you and David."

"You know he is a confirmed bachelor."

"I know he's said that repeatedly, but he's only sixty, and I would think he might enjoy the company of a woman while he's here, and Elizabeth fits that role perfectly. Besides, she could be just the kind of calming influence he needs to allow him to relax. Kinda like I help you relax." She put her arms around his neck and looked lovingly up into his eyes.

"Okay," Jack agreed reluctantly, "but, if he gets upset, or if things get weird, I'm going to make sure they both know this was all your doing."

****

The hotel room wasn't anything special, but given the typical clientele, Elaina wasn't surprised. She told the manager that she wanted to prepay for five nights, but she was told that she'd actually save about thirty dollars if she'd book the room for a full week instead of by the day.

When Elizabeth drove her dark blue suburban up to the house late the next afternoon, Elaina and Amy both came bounding out of the front door to greet her. They quickly went inside where Lucinda had prepared some fruit and iced tea. The guys had all gone into town, giving the women a chance to chat without interruption.

Elaina showed her friend around the house and then insisted they go down to the beach. Amy said she wanted to wait for David, so the two of them made their way across the wooden bridge and down to the beach. The sunset was a bit disappointing she thought, but Elizabeth was impressed by everything she saw.

"This is an amazing place you have here," she said.

"I fell in love with it the first time we saw it," Elaina explained, "and every time I come down here to the beach I am so thankful to be here. I just feel so at home."

"I'm so happy for you," Elizabeth said with a genuine warmth. While she loved her place in Costa Rica as much as Elaina loved this place, she felt a twinge of jealousy, knowing her friend had someone to share it with.

Elaina pointed down the beach toward the town, saying, "there is your hotel. As you can see it's less than a three minute walk."

"I probably better go get checked-in, don't you think?"

"I thought we'd walk down there together. Federico will meet us down there with your luggage."

"He doesn't need to do that," Elizabeth protested.

"He may not need to, but he already did," she laughed. "Let's go."

As they made their way down the beach, carrying their sandals, Elizabeth decided to ask about Jack's brother. "So, before I say something stupid and embarrass myself when I meet Jack's brother, what should I know about him?"

"Well, first of all he is brilliant."

"Uh-oh!" Elizabeth replied, "Sounds intimidating."

"Just to talk to him you would never know it. He has two PhDs, and he's into aerospace and bioengineering, and all that kind of stuff, but he doesn't talk about any of that stuff unless you ask him."

"Good. I'll make a point of not asking about anything like that," she laughed.

"He is also a confirmed bachelor, but I'm not sure why. I suspect he's just never found the right woman."

"He's not...?"

"No, no, I don't think so."

"Like a said, I just don't want to say something that might embarrass me or get me in trouble."

"He can be a little shy when he's around people he doesn't know, but he can be very engaging once he gets to know you."

"Just as long as he doesn't start asking me about nuclear physics or geometry, I'll try and hold my own."

Both women laughed out loud as they approached the beachside entrance to the small hotel. Federico was waiting for them in the lobby with her two small suitcases. The clerk at the desk had the registration papers ready for her to sign, but refused to accept her credit card as Elaina had instructed.

"Wait a minute," she protested, "I told you I would only come if I could stay in a hotel. I certainly don't intend for you to pay for it."

"Don't be silly," Elaina scolded, "We invited you to come up here as our guest. That was part of the deal."

"I wouldn't have come if I had known you were going to be footing the bill for a hotel room."

"Just like Federico bringing your luggage, it's already done, so get over it." Elaina laughed, satisfied that her plan was working out exactly as she'd hoped, but, from this point forward, it would be up to Elizabeth.

****

Jack had suggested to Lucinda that his brother loved Mexican food, and wondered if she could fix something he might like. So far, she had not prepared anything resembling the Tex-Mex food they had grown to love, like the cheesy casserole they had enjoyed several times at Domingo and Felicia's home. The housekeeper said, "you leave everything to me, señor."

That evening she served a salad of avocado slices, fresh tomatoes, jicama, and papaya with a light oil and vinegar dressing. The main course was composed of chicken enchiladas covered with a sour cream sauce, along with some locally grown peppers, stuffed with shrimp and cheese, then rolled in cornmeal and pan fried to a crispy, golden brown. As with almost every meal, she served them gallo pinto patties. For dessert she made crispy sopapillas, covered with powdered sugar and honey.

"When I asked you the other day about Mexican food," Ben said, directing his comments at his brother across the table, "you said I would be surprised by what I found here in Nicaragua, and you were right. That was one of the best meals I've had in years." He turned toward Lucinda and spoke to her in fluent Spanish. "Thank you so much señora. That was a wonderful meal. I hope before I leave to go back to Japan that you will show me how to make those stuffed peppers."

"I didn't know you could speak Spanish," Jack said, shocked at what he was hearing.

"Don't you remember that Spanish tutor that came over to our house three days a week."

"Of course I remember, but that was what, almost fifty years ago? Do you have somebody in Japan that you've been conversing with?"

"No," Ben replied. "I think the last time I actually spoke Spanish was probably ten years ago, when I was living in California."

"And, it just came back to you, just like that?"

"Yes," Ben stated as if it were nothing special. "I learned the language. I don't know why you think I should have to learn it again."

"Well, most of us mortals have brains that tend to lose things like language unless we use them regularly."

"I suspect it's that scotch you drink that killed part of Wernicke's area in your brain where language comprehension is processed."

"I told you," Elaina said, directing her comment toward Elizabeth.

"What?" Ben asked, not even realizing he was exposing his considerable wealth of knowledge.

David smiled and said, "Wow, Uncle B, I only learned about that in med school on the Neurology service a few months ago. Did you go to medical school?"

"No, David. I just read a lot."

"I read quite a bit too," Elizabeth said, trying to sound serious, "but, I don't think Werner's area, or whatever part of the brain you were talking about, has ever even been mentioned in the books I read."

Everyone laughed except Ben and Elizabeth. "I don't know what it is that you all find so funny," he said

"I don't think they're laughing at you," she said. "I think they are laughing at my relative lack of education."

"No," Elaina said quickly. "I was laughing because you said exactly what I was thinking."

"Me too," Amy added.

"This whole conversation is making me laugh," Jack said. "I'm just impressed that you retained those language skills. Speaking of retaining skills," he quickly made an effort to change the subject. "Elaina promised to play some Christmas music for us. It cost a pretty penny to ship that piano down here, so let's hear something."

Elaina made her way over to the piano bench and lifted the fall, exposing the keys. As she started to play, Elizabeth was quick to recognize the familiar melody. She spontaneously began singing along. Her voice had a confident, polished quality that suggested many years of training. Everyone else remained quiet, taking in the beautiful blend of piano and vocal tones. Elaina smiled broadly as her playing became more an accompaniment to Elizabeth's nearly professional performance than what she had first assumed would be an instrumental version of one of her favorites, Have Yourself a Merry Little Christmas.

The final verse was especially moving for Jack, given what all had happened over the last few months. He shared the wish of always being together, as he looked at the shining star on the top of the tree. As Elizabeth finished the final lyrics, she allowed her voice to lead Elaina's playing in a steady decrescendo and retard. When she finally lifted her hands from the keys, Elaina began applauding vigorously, and the others joined in enthusiastically. Everyone accept for Ben.

"That was incredible!" Amy said, with David and Jack quickly agreeing.

"Thank you," Elizabeth replied shyly.

Ben stood almost motionless, mesmerized by what he had just witnessed. All eyes seemed to move in unison toward him, anticipating he would offer his own appreciation, but he remained speechless. Jack was quite certain he had never before seen his brother awe struck. When Elizabeth finally raised her gaze to meet his, he shook his head quickly, but almost imperceptibly as if responding to a feathery touch.

"Where did you learn to sing like that?" He asked in amazement.

"I took voice lessons when I was in high school, and I majored in music at Baylor, back in the late seventies."

"I have never heard anything so beautiful in my life."

"Oh, come on," Elizabeth objected.

"Would you please sing something else?"

"Now you're putting me on the spot," she replied.

"Absolutely," Jack insisted. "We all want to hear more."

She turned to Elaina, who simply shrugged and asked, "What will it be?"

"Do you know the Christmas Song?"

"Of course," Elaina replied, immediately beginning the intro to the song she'd first heard as a small child. It had been recorded by countless artists over the years, but that original version by Nat King Cole was still her favorite.

"Chestnuts roasting on an open fire..." Elizabeth began. She seemed so completely comfortable as she flawlessly recalled the familiar lyrics and timeless melody. As she completed the final refrain that wished everyone a Merry Christmas, she smiled seductively and looked across the room, directly into Ben's eyes. He scarcely even blinked, as it became clear to everyone in the room that he was thoroughly hypnotized, as if by a sirens song.

Elizabeth continued to stare at him for a few moments, waiting for him to say something, but not uncomfortable with the silence. Elaina rose from the bench as all eyes were darting back and forth between Ben and Elizabeth. "Why don't we take a walk down to the beach?" she said, sensing that this siren and her new conquest might like some time alone.

Elaina and Jack led the way, followed by Amy and David, with Elizabeth and Ben lagging a few steps behind.

"You have the most beautiful voice I've ever heard," Ben said, once the others were well ahead, beyond where they could hear.

She stopped immediately, and turned to face him. "Do you really mean that, or are you just trying to flatter this old woman?"

They stood face to face in the middle of the wooden bridge that traversed the shimmering lagoon. As she looked up into his dark eyes again, the nearly full moon over head reflected off her face, giving it a softer, more youthful glow than the harsher lights inside the house.

"Yes." His reply was so faint she wasn't sure she heard him. Then his voice seemed to regained most of it's former strength as he added. "I'm not one who gives compliments, and I am certainly not prone to flattering anyone."

"Well, I'm not someone who is used to receiving compliments." Her voice was less confident as her eyes dipped, followed by a drop of her head.

Ben leaned forward slightly and used his right hand to lift her chin until she was looking at him again. "I think you should be receiving compliments everyday," he said, in an almost seductive voice that was completely out of character.

"That's one of the nicest things anyone has ever said to me."

She stood silently, anticipating he might draw her into a passionate embrace, not realizing that Ben had no experience in matters of the heart. Instead, he looked toward the beach and said, "we better catch up with the others. Otherwise we might get lost."

Elizabeth couldn't imagine anything she'd like better than getting lost on this secluded beach with this brilliant, yet naive and vulnerable man.

CHAPTER 18

On Christmas morning, David and Amy were up early, just like when they were kids, but this time for a different reason. Amy was kneeling desperately over the commode. When Lucinda came in through the front door, she heard the muffled sounds of the young woman's distress coming from the guest room. She moved quickly into the kitchen and started making a large pot of coffee.

"Good morning señor Ben," Lucinda said as he walked deliberately from his bedroom toward the french doors leading out to the deck. "*Feliz Navidad.*"

"Merry Christmas to you as well," he replied. "I will be back in half an hour or so."

Ben was headed to Elizabeth's hotel, via the beach. He had escorted her back to her room last night and he believed it was his obligation to accompany her back to the house this morning.

As Ben quickly disappeared across the bridge, Elaina came into the kitchen to check on the progress of her traditional Christmas breakfast dish. She had shown Lucinda how to prepare the layered casserole of scrambled eggs, ground sausage and mild salsa, topped with shredded cheese.

"It is almost ready señora." Lucinda said.

"Have you seen David and Amy yet?"

"No, señora. They are both still in their room." She wanted to tell her how she knew, but knew it was none of her business. She simply smiled.

David suddenly appeared from around the corner with a concerned look on his face. "Do you have any hot tea, Mom?" he asked.

"Sure, sweetie," she replied, "is something wrong?"

"No, Amy just has an upset stomach. I think she must have eaten something that didn't agree with her." He didn't tell her that this was the third morning since they arrived that she had been sick.

Lucinda went to the cupboard for the tea, and when she returned with the small bag of Earl Grey she was smiling broadly. Elaina looked at her rather quizzically as she waited for the microwave to finish heating the mug of water. The housekeeper returned to the oven to check on the casserole while David's mother prepared the hot tea.

"Is there anything else I can get for her," she asked as she handed David the mug filled with the steaming liquid.

"No, I think she'll be fine with just this tea to settle her stomach."

As he returned to the guest room, Elaina caught a glimpse of Lucinda smiling once more, seemingly amused by her daughter-in-law's condition. She offered a reproachful stare, and Lucinda quickly returned to her duties.

"When do we eat?" Jack asked playfully as he joined his wife in the kitchen, His hair was still damp from his morning shower, and he was wearing what had become his retirement uniform; a pair of faded blue jeans, a white tee shirt and a pair of leather sandals.

****

"Are you almost ready?" Ben called out impatiently. He was not used to waiting on anyone, much less a woman who seemed to take forever getting ready just to walk up the beach.

"Just a minute," Elizabeth called back from behind the bathroom door. She too was unaccustomed to being harassed in the morning, or any time for that matter. Having someone, other than the orphans, that even cared whether she got up in the morning was somehow revitalizing.

She quickly finished dressing after she put on make-up for the first time in more than six months. The last time she fixed her face and hair was for a big fund raiser at her friend's house in Costa Rica. She silently wished she'd not let the gray dominate the way it now did, but if he didn't like her the way she was, well that was just too bad. As she came out into the room, she said, "I'm ready."

Ben quickly stood up from the desk chair, staring at her to the point where she became uncomfortable. "Is there something wrong?" she said looking down at the black denim slacks and bright red and white blouse. It was the nicest outfit she'd brought from home.

"No," Ben replied slowly. "I think you look terrific."

"Why, thank you. You don't look so bad yourself."

She walked over toward him, realizing she was becoming more attracted to him each time they were alone together. As she stood directly in front of him, she desperately wanted him to reach out and take her in his arms and kiss her. As she stared up into his eyes, she saw the reflection of an innocent teenager. Someone who didn't know what to do with his own feelings.

"Are you ready?" she asked, sounding more seductive than she intended.

Ben didn't respond. He simply stood there with a look of frightened anticipation. It was all she could do to keep from throwing herself into his arms, just to let him know that she was the one who was indeed ready. Instead, she simply smiled, fearing he would reject her advance, and end the fairytale she was living in her mind.

"Let's go," she said, "we're going to be late for Elaina's brunch."

Ben didn't take his eyes off her as she walked ahead of him out the door and into the dimly lit hallway. As they made their way to the beach, they walked side by side, close enough to touch one another, but neither made any effort to do so.

The hotel was constructed on a slightly raised foundation, with a short stairway leading down to a flagstone walkway that led out to the beach. At the end of the walk was a very narrow set of wooden steps going down to the volcanic sand. Elizabeth took the lead, and as she reached the last wooden plank there was an audible crack as the old pine tread gave way, causing her to stumble and twist around, falling backward onto the soft ground.

Ben immediately leaped down the last two steps and knelt down next to her, reaching instinctively for her arm. "Are you okay?" he asked, sounding more concerned than seemed necessary, given the minimal chance of actual injury.

Elizabeth laughed, mostly from embarrassment, as she turned quickly toward him and said, "The only thing I've hurt is my pride."

Ben quickly helped her to her feet, and innocently began brushing the dark gray volcanic sand from the back of her legs. Without the slightest thought, he used the palm of his right hand to gently sweep the sand off the material that covered her still shapely bottom and the back of her thighs. Her first instinct was to turn away from this obvious advance, but instead she hesitated. This was the physical contact she had been longing for, despite his obvious lack of romantic intent.

"Are you sure your okay?" Ben asked as he reached for her left arm and turned her toward him.

"I'm fine," she said, as she looked down at his hand holding the bare skin above her elbow. "Thank you," she added with a broad smile as she looked up into his still concerned eyes. Why doesn't he kiss me, she wondered. Then he would be able to see for himself exactly how I feel, but Ben's gaze continued to betray his lack of confidence.

"Good" he said, "You had me worried for a minute."

As they walked quietly down the beach, Elizabeth couldn't help herself, She wanted his touch again, so she moved slightly closer to his side. When she was almost close enough to brush against his arm, she faked another slight stumble in the soft sand, bumping into him, trying successfully to make it appear accidental.

"Sorry," she said, regaining her balance.

Ben reached out to help steady her, grabbing her by the wrist a bit more firmly that necessary, but she made no effort to escape his grasp, and he held it long after her gait was steady. As he slowly released her wrist, his fingers seemed to automatically slide down to touch hers. He allowed himself to hold on for a moment, anticipating she would pull away now that she no longer required his assistance. Instead, she spread her fingers, allowing them to intertwine with his. Each hand gripped the other firmly for a moment before relaxing into a more comfortable, tensionless bond.

Elizabeth looked up toward him to gage his response, but Ben stared silently down the beach as if nothing was happening. She recalled vividly the first time a boy had held her hand in a movie theater. They were both just thirteen, and that boys adolescent demeanor, nearly forty-three years ago, had been just as casual and detached as Ben's was now. It seemed the ability to display affection was a learned behavior for the male members of the species, so at least for now, she was content to walk quietly down the beach, hand in hand.

****

"It's time to open presents," Elaina announced once everyone had finished eating. Amy had made it to the table a little after the others, but all in all she looked like whatever caused her upset stomach had been cured by the hot tea and honey.

Lucinda and Federico had reluctantly agreed to join in the traditional family gathering around the tree. Lucinda had prepared a sugary candy, similar to Mexican pralines, but instead of pecans, the chewy sweet treats were filled with coconut. Her husband had helped prepare them, and he had individually wrapped each prize in clear cellophane, which were tied neatly with small red ribbons.

Elaina had gone shopping a few weeks earlier in Managua and found something suitable for each of them. She handed Federico a large box, neatly wrapped in green paper. As he excitedly tore through the paper, he told her he had never received a gift that was wrapped. He opened the box and pulled out a new pair of leather work boots and some work gloves. She had no way of knowing that he would likely never wear the gloves, but he put the boots on as fast as he could manage. He stood up and proudly walked around the living room. The scene reminded Elaina of the Christmas when Jack gave David his first pair of bright red cowboy boots.

Lucinda was overcome as she held up the pink and purple cotton dress, followed by the large white apron with her name embroidered across the front. She put the dress neatly back in the box for use on Sunday's, then donned the apron immediately. "*Muchas gracias señora Elaina y señor doctor Jack,*" they both said through their bright smiles.

Elaina pulled another small box out from under the tree and handed it to Elizabeth.

"You didn't need to buy me anything," she protested.

"It's not much," Elaina said, "Just something Jack and I knew you could use."

She carefully unwrapped the package by pulling the taped edges apart rather than tearing through the paper. Her mother had been one of those women who saved everything, including wrapping paper, and that habit had obviously been passed down. As she opened the box, it contained still another smaller box surrounded by tissue paper. She carefully opened the second package and found a leather bound book containing bilingual children's bible stories.

"This is exactly what I have been looking for," she said excitedly. "I've looked everywhere in Costa Rica. Where did you find it?"

"I also looked at the book store in Managua, and didn't find anything, so when I saw this one on the Zondervan web site I ordered it directly from them. "I was planning to mail it to you along with that envelope," Elizabeth explained, "but, when you said you would come up for a visit, I decided to wait until today."

She carefully opened the white envelop and immediately started to cry. "Oh, Elaina, you didn't..."

"It is the least we can do," Elaina said, as a tear began to form in her own eye.

Elizabeth clutched the check to her chest and rose from the sofa. She made her way over to where her friend was sitting and threw her arms around her. "Thank you so much. I can promise you this will be put to good use."

"What is it?" Amy asked.

"It is a check to the orphanage for five thousand dollars!" Elizabeth said, through her joyful tears. "We were just talking last week about the cost of air conditioning our two classrooms. The director said he had received a bid of four thousand dollars, so in his words, 'it would take a miracle.' So, I guess this qualifies."

"We were so moved by your efforts in that orphanage," Elaina said, as she reached out to take Elizabeth's hand.

"It is truly God's work you are doing down there," Jack added.

Ben sat silently, amazed once more by still another side of the woman he felt attracted to more than ever. As she sat back down next to him, he instinctively reached for her hand, and she welcomed his touch.

"Well Ben," Jack said, "I couldn't think of anything to get you that you might be able to use back in Tokyo, so I decided to buy you something that you likely will never use. I hope it will, at the very least, broaden your knowledge of a topic, which many of us consider extremely important." He handed his brother a small package, trying his best to avoid smiling.

"Thank you... I think," Ben replied as he began removing the wrapping paper. "What in the world?"

"You don't have to drink scotch to appreciate the extraordinary nature of what the Scots call the water of life," Jack pronounced.

Ben carefully examined the book, and held it up for everyone to see. "It's a book titled *The Making of Scotch Whisky: A History of the Scotch Whiskey Distilling Industry* by Michael Moss. I can't imagine how I have managed to survive to this day without the knowledge I'm certain is contained in these pages," he said sarcastically.

Jack laughed and said, "read the inscription."

Ben turned to the inside cover and read, "To my learned brother. One can only hope that before your earthly days come to an end, you will find a way for that brilliant mind to reconcile indulging in at least one of the great pleasures life has to offer. On that list, a fine malt whisky ranks just below the love of a good woman."

Jack laughed again, knowing he had embarrassed his younger brother for the first time he could recall. Ben's face assumed a boyish smile as his cheeks gained an uncommon color.

"It has taken me fifty years, but I believe I've finally gotten you back for that practical joke you played on me at the University of Minnesota hospital."

Ben nodded in agreement, and said, "Indeed you did." He didn't dare look at Elizabeth for fear of revealing how much he had been thinking about the possibility of actually enjoying the thing his brother had named at the top of his list of life's greatest pleasures.

When the laughter subsided, Elizabeth asked about the prank Jack was referring to, but Ben just said, "I'll explain later."

Jack turned to her and said, "We're just having a little fun with Ben. Something he could stand to have more of."

Jack reached under the tree again and retrieved a small box and handed it to David. "This is from your mother and me, and its for both of you."

David had been standing next to Amy's chair. She scooted over to make room for him to sit next to her as he shook the box carefully in an effort to guess what was in it. From the extremely light weight and absence of any sound when he shook it he guessed, "It's either a tie, or it's money."

"Well, it's not a tie. Like I said it's for both of you."

He quickly removed the colorful wrapping paper from the long flat box. He pulled out an envelope, and opened it to find an official looking document. "What is this?" David asked, never having seen one before.

"That is the deed to my mother and dad's old house in Hurst," Jack said.

Amy almost squealed as she exclaimed, "A house?"

Jack added, "It is currently leased to a very nice older couple. It generates eighteen hundred dollars a month, and after taxes and maintenance costs it nets about thirteen fifty. Your mom and I figured you could use some extra income." Jack quickly added, "Now, if you decide to sell it, it's worth about a hundred and seventy-five thousand, but if you want my advice, I'd hang on to it and keep it leased. They say there's nothing like a steady passive income."

"This is unbelievable," David said. "First a new truck, and now a house? I don't know what to say."

"We know times are a little tough for y'all right now, and we hope this will help you kids get on your feet," Elaina said.

"You have no idea how much this means, Dad," David said. His unsteady voice emphasized the emotion of his words. "Especially now."

David turned to Amy and nodded his approval. She smiled as him, then looked directly at Elaina saying, "Right before we left to come down here I found out I'm pregnant."

Elaina's eyes widened as she almost screamed, "Really? You're going to have a baby?"

"That's what the doctor said last Thursday," David replied.

Elaina jumped to her feet and half stumbled over Jack's feet as she ran to the young couple. "This is the greatest Christmas present ever," she cried as she hugged them both. "When?"

"My due date is July tenth," Amy said proudly. "That is just a week or so after David starts his internship."

"Wherever that is," David added.

Elaina was so excited. She looked back toward Jack and said, "We're going to have a baby!"

He just smiled and nodded his head. He knew how much this meant to her. After they were married in 1990, they had tried to have another child, but for reasons that remained unknown to either of them, she had been unable to conceive. They had talked about adopting, but she wanted to keep trying to have Jack's baby. By the time it was clear that wasn't going to happen, she felt she was too old for the task of raising another child.

"I'm going to be a grandmother," she said to Elizabeth, trying to grasp the reality of the statement.

"That is wonderful," Elizabeth replied. She was once more truly excited for her friend, but again had to conceal her jealousy. Her son, Tommy, was now in his mid-thirties and had never married. She hated to admit it, but given his lifestyle, she knew he never would.

As Elaina's eyes met Lucinda, she saw that same smile she'd seen earlier in the day. "How did you know?" she asked her in Spanish."

"I knew the minute she came into this house," Lucinda replied. "She had a look about her, that comes to a woman only one way. When I heard her every morning in the bathroom, struggling with the sickness, I was sure."

****

"Are you ready?" Elaina called through the door.

"Almost," Elizabeth replied. She was finishing fixing her hair after changing into one of Elaina's dresses. Fortunately, they were close to the same size, despite the fact that Elizabeth was a couple of inches taller. She hadn't brought any nice clothes with her from her home, and she wasn't about to show up at the home of Franco Gutierrez wearing blue jeans or capris and a tee shirt. "What do you think?" she asked as she came out of Elaina's bathroom.

"You look great," Elaina replied. "That dress looks like it fits you better than it does me."

"Okay then, I guess I'm ready."

The Gutierrez estate was located southwest of the city, only about forty-five minutes from El Transito, and when they arrived at the gate just after sunset, the guard recognized Jack and quickly allowed them through.

"Was that a machine gun that guy was carrying?" Elizabeth asked, almost in a whisper.

"Yes," Jack replied. "Franco apparently has more than a few enemies. He didn't bother to add how the photo of him talking to that same guard had been instrumental in his losing his bid to become a United States Congressman.

As they made the final turn out of the heavily wooded area from the gate to the broad driveway that skirted the expansive front lawn, the huge house came into view. "Oh my God," Elaina gasped, "now I know why I couldn't find any outdoor lights. They're all here!"

The house was elaborately adorned with strings of white lights, outlining the roof, the perimeter walls and around every window and doorway. The driveway was defined by bright green lights, and the fountain was turned off and was outlined with red lights, while another group of white lights replaced the flowing water.

"That is spectacular," Elizabeth said.

"I suspect they had to run at least one additional electric service line to the house, just to supply the power to run all those lights," Ben offered, ever the practical scientist.

"I don't think he cares anything about that," Amy said. "I just wonder if anyone other than his family has even seen it."

"You have," Jack said, reminding her how fortunate they were to have been invited for this Christmas dinner.

The same three men that had greeted them the first time they visited this house came out to open the doors and Maria was there to greet them at the front door. "Señor Gutierrez will be with you in just a moment," she said without her usual smile. The seriousness in her voice made Elaina slightly uncomfortable.

"What's wrong?" Jack asked when we saw the look on Elaina's face.

"I don't know. Maria just seemed..."

"Hello my friends. Please come in," Franco said. His voice had a more business quality than Jack had heard before.

"Hi Franco," Jack said cautiously, as he shook his hand. "Is everything okay?"

"Yes, of course," Franco replied, trying his best to sound more festive. "Just a problem at one of my construction sights. Nothing for you to concern yourself over." He then turned to Elaina and greeted her, but she clearly detected an unusual tension in his more formal embrace.

"Hi, Mr. Gutierrez," Amy said as she stepped forward with David by her side.

Franco's smile warmed as he took her hand and gently drew her toward him, "Please, Amy, call me Franco. I'm so glad to see you again." He then turned to David and extended his hand, as he smiled and said, "and, the other Dr. Roberts."

"Well, not for a few more months," David corrected. "Thank you so much for having us all over this evening."

"Of course, of course," Franco said, again seeming to force a smile.

Jack stepped over next to Ben and Elizabeth. "This is my brother Ben Roberts and our dear friend, Elizabeth Burke." Jack didn't mean to imply that they were a couple, but the nature of his introduction certainly suggested as much.

Franco shook Ben's hand more formally and said, "Welcome, please come in. " He then turned to Elizabeth who was beyond nervous just meeting this man whom she'd been told was the most influential person in Central America.

"It is very nice to meet you, Mr. Gutierrez," she stammer just a bit.

"Please, I insist you call me Franco." His smile seemed to soften again as he used their handshake to gently guide her toward the main living room.

"Elaina told me what a magnificent home you have, but I wasn't prepared for this," she said, overwhelmed by the huge room and the massive painting on the ceiling.

"I'm sorry, but will you excuse me for just a moment," Franco said. "I have a brief matter I must attend to. Maria will get you whatever you'd like to drink."

Just as Franco turned back toward his study, Gabriella came into the room from the opposite side of the house, with Christina at her side. After the usual introductions she invited everyone to sit down again in the formal living area. Jack detected the same air of concern in Gabriella that he'd felt coming from Franco.

"I fear we may have come at a bad time," he said.

"No," she protested, "it has just been…" She didn't think it was her place to explain any further. "We are so glad you are here to help us celebrate Christmas."

Jack smiled cautiously, knowing that something was obviously bothering her, as well as her husband, but decided not to probe any further. "So how are you?" he asked Christina. She was now a rather gangly eight year old, who now seemed far more shy and reserved than she had when she was a young child.

"I'm fine, sir," she replied in her best English. She didn't leave her mother's side until Elaina held out her arms, asking for a hug. With Gabriella's encouragement she ran over to receive Elaina's welcome embrace.

"This is Christina," she explained to Elizabeth and Ben. She looked down at the beautiful young girl and said, "She is the reason we became friends with Franco and Gabriella."

As Franco returned to the group, it was clear he was even more upset. He looked at his wife whose face reflected her own concern. He frowned and shook his head slightly.

"What's wrong?" Jack asked. He had never seen his friend in such a somber mood.

"It is nothing," Franco said, trying to hide his concern.

"I have known you for many years, and something is obviously upsetting you," Jack said, in a sympathetic tone.

Franco knew that the festive evening Gabriella had planned was already ruined, so he might as well tell his friend about the accident. "Last night, one of my construction crews was involved in a major accident. One man was killed and four others are in serious condition in a hospital in Nicoya, Costa Rica."

"Oh my," Elaina gasped.

"What happened?" Jack asked.

"They were constructing a new hotel in the resort town of Timarindo, and I am told they were in the process of setting a major steel cross beam on the third story when an unexpected earthquake suddenly shook the area. The beam was not yet secured, and when the structure swayed, the beam slipped out of its support brackets, falling to the ground. It landed directly on the man who was supervising the job, killing him instantly. Four other men who were on the structure fell to the ground, sustaining major injuries."

"Do they have the facilities to care for them there?" David asked.

"Not really," Franco replied. "They considered transporting them back here to Managua, to the government hospital, but our facility is not much better than what they have there. I spoke with the local surgeon and he explained that the men are too badly injured to transport them at this time. He didn't hold out much hope that any of them would survive."

"That's terrible," Jack replied.

"I am planning to go down there tomorrow to see if there is anything I can do," Franco added.

"I would like to go with you, if that would be okay," Jack added quickly. He didn't even consider the fact that his brother would be leaving to go back to Japan in just a few days.

"I would very much appreciate your expertise," Franco replied. "I will be taking my private plane."

"Could I go, too?" David asked, never wanting to miss an opportunity to be a part of anything if his dad was involved.

"I don't see why not," Franco replied. "I was planning to fly down in the morning and return tomorrow evening."

David looked toward Amy in the hope of gaining her approval, even though he had already committed. She nodded without hesitation.

"You should spend the night here rather than driving all the way back to El Transito," Franco said. His mood seemed to lighten somewhat as he found something he thought he could control.

Elaina interrupted, "No, we can't stay." She turned to Jack and said, "None of us brought any of the stuff we need to spend the night, and besides, we really should get back home tonight. I have several things I need to do tomorrow."

In reality she didn't have any plans, but she was not comfortable imposing further on their host. Her words had a definitive tone that stopped Jack and

Franco from objecting further. Instead Jack asked Franco, "What time would you like for us to meet you at the airport?"

"I will come by and pick you up around seven in the morning."

"You don't need to do that."

"It is not that far out of my way," Franco exaggerated. "And, it will be much easier accessing the plane if we all arrive together."

"Okay, David and I will be waiting at the house."

After dinner, Jack and Franco retired to his study and they were quickly joined by David, as the women began discussing Amy's pregnancy and how grown up Christina had become. Ben sat quietly next to Elizabeth, holding her hand. They were becoming increasingly more comfortable in each other's company, but he seemed thoroughly bored as he shifted his weight repeatedly.

"Would you like to take a walk?" Elizabeth asked during a lull in the conversation.

"Sure," he agreed, and stood and moved quickly toward the back door.

Once they were out on the patio, she turned to him and asked, "Did you want to go with Jack and David tomorrow?"

"No, I would rather stay... with you." Ben's voice was almost childlike as he made it clear he didn't care to leave her, even if it was just for a day.

"That is so sweet."

"I only have a few more days before I'm scheduled to return to Japan, you know?"

"Yes, I know. I really need to get back home, too. I'm a little worried about that earthquake. The coastal region Franco mentioned is not that far from where I live." Over the last year and a half she'd felt a few minor tremors, but nothing that she would call a real earthquake. "I haven't heard anything from my friends back home, and I'm sure they would have called if there was any damage around where I live."

"Tell me about your house," Ben said, looking for a possible topic of conversation.

Elizabeth willingly went into an extensive description of the home she loved, as they walked, hand in hand, next to the pool and out into the garden. It wasn't long before they were well beyond where they could be seen from the house. A warm breeze stirred the trees around them, and the clouds drifted slowly across the moonlit sky, casting faint shadows across the flagstone path.

"I'm sure Costa Rica must be similar to Nicaragua. This is not at all what I envisioned when I agreed to come here to visit my brother," Ben said, as he looked around the grounds behind the huge mansion.

"I know what you mean," she replied. "For several years I refused to even consider going to visit my friends in Costa Rica, but they just kept badgering me, telling me how beautiful it was, until I finally said okay. When I got down there I absolutely fell in love with the place."

Ben found himself smiling, just listening to her talk about her new home and new country, especially when she added, "You should come down and see where I live."

He stopped and turned toward her, instinctively reaching forward, taking her other hand in his. "I would really like that."

Elizabeth smiled up at him, sensing just how truly naive he was when it came to women. She knew she risked rejection and perhaps humiliation, but she needed to know where this relationship was going. He clearly wasn't comfortable, so she decided to make the first move. She pulled her hands free and reached up, placing one on either side of his face. When he didn't pull away, she leaned forward and whispered, "I'd really like that, too." She kissed him softly at first, then pulled back to gauge his response. Ben's eyes had closed and he had a faint smile, so she repeated her advance, this time with a bit more aggression. As their lips touched again, she felt his arms reaching around her back. She allowed him to pull her body close to his as she put her arms around his neck.

As they broke the unfamiliar contact between their lips, Ben said "I'm not very experienced at ..."

"I know," she interrupted. "It's okay ..." He stopped her from saying anything more by resuming their kiss. He was somewhat clumsy, but tender, as she allowed him to assume the lead in this new romantic interplay. She found herself recalling an encounter with a boy back in high school. They were sitting on her parent's sofa, neither one knowing exactly what to do, but loving the feeling of being part of something new and exhilarating.

Ben pulled back again and looked into her eyes. He spoke softly as he innocently said, "I really liked that."

She grinned slightly, then said, "me too. I hope you're not finished."

He pulled her tighter to him and resumed their kiss, this time with more passion. She allowed her mouth to open slightly for the first time, which seemed to startle him as first. But he soon followed her lead as they melted into a more intimate oral embrace.

Ben and Elizabeth stood in the garden for nearly half an hour, before she finally said, "I think we better go back to the house."

"Okay," was his sad reply, the disappointment in his voice was obvious. He was really enjoying this new kissing experience. He placed his arm around her waist, drawing her near to him as they walked back up toward the lights of the pool until he saw Elaina waiting patiently at the door. He reflexively released his hold, creating some space between them, hoping his sister-in-law wouldn't suspect what she already knew.

"I thought I was going to have to come find you two," she said with a smile, satisfied that her earlier plan was finally working the way she had hoped. "We're about ready to leave."

On the way back to El Transito, Ben and Elizabeth sat quietly in the third row seat of the big Toyota, holding hands in the darkness. Amy laid her head against David's shoulder and was quickly asleep.

"So, what did you guys talk about?" Elaina asked.

"Not much," Jack replied. "I know Franco is really upset by the accident, so I was just trying to get his mind off it by talking about other stuff."

"Gabriella said he hadn't slept all night last night, and he originally planned to fly down to Costa Rica this morning to check on those men, but she told him he needed to be with his family on Christmas day. That's why he decided to wait until tomorrow to go."

"I'm certain he feels responsible for those men." Jack's voice was filled with a deep sadness for the man who had become one of his closest friends.

"Why?" she asked. "He couldn't very well control an earthquake."

"I know, but that doesn't change the fact that those men work for him and I'm sure he's thinking there was probably something he could have done to prevent their injuries."

"You men and your control issues," she sighed. "Sometime things just happen."

"Yeah, I know, and I'm sure it was, as you always say, for a reason, but, it's hard to find a reason for something like that. And, it doesn't matter whether there is a reason or not, guys like Franco always feel responsible." In this case Jack was talking about Franco, but she knew he wasn't any different. Long ago she had learned to accept the fact that he was, by his own admission, a control freak, and along with it came the tendency to blame himself for anything that didn't go perfectly.

By the time they got back to the house, it was after eleven, and Jack and David both said they were going to bed, anticipating an early morning and a long day ahead. Amy quickly followed David into the guest room.

"I'm going to walk Elizabeth back to her hotel," Ben said to Elaina, causing a smile to come across her face.

"Okay," she replied. "I'm going to bed too. I'll leave the light on over the stove and the back door unlocked."

Ben and Elizabeth walked out on to the deck, down the walkway and across the wooden bridge over the lagoon. When they reached the other side, Elizabeth took off her shoes and continued barefoot in the sand, while Ben continued in his loafers. They walked along holding hands like a couple of school kids, but as they made the familiar turn around the huge rock that had hidden the beach from view, Elizabeth broke the bond and hurried on ahead.

The half moon was low in the western sky, creating a shimmering band of brightness reflecting off the still, black water of the cove. In the darkness, Ben watched as this woman he barely knew ran playfully toward the water's edge, stealing the heart he scarcely knew he had. "Don't go too close to the water," he warned in a paternal voice, but not certain why.

She turned around in response to his voice, but continued to walk quickly backward toward the gentle surf and half shouted, "I feel like getting my feet wet. You wanna come?"

"No way, I'm not an ocean person."

"Oh, come on," she urged as she held the skirt of Elaina's dress up just above her knees and waded ankle deep into the warm water.

"I don't think so," Ben replied tentatively.

"What's the matter, are you chicken?" she teased as she kicked water a few feet into the air.

"I told you, I'm not an ocean person," he admitted.

Ben's only experience with the surf had been memorable for all the wrong reasons. When he was five years old his dad took the family to Stewart Beach on Galveston island. He had immediately been fascinated by the sight of the water, and as soon as he put on his swimming trunks he raced ahead of everyone else to the waters edge where he encountered one of the countless floating mollusks that had arrived on the tide earlier that morning. The purplish-blue, air-filled creature, commonly known as a Portuguese Man-of-War, was bobbing on the surface, and his curious mind would not be satisfied until he discovered for himself what it was. He reached out and grabbed it's irregular dorsal fin, plucking it off the top of the water, and as he did, the long tentacles that had extended beneath the surface brushed against the side of his bare legs. Within seconds he began to feel the effects of the chemical toxin that had been deposited on his young skin. He screamed in pain and through the monster back into the surf, causing one of the stringy appendages to rake across the front of his abdomen, adding to the incredible stinging sensation he was feeling. Almost immediately every point of contact with the tentacles elicited a raised, red streak on his skin. Fortunately a beach patrol officer had seen the incident from up on the seawall. and he ran to the young boys aid. He took him into a nearby restaurant and washed the areas with hot water. While the water was uncomfortable, the toxin was quickly rendered harmless by the heat and the pain soon subsided. His tender skin continued to show evidence of the attack for nearly a week, and even now, if he looked very closely he could still see the faint increased pigmentation in the skin in those small areas. While he now understood exactly what had happened, and why the shallow ocean posed no real threat, the psychological scar still lived in his subconscious fifty-five years later.

"Well, if you want me to get out, you'll just have to come out here and get me."

Her voice took on a sultry quality, designed specifically to tempt him, and it worked. He slowly pulled off his shoes and socks and laid them on the sand, then rolled up his trousers to the knee. He walked cautiously to the waters edge where he paused , no more than ten feet away from her as the tiny waves lapped against her lower calves.

"Come on," she said, growing impatient for his touch.

He took one tentative step into the darkness, as if it were a steaming hot bath, but once he got passed that first contact, he grew bolder and moved quickly into the salty water until he was standing in front of her. She continued to hold the hem of her skirt up with her elbows out away from her body, allowing him to slip his arms through and around her narrow waist. She laughed as he suddenly pulled her roughly into him, causing her to loose her grip on the skirt, allowing it to drop into the blackness around her legs. She threw her arms around his neck as he kissed her with more passion than she thought he possessed. Until that moment, she hadn't been sure exactly what it was she was feeling for this man, but the warmth she felt come over her entire body, as they stood there, wrapped in each other's arms, was unmistakable. It was a familiar sensation from what seemed a lifetime ago, A feeling she'd been certain had been lost forever.

He didn't say anything as he pulled her around until he was facing the shore and she was looking out toward the open ocean. He held her shoulders steady, just far enough away to see her face. The reflection of the moonlight off the moving surface of the water, danced across her skin, and made her blue eyes seem to sparkle.

"What are you thinking," she asked, more to break the silence than as an actual question.

"I was just thinking how beautiful you are," Ben said, his voice sounding more analytical than she'd hoped for, but at least the words were correct.

"Why, thank you," she replied as her gentle smile turned to a more cunning grin.

"Do you mind if we get out of the water now?" he asked.

She didn't answer, but simply took his hand and led him up on to the sand. With his free hand, he picked up his shoes and socks along with her sandals, as they began a slow stroll down the beach to her hotel.

"Would you like to get a cup of coffee?" he asked as they walked onto the hotel grounds.

"No," she said, pausing for effect before smiling and saying, "but, I would like a nightcap."

"Is the hotel bar open?"

"Are you kidding? This is a surfer hang-out. I don't think the bar ever closes."

They found a quiet table on the patio, well away from a small, but rather rowdy group of twenty somethings who had obviously been there for a while. When the waitress came to their table, Elizabeth ordered a vodka tonic with extra limes. When the woman turned to Ben, he wasn't sure what to say. Finally he said, "bring me a twelve year old Glenlivet scotch whiskey, neat."

Elizabeth smiled and let her head drop slightly. "I didn't think you drank alcohol."

"I don't, but my brother insists I expand my experience. He tells me I'm missing some of life's great pleasures."

When their drinks came, Elizabeth watched as he carefully sampled the straight whiskey. The look on his face told her all she needed to know. "I don't know what my brother thinks is so incredible about this liquid. It tastes rather smokey and burns the back of my tongue."

"I'm not especially fond of scotch either," she said. "Why don't you try this?" She handed him the tall glass containing the sparkling clear drink with several small wedges of lime suspended amid the ice cubes.

He took it from her hand and approached it with the same caution he had exercised in sampling the scotch. "This tastes more like a lime soda. Does it have alcohol in it?"

"Of course," she laughed.

"I think I could actually drink this." He handed it back to her, then turned to catch the attention of the waitress. When she returned to their table he said, "Please bring me one of those," as he pointed to Elizabeth's drink.

They sat quietly watching the drunken behavior of the other patrons, as they attempted to engage in some form of drinking game. "I would hope that I would have enough self control to avoid becoming that inebriated," Ben said as he took a generous sip of the citrusy drink.

"They're just having fun," she replied with a chuckle.

"That is something else my brother tells me I'm missing, but if that's what he's talking about, I think I'll pass."

She smiled as they watched the actions of the younger men, and wondered if he had ever allowed himself the freedom to do anything without first analyzing all the potential implications. His demeanor seemed so cool and calculating, yet at the same time quite vulnerable. He picked up the small glass of scotch that was still sitting in front of him and took another more generous sip.

"You know, this is not half bad," he said as he nodded his head slightly.

She laughed and said, "I think we should go before you decide to go challenge those guys to a drinking game."

He didn't think she was especially funny, but agreed he'd probably had enough. The waitress brought their check and Ben left more than enough cash on the table to cover the cost. As he stood, he didn't feel the effects of the alcohol at first. He was still thinking very clearly, but his legs seemed to react more slowly somehow. He bumped into the edge of the table as he stumbled slightly. She caught him by the arm and laughed again, drawing a questioning look as he quickly regained his balance. As they walked back to her room he said, "I'm not sure that I would classify the effects of alcohol among life's great pleasures."

She couldn't help laughing again, as they reached her door. "Are you laughing at me?" he asked in a very serious tone.

"No, no," she replied. "I was actually thinking how much I agree with you." She unlocked the door and turned toward him. His face reflected an innocent charm as he stood motionless in front of her. The previous evening, when he had walked her to her door, he had turned to leave as soon as she opened it, but not this time. They stood in the doorway for several moments before he reached for her hands as he had in Franco's garden, and drew her willingly to him. Her lips were more familiar now, and he felt less inhibited as the alcohol boosted his confidence. He found himself holding her tighter to him, fearing that she would somehow slip away if he relaxed.

Their embrace was interrupted by the sound of a small group of the drunken surfers coming up the narrow hallway toward them. "Let's go inside," she said, quickly stepping into the small, darkened room. He closed the door behind them, and stood silently for a moment, listening to the raucous banter of the strangers. It gradually faded as they stumbled down the hall.

When he turned around, he saw her silhouette standing near the bed a few feet away. A strange boldness and unexpected desire came over him, compelling him to advance toward what he hoped would be the other great pleasure his brother had mentioned.

He pulled her back into his arms, but didn't resume their kiss. Instead he looked into her cautiously smiling face, reflected in the faint light from a nearby street lamp that filtered in through the open window. "I suspect you know I'm not very experienced in this sort of thing."

"It's been a very long time for me," she whispered.

Other than a couple of blind dates that were both unmitigated disasters, she hadn't been alone with a man since her husband left her for another woman a dozen years ago. Ben had been so much younger than any of the other college students, he never experienced the dating scene. Later as he pursued his post-graduate degrees, he was too busy to even consider a social life. While at the Jet Propulsion Laboratory in Southern California, he went out with a couple of girls that his co-workers arranged, but he showed little interest. It wasn't until he went to Tokyo at age fifty-four that he had his first real experience with a woman.

In Japan, he lived a largely secluded life, but on occasion, Naryama and some of his business associates invited him to accompany them out on the town. He discovered the business world was quite different. Most of the men routinely drank heavily after a late dinner, then sought out the company of ladies of the evening. While Ben had always flatly refused the sake and other intoxicating drinks, he had been with a prostitute a couple of times, but he didn't find the experience particularly fulfilling. They were purely physical acts that he thought were rather pointless. There was none of the emotional energy he was feeling now, standing here with Elizabeth.

"Do you want me to leave?" Ben asked, releasing his grasp on her slightly, not sure what she meant by her reference to how long it had been.

"No," she replied quickly, moving her face closer to his. Then she whispered "I want you to... I... want you to stay with me tonight."

Ben kissed her more passionately, as she pulled herself tightly to him, pressing her pelvis aggressively into him. Their mutual arousal was now obvious as he slowly guided her to the edge of the bed.

****

The smells of fried bacon and fresh coffee wafted through the house as Jack joined Elaina and David in the kitchen. "Where's Ben," he asked as he sat down at the table.

"I haven't seen him this morning," she replied with a sly smile. Ben was typically an early riser and had been the first to sample Lucinda's coffee every morning since he'd arrived.

When Jack looked questioningly toward Lucinda, she simply shrugged, indicating she hadn't seen him either.

"You don't think he's still sleeping do you?" he asked, but quickly realized that wasn't the case as he looked down the hall and could see his bedroom door was standing open.

"The last time I saw him was last night when he left to walk Elizabeth back to her hotel," David said casually. "Maybe he decided to stay down there with her."

Jack looked at his son with a shocked expression, "I can't imagine..."

"I thought they seemed pretty tight," David added with a smile.

Jack's obvious surprise continued as he asked Elaina, "Do you think ...?"

"Like your son said, they seemed pretty, how was it you described it? - tight?"

David laughed, more at his dad's reaction than the thought of his uncle being romantically involved with the same woman who had, more or less, sanctioned his own sexual activities with Amy.

Before Jack could respond further he heard Franco's limo coming down the gravel driveway. "We better go," he said, leaning over to kiss Elaina. We'll be back some time this evening."

David quickly went down the hall and into the guest room where he found Amy just beginning to stir. "I'll be back this evening, okay?"

"I'll be here," she said, trying to take a few deep breaths to help control the nausea.

"I love you," he said as he kissed her on the forehead.

"I love you, too," she replied before adding, "you be careful down there."

"I will," he said with a boyish smile, then quickly ran out the door to join his dad and Franco. As he approached them, he couldn't help thinking how out of place the huge black limo with the uniformed driver appeared. The same thought returned to him as they made their way slowly through the streets of El Transito, all of which were in desperate need of repair. He watched as groups of barefoot children stopped their play and stared wide-eyed at the strange vehicle.

When they arrived at the airport, the limo was allowed to pass through a separate gate manned by two uniformed military guards. They drove to a private hanger where Franco's gleaming white jet sat ready for immediate departure. David's eyes grew as wide as those of the children he'd seen earlier when he saw the writing on the side of the airplane. It read Gutierrez Enterprises, Ltd. He stared a the colorful logo of an eagle soaring over twin volcanic peaks that covered most of the plane's tail, until Jack called out, "Let's go, buddy."

The interior of the luxury jet had been returned to it's standard, six passenger configuration, and David took the middle seat on the left side, while his dad sat behind him, across from Franco. In less than ten minutes they were airborne, headed due south toward a small landing strip in the mountainous regions of western Costa Rica.

"It will only take about twenty minutes for us to get to Nicoya," Franco said. "One of my men will meet us at the airport and take us to the hospital. After lunch I plan to visit the construction site. Its about a forty minute drive from Nicoya to the coast."

"Has your company experienced any previous accidents like this?" Jack asked.

"We have had a few incidents over the years, but never anything like this. A few years ago we had one of our older workers suffer a heart attack on the job, and he died the following day in the hospital, but other than that we have had no fatalities."

"Hopefully, your other men will recover." Jack wanted to sound optimistic, but he had no way of knowing the severity of their injuries, or the capabilities of the people who were caring for them. In the US, industrial accidents like this occurred with considerable frequency, but the system of ambulances and evacuation helicopters made it possible for most victims to reach a modern hospital with an experienced trauma team within a matter of minutes. The possibility of survival following any major accident depended on both variables, and here in Central America both were questionable.

The pilot had scarcely finished climbing out through twenty-eight thousand feet when he came on the intercom and announced, "We will be landing in about ten minutes, sir. The air is going to be a bit bumpy on our approach over the mountains. Please keep your seat belts fastened."

David was familiar with the clear air turbulence the pilot was referring to, having experienced it during their landing in Managua nearly a week earlier, however, he had never flown in a small jet like this one. As he looked out to his left, he could see the twin volcanic peaks of Concepcion and Maderas speeding passed, both seemingly suspended in the blue waters of Lake Nicaragua. As the plane began it's gradual descent, he could see another cone shaped peak coming into view.

Miravalles was geologically quiet, but the air around the inactive volcano was anything but still. As the pilot maneuvered the plane through the cloudless sky, they first encountered some choppy air, followed by a sudden drop of more than one hundred feet. The plane rocked forcefully from side to side, then seemed to rise suddenly, pushing him deep into his seat. David had experienced these kinds of random violent movements on the roller coasters of Six Flags back home, but at least there he could anticipate the direction of each dip or turn based on the tracks ahead. On this ride, the movements were totally unpredictable and far more frightening.

During one sudden drop, the plane shuddered and rocked over to the left giving David a clear view of the ground out the window before the pilot made the necessary correction. Without warning an opposite movement had him looking up into the deep blue sky before the wings leveled off again. He couldn't help but let out an audible groan as they suddenly dropped again toward the ground.

"You okay up there buddy?" Jack asked. He knew his son was gripping the arms of his chair tightly, blanching the knuckles of his hands, because he was doing much the same.

"Yeah, I'm okay, but I'm glad Amy didn't ask to come along."

Jack laughed, then groaned himself, as the plane rose suddenly on a thermal current. In the distance, David could see yet another volcanic peak rising from the lush green vegetation. Arenal was also considered inactive, but it had erupted as recently as fifteen years ago.

The pilot banked the jet to the west, away from the line of peaks that extended the length of Central America, and toward the Pacific Ocean. The air remained bumpy as they crossed the lower mountains of northwestern Costa Rica. As they made their final approach into Nicoya, there was one final sudden drop in altitude that took David's breath away. The plane quickly recovered, and soon he could hear the sound of the landing gear being lowered as their airspeed slowed significantly. Soon the familiar screech of the tires on concrete was welcomed by everyone on board.

When the plane was finally parked near a small private hanger, David released his seat belt and attempted to stand. He didn't realize how rubbery his legs were, as he seemed to collapse back into his chair. "Wow, that was quite a ride," he exclaimed.

Franco laughed and said, "You feel every bump in these small planes, much more than the larger commercial jets. I trust you are okay?"

"Yes , sir," he replied, "I'm okay, now."

****

The one story hospital was located on the main road that ran through the center of Nicoya. The three men made their way through the main entrance into a crowded waiting room. On the wall to their right was a sign designating that part of the building as an outpatient clinic, which also served as the emergency room. To the left was a hallway leading to the inpatient rooms.

As they made their way down the rather narrow corridor, the stark white walls smelled of fresh paint. They passed several doorways on their right. One labeled "Administración", another "Radiología", and then another "Laboratorio". Another long hallway extended to the right, beyond what was apparently the nurses station for the inpatient rooms that extended down either side. A solitary clerk sat with her back toward them, and Franco started to interrupt her, but Jack motioned for him to follow him toward a set of double doors at the end of the main corridor. The sign over the entrance read "Unidad de Cuidados Intensivos".

"I would assume your guys are in the ICU," he said.

"Yes, that is what I was told," Franco replied as he followed Jack's lead.

They approached the automatic doors, but they remained closed, and there were no handles that would allow them to be opened. Jack pushed the red button next to the small intercom on the wall next to the door, and in a moment a voice crackled through the speaker, "May I help you," the woman asked in a robotic tone.

"We are here to see the men who were brought in from the accident in Tamarindo," Franco replied loudly, not certain whether she could hear him through the old communication device.

"Visiting hours are from nine to ten, and two to three," the woman said without emotion.

"I am Franco Gutierrez," he insisted. "I have come from Managua to check on my employees. Please open this door immediately." Franco was not used to being kept waiting, especially by some minor functionary who was merely following some arbitrary set of rules.

Like everyone else in this part of the world, the clerk knew the name as well as the reputation, but she had her orders. "Just a moment, please." She called across the desk to get the attention of the head nurse. There is a man outside the door, demanding to see the trauma victims.

"I'll take care of it," she said, sounding frustrated by the interruption. She moved toward the entrance to the unit and touched a large silver colored button on the wall. The doors swung open, revealing the three men who quickly stepped through into the large room, containing six beds around the perimeter, all but one of which were occupied.

"Can I help you?" the nurse asked as the doors silently closed behind them.

"Four of my employees were brought here about thirty-six hours ago following an accident at one of my construction sites in Tamarindo. Can you tell me how they are doing?"

The nurse took a step toward Franco and extended her hand. "I am Mrs. Campos, the nurse in charge of this unit. Who are you?"

"My name is Franco Gutierrez, and this is my good friend Dr. Jack Roberts and his son, David."

The nurse was stunned by the presence of this famous man in her unit. She was unaware of his connection with the severely injured patients, not having known any of the specifics of the accident. "It is nice to meet you, Mr. Gutierrez," she said somewhat timidly, all but ignoring the other two men. "What can I do for you?"

"I have come to check on my four employees who were involved in the accident in Tamarindo."

Her face darkened and her eyes dropped slightly as she said, "I'm sorry to have to tell you that two of those gentlemen died last night. Their injuries were simply too severe."

Franco's shoulders slumped perceptibly before he gathered himself. "What about the other two?"

"One of the men just went into surgery again this morning. Dr. Velasquez took him back to the OR to wash out his abdomen again. He suffered a ruptured small intestine and a fractured liver, and the surgeon is doing what he can to save him."

"What about the other man?"

"He is over there, in bed three," she said, pointing at one of the occupied beds. "Dr. Velasquez operated on him for three and a half hours last night for a ruptured spleen, pelvic fracture and ruptured bladder. His blood pressure is still low and he remains on the ventilator."

"Is there anything I can do to help?" Jack offered.

"Not unless you're a surgeon," she said. "Dr. Velasquez has been operating almost continuously since these men arrived late in the evening on Christmas Eve. It's been nearly forty hours now," she said, looking down at her watch. "I'm sure he is extremely tired, but he is the only surgeon in this part of the country."

"I am a surgeon, and I would be happy to help. Just tell me where the operating room is, and I'll see if Dr. Velasquez wants me to lend him a hand."

"Right this way," she said, without hesitating.

Jack turned to follow her out through the double doors, then looked back toward David and said, "Come with me."

They walked briskly down an adjacent corridor to another set of doors marked "Cirugya". She tapped the silver button on the wall, and the doors swung open. Once inside, she found the supervisor and quickly explained that these two men were American surgeons who were offering to assist Dr. Velasquez.

The supervisor looked suspiciously at Jack, then said, "wait here please." In a few moments she returned from the operating room and said, "Dr. Velasquez said he needs a vascular surgeon."

"I have been a cardiac surgeon for more than thirty-five years, just show me where to change into some scrubs."

She continued to look at the American doctor with a questioning expression, but her surgeon had sounded desperate as he struggled to gain control of the bleeding his patient was experiencing. Somewhat reluctantly, she showed Jack and David the rather dimly lit change room, where they quickly put on the dark green scrubs, shoe covers and caps. When they emerged back into the surgical corridor the nurse handed them each a mask and showed them to the operating room.

"I'm sorry," she said, "I didn't catch your name."

"I'm Jack Roberts, and this is my son, David. He is a third year medical student back in Texas."

"Dr. Velasquez?" she called out to the surgeon who was hunched over the body on the operating table, working feverishly to control a major bleeding vessel.

"What?" he barked, obviously feeling frustration and near paralyzing exhaustion.

"This is Dr. Roberts. He says he is a cardiac surgeon and is offering to help."

The surgeon, who looked to be in his mid-thirties, looked up and said, "I could certainly use a hand. The left renal artery has torn away from the aorta, and I am not able to gain control of it."

"Just keep your finger on it, and I'll be right there."

Jack ran to the scrub sink and quickly went through an abbreviated version of the routine he had repeated thousands of times. He returned to the room and quickly dried his hands. As the nurse helped him put on his sterile gown and gloves he asked, "do you know the mechanism of injury?"

Velasquez looked up as Jack approached the left side of the table. The fatigue was obvious in his eyes as he said, "I operated on him early yesterday morning and repaired a ruptured area of the small bowel and packed off a fracture of the left lobe of the liver. At that time I didn't appreciate the injury to the left renal artery." As he finished his statement he looked back into the abdomen where his left hand was holding pressure against the artery to the left kidney. "He must have partially avulsed the vessel, but his pressure was so low when he came in it wasn't bleeding. I brought him back this morning to remove the liver packing and saw the expanding collection of blood in the retroperitoneum. It must have started bleeding when his pressure finally came up during the night."

"Let me take a look," Jack said as he took the suction in his left hand, and urged his colleague to remove his hand. When he did there was a sudden rush of bright red blood that quickly filled the small space before Jack could place his own finger over the hole in the aorta. He immediately determined that the artery had been ripped off the side of its parent vessel. Even under ideal circumstances this would be a difficult repair, and these were hardly ideal circumstances.

"I don't see any way we can save this kidney," Jack announced. He then turned to the anesthesiologist and asked, "Do you have blood available to give him?"

"I have given all we have," he replied. "We have sent for more, but it will be several hours before it arrives from San José."

"How is his pressure right now?"

"It is one hundred over fifty, and his heart rate is one hundred ten. I am giving fluids as rapidly as I can."

"Okay," Jack said, "We should be able to get this under control in a few minutes. You might start him on a dopamine drip and back off just a bit on the fluids. I don't want to see him go into pulmonary edema."

Jack was suggesting the use of a medication to support his blood pressure that would promote better blood flow into his remaining good kidney and allow the use of less intravenous fluids. Hopefully they had that medication available because this man was now at high risk of multi-organ failure, starting with his lungs. Giving too much fluid at this point could prove irreversible, even if he was able to stop the bleeding.

"Do you have any vascular clamps?"

"Yes," the scrub nurse replied. She brought a tray of clamps up from the table behind her, showing Jack precisely what he had available. Jack pointed to a couple of large vascular clamps, a needle holder and a pair of forceps he thought he could use.

"How about some vascular suture?"

"I have both two-o and three-o prolene."

"Do you have any Teflon pledgets?"

"I don't know what that is." Her reply was not what Jack had hoped for.

"Do you have a vascular graft?"

"Yes, sir. I think so." she said, then turned to the circulating nurse and asked her to go to the store room and bring her the small basket of tubular plastic grafts that could be used to replace various diseased blood vessels. Another surgeon had visited their hospital once, long before Dr. Velasquez came to town, and he had insisted they order them, but they had never been used. She wasn't certain whether the sterilization had expired or not.

As he waited for the nurse to return, Jack looked up into the face of the other doctor. Now that he no longer held the patient's life in his hands, the surgeon had closed his eyes, and Jack feared he was on the verge of collapsing. "David, go scrub your hands and come help me," he said. There was no reaction from Velasquez, so with his free hand he reached across the table and gently took hold of his arm. "You need to go sit down my friend. I've got it from here."

Velasquez was totally exhausted. Now, relieved of his duty, he staggered back from the table. He made it as far as the wall, but as he leaned against it he slowly sank to the floor. He had put forth an almost superhuman effort, finally exceeding the limits of what his body could endure.

David put on the gown and gloves the way he had been instructed during his recent rotation on obstetrics service at Parkland. He stepped up to the table and asked, "what do you want me to do?"

"Just hold that retractor and keep the bowel out of the way, and use the suction to keep the area free of blood the best you can."

Jack placed one of the large vascular clamps completely across the aorta above the left renal artery and a second one across the same huge vessel below the injury. He placed a third clamp across the renal artery before removing his finger from the sight of the injury.

"When this guy fell from the platform and hit the ground, his body stopped suddenly, but the motion of the kidney continued, causing the vessel to be torn by the force," Jack explained. As he suspected, there was no possibility of repairing this injury, so he quickly divided the remaining portion of the vessel and used the sutures to close the hole in the side of the aorta. He reinforced the sutures with small pieces of woven Dacron material he had trimmed from one end of one of the grafts the nurse had located.

As soon as the hole was closed he removed the clamps from the aorta to restore the flow of blood to the lower part of the man's body. The removal of the kidney was routine, and Jack managed to finish the operation in less than twenty minutes. He looked around the rest of the abdominal cavity and saw that the liver was not bleeding and the repair of the ruptured intestine appeared to be intact.

"This reminds me so much of my days on the trauma service back when I was a resident."

David watched as his dad quickly closed the long midline incision. He helped by cutting the sutures as Jack tied them. Under other circumstances Jack would have insisted that the student tie the sutures, but this was not a training opportunity. Getting this man off the operating table as quickly as possible was the sole objective. When the dressing was finally applied, he helped his dad remove the sterile drapes and move the patient on to a stretcher for transfer to the recovery room. As David helped the anesthesiologist roll the patient out, his dad went over to check on Dr. Velasquez.

He couldn't just leave him sleeping on the floor, but it was clear his colleague wasn't going to stand on his own. "Can you find me a wheelchair?" he asked the scrub nurse. In a few minutes she returned and helped Jack lift the still groggy surgeon into the chair, then wheeled him out of the room that had been the sight of his ultimate effort.

"Where is Dr. Velasquez?" asked the recovery room nurse.

"He is asleep in one of the patient rooms." Jack offered with sympathy. "He is completely exhausted. He needs to sleep for a few hours."

Jack wrote some orders for the nurses to follow, and once he was sure the patient was stable he made his way back to the intensive care unit. He found Franco sitting quietly beside the bed of his other surviving employee. As he approached Franco rose to his feet and asked, "how is he?"

"Barring any further setbacks, I think he may survive."

"I'm afraid this man is not doing as well," Franco said sadly. "The nurse tells me his blood pressure is continuing to drop."

Jack stepped over to the patient's bedside and did a quick assessment of the unconscious trauma victim. Unlike what he was used to, there was no electronic monitor to display his pulse rate and blood pressure. Instead, the nurse recorded the vital signs on a clipboard that was suspended from the foot of the bed. He saw that his blood pressure had been steadily dropping since he arrived back in the ICU nearly six hours earlier. Over the same period his pulse rate had steadily increased. His urine output was also very low. Jack examined his abdomen, and it was obviously distended and very tight. He turned and spoke as much to himself as to the nurse. "This man has developed abdominal compartment syndrome. Unless we decompress his abdomen soon, he is going to die."

"What do you mean?" Franco asked.

"His internal injuries have caused fluid to accumulate in his abdominal cavity and at the same time the intestines are acutely swollen. There just isn't enough room in there, and as the pressure builds it impairs blood flow to the liver, kidneys and intestine. If it's allowed to continue, all those organs will begin to fail and he will die."

"Can you do something to stop it?"

"He needs to go back to the OR, and Dr. Velasquez is in no condition to operate on him or anyone else right now."

"Why don't you do it?"

"I would, but I don't have privileges to practice in this hospital. In fact I probably violated Costa Rican law even helping with the previous operation. If I were to take over the care of this patient it would certainly be outside the medical practice laws of this country." Jack just shook his head, not sure how he would even go about getting the hospital personnel to agree to let him take this patient to the OR. "But, if I don't, he's not likely to live."

Franco stepped out into the hallway and pulled out his cell phone to make a call back to Nicaragua. After a couple of minutes he returned to the room, where

Jack was reassessing the patient's abdomen. David had joined his dad at the bedside and was getting yet another first hand lesson in trauma surgery, as Jack explained the reason for his rapidly deteriorating condition.

"So, why don't we just take him back to the OR?" David asked in frustration.

"Without a license to practice in this country, it would be considered assault"

"Even if it's the only way to save his life?" David asked.

"The laws are very clear, and they're written to keep unqualified people from calling themselves doctors and doing things that could potentially harm the most vulnerable."

"But you're probably more qualified than anyone in this country," David said disgustedly.

"They don't know that, and..."

"Dr. Roberts?" the nurse asked as she interrupted Jack in mid-sentence. "There is a phone call for you at the desk."

Jack looked at her with a questioning expression, then he followed her to the nurses station in the center of the room.

"This is Jack Roberts," he said.

"Dr. Roberts, this is Juan Diego-Mendez, the Minister of Health here in San José. I understand you are an American surgeon, is that correct?"

"Yes, sir."

"I also understand that there is a patient in the hospital there in Nicoya in need of life saving surgery."

"That is correct. Unfortunately, Dr. Velasquez has been operating on a group of trauma victims for nearly two days without any rest, and he is not capable of performing the procedure."

"Based on a call that I received from my friend, the Nicaraguan Minister of Health, I would like to extend an emergency temporary medical license to you."

"That is very kind of you, sir. I'm not certain this man will survive, even with an operation, but it is the only chance he has."

"If you will give the phone back to the nurse, I will tell her of my decision."

"Thank you, Minister," Jack said before handing the phone back to the nurse in charge.

As he returned to the bedside, he spoke to his son. "Well, once again, Mr. Gutierrez here has proven that at times it's far more important who you know, than what you know."

"What do you mean?" David asked, as he noticed his dad smiling at Franco.

"Our friend here has pulled a few political strings and secured an emergency temporary license for me to take care of this patient." He pointed an accusing finger in his Franco's direction.

Within less than thirty minutes the patient was back in the operating room, and Jack opened his abdomen with David assisting again. He was glad to see there wasn't any active bleeding, and as soon as the incision was open his blood pressure and pulse rate improved dramatically.

The problem would almost certainly recur if he simply sewed the muscle layers back together, and he was certain that they didn't have any of the new biologic mesh materials that would allow him to cover the internal organs without tension. Instead, he chose to bridge the gap using a plastic IV bag. He emptied the sterile fluid into a basin on the back table, and split the clear polyethylene material along one side. He then sewed the plastic to both sides of the incision. He made no attempt to close the skin incision, but instead just covered the area with a sterile towel. and a loose abdominal binder. He anticipated Velasquez would bring him back to the OR in a few days to close the abdomen, once the swelling had resolved.

Jack looked across the table and said, "I'd say you've had a rather educational day."

"Thanks so much for allowing me to be a part of this," David said. "I can't imagine how you must feel, having personally saved the lives of these two men."

"This isn't about me, son. This is God's work we do. I just wish there was something that could have been done to save those other two men who died last night."

CHAPTER 19

"Come out here!" David exclaimed, calling into the house through the back door. "You guys have to see this."

Amy and Elaina were busy looking at baby furniture on Jack's computer in the guest room, but they reluctantly left the digital images of cribs and strollers and walk out on to the deck. Even through the windows they could see the source of David's excitement, but once the view was unobstructed the magnificence of the sunset was beyond description.

"Oh my God," Amy gasped. "That's incredible."

"We have gorgeous sunsets here almost every day," Elaina said slowly, "but, I don't think I've ever seen one like that. It's overwhelming."

"You should take a picture," Amy said, breaking the spell the colorful spectacle seemed to have cast on her young husband.

"Absolutely," he said before running into the house to retrieve his camera. When he returned he set it up carefully on the railing. He hadn't brought his tripod, so the wooden railing would have to do. He quickly began taking images in rapid succession, each one only minimally different than the one before.

"Why don't you just video it instead of taking all those still pictures?" Amy asked.

"That would be boring," he said. Then after taking two more pictures he said, "I've got an idea." He pulled out his cell phone and selected the stop watch application. For the next thirty minutes the camera remained stationary as he took one image after the other every two seconds. "This is going to be so cool," he added.

In the fading light of the late December evening, David took the last image of the most amazing combination of colors and shapes he had ever witnessed. As soon as the final image was stored on the camera's sim card, he made his way back into the house.

"Aren't you going to eat supper with us?" Elaina called to him.

"Yeah, I'll be there in just a minute." He disappeared into his room and began the process of downloading all nine hundred images into his MacBook Pro lap top. Since it was going to take a few minutes, he decided to join the rest of the family at the dinner table.

"What were you doing out there on the deck?" Jack asked.

"You'll see," David replied.

Jack then added, "I thought you might like to know, I got a call this afternoon from Dr. Velasquez down in Costa Rica. He said both of our patients are doing great. He's anticipating taking that second guy back to the OR tomorrow to close his abdominal wound, now that the swelling has resolved."

"That's great," David responded. "It's only been three days."

"Typically those situations resolve pretty quickly, provided you get to them before the liver and kidneys are damaged."

"Where's Uncle B?" David asked.

"He's down at Elizabeth's hotel, helping her pack her suburban," his mom explained. "She's planning to leave in the morning to go back to Costa Rica."

"When is he planning to leave for Japan?" David asked.

"I don't know. He didn't say."

"He really seems to like Elizabeth, huh?" David offered.

"I think the feeling is mutual," Elaina agreed. "They seem to have hit it off right from the start."

"I'm really glad," David said in a satisfied tone.

"Yeah, I think he needs someone like her in his life." Elaina didn't mention that getting the two of them together had been her plan all along, but from the tone in her voice it was clear she was happy about the way things were working out.

"Like you always say," David said, as he looked up at his father, "life is about achieving balance, right?"

"Absolutely," Jack smiled, satisfied that the lesson seemed to have been well learned. "I think you're about to have that concept tested in your own lives, very soon."

Amy and David looked at each other and nodded, believing they understood exactly what would be required of them during the last few months of medical school and the transition to internship. What they weren't factoring in was the challenges of her pregnancy.

****

"I'm not comfortable with you driving back to Costa Rica by yourself," Ben announced as they sat in the hotel bar watching the sun go down and sipping on yet another vodka and tonic with extra limes.

"Don't be silly," she laughed, "I drove up here by myself, didn't I?"

"Yes, but that was before I knew you." Since that first night together in her room, Ben had been struggling with how to deal with their rapidly approaching separation. He couldn't rationalize changing his plan to fly back to Tokyo on Tuesday, but he also couldn't imagine watching her leave on Monday without him. He had never experienced these kinds of emotional distractions. He was finding it difficult to concentrate on anything except this woman. What was wrong with him, he wondered.

"I'll be just fine," she said. "It's only about six hours, assuming I don't have any problems getting across the border."

"But what if you have car trouble? Even just a flat tire?"

"I can change a tire," she insisted.

"I just can't imagine you on the side of the road, jacking up that huge truck and trying to remove the lug nuts. Even if you were able to get the tire off, I don't think you could lift the spare to get it onto the hub, and ..." He just shook his head and looked back out toward the ocean.

"So what do you propose I do?"

"I think I should go with you." For several days he'd been trying to find of way to ask her if he could go back to Costa Rica with her. He hadn't anticipated it would come out in such a demanding sounding way.

Elizabeth smiled and sat back in her chair. "Why didn't you just ask if you could come home with me?"

Ben sighed and said, "Because, I was afraid you'd say no."

She smiled broadly and reached forward to take his hand away from this drink. "I can't imagine anything I'd like better."

****

"Come take a look at this, dad," David called from the guest room.

Jack put down the book he was reading and walked toward his son's voice. "What have you got?"

David just sat back as he pushed the play button on the QuickTime movie he had just completed. The incredible sunset they had just witnessed that evening seemed to come alive. The huge black rocks in the foreground created an irregular horizon the served as a sharp contrast to the rays of yellow and orange against a complex network of irregular clouds. As the thirty minutes was compressed into thirty seconds the brilliant rays that seemed to emanate from behind the rocks seemed to flicker back and forth as they gradually faded away, leaving behind the pink, red and orange clouds against the cerulean blue background. The whole image was reflected in the still water of the lagoon in the foreground. As the celestial blue rapidly melted into a pale yellow then to a deep purple, the colors in the clouds near the horizon also morphed into more subtle shades of magenta, lavender, and garnet. Eventually most of the colors faded to deep blues and grays, but the tops of the highest clouds retained their peach and orange hues, capped with a narrow, glorious golden ribbon.

"Wow!" Jack exclaimed. "That was beautiful."

"I'm going to post it on YouTube and then link it to my Facebook page. It will be interesting to see what kind of response I get."

Like most young people, David had more than eight hundred Facebook friends, and given the holiday season, most of them were spending even more time online than usual. Within thirty minutes of posting his video, he had more than one hundred "Likes" and almost that many of his friends had shared what had come to be called "The Greatest Sunset - EVER."

"You're not going to believe this," David said as he sat down at the breakfast table the next morning.

"What?" Jack asked.

"That video of the sunset... It's been viewed more than nine thousand times."

"Really? How did that happen?"

"Hey, it's the Internet. Once it was up on YouTube it became available to the whole world. My Facebook friends shared it with their friends, and within a few hours people were watching it all over the world."

"How do you know that?" Jack asked, not believing what his son was saying.

"I went to my YouTube account and used the analytics to see how many times it was watched, the age and gender of the people watching it, and what country they live in."

"I had no idea you could do that." Jack was clearly aware of social media, but since his campaign he hadn't bothered to even look at his old Facebook or Twitter accounts.

"Anybody can track what's going on with anything they upload on the web. Its really pretty easy,' David said.

"How much time do you spend online in any given day?" Jack asked.

"I don't know, a couple of hours, I guess."

His father was stunned. "I can't believe you're wasting that much time everyday."

"I'm not wasting my time," David objected. "I use the Internet to look stuff up, and to buy stuff, and to communicate with people about all sorts of things. It's not like I'm sitting around playing video games all day."

"What about school?"

"A few of the younger professors have their lectures online, but most of the older ones don't even do email. It's really inconsistent. I wish it was all online. Things would be a lot easier."

Jack hadn't asked about the availability of medical school lessons online. He was more concerned that his son was spending too much time on the computer and not enough time reading. "Don't you think those two hours a day on the Internet could be better spent reading and studying?"

David just looked at his dad for a moment, trying to understand why his dad thought he was wasting time, then he responded. "The time I spend on the Internet makes me more productive than I could ever be if I had to get in the car and drive to the bookstore or the computer store every time I need something. And I can't imagine how long it would take me to sit down and write a letter and mail it to people I need to communicate with. My computer and the Internet have made it possible for me to be far more productive than I could ever be otherwise."

"I guess I can see that," Jack admitted reluctantly.

"Some of my friends are online almost all the time. They tell me that virtually everything they need to do their jobs is available on the web. Like I said, I wish medical school was that way."

"I don't know. I think there's a lot to be said for listening to a live lecture or sitting down with a textbook."

"There's nothing that says those things can't be done online, dad," David said, sounding a bit frustrated. "I just think the old professors don't want to change. They've been teaching the same way forever, and to tell the truth, its not all that inspiring."

"Those teaching techniques have worked pretty well for a long time," Jack replied.

"That may be," David said, "but, it doesn't mean they can't be improved. With all the cool digital technology that's available, I think medical school could be taught much more effectively than it is now."

What David was saying began to strike a cord with his dad. He had often said that this new generation was more interested in being entertained than they were in being educated. The fact that thousands had already taken the time to watch David's latest video online was clear evidence of that truth.

"You're probably right," Jack admitted, "but I don't know how you'd go about making pharmacology entertaining."

"I do," David announced. "I think it would be easy to use 3-D animations to show the various molecular structures and how they interact with either normal or abnormal physiologic processes. For me, seeing something like that would be far more effective. Of course, I'm a visual learner."

Jack smiled broadly as he heard his son saying almost exactly what he was thinking. The reason why he had hated pharmacology but loved anatomy was the visual nature of what was being taught. "I remember to this day looking through that huge window, watching Dr. Lillihei replace that aortic valve. The heart didn't look anything like what I had imagined. It was inspiring because I could see it."

"That's what I'm talking about," David said, trying to emphasize his point. "I learned more about the physiology of trauma the other day, watching you down in Costa Rica than I ever could listening to some lecture."

"That may be," Jack said, "but not everyone can have that sort of opportunity."

"Why not? Nearly ten thousand people have already been able to experience that sunset yesterday, and potentially be inspired by it. And, they didn't even need to leave their homes." David paused for a moment as he made a few key strokes on his computer, then he added, "now it's up to fifteen thousand."

Jack just shook his head and smiled at his son's compelling argument.

****

The dark blue suburban pulled up to the front of the house, and Ben got out of the drivers side, as Elizabeth opened the passenger side door.

"Are you all set?" Elaina asked as they entered the house.

"Not quite," she said with a hesitating grin.

"I need to get my stuff together," Ben offered as he made his way passed her and into the room he hadn't slept in for the last five nights.

"What?" Elaina asked with sly smile.

"He's going to drive down to Costa Rica with me," Elizabeth said dryly. She was trying unsuccessfully to hide her excitement.

Jack came in from the backyard where he had been talking to Federico about his plan to put a railing on the bridge over the lagoon. "Are you leaving us?" he asked Elizabeth, already knowing she was planning to depart that morning.

"Yes," she said, "as soon as your brother gets his things together."

Jack's eyes widened as he exclaimed, "Ben's going with you?"

"It was his idea," she replied. "I told him I would be just fine, but..."

"I just want to make sure she gets home safe," Ben announced without emotion as he came out of the spare room that also served as Jack's office, carrying his suitcase and briefcase.

"So, how are you getting back to Tokyo?"

"I'll get a flight out of San José."

Jack wanted to ask when, but he thought better of it, not wanting to put either of them on the spot. "Well, I guess we'll see you when we see you."

"I'll be in touch," Ben assured his brother, "and I'll let you know if I hear anything more concerning those clinical trials."

Ben stepped forward and gave his brother a clumsy, one armed embrace before repeating the same with David and then Amy. When he approached Elaina he put his suitcase and briefcase on the floor before leaning over to give her a big hug. He whispered softly in her ear, "Thank you. I know you were behind this."

As he released her she held his arms briefly and said, "I am so happy for you." Then she kissed him quickly on the cheek before turning to hug Elizabeth.

"Thanks for allowing me to join your family Christmas. It really means a lot."

Elaina thought about suggesting once more that she was part of the family, but thought she'd better wait until Ben made that decision. Instead, she just said, "You guys be careful."

"I'll call you when we get there this evening," Ben offered as he put his things in the back seat, before opening her door. Jack couldn't help but smile again as he watched his brother's actions. almost as if he were watching a couple of teenagers going off to their first prom together.

The small group watched as Ben pulled away, disappearing quickly down the gravel driveway and onto the street. Elaina turned to Jack and said, "Are you still mad at me for inviting her?"

He laughed slightly and said, "No, I think you're brilliant. They are perfect for each other."

****

"You told me a little bit about your son," Ben said as they made their way onto the Pan American Highway, "but you haven't said anything about his father."

She hadn't anticipated being interrogated about her past during their six hour drive, so she decided to keep her answers short and sweet. That way, hopefully he would soon grow tired of asking. "He was a tax attorney."

"So what happened? Why did you get a divorce?"

"Twelve years ago I caught him cheating on me with his secretary, and so I threw him out."

"How long had you been married?"

"Twenty years."

"Is Tommy your only child?"

"Yes," her voiced developed a sad tone as she added, "I was pregnant one other time, about two years after Tommy was born, but my little girl was still born."

"I know that must have been difficult for you," Ben said, not recognizing just how devastated Elizabeth had been when the doctor told her he could not hear the baby's heartbeat after she'd carried her for almost thirty weeks.

"Yes, it was. Do you think we could talk about something else?"

"Of course," Ben said, realizing he had accidentally opened an old wound. "What would you like to talk about?"

"Why don't you tell me about you?"

"Okay, what would you like to know?"

"Well you could start by telling me what it's like being so smart."

"I don't think about it," he said. "I have no other perspective beyond my own, so to me it is normal."

"Well, trust me. It's anything but normal."

"Only recently did I come to understand why you might feel that way."

"How's that?"

"After listening to you singing the other day, I realized what it feels like to be around someone who can do something I can't imagine doing myself."

She laughed, saying, "Singing hardly compares to astrophysics."

"I know," Ben replied, seriously. "Singing is much harder."

She laughed again, even more loudly, while Ben's face remained stoic. He was very serious, and every time she looked over at him she laughed even harder.

"I don't know what it is you find so funny. I'm being completely serious."

"I know you are," she said, through her sympathetic smile. "I'm sorry. I wasn't laughing at you. I just disagree with your comparison."

"You have your talents and I have mine. I don't see the difference."

"Okay, you win," she offered in hopes of returning to a more rational discussion. "I started this with my silly question."

"I don't think you're silly. I think your very intelligent. That's part of why I like being with you."

"You're very sweet," she said, her smile turning to a soft pout, as she reached across the console with her left hand and gently touched his right arm. "Why don't you tell me about your childhood?"

Ben began relating the story of his congenital heart problem, and how he had undergone an operation as a one week old baby, and another at age nine. He obviously had know recollection of the first procedure in Baltimore, but he remembered vividly his experience in Minneapolis. He then explained how he had been home schooled by a collection of tutors, allowing him to complete the entire high school curriculum when he was just thirteen.

Elizabeth sat quietly listening to Ben talk about his relationship with his brother, and the love and admiration he had for him was obvious. As he started talking about beginning college at Stanford, she was surprised at the sadness in his voice. "Was it hard for you to be so far away from your family?'

"Yes, it was," he replied. "I've never told anyone this before, but for the first year I was there, I cried myself to sleep almost every night." Ben wasn't sure why he was telling her this long held secret, but for some reason he was no longer embarrassed by it.

"Were you living alone on campus?"

"No, I was living with one of the physics professors and his wife. They had agreed to act as my guardians, and they made sure I got back and forth to my classes. They were both very helpful in that regard." His voice was hesitating, and betrayed the fact that there was clearly more to the story.

"So, you were only thirteen and going to Stanford studying astrophysics, living with a couple of strangers?" She wanted to add, no wonder you didn't develop a social life, but thought better of it.

"Yes, I had a very unusual childhood, and by the time I got my PhD in aerospace engineering I was still only eighteen. I got an offer from the guys at JPL. They insisted that I come to work there on the Mariner projects."

"What is JPL?" she asked innocently.

"The Jet Propulsion Laboratory," he said, not realizing she had no idea what he was talking about, other than it sounded incredibly important. "I started working on the Mariner spacecraft project."

She seemed fascinated by the way he spoke so casually about space probes she only vaguely remembered from her own childhood. "I was only twelve years old," she said in amazement.

Her interruption made him stop and smile. Then, sensing her interest, he continued. "When I first got to JPL in 1970, they were about to launch two spacecraft, Mariner eight and nine, that were designed to fly around Mars and map the surface for future landing missions. Unfortunately, eight was destroyed during launch, so only one probe ultimately had to do the work designed for two. Mariner nine was successful, to a degree, but it could have been so much more effective had it had it's partner. Ultimately it was turned off once it had sent back all the information it was capable of providing, but its still out there, just circling Mars. Eventually it's orbit will decay and it will crash into the Martian surface."

Elizabeth smiled softly, wondering if he were subconsciously referring to himself, and a lifetime of living and working alone. "Speaking of partners, why didn't you ever ..."

"Why didn't I ever get married?"

She nodded and innocently said, "I was just wondering."

"I have spent my entire life either going to school or working. There was never any time to pursue anything else. I went on a few dates with a co-worker while I was at JPL, but other than work, we had nothing in common, and she was eight years older than me." His voice was casual, but again it reflected an inner sadness that she found tragic. "I guess the biggest reason was the right woman never came along."

"I'm sorry," she half whispered, as if she was about to cry.

"Don't be," he insisted. "I've had a very rewarding life. I don't think I would change anything, even if I could."

Ben went on to tell her how he became bored with the precision mathematics of space flight, so he decided to leave JPL after just a couple of years. He went back to school, this time at MIT. He received a grant from the National Institutes of Health to study the budding new field of Bioengineering. By the time he was twenty-four he had received his second PhD, and was quickly hired by one of the big medical device manufacturers in Southern California.

"Over the next twenty-five years I worked for more than a dozen different companies," he said. "I helped develop everything from new hip prostheses to those intrauterine devices that prevent pregnancy."

"How did you end up in Japan?" she asked.

"About eight years ago I was working for a company that was developing robotic technology for use in surgery, and I was approached by a man by the name of Shinti Naryama. I don't know how he found me, but he told me about a concept he wanted to pursue that involved robotically controlled catheters to perform surgery inside the heart. It sounded crazy, but after thinking about it I told him I thought it might be possible. He offered me a significant stake in the company and total control of the development process if I would move to Tokyo, and I've been there since."

"I know what it's like to move off to a foreign country, all alone," she said. "I moved down here to Costa Rica by myself, five years ago. I had a couple of friends, and I knew enough Spanish to get by, but I didn't really know anything about the country or the culture."

"You are obviously a very courageous woman," Ben replied.

She had never thought of herself as courageous. Impulsive and reckless were words she would use to more accurately describe her actions. "I don't think so."

"Well, I do," he replied. "I greatly admire the fact that you took the initiative to set out on your own, to live the life you wanted to live. Not many people are willing to do that."

As he was describing her life, she wondered if he had any idea how lonely she felt most of the time. When she made the move to her tropical paradise, she was sure she'd have visitors coming and going all the time. She soon discovered that wasn't the reality she had experienced. Her son came down for one week each summer, but only because she paid for his airfare. Her old friend from high school had come down once, but didn't stay long because of the heat, and Jack and Elaina had visited once, a year and a half ago. No one else had even seen her house, despite numerous invitations to friends back in Texas. If it weren't for her work at the orphanage she certainly would have sold the place and moved back to Brownsville two years ago.

****

It was the last night in Nicaragua for David and Amy, and Jack had asked Domingo, Felicia and their son, Rafael, to join them for a New Years Eve party, one day early. The young neurosurgery chief-resident had come home for a few days over the holiday, and his parents were anxious to show him off to the Roberts family.

"Come in, please. Make yourselves at home," Elaina said, as the trio came to the front door. Rafael was now a dashing thirty-one year old man, with jet black hair and dark eyes. He was several inches taller than his father, standing nearly five ten, and he had a more muscular physique than the last time she had seen him. She hugged him warmly and said, "What's it been Rafael, ten or eleven years?"

"I believe the last time was when I was home for a month during the summer after my third year of college. You and Dr. Roberts were visiting my parents."

"Please, it's Elaina and Jack."

"Very well, if you insist."

"I would like to introduce you to our son, David, and his wife, Amy."

"It is very nice to finally meet you," David said, as he shook Rafael's hand.

Rafael's face had a quizzical expression as he said, "It is good to meet you as well."

"I feel like I already know you. Your mother told me all about you, and I actually stayed in your room on two separate occasions when I was down here with my mom and dad."

He nodded his understanding before saying, "Please, call me Raffy,"

"Raffy, this is my wife Amy."

"It's my pleasure," Raffy said, as he took Amy's hand, bowing his head slightly in a very formal way.

Amy just smiled, wondering whether this guy had any kind of a social life. Throughout the evening he never seemed to relax. His eyes were so intense and his posture so rigid, she wondered if he was always so up tight.

David and Raffy spent much of the evening discussing the rigors of medical school and residency. David told him that he had submitted his choices for the surgical internship matching program, but didn't know yet where he'd be going for his training.

"You should come to Johns Hopkins," Raffy said, without the hint of a smile. "It is the best surgical program in the world."

"I suspect there are a few other programs that might argue that point," David replied, with a smile.

"I'm afraid they would be wrong," Raffy replied sharply. "At least in neurosurgery, Hopkins is rated as having the best faculty, the best facility and the highest percentage of surgeons who pass their boards."

David had done his own research and based on the criteria Raffy was using he knew that programs like Hopkins, Duke and Harvard always scored very high, but he also understood that hands on experience was extremely important for any surgeon who wanted to go out into practice. The residents in most of those programs spent far more time in the classroom and the research lab than they did in the operating room. But, he knew better than to argue that point with anyone who carried the considerable academic bias Raffy had already shown.

"So, what are you going to do when you finish your residency?"

Raffy took a noticeably deeper breath before answering, "I have been offered a position as an assistant professor in the department of neurosurgery at Hopkins, but I promised my father I would return here to Managua." His expression changed to one of slight disgust as he continued, "I'm obligated to come back here this summer, but I don't intend to stay more than a couple of years. I'm not going to get stuck in this place for the rest of my life."

David didn't know what to say. He understood why Raffy wanted to stay at Hopkins, but he also knew that he'd made a promise to his father many years ago. David couldn't imagine disappointing his own dad, no matter what the reason.

THE CONFLICT

****

Ben had told Jack and Elaina he would call once they arrived in La Garita, but his mind was elsewhere when he and Elizabeth were alone in her home. They had arrived just as the sun was setting, but by the time he unloaded her truck and helped her fix them each a vodka tonic, the deep blue moonless sky was rapidly growing darker, except for a soft orange glow over the western horizon. She turned off the lights in the house and suggested, "Why don't we take our drinks out on the deck?"

The night air was cool, as the stars were rapidly revealing themselves from east to west. Below the blanket of twinkling lights it was soon too dark for Ben to see the perimeter of her property, but he could still sense the cliff just beyond the small backyard. On the hills in the distance there were a few scattered lights, and within a few minutes the last traces of the dying sun were gone and most of what he could see was blackness.

Reluctantly, he broke the silence as they stood leaning against the railing. "I love the peaceful isolation of this place," his voice lacked the air of finality that she had come to expect. It had a softer, more gentle tone than she had heard, even during their romantic interludes.

"I love it, too," she said, as she felt his arm move around her waist, drawing her closer to him. "I sit out here every evening and watch the sun go down and the stars come out. It is beautiful, but ..." she allowed her voice to trail off, not willing to share her true feelings.

"But... I suspect it gets pretty lonely, doesn't it?" He knew instinctively what she wanted to say, because he had experienced that same feeling, sitting in his apartment in Tokyo, night after night, reading journals and working out his latest design concept, all alone.

She didn't reply. Instead she turned toward him, and placed her arms slowly around his neck. He responded by kissing her softly. Both of them sensed something more than the physical relationship they had shared back in her hotel room. They shared an excitement, that perhaps this was a turning point in each of their lives, but at the same time they were each frightened by the possibility of over estimating the reaction of the other. They stood motionless for several minutes except for their shallow breathing, their bodies and their minds held together in a common dream that neither was willing to speak.

"Would you like to sit down for a while?" Elizabeth asked in a whisper.

"Sure. Whatever you'd like to do."

She guided him over to the corner of the deck outside her bedroom where they sat down in the wide swing that was suspended by a pair of chains from the ceiling. Once he was comfortable she moved as close as possible, momentarily recalling what she'd thought as she watched David and Amy sitting across from her in the restaurant. There was no such thing as too close.

"I could get used to this," Ben said slowly, as he gently put his arm around her again. He was careful not to move too quickly for fear of disturbing the magnetic bond that was building between them.

"I could get used to having you around," she said, almost too softly for him to hear.

"This is going to be difficult," he said. A bit of a calculating tone had returned to his voice.

"I know it is for you," she replied, "but, for me the only thing that will be difficult is when you leave to go back to Japan."

"My work over there is essentially complete. I'm just trying to find someone to do the clinical trials using MATRICS."

He had explained the system to her during the drive earlier that day. She wasn't sure she understood it completely, but it was clear he was passionate about the project and would continue to follow it through to completion. "I wish there was something I could do to help," she said, in a sad, and almost childlike voice.

As she looked up into his darkened face, out of the corner of her eye she saw a tiny bright light streak across the sky beyond his view. "I just saw a shooting star," she exclaimed.

"What you saw was likely a tiny meteor, falling through the outer stratosphere. They are actually quite common. Most of them are smaller than a golf ball and they quickly burn up due to friction as they enter the atmosphere." Ben's analytical mind had responded automatically.

"Oh," she replied, "I thought it was some mystical sign." She couldn't help the sarcasm in her voice.

"Sorry," Ben replied, recognizing he had changed the mood. "I told you, I'm not very good at this."

"Not very good at what?" she asked, trying to lead him without letting him know he was being led.

He leaned over and kissed her again, this time more aggressively and her mouth responded as he had hoped it would. He moved his hand down to her bottom to pull her closer and she willingly allowed herself to be drawn on to him.

"I'm not very good at this romance stuff," he said as he allowed their mouths to separate.

"I think you're doing pretty well," she said. "In fact, if I were giving you a grade, I think I'd give you an A plus."

"I don't want a grade," Ben said softly. "I just want you."

THE CONFLICT

****

The following day Ben made two calls, first to Naryama to let him know he wouldn't be back in the office for another week, and the other to break the news to his brother.

"Hi Ben," Jack said, as he pushed the hands free answer button on the steering wheel. "We were just talking about you."

"Really?" Ben's voice could be heard through the car's speakers as the bluetooth wireless connection had automatically linked the two electronic devices.

"Yeah, Elaina and I just dropped the kids off at the airport, and we're headed back to the house. She asked me if I heard from you last night and I told her no. I figured you probably fell off that cliff behind Elizabeth's house." He laughed out loud, knowing his brother was actually afraid of heights.

"Well, in a way you were right," he said. "I did fall." there was a long silence as Jack anticipated his brother telling him about some accident. Instead what he heard was even more shocking. "I fell in love, with the most amazing woman in the world."

"What?" Jack's mouth fell open, never expecting to hear those words coming from his brother.

"Yes, I know, I've said repeatedly that I had no interest in getting involved in any type of a relationship, but this is different."

Jack chuckled to himself, but his reaction was obvious to his brother. "It doesn't sound all that different to me."

"Well, maybe not to you, but it definitely feels very different to me."

"So what are you planning to do?"

"I'm going to stay her with Lizzy for another week."

"Lizzy?" Jack asked with another audible laugh.

"Yes, that's what she asked me to call her, but you still need to call her Elizabeth. If you don't mind." Ben paused momentarily to make sure he'd made his point before continuing. "I need to go back to Tokyo and wrap some things up. I think that will take four or five weeks, then I will be coming back here."

"So, you're going to move in with Elizabeth?" he half shouted.

"Yes. Isn't that what people do under these circumstances?"

"But, this is so sudden." Jack said, conveniently forgetting how it was when he met Elaina.

"We discussed it last night and then again this morning. We decided neither of us is getting any younger, so if we're going to have a life together we had better get started."

"I... don't know what to say," Jack stumbled with his words as he was trying to digest what his brother was telling him. "So, are you ...?"

"Yes, we are going to get married when I return from Tokyo."

This time Jack was speechless, while Elaina sat quietly in the passenger seat of the big Toyota, with a knowing smile across her face. Finally she spoke up, "Congratulations, Ben. We are very happy for you."

"Thank you, Elaina. Lizzy and I both owe you."

"You don't owe me anything. I'm just excited things worked out."

After another brief exchange, Jack wished his brother well before hitting the end button on his cell phone. He glanced over at his wife who innocently responded to his unspoken accusation with a single word, "What?"

****

In the first half of his third year of medical school, David had been through six clinical rotations, including six weeks each on the Internal Medicine and Obstetrics and Gynecology services, and three weeks of Pathology, Psychiatry and Emergency Medicine. His only elective was the three weeks he spent on the Cardiology service, right before the holiday break. Now that he and Amy were back in Dallas, he couldn't wait to get back to Parkland and start his six week rotation on General Surgery. After that he was scheduled to do three weeks each of Radiology and Orthopedics, followed by six weeks of Family Medicine. He would complete his clinical year with two, three week electives. He had naturally selected Pediatrics and Cardiothoracic Surgery.

Amy continued to battle morning sickness, which didn't seem to be getting any better. It didn't help that David somehow felt obligated to tell everyone they knew about her struggles. Her obstetrician told her it would likely improve by the end of her first trimester, and she shouldn't worry about it at this point. Dr. Fletcher-Brown was a young woman who had been out of residency only a year and a half. She had stayed on at the medical school as a junior faculty member, because her husband was a surgery resident, with eighteen more months of residency before he was finished.

"Will all this vomiting I'm doing every morning harm my baby," Amy asked. She had expressed the same concern to David, but he reassured her that as long as she stayed well hydrated and ate nutritious foods, the baby would be fine. But, he was just a medical student. What did he know.

"It is important for you to stay well hydrated through the course of the day," Dr. Fletcher-Brown said, "and you need to eat a good nutritious diet and make sure to take your prenatal vitamins. If you do that, your baby will be just fine."

She laughed to herself, prompting the doctor to ask, "what so funny."

"That is exactly what my husband said, right before he went off on a lecture about hyperemesis gravidarum."

"I don't think you need to concern yourself about that," she said. "HG occurs in less than two percent of pregnancies, and you are otherwise in excellent health, so I think the risk is minimal. You are approaching the end of your first trimester, and I feel sure the morning sickness will begin to subside soon."

"I hope so," Amy said with a tentative smile. "Thank you, doctor"

"I will see you again next month, okay?"

As Amy made her way back out to the front of the clinic to make her next appointment, she looked out into the waiting room, crowded with young women in various stages of pregnancy. She had yet to start showing, and was a bit jealous of those women who's pregnant status was obvious. As she finished making her appointment, a nurse came up behind her and called out another patient's name. Across the room a woman about her age struggled to push herself up out of one of the large arm chairs. As she slowly rose to her feet, the only thought that came to Amy's mind was how huge the woman's abdomen was, and how uncomfortable she looked. She decided it must be twins or maybe even triplets,. Surely, no single baby could be that big. Thank God her first sonogram had confirmed only one fetus. So far she didn't know her baby's gender, but it didn't really matter. All she wanted was a healthy child.

****

"What do you think we should get Ben and Elizabeth for their wedding?" Elaina asked.

"I have no idea," Jack replied.

"Well its coming up next month, and we have to get them something nice."

"How about one of those African fertility idols," Jack laughed.

"I'm serious," she replied.

"Me too! I think it would be great to have a niece or nephew."

"You aren't the least bit funny," she said shaking her head in disgust. "I thought about a painting I saw the last time I was in town."

Now it was Jack's turn to shake his head. "Not personal enough." He paused another moment before suggesting, "How about a case of scotch."

"Don't be ridiculous."

"Okay, then, how about a set of crystal glasses. It appears that Ben has decided he kinda likes that vodka and tonic, so if they're not going to drink good scotch, at least they should have some decent highball glasses."

"That's a great idea," she said. "I saw a set of Baccarat crystal the other day that would be perfect."

Jack flashed his crooked smile at her as she thought about exactly which pieces she planned to get. When she looked back at him, her expression turned to a question. "What is it?" she asked.

"I was just thinking."

"About what?"

"Just another gift idea," he said casually, continuing to offer no insight into the source of what was now a sheepish grin.

"You are not buying them a fertility idol," she insisted.

"No, no. I was just kidding about that. I have something else in mind. You get them the crystal, but I'm going to get Ben something just from me."

****

The six hour drive down the Pan American highway into Costa Rica was uneventful. While he'd only owned the Land Cruiser for four months, it already had nearly eight thousand miles on it. Elaina's BMW sat under the covered car port most of the time, since Jack did most of the driving, and he preferred the size and stability of the much larger vehicle.

He had no trouble finding La Garita, but from there he wasn't quite sure how to get to Elizabeth's neighborhood. Elaina suggested he just call her and get directions.

"I can find it. Just give me a minute," he said, looking at a map of the area he had printed off the Internet before they left home.

She had always known him to be stubbornly self reliant, but since their move to El Transito that trait seemed to have moved to a whole different level. Perhaps it was because he had so much free time on his hands, but Jack now assumed control of virtually every situation. When Federico said he planned to build a hand railing for the bridge across the lagoon, Jack sat down at his computer and drew up an elaborate drawing of what he wanted the structure to look like, complete with a list of all the materials they would need. The next day, he took Federico into town with him to buy all the lumber and brackets, the bolts and nuts to fasten them together, a battery operated power saw and an electric drill that used the same battery pack. For the next week he and Federico worked eight to ten hours a day to complete the project. What had started out as Federico's idea had become Jack's obsession.

After they had driven up and down three different streets, each one he'd been certain was the right one, he finally gave into her continued request and called

Elizabeth. From his description she knew exactly where they were and gave him the simple directions to the house that was no more than a kilometer away.

Elizabeth came running out to greet them. The smile on her face was infectious, and there was something else about her than seemed different. Jack couldn't put his finger on it, but Elaina knew immediately. She had colored her hair, to cover the gray once more, and she was wearing a bit of mascara and a touch of lip stick and eye shadow. She looked at least five years younger then when they last saw her, only six weeks earlier.

"Come in, come in," she said enthusiastically. "It is so good to see you both."

Jack retrieved their bags from the back of the truck, but left the two large boxes, one wrapped in silver paper with a white ribbon and bow, and the other was simply wrapped in plain blue paper, without a bow or label.

"Where's the groom to be?" Jack asked as they entered the house.

"He went into San José to pick up the cake I ordered for tomorrow." The excitement in Elizabeth's voice was obvious. It was as if she were a twenty year old again, preparing for an elaborate church wedding, instead of the rather modest ceremony they had planned. It would take place right here, in her home, with only a few friends and family.

"You guys will be in the guest room," she said, pointing toward the familiar room they'd occupied when they visited a few years earlier. As Jack started to carry their bags in that direction, a young man came out of the adjacent room, apparently unaware that her other guests had arrived.

Both men stopped abruptly before realizing the identity of the other. "Jack this is my son, Tommy," Elizabeth stated quickly. "Tommy, this is Jack Roberts, Ben's brother."

Jack sat the suitcases down and stepped forward to shake the younger man's hand. Tommy smiled timidly and extended his hand to the older and much taller man. As Jack took his hand he immediately detected a somewhat frail, almost feminine quality that made him subconsciously soften his own grip to avoid injuring him. "It's very nice to finally meet you," Jack said confidently.

"Yeah, Mom has told me a lot about you as well." he said, forcing a smile as he pulled his hand away. He turned toward Elaina and his demeanor immediately seemed more comfortable. "So, you must be Elaina," he said more confidently.

"That's me," she replied casually, as she stepped forward to shake his hand. "Your mom told me she hoped you would come."

"Yeah, I got here yesterday. I couldn't miss my mom getting married, even though it is rather sudden." That statement was one he had used several time since he'd first learned of her plan, and was his, not so subtle way of expressing his concern.

Jack had initially had a similar reaction, but he didn't think it appropriate for her son to express it openly. Instead, he felt an obligation to defend their action, saying, "When two people fall in love, it often is rather sudden."

Tommy's reaction was to laugh, then say, "I guess so," but the tension between the two men was palpable. "I think I'm going to take a walk before dinner," he said, giving his mom a kiss on the cheek as he headed up the stairs toward the front door.

When he was gone, Elizabeth turned to her guests and her expression had turned to one of sympathetic concern. "He's not at all happy about this."

"Why not," Elaina asked mirroring Elizabeth's mood change. "I would think he'd be excited for you."

"Tommy has always been a very sensitive person, and ever since his father and I got divorced, he has been very protective of me."

Jack wisely didn't say what he was thinking about the mother-son relationship. Instead he picked up the suitcases and carried them into their room, leaving the two women to rationalize the immature behavior of Elizabeth's son.

****

On the deck that overlooked the huge canyon to the south, mountains to the east and the Pacific Ocean in the distance to the west, the pastor of the local non-denominational Christian church in La Garita stood with his back to the railing. A local musician sat in a chair where the swing had been the day before. He played a baroque guitar version of Stanley Myers beautiful "Cavatina", as a half dozen of Elizabeth's neighbors and friends filed out on to the deck. They were seated in the single row of chairs against the wall of the house to the left, leaving a single seat open nearest the door. A second small group of employes and several of the older children from the orphanage in Atenas took seats arranged against the wall on the right side. The deck seemed more narrow with so many people gathered there, but the cozy confines offered exactly the intimate setting Elizabeth had wanted.

Tommy took his seat nearest the doorway, then Ben walked passed the guitarist, having come out onto the deck through the master bedroom door around the corner. He was followed closely by his brother. Jack wore a dark blue suit and matching tie, while Ben was wearing a cream colored, linen suit with the bright yellow tie Elizabeth had selected for him. The single yellow rose on his lapel matched the tie perfectly. Ben was more nervous than his brother had ever seen him, as the two men took their positions to the right of the pastor.

THE CONFLICT

They waited impatiently as the guitarist finished the final measures of the classical melody while Ben was noticeably wringing his hands.

Everyone sat in quiet anticipation as the pastor nodded to the musician who broke the silence with the first cords of the processional piece Elizabeth had selected. She had always loved the harmonic simplicity of Pachelbel's Canon in D Major. Elaina made her way slowly down the long stairway wearing a modest light blue cotton dress and white sandals. As she came through the door she smiled broadly first at Jack and then at Ben, who forced as brief boyish grin.

As the complexity of the music gradually increased, eleven year old Hermina walked carefully down the stairs carrying a bouquet of yellow roses that complimented the new blue dress that matched the one worn by the maid of honor. Her smile was so intense, it completely obscured the dark, raised scars that had been the result of the fire, which had taken the other members of her family six years ago. She took her position next to Elaina and with her hands she motioned for everyone to stand.

Elizabeth almost floated down the stairs in the bright yellow satin dress. The full skirt spread out from her narrow waist, extending nearly to the floor. The bodice was tightly fitted with only a hint of cleavage showing above the wide scoop neckline. Her hair was neatly piled on to her head and held in place with a small arrangement of yellow rose buds. It had been her intent to present herself to Ben as a true "yellow rose of Texas", and by all accounts she had managed to do exactly that.

When he finally saw her gracefully negotiating the last few steps, and then slowly walking toward him, his nervousness simply evaporated as his face exploded into the widest grin she had ever seen. As she stood in front of him, he took her hands and stared up and down the full length of her body before gently turning her to face the preacher.

The ceremony was short, with an exchange of traditional vows and rings, and as the preacher pronounced them husband and wife, the audience stood and applauded vigorously as Ben kissed his new partner. He was surprised by the salty taste of the tears that were joyfully streaming down her cheeks.

"Ladies and gentlemen, I present to you Dr. and Mrs. Benjamin Roberts." As the preacher finished his pronouncement the guitarist began a stirring rendition of Beethoven's "Ode to Joy". Instead of walking arm in arm away from the make-shift alter, they simple walked together to greet each of their guests, in what amounted to an immediate informal reception. Hermina stood along side of Elaina, holding her hand and dreaming of a day when she too might be a beautiful bride.

One of Elizabeth's friends walked up to Elaina and said, "that was a wonderful wedding."

"Yes, is certainly was," she agreed. "I'm afraid we haven't been introduced yet."

"My name is Danielle Mulder. I am one of Elizabeth's neighbors," she replied with a distinctly European accent.

"I'm Elaina Roberts, and this is my husband Jack." She pulled on Jack's hand to gather his attention.

"Ah, yes," she replied, "Elizabeth has told me all about both of you." She turned her attention toward Jack and said, "and I read about the part you played in the recent industrial accident over in Tamarindo. What a terrible tragedy."

"Yes, it was," he agreed as he shook the older woman's hand.

"From what I understand, it would have been even worse had it not been for you."

"That is kind of you to say, but Dr. Velasquez deserves most of the credit for saving the lives of the two men who ultimately survived."

"Perhaps, but that is not the story that he tells."

Jack was unaware of the extensive national news coverage that the accident had received, including a lengthly interview with the surgeon at the hospital in Nicoya. He had credited Jack not only with saving the lives of two of the workers, but also saving him from his own physical collapse.

"I don't know what he had to say, but he did a great job given the resources he has to work with." Jack knew that the two men who had died after reaching the hospital had suffered injuries that likely would have been fatal no matter where they were treated. One had a rather massive head injury that would have challenged even the best neurosurgeons, while the other had suffered an avulsion of the aortic root. The same type of sudden deceleration that had torn the renal artery of one of the survivors, had been responsible for literally tearing the main artery from its attachment to the heart.

"Well, I'm glad you were there to help," she said, and if there is ever anything I can do to assist you in improving the level of healthcare in this region, I trust you will call on me."

She didn't tell him that she still received virtually all her personal care back in Amsterdam. The thought of receiving medical attention in the third world scared her, so she just didn't think about it.

"I would like for you to meet my good friend Sherman Masterson," she said as she drew a very distinguished appearing elderly gentleman into their small circle. "Sherman and I live together in my villa up on the side of the mountain."

"Good afternoon," the older man said, in a formal, yet somehow detached manner as he reached clumsily forward to shake Jack's hand.

"Sherman, this is Dr. Roberts. You remember Elizabeth telling us about him don't you?"

From the way she was talking and the rather delayed resp(
obvious that the older man was suffering from some form of ea(
is a pleasure meeting you Mr. Masterson."

"Please, call me Sherm," he replied, in what was obviously a p(
repeated countless times in his seventy-eight years.

"Sherman was a Federal judge in the United States until about ten (
when he retired," she stated, purposely failing to reveal that for the last t(
years he had been under treatment for progressive Alzheimer's syndrome (
physician in the Netherlands.

"This is certainly a beautiful place to retire," Jack said, as he tried to tactfully pull his hand away.

"Please, call me Sherm."

Elaina smiled pitifully at the old man, and Jack couldn't help but think of his mother who had suffered much the same fate, but without a companion to care for her.

CHAPTER 20

"Why am I still throwing up all the time?" Amy asked.

The young Dr. Fletcher-Brown's reply seemed rather cold, almost as if she were reading from a textbook. "We don't really understand exactly what causes morning sickness, but it's related to your changing hormone levels. It is highly unusual for it to persist this long."

"In the beginning it was only in the mornings, but now I find myself throwing up several times a day."

Are you able to keep down your neonatal vitamins?"

"Yes, but I have to take them at lunchtime. That's the only meal I seem to be able to eat without throwing-up."

"I'm going to prescribe you some Diclegis, which should help."

"Is it safe?" Amy's response was immediate, and reflected a concern David had raised when they first found out she was pregnant. "Everybody tells me that I shouldn't take any medicines, because they could cause birth defects."

The doctor's reply seemed rather dismissive of Amy's concerns. "This is the most effective medication we have for the treatment of morning sickness, and it has been fully tested and found to be totally safe during pregnancy."

She remained hesitant, recalling David's warnings. "My husband had a congenital heart problem, and I don't want to run the risk of that happening to my baby."

"Like I said, Diclegis has been tested and shown to be very safe, and in my opinion the biggest risk to your baby is inadequate nutrition. If you continue to have trouble keeping food and fluids down, you'll end up having a low birth weight baby, and that is associated with far more problems than any medication."

So far Amy had only gained three pounds, which was two and a half pounds less than the minimum expected, and almost five pounds under the average predicted weight gain by sixteen weeks. She had always heard that pregnant women had a certain glow about them, but her skin was anything but glowing. The area around her eyes had taken on a subtle grayness that had her coworkers wondering if she was getting enough sleep.

The young mother to be shook her head slowly as she replied, "I still think I'd rather not take any medicine right now, if that's okay."

The young doctor frowned noticeably, but offered no further suggestions. While the protocol called for this medication to be prescribed, she knew she couldn't force her to take it. She would just make certain to document in the chart how the patient refused her recommendation so she wouldn't be sighted by the quality assurance committee for not following the best practice protocol.

"You're sixteen weeks, and I've never seen morning sickness persist beyond eighteen weeks. Hopefully this problem will begin to subside soon, but I need to see you again in one week." Her tone had turned even more detached as she felt pressured by her busy clinic schedule to cut the discussion off. She also feared that this patient might actually have true Hyperemesis Gravidarum, something she had yet to encounter in her limited tenure on the faculty.

****

It was after eight when David finally made his way up the stairs to their apartment. "I'm home," he called out, assuming Amy was in the bedroom, then he walked over to the refrigerator to see if he could find anything to eat. There was a small container of sliced ham, but there were only two small pieces left. He quickly ate them without bothering to make a sandwich, and continued to look for anything else that might satisfy him. Not finding much else, he closed the refrigerator and turned toward the small pantry, but as he opened it, he heard the all too common sound of Amy retching in the bathroom. He couldn't help but sigh to himself as he quickly made his way to her.

"Is there anything I can do?" he asked, finding her sitting on the floor, leaning over the commode.

"You could get me a cold wash cloth," she replied between aborted efforts to throw up. Her stomach was already completely empty. She had lost all the cold cereal she'd eaten for supper an hour ago.

As he ran the cool water through the small terry cloth rag, he asked, "what did the doctor have to say?"

"She said this will probably start to subside soon," but she had barely gotten the words out of her mouth before she returned to the commode with another violent attempt to empty her stomach.

"Isn't there something they can do?"

She tried to get me to take come kind of medicine, but I told her I didn't want to risk it."

David's experience with pregnancy was limited to the six weeks he'd spent on the OB-Gyn service the previous fall, but he knew what Amy was experiencing wasn't typical morning sickness. "What was the name of the medicine she wants to give you?"

"I don't know," Amy said as she attempted to get up off the floor, only to sink down once more, feeling another wave of nausea, but this time there was only a slight involuntary lurch forward of her chin without any sound. She wiped her mouth again with the cloth and stood up, making her way slowly into the bedroom where, with David's help, she laid down exhausted from the effort.

He stood next to the bed, feeling more helpless than he had ever felt. He reached over and took her hand, but her response was weak and listless. He felt he had to do something, so he asked, "Would you like for me to make you some hot tea?"

She opened her eyes slowly, and in the dim light of the open bathroom door he could see the darkness around her eyes and the pallor of her cheeks. "I don't know if I can keep it down," she replied weakly.

"I'll be right back," he said as he left to prepare the tea. While the water was heating in the microwave, he pulled out his phone and went to the Epocrates app and did a quick search for anti-nausea medications. He found a specific article on the treatment of morning sickness. He thought the name of condition was rather ironic, given the current time of day.

He carried the mug of hot tea back into the bedroom and sat it down on the night stand to cool. "Was the medicine she wanted to give you Diclegis?"

"I don't know, but that sounds like it."

'Well, according to this report, that drug should be safe to take, and I think we have to do something." David's voice sounded more desperate than he'd intended. He didn't want her to sense his growing fear. "I'll call your doctor in the morning and ask her about it."

Amy started to tell him she was sure the doctor wanted her to start taking it, but she didn't really have the strength to continue any conversation.

The next morning David was busy with three new admissions, and it was almost noon before he had the chance to call the obstetrics clinic. The secretary told him that Dr. Fletcher-Brown was performing a C-section and wouldn't be back in the clinic until two o'clock. He had a conference from two to three then he had to prepare for afternoon rounds, so rather than call her back he decided to try and find her, and talk to her in person. He made his way over to labor and delivery, where the head nurse told him the doctor was almost finished with the C-section. He took a seat in the nurses station and waited for her to appear.

Almost finished turned into thirty minutes, but eventually he spotted the young staff physician as she came out of the sterile corridor. He jumped to his feet and caught her just before she disappeared into the women's locker room. "Excuse me, Dr. Fletcher-Brown?"

She stopped and turned with an angry expression at the interruption. "Yes?" she answered abruptly.

"I'm David Roberts, Amy's husband. You saw her yesterday in your clinic." He knew it was highly irregular for a student to interrupt a faculty member, but in this case he was acting as the husband of one of her patients instead of a lowly medical student.

"I remember Amy very well. She refused the Diclegis I suggested, and from what she said, I assume it was on your recommendation." Her contempt for the opinion of a student was obvious.

"I don't know what to say, other than I'm sorry she took what I said when we first found out she was pregnant as an absolute."

"Well, I tried to convince her the drug is perfectly safe, but she wouldn't listen. You've rotated on this service before haven't you?"

"Yes, ma'am."

"Then you should know that the best practices guidelines all call for the use of medications to control morning sickness in an effort to avoid low birth weight infants."

"That's why I came here to find you. I was hoping you would give her a prescription for Diclegis and I'll get her to start taking it right away."

She looked at him with an arrogant disgust before saying, "Alright. Let me change and I'll meet you out at the desk."

After a few minutes the doctor reappeared wearing a plain white blouse and black slacks, covered with a knee length white coat. As she sat down to write the prescription, David said, "I'm really worried there is something more going on than just morning sickness."

"Really?" she said, again with an air of contempt for his opinion.

"She's throwing up almost all day, and I'm afraid she's becoming dehydrated. I'm afraid she might have Hyperemesis Gravidarum."

"I'm not," she said as she tore the completed prescription from the pad. She thrust it toward him and said, "and I would suggest you leave the diagnosing up to me."

"Absolutely," he said in a voice that was far more contrite than he felt. "Thank you."

****

Amy continued to try and work despite what had become a debilitating problem. The medication that Dr. Fletcher-Brown prescribed had scarcely slowed it down, and at her next doctor's appointment she had actually lost a pound. However, her concerns all seemed to melt away when the doctor showed her the sonogram of the seventeen week fetus she was carrying. Before she even got dressed, she took a picture of the sonogram with her cell phone and texted it to David with the caption, "IT'S A BOY!!!"

It didn't take long for David to post the photo on his Facebook page with the same caption, and within a few hours everyone knew, even his mom and dad had access to their news and "Liked" the post. The comments from many of their friends included congratulations and questions about whether they had decided on a name, but surprisingly no one asked how Amy was doing.

Her excitement of the early morning news carried over for the rest of the day, but as she returned to work she began feeling queazy yet again. She tried some soup and crackers from the cafeteria, but found herself running to the bathroom less than thirty minutes later.

"You really should go home," her supervisor said, as she returned to her desk, looking a bit pale and exhausted.

"I'll be okay.". She knew that her work was slipping, and that she probably shouldn't even be there. For the last six weeks, since returning from Nicaragua, she had called in sick at least two days a week, and on the days she was there she couldn't stay at her desk more than twenty minutes at a time before having to literally run to the nearby ladies room.

After a few seconds she took a small sip from the bottle of gatorade on her desk. "I think things are getting better," she lied, trying to reassure the man who had the power to make her take a leave of absence. To her, that would be a disaster because as long as her husband was still in school, her's was their only income. David had tried to assured her that they could get by on the rental income from his grandmother's house and the five thousand dollars he'd gotten from the sale of his old Honda.

The next afternoon, as he was headed into the weekly morbidity and mortality conference, David's cell phone vibrated.

"Hello, Mr. Roberts," the panic in the man's voice was obvious.

"Yes?" he replied.

"This is Kyle Durbin, Amy's boss. Your wife has passed out here in the office. I have called 9-1-1 and the Paramedics ..."

David didn't wait for him to complete his statement, half shouting, "I'll be right there!"

He turned to one of his classmates and said, "it's Amy. I gotta go. Cover for me would you?"

Before his friend could respond, David turned and ran down the hall and into the stairwell where he descended the five flights of stairs, taking the steps three at a time until he burst out into the main lobby of the hospital. Once out the door he turned and ran the block and a half to the office building that housed the research department. He raced up the three flights of stairs to Amy's floor, arriving well ahead of the EMTs. One of her co-workers was helping his wife as she tried to sit up.

"No, keep her laying down," David insisted as he approached, quickly seizing control. Just lay back down, Baby," he said, gently laying her head back down on the thin carpet.

"But I need to get back to my desk," she insisted in an incoherent mumble.

"No, we're taking you to the ER. You need some fluids."

****

"Hello, Mom?" David said with just a hint of fear in his voice.

"Yes, sweetie, what's the matter?" Elaina asked, fearing the worst.

"It's Amy. We had to take her to the Emergency Room. She passed out at work."

"Is the baby ...?" she inquired, desperately hoping she hadn't lost the pregnancy.

"The baby's okay, as far as I know, but I'm really worried about Amy. Is Dad around where I can talk to him?"

"Sure, let me get him." She turned quickly and made her way out onto the deck where she found Jack busily working on something on his laptop. She handed him her cell phone and said, "it's David, something has happened to Amy."

"What's the matter son?" Jack asked, without any greeting.

"Amy passed out at work and we have her in the ER. She looks really dehydrated. The EMTs weren't even able to find a vein to start an IV, so the resident is now trying to get an IV started."

"Did she have a miscarriage?"

"No, like I told Mom, I think the baby is fine. I'm just worried about Amy! She's been so sick lately. Throwing up all the time."

"Sounds like Hyperemesis Gravidarum," Jack concluded, despite the fact he didn't yet have all the facts.

"That's what I told her doctor a week ago, but she told me I didn't know what I was talking about."

"How long has this been going on?"

"Ever since we were down there with you guys over the holiday's"

"Wow! That's been a month and a half." Jack said, showing his increasing concern. "Have they been treating her with anything?"

"She finally started taking Diclegis last week, but it hasn't seemed to help."

A number of thoughts were racing through Jack's mind as he couldn't help but create his own differential diagnosis, based on the information available to him. "Be sure to tell them that you guys recently traveled here to Nicaragua. I doubt she picked up any kind of parasite, but it's certainly possible. She's not had any diarrhea, has she?"

"Not that I know of," David replied. "Listen, I gotta go, they're calling me back to her room. I'll call you later and let you know."

"Okay," Jack said as he heard his son's phone disconnect.

****

"She's so dry, I'm not able to find an adequate vein in either arm," the surgical resident said as David came into the small alcove with scarcely enough room for the stretched and the small bedside table. The young, dark skinned doctor was writing something on the ER record, and on the table he could see four, used, intravenous catheters, and a blue rubber tourniquet. Amy was lying on the stretcher with both arms exposed, and four separate bandaids covered the sites where the resident had attempted to access her veins.

"I'm going to need to start a central line," the doctor spoke with a very distinct accent. David was certain he was from either India or Pakistan. "You will need to sign that permit before I can proceed." His tone was detached, but at the same time David detected a hint of apprehension.

"What route are you planning to use?" he asked. The resident seemed slightly frustrated by what he perceived as an inappropriate questioning of his decision. The fact that David was a medical student was obvious, based on his short white jacket and name tag, but he was in no mood to indulge in a discussion of the various major veins that could be used to establish venous access.

"I'm going to place an internal jugular line," he replied. "It should only take a few minutes."

"Have you done many of those?" David asked. He was well aware that there was less risk of collapsing her lung with that technique, compared to the traditional subclavian approach, but he also knew that there was also a slight risk of sticking the needle into the carotid artery if the resident wasn't familiar with the anatomy.

"Yes, hundreds," the young doctor exaggerated. At most, he had placed no more than twenty or thirty central lines in his year and a half of training, but admitting his relative inexperience to a medical student was, in his mind, unacceptable.

David hesitated as he picked up the clip board with the consent form awaiting his signature. Sensing his concerns, the resident added, "I'll be using ultrasound to locate the vein. It's a piece of cake."

He sighed deeply, having heard that phrase used many times to describe a routine procedure. He had even used it himself the previous week when he was explaining to one his patients that he was going to draw his blood. The older man had looked up at him rather anxiously and said, "Maybe for you ..."

Reluctantly he scribbled his signature along the designated line and handed the clip board to the nurse who had come in to assist with the procedure. As she accepted the mandatory document, her voice sounded rather robotic as she said, "I need for you to go back out to the waiting room. I will allow you to come back when Dr. Bazjani has finished."

David made his way over to Amy's side and took her hand in his. It was cooler than normal and her palm was moist. He could see the fear in her face, as he tried to comfort her. "It's going to be okay, Baby," he said softly. "I'll be right outside."

She wanted him to stay with her, but before she could gather the strength to say anything, he leaned over and kissed her on the forehead and released her hand. He pulled the vinyl curtain closed behind him as he slowly walked back out into the crowded waiting room.

It was far different being on this side of the wall. He had quickly grown accustomed to being where the action was. Sitting here in one of the hard plastic chairs, among the herd of waiting family members, all equally helpless, was a revelation to him. Likely none of them had any idea what was actually happening to their loved ones back in what the residents affectionately called *The Pit*. He, on the other hand, knew precisely what was happening to his wife, and it scared him more than anything he could remember.

In his mind's eye he could see the resident as he put on the paper mask along with the sterile gown and gloves that came in the prepackaged central line kit. The nurse had already exposed and prepped Amy's upper chest, right shoulder and the side of her neck. As if he were there, he could see them place the large sterile drape over the entire area with only a six inch diameter hole in the middle through which the resident would work. He could almost feel her fear rising, as the drape was positioned, covering her face. Involuntarily, she was tensing every muscle in her young body, in anticipation of what was to come. He could see her lying there, motionless, for what seemed like hours, waiting for the doctor to draw the local anesthetic into the small syringe and prepare the catheter for insertion into the large vein in her neck. His own palms began to moisten as he imagined the nurse pushing a large pedal on the side of the stretcher causing it to suddenly tilt dramatically, with her head now well below her feet. He hoped the doctor would explain that this position was necessary to dilate the vein and make it easier to find with the needle, but in his mind he doubted he was offering any reassurance. Instead, he heard only the words, "There is going to be a little stick here in the side of your neck," followed immediately by the sudden puncture of the skin from a hidden source. She didn't cry out initially, but as the lidocaine was injected the burning sensation caused her to reflexively pull away. "I need for you to hold very still" was all the resident said in frustration as he nearly stuck himself with the needle.

    David imagined the nurse handing him the small ultrasound probe that he accepted using the sterile plastic cover. He applied a small amount of sterile lubricant to her neck, and then began searching for the vein. It was just inside and slightly below the long muscle on the side of her neck, but the resident was pressing the probe down too hard to see it. By compressing the low pressure vein, it was easily collapsed, making the carotid artery the only vascular structure visible on the portable monitor. He wanted to shout through the wall, That's not it, but he knew his objection would serve no purpose.

    As he watched the scene unfold, his mind wouldn't allow such an injury to occur. He imagined the young doctor lightening his pressure, providing a clear view of the large vein. "Okay," he thought, "anybody could hit that." He found himself coaching the doctor through a procedure he had only done twice himself. The needle penetrated the skin, temporarily distorting the ultrasound image before the bright reflection of the metallic device came into view. As the needle was advanced he could see the way it indented the wall of the vein before suddenly penetrating it. Finally, the tip was in the right spot, so he laid the ultrasound probe on her chest and used both hands to pull back on the syringe, drawing a sizable amount of dark red blood from the internal jugular vein.

    "The rest is easy," David told himself, but he imagined the doctor fumbling to detach the syringe from the hub of the needle. He was afraid he was about to pull the needle out of the vein, which would mean he'd have to start over, but, eventually the connection was freed, and he held the needle with one hand as he placed the blood filled syringe back into the kit, and retrieved the guide wire.

Couldn't this guy see the blood that was pouring out of the end of the open needle. It was flowing down through the gap between the drape and her neck, on to the sheet and into her golden hair. Finally, the bleeding was stopped as he threaded the end of the wire through the needle and into the large vein. He advanced it another six inches or so to ensure that it was into the superior vena cava. He picked up the ultrasound probe again and reexamined the area. There was now a bright reflection inside the vein that extended beyond the limit of what he could see. He tossed the ultrasound probe on to her chest, causing her to flinch once more. He could hear the resident say, "hold still, please," admonishing her for reacting in the darkness.

David felt an unconscious sigh of relief, knowing that the guide wire was now in place, and the risk of unintended injury was over, but the catheter was still not in the vein. The vision of the resident using a tiny scalpel to cut the skin at the point where the wire was protruding made him recoil slightly. No one had ever laid a knife on his wife's beautiful skin before, and he wished it weren't happening now. He knew from their countless romantic interludes that the side of her neck was particularly sensitive, but she wasn't feeling anything due to the local anesthetic.

The resident then threaded a tapered hard plastic tube over the wire and plunged it down over the wire through the opening he'd created in the skin, and into the vein. She clearly felt the pressure and groaned softly. This dilated the tract enough to allow the softer and more flexible, intravenous catheter to pass over the wire. He removed the dilator and then placed the end of the wire into the tiny opening in the end of the catheter. While he was making this final exchange, dark red blood was once again oozing out of the side of her neck from around the wire. Finally, he pushed the catheter into the vein, eventually allowing the tip to rest just above the right atrium of Amy's heart. He removed the wire and cast it carelessly back toward the kit, but it ended up on the floor.

"We are almost finished," he could hear the resident say, and he sensed the tension begin to leave her body. The final step was to secure the catheter to the skin with a black silk suture. He was anticipating the resident would use another injection of local anesthetic, but instead he drove the small curved needle directly through her skin an inch above the point where the catheter had been placed. Again she winced, but didn't cry out as he pulled the thread through the skin and tied it around the base of the catheter. When he had cut the suture he placed a sterile gauze over the sight of his work and turned to the nurse, saying, "flush all three lines with saline, and put a dressing on it, would you? I'll have the secretary order the chest x-ray." David only hoped that when they came in with portable x-ray machine that the technician would shield her abdomen from the radiation with a lead apron. "Surely they would, wouldn't they?" he said audibly to himself.

The images in his mind could not have been more real had he been in the room. He expected the resident to come find him in the waiting room any minute, but no one came. He sat silently for thirty more minutes, worrying about a thousand things that might have gone wrong. Another fifteen minutes passed and still no word. He stood up and started pacing back and forth, unable to get the negative thoughts out of his mind.

Finally, after an hour he was no longer willing to follow the unwritten protocol. He used his name badge to open the controlled access door and entered the inner sanctum of the Emergency Department once again. He quickly found Amy alone, right where he had left her. The IV fluids were now running in through the tubing connected to the catheter in the left side of her neck. On the right side was a large bulky gauze dressing covering what was clearly an unsuccessful attempt to place the catheter.

"What happened?" he asked as she finally opened her eyes at the touch of his hand.

"Oh, God, David. I thought he was going to kill me. Didn't you here me screaming for you?"

"No Baby," he replied, the anger building in his gut. Clearly, what he had imagined was not her reality.

"He stuck me over and over again. I don't know how many times." She was now crying between her words. "The nurse asked him if he wanted her to get the chief resident, but he said no, insisting he could do it. Finally, the chief resident came in and took over. He put it over here on the other side in the first stick. That didn't hurt at all."

David hoped he would never run into that other guy again. He looked more closely at the swollen right side of her neck and hoped that whatever damage that incompetent jerk had done was temporary. "Have you seen Dr. Fletcher-Brown yet?"

"No," she said, trying to gain control of her emotions. "They said she would be coming by when she finished seeing patients in her clinic, but I did see the OB resident. She came in and did a pelvic exam and told me everything looked okay." Amy looked up into his face, and as her tears resumed her voiced cracked with the words, "David, I'm scared."

He leaned forward and wrapped his arms over her shoulders, drawing himself as close as he could as he said, "I know, Baby. It's going to be okay."

****

"What a fiasco!" David said as he finished describing to his dad Amy's experience in the emergency room.

"I'm really sorry you guys had to go through that." Jack wanted to add his own assessment of the situation, but he knew it would only inflame things further. "At least she's getting the IV fluids she needs. What did her OB doc have to say?"

"She was pretty upset by what had happened, but the guy in the ER wasn't part of her service. He's a surgery resident, so there wasn't anything she could do about it."

"I was asking what she's planning to do for Amy, now."

"She said she was going to hold all oral intake for the next twenty-four hours and try her on IV Reglan. She said that has been reported to work pretty well, and its safe for the baby."

Jack was very familiar with that drug, having used it frequently in older patients who had poor intestinal motility after major vascular operations, but he also knew it could cause significant neurologic side effects if it was used over an extended period of time. He decided not to worry his son any further with those concerns. "Well, your mom and I will continue to keep both of you in our prayers, and hopefully things will start improving soon."

"I sure hope so," David replied in frustration. "One thing I will say, she hasn't thrown up anymore since we arrived in the ER, but she hasn't had anything to drink either."

Once their conversation was over he returned to Amy's side, and saw that she was finally sleeping. He stepped out into the hallway of the OB floor and called the number of his faculty advisor. The older doctor listened patiently as David explained what was going on, and why he'd had to leave the morbidity and mortality conference that afternoon. He said he understood, but he suggested that if he still planned to graduate in June, he would need to make sure he didn't miss anymore required conferences.

"I understand, sir," was all he could say, as their conversation concluded abruptly.

He chose another number from his contacts and the call was quickly answered. "Hello," the familiar voice replied.

"Mrs. Callahan, this is David."

****

For the next ten days, Amy remained hospitalized. During the first week she seemed fine as long as she didn't try to take anything by mouth, but as soon as she took in more than just a sip of water, the violent retching returned. She was placed on total parenteral nutrition, and was receiving nearly three thousand calories of amino acids, carbohydrates and fats through the IV in her neck. Her weight loss stopped, and she actually gained about five pounds, most of which was simply water being replenished into her system.

Everyday, her mom drove over to Parkland from Fort Worth to stay with her, while David slept in her room every night when he wasn't on call at the hospital. Eventually, the combination of Vitamin B6 and Reglan seemed to provide relief from the constant nausea, and she was able to start taking small meals of bland foods like oatmeal and mashed potatoes. The day before she was discharged, her intravenous medicines were switched to pills, and she was able to eat some scrambled eggs and toast for breakfast and a small chicken breast for lunch.

That evening Dr. Fletcher-Brown came by to check on her again. After looking over the chart she said, "I think we can let you go home in the morning, but I want you to stay off work for the rest of your pregnancy."

"But ..." Amy started to protest before being interrupted by David.

"I'll make sure of that," he said.

"There is some evidence that HG can be triggered by excess stress, so I want you to stay home. I'm not going to require bed rest, but I want you to take it easy. You understand?" Her tone had turned somewhat maternal, as she was making her points.

While she hadn't openly admitted that David's diagnosis had been correct, she had been far more collegial toward him during Amy's time in the hospital. Now using HG, the short hand name for Hyperemesis Gravidarum in her instructions, she made it clear she had accepted his assessment, even if she thought it was likely just a lucky guess on his part.

"If your symptoms come back, I need to know about it right away. We can't afford to allow you get as far behind as you were when you came in to the ER."

"I will. I promise," Amy said as she nodded in agreement.

"According to your original dates, you are scheduled to deliver around the fifteenth of July. That's another twenty weeks. Hopefully, we can avoid any further need for hospitalization between now and then."

"I'll do my best," Amy said as she thanked the doctor as she and the nurse walked out of her room.

"Well that's great news," David said.

"I don't know how you can say that," she protested. "There is no way we can make it if I'm off work for four and a half months."

"Well, there is no way you're going back to work, so we'll find a way," David stated without allowing her any opportunity to respond. "Come July, I will start getting paid as an intern, and I'm sure we can get by until then. The monthly income from the rent house is almost exactly the same as our rent and utilities. We'll be fine."

"What about all the things we need for the baby's room?"

"I thought that's what baby showers were for," he said with a grin. "My mom said she wants to help your mom put on a big event right before graduation. They are going to come back up here around the first of June, and they are planning to stay for a couple of weeks. You just need to talk to your mom and decide on a date."

****

The next three months went by much more rapidly for David than they did for Amy. She found out just how stupid daytime television programs were, while he was flying through his last few rotations. The highlight came on March twenty-fourth, "National Match Day." Back in late January David had submitted his list of choices where he wanted to do his internship, and his choice was made even more certain given Amy's condition. He saw no reason to move anywhere. He was well liked by the faculty, and from everyone he'd talked to, it was clear that Southwestern was still among the best surgical training programs in the country. The only time he had questioned that assessment was the day Amy came to the Parkland ER and that surgical resident had assaulted his wife.

When the results were released, David was one of twenty-four individuals accepted into the surgical internship program of the University of Texas Southwestern. A huge side benefit would be that Amy could keep her doctor, in whom she'd developed a solid trust. She had also been assured that her job would still be there when she finally decided to go back to work.

The best news of all was really no news. Amy's nausea had completely subsided. Sh was even able to stop taking the Reglan, but her doctor recommended she continue taking the Diclegis. A little extra vitamin B6 couldn't hurt.

There was one significant issue that she hadn't anticipated. The bill for her ten day hospitalization was far more than they had expected. When Amy opened the mail, she nearly passed out again. She didn't show it to David for several days, but eventually it would have to be dealt with.

"I know you said everything would be okay, but there's something you need to see," she said, one evening when he seemed to be in a good mood. She handed him the envelop from Parkland Memorial Hospital.

He looked at the document and said, "I don't know what you're so concerned about. It says right here, this is not a bill." He pointed to the bold letters on the top right of the first page of the five page document with printing

THE CONFLICT

on both sides of each sheet of paper. He quickly flipped through the itemized list of every item that had been used during her stay. The subtotal included daily charges for a private room, twenty-two thousand dollars. The emergency department charges included the central line debacle, and the charge was thirty-five hundred dollars. The total from radiology was twelve hundred and the lab charge was twenty-one hundred. The charge for medications included eight days of total parenteral nutrition as well as all the intravenous fluids and drugs. It was a whopping eighteen thousand five hundred dollars. A miscellaneous category totaled four hundred dollars. The grand total was almost forty-eight thousand dollars.

"This is how much they submitted to Humana, but it's not realistic. Our insurance company isn't about to pay them that much. We'll need to wait and see how much they actually approve and how much of it they pay."

"This is just crazy," Amy offered. "I have a degree in finance from a prestigious university, and I have never seen any economic model in business that works like that."

"I don't understand it all either, but our insurance policy has a two thousand dollar deductible, and that's all we should be out for the entire year. You've already paid Dr. Fletcher-Brown over five hundred dollars, so the most we'll owe is fifteen hundred or so."

What they both failed to recognize at the time was the major change in their group policy, which had taken effect beginning in January, 2014. The long awaited implementation of the Affordable Care Act required Humana, and every other company, to sell insurance to anybody, even those with pre-existing conditions. The new policies were also required to pay for a variety of things that were not previously covered. As a result, Humana had increased the premiums the university paid to ensure it's employees by thirty-five percent. The young couple didn't care about that, because it wasn't coming out of their pocket, but the increase in their annual deductible, now up to five thousand dollars, was certain to capture their attention.

****

"Hello, Jack? This is Ron McGinnis."

"Hi Ron, how are you?" Jack said, recognizing his long time accountant's voice.

"I'm just fine. I haven't heard from you in quite a while."

It suddenly dawned on him why Ron would be calling. It was the middle of March, and Ron was needing all of his personal financial information to prepare their 2013 federal income tax return. Jack knew he was going to have a tax problem this year, having sold the house and all his business assets. That was the reason he left the one point four million he had gotten from the sale of the house and the eight hundred thousand for the liquidation of his practice back in the bank in Fort Worth.

He briefly explained to Ron why he and Elaina had moved to Nicaragua, and how he had liquidated virtually everything he owned. "I'll get all the documentation to you in the next couple of days." He planned to get Mary Anne to send all the receipts from the sale of the practice assets, and he would fax him the closing statement from the sale of the house.

"Wow! You've had a busy last few months, haven't you." Ron said.

"Yes, we've made a lot of changes, but things are finally settling down now."

"Okay, I'll get everything together and get back to you in a week or so. We'll have write-offs that will help minimize what we have to show as profit from the sale of the house and your business assets, and those are all handled as long term capital gains. I think we'll probably be okay, but I'll get back to you in a week or so with the bad news."

"That'll be fine," Jack said knowing he would need to write a big check to the government of the country where he no longer resided. He rationalized it based on the fact he was still a US citizen. "This is probably a silly question," he added, "but are my health insurance premiums deductible?"

"They could be," Ron replied. "They are considered medical expenses, and if your total medical expenses exceed seven percent of your taxable income you can deduct any amount in excess of the seven percent."

Jack laughed and replied, "So, in other words, no."

"I'm afraid not." He had been doing Jack's taxes for more than twenty years and he had a good idea what his taxable income would likely be, based on the last few returns. "You didn't have any other major transactions in 2013, did you?" Ron asked, because he had several clients who conveniently failed to mention the sale of a piece of property or some other asset until after he'd prepared their return.

Jack suddenly remembered the Apple stock. He wasn't sure how that would be handled from a tax standpoint since he hadn't shown the proceeds of the sale in any US bank account. "As a matter of fact, I did sell some stock that I had held for a long time," he replied tentatively.

"Had you owned it for more than a year?" Ron asked.

"Yes, actually more than ten years."

"We certainly don't need to be showing any more taxable income than necessary, but it sounds like the stock sale will also be considered capital gains. How much was it?

Jack hesitated for a moment before saying, "It was just over fifteen million."

There was a moment of silence before Ron repeated the number back very slowly. "Did you say fifteen million?"

"Yeah, I liquidated my entire holding of Apple stock, but I moved it into my Swiss bank account. I was afraid the feds were going to seize all my assets."

"Well, they aren't going to seize all your assets, but they're sure going to seize a big chunk of them."

"How big?" Jack asked, afraid of what he was about to hear.

"That depends. How much did you originally pay for it?"

"I accumulated it over a number of years, but I think all together I had about a hundred thousand invested."

Again there was silence as Ron was trying to get his mind around the idea that one of his own clients had essentially won the lottery. "So, virtually all of it was profit?"

"I did have to pay the brokerage firm almost a half million in commission on the sale, so the actual profit was only about fourteen and a half," Jack explained, trying to minimize the number any way he could. "Like I said, I had the funds wired directly to my Swiss account. Do you think the IRS even knows about it?"

"Oh, they know, trust me. A transaction of that size would immediately catch their attention. I hate to have to tell you this, but just using a rough estimate in my head, you're going to owe the IRS in excess of three million bucks."

Now it was Jack's turn to remain silent. After a few seconds he said, "I thought the long term capital gains rate was only fifteen percent?"

"It was, in 2012, but last year it went up to twenty percent, and they added another three point eight percent Medicare tax."

"You're kidding. Even on capital gains?" Jack said in frustration. "Isn't there anyway around it?"

"Not unless you want to go to jail."

"Trying to stay out of jail is what started all this." Jack could only laugh disgustedly at himself.

****

Throughout the months of March, April and May, Jack worked three or four days a week in Domingo's clinic, helping him see the hundreds of children with bronchitis and ear infections along with the occasional laceration or minor fracture. It kept him busy, but it was not the kind of work he was used to doing, and not something he could see himself doing for another eight to ten years.

"I'm not going to be here the first half of June," he told Domingo. "Elaina and I are going back to Texas for David's graduation."

"That's right!" Domingo replied. "I had almost forgotten it was coming up next month. I know you are both very proud."

"Yes, we are," Jack agreed, "much the way you and Felicia were seven years ago when Rafael graduated."

"That was indeed a great day for us, and I am so looking forward to him coming back here to Managua the first of July."

"He's not coming back to live with you, is he?"

"Only until he finds his own place."

"I know you are looking forward to having him nearby, and it will be great for the entire country to have a new, well trained neurosurgeon in the area." Jack had met one older neurosurgeon during one of his earliest trips to Nicaragua, but he had no knowledge of his training or capabilities. Rafael would be a major addition to any medical community, especially this one.

"Yes, I don't think he is very happy about the idea of returning here, and he may not stay for long, but I made him promise me he would return to his home country when he finished his training, and to his credit he is doing just that. I am very proud of him."

"As well you should be, my friend."

****

"I am so grateful to you both," Amy said as she hugged her mother and her mother-in-law at the conclusion of the huge baby shower they'd co-hosted at the Callahan's home in Fort Worth.

"We are so happy for you, dear," Joanne Callahan said, as she held her daughter close.

Elaina agreed, adding, "I'm not sure who is more excited, you, your mother, or me."

Amy then looked around the room, surveying the piles of baby clothes, and beyond them was the new crib and stroller. On the other side of the room she saw a half dozen cases of disposable diapers, two smaller boxes of Pedialyte and three larger boxes of canned formula. She anticipated returning the formula, since her intent was to breast feed her son, but she thought having a store credit at Babies-"R"-Us was probably better anyway.

"It looks to me as though you're pretty well set," her mom said. "I just love the crib."

Elaina smiled, "It looked so much like David's old crib, when I saw It I couldn't resist getting." She turned toward Amy and added, "If there's one you'd rather have, we can easily exchange it. It wouldn't hurt my feelings, I promise."

"No, I love it," Amy replied. "I love everything. I can't tell you how excited I am about all of this. Ya'll did such a great job putting this together. Getting all my old high school friends to come. It was just perfect."

"Now, only one more minor event before the big day," Elaina said with a big smile.

"I would hardly call David's graduation from medical school a minor event," Amy scoffed playfully.

"Well, there was a time I would have agreed with you," Elaina replied, "But, compared to the birth of my first grandbaby, it doesn't come close."

They all laughed as they hugged each other once more.

****

Near the conclusion of the graduation exercise, all the new doctors stood and recited a highly modernized version of the ancient "Oath of Hippocrates" committing themselves to the work that lay ahead of them. As Jack listened to the words, he was troubled by the subtle changes that had been made from the original version. He had no problem with the deletion of the swearing to Apollo, the physician, and all the other gods and goddesses of ancient Greece. He had always thought that part was a bit absurd, but in this version, there was only one reference to a superior being, and it was a rather tangential reference to the new doctors promising not to play god. He was also disturbed by a rather puzzling phrase that required the physician have the "utmost respect for human life from its beginning", which sounded like something out of a secular brochure that would allow for individual interpretation.

To Jack, and others of his generation, the Hippocratic Oath was the moral and ethical foundation of the profession, and he wondered why others now felt compelled to modify something that had survived more than twenty-five hundred years. Perhaps the changes in the modern social environment demanded that the practice of medicine be reduced to a less virtuous status, or maybe the economic pressures of doing everything possible for each individual patient as required by the previous version, were now simply too much for any society to bear. Was this societies way of reining in those who would be committed otherwise? He didn't know the answers to these questions and chose not to dwell on them given the joy of the occasion, but he was nevertheless saddened by what he perceived to be a cheapening of his profession. One he had always considered to be a calling.

When the oath was finished there was a rousing applause for all the graduates, after which they filed out into the massive foyer of the giant Morton H. Meyerson Symphony Center as the pipe organ filled the massive auditorium with the theme from the movie "Star Wars". Apparently the graduates had voted against the traditional "Pomp and Circumstance".

"Well, Dr. Roberts," Jack said, trying his best to conceal his incredible pride, "your life is never going to be the same. It doesn't really belong to you any more. It belongs to medicine."

David hugged his dad firmly before stepping back and saying, "That may be true, but a wise man once told me that I should seek a perfect balance in my life, and I intend to try and do just that." he looked over at Amy and winked at her smiling face.

Jack laughed and said, "I hope you have better luck with that than I have."

"We are so incredibly proud of you, son," Elaina said as she raised up on her toes to hug her son through his dark blue graduation robe. The tears were streaming down her face as she refused to turn him loose, saying, "I have dreamed of this day almost since the day you were born. I know you are going to become a great surgeon."

David held her back at arm's length and smiled into her joyful face. "You know I couldn't have done it without your support. You and Dad have made it possible for me to achieve more than I could have ever hoped for, and I love you both so much."

She threw her arms around him again and replied through her tears, "we love you too son, more than anything."

They made their way over to a designated area with the seal of the university as a photo backdrop, where David posed for pictures, first with Amy who was now eight months pregnant, and then with his mom, then his dad, and finally the entire group. While this was clearly his moment, Amy stole the show. She had finally developed that radiant glow of a woman heavy with child, and her face was made even lovelier by the pride she had in her man.

Jack stood back, beaming with pride in his only son, but in the back of his mind he couldn't help fearing what the future might hold.

Thank you for reading *A Surgeon's Heart: The Conflict*, the second volume in this series. To see what's in store for Jack, Elaina, David and Amy, look for the next volume available in the summer of 2014 ...

A Surgeon's Heart: The Crisis

To learn more about this entire series by R.W. Sewell, M.D., including volume one, *A Surgeon's Heart: The Calling*, go to www.asurgeonsheart.com. Feel free to contact the author and offer your comments.

ABOUT THE AUTHOR

Robert Walter Sewell was born November 20, 1950, in Independence, Missouri, and moved to Texas with his parents at the age of twelve. He has lived in Texas since, attending Thomas Jefferson High School in Port Arthur and Lamar University in Beaumont, where he received a bachelor's degree in biology. He went on to the University of Texas Medical Branch at Galveston, where he achieved his medical degree in 1974. He was accepted into the general surgery residency program at the University of Texas Health Science Center in San Antonio and completed his surgical training in 1979.

After finishing his residency, Dr. Sewell immediately began his surgical practice in the Mid-Cities between Dallas and Fort Worth in North Texas. He moved his practice to its current location in Southlake, Texas, in 2003, and remains an active surgeon today, with an emphasis on minimally invasive general surgery at the Texas Health Harris Methodist Hospital Southlake.

As a recognized specialist in the field of laparoscopic surgery, Dr. Sewell has lectured on various minimally invasive procedures throughout the United States and around the world. He is a member of the American Society of General Surgeons (ASGS) and was elected president of that organization in February 2008. He is also a fellow of the American College of Surgeons (FACS) and has served as a governor since 2013. Dr. Sewell maintains memberships in the Association of American Physicians and Surgeons, the Texas Medical Association, the Tarrant County Medical Society, as well as the prestigious Texas Surgical Society.

Along with his wife, Donna, Dr. Sewell resides in Colleyville, Texas, where he enjoys golf, photography, computer graphics, video production, gardening and, of course, writing.

Made in the USA
San Bernardino, CA
13 May 2014